READER'S DIGEST
SELECT EDITIONS

The condensations in this volume
are published with the consent of the authors
and the publishers © 2009 Reader's Digest.

www.readersdigest.co.uk

The Reader's Digest Association Limited
11 Westferry Circus Canary Wharf London E14 4HE

Printed in Germany
ISBN 978 0 276 44434 0

SELECTED AND CONDENSED
BY READER'S DIGEST

THE READER'S DIGEST ASSOCIATION LIMITED, LONDON

CONTENTS

If you're looking at a woman who might just be a suicide bomber, there are eleven telltale signs. Jack Reacher can see all of them in the nervous, bundled-up figure sitting opposite him on the New York subway. That's the electric beginning to this thriller, which builds to a vortex of suspense as Reacher uncovers Pentagon secrets that will force him into conflict with some age-old enemies of America. This Select Editions choice, for sure, will be one of the most dynamic blockbusters of the year.

Harry Ballantyne and Richard King, both key players in the world of fine art dealing, started out as friends at Oxford, then became rivals and, finally, arch enemies. Which probably wouldn't matter, except that their grandchildren, James and Artemis, have fallen in love. This beguiling saga of a feud between two families spans five decades and unravels a mystery that begins one summer day, when three students visit the Essex home of the artist, Alfred Munnings.

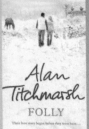

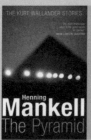

THE PYRAMID

HENNING MANKELL

335

Kurt Wallander is now firmly established as one of the world's most famous fictional detectives, especially since his appearance in three television dramas filmed for the BBC in Sweden, his creator's native country. Chronologically, *The Pyramid* comes first in the Wallander bibliography and is a memorable introduction to the newly divorced detective, as he tries to find the link between three very different crimes, and has to travel to Egypt to rescue his elderly father from the Cairo police.

In 1947, Guernsey is just emerging from German Occupation. Food and books are scarce, and the members of a book club, formed to outwit the Germans, are hungry for contact with the outside world. Enter Juliet Ashton, a budding, London-based author. In an exchange of letters with the islanders, she hears stories hilarious, moving and tragic, which draw her to a new and joyous life on the island.

THE GUERNSEY LITERARY AND POTATO PEEL PIE SOCIETY

MARY ANN SHAFFER

455

Gone
Tomorrow
Lee Child

If you're an ex-military policeman, you know how to recognise a suicide bomber. There are very definite telltale signs.

So Jack Reacher, riding the New York subway at two o'clock in the morning, has no doubts about his conclusion that the bundle of nerves huddled a few feet from him is a dangerous, and very imminent, threat.

He has just seconds to decide what to do.

Chapter One

Suicide bombers are easy to spot. They give out all kinds of tell-tale signs. Mostly because they're nervous. By definition they're all first-timers.

Israeli counterintelligence wrote the defensive playbook. They told us what to look for. They used observation and psychological insight and came up with a list of behavioural indicators. I learned the list from an Israeli army captain twenty years ago. He swore by it. Therefore I swore by it too, because at the time I was on three weeks' detached duty mostly about a yard from his shoulder, in Israel itself, in Jerusalem, on the West Bank, in Lebanon, in Syria, in Jordan, on buses, in stores, on crowded sidewalks. I kept my eyes moving and my mind running free down the bullet points.

Twenty years later I still know the list. And my eyes still move. Pure habit. From another bunch of guys I learned another mantra: Look, don't see, listen, don't hear. The more you engage, the longer you survive.

The list is twelve points long if you're looking at a male suspect. Eleven, if you're looking at a woman. The difference is a fresh shave. Male bombers take off their beards. It helps them blend in. The result is paler skin on the lower half of the face. No recent exposure to the sun.

But I wasn't interested in shaves.

I was working on the eleven-point list. I was looking at a woman.

I was riding the subway, in New York City. The 6 train, the Lexington Avenue local, heading uptown, two o'clock in the morning. I had got on at Bleecker Street from the south end of the platform into a car that was empty except for five people. I was sprawled on a two-person bench north of the end doors on the track side of the car. The other five passengers were all south of me on the long bench seats, three on the left and two on the right.

The car's number was 7622. I once rode eight stops on the 6 train next to a crazy person who talked about the car we were in with the same enthusiasm that most men reserve for sports or women. Therefore I knew that car number 7622 was an R142A model, the newest on the New York system, built by Kawasaki in Kobe, Japan. I knew it could run two hundred thousand miles without major attention. I knew its automated announcement system gave instructions in a man's voice and information in a woman's, because the transportation chiefs believed such a division of labour was psychologically compelling. I knew that each R142A car was a fraction over fifty-one feet long and a little more than eight feet wide. I knew that the no-cab unit had been designed to carry a maximum of forty people seated and up to 148 standing. The crazy person had been clear on all that data. I could see for myself that its wall panels were moulded from graffiti-resistant Fibreglass. I could see its twin strips of advertisements where the wall panels met the roof. I could see small, cheerful posters touting television shows and language instruction and easy college degrees.

I could also see a police notice advising me: If you see something, say something.

The nearest passenger to me was a Hispanic woman. She was across the car from me, on my left, all alone on a bench built for eight. She was small, somewhere between thirty and fifty, and she looked hot and tired. She had a well-worn supermarket bag looped over her wrist and she was staring at the empty place opposite with eyes too weary to be seeing much.

Next up was a man on the other side, maybe four feet farther down the car. He was all alone on his own eight-person bench. Dark hair, lined skin. He was sinewy, worn down by work and weather. He was leaning forward with his elbows on his knees. Not asleep, but close. He was about fifty, dressed in baggy jeans that reached only his calves, and an oversized NBA shirt with a player's name on it that I didn't recognise.

Third up was a woman who might have been West African. She was on the left, south of the centre doors. Tired, inert, her black skin made dusty and grey by fatigue and the lights. She was wearing a colourful batik dress with a matching square of cloth tied over her hair. Her eyes were closed. I know New York reasonably well. It was an easy guess that any three people already seated on a late-night northbound 6 train south of Bleecker were office cleaners heading home from evening shifts round City Hall, or restaurant service workers from Chinatown or Little Italy.

The fourth and the fifth passengers were different.

The fifth was a man. He was maybe my age, on the two-person bench diagonally opposite me, all the way across and down the length of the car. He was dressed casually but not cheaply. Chinos and a golf shirt. His eyes were fixed in front of him. Their focus changed and narrowed constantly. They reminded me of a ballplayer's eyes. They had a canny, calculating shrewdness in them.

But it was passenger number four that I was looking at.

If you see something, say something.

She was seated on the right side of the car, all alone on the farther eight-person bench, across from and about halfway between the West African woman and the guy with the ballplayer's eyes. She was white and in her forties. She was plain. She had black hair, neatly but unstylishly cut. She was dressed all in black. The guy nearest to me on the right was still sitting forward, and the V-shaped void between his bent back and the wall of the car made my line of sight uninterrupted except for the stainless-steel grab bars.

Not a perfect view, but good enough to ring every bell on the eleven-point list. The bullet headings lit up like cherries on a Vegas machine. According to Israeli counterintelligence I was looking at a suicide bomber.

I dismissed the thought immediately. The timing was wrong. The New York subway would make a fine target for a suicide bombing. The 6 train would be better than most. It stops under Grand Central Terminal. Eight in the morning, six at night, a crowded car, wait until the doors open on packed platforms, push the button. A hundred dead, a couple of hundred injured, infrastructure damage, a major transportation hub shut down for weeks. A significant score, for people whose heads work in ways we can't quite understand.

But not at two o'clock in the morning.

The train stopped at Astor Place. The doors hissed open. No one got on. No one got off. The train moved on.

The bullet points stayed lit up.

The first was a no-brainer: inappropriate clothing. By now explosive belts are as evolved as baseball gloves. Take a three-foot by two-foot sheet of heavy canvas, fold once longitudinally, and you have a continuous pocket a foot deep. Wrap the pocket round the bomber, and sew it together at the back. Insert a stockade of dynamite sticks into the pocket all the way round, wire them up, pack nails into the voids, sew the top seam shut, add crude shoulder straps to take the weight. Effective, but bulky. The only practical conceal-ment, an oversized garment like a padded winter parka.

But this was September, and it was as hot as summer. I was wearing a T-shirt. Passenger number four was wearing a North Face down jacket, black, puffy and zipped to her chin.

If you see something, say something.

The second point is: a robotic walk. Not relevant with a seated suspect. Bombers walk robotically because they're carrying forty extra pounds of weight, and because they're drugged. Martyrdom's appeal goes only so far. Most bombers are browbeaten simpletons with a slug of raw opium paste held between gum and cheek.

The train stopped at Union Square. No one got on. No one got off. The train moved on.

Points three to six are: irritability, sweating, tics and nervous behaviour. In my opinion sweating is as likely to be caused by physical overheating as by nerves. Also, the inappropriate clothing, and the dynamite. Dynamite is wood pulp soaked with nitroglycerine and moulded into baton-sized sticks. Wood pulp is a good thermal insulator. But the irritability and the tics and the nervous behaviour are valuable indicators. These people are in the last weird moments of their lives, anxious, scared of pain, woozy with nar-cotics. Brave talk in clandestine meetings is one thing. **Action** is another.

Passenger number four looked exactly like a woman heading for the end of her life.

Therefore point seven: breathing.

She was panting, low and controlled. Like a technique to conquer the pain of childbirth, or like a last desperate barrier against screaming with dread and fear and terror.

Point eight: suicide bombers stare rigidly ahead. Video evidence and eyewitnesses have been entirely consistent in their reports. No one knows why, but they all do it.

Passenger number four was staring at the window opposite so hard she was almost burning a hole in the glass.

Points one to eight, check.

Points nine, ten and eleven were all present too, and they were the most important points of all.

Point nine: mumbled prayers. To date all known attacks have been inspired, or validated, by religion, almost exclusively the Islamic religion, and Islamic people are accustomed to praying in public. Surviving eyewitnesses report long incantations repeated more or less inaudibly, but with visibly moving lips. Passenger number four was really going at it.

The train stopped at 23rd Street. The doors opened. No one got off. No one got on. The train moved on.

Point ten: a large bag.

Dynamite is a stable explosive, as long as it's fresh. It needs to be triggered by blasting caps. Blasting caps are wired with detonator cord to an electricity supply and a switch. The big plungers in old Western movies were both things together. Not practical for portable use. For portable use you need a battery, and you want one of the big, square, soup-can sized cells sold for serious flashlights. Too big and too heavy for a pocket, hence the bag. The battery nestles in the bottom of the bag, wires come off it to the switch, then they head on out through an unobtrusive slit in the back of the bag, and loop up under the hem of the inappropriate garment.

Passenger number four was wearing a black canvas messenger bag, looped in front of one shoulder and behind the other, and hauled round into her lap. The way the stiff fabric bulged and sagged made it look empty apart from a single heavy item.

The train stopped at 28th Street. No one got on. No one got off. The train moved on.

Point eleven: hands in the bag.

Twenty years ago point eleven was a recent addition. Israeli security forces and some brave members of the public had adopted a new tactic. If your suspicions were aroused, you didn't run. No point, really. You can't run faster than shrapnel. What you did instead was grab the suspect in a desperate bear hug. You pinned their arms to their sides. You stopped them reaching the button. Several attacks were prevented that way. Many lives were saved. But the bombers learned. Now they are taught to keep their thumbs on the button at all times, to make the bear hug irrelevant. The button is in the bag, next to the battery. Hence, hands in the bag.

Passenger number four had her hands in her bag.

The train stopped at 33rd Street. No one got off. A lone passenger entered the next car.

The train moved on.

I stared at passenger number four. Pictured her slim, pale thumb on the hidden button. I pictured a tangle of wires. A thick detonator cord, exiting the bag, tucked under her coat, connecting twelve or twenty blasting caps in a long, lethal, parallel ladder. Dynamite is unbelievably powerful. In a closed environment like a subway car the pressure wave alone would crush us all to paste.

I stared at the woman. I was thirty feet away. Her thumb was already on the button. She was good to go, and I wasn't.

I stared on at her. Too hard.

She felt it. She turned her head, slowly, smoothly.

Our eyes met. Her face changed.

She knew I knew.

WE LOOKED straight at each other for ten seconds. Then I got to my feet. I would be killed thirty feet away, no question. I couldn't get any deader by being any closer. I handed myself from one grab bar to the next. Passenger number four stared at me all the way, frightened, panting, muttering. Her hands stayed in her bag.

I stopped six feet from her. I said, 'I really want to be wrong about this.'

The large object in her bag shifted slightly.

I said, 'I need to see your hands.'

She didn't reply.

'I'm a cop,' I lied. 'I can help you.'

She didn't reply.

I let go of the grab bars and dropped my hands to my sides. It made me smaller. Less threatening. I stood as still as the moving train would let me. I did nothing. I had no option. She would need a split second. I would need more than that. I could have grabbed her bag and tried to tear it away from her. Except that I wouldn't have got near her. She would have hit the button before my hand was halfway there.

I could have tried to incapacitate her. But a swing from six feet away would have taken most of half a second. She had to move her thumb an eighth of an inch. She would have got there first.

I asked, 'Can I sit down? Next to you?'

She said, 'No, stay away from me.'

No obvious accent. Up close she didn't look deranged. Just resigned, and scared, and tired. She was staring up at me with the same intensity she had been using on the window.

'It's late,' I said. 'You should wait for rush hour.'

She didn't reply. Her hands moved, inside her bag.'

'Just one. Show me one hand. You don't need both of them in there.'

The train slowed hard. I staggered back and reached up to the grab bar close to the roof. Grand Central, I thought. I glanced out of the window, expecting lights and white tiles, but we were stopping in the tunnel.

I turned back. 'Show me one hand,' I said again.

The woman was staring at my waist. With my hands high my T-shirt had ridden up and the scar on my stomach was visible. Raised white skin. Crude stitches. Shrapnel, from a truck bomb in Beirut, a long time ago. I had been a hundred yards from the explosion.

I was ninety-eight yards closer to the woman on the bench.

I said, 'Show me one hand.'

She asked, 'Why?'

'I don't know,' I said. I was just talking for the sake of it. Which is uncharacteristic. Mostly I'm a very silent person. It would be statistically very unlikely for me to die halfway through a sentence.

The woman moved her hands. I saw her take a solo grip inside her bag with her right hand and she brought her left out slowly. Small, pale. Plain nails, trimmed short. No rings.

'Thank you,' I said.

She laid her hand palm-down on the seat next to her. I lowered my hands. The hem of my shirt fell back into place.

I said, 'Now show me what's in the bag.'

She didn't reply.

I said, 'I won't try to take it away from you.'

The train moved on again. A gentle cruise into the station.

I said, 'I think I'm entitled to at least see it.'

She made a face, like she didn't understand.

'Because I'm involved here. Maybe I can check it's fixed right. For later. Because you need to do this later. Not now.'

'You said you were a cop.'

'We can work this out,' I said. 'I can help you.' The train was creeping along. White light up ahead. The woman's right hand was moving. She was shaking it free of the bag.

I watched. Her right hand came out.

Not a battery. No wires. No button. No plunger.

Something else entirely.

The woman had a gun in her hand. She was pointing it between my groin and my navel. All kinds of necessary stuff in that region. Organs, spine, intestines, arteries and veins. The gun was a Ruger Speed Six. A big old .357 Magnum revolver, capable of blowing a hole in me big enough to see daylight through.

But overall I was a lot more cheerful than I had been a second before. Bombs don't need aiming, and guns do. The Speed Six weighs north of two pounds fully loaded. A lot of mass for a slim wrist to control. And Magnum rounds produce searing muzzle flash and punishing recoil. A split second before pulling the trigger her arm would clench and her eyes would close and her head would turn away. She had a decent chance of missing, even from six feet. If she missed, she wouldn't get a second shot.

I said, 'Take it easy.' Her finger was bone-white on the trigger, but she hadn't moved it yet. The Speed Six is a double-action revolver, which means that the first half of the trigger's pull moves the hammer back and rotates the cylinder. The second half drops the hammer and fires the gun. I stared at her finger. Sensed the guy with the ballplayer's eyes, watching. I guessed my back was blocking the view from farther up the car.

I said, 'Put the gun down and talk.'

She didn't reply. I was concentrating on the vibrations coming up through the floor. Waiting for the car to stop. My crazy fellow passenger had told me that the R142As weigh thirty-five tons. They can do sixty-two miles an hour. Therefore their brakes are very powerful. They clamp and jerk and grind.

I figured the same would apply even after our slow crawl. Maybe more so, relatively speaking. The gun was essentially a weight on the end of a pendulum. A long, thin arm, two pounds of steel. When the brakes bit down, momentum would carry the gun onwards. Newton's Law of Motion. I was ready to fight my own momentum and push off the bars and jump downtown. If the gun jerked five inches north and I jerked five inches south I would be in the clear.

She asked, 'Where did you get your scar? Were you shot?'

'Bomb,' I said.

She aimed at where the scar was hidden by my shirt.

The train rolled on. Into the station. Infinitely slow. Grand Central's platforms are long. The lead car was heading all the way to the end. I waited for the brakes to bite. I figured there would be a nice little lurch.

We never got there.

The gun moved vertical. For a split second I thought the woman was surrendering. But the barrel kept on moving. The woman raised her chin high, like a proud, obstinate gesture. She tucked the muzzle into the soft flesh beneath it. Squeezed the trigger halfway. The cylinder turned and the hammer scraped back across the nylon of her coat.

Then she pulled the trigger the rest of the way and blew her own head off.

Chapter Two

The doors didn't open for a long time. Maybe someone had used the emergency intercom or maybe the conductor had heard the shot. The system went into full-on lockdown mode.

The waiting wasn't pleasant. The woman's body had collapsed into a slumped position on the bench. Her right index finger was still hooked through the trigger guard. The gun was on the seat next to her.

The sound of the shot was still ringing in my ears. I could smell the woman's blood. I ducked forward and checked her bag. Empty. I unzipped her jacket and opened it up. Nothing there.

I found the emergency panel and called through to the conductor myself. I said, 'Suicide by gunshot. Last but one car. It's all over now. We're secure. No further threat.'

I didn't get a reply from the conductor. But a minute later the conductor's voice came through the train PA. He said, 'Passengers are advised that the doors will remain closed for a few minutes due to an evolving incident.' He spoke slowly. He was probably reading from a card. His voice was shaky.

I sat down three feet from the corpse and waited.

Eventually six officers came down the stairs. They had drawn their weapons. NYPD patrolmen, probably out of the 14th Precinct on West 35th Street, the famous Midtown South. They ran along the platform and started checking the train from the front. I got up and watched through the windows. I could see the cops opening doors car by car, checking, clearing the passengers out. It was a lightly loaded night train and it didn't take long for them to reach us. They checked through the windows and saw the body and the gun and tensed up. The doors hissed open and they swarmed on board.

One cop blocked each of the doorways and the other three moved straight towards the dead woman. They stopped and stood off about six feet. Didn't check for a pulse or any other sign of life.

A big cop with sergeant's stripes turned round. He had gone a little pale. He asked, 'Who saw what happened here?'

There was silence at the front of the car. The Hispanic woman, the man in the NBA shirt and the African lady. They were saying nothing. The guy in the golf shirt said nothing. So I said, 'She took the gun out of her bag and shot herself.'

'Just like that?'

'More or less.'

'Why?'

'How would I know?'

'Where and when?'

'On the run-in to the station. Whenever that was.'

The guy processed the information. Suicide by gunshot. The subway was the NYPD's responsibility. The deceleration zone between 41st and 42nd was the 14th Precinct's turf. His case. He nodded. Said, 'OK, please all of you exit the car and wait on the platform. We'll need names and addresses and statements from you.'

We got out into a gathering crowd on the platform. Transport cops, more regular cops arriving, subway workers. Five minutes later a paramedic crew clattered down the stairs with a gurney. I didn't see what happened after that because the cops started making ready to find a passenger each for further enquiries. The big sergeant came for me. He led me deep into the station and put me in a hot, stale, white-tiled room that could have been part of the transport police facility. He sat me down alone in a wooden chair and asked me for my name.

'Jack Reacher,' I said.

He wrote it down and didn't speak again. Just hung around in the doorway and watched me. And waited. For a detective to show up, I guessed.

THE DETECTIVE WHO SHOWED UP was a woman. She was wearing trousers and a grey shirt. It was untucked and I guessed the tails were hiding her gun. Inside the shirt she was small and slim. Above the shirt she had dark hair tied back and a small oval face. She was in her late thirties. An attractive woman. I liked her immediately. She looked friendly. She showed me her gold shield and handed me her business card. It had numbers on it for her office and her cellphone. It had an NYPD email address. The name was Theresa Lee.

She said, 'Can you tell me exactly what happened?' She spoke softly, in a voice brimming with care and consideration.

So I told her exactly what had happened, all the way through the eleven-point list, my approach, the fractured conversation, the gun, the suicide.

Theresa Lee wanted to talk about the list.

'We have a copy,' she said. 'It's supposed to be confidential.'

'It's been out in the world for twenty years,' I said. 'Everyone has a copy. It's hardly confidential.'

'Where did you see it?'

'In Israel,' I said. 'Just after it was written.'

'How?'

So I ran through my résumé for her. The abridged version. The US Army, thirteen years a military policeman, the elite 110th investigative unit, service all over the world, plus detached duty here and there. Then the Soviet collapse, the peace dividend, the smaller defence budget, suddenly getting cut loose.

'Officer or enlisted man?' she asked.

'Final rank of major,' I said.

'And now?'

'I'm retired.'

'You're young to be retired.'

'I figured I should enjoy it while I can.'

'What were you doing tonight?'

'Music,' I said. 'Those blues clubs on Bleecker.'

'And where were you headed on the 6 train?'

'I was going to get a room somewhere or head over to the Port Authority to get a bus.'

'Where do you live?'

'Nowhere.'

'Where's your luggage?'

'I don't have any.'

Most people ask follow-up questions after that, but Theresa Lee didn't. Instead her eyes changed focus again and she said, 'I'm not happy that the list was wrong. I thought it was supposed to be definitive.' She spoke inclusively, cop to cop.

'It was only half wrong,' I said. 'The suicide part was right.'

'I suppose so,' she said. 'The signs would be the same, I guess. But it was still a false positive.'

I asked, 'Do we know who she was?'

'Not yet. But we'll find out. They found keys and a wallet at the scene. But what was with the winter jacket?'

I said, 'I have no idea.'

She went quiet. Then she asked, 'Are you OK?'

I took it to be an enquiry as to whether I was shaken up. I said, 'I'm fine,' and she looked a little surprised and said, 'I would be regretting the approach, myself. On the train. I think you tipped her over the edge. Another couple of stops and she might have got over whatever was upsetting her.'

We sat in silence for a minute after that and then the big sergeant stuck his head in and nodded Lee out to the corridor. I heard a short whispered conversation, then Lee came back in and asked me to go to West 35th Street with her. To the precinct house.

'To get your statement typed up, to close the file.'

So I shrugged and followed her out of Grand Central to Vanderbilt Avenue, where her car was parked. It was an unmarked Ford Crown Victoria, battered and grimy, but it got us over to West 35th just fine. She led me upstairs to an interview room. She stepped back and let me go in ahead of her. Then she closed the door behind me and locked it from the outside.

THERESA LEE CAME BACK twenty minutes later with the beginnings of an official file and another guy. She put the file on the table and introduced the other guy as her partner. She said his name was Docherty. She said he had come up with a bunch of questions that maybe should have been asked and answered at the outset.

'What questions?' I asked.

Docherty said, 'Run through it all again.'

So I did, and Docherty fussed a bit about how the Israeli list had produced a false positive, the same way that Lee had. For five minutes we were three people discussing an interesting phenomenon.

Then the tone changed.

Docherty said, 'We're homicide detectives. We have to look at all violent deaths. You understand that, right? Just in case.'

I said, 'Just in case of what?'

'Just in case there's more than meets the eye.'

'There isn't. She shot herself.'

'Says you.'

'No one can say different. That's what happened.'

Docherty said, 'Maybe *you* shot her.'

I said, 'I didn't.'

Theresa Lee gave me a sympathetic look.

I said, 'What is this? There were witnesses.'

Lee shook her head. 'They didn't see anything. Their view was blocked by your back. Plus they were half asleep, and plus they don't speak much English. Basically, I think they wanted to get going before we started checking green cards.'

'What about the other guy? He was in front of me. He was wide awake. And he looked like an English speaker.'

'What other guy?'

'The fifth passenger. Chinos and a golf shirt.'

Lee opened the file. Shook her head. 'There were only four passengers, plus the woman.'

Lee took a sheet of paper out of the file and reversed it and slid it halfway across the table. It was a list of witnesses. Mine, plus a Rodriguez, a Frulov and an Mbele.

I said, 'He must have slipped away.'

Docherty asked, 'Who was he?'

'Just a guy. My age, not poor.'

'Did he interact in any way with the woman?'

'Not that I saw.'

Docherty shrugged. 'So he's just a reluctant witness. Probably cheating on his wife. Happens all the time.'

'He ran. But you're looking at me instead?'

'You just testified that he wasn't involved.'

'I wasn't involved either.'

'Says you.'

I said, 'This is a waste of time.' And it was. It was such an extreme, clumsy waste of time that I suddenly realised it wasn't for real. It was stage-managed. I realised that in fact, in their own peculiar way, Lee and Docherty were doing me a small favour.

There's more than meets the eye.

I said, 'Who was she?'

Docherty said, 'Why should she be someone?'

'Because you made the ID and the computers lit up like Christmas trees. Someone called you and told you to hold on to me until they get here. You didn't want to put an arrest on my record so you're stalling me with all this bull.'

'We didn't particularly care about your record. We just didn't want to do the paperwork.'

'So who was she?'

'Apparently she worked for the government. A federal agency is on its way to question you. We're not allowed to say which one.'

THEY LEFT ME locked in the room. Grimy, hot, no windows. The table, and three chairs. Two for the detectives, one for the suspect. Back in the day, maybe the suspect got smacked around and tumbled out of the chair. Maybe he still did. It's hard to say exactly what happens, in a room with no windows.

I timed the delay in my head. The clock had already been running about an hour since Theresa Lee's talk in the Grand Central corridor. So I knew it wasn't the FBI. Their New York field office is the largest in the nation, based down in Federal Plaza, near City Hall. The FBI would have arrived long ago. That left a bunch of other three-letter agencies. CIA, DIA.

Central Intelligence Agency, Defense Intelligence Agency. Maybe others recently invented.

After a second hour I figured they must be coming from DC, which implied a small specialist outfit. Anyone else would have a field office closer to hand. I gave up speculating and tipped my chair back and put my feet on the table and went to sleep.

At five in the morning three men in suits came in and woke me up. They were polite and businesslike. Their suits were mid-priced and pressed. Their eyes were bright, their haircuts short. Their bodies were stocky but toned. My first impression was recent ex-military. True believers, doing important work. I asked to see ID, but they quoted the Patriot Act and said they weren't obliged to identify themselves. Probably true, and they certainly enjoyed saying so. I considered clamming up in retaliation, but they saw me considering, and quoted some more of the Act at me, which left me in no doubt that a world of trouble lay at the end of that road. I am afraid of little, but hassle with today's security apparatus is best avoided. So I told them to ask their questions.

They started out by saying that they were aware of my military service and very respectful of it. Then they said that they would be observing me very closely and would know whether I was telling the truth or lying. Which was total bull, because only the best of us can do that, and these guys weren't the best of us, otherwise they would have been in very senior positions, meaning that right then they would have been at home and asleep in a Virginia suburb, rather than running up and down I-95 in the middle of the night.

But I told them again to go ahead.

They had three areas of concern. The first: did I know the woman who had killed herself on the train? Had I ever seen her before?

I said, 'No.' Short and sweet, quiet but firm.

They didn't follow up. Which told me roughly who they were and what they were doing. They were somebody's B team, sent to dead-end an open investigation. They wanted a negative answer to every question, so the file could be closed and put to bed.

The second question: did I know a woman called Lila Hoth?

I said, 'No,' because I didn't. Not then.

The third question was more of a dialogue. The lead agent opened it. 'You approached the woman on the train.'

I didn't reply. I was there to answer questions.

The guy asked, 'How close did you get?'

'Six feet,' I said. 'Give or take.'

'Close enough to touch her?'

'No.'

'If you had extended your arm, and she had extended hers, could you have touched hands?'

'Maybe,' I said.

'Did she pass anything to you?'

'No.'

'Did you take anything from her after she was dead?'

'No.'

'Did you see anything fall from her hand, or her bag?'

'No.'

'Did she tell you anything?'

'Nothing of substance.'

The guy asked, 'Would you mind turning out your pockets?'

I had nothing to hide. I went through each pocket and dumped the contents on the table. A folded wad of cash and a few coins. My old passport. My ATM card. My toothbrush. The MetroCard. And Theresa Lee's card.

The guy nodded to one of his underlings, who stepped up close to pat me down. He found nothing more.

The main guy said, 'Thank you, Mr Reacher.'

And then they left, as quickly as they had come in. I was surprised, but happy enough. I put my stuff back in my pockets and then I wandered out. I saw Theresa Lee at a desk and Docherty walking a guy across the squad room to a cubicle in the back. He had on a creased grey T-shirt and a pair of red sweat pants. He had left home without combing his hair. Theresa Lee saw me looking and said, 'Family member.'

'The woman's?'

Lee nodded. 'She had contact details in her wallet. That's her brother. He's a cop himself. Small town in New Jersey.'

'Poor guy.'

'I know. We didn't ask him to make the formal ID. She's too messed up.'

'So are you sure it's her?'

Lee nodded again. 'Fingerprints.'

'Who was she?'

'I'm not allowed to say.'

'Am I done here?'

'The feds finished with you?'

'Apparently.'

'Then beat it. You're done.'

I made it to the top of the stairs and she called after me. 'I didn't mean it about tipping her over the edge.'

'Yes, you did,' I said. 'And you might have been right.'

I stepped out to the dawn cool and turned left on 35th Street and headed east. *You're done.* But I wasn't. Right there on the corner were four more guys waiting to talk to me. Similar types as before, but not federal agents. Their suits were too expensive.

YOU SEE FOUR GUYS bunched on a corner waiting for you, you either run like hell in the opposite direction, or you keep on walking without breaking stride. You look ahead with neutrality, you check their faces, you look away, like you're saying *is that all you got*?

Truth is, it's smarter to run. The best fight is the one you don't have. But I have never claimed to be smart. Just obstinate, and occasionally bad-tempered. I keep walking.

The suits were all midnight blue and looked like they came from the kind of store that has a foreign person's name above the door. The men inside the suits looked capable. They were certainly ex-military, or ex-law enforcement, or ex-both.

They separated into two pairs when I was still four paces away. Left me room to pass if I wanted to, but the front guy on the left gave a kind of dual-purpose *please stop* and *we're no threat* gesture. I spent the next step deciding. You can't let yourself get caught in the middle of four guys. Either you stop early or you barge on through. At that point my options were still open. Easy to stop, easy to keep going. If they closed ranks while I was still moving, they would go down like bowling pins. I weigh 250 pounds and was moving at four miles an hour.

Two steps out, the lead guy said, 'Can we talk?'

I stopped walking. Said, 'About what?'

'You're the witness, right?'

'But who are you?'

The guy answered by peeling back the flap of his suit jacket, slow and unthreatening. No gun, no holster, no belt. He put his right fingers into his left inside pocket and came out with a business card. Handed it to me. The first line said: *Sure and Certain, Inc.* The second line said: *Protection, Investigation, Intervention.* The third line had a telephone number, with a 212 area code. Manhattan.

'Who are you working for?'

'We can't say.'

'Then I can't help you.'

'Better that you talk to us than our principal. We can keep things civilised.'

'Now I'm really scared.'

'Just a couple of questions. Help us out.'

'What questions?'

'Did she give anything to you?'

'Who?'

'You know who. Did you take anything from her?'

'And? What's the next question?'

'Did she say anything?'

'She said plenty. I didn't hear very much of it.'

'Did she mention names?'

'She might have.'

'Did she say the name Lila Hoth?'

'Not that I heard.'

'Did she say John Sansom?'

'No.'

'Did she give you anything?'

'Tell me what difference it would make.'

'Our principal wants to know.'

'Tell him to come ask me himself.'

I walked on, through the alley they had created. But one of the guys on the right tried to push me back. I spun him out of my way. He came after me again and I shoved him so that he stumbled ahead of me. His jacket had a single centre vent. I caught a coat tail in each hand and tore the seam all the way up the back. Then I shoved him again. He stumbled ahead. His jacket was hanging off him by the collar, open at the back, like a hospital gown.

Then I ran three steps and stopped and turned round. It would have been more stylish just to keep on walking slowly, but also much dumber. Insouciance is good, but being ready is better. The four of them wanted to come and get me. But they were on West 35th Street at dawn. At that hour virtually all the traffic would be cops. So they just gave me hard looks and moved away. *You're done.*

But I wasn't. I turned and a guy came out of the precinct house. Creased grey T-shirt, red sweat pants, grey hair sticking up. The brother. He caught up with me and told me he had seen me inside and had guessed I was the witness. Then he told me his sister hadn't committed suicide.

I TOOK THE GUY to a coffee shop on Eighth Avenue. A long time ago I was sent on a one-day MP seminar at Fort Rucker, to learn sensitivity around the recently bereaved. Sometimes MPs had to deliver bad news to relatives. My skills were widely held to be deficient. I used to walk in and just tell them. So I was sent to Rucker. I learned good stuff there. I learned to take emotions seriously. Above all I learned that diners and coffee shops were good environments for bad news. The public atmosphere limits the likelihood of falling apart, and the process of ordering and sipping punctuates the flow of information in a way that makes it easier to absorb.

We took a booth next to a mirror. The place was about half full. We ordered coffee. I wanted food too, but I wasn't going to eat if he didn't. Not respectful. He said he wasn't hungry. I sat quiet. Let them talk first, the Rucker psychologists had said.

He told me that his name was Jacob Mark. He said I could call him Jake. I said he could call me Reacher. He told me he was a cop. I told him I had been one once, in the military. He told me he wasn't married and lived alone. I said the same went for me. Up close and looking past his physical disarray he was a squared-away guy. He was in his forties, already very grey, but his face was youthful and unlined. I liked him, and I felt sorry for his situation.

He told me his sister's name was Susan Mark. At one time Susan Molina, but many years divorced and reverted. Now living alone. He talked about her in the present tense. He was a long way from acceptance.

He said, 'She can't have killed herself. It's just not possible.'

I said, 'Jake, I was there.'

The waitress brought our coffee and we sipped in silence for a moment. Passing time, letting reality sink in. The Rucker psychologists had been explicit: the suddenly bereaved have the IQ of labradors. Indelicate, because they were army, but accurate, because they were psychologists.

Jake said, 'So tell me what happened.'

I asked him if his department had a copy of the Israeli list. He said that after the Twin Towers every police officer had been required to learn every point on every list.

I said, 'Your sister was behaving strangely, Jake. She rang every bell. She looked like a suicide bomber.'

'Bull,' he said, like a good brother should.

'Obviously she wasn't,' I said. 'But you would have thought the same thing. You would have had to, with your training.'

'So the list is more about suicide than bombing.'

'Apparently.'

'She wasn't an unhappy person.'

'She must have been.'

He didn't reply. We sipped a little more. People came and went.

I said, 'Tell me about her.'

He asked, 'What gun did she use?'

'An old Ruger Speed Six.'

'Our dad's gun. She inherited it.'

'Where did she live? Here, in the city?'

He shook his head. 'Annandale, Virginia.'

'Did you know she was up here?'

He shook his head again.

'Why would she come?'

'I don't know.'

'Why would she be wearing a winter coat?'

'I don't know.'

I said, 'Some federal agents came and asked me questions. Then some private guys found me, just before you did. They were all talking about a woman called Lila Hoth. You ever hear that name from your sister?'

'No.'

'What about John Sansom?'

'He's a congressman from North Carolina. Wants to be a senator. Some kind of hard-ass.'

I remembered vaguely. Election season was gearing up. I'd seen newspaper and television coverage. Sansom had been a late entrant to politics and was a rising star. He was seen as tough and uncompromising. And ambitious. He had done well in business and before that he'd done well in the army. He hinted at a Special Forces career, without supplying details.

'Did your sister know him?'

'I can't see how.'

I asked, 'What did she do for a living?'

He wouldn't tell me.

He didn't need to tell me. Her fingerprints were on file and three shiny pink ex-staff officers had hustled up the highway but had left within minutes. Which put Susan Mark in the defence business, but not in an elevated position. And she lived in Annandale, Virginia, an easy commute to the world's largest office building.

'She worked at the Pentagon,' I said.

Jake said, 'She wasn't supposed to talk about her job.'

I shook my head. 'If it was really a secret, she would have told you she worked at Wal-Mart.'

He didn't answer. I said, 'I had an office in the Pentagon once. I'm familiar with the place. Try me.'

He paused, then said, 'She was a civilian clerk. But she made it sound exciting. She worked for an outfit called CGUSAHRC.'

'It's not an outfit,' I said. 'It's a guy. CGUSAHRC means Commanding General, United States Army, Human Resources Command. It's a personnel department. Paperwork and records.'

Jake didn't reply.

I asked, 'Did she tell you anything about it at all?'

'Not really. Maybe there wasn't much to tell.' He said it with a hint of bitterness.

I said, 'People dress things up, Jake. It's human nature. Did she enjoy her job?'

'She seemed to. She had the right skills for a records department. Great memory, very organised, good with computers.'

I started to think about Annandale again. Under the present circumstances it had just one significant characteristic.

It was a very long way from New York City.

Jake said, 'What?'

There's more than meets the eye.

I asked, 'How long have you been a cop?'

'Eighteen years.'

'Have you seen many suicides in Jersey?'

'One or two a year, maybe.'

'Anyone see any of them coming?'

'Not really. They're usually a big surprise.'

'Like this one.'

'You got that right.'

'But behind each one there must have been a reason.'

'Always. Financial, sexual, something about to hit the fan.'

'So your sister must have had a reason.'

'I don't know what,' he said. 'What are you saying?'

'I'm saying that I never heard of a suicide where the person travels hundreds of miles from home and does it while the journey is still in progress.'

'So?'

'Think like a cop, Jake. Not like a brother. What do you do when something is way out of line?'

'You dig deeper.'

'So do it.'

'It won't bring her back.'

'But understanding a thing helps a lot.' Which was also a concept they taught at Fort Rucker. But not in the psychology class.

I got a refill of coffee and Jacob Mark picked up a packet of sugar and turned it over and over in his fingers. I could see his head working like a cop and his heart working like a brother. It was all right there in his face.

He asked, 'What else?'

'There was a passenger who took off before the NYPD got to him. The cops figured he was maybe cheating on his wife.'

'Possible. And?'

'Both the feds and the private guys asked me if your sister had handed me anything. I'm guessing something small.'

'Who were the feds?'

'They wouldn't say.'

'Who were the private guys?'

I took the business card out of my back pocket. Jake read it slowly. *Sure and Certain, Inc.* The telephone number. He took out a cellphone and dialled. I heard a chirpy three-note tone and a recorded message. Jake closed his phone. 'Not in service. Fake number.'

I took a second refill of coffee. Jake slid the business card back to me and said, 'I don't like this.'

I said, 'I wouldn't like it, either.'

'We should go back and talk to the NYPD.'

'She killed herself, Jake. They don't care how or why.'

'They should.'

'Maybe so. But they don't. Would you?'

'Probably not.' I saw his eyes go blank. 'You got a theory?'

I said, 'It's too early for a theory. All we got so far is facts.'

'What facts?'

'The Pentagon didn't entirely trust your sister.'

'That's a hell of a thing to say.'

'She was on a watch list, Jake. As soon as her name hit the wires, three feds saddled up.'

'They didn't stay long.'

I nodded. 'Which means they weren't very suspicious. Maybe they had a small thing on their minds. They came to rule it out.'

'What kind of thing?'

'Information,' I said. 'That's all the Human Resources Command has got.'

'They thought she was passing information?'

'Maybe she was seen in the wrong office, opening the wrong filing cabinet. Maybe they figured there was an innocent explanation, but they wanted to be sure. Or maybe something went missing and they didn't know who to watch, so they were watching them all.'

'What kind of information? Like a copied file?'

'Smaller,' I said. 'A folded note, a computer memory. Something that could be passed from hand to hand in a subway car.'

'She was a patriot. She loved her country. She wouldn't do that.'

'She didn't pass anything to anyone.'

'So we've got nothing.'

'We've got your sister hundreds of miles from home with a loaded gun.'

'And afraid,' Jake said.

'Wearing a winter jacket in ninety-degree weather.'

'With two names floating around,' he said. 'John Sansom and Lila Hoth.'

He went quiet again and I sipped coffee. The traffic was getting slower on Eighth. The morning rush was building.

Jake said, 'Give me somewhere to start.'

I shrugged. 'You ever met any ex-Special Forces guys?'

'Maybe four or five, counting the Troopers I knew.'

'You probably didn't. Most Special Forces careers never happened. Most of them never made it out of the infantry. Some of them were never in the army at all. People dress things up.'

'Like my sister. What's your point?'

'We've got two random names, and election season starting, and your sister in HRC.'

'You think John Sansom is lying about his past?'

'Probably not,' I said. 'But it's a common area of exaggeration. And politics is a dirty business. So it's a no-brainer to assume that people are fact-checking his actual biography. It's a national sport.'

'So maybe Lila Hoth is a journalist. Or a researcher.'

'Maybe she put the squeeze on an HRC clerk for Sansom's service record. Maybe she picked your sister.'

'Where was her leverage?'

I said, 'That's the first big hole in the story.' Susan Mark had been desperate and terrified. It was hard to imagine a journalist finding that kind of leverage. 'Was Susan political?'

'Why?'

'Maybe she didn't like Sansom. Maybe she was cooperating.'

'Then why would she be so scared?'

'Because she was breaking the law,' I said.

'And why was she carrying the gun?'

'Didn't she normally carry it?'

'Never. It was an heirloom. She kept it in her sock drawer.'

The gun was the second big hole in the story. People take their guns out of their sock drawers for a variety of reasons. Protection, aggression. But never just in case they feel a spur-of-the-moment impulse to off themselves far from home.

Jake said, 'Susan wasn't very political. There can't be a connection with Sansom.'

'Then why did his name come up?'

'I don't know.'

I said, 'Susan must have driven up. Can't take a gun on a plane. She must have come through the Holland Tunnel and parked way downtown.'

Jake didn't reply. My coffee was cold. The waitress had given up on refills. We were an unprofitable table. I pictured Susan Mark twelve hours earlier, getting ready for a busy night. Dressing. Finding her father's gun, loading it, packing it into the bag. Climbing into her car, taking the Beltway, hitting 95, heading north, eyes wide and desperate, drilling the darkness ahead.

Suddenly I could hear Theresa Lee in my head. *You tipped her over the edge.* Jake saw me thinking and asked, 'What?'

'Let's assume the leverage,' I said. 'Let's assume it was compelling. So let's assume Susan was on her way to deliver whatever information she was told to get. And let's assume these were bad people. She didn't trust them to release whatever hold they had over her. She was in and didn't see a way of getting out. And she was very afraid of them. So she took the gun. Possibly she thought she could fight her way out, but she wasn't optimistic.'

'So?'

'She never intended to shoot herself.'

'But what about the list? The behaviours?'

'Same difference,' I said. 'She was on the way to where she expected someone else to end her life, either literally or figuratively.'

Jacob Mark said, 'It doesn't explain the coat.' But I thought he was wrong. I thought it explained the coat pretty well. And it explained the fact that she parked downtown and rode up on the subway. I figured she was looking to come upon whoever she was meeting from an unexpected angle, armed, dressed all in black, ready for some conflict in the dark. Maybe the parka was the only black coat she owned.

And it explained everything else, too. The sense of doom. Maybe the mumbling had been her way of rehearsing pleas, or threats. Maybe repeating them over and over again had made them more convincing to her.

Jake said, 'She can't have been on her way to deliver something, because she didn't have anything with her.'

'She might have,' I said. 'In her head. You told me she had a great memory.'

He tried to find a reason to disagree. He failed.

'Classified information,' he said. 'I can't believe it.'

'She was under pressure, Jake.'

'What kind of secrets does a personnel department have anyway, that are worth getting killed for?'

I didn't answer. Because I had no idea. In my day HRC had been called PERSCOM. Personnel Command, not Human Resources Command, and all the interesting information had been elsewhere.

Jake moved in his seat. He said, 'So why did she up and kill herself before she got where she was going?'

I said, 'She was in breach of all kinds of trusts. And she must have suspected some kind of surveillance. Every cop was a potential danger. Every guy in a suit could have been a federal agent. On the train, any one of us could have been getting ready to bust her. And then I approached her.'

'And?'

'She flipped. She thought I was about to arrest her. The game was over.'

'Why would she think you were going to arrest her?'

'Jake, I'm sorry, but I told her I was a cop.'

'Why?'

'I thought she was a bomber. I was trying to get through the next three seconds without her pushing the button.'

He asked, 'What exactly did you say?'

So I told him.

I think you tipped her over the edge.

'I'm sorry,' I said again.

For the next few minutes I was getting it from all sides. Jacob Mark was glaring at me because I had killed his sister. The waitress was angry because she could have sold about eight breakfasts in the time we had two cups of coffee. I took out a twenty-dollar bill and trapped it under my saucer. That solved the waitress problem. The Jacob Mark problem was tougher. Eventually he said, 'I got to go. I got things to do. I have to find a way to tell her family.'

I said, 'Family?'

'Molina, the ex-husband. And they have a son, Peter.'

'Susan had a son?' I said, 'Jake, we've been talking about leverage, and you didn't think to mention that Susan had a kid?'

He said, 'He's not a kid. He's twenty-two years old. He's a senior at the University of Southern California. He plays football. And he's not close to his mother. He lived with his father after the divorce.'

I said, 'Call him.'

'It's four o'clock in the morning in California.'

'Call him now.'

So Jake took out his cell again. He looked one kind of worried through the first five rings, and then another kind after the sixth. He lowered the phone slowly and said, 'Voicemail.'

I said, 'Go to work. Call the LAPD or the USC campus cops and ask for some favours. Get someone to check whether he's home.'

'They'll laugh at me. It's a college jock not answering his phone at four in the morning.'

I said, 'Just do it.'

Jake said, 'Come with me.'

I shook my head. 'I'm staying here. I want to talk to those private guys again.'

'You'll never find them.'

'They'll find me. I never answered their question about whether Susan gave me anything. I think they'll want to ask it again.'

Chapter Three

We arranged to meet in five hours, in the same coffee shop. Then I walked south on Eighth, slowly, like I had nowhere special to go, which I didn't. I was tired from not sleeping much but wired from all the coffee, which got me thinking about time. Just as two in the morning was the wrong time for a suicide bombing, it was also a weird time for Susan Mark to be heading for a rendezvous and delivering information.

So I stood at the newspaper rack outside a deli and leafed through the tabloids. I found what I was half expecting buried deep inside the *Daily News*. The New Jersey Turnpike had been closed northbound for four hours the previous evening. A tanker wreck.

I pictured Susan Mark trapped on the road between exits. A four-hour delay. Disbelief. Mounting tension. A deadline, approaching. A deadline, missed. Threats and penalties. *You tipped her over the edge.* Maybe so, but she hadn't needed a whole lot of tipping.

I set off strolling again. I figured the guy with the torn jacket would have gone to change, but the other three would be close by. I made no attempt to channel them to a place of my choosing. I just walked. Their call.

THEY APPROACHED ME a block south of Madison Square Garden. Construction shunted pedestrians along a fenced-off lane in the gutter. I got a yard into it and one guy stepped ahead of me and one fell in behind and the leader came alongside me. Neat moves. The leader said, 'We're prepared to forget the thing with the coat. But we need to know if you have something that belongs to us.'

'To you?'

'To our principal.'

'Who are you guys?'

'I gave you our card.'

'There are more than three million possible combinations for a seven-digit phone number. But you didn't choose randomly. You picked one you knew was disconnected. That's tough to do. So I guessed you had access to a list of numbers that never work. Phone companies keep a few, for when a number shows up in movies or on TV. So then I guessed you know people in the movie and TV business. Probably you rent out as sidewalk security when there's a show in town. Therefore the closest you get to action is fending off autograph hunters. I'm sure you had something better in mind when you set up in business.'

The guy said, 'Can we buy you a cup of coffee?'

I was done with sitting down, so I agreed to go-cups only. We stopped in at the next Starbucks. I got a tall house blend, black.

We carried on down Eighth. But four people made an awkward group, so we ended up on a cross street, with me leaning on a railing, and the other three in front of me. The guy who did all the talking said, 'You're seriously underestimating us.'

'OK,' I said.

'You're ex-military, right?'

'Army,' I said.

'You've still got the look.'

'You too. Special Forces?'

'No. We didn't get that far.'

I smiled. An honest man.

The guy said, 'We got hired as the local end for a temporary operation. The dead woman was carrying an item of value. It's up to us to recover it.'

'What item? What value?'

'Information.'

I said, 'I can't help you.'

'Our principal was expecting digital data, on a computer chip, like a USB flash memory stick. We said no, that's too hard to get out of the Pentagon. We said it would be verbal. Read and memorised.'

I said nothing. Thought back to Susan Mark on the train. The mumbling. Maybe she wasn't rehearsing pleas. Maybe she was running through the details she was supposed to deliver.

The guy said, 'The woman spoke to you on the train.'

'Yes,' I said. 'She did.'

'So the assumption is that whatever she knew, you know.'

'Possible,' I said.

'Which gives you a problem. Data on a computer chip, no big deal. Something in your head would need to be extracted.'

I said nothing.

The guy said, 'We go back empty, sure, we'll get fired. But Monday morning we'll be working again, for someone else. But you're exposed. Our principal brought a whole crew. Right now they're on a leash, because they don't fit in here. But if we're gone, they're off the leash. And you really don't want them talking to you.'

'I don't want anyone talking to me. Not them, not you. I don't like talking.'

'This is not a joke.'

'You got that right. A woman died. The woman worked at the Pentagon. That's national security. You should talk to the NYPD.'

The guy shook his head. 'I'd go to jail before I crossed these people. You hear what I'm saying?'

I drained my cup and tossed it into a trash can. 'Call your principal and tell him the woman's information was all on a memory stick, which is right now in my pocket. Then resign by phone and go home and stay the hell out of my way.'

I crossed the street and headed for Eighth. The leader called after me, loud. He said my name. I turned and saw him holding his cellphone at arm's length. It was pointing at me. Then he lowered it and all three guys moved out of sight before I realised I had been photographed.

RADIO SHACK STORES open early. I stopped in at the next one I saw and a guy stepped forward to help me. I asked him about cellphones with cameras. I told him I wanted to see how good the still pictures came out. He picked up a random phone and I stood in the back of the store and he snapped me from the till. The resulting image was small and lacked definition. My features were indistinct. But my overall size and shape and posture were captured fairly well. Well enough to be a problem. Truth is, my face is plain and ordinary. Very forgettable. My guess is most people recognise me by my silhouette, which is not ordinary.

I told the guy I didn't want the phone. But I bought a memory stick from him. A USB device, for computer data. Smallest capacity he had, lowest price. It was for window-dressing only. The stick came with a choice of two soft neoprene sleeves, blue or pink. I used the pink. A pink sleeve equals a woman's property. I thanked the guy for his help.

I walked two and a half blocks east on 28th Street. I went down into the subway at Broadway and swiped my card. Then I sat on a wooden bench and let nine downtown trains go by. Partly to kill time until businesses opened, and partly to check I hadn't been followed.

Eventually I got restless. I stood up and looked at the posters on the wall. One was an official notice prohibiting something called subway surfing. There was an illustration of a guy clamped like a starfish on the outside of a subway car's door. Apparently the older stock on the New York system had toe boards under the doors, designed to bridge part of the gap between the car and the platform, and small rain gutters above the doors, designed to stop dripping water getting in. My crazy co-rider had told me the new

R142As had neither feature. But with the older cars it was possible to wait on the platform until the doors closed, and then jam your toes on the toe board, and hook your fingertips in the rain gutter, and hug the car, and get carried through the tunnels on the outside. Subway surfing. A lot of fun for some, maybe, but now illegal.

I turned back to the track and got on the tenth train to pull in. It was an R train. It had toe boards and rain gutters. But I rode inside, two stops to the big station at Union Square.

I came up in the northwest corner of Union Square and headed for a huge bookstore I remembered on 17th Street. Campaigning politicians usually publish biographies ahead of election season, and news magazines are always full of coverage. I could have looked for an Internet café instead, but I'm not proficient with the technology and anyway Internet cafés are much rarer than they were. Now everyone carries small electronic devices named after fruits or trees. Internet cafés are going the same way as phone booths, killed by new wireless inventions.

The bookstore had tables at the front of the ground floor. They were piled high with new titles. I found what I wanted on the back side of the second table. John Sansom's book was called *Always on a Mission*. I took it and rode up on the escalator to the third floor, where the magazines were. I picked out all the news weeklies and carried them with the book to the military history shelves. I confirmed that the army's Human Resources Command didn't do anything that the Personnel Command hadn't done before it. Paperwork and records, like always.

Then I sat on a windowsill and read the stuff I had picked up.

The news weeklies all had campaign reports. The House and Senate contests got a few lines each. We were fourteen months ahead of the elections themselves, and Sansom was polling well throughout his state. He was raising lots of money, his blunt manner was seen as refreshing, and his military background was held to qualify him for just about everything. Clearly most journalists liked the guy. And they had him earmarked for bigger things.

His book cover was made up of his name and the title and two photographs. The larger was a grainy action picture blown up to form a background. It showed a young man in worn battledress and full camouflage face paint. Laid over it was a newer studio portrait of the same guy, in a business suit. Sansom, obviously, then and now. His whole pitch, in a single visual.

The recent picture showed him to be a small, lean guy, maybe five-nine and a hundred and fifty pounds. Full of endurance and wiry stamina, like the best Special Forces soldiers always are.

The cover flap featured his full name and military rank: Major John T. Sansom, US Army, Retired. Then it said he was the winner of the Distinguished Service Cross, the Distinguished Service Medal and two Silver Stars. Then it said he had been a successful CEO of Sansom Consulting. Again, his whole pitch, right there. I wondered what the rest of the book was for.

I skimmed it and found it fell into five main sections: his early life, his time in the service, his subsequent marriage and family, his time in business and his political vision for the future. The early stuff was conventional for the genre. No money, his mom a pillar of strength, his dad working two jobs to make ends meet. Almost certainly exaggerated.

I skipped ahead to where he met his wife. She was wonderful, their kids were great. I didn't understand much of the business part. Sansom Consulting had made suggestions, basically, then bought into the corporations they were advising, and then sold their stakes and got rich. Sansom himself had made what he described as a fortune. I wasn't sure how much he meant. I feel pretty good with a couple of hundred bucks in my pocket. I suspected Sansom came out with more than that, but he didn't specify how much.

I looked at the part about his political vision for the future. It boiled down to giving the voters everything they wanted. But all in all Sansom came across as a decent guy.

There were photographs in the middle of the book. All except one were bland snapshots tracing Sansom's life to the present day.

But the photograph that was different was bizarre.

It was of Donald Rumsfeld, in Baghdad, shaking hands with Saddam Hussein, the Iraqi dictator, back in 1983. Donald Rumsfeld had twice been Secretary of Defense, but at the time of the picture had been a special presidential envoy for Ronald Reagan. He had gone to kiss Saddam's ass and give him a pair of solid gold spurs as a symbol of America's everlasting gratitude. Sansom had captioned the picture: *Sometimes our friends become our enemies, and sometimes our enemies become our friends.*

I turned back to his service career. That was my area of expertise.

Sansom joined the army in 1975 and left in 1992. A seventeen-year window, four years longer than mine. A good era, basically. It looked like Sansom had enjoyed it. He described basic training accurately, described Officer Candidate School well, was entertaining about his early infantry service. He was open about being ambitious. He picked up every qualification available to him and moved to the Rangers and then the nascent Delta Force. As usual he dramatised Delta's induction process, the endurance, the exhaustion. As usual he didn't criticise its incompleteness. Delta is full of guys who can stay awake for a week and walk a hundred miles and shoot the balls off a tsetse fly, but it's relatively empty of guys who can do all that and then tell you the difference between a Shiite and a trip to the latrine.

But overall I felt Sansom was pretty honest. Truth is, most Delta missions are aborted before they even start, and most that do start fail. Sansom was straightforward about the excitement, and frank about the failures.

Then there was fairly routine stuff in West Africa, plus Panama, plus some SCUD hunting in Iraq during the first Gulf War in 1991. His was maybe the first unexaggerated Special Forces memoir that I had ever seen. More than that, even. It was downplayed.

Which was interesting.

I TOOK A LOT OF CARE getting back to the coffee shop on Eighth. *Our principal brought a whole crew.* And by now they all knew roughly what I looked like. The Radio Shack guy had told me how pictures could be phoned from one person to another. I had no idea what the opposition looked like. But nobody showed any interest in me. Not that I made it easy. I took the 4 train to Grand Central, took the shuttle to Times Square, walked an illogical loop from there to Ninth Avenue, and came towards the diner from the west, past the 14th Precinct.

Jacob Mark was already inside. He was in a back booth, cleaned up, hair brushed. I slid in opposite him.

'Did you talk to Peter?' I asked him.

He shook his head. 'But I think he's OK.'

The waitress came by. The same woman from the morning. I was too hungry to be sensitive about whether or not Jake was going to eat. I ordered a big platter, tuna salad with eggs. Plus coffee. Jake got a grilled cheese sandwich and water.

I said, 'Tell me what happened.'

He said, 'The campus cops helped me out. Peter's a football star. He wasn't home. So they rousted his buddies and got the story. Turns out Peter is away somewhere with a woman.'

'What woman?'

'A girl from a bar. Peter and the guys were out four nights ago. The girl was in the place. Peter left with her.'

I asked, 'Who picked up who?'

'This is what makes me feel OK. He did all the work. So it wasn't Mata Hari or anything.'

'Description?'

'A total babe. And these are jocks talking, so they mean it. A little older, maybe twenty-five. You're a college senior, that's an irresistible challenge, right there.'

'Name?'

'The others kept their distance. It's an etiquette thing.'

'Their regular place?'

'On their circuit.'

'Hooker? Decoy?'

'No way. These guys can tell.'

'I hear you,' I said.

Jake said, 'But?'

'Susan was delayed four hours on the Turnpike. I'm wondering what kind of a deadline could have passed, to make a mother feel like killing herself.'

The waitress came by with the food. It looked pretty good, and there was a lot of it.

Jake asked, 'Did the private guys find you?'

I nodded and told him the story between forkfuls of tuna.

He said, 'They knew your name? That's not good.'

'Not ideal. And they knew I talked to Susan on the train.'

'They took your picture? That's not good, either.'

'Not ideal,' I said again.

'Any sign of this other crew they were talking about?' he asked.

I checked the window, and said, 'So far, nothing.'

'What else?'

'John Sansom isn't exaggerating about his career.'

'Dead end, then.'

'Maybe not,' I said. 'He was a major. That's one automatic promotion plus two on merit. I was a major, too. I know how it works. Plus this guy won three of the top four medals available to him, one of them twice. So he must have done something special. Four somethings, in fact.'

'Everybody gets medals.'

'Not those medals. I got a Silver Star myself, which is pocket change to this guy. And I got a Purple Heart, too, which Sansom apparently didn't. No politician would forget about a wound in action. But it's relatively unusual to win a gallantry medal without a wound. Normally the two things go hand in hand.'

'So?'

'So I think he's leaving stuff out, not putting stuff in.'

'Why would he?'

'Because he was on at least four secret missions, and he still can't talk about them. Which makes them very secret indeed, because the guy is in an election campaign, and the urge to talk must be huge.'

'So maybe Susan was asked for details.'

'Impossible,' I said. 'Delta's orders and operational logs and after-action reports are destroyed or locked up for sixty years at Fort Bragg.'

'So how does this help us?'

'It eliminates Sansom's combat career, that's how. If Sansom is involved, it's in some other capacity.'

'What capacity?'

I put my fork down and drained my cup and said, 'I don't want to stay in here. It's ground zero for this other crew. It's the first place they'll check.'

I left a tip on the table and headed for the till. This time the waitress was pleased. We were in and out in record time.

MANHATTAN IS BOTH the best and the worst place in the world to be hunted. The best, because it is teeming with people. The worst, because it is teeming with people, and you have to check every one of them, just in case, which is tiring, and frustrating, and fatiguing, and eventually drives you crazy, or makes you lazy. So for the sake of convenience we went back to West 35th and walked up and down opposite the row of parked cop cars, which seemed like the safest stretch of sidewalk in the city.

'What capacity?' Jake asked again.

'What did you tell me were the reasons behind the suicides you saw in Jersey?'

'Financial or sexual.'

'And Sansom didn't make his money in the army.'

'You think he was having an affair with Susan?'

'Possible,' I said.

'I don't see it. He's married. Susan wasn't like that.'

'Maybe Sansom had an affair long ago, with someone else, when he was still in the army.'

'He wasn't married then.'

'But there were rules. Maybe he was banging a subordinate. That resonates now, in politics.'

'So you think there are rumours about Sansom, and Susan was asked to confirm them?'

'She couldn't confirm the behaviour. That kind of stuff is in a different set of files. But maybe she could confirm that person A and person B served in the same place at the same time. That's exactly what HRC is good for.'

'So maybe Lila Hoth was in the army with him. Maybe someone is trying to link the two names, for a big scandal.'

'I don't know,' I said. 'It sounds pretty good. But I've got a local tough guy too scared to talk to the NYPD, and I've got all kinds of dire threats, and I've got a story about some barbarian crew ready to slip the leash. Politics is a dirty business, but is it that bad?'

Jake didn't answer.

I said, 'And we don't know where Peter is.'

'Don't worry about Peter. He's a defensive tackle. He's three hundred pounds of muscle. He can take care of himself.'

I said, 'So what do you want to do now?'

Jake shrugged and stomped around, up and down the sidewalk, an inarticulate man further stymied by the complexity of his emotions. He stopped and leaned on a wall, across the street from the 14th Precinct's door. Gazed at the parked cars opposite. I saw the vehicle that Theresa Lee had used. One of the unmarked Crown Vics farther along the row was newer than the others. Shinier. It was black with two short, thin antennas on the boot lid, like needles. Federal, I thought.

Jake said, 'I'm going to tell her family, and we're going to bury her, and we're going to move on. Maybe there's a reason. Better not to know. No good can come of it. Just more pain.'

'Your choice,' I said.

He nodded, shook my hand and moved away. I wondered when I would see him again. Between three days and a week, I thought.

I was wrong.

I WAS STILL DIRECTLY ACROSS the street from the 14th Precinct's door when Theresa Lee came out with two guys in blue suits. She looked tired. She saw me on the far sidewalk and smacked the guy next to her and said something and pointed straight at me.

The guys in the suits hustled across the street, dodging cars, coming at me from the left and the right simultaneously. I guessed the Crown Vic with the needle antennas was theirs. The left sides of their suit coats bulged more than the right. Right-handed agents with shoulder holsters. They were late thirties, early forties. In their prime.

FBI, I thought. They didn't show me ID. They just assumed I knew what they were.

'We need to talk to you,' the guy on the left said.

'I know,' I said.

'How?'

'Because you just ran through traffic to get here.'

'Do you know why?'

'No idea. Unless it's to offer me counselling because of my traumatic experience.'

The guy gave a little wry smile. 'OK, here's my counsel. Answer some questions and then forget you were ever on that train.'

'What train?'

The guy started to reply, and then stopped, late to catch on that I was yanking his chain. He asked, 'What's your phone number?'

I said, 'I don't have a phone number.'

'Not even a cell?'

'Especially not even,' I said. 'I'm that guy. You found me.'

'What guy?'

'The only guy in the world who doesn't have a cellphone.'

The guy went quiet. Theresa Lee was still on the sidewalk outside the 14th Precinct's door. She was standing in the sun and watching us from across the street. The other guy said, 'It was just a suicide on a train. Upsetting, but no big deal. Are we clear?'

I said, 'Are we done?'

'Did she give you anything?'

'No.'

The guy asked, 'You got plans?'

'I'm leaving town.'

'Heading where?'

'Someplace else.'

The guy nodded. 'OK, we're done. Now beat it.'

I stayed where I was. I let them walk away, back to their car. They got in and waited for a gap in the traffic and eased out and drove away.

Theresa Lee was still on the sidewalk. I crossed the street and stepped onto the kerb near her. I asked, 'What was that all about?'

She said, 'They found Susan Mark's car parked down in SoHo. It was towed this morning.'

'And? What did they find?'

'A piece of paper, with what they think is a phone number on it. It had a 600 area code, which they say is a Canadian cellular service. Then a number, then the letter D.'

'Means nothing to me,' I said.

'Me neither. Except I don't think it's a phone number.'

'So what was it?'

She pulled a small notebook out of her back pocket. She opened it and showed me a page with *600-82219-D* written on it in neat handwriting. Her handwriting, I guessed.

'It's like a code or a serial number. Or a file number,' Lee said

'Maybe it's not connected. Trash in a car, it could be anything. Was there luggage in the car?'

'No. Nothing except the usual crap that piles up in a car.'

'So it was supposed to be a quick trip. In and out.'

Lee didn't answer. She yawned and said nothing. She was tired.

'Are you closing the file?'

'It's already closed.'

'You happy with that?'

'Why shouldn't I be?'

'Statistics,' I said. 'Eighty per cent of suicides are men. And where she did it was weird.'

'But she did it. You saw her. There's no doubt about it.'

She glanced up and down the street, wanting to go, too polite to say so. I said, 'Well, it was a pleasure meeting you.'

'You leaving town?'

I nodded. 'I'm going to Washington, DC.'

I TOOK THE TRAIN from Penn Station. DC was as hot as New York had been, and damper. The sidewalks ahead of me were dotted with knots of tourists. My destination was unmistakable and right there in front of me. The US Capitol. Beyond it across Independence Avenue were the House offices. At one time I had a rudimentary grasp of Congressional politics. I knew that the Rayburn Building was full of old hacks. I figured a relatively new guy like Sansom would have been given space in the Cannon Building. Prestigious, but not top-drawer.

The Cannon Building was on Independence and First. It had all kinds of security at the door. I asked a guy in a uniform if Mr Sansom of North Carolina was inside. The guy checked a list and said yes, he was. I asked if I could messenger a note to his office. The guy said yes, I could. He supplied a pencil and special House notepaper and an envelope. I addressed the envelope to: *Major John T. Sansom, US Army, Retired*, and added the date and the time. On the paper I wrote: *Early this morning I saw a woman die with your name on her lips.* Not true, but close enough. I added: *Library of Congress steps in one hour.* I signed it: *Major Jack-none-Reacher, US Army, Retired.* I sealed the envelope and handed it in and went back outside to wait.

THE SIXTY-MINUTE DEADLINE came and went. Ten minutes after the hour was up I saw a mismatched couple climb out of a Town Car and look around. I recognised Sansom's wife from the pictures in Sansom's book. She had expensive salon hair and good bones and a lot of tone. The guy with her looked like a Delta veteran in a suit. He was small, but hard and wiry and tough. The same physical type as Sansom himself.

The two of them glanced around at the people in the vicinity. I raised a hand in greeting. I didn't stand. Less threatening to stay seated. More conducive to conversation. And I was tired.

They stopped two levels below me and introduced themselves. Mrs Sansom called herself Elspeth, and the guy called himself Browning, and said it was spelled like the automatic rifle, which I guessed was supposed to put it in a menacing context. He wasn't in Sansom's book. He went on to list his pedigree, which started out with military service at Sansom's side, and went on to include civilian service as head of security during Sansom's business years, and then head of security during Sansom's House terms. The whole presentation was about loyalty. The wife, and the faithful retainer.

Mrs Sansom said, 'We've won plenty of elections and we're going to win plenty more. People have tried what you're trying a dozen times. They didn't succeed and you won't, either.'

I said, 'I'm not trying anything. And I don't care about who wins elections. A woman died, that's all, and I want to know why.'

'What woman?'

'A Pentagon clerk. She shot herself in the head, last night, on the New York subway.'

Elspeth Sansom glanced at Browning and Browning nodded. 'I saw it on-line. The *New York Times* and the *Washington Post*. It happened too late for the printed papers.'

Elspeth Sansom looked back at me and asked, 'What was your involvement?'

'Witness,' I said.

'And she mentioned my husband's name?'

'That's something I'll need to discuss with him. Or with the *New York Times* or the *Washington Post*.'

'Is that a threat?' Browning asked.

'I guess it is,' I said. 'What are you going to do about it?'

'Always remember,' he said. 'You don't do what John Sansom has done in his life if you're soft. I'm not soft either. And neither is Mrs Sansom.'

'Terrific,' I said. 'We've established that none of us is soft. In fact, we're all hard as rocks. Now, when do I get to see your boss?'

Elspeth Sansom said, 'Seven o'clock this evening.' She named what I guessed was a restaurant, on Dupont Circle. 'My husband will give you five minutes.' Then she said, 'Don't come dressed like that, or you won't get in.'

They got back in the Town Car and drove away. I had three hours to kill. I found a store and bought a pair of blue trousers and a blue checked shirt. Then I walked on down to a hotel I saw two blocks south on 18th Street. It was a big place, and quite grand, but big grand places are usually the best for a little off-the-books convenience. I took an elevator up to a random floor and walked the corridor until I found a maid servicing an empty room. It was past four o'clock in the afternoon. Check-in time was two. Therefore the room was going to stay empty that night. Big hotels are rarely a hundred per cent full. And big hotels never treat their maids very well. Therefore the woman was happy to take thirty bucks in cash and move on to the next room on her list and come back later.

In the bathroom there were two clean towels still on the rack, a cake of soap still wrapped next to the sink and half a bottle of shampoo. I brushed my teeth and took a long shower. I dried off and put on my new trousers and shirt. I swapped my pocket contents over and left my old garments in the bathroom trash. I was back on the street inside twenty-eight minutes.

I walked up to Dupont and spied out the restaurant. Afghan cuisine, outside tables in a front courtyard, inside tables behind a wooden door. I walked on P Street west to Rock Creek Park, and clambered down close to the water. I sat on a broad flat stone and listened to the stream below me. When the clock in my head hit five to seven I headed for the restaurant.

THE AFGHAN PLACE had paper lanterns strung over the courtyard. Most of the courtyard tables were already full. But not with Sansom and his party. I guessed he was inside, behind the wooden door.

I walked past the hostess station and called, 'I'm with the congressman.' I pushed through the door and scanned the inside room.

Sansom wasn't in it. No sign of him, no sign of his wife, no sign of Browning, no pack of eager staffers or campaign volunteers.

I backed out again and the woman at the hostess station looked at me quizzically and asked, 'Who were you joining?'

I said, 'John Sansom.'

'He isn't here.'

'Evidently.'

A young man at a table next to my elbow said, 'North Carolina Fourteenth? He left town. He's got a fundraiser breakfast tomorrow in

Greensboro. Banking and insurance. I heard him tell my guy all about it.' His last sentence was directed at the girl opposite him, not at me. Maybe the whole speech was. *My guy.* Clearly the kid was a hell of an important player, or wanted to be.

I stepped back to the sidewalk and stood still for a second and then set out for Greensboro, North Carolina.

I SLEPT ALL THE WAY. The bus arrived in Greensboro close to four o'clock in the morning. I walked until I found the kind of diner I wanted. I was looking for phone books and free local newspapers. The place I picked was just opening for business. A guy was greasing a griddle. Coffee was dripping into a flask. I hauled the Yellow Pages to a booth and checked 'H' for hotels.

I figured a fundraising breakfast would take place in a fairly upscale location. I guessed the Hyatt or the Sheraton. Greensboro had both. Then I started leafing through the free papers, looking for confirmation. Free papers carry all kinds of local coverage.

I found a story about the breakfast in the second paper I opened. I was wrong about the hotels. Not the Hyatt, not the Sheraton. Instead Sansom was fixed up at a place called the O. Henry Hotel, which I guessed was named after the famous North Carolina writer. There was an address given. The event was planned to start at seven in the morning. The guy behind the counter brought me a mug of coffee without asking. I took a sip. Nothing better than a fresh brew in the first minute of its life. Then I ordered the biggest combo on the menu.

I TOOK A CAB to the O. Henry Hotel. I wanted to arrive in style. I got there at a quarter past six. The lobby was rich and full of clubby leather armchairs. I walked to the reception desk with as much panache as was possible for a guy in a creased nineteen-dollar shirt. The young woman behind the counter looked up at me and I said, 'I'm here for the Sansom breakfast.'

The young woman didn't reply. She struggled to find a reaction, like I was embarrassing her with too much information. I said, 'They were supposed to leave my invitation here.'

'Who was?'

'Elspeth,' I said. 'Mrs Sansom, I mean. Or their guy.'

'Mr Springfield?'

I smiled to myself. Springfield was a manufacturer of autoloader rifles, the same as Browning was. The guy liked word games.

I asked, 'Have you seen them yet this morning?' Sansom had probably stayed in the hotel overnight. But I couldn't be sure.

The woman said, 'They're still upstairs, as far as I know.'

I said, 'Thanks,' and walked back into the lobby. I waited until she started concentrating on her computer screen, then I drifted towards the elevators and hit the up button.

I figured that Sansom would be in a big suite, and that they would all be on the top floor, so I hit the highest number the elevator offered. I stepped out into a carpeted corridor and saw a uniformed cop standing outside a double mahogany door. A token presence. I nodded to him and said, 'Jack Reacher for Mr Sansom,' and knocked on the door. He didn't react.

The suite door opened. Sansom's wife stood there, dressed, coiffed, made up and ready for the day.

'Hello, Elspeth,' I said. 'Can I come in?'

I saw an expert, politician's-wife calculation run behind her eyes. First instinct: throw the bum out. But there was a cop in the corridor, and probably media in the building. And local people talk. So she swallowed and said, 'Major Reacher, how nice to see you again,' and stood back to give me room to pass.

The suite was large. There was a living room with a breakfast bar and an open door that must have led to a bedroom. John Sansom stepped out of the bedroom to see what the fuss was all about.

He was in trousers and a shirt and a tie and socks. No shoes. He looked small. Wiry build, narrow through the shoulders. His hair was cut short. His skin was tanned, in an active, outdoors way. He glowed with wealth and power and energy and charisma. It was easy to see how he had won plenty of elections. He looked at me and then looked at his wife and asked, 'Where's Springfield?'

Elspeth said, 'He went downstairs to check on things.'

Sansom glanced at me and said, 'You don't give up.'

I said, 'I never have. You got ten minutes?'

'I can give you five.'

'You got coffee?'

'You're wasting time.'

'We've got plenty of time. More than five minutes, anyway. You need to lace your shoes and put a jacket on. How long can that take?'

Sansom stepped over to the breakfast bar and poured me a cup of coffee. He gave it to me and said, 'Now cut to the chase.'

'Did you know Susan Mark?' I asked him.

He shook his head. 'Never heard of her before last night.'

I was watching his eyes, and I believed him. I asked, 'Why would an HRC clerk be coerced into checking you out?'

'Is that what was happening?'

'Best guess.'

'I have no idea. HRC is the new PERSCOM, right? What have they got there? Dates and units. My life is public record anyway.'

'Your Delta missions were secrets.'

The room went quiet. Sansom asked, 'How do you know that?'

'You got four good medals. You don't explain why.'

'That damn book,' he said. 'The medals are a matter of record, too. I couldn't disown them. It wouldn't have been respectful. Politics is a mine-field. Damned if you do, damned if you don't. Either way round, they can always get to you.'

I said nothing. He looked at me and asked, 'How many people are going to make the connection? Besides you, I mean?'

'About three million,' I said. 'Everyone in the army, and all the vets with enough eyesight to read. They know how things work.'

He shook his head. 'Not that many. Most people don't have enquiring minds. And even if they do, most people respect secrecy in matters like that. I don't think there's a problem.'

'There's a problem somewhere. Otherwise why was Susan Mark being asked questions?'

'Did she actually mention my name?'

I shook my head. 'That was to get your attention. I heard your name from a bunch of guys I'm assuming were employed by the person asking the questions.'

'And what's in this for you?'

'Nothing. But she looked like a nice person, caught between a rock and a hard place.'

'And you care?'

'You do, too, if only a little bit.'

Sansom was quiet, then he said, 'The FBI briefed me, too. They say the NYPD feels you're reacting to this with a measure of guilt. Like you pushed too hard on the train. And guilt is never a sound basis for good decisions.'

I said, 'That's just one woman's opinion.'

'Was she wrong?'

I said nothing.

'I'm not going to tell you about the missions.'

I said, 'I don't expect you to.'

'But?'

'How much could come back and bite you in the ass?'

'Nothing in this life is entirely black and white. You know that. But no crimes were committed. And no one could get to the truth through an HRC clerk, anyway. This is amateur muckraking journalism at its worst.'

'I don't think so,' I said. 'Susan Mark was terrified and her son is missing.'

Sansom glanced at his wife. He said, 'We didn't know that.'

'It hasn't been reported. He's a jock at USC. He left a bar with a girl five days ago. Hasn't been seen since.'

'And you know this how?'

'Through Susan Mark's brother. The boy's uncle.'

'And you don't buy the story?'

'Too coincidental.'

'Not necessarily. Boys leave bars with girls all the time.'

'You're a parent,' I said. 'What would make you shoot yourself, and what would make you not?'

The room went quieter still. John Sansom got the kind of faraway look in his eyes that I had seen before from good field officers reacting to a tactical setback. Rethink, redeploy, reorganise, all in a fast second or two. He said, 'I'm sorry about the Mark family's situation. And I would help if I could, but I can't. There's nothing in my Delta career that could be accessed through HRC. Either this is about something else entirely, or someone is looking in the wrong place.'

'Where else would they look?'

'You know where. And they wouldn't even get close. So this is not about Special Forces.'

'So what else could it be about?'

'Nothing. I wouldn't have got into politics if I had the tiniest thing to hide. And now we really have to go.'

'OK,' I said. 'You ever heard the name Lila Hoth?'

'Lila Hoth?' Sansom said. 'No, I never heard that name.'

I was watching his eyes, and I felt he was telling the truth. And lying. Both at the same time.

Chapter Four

I went back to New York the same way I had left it. The trip took all day and some of the evening. I spent the travel time thinking, first about what Sansom had said, and secondly about what he hadn't. *Nothing in this life is entirely black and white. But no crimes were committed. And no one could get to the truth through an HRC clerk, anyway*. No denial of questionable activity. Almost the opposite. But he felt he hadn't strayed outside the envelope. Certainly my own career would not withstand extended scrutiny. In general I'm happy that the details stay locked away. I know my details. But what were Sansom's? Something damaging to him, obviously. But damaging in a wider context, too, or why else would the feds be involved in the first place?

And who the hell was Lila Hoth?

I asked myself these questions all the way through the bus ride, and all the way though the stopover at Union Station, and then I gave them up when the train I made rolled through Baltimore. By then I was thinking about where in New York City Susan Mark had been headed. She had driven in from the south and had planned to ditch her car and arrive at her destination by subway. She wouldn't have worn her winter coat in the car. Too hot. She probably had it in the boot, with the bag and the gun. Therefore she chose to get herself battle-ready at a distance and in relative privacy.

But not too far from her ultimate destination. Because she was seriously late. Therefore if she was headed way uptown, she would have parked in midtown. But she had parked in SoHo. Probably joined the train at Spring Street, one stop before I had. She was still sitting tight past 33rd Street.

Then things had unravelled. If they hadn't, I figured she would have got out at 51st Street. Maybe 59th. But no farther. Sixty-eighth was a whole new neighbourhood. So the 59th Street station was her upper limit. But I felt she would have aimed to approach from the south, overshoot, come back from the north. And hope her opponents were facing the wrong way.

So I drew a box in my head, 42nd Street to 59th, and Fifth Avenue to Third. Sixty-eight square blocks. Containing what?

About eight million different things.

I stopped counting them well before we hit Philadelphia. By then I was distracted by the girl across the aisle. A total babe, as a USC jock might say. Which got me thinking about Peter Molina again, and the apparent contradiction in someone expert enough to use him for leverage against a source that was worthless.

Our principal brought a whole crew. New York City has six main public transportation gateways: Newark, LaGuardia and JFK airports, plus Penn Station and Grand Central, plus the Port Authority bus depot. Total manpower required to make an attempt at surveillance would run close to forty people. Eighty to allow for round-the-clock coverage. And eighty people was an army, not a crew. So I got off the train with no more than normal caution.

Which, fortunately, was enough.

I SAW THE WATCHER IMMEDIATELY. He was leaning on a pillar in the centre of the Penn Station concourse. He had a clamshell phone in his hand, open, held low against his thigh. He was a tall guy, but reedy. Maybe thirty. He had a shaved head and ginger stubble. He was dressed in a shirt with a floral pattern and over it was a leather jacket that looked orange under the lights. He was staring at the oncoming crowd with eyes that had long ago grown tired.

I moved with the flow. The watcher was about thirty feet away, ahead and on my left. He was letting people walk through a fixed field of vision. It was going to be like stepping through a metal-detector hoop at the airport.

I passed through the watcher's point of focus. He didn't react. Then his eyes widened and he raised his phone and flicked the lid to light the screen. He glanced at it. Glanced back at me. I was about four feet away from him.

Then he fainted. I lunged forward and caught him and lowered him gently to the ground. That was what people saw, anyway. If they had replayed the brief sequence in their heads they might have noticed that I had lunged slightly before the guy had started to fall. That whereas my right hand was certainly moving to catch him, it was only moving a second after my left hand had already stabbed him in the solar plexus, very hard, but hidden.

But people see what they want to see. They always have, and they always will. I crouched over the guy like the responsible member of the public I was pretending to be. A woman crouched down next to me. Other people looked down. The guy in the leather jacket was twitching with chest spasms and gasping for air. A hard blow to the solar plexus will do that. But so will a heart attack and any number of other medical conditions.

The woman next to me asked, 'What happened?'

I said, 'I don't know. He just keeled over. His eyes rolled up.'

'We should call an ambulance.'

I said, 'I dropped my phone.'

The woman fumbled in her purse. I said, 'Wait. He might have had an episode. We need to check if he's carrying a card.'

'An episode?'

'An attack. Like a seizure.'

The woman reached out and patted the guy's jacket pockets, on the outside. Nothing there. She folded the jacket back and checked inside. There was an inside label, quite ornate, with Cyrillic writing on it. The guy's inside pockets were empty, too.

'Try his trousers,' I said. 'Quick.'

The woman said, 'I can't do that.'

Some executive dropped down and stuck his fingers in the guy's trouser pockets. Nothing there. Nothing anywhere. No wallet, no ID.

'We better call the ambulance,' I said. 'Do you see my phone?'

The woman looked around and came up with the clamshell cell. The lid got moved on the way and the screen lit up. My picture was right there on the screen. The woman glanced at it. I knew people kept pictures on their phones. I've seen them. Their partners, their dogs, their cats, their kids. Maybe the woman thought I was a big-time egotist who used a picture of himself. But she handed me the phone anyway. By that time the executive was already dialling the emergency call. So I said, 'I'll go find a cop.'

I forced my way into the tide of people again and let it carry me out of the door, to the sidewalk, and away.

NOW I WASN'T that guy any more. No longer the only man in the world without a cellphone. I stopped in the hot darkness three blocks away on Seventh Avenue and looked over my prize. I checked for calls dialled. There were none recorded. I checked calls received, and found only three, all within the past three hours, all from the same number. I guessed the watcher was supposed to delete information on a regular basis, but had got lazy. I guessed the calls had come in from some kind of a dispatcher. Maybe even the boss. If it had been a cellphone number, it would have been no good to me. Cellphones can be anywhere.

But it was a 212 number. A Manhattan land-line number.

Which would have a fixed location.

I hit the green button and the phone brought up the number. I hit the green button again and the phone started dialling. There was a ring tone. A woman's voice said, 'This is the Four Seasons, and how may I help you?'

I said, 'The hotel?'

'Yes, and how may I direct your call?'

I said, 'I'm sorry, I have the wrong number.' I clicked off.

The Four Seasons Hotel. I had never been in it. It was above my current pay grade. It was on 57th Street between Madison Avenue and Park Avenue. Right there in my sixty-eight square-block box. A short walk for someone getting off the 6 train at 59th Street.

I thought for a moment, looked around very carefully and then reversed direction and headed for the 14th Precinct.

I EXPECTED THERESA LEE to be there within about an hour. I expected to wait for her in the lobby. What I didn't expect was to find Jacob Mark already there. He looked up at me with no surprise and said, 'Peter didn't show up for practice.'

Jacob Mark talked for about five straight minutes. He said that the USC football people had waited four hours and then called Peter's father, who had called him. He said that for a star senior on a full scholarship to miss practice was completely unthinkable. Plus Peter was going to the NFL, the National Football League, and pro teams look for character. So missing practice was the same thing as trashing his meal ticket.

I listened without paying close attention. Close to forty-eight hours since Susan Mark had missed her deadline. Why hadn't Peter's body been found?

Then Theresa Lee showed up with news.

But first she had to deal with Jacob Mark's situation. She took us up to the second floor squad room and heard him out and asked, 'Has Peter been officially reported missing?'

Jake said, 'I want to do that right now.'

'You can't,' Lee said. 'At least, not to me. He's missing in LA, not in New York.'

'The USC people don't take missing-persons reports,' Jake said. 'And the LAPD won't take it seriously.'

'Peter's twenty-two years old. It's not like he's a child.'

'He's been missing more than five days.'

'Duration isn't significant. He doesn't live at home. And who is to say he's missing? Presumably he goes out for long periods without contacting his family.'

'But he missed football practice. That doesn't happen.'

'It just did, apparently.'

'This is different. Susan was being threatened,' Jake said.

'By who?'

Jake looked at me. 'Tell her, Reacher.'

I said, 'Something to do with her job. There was a lot of leverage. A threat against her son would be consistent.'

'OK.' Lee looked round the squad room and found her partner, Docherty. 'Go make a full report. Everything you know.'

Jake nodded gratefully and headed towards Docherty. I waited until he was gone and asked, 'Are you reopening the file now?'

Lee said, 'No. The file is staying closed. Because there's nothing to worry about. But the guy's a cop and we have to be courteous. And I want him out of the way for an hour.'

'Why is there nothing to worry about?'

She said, 'We know why Susan Mark came up here.'

'How?'

'*We* got a missing-persons report,' she said. 'Apparently Susan was helping someone with an enquiry, and when she didn't show, the individual concerned came in to report her missing.'

'What kind of enquiry?'

'I wasn't here. The day guys said it sounded innocent enough.'

'And Jacob Mark shouldn't know this? Why?'

'We need a lot more detail. And getting it will be easier without him there. He's too involved. He's a family member.'

'Who was the individual concerned?'

'A foreign national briefly here in town for the purpose of conducting the research that Susan was helping with.'

'Wait,' I said. 'Briefly here in town? Staying in a hotel?'

'Yes,' Lee said.

'The Four Seasons?'

'Yes,' Lee said.

'What's his name?'

'It's a her, not a him,' Lee said. 'Her name is Lila Hoth.'

IT WAS VERY LATE in the evening but Lee called anyway and Lila Hoth agreed to meet us at the Four Seasons. We drove over in Lee's car. The lobby was all pale sandstone and brass and golden marble. Lee showed her badge and the clerk called upstairs.

Lila Hoth's room was a suite. Theresa Lee knocked. The right-hand panel opened and a woman stood in the doorway. She was easily sixty, short and thick and heavy, with steel-grey hair cut plain and blunt. Dark eyes, hooded. A white slab of a face, meaty, immobile and bleak. A guarded, unreadable expression. She was wearing an ugly brown housecoat.

Lee asked, 'Ms Hoth?'

The woman ducked her head and moved her hands.

I said, 'She doesn't speak English.'

Lee said, 'She spoke English earlier on.'

The light behind the woman dimmed briefly as a second figure headed our way. Another woman. Maybe twenty-five. And very, very beautiful. Rare and exotic. She smiled a little shyly and said, 'It was me speaking English. I'm Lila Hoth. This is my mother.'

She spoke fast in a foreign language, Eastern European, quietly into the older woman's ear. The older woman brightened and smiled. We introduced ourselves. Lila Hoth spoke for her mother. She said her name was Svetlana Hoth. We all shook hands. Lila Hoth was stunning. She was tall but not too tall, and she was slender but not too slender. She had dark skin, like a perfect beach tan, and long dark hair. Huge eyes, the brightest blue I had ever seen. She moved with a kind of lithe economy. She was wearing a simple black cocktail dress that probably cost more than a car.

We followed her inside and her mother followed us. The suite was made up of a living room in the centre, and bedrooms either side. The living room included a dining table. There were the remnants of a room-service supper on it. There were shopping bags in the corners of the room. Two from Bergdorf Goodman, and two from Tiffany. Theresa Lee pulled her badge and Lila Hoth stepped away to a credenza and came back with their passports. She thought official visitors in New York needed to see papers. Lee flipped through them.

Then we all sat down. Svetlana Hoth stared ahead, excluded by language. Lila Hoth said, 'I am so sorry about what happened to Susan Mark.'

She spoke English very well. A little accented, a little formal.

I said, 'We don't know what happened to Susan Mark. Beyond the obvious facts, I mean.'

Lila Hoth nodded, courteously, delicately. She said, 'You want to understand my involvement.'

'Yes, we do.'

'It's a long story. But let me say that nothing in it could explain the events on the subway train.'

Theresa Lee said, 'So let's hear the story.'

And so we heard it. Lila Hoth was twenty-six years old. She was Ukrainian. She had been married at the age of eighteen to a Russian. The Russian had grabbed oil leases and coal and uranium rights from the crumbling state. He had become a single-figure billionaire. A rival had shot the Russian in the head, one year ago. The newly widowed Lila Hoth had moved to London with her mother.

She said, 'My father died before I was born. My mother is all I have left. So, of course, I offered her anything she wanted. Houses, cars, holidays, cruises. All she wanted was a favour. She wanted me to help her track down a man from her past.'

I asked, 'Who was the man?'

'An American soldier named John. That was all we knew. But then it emerged that he had been very kind to her.'

'Where and when?'

'In Berlin. It was in 1983. I thought trying to find the man was a hopeless task. I thought my mother was becoming a silly old woman. But I was happy to go through the motions. And don't worry, she doesn't understand what we're saying.'

Svetlana Hoth nodded at nothing in particular.

I asked, 'Why was your mother in Berlin?'

'She was with the Red Army,' her daughter said.

'Doing what?'

'She was with an infantry regiment. She was a political commissar. All regiments had one.'

I asked, 'So what did you do about tracing the American?'

'My mother was clear that her friend John had been in the army. That was my starting point. So I telephoned from London to your Department of Defense and asked what I should do. I was transferred to the Human Resources Command. They have a press office. The man I spoke to was quite touched. Possibly he saw a public-relations aspect. He said he would make enquiries. Personally I thought he was wasting his time. John is a very common name. And as I understand it, most American soldiers rotate through Germany, and most visit Berlin. Weeks later, a clerk called Susan Mark telephoned me. She told me that some names that sound like John are contractions of Jonathan. She wanted to know if my mother had ever seen the name written down. I asked my mother and told Susan Mark we were sure it was John with the letter H. The conversation with Susan was very pleasant, and we had many more. We almost became friends. She told me a lot about herself. She was a very lonely woman.'

Lee asked, 'And then what?'

'Eventually Susan said she had arrived at some preliminary conclusions. I suggested we meet here in New York, almost as a way to consummate our friendship. You know, dinner and maybe a show. As a way of saying thank you for her efforts. But she never arrived.'

I asked, 'What time were you expecting her?'

'About ten o'clock. She said she would leave after work.'

'Too late for dinner and a show.'

'She planned to stay over. I booked a room for her.'

'When did you get here?'

'Three days ago.'

'How?'

'British Airways from London.'

I said, 'You hired a local crew.'

Lila Hoth nodded. 'Just before we got here. It's expected. And sometimes useful.'

'Where did you find them?'

'They advertise. In the Moscow papers, and in the expatriate papers in London. It's good business for them, and it's a kind of status check for us. If you go overseas unassisted, you look weak.'

'They told me you brought a crew of your own.'

She looked surprised. 'I don't have a crew of my own,' she said. 'Why on earth would they say that? I don't understand it.'

'They said you brought a bunch of scary types.'

For a second she looked mystified. Then comprehension dawned in her face. She said, 'When Susan didn't arrive, I sent them out looking. I thought, I'm paying them, they might as well do some work. I offered them a bonus. So perhaps those men were making up a story for you. Perhaps they were inventing a scary alternative. To make sure they got their extra money. So that you would be tempted to talk to them.'

I said nothing.

Then something else dawned in her face. She said, 'I have no crew, as you call it. Just one man. Leonid, one of my husband's old team. He's at Penn Station. He's waiting for you. The police told me that the witness had gone to Washington. I assumed you would take the train, and come back the same way. Did you not?'

I said, 'Yes, I came back on the train.'

'Then Leonid must have missed you. He had your picture. He was supposed to ask you to telephone me. He must still be there.'

She stood up and headed for the phone. Which gave me a temporary tactical problem. Leonid's cell was in my pocket.

Lila Hoth hit nine for a line and dialled.

I put my hand in my pocket and used my thumbnail and found the catch and unlatched the battery. Separated it from the phone.

Lila Hoth waited, and then hung up. 'He's hopeless.'

I said, 'The local crew mentioned John Sansom's name.'

She sighed. 'I briefed them when we arrived. I told them the story. I think all of us felt that we were wasting our time, humouring my mother.

One of the men was reading the newspaper about Sansom. He said, here's an American soldier called John, of roughly the right vintage. He said, maybe Sansom is the guy you're looking for. For a day or two, we would say, let's just call John Sansom. I was only joking, because what are the chances? A million to one, perhaps. And they were joking too, but later they became quite earnest about it. Perhaps because of the impact it would have, because he is such a famous politician.'

'What impact? What did your mother do with this guy called John?'

Svetlana Hoth stared on into space. Lila Hoth said, 'My mother has never spoken in detail about it. Certainly it can't have been espionage. My mother is still alive. Therefore she was never suspected. And her American friend was not a traitor, either. Liaising with foreign traitors was a KGB function, not army. It was likely personal help, either financial or political. Those were bad times for the Soviet Union. But possibly it was romantic.'

'But you think Sansom isn't actually involved?'

'No, that was a joke that got out of hand. Unless, of course, it really is a million-to-one thing. Which would be extraordinary, don't you think? To joke about something and have it turn out to be true?'

I said nothing.

Lila Hoth said, 'Now may I ask you a question? Did Susan Mark give you the information intended for my mother?'

I said, 'Why would you think she gave me information?'

'Because the people I hired here told me you told them that she had. Computerised, on a USB memory stick. They gave me that message, and transmitted your photograph, and resigned their commission. I'm not sure why. I was paying them very well.'

I stuck my hand in my pocket. Found the Radio Shack stick. I held it up and watched Lila Hoth's eyes carefully.

She looked at the stick the way a cat looks at a bird.

Theresa Lee moved in her chair and looked at me.

I said, 'Susan Mark was terrified on the train. She didn't look like a person coming to town to meet a friend for dinner and a show.'

Lila Hoth said, 'I told you, I can't explain that.'

I put the memory stick back in my pocket. Said, 'Susan didn't bring an overnight bag.'

'I can't explain it.'

'And she was carrying a loaded gun.'

'I can't explain it. I'm sorry.'

'And her son is missing. Last seen leaving a bar, with a woman of your age and roughly your description.'

'What bar?'

'Somewhere in LA. In California.'

'I haven't been to Los Angeles. I've been in New York for three days on a tourist visa and I occupy three rooms in a hotel. I have no crew, as you call it. I have never been to California.'

I said nothing.

She said, 'And it's probably true that Peter is away somewhere with a girl. Yes, I know his name. Susan told me. We talked about all our problems. She hated her son. He is just a shallow fraternity boy. He rejected her in favour of his father. And do you know why? Because Susan was adopted. Her son thought of her only as a person born out of wedlock. He hated her for it. I know more about Susan than anybody. I was her friend.'

I sensed that Theresa Lee needed to get going and I certainly wanted to be out of there before Leonid showed up. So I shrugged as if I had nothing more to say. Lila Hoth asked if I would give her the stick that Susan Mark had given to me. I didn't answer. We just shook hands all round. The door closed behind us and we walked through the corridor and the elevator opened. We stepped in and Lee said, 'Well, what did you think?'

'I thought she was beautiful,' I said.

'Apart from that. Did you believe her?'

'Did you?'

Lee nodded. 'I believed her. Because a story like that is easy to check. Like, does the army have press officers?'

'Hundreds of them.'

'So all we have to do is find the one she spoke to. We could even track the phone calls from London.'

I said, 'A foreign number into the DoD? They're already part of an intelligence analysis somewhere.'

'And we could track Susan Mark's calls out of the Pentagon. If they talked as often as Lila claimed, we'd see them easily.'

'So go for it. Check.'

'I guess I will,' she said. 'She must know I could. She knows British

Airways and Homeland Security can track her in and out of the country. She knows we can ask Jacob Mark whether his sister was adopted. It's all so easy to confirm. Plus she came into the precinct house and involved herself voluntarily. And she just showed me her passport. Which is the opposite of suspicious behaviour. But if it's all so innocent, why are there feds involved?'

'If the story is true, then an American soldier met a Red Army political commissar back during the Cold War. The feds want to be sure it's innocent.'

We left the hotel and got into Lee's car. She said, 'You aren't agreeing with me all the way, are you?'

I said, 'If the Hoth family business is innocent, so be it. But something wasn't innocent. And we're saying that the other something brought Susan Mark to the exact same place at the exact same time. Which is a hell of a coincidence. How many times have you known a million-to-one chance turn out a winner?'

'Never.'

'Me neither. But I think it's happening here. John Sansom is a million to one against, but I think he's involved.'

'Why?'

'I spoke to him.'

'In Washington?'

'Actually I had to follow him to North Carolina. Then I asked him if he had heard the name Lila Hoth. He said no. I was watching his face. I believed him, and I thought he was lying, too.'

'How?'

'Maybe he had heard the name Hoth, but not Lila. Maybe he had heard the name Svetlana Hoth.'

'What would that mean?'

'Maybe more than we think. Why would Susan Mark bust a gut on a case like this?'

'She had sympathy.'

'Because she was adopted. Born out of wedlock, wondering about her real folks from time to time. Sympathetic to other people in the same situation. Like Lila Hoth, maybe. Some guy was very kind to her mother before she was born? There are a lot of ways to interpret a phrase like that.'

'For example?'

'Maybe John Sansom is Lila Hoth's father.'

LEE AND I went straight back to the precinct. Jacob Mark looked happier. Docherty had a patient expression on his face. Lee and I walked over and Jake said, 'Peter called his coach.'

I asked, 'When?'

'Two hours ago. The coach called Molina, who then called me.'

'So where is he?'

'He didn't say. He left a message. His coach never picks up during dinner.'

'But Peter's OK?'

'He said he won't be back anytime soon.'

'Are you happy that the message was for real?'

'The coach knows his voice.'

'Anyone try calling him back?'

'All of us. But his phone is off again.'

'May I ask you a question about another subject?'

'Shoot.'

'Was your sister adopted?'

Jake paused. Nodded. 'We both were. Three years apart. Susan first.' Then he asked, 'Why?'

Lee said, 'It seems that Susan came here to meet a friend.'

'What friend?'

'A Ukrainian woman called Lila Hoth.'

Jake glanced at me. 'We've been through this. I never heard that name from Susan.'

Lee asked, 'How many people knew that Susan was adopted?'

'She didn't advertise it. But it wasn't a secret.'

'How would you describe Susan's relationship with her son?'

Jake was quiet. Then he said, 'I guess you could call it a love–hate relationship. Susan loved Peter, Peter hated her.'

'Why?'

More hesitation. 'Peter wanted to live in a Ralph Lauren advertisement. He wanted his father to have an estate in Kennebunkport, and his mother to have the remnants of an old fortune. Susan was the daughter of a drug-addicted teenage whore from Baltimore, and she made no secret of it. Peter handled it badly. They never really got past it, and then the divorce came, and Peter chose sides.'

'Did Susan like Peter as a person?'

Jake shook his head. 'No. Which made things even worse. Susan had no sympathy for jocks and letter jackets. But that stuff was important to Peter.'

I said, 'You told me Susan wasn't an unhappy person.'

Jake said, 'And she wasn't. I know that sounds weird. But adopted people have different expectations of family. Believe me, I know. Susan was at peace with it. It was a fact of life, that's all.'

'Was she lonely?'

'I'm sure she was.'

Lee asked him, 'Have you got kids?'

'No,' Jake said. 'I'm not even married. I tried to learn from my big sister's experience.'

Lee stayed quiet and then said, 'Thanks, Jake. I'm sorry I had to bring all that bad stuff up.' Then she walked away and I followed her and she said, 'I'll check the other things too, but my guess is that Lila Hoth will pan out. She's two for two so far, on the adoption thing and the mother–son thing. She knows stuff only a genuine friend would know.'

I nodded agreement. 'You interested in Sansom?'

'Not even a little bit. Are you?'

'I feel like I should warn him, maybe.'

'About what? A million-to-one possibility?'

'Call it a brother officer thing. Maybe I'll head back to DC.'

'No need. He's coming here. Tomorrow midday, for a fundraiser lunch at the Sheraton. We got a memo.'

Then she walked away, leaving me in the empty squad room. Leaving me feeling a little uneasy. Maybe Lila Hoth really was as pure as the driven snow, but I couldn't shake the sensation that Sansom was walking into a trap.

IT HAS BEEN a long time since you could sleep well in New York for five dollars a night, but you can still do it for fifty, if you know how. The key is starting late. I walked down to a hotel I had used before, near Madison Square Garden. It was a big place, once grand, now just a faded old pile. After midnight a lone night porter is responsible for everything including the desk. I walked up to him and asked if he had a room available. He made a show of tapping on a keyboard and looking at a screen and then he said yes, he did. He quoted a price of a hundred and eighty-five dollars. I asked if I could see the room before I committed. The guy took me up in the elevator.

He opened a door with a pass card attached to his belt by a curly plastic cord.

The room was OK. I took out two twenties and said, 'Suppose we don't worry about that whole registration process?'

The guy said nothing. I took out another ten and said, 'For the maid, tomorrow.'

He took the money. 'Be out by eight,' he said and walked away.

I SLEPT WELL and woke up feeling good and I was out five minutes before eight. I got breakfast in the back booth of a place on 33rd. The battery on Leonid's cell was still half charged. I figured I had enough juice for a few calls. I dialled 600 and then aimed to dial 82219 but before I got halfway through the sequence a voice told me my call could not be completed as dialled. I tried 1-600 and got the same result. I tried 011 for an international line, and then 1 for North America, and then 600. The outcome was no better.

So, 600-82219-D was not a phone number. Which the FBI must have known. So they had buried their real questions for me behind a smoke screen.

What else had they asked me?

They had gauged my level of interest, they had asked yet again if Susan had given me anything, and they had confirmed that I was leaving town. They wanted me incurious, empty-handed and gone.

Why? I had no idea.

And what was 600-82219-D, if it wasn't a phone number?

The 600 part rang a faint bell. But I couldn't get it.

I finished my coffee and headed north towards the Sheraton.

The hotel was a huge glass pillar with a plasma screen in the lobby that listed the day's events. The main ballroom was booked for lunch by a group calling itself FT. Plausible cover for a bunch of Wall Street fat cats looking to buy yet more influence. Their affair started at noon. I figured Sansom would try to arrive by eleven. Which gave me two more hours to kill.

I found a clothing store. I wanted another new shirt. I didn't like the one I was in. It was a symbol of defeat. *Don't come dressed like that, or you won't get in.* Elspeth Sansom had suckered me completely. I had bought a shirt I didn't need or want. If I was going to see her again I didn't want to be wearing a badge of my failure and her success.

I chose an insubstantial thing made from thin khaki poplin and paid eleven bucks for it. Cheap, and it should have been. It had no pockets and the sleeves ended halfway down my forearms. But it was a satisfactory garment. And it was purchased voluntarily.

By ten thirty I was back in the Sheraton's lobby.

By ten forty I had figured out what 600-82219-D meant.

Chapter Five

I followed signs to the Sheraton's business centre, but I couldn't get in. You needed a room key. In three minutes another guy showed up, opened the door and I stepped in after him.

There were four identical work stations in the room. Each had a computer and a printer. I sat down far from the other guy. I checked the screen icons and found that if I held the mouse pointer over them, then a label popped up. I identified the Internet Explorer application and clicked on it twice. The hard drive chattered and the browser opened up. Much faster than the last time I had used a computer. Maybe technology really was moving on. Right there on the home page was a short cut to Google. I clicked on it. I typed *Army Regulations* in the dialogue box and hit enter.

For the next five minutes I clicked and scrolled and read.

I got back to the lobby ten minutes before eleven. I went out to the sidewalk. I figured Sansom would come in through the front door. The whole point was for him to be seen.

Sansom arrived in a Town Car at five past eleven. Springfield climbed out of the front passenger seat, and then Sansom and his wife climbed out of the back. They scanned faces and saw mine. Springfield headed in my direction but Elspeth waved him off with a small gesture. I guessed she had appointed herself damage-control officer as far as I was concerned. She shook my hand like I was an old friend. She didn't comment on my shirt. Instead she leaned in close and asked, 'Do you need to talk to us?'

It was a perfect politician's-wife enquiry. She was saying, *We know you have information that might hurt us, and we hate you for it, but we would be truly grateful if you would be kind enough to discuss it with us first, before you make it public.*

I said, 'Yes, we need to talk.'

Springfield scowled but Elspeth smiled and led me inside. The hotel staff showed us to a private lounge with bottles of sparkling water and pots of weak coffee. Elspeth played host. Sansom took a call on his cell from his chief of staff back in DC about their afternoon agenda. It was clear that Sansom was heading back to the office after lunch.

Sansom clicked off and the room went quiet. Then Elspeth Sansom asked, 'Is there any news on the missing boy?'

I said, 'He skipped football practice, which apparently is rare.'

'At USC?' Sansom said. He had a good memory. I had mentioned USC only once. 'Yes, that's rare.'

'But he called his coach and left a message. Apparently he's with a woman.'

Elspeth said, 'That's OK, then.'

'I would have preferred a live real-time conversation. Or a face-to-face meeting. I'm a suspicious person.'

'So what do you need to talk about?'

I turned to Sansom and asked him, 'Where were you in 1983?'

He paused a beat and said, 'I was a captain in 1983.'

'That's not what I asked you. I asked where you were. Were you in Berlin?'

'I can't tell you that.'

'You ever heard the name Svetlana Hoth?'

'Never,' Sansom said.

'Did you win a medal in 1983?'

He didn't answer. Then Leonid's cell rang in my pocket. I fumbled the phone out and looked at the small window on the front. A 212 number. The Four Seasons hotel. Lila Hoth, presumably.

I pressed buttons until the ringing stopped. I looked at Sansom and said, 'I'm sorry about that.'

He shrugged, as if apologies were unnecessary.

'You know what 600-8-22 is?'

'An army regulation, probably.'

I said, 'We figured all along that only a dumb person would expect HRC to have meaningful information about Delta operations. But I think a really smart person might expect it, with a little lateral thinking.'

'In what way?'

'Suppose someone knew for sure that a Delta operation had taken place. Suppose they knew for sure it had succeeded.'

'Then they wouldn't need information, because they've already got it.'

'Suppose they wanted to confirm the identity of the officer who led the operation?'

'They couldn't get that from HRC.'

'But what happens to officers who lead successful missions?'

'You tell me.'

'They get medals,' I said. 'The bigger the mission, the bigger the medal. And army regulation 600-8-22, section one, paragraph nine, subsection D requires the Human Resources Command to maintain a historical record of every award decision.'

Sansom said, 'But if it was a Delta mission, then all the details would be omitted.'

I nodded. 'All the record would show is a name, a date and an award. Which is all a smart person really needs, right? An award proves a mission succeeded, the lack of a citation proves it was a covert mission. Pick any month, say early in 1983. Not much was happening. How many DSMs were handed out? How many DSCs? I bet they were as rare as hens' teeth.'

Elspeth said, 'I don't understand.'

Sansom answered for me. 'If someone knew that a Delta mission had taken place and succeeded, and when, then whoever got the biggest unexplained medal that month probably led it. In peacetime a big award would stick out like a sore thumb.'

'So who is asking?' Elspeth said.

I said, 'An old battle-axe called Svetlana Hoth, who claims to have been a Red Army political commissar. She says she knew an American soldier named John in Berlin in 1983. She says he was very kind to her. And the only way that enquiring about it through Susan Mark makes any sense is if there was a mission involved and the guy named John led it and got a medal for it. The FBI found a note in Susan's car. Someone had fed her the regulation to tell her exactly where to look.'

Sansom didn't respond. So I asked him straight out, 'Were you on a mission in Berlin in 1983?'

Sansom seemed to lose patience with me, and he said, 'You seem like a smart guy. Think about it. What possible kind of operation could Delta have been running in Berlin in 1983?'

I said, 'I don't know. And I don't really care. I'm trying to do you a favour here. One brother officer to another. Because my guess is something is going to come back and bite you in the ass and I thought you might appreciate a warning.'

Sansom calmed down and said, 'I appreciate the warning. And I'm sure you understand that I'm not allowed to deny anything. Because denying something is the same as confirming something else. But I'll go out on a limb. I was not in Berlin in 1983. I never met any Russian women in 1983. I don't think I was very kind to anyone, the whole year long. This person is looking for someone else. It's as simple as that.'

Sansom's little speech hung in the air for a moment. Then Elspeth checked her watch and her husband said, 'You'll have to excuse us now. We have some really serious begging to do. Springfield will see you out.' I figured he wanted to set up a little quiet time for Springfield and me. So I stood up and headed for the door.

Springfield followed me to the lobby. I stopped and waited and he caught up with me and said, 'You need to leave this whole thing alone. Just let it go. You can't afford to turn over the wrong rock.'

'Why not?'

'Because you'll be erased if you do. You'll just disappear. That can happen now, you know. This is a whole new world.'

I asked, 'Why, if he wasn't even there?'

'Because to prove that he wasn't there you'll start asking where he was instead. Better that you never know.'

I nodded. 'This is personal to you too, isn't it? Because you were right there with him. You went wherever he went.'

He nodded back. Then he turned and headed for the elevators.

I stepped out to Seventh Avenue and Leonid's phone started ringing in my pocket again. I answered the phone. Lila Hoth's voice, soft in my ear, said 'Reacher?'

I said, 'Yes.'

'I need to see you, quite urgently. I think my mother might be in danger. Myself also, possibly.'

'From what?'

'Three men were asking questions at the desk. While we were out. I think our rooms have been searched.'

'Why talk to me about it?'

'Because they were asking about you, too.'

I asked, 'You're not upset about Leonid?'

She said, 'I think that was just a misunderstanding. Please come.' She spoke politely, a little diffidently. But something in her voice made me aware that she was so beautiful that the last time any guy had said no to her was probably a decade in the past.

Just let it go, Springfield had said, and I should have listened to him. But instead I told Lila Hoth, 'I'll meet you in your hotel lobby, fifteen minutes from now.' Then I headed for the Sheraton's taxi line.

I FOUND LILA HOTH and her mother at a corner table in a panelled space that seemed to be a tearoom. Leonid wasn't there. I checked and saw no one else worth worrying about. So I slid into a seat, next to Lila, across from her mother. Lila was wearing a black skirt and a white shirt. Her eyes were as blue as a tropical sea. Svetlana was in another shapeless housecoat. She nodded as I sat down. Lila extended her hand and shook mine quite formally.

Lila got straight to the point. 'Did you bring the memory stick?'

I said, 'No.' It was in my pocket.

'Where is it?'

'Somewhere else.'

She asked, 'Why did those men come here?'

'Because you're poking around in something that's a secret.'

'But the press officer at the Human Resources Command was enthusiastic about it.'

'That's because you lied to him. You told him it was about Berlin. But it wasn't. Berlin in 1983 was a Cold War tableau, frozen in time. There was no real US Army involvement. For our guys it was just a tourist destination. Probably ten thousand guys called John passed through, but they didn't fight and they didn't win medals. So tracking one of them down would be next to impossible. Susan Mark can't have told you anything about Berlin that made it worth coming over here.'

'So why did we come?'

'Because during those first phone calls you made her your friend and then you told her what you really wanted. And exactly how to find it. Not Berlin. Something else entirely.'

Lila Hoth sat quiet for a beat. Rethink, redeploy, reorganise.

She said, 'I asked Susan for help. She agreed, quite willingly. Clearly her actions created difficulties for her with other parties. And I regret what happened, very much.'

I said, 'What other parties?'

Lila Hoth said, 'Her own government, I think.'

'Why? What did your mother really want?'

Lila said she needed to explain the background first.

LILA HOTH HAD BEEN just seven years old when the Soviet Union had fallen apart, so she spoke with a kind of historical detachment. She told me that the Red Army had deployed political commissars very widely. Every infantry company had one. She said that command and discipline were shared between the commissar and a field officer. Rivalry was common and bitter, especially when it came to tactical common sense versus ideological purity.

Svetlana Hoth had been a political commissar assigned to an infantry company. Her company had gone to Afghanistan soon after the Soviet invasion of 1979. Initial combat operations had been satisfactory for the infantry. Then they had turned disastrous. Moscow reacted, belatedly. Tactical common sense had suggested retrenchment. Ideology had required renewed offensives. Morale had required unity of ethnicity and geographical origin. Companies had been reconstituted to include sniper teams. Expert marksmen were brought in, with their companion spotters. Thus pairs of ragged men used to living off the land had arrived.

Svetlana's sniper was her husband.

His spotter was Svetlana's younger brother.

The situation had improved. Offensive requirements were satisfied by regular night-time sniper operations. Soviet snipers had long been the best in the world. The Afghan mujahideen had no answer to them. Late in 1981 Moscow had shipped a new-model rifle. It was top secret. It was called the VAL Silent Sniper.

I nodded. Said, 'I saw one once.'

The VAL was a great weapon. It was a very accurate silenced semiautomatic rifle. It came with a choice of powerful day telescopes or electronic night scopes. You could be killed with no warning, silently, suddenly.

The stable situation lasted a year. The Soviet infantry's military reward for good performance was to be handed ever more dangerous tasks. Svetlana's company was ordered to push up the Korengal Valley. The Hindu Kush mountains reared up on one side, and the Abas Ghar ridge blocked the other. The six-mile trail in between was a major mujahideen supply line out of the North-West Frontier, and it had to be cut.

Lila said, 'The British wrote the book over a hundred years ago, about operations in Afghanistan. They said, when contemplating an offensive, the very first thing you must plan is your inevitable retreat. And they said, you must save the last bullet for yourself, because you do not want to be taken alive, especially by the women. The company commanders had read that book. The political commissars had been told not to. They had been told that the British had failed only because of their political unsoundness. Soviet ideology was pure, and therefore success was guaranteed.'

The push up the Korengal Valley had succeeded for the first three miles. A fourth had been won against opposition that had seemed ferocious to the grunts but strangely muted to the officers.

The officers were right. It was a trap.

The mujahideen waited until Soviet supply lines were stretched four miles long and then they dropped the hammer. Helicopter resupply was interdicted by a constant barrage of US-supplied ground-to-air missiles. Coordinated attacks pinched off the salient at its origin. Late in 1982 thousands of Red Army troops were essentially abandoned in a long thin chain of improvised encampments. The winter weather was awful.

Then harassment raids started.

Prisoners had been taken. Their fate was appalling.

Lila quoted lines that the British writer Rudyard Kipling had put in a doom-laden poem: *When you're wounded and left on Afghanistan's plains, and the women come out to cut up what remains, jest roll to your rifle and blow out your brains, an' go to your Gawd like a soldier.* Then she said Soviet infantrymen would go missing and hours later the wind would carry the sound of their screaming, from unseen enemy camps close by. Most corpses were never recovered. But sometimes bodies would be returned, missing hands and feet, or whole limbs, or heads.

Lila had not witnessed these events, but it sounded like she had. It struck me that she would make a fine storyteller. She had the gift of narrative.

She said, 'They liked to capture our snipers best of all. My mother was worried about my father, obviously. And her brother. They went out most nights, into the low hills, with the electronic scope. Not too far, just enough to find an angle. Far enough to be effective, but close enough to feel safe. But nowhere was really safe. Their orders were to shoot the enemy. Their intention was to shoot the prisoners. They thought it would be a mercy. My mother was pregnant by then. With me. I was conceived in a rock trench under a greatcoat that dated back to the end of World War Two.'

I said nothing. Svetlana stared on.

Lila said, 'For the first month my father and my uncle came back every morning, safe. They were a good team.'

Lila paused a beat. Then she changed the subject. 'There were Americans in Afghanistan at that time. Soldiers. Not many, but some. The Soviet Union was their enemy, and the mujahideen were their allies. It was the Cold War by proxy. It suited President Reagan to have the Red Army worn down. It was a part of his anticommunist strategy. And he enjoyed the chance to capture some of our new weapons for intelligence purposes. So teams were sent. Special Forces. And one night in March of 1983, one of those teams found my father and my uncle and stole their VAL rifle.'

I said nothing.

Lila said, 'But what was worse was that the Americans gave my father and my uncle to the tribeswomen. My mother heard their screams all the next day and far into the night.'

I said, 'I'm sorry, but I don't believe you.'

Lila Hoth said, 'I'm telling you the truth.'

I shook my head. 'I was in the US Army. I was a military cop. Broadly speaking I knew where people went, and where they didn't. And there were no US boots on the ground in Afghanistan. Not back then.'

'But you had a dog in the fight.'

'Of course we did. Like you did when we were in Vietnam.'

'But you admit that material help was provided, surely. To the mujahideen. And whenever did the United States provide military aid without also sending what they called military advisers?'

I said, 'Even if you're right, why not assume your father and your uncle were captured directly by the mujahideen?'

'Because their rifle was never found. And my mother's position was never fired on at night by a sniper. My father had twenty rounds in his magazine, and he was carrying twenty spare. If the mujahideen had captured him directly, then they would have killed forty of our men, or tried to, and then they would have abandoned the gun. My mother's company would have found it eventually. The mujahideen were intelligent. They had a habit of doubling back to positions we had previously written off as abandoned. But over a period of time our people saw all their places. They would have found the VAL. They accounted for all their other captured weapons that way. But not that VAL. The only logical conclusion is that it was carried straight to America, by Americans.'

I said nothing.

Lila Hoth said, 'I'm telling you the truth.'

We all sat quiet for a moment. A discreet waiter came by and offered us tea. Lila asked for a flavour I had never heard of, and then she translated for her mother, who asked for the same thing. I asked for regular coffee, black. I waited until the guy had retreated and asked, 'How did you figure out who you are looking for?'

Lila said, 'My mother's generation expected to fight a land war with you in Europe, and they expected to win. Their ideology was pure, and yours wasn't. After a swift and certain victory, they expected to take many of you prisoner. In that phase, part of a political commissar's duties would have been to classify enemy combatants. To aid them in that task, they were made familiar with the structure of your military.'

'Made familiar by who?'

'By the KGB. They knew who did what. They even knew names. Not just the officers. For incursions into the Korengal Valley, my mother reasoned that there were only three realistic options. Either SEALs from the Navy, or Recon Marines from the Corps, or Delta Force from the Army. Contemporary intelligence argued against the SEALs or the Marines. But there was significant radio traffic out of Delta bases in Turkey, and out of staging posts in Oman. Our radar picked up unexplained flights. It was a logical conclusion that Delta was running the operations.'

The waiter came back with a tray. He made a big show of serving the tea. My coffee came in a nice cup. When he was gone again Lila said, 'My mother estimated that the raid would have been led by a captain. A lieutenant would have been too junior and a major would have been too senior. The KGB had personnel lists. There were a lot of captains assigned to Delta. But there had been some radio analysis. Someone heard the name John.'

I nodded.

Lila said, 'My mother knew all about your army's medals. She knew that the VAL rifle would be worth a major award. But which award? Remember, most of your major awards specify gallantry or heroism while in action against an armed enemy of the United States. Whoever stole the VAL from my father was not eligible for those awards, because technically the Soviet Union was not an enemy of the United States. Not in the military sense. There had been no declaration of war.'

I nodded again.

Lila said, 'Capturing the VAL was a big coup. Its acquisition would have been rewarded with a big medal. My mother concluded it would be the Distinguished Service Medal. The applicable standard is exceptionally meritorious service to the United States Government in a duty of great responsibility. It is independent of formal combat activities. Below the rank of brigadier general it is awarded only very rarely. It's the only significant medal a Delta captain could have won that night in the Korengal Valley.'

I agreed. Svetlana Hoth was a pretty good analyst. I said, 'So you went looking for a guy called John who had been a Delta captain and won a DSM, both in March of 1983. And you made Susan Mark help.'

'I didn't *make* her. She was happy to help.'

'Why?'

'Because she was upset by my mother's story. And she was a little upset by my story, too. I'm a fatherless child, the same as her.'

I asked, 'How did John Sansom's name come up even before Susan reported back? I don't believe that it was from a bunch of New York private eyes sitting around reading the newspaper and making jokes.'

'It's a very rare combination,' Lila said. 'John, Delta, DSM, but never a general. We noticed it in the *Herald Tribune*, when his Senate ambitions were announced. We were in London. You can buy that paper all over the world. John Sansom might well be the only man in your army's history who matches those criteria four out of four. But we needed final confirmation.'

'Before what? What do you want to do to the guy?'

'Do?' Lila said. 'We don't want to *do* anything. We just want to talk to him, that's all. We want to ask him why? Why would he do that, to two other human beings?'

She finished her tea, and put her cup down on her saucer. Bone china clinked politely on bone china.

I asked, 'Why was your husband killed?'

'*My* husband?' Lila paused. 'It was the times.'

'Same for your mother's husband.'

'No. I told you, if Sansom had shot him in the head, or stabbed him, it would have been different. But he was cruel instead.'

I said nothing.

'Will you give me Susan's information?'

'No point,' I said. 'Because you wouldn't get near John Sansom. If any of what you say happened, then it's a secret. There are already federal agencies at work on this. You just had three guys asking questions. At best, you'll be deported. And at worst, you'll just disappear.'

Lila Hoth didn't speak.

'My advice?' I said. 'Forget all about it. Your father and your uncle were killed in a war.'

'We just want to ask him why.'

'You already know why. There had been no declaration of hostilities, therefore he couldn't kill your guys.'

'Did Susan really have the confirmation? Just tell me, yes or no. I won't do anything without actually seeing it. I can't.'

'You won't do anything, period.'

'Is there anything I can do to change your mind?'

'No,' I said.

The waiter brought the bill. Lila Hoth signed it.

I dumped Leonid's phone on the table. I got ready to leave.

Lila said, 'Please keep the phone.'

I said, 'Why?'

'Because my mother and I are staying. Just a few more days. And I would like to be able to call you, if I wanted to.'

Then she said, 'Even if you're not a friend', and I heard the tiniest bat-squeak of a threat in her voice.

I put the phone back in my pocket, stood up and walked away. I figured I could get to the Sheraton before Sansom finished lunch.

I DIDN'T GET TO THE SHERATON before Sansom finished lunch, partly because the sidewalks were clogged with people, and partly because it had been a short lunch. I didn't make it onto the same Amtrak as him, either, which meant I trailed him back to DC an hour and a half in arrears.

The same guard was at the Cannon Building's door. There was a gaggle of House pages inside the lobby and one of them called ahead and then walked me to Sansom's quarters.

A door off the corridor, lots of flags, lots of eagles, a reception desk with a young woman behind it. Springfield was leaning on the corner of her desk. He saw me and came to the door.

'Cafeteria,' he said.

We got there down a flight of stairs. It was a wide, low room full of tables and chairs. Sansom was nowhere in it. Springfield grunted like he wasn't surprised and concluded that Sansom had returned to his office while we were out looking for him, by an alternate route, possibly via a colleague's billet. He said the place was a warren. We walked back the same way we had come and Springfield stuck his head round an inner door and then backed away and motioned me inside.

Sansom was in a red leather chair behind a desk, with papers spread out in front of him. He had the airless look of a man who had been sitting still for a long time. He hadn't been out. The cafeteria detour had been a charade to allow someone to make an exit without me seeing him. I sat down in the visitor chair and found it still warm. Behind Sansom's head was a large framed print of the same picture I had seen in his book. Donald Rumsfeld and Saddam Hussein, in Baghdad. Next to it was a cluster of smaller pictures, some of Sansom standing with groups of people.

Sansom said, 'So?'

I said, 'I know about the DSM in March of 1983.'

'How?'

'Because of the VAL Silent Sniper. The battle-axe I told you about is the widow of the guy you took it from. Which is why you reacted to the name. You probably took his dog tags. You've probably still got them.'

There was no surprise. No denial. He just said, 'No, those tags were locked up with the after-action reports, and everything else.'

I said nothing.

Sansom said, 'His name was Grigori Hoth. He was about my age at the time. He seemed competent. His spotter should have heard us coming.'

There was a long silence. Then the situation seemed to hit home and Sansom's shoulders fell. He sighed and said, 'What a way to get found out, right? Medals are supposed to be rewards, not penalties.'

I didn't reply.

He asked, 'What are you going to do?'

I said, 'Nothing. I don't care what happened in 1983. And they lied to me. First about Berlin, and they're still lying. They claim to be mother and daughter. But I don't believe them.'

'So who are they?'

'I'm prepared to accept that the older one is for real. She was a Red Army political commissar who lost her husband and her brother in Afghanistan.'

'Her brother?'

'The spotter.'

'But the younger woman is posing?'

'As a billionaire expatriate widow from London.'

'But? What is she really?'

'I think she's a journalist. She's got the right kind of enquiring mind. She's a hell of a storyteller. But she talks too much.'

'For example?'

'She made out that the political commissars were in the trenches. She claims she was conceived on a rock floor under a Red Army greatcoat. Commissars stayed well away from the action. They clustered together back at HQ, writing pamphlets.'

'And you know this how?'

'You know how I know it. We expected to fight a land war with them in Europe. We expected to win. We expected to take millions of them prisoner. MPs were trained to handle them all. The 110th was going to direct operations. We were taught more about the Red Army than we were about the US Army. Certainly we were told exactly where to find the commissars. We were under orders to execute them all immediately.'

'What kind of journalist?'

'Television, probably.'

'What country?'

'Ukraine.'

'What angle?'

'Investigative, historical, with a little human interest.'

'Why? What's the message? They want to embarrass us now?'

'No, I think they want to embarrass the Russians. There's a lot of tension right now between Russia and Ukraine. I think they're saying that big bad Moscow shouldn't have put the poor helpless Ukrainians in harm's way.'

'So why haven't we seen the story already?'

I said, 'They're looking for confirmation.'

'Are they going to get confirmation?'

'Not from you, presumably. And no one else knows anything for sure. Susan Mark didn't live long enough to say yea or nay. So the lid is back on. I advised them to forget it and head home.'

Sansom nodded. Then he got a sheepish look on his face and asked, 'So what do you think of me now?'

'I think you should have shot them in the head.'

He paused and said, 'We had no silenced weapons.'

'You did. You had just taken one from them.'

'Rules of engagement.'

'You should have ignored them. The Red Army didn't travel with forensics labs. They would have had no idea who shot who.'

'So what do you think of me?'

'I think you shouldn't have handed them over. That was going to be the point of the story, on Ukrainian TV. Get the old woman next to you and let her ask you why.'

Sansom shrugged. 'I wish she could. Because the truth is, we didn't hand them over. We turned them loose. It was a calculated risk. They'd lost their rifle. Everyone would have assumed that the mujahideen had taken it. Which was a major disgrace. It was clear that they were very scared of their officers and their political commissars. So they would have been falling over themselves to tell the truth, that it was Americans, not Afghans. But the truth would have sounded like a pathetic excuse. It would have been discounted immediately. So I felt it was safe enough to let them go.'

I said, 'So what happened?'

Sansom said, 'I guess they were too scared to go back. I guess they just wandered, until the tribespeople found them. Grigori Hoth was married to a political commissar. He was scared of her. And that's what killed him.'

I said nothing.

He said, 'Not that I expect anyone to believe me. You're right about tension between Russia and Ukraine. But there's tension between Russia and ourselves, too. Right now. If the Korengal part of the story gets out, things could blow up big.'

Sansom's desk phone rang. It was his receptionist. I could hear her voice through the earpiece. Sansom hung up and said, 'I have to go. I'll call a page to see you out.' He walked out of the room. He left me all alone, sitting in my chair, with the door open. Springfield had gone, too. No page showed up.

After an interval I headed over to the wall behind the desk. I studied the pictures. I counted faces I knew. Four presidents, nine politicians, five athletes, two actors, Donald Rumsfeld, Saddam Hussein, Elspeth and Springfield.

Plus someone else.

In all of the election-victory pictures, right next to Sansom, was a guy smiling widely. Sansom's chief of staff, presumably.

He was grinning, but his eyes were cold. They had a calculating shrewdness in them. They reminded me of a ballplayer's eyes.

I knew who had been sitting in Sansom's visitor chair.

I knew Sansom's chief of staff. I had seen him before. I had seen him wearing chinos and a golf shirt, riding the 6 train late at night in New York City.

Then a page bustled in and two minutes later I was back on Independence Avenue. Fourteen minutes after that I was back inside the station, waiting for the next train back to New York. Fifty-eight minutes after that I was on it, leaving town. And at that point I knew everything I was ever going to know. But I didn't know that I knew. Not then.

Chapter Six

The train rolled into Penn and I got a late dinner in a place across the street from where I had got breakfast. Then I walked to the 14th Precinct. The night watch had started. Theresa Lee and her partner Docherty were in place. The squad room was quiet, like all the air had been sucked out of it. Like there had been bad news.

I headed to the back of the room. Docherty was on the phone. Theresa Lee looked up as I approached and said, 'I'm not in the mood.'

'For what?'

'Susan Mark.' She paused and sighed. 'What have you got?'

'I know who the fifth passenger was.'

'There were only four passengers.'

'And the earth is flat and the moon is made of cheese.'

'Did this alleged fifth passenger commit a crime somewhere between 30th Street and 45th?'

'No,' I said.

'Then the file stays closed.'

Docherty put his phone down and glanced at his partner.

I asked, 'What happened?'

Lee said, 'Multiple homicide over in the 17th. A nasty one. Four guys under the FDR Drive, beaten and killed.'

'With hammers,' Docherty said. 'From the Home Depot on 23rd Street. Just purchased. Found at the scene.'

I asked, 'Who were the four guys?'

'No one knows,' Docherty said. 'That seems to have been the point of the hammers. Their faces are pulped, their teeth are smashed out and their fingertips are ruined.'

'Old, young, black, white?'

'White,' Docherty said. 'Not old. In suits. They had phoney business cards in their pockets.'

Docherty's desk phone rang and he picked it up. I said to Lee, 'Now you're going to have to reopen the file.'

She asked, 'Why?'

'Because those guys were the local crew that Lila Hoth hired.'

She said, 'What are you? Telepathic?'

'I met with them twice.'

'Nothing says these are the same guys.'

'They gave me one of those phoney business cards.'

'All those crews use phoney business cards.'

'They said Lila Hoth's name.'

'No, some crew said her name. New York is full of private guys. They all look the same and they all do the same stuff.'

'They said John Sansom's name, too. In fact, they were the first place I heard his name.'

'Then maybe they were his crew, not Lila's. Would he have been worried enough to have his own people up here?'

'He had his chief of staff on the train. That's who the fifth passenger was.'

'There you go, then.'

'You're not going to do anything?'

'I'll inform the 17th, for background.'

I said, 'I'm going to the Four Seasons.'

THE LOBBY WAS QUIET. I walked in and rode the elevator to Lila Hoth's floor. Paused outside her suite.

Her door was open an inch.

I pushed the door and listened. No sound inside.

I stepped in. Ahead of me the living room was empty. Empty, as in no people in it. Also empty as in checked-out-of.

The bedrooms were the same. The closets were empty.

I stepped back to the corridor. I rode back to the lobby and walked to the desk. A guy looked up and asked how he could help me. I asked him when exactly the Hoths had checked out.

'The who, sir?' he asked back.

'Lila Hoth and Svetlana Hoth,' I said.

The guy hit a couple of keys on his keyboard. He scrolled up and down and said, 'I'm sorry, sir, but I can't find a record of any guests under that name.'

I told him the suite number. He hit a couple more keys and he said, 'That suite hasn't been used at all this week.'

I said, 'I was in it last night. It was being used then. I met the occupants today, in the tearoom. There's a signature on a bill.'

The guy called up tearoom bills charged to guest accounts. There was no record of any charge.

Then I heard small sounds behind me. The scuff of soles on carpet, the rattle of drawn breath, the sigh of fabric moving through the air. And the clink of metal. I turned and found myself facing a semicircle of seven men. Four were uniformed NYPD patrolmen. Three were federal agents.

The cops had shotguns.

The feds had something else.

SEVEN MEN. Seven weapons. The police shotguns were Franchi SPAS-12s. From Italy. Probably not standard NYPD issue.

Two of the feds had Glock 17s in their hands. Nine-millimetre automatic pistols from Austria, boxy, reliable.

The fed leader was holding a weapon I had seen before only on television, the National Geographic channel. A wildlife documentary. Gorillas. A bunch of zoological researchers was tracking an adult male silverback. They wanted to put a radio tag in its ear. The creature weighed close to five hundred pounds. They got it down with a dart gun loaded with primate tranquilliser.

That was what the fed leader was pointing at me. A dart gun.

The National Geographic people had taken great pains to reassure their viewers that the procedure was humane. The dart was a tiny feathered cone, with a surgical steel shaft. The tip of the shaft was a sterile ceramic honeycomb laced with anaesthetic. The gorilla had been groggy after eight seconds, and in a coma after twenty. Then it had woken up in perfect health ten hours later. But it had weighed twice what I weigh.

The fed leader was sighting down the barrel of his dart gun and aiming directly at my left thigh. Behind the seven men I could see a paramedic crew in a corner. They had a wheeled gurney ready.

The fed leader shot me. With the dart gun. I heard a blast of compressed gas and felt pain in my thigh.

I looked down. The dart's feathered butt was tight against my trousers. I pulled it out. The shaft was smeared with blood. But the tip was gone and the liquid was already inside me. The seven men in front of me seemed to slide sideways. The edge of the counter hit me on the shoulder. Either it was rising up or I was sliding down. I was trying to count seconds. I wanted to get to nine. I wanted to outlast the silverback.

My ass hit the ground. My vision brightened, full of whirling silver shapes. Then I started a sequence of crazy dreams. Afterwards I realised that the start of the dreams marked the point where I officially lost consciousness, lying on the Four Seasons' lobby floor.

I SURFACED EVENTUALLY. I was on a narrow bed. My wrists and my ankles were fastened to the rails with plastic handcuffs. I was still fully dressed, apart from my shoes. I moved my toes. Then I moved my hips. I could feel my pockets were empty. They had taken my stuff.

I scraped my chin across my shirt. Stubble. Maybe eight hours' worth. The gorilla on the National Geographic channel had slept for ten. Score one for Reacher.

I raised my head again. I was inside a cell, and the cell was inside a room. No window. Bright electric light. A row of three cages made of new spot-welded steel, sitting in a line inside a big old room made of brick. The cells were each about eight feet square and eight feet tall. They were roofed with bars, the same as their sides. They were floored with steel treadplate. The treadplate was folded up at the edges, to make a shallow inch-deep tray. There were no bolts through the floors. The cells were not fixed down.

I was in the centre cage of the three. I had the bed I was strapped to, and a toilet. That was all. The other two cages looked the same. Leading away from each of the cells were recent excavations in the outer room's floor. Narrow trenches, three of them, dug up and smoothed over with new concrete. Sewer lines to the toilets, I guessed, and water lines to the taps.

The other two cages were empty. I was all alone.

In the far corner of the outer room there was a surveillance camera. I guessed there would be microphones, too.

A guy walked in with a hypodermic syringe. Some kind of a medical technician. He looked at me through the bars.

I asked him, 'Is that a lethal dose?'

The guy said, 'No. It's a painkiller. For your leg.'

'My leg is fine. Just back off.'

So he did.

I dropped my head back on the bed. I stared up through the bars at the ceiling and prepared to settle in. But less than a minute later two of the federal agents came in through the wooden door. Not the leader. One of them had a Franchi 12 with him. The other guy had some kind of a tool in his hand and a bunch of thin chains. The guy with the shotgun stepped up close to my bars and poked the barrel through and jammed the muzzle into my throat. The guy with the chains unlocked my gate by spinning a dial left and right. A combination lock. The tool in his hand was some kind of a cutter.

The guy with the chains laid them in place. One would cuff my wrists to my waist, one would chain my ankles, and the third would connect the first two together. Standard-issue prison restraints. I would be able to shuffle along a foot at a time and lift my hands as far as my hips. The guy got the chains fastened, and then he cut off the plastic cuffs. He backed out of the cage and left the gate open.

I guessed I was supposed to slide off the bed and stand up. So I stayed where I was. You have to ration your opponents' victories.

But the two feds had had the same training I'd had. They walked away, and the guy with the chains called back, 'Coffee and muffins through here, any old time you want them.' Which put the onus right back on me, exactly like it was designed to. So I waited just a token interval and then I shuffled out of the cage.

The door led to a room with a large wooden table in the centre. Three chairs on the far side, full of the three feds. One chair on my side. On the table, lined up neatly, was the stuff from my pockets. My roll of cash and a few coins. My old passport. My ATM card. My toothbrush. My MetroCard. Theresa Lee's NYPD business card. The phoney business card that Lila Hoth's local crew had given to me. The computer memory I had bought at Radio Shack, with its pink neoprene sleeve. Plus Leonid's clamshell cell-phone. Nine separate items.

To the left of the table was another door. To the right of the table was a low chest of drawers. On it were napkins and foam cups and a vacuum bottle and a plate with two blueberry muffins. I shuffled over in my socks and poured a cup of coffee. I carried the cup low and two-handed to the table. Sat down. Dipped my head and sipped. The coffee was pretty bad.

The fed leader moved his hand and stopped it behind my passport.

He asked, 'Why is it expired?'

I said, 'Because no one can make time stand still.'

'I meant, why haven't you renewed it?'

'No imminent need.'

'When was the last time you left the country?'

I said, 'I would have talked to you. You didn't need to shoot me with a dart like I had escaped from the zoo.'

'You had been warned many times.'

I said, 'No ID, no names, no charges, no lawyer. Brave new world, right?'

'You got it.'

'Well, good luck with that,' I said.

He asked, 'Where were you born?'

'I was born in West Berlin,' I said.

'And your mother is French?'

'She was French. She's dead.'

'I'm sorry. Are you sure you're an American citizen?'

'What kind of a question is that?'

'You were born overseas to a foreign parent.'

'I was born on a military base. That counts as US sovereign territory. My parents were married. My father was an American citizen. He was a Marine.'

'Can you prove all of that? Whether or not you're a citizen could affect what happens to you next.'

'How much patience I have will affect what happens to me next.'

The guy on the left stood and walked into the third room. I glimpsed desks, no people. The door closed behind him.

The main guy asked, 'Was your mother Algerian?'

I said, 'I just got through telling you she was French.'

'Was she a Muslim?'

'Why do you want to know?'

'I'm making enquiries.'

The guy used his index finger to push the computer memory an inch towards me. He said, 'You concealed this from us when we searched you. Susan Mark gave it to you on the train.'

'Susan Mark gave me nothing. I bought that at Radio Shack.'

The guy shrugged and pulled the stick back, and then moved the phoney business card and Leonid's cellphone both forward an inch. He said, 'You've been working for Lila Hoth. The card proves you were in communication with the crew she hired, and your phone proves she called you at least six times. The Four Seasons' number is in the memory.'

'It's not my phone.'

'We found it in your pocket.'

'Lila Hoth didn't stay at the Four Seasons, according to them.'

'Only because we told them to cooperate.'

'I wasn't working for her.'

'Your phone proves that you were. Where is Lila Hoth now?'

'Don't you know? I assumed you scooped her up when she checked out.'

The guy said nothing.

'You searched her room. I assumed you were watching her.'

The guy said nothing.

'You missed her, right? Terrific. A foreign national with some kind of weird Pentagon involvement, and you let her go?'

'It's a setback,' the guy said. He seemed embarrassed.

I asked, 'Who is she?'

'The most dangerous person you ever met.'

'She didn't look it.'

'That's why.'

I said, 'I have no idea where she is.'

The guy moved the phoney business card and the cellphone back and advanced Theresa Lee's card. 'How much does Lee know?'

'What does it matter?'

'We have a fairly simple sequence of tasks in front of us. We need to find the Hoths, we need to recover the real memory stick, but above all we need to contain the leak. So we need to know how far it has spread. So we need to know who knows what.'

'Nobody knows anything. Least of all me.'

'We're all on the same side here.'

'Doesn't feel that way to me.'

'You need to take this seriously.'

'Believe me, I am. I don't know who knows what.'

I heard the door on my left open again. The leader nodded some kind of consent. I turned and saw the guy from the left-hand chair. He had a gun in his hand. The dart gun. He raised it and fired. The dart caught me high in the upper arm.

I WOKE UP AGAIN, but I didn't open my eyes. I felt like the clock in my head was back on track, and I wanted to let it calibrate undisturbed. Right then it was showing six o'clock in the evening. Which meant I had been out about another eight hours. I was very hungry and very thirsty. My arm hurt the same way my leg had. I still had no shoes. But my wrists and my ankles were no longer fastened to the rails of the bed.

I opened my eyes and discovered two things. One: Theresa Lee was in the cage to my right. Two: Jacob Mark was in the cage to my left. Both of them were cops. Neither one had shoes on.

That was when I started to worry.

They were both looking at me. Lee was wearing blue jeans and a white shirt. Jake was wearing a police officer's uniform, minus the belt, the gun, the radio and the shoes. I sat up on my bed and swung my feet to the floor. Then I stood up and stepped over to the sink and drank from the tap. New York City, for sure. I recognised the taste of the water. I looked at Theresa Lee and asked her, 'Do you know exactly where we are?'

She said, 'We have to assume this place is wired for sound.'

'I'm sure it is. But they already know where we are.'

Lee said nothing. She looked uneasy.

'What's on your mind?' I asked her.

'Those clubs on Bleecker are nearer Sixth Avenue than Broadway. You had the A train right there. Or the B or the C or the D. So why were you on the 6 train at all?'

'I had nowhere to go. I came out of a bar and turned left and walked. I can't explain it any better than that.'

She said, 'You have no bags. I never saw a homeless person with nothing. Most of them haul more stuff around than I own. They use shopping carts.'

'I'm different. And I'm not a homeless person. Not like them.'

She said nothing.

I asked, 'Were you blindfolded when they brought you here?'

She looked at me for a long moment and then she shook her head and sighed. She said, 'We're in a closed firehouse in Greenwich Village. On West 3rd. Street level and above is disused. We're in the basement.'

'Do you know exactly who these guys are?'

'They didn't show ID. Not today, and not that first night either, when they came to talk to you at the precinct.'

'But?'

'Not showing ID can be the same thing as showing it, if you're the only bunch that never does. We've heard some stories.'

'So who are they?'

'They work directly for the Secretary of Defense.'

'That figures,' I said. 'The Secretary of Defense is usually the dumbest guy in the government.'

Lee glanced up at the camera, as if I had insulted it. She asked, 'Do you know what they want?'

'Some of it.'

'Don't tell us. But is it big enough for the White House?'

'Potentially, I guess. When did they come for you?'

'This afternoon. Two o'clock. I was asleep.'

'Did they have the NYPD with them?'

Lee nodded, and hurt showed in her eyes.

I asked, 'Did you know the patrolmen?'

She shook her head. 'Hotshot counterterrorism guys. They write their own rules and keep themselves separate. They ride around in special cars all day long. Fake taxis, sometimes. One in the front, two in the back. Big circles, up on Tenth, down on Second.'

'What time is it now? About six after six?'

She looked at her watch, and looked surprised. 'Dead on.'

I turned. 'Jake?' I said. 'What about you?'

'I've been here since noon.'

'Any word from Peter?'

'Nothing.'

'I'm sorry. Have these guys talked to you yet?'

Both of them shook their heads.

I asked, 'Are you worried?'

Both of them nodded. Lee asked, 'Are you?'

'I'm sleeping well,' I said. 'But I think that's because of the tranquillisers.'

AT SIX THIRTY they brought us food. Plus bottles of water. I drank my water first and refilled the bottle from the tap.

At seven o'clock they took Jacob Mark away for questioning. No restraints. Theresa Lee and I didn't talk much. Mostly I reran conversations in my head. John Sansom, Lila Hoth, the guys in the next room. There were strange half-comments, little off-key implications. I didn't know what any of them meant. But knowing that they were there was useful in itself.

At seven thirty they brought Jacob Mark back and took Theresa Lee away. No restraints. Jake sat on his bed with his back to the camera. I looked at him. An enquiry. He rolled his eyes. Then he kept his hands in his lap, out of sight of the camera, and made a gun with his right thumb and forefinger. He tapped his thigh and looked at mine. I nodded. The dart gun. He put two fingers down between his knees and held a third in front and to the left. I nodded again. Two guys behind the table, and the third to the left with the gun. On guard. I massaged my temples and while my hands were still up I mouthed, 'Where are our shoes?' Jake mouthed back, 'I don't know.' After that we sat in silence.

At eight o'clock they brought Theresa Lee back and took me away again.

NO RESTRAINTS. Clearly they thought I was afraid of the dart gun. Which I was, to a degree. I didn't want to waste any more time.

The room was populated exactly as Jacob Mark had semaphored it. My possessions were on the table. Nine items. Which was good, because I needed to take at least seven of them with me.

The guy in the centre chair said, 'Sit down, Mr Reacher.'

I moved towards my chair and felt all three of them relax. They were into their third straight hour of interrogation. And interrogation is heavy work. So the three guys were tired enough to have lost their edge. As soon as I headed for my chair, they thought their troubles were over. They were wrong.

Half a step short of my destination I raised my foot to the edge of the table and straightened my leg and shoved. Shoved, not kicked, because I had no shoes on. The table hit the two seated guys in the stomach and pinned them against their chair backs. I was already moving to my left. I came up from a crouch at the third guy and tore the dart gun up and out of his hands and kneed him hard in the groin. He gave up on the gun and folded forwards and I high-stepped and changed feet and kneed him in the face. Like a folk dance from Ireland. I levelled the gun and shot the main guy in the chest. Then I went over the table and battered the other guy in the head with the dart gun's butt, until he stopped moving.

Four noisy, violent seconds. The table, the dart gun, the main guy, the second guy. Smooth and easy. The two guys I had hit were unconscious. The main guy was on his way under, chemically assisted.

Then I turned and watched the door to the third room. But the door stayed closed. I checked under the third guy's jacket. No Glock. No firearms in any closed room with a prisoner present. I checked the other two guys. Same result.

I checked pockets. All empty.

I picked up the dart gun again. Moved to the third room's door.

The third room was unoccupied.

It had another door. I crossed to it and eased it open.

A stairwell. I closed the door again and checked the office furniture.

Three desks, five cabinets, four lockers, all made of steel, all locked. With combination locks.

I stood still for a long moment I was disappointed about the locks. I wanted to find their stores and reload the dart gun and shoot the other two agents with it. And I wanted my shoes.

I padded back to the cells. Jacob Mark and Theresa Lee looked up, looked away, looked back. Classic double takes.

Lee asked, 'What happened?'

I said, 'They fell asleep.'

'So now you're really in trouble.'

I checked the locks on the cell gates. The knobs turned both ways. I spun them. Didn't feel any tumblers falling.

I asked, 'Do you want me to get you out?'

Lee said, 'Why wouldn't I?'

'Because then you'd really be in trouble. Jake? What about you?'

'How can you get us out?'

'It will be difficult. So I need to know whether to start.'

Jake said, 'OK, I want out.'

I looked at Theresa Lee. 'I was telling Sansom about how we studied the Red Army. You know what they were most afraid of? Not us. They were most afraid of their own people. Their worst torment was spending their whole lives proving their own innocence, over and over again.'

Lee nodded. 'I want out,' she said.

'OK,' I said. I estimated dimensions and weights by eye.

'Sit tight,' I said. 'I'll be back in less than an hour.'

FIRST STOP was the next room. The three federal agents were still out cold. The main guy would stay that way for eight solid hours. Or maybe much longer, because his body mass was less than two-thirds of mine. The other two would be waking up earlier. So I ducked through to the anteroom and tore all of the computer cords out of the walls and used them to truss the two guys up. I peeled my socks off and used them for a gag on the guy with the head wound.

I reloaded my pockets with my possessions from the table and then I left the building.

The staircase led up to the first floor and came out in the back of what had once been the place where the fire trucks parked. The personnel door was fitted with a new lock, but it was designed to keep people out, not in. On the inside was just a simple lever. On the outside was a combination dial. I found a heavy brass hose coupler and used it to wedge the door open a crack. I left it that way for my return and stepped out to an alley, and two paces later I was on the West 3rd Street sidewalk.

Nobody looked at my bare feet. I flagged a cab and it took me to the Home Depot on 23rd Street. The store was getting ready to close up, but they let me in. I found a five-foot crowbar, thick and strong. The trip back to the tills took me through the gardening section and I decided to pick up a pair of rubber gardening clogs. They were ugly, but better than literally nothing. I paid with my ATM card, which would leave a computer trail, but there was no reason to conceal the fact that I was buying tools. That purchase was about to become obvious in other ways.

Within a minute I was on my way back south in a cab. I got out on 3rd, near, but not right next to, the firehouse.

Ten feet ahead I saw the medical tech step into the alley. The guy looked clean and rested. Staff rotation, I figured. The agents held the fort all day, and then the medical guy took over at night.

I put the crowbar in my left hand and made it to the personnel door before the guy was all the way through it. I shoved him inside. He went down on one knee. I held him at arm's length and eased the brass coupler aside with my toe and let the door close. He raised his hands in a gesture of surrender. Then we got to the second room and he saw the three guys on the floor and sensed what was in store for him. He looked at me, a huge, determined man in ludicrous shoes, holding a big metal bar.

I asked him, 'Do you know the combinations for the cells?'

He said, 'No.'

'Where is your equipment?'

'In my locker.'

'Show me,' I said. 'Open it.'

We went back to the anteroom and he led me to a locker and spun the combination dial.

His locker had a bunch of shelves inside, piled high with all kinds of medical stuff. And a box of wrapped darts.

I asked, 'What exactly is in the darts?'

The guy said, 'Local anaesthetic to help the wound site, plus barbiturate.'

'How much barbiturate? Enough for a gorilla?'

'Reduced dose. Calculated for a normal human.'

I asked him, 'Are there side effects?'

'None.'

'You sure? You know why I'm asking, right?'

The guy nodded. He knew why I was asking. I found the gun and loaded it.

I said, 'You want to lie down on the floor? You know, to save bumping your head.'

The guy got down on the floor.

I asked him, 'Any preference as to where? Arm? Leg?'

He said, 'It works best into muscle mass.'

'So roll over.' He rolled over and I shot him in the ass.

I reloaded the thing twice more and put darts into the two agents that were liable to wake up. Which gave me at least an eight-hour margin, unless there were other unanticipated arrivals. Or unless the agents were supposed to call in with status checks every hour. I carried the crowbar through to the cell block.

I stepped round to the back of Lee's cell and jammed the flat end of the crowbar under the bottom of the structure. Then I leaned my weight on the bar and felt the whole thing move, just a little.

Lee said, 'This thing is a self-contained freestanding cube. You might tip it over, but I'll still be inside.'

I said, 'Actually it's not freestanding.'

'It's not bolted to the floor.'

'It's clamped down by the sewer connection. Under the toilet. If I tip it up and the sewer connection holds, then the floor will tear off, and you can crawl out.'

'Go for it.'

Two rooms away I heard a telephone start to ring.

I knelt down and eased the tip of the crowbar under the bottom horizontal rail of the cell. Then I kicked it sideways a little until it was directly below one of the upside-down T-welds, where the force would be carried upwards through one of the vertical bars.

Two rooms away the telephone stopped ringing.

I looked at Lee and said, 'Stand on the toilet seat.'

She climbed up and balanced. I took up all the slack in the crowbar and then leaned down hard and bounced, once, twice, three times. A bright bead of metal pinged loose and skittered away.

'That was a spot,' Lee called. 'As in spot-weld.'

I moved the crowbar and found a similar position twelve inches to the left. Wedged the bar tight, took up the slack and bounced. Same results.

A second phone started to ring. A different tone.

I stood back. Moved the crowbar again. Repeated the procedure, and was rewarded with another broken weld. Three down, many more to go. But now I had approximate hand-holds in the bottom rail, where the crowbar had forced shallow U-shaped bends into the metal. I squatted facing the cell and shoved my hands palms-up into the holds.

Two rooms away the second telephone stopped ringing.

And a third started.

I heaved upwards. I got the side of the cell about a foot off the ground. The treadplate floor shrieked and bent like paper. But the welds held. I looked up at Lee and mouthed, 'Jump.' She jumped high off the toilet and smashed her bare feet down together right where two welds were under pressure. The welds broke immediately and the floor bent down into a radical V-shaped chute. Like a mouth. About a foot wide and a foot deep. Good, but not good enough.

All three phones started to ring simultaneously.

After that it was just a question of repeating the triple procedures over and over again. It took us eight minutes to get the job done. Lee came out on her back, feet first, like a limbo dancer. Then she stood up and hugged me hard.

I repeated the whole procedure for Jacob Mark.

Two rooms away phones rang and stopped.

WE GOT OUT FAST. Theresa Lee took the lead agent's shoes. They were big on her, but not much. Jacob Mark took the medical technician's whole outfit. He figured that an incomplete out-of-town cop's uniform would be conspicuous on the street, and he was probably right.

Then we headed out to the 3rd Street sidewalk and hustled straight for Sixth Avenue.

We crossed Sixth and then found refuge on Cornelia Street, which was dark and quiet, except for diners at sidewalk café tables. We headed up the street and took stock. Lee and Jake had nothing. All their stuff was locked in the firehouse basement. I had what I'd reclaimed from the table, the important components of which were my cash, my ATM card, my MetroCard and Leonid's cellphone. The cash amounted to forty-three dollars. The MetroCard had four rides left on it. Leonid's cell was almost out of battery. We agreed it was certain that my ATM number and Leonid's phone number were already flagged up in various computer systems. But I wasn't worried. If we escaped from West 3rd and days later withdrew cash in Oklahoma City, then that data would be significant. If we withdrew cash immediately a couple of blocks from the firehouse, it told them nothing they didn't already know.

So we found an ATM and I withdrew all the cash I could, which was three hundred bucks.

We moved on again and Lee bought an emergency cellphone charger. She plugged it into Leonid's phone and called Docherty, her partner. It was ten past ten, and he would be getting ready for work. He didn't pick up. Lee left a message and then switched off the phone. She said cellphones had GPS chips in them. I didn't know that. She said the way to use a cell on the run was to keep it switched off except for brief moments just before leaving one location and moving on to the next. That way the GPS trackers were always one step behind.

So we moved on again. We found a noisy bistro in the heart of NYU territory. The place was dark and packed with undergraduates. I was hungry and still dehydrated. I drank whole glasses of tap water and ordered a kind of shake made of yoghurt and fruit. Plus a burger and coffee. Jake and Lee said they were too shaken to eat. Then Lee said, 'You better tell us what exactly is going on.'

I said, 'I thought you didn't want to know.'

'We just crossed that line.'

'They didn't show ID. You were entitled to assume the detention was illegal. In which case busting out wasn't a crime.'

She shook her head. 'I knew who they were.'

I looked at Jake, to see whether he wanted to be included. He shrugged, as if to say in for a penny, in for a pound. I told them what I knew. March of 1983, Sansom, the Korengal Valley. All the details, and implications.

Jake said, 'So how big of a deal do you think this is?'

'Huge,' Lee said. 'For us, anyway. Because overall it's still small. Which is ironic, right? See what I mean? If three thousand people knew, there's not much anyone could do about it. But right now only the three of us know. And three is a small number. Small enough to be contained. They can make three people disappear without anyone noticing.'

'How?'

'It happens, believe me. Who's going to pay attention? You're not married. Me neither.' She looked at me. 'Reacher, are you married?'

I shook my head.

She paused a second. 'No one left behind to ask questions.'

Jake said, 'This is insane. We have rights.'

'We used to.'

Jake said nothing in reply to that. I finished my coffee. Lee called for the bill and waited until I had paid it, and then she turned Leonid's phone back on. There was a text message waiting.

'It's from Docherty,' she said.

She read and scrolled. It was a long message. And it was full of bad news, according to Lee's face. She shut it down and handed it back to me. 'You were right. The dead guys under the FDR Drive were Lila Hoth's crew. The 17th broke into their offices and found billing records made out to Lila Hoth, care of the Four Seasons Hotel. But here's the thing. Those billing records go back three months, not three days. And Homeland Security has no record of two women called Hoth ever entering the country. And Susan Mark never called London.'

Chapter Seven

Use the phone and move on immediately was the rule. We took Broadway north. We hustled as far as Astor Place and then burned three of my four remaining MetroCard rides on the 6 train north. Where it all began. It was eleven in the evening. We sat together on one of the eight-person benches. Jake asked, 'So which is it? Are the Hoths phoney or is the government already covering its ass by erasing data?'

I said, 'The Hoths are phoney.'

'You think or you know?'

'It was too easy at Penn station. Leonid let me see him. Then he let me hit him. Because I was supposed to take the phone and find out about the Four Seasons. They manipulated me. There are layers upon layers here. They lured me to the hotel and tried a sweet, easy approach. They even had a back-up plan, which was coming to the precinct house and making the missing-persons report. Either way I would have showed up eventually.'

'What do they want from you?'

'Susan's information.'

'Which was what?'

'I don't know.'

'Who are they?'

'Not journalists,' I said. 'I was wrong about that.'

'Where are they now? They bailed out of the hotel.'

'They always had somewhere else. I don't know where they are now. Here in the city, probably. Maybe a town house. Because they have a crew with them. Bad people. Those private guys were right. How bad, they found out the hard way. With the hammers.'

The train stopped at 23rd Street. The doors opened. No one got on. No one got off. Theresa Lee stared at the floor. Jacob Mark looked across her at me and said, 'If Homeland Security can't even track Lila Hoth into the country, then they also can't tell if she went to California. Which means it could have been her with Peter.'

'Yes,' I said. 'It could have been.'

The doors closed. The train moved on.

Theresa Lee looked up from the floor and turned to me. 'What happened to those four guys was our fault. With the hammers. Your fault, specifically. You told Lila you knew about them. You turned them into a loose end.'

I said, 'Thanks for pointing that out.'

You tipped her over the edge. Your fault, specifically.

We got out at 33rd Street. Park Avenue was busy. Two cop cars came past in the first minute. We doubled back south and took a quiet cross street towards Madison. I was feeling pretty good. I had spent sixteen hours asleep. But Lee and Jake looked beat. They had nowhere to go and weren't used to it. Obviously they couldn't go home.

I liked the look of the block we were on. New York has hundreds of micro-neighbourhoods. Park and Madison are slightly seedy in parts. The cross streets are a little down at heel. We hid out under sidewalk scaffolding until the clock passed midnight and then we snaked back and forth until we found the right kind of hotel. It looked a little run-down. Smaller than I would have liked.

But it was a decent target for the fifty-dollar trick.

In the end we had to pay seventy-five, probably because the night porter suspected we had a sexual threesome in mind. The room he gave us was small, in the back of the building, and had twin beds.

Lee said, 'We can't live like this indefinitely.'

'We can if we want to,' I said. 'I've lived like this for ten years.'

'OK, a normal person can't live like this indefinitely. We need help. This problem isn't going to go away.'

'So who the hell will help us?' Jake asked.

'Sansom,' I said. 'He's got a lot to lose. We can use that.' I took Leonid's phone out of my pocket and dropped it on the bed next to Theresa Lee. 'Call Sansom's office and demand to speak with him personally. Tell him you're a police officer in New York and that you're with me. Tell him we know his guy was on the train. Then tell him we know the DSM wasn't for the VAL rifle. Tell him we know there's more.'

Lee asked, 'What makes you think there's more?'

I said, 'Sansom won four medals, not just one. He must have done all kinds of things.'

'Like what?'

'Whatever needed doing. Think about it. Stumbling into a Soviet sniper team in the dark was a totally random chance. Would they have sent an ace like Sansom walking around in the hills, hoping for the best? There must have been something else going on.'

'That's pretty vague.'

'I spoke to Sansom in DC. He seemed sour about the whole thing. Gloomy, and kind of troubled.'

'It's election season.'

'But grabbing up the rifle was kind of cool, wasn't it? Nothing to be ashamed of. So his reaction was wrong.'

'Still vague.'

'He knew the sniper's name. I figured he had the dog tags as souvenirs. He said no, those tags were locked up with the after-action reports and everything else. It was like a slip of the tongue. *And everything else*? What did that mean?'

Lee said nothing.

I said, 'We talked about the fate of the sniper and the spotter. Sansom said he had no silenced weapons. Which was like another slip of the tongue. Delta would never set up for clandestine night-time incursions without silenced weapons. Which suggests that the VAL episode was an accidental by-product of something else.'

I continued, 'He's worried about Russia, or the Russian Federation. He said things could blow up big, if the Korengal part of the story gets out. You hear that? The Korengal *part of* the story? It was effectively an admission that there's more.'

Jacob Mark asked, 'What kind of more?'

'I don't know. But whatever it is, it's information-intensive. Right from the start Lila Hoth was looking for a USB memory stick. And the feds assume there's one out there somewhere. They said their task is to recover the real memory stick. Real, because they assumed mine was a decoy.'

'But Susan didn't have anything with her.'

'True. But everybody assumes she did.'

'What kind of information?'

'I have no idea. Except that Springfield, Sansom's security guy, was uptight. He said, you can't afford to turn over the wrong rock.'

'So?'

'What happens when you turn over a rock?'

'Things crawl out.'

'Exactly. Present tense. This is about things that are alive today.'

I saw Theresa Lee thinking it through. She said, 'Sansom's kind of careless, isn't he? He made some slips of the tongue.'

'I'm not so sure. He read my record. I think maybe he was looking for help. Maybe he was dropping a couple of breadcrumbs, and waiting to see if I would follow them.'

'Because?'

'Because he wants the lid back on.'

'Doesn't he trust Springfield?'

'With his life. But Springfield is just one guy.'

'So he's bound to help us.'

'Not bound,' I said. 'But he might be inclined. Which is why I want you to call him. I'll meet you at ten, in Madison Square Park.'

'Where are you going?'

'To look for Lila Hoth. I'm sure they're out looking for me.'

'I'm sure the cops are out looking for you, too. And the Defense Department, and the FBI.'

'Busy night all round.'

NEW YORK CITY. One o'clock in the morning. The best place and the worst place in the world to be hunted. There were still people around. I chose 30th Street and crossed to Park and then Lex. I was never trained in the art of staying invisible. But I get by.

I paid a lot of attention to cars. No way to find an individual in New York City except by cruising the streets. The NYPD's cruisers were easy to spot. Every time I saw one coming I paused in the nearest doorway and laid myself down. Just another homeless guy. Unmarked cop cars were harder to spot. But budgets restrict choice to a specific handful of makes and models. And they're dirty, they sag.

Except for unmarked federal cars. Same makes, same models, but often new and clean and polished.

I figured Lila Hoth's crew would have rentals, new and clean. I took all reasonable precautions to stay out of law enforcement's way, and I made all reasonable efforts to let Hoth's people see me.

I walked for half an hour, but nothing happened.

Until I looped round to 22nd and Broadway.

I saw in the corner of my eye a black Crown Vic come through the 23rd Street light. Clean, shiny, the spike of needle antennas on the trunk lid shown up by the headlights of a car thirty yards behind it. It slowed to a walk.

Broadway is double-wide on that block. Six lanes, all headed south. I was on the left-hand sidewalk. Next to me, an apartment house. On my right, six lanes away, the Flatiron Building.

Dead ahead, a subway entrance.

The Crown Vic stopped in the second of the six lanes. Headlights showed two guys silhouetted in the front seats.

I sat down on a low brick wall that ran in front of the apartment house. Next to the kerb was a subway grate. The subway entrance ten feet from me was the south end of the 23rd Street station. The N, the R and the W trains. The uptown platform. I made a bet with myself that it was a HEET entrance. A high entry–exit turnstile. Not a money wager. Something far more important. Life, liberty and the pursuit of happiness.

At one thirty in the morning the subway was well into its night-time hours. Twenty-minute gaps between trains. I heard no rumbling below. There was no rush of air.

The Crown Vic turned sharply across four lanes and stopped on the kerb alongside me. The two guys stayed inside. It was a federal car, for sure. The sidewalk wasn't busy, but it wasn't deserted.

The two guys got out of their car. The passenger stood with the driver in the gutter by the Crown Vic's hood, maybe twenty feet away across the sidewalk. They had their shields clipped on their breast pockets. FBI, I guessed. The passenger called, 'Federal agents.' I didn't respond.

The subway grates stayed still and silent.

The passenger called, 'Jack Reacher?'

I didn't answer. When all else fails, play dumb.

My shoes were rubber, and much less tight and firm than I am used to. But I felt the first faint subway rumble through them. A train, either starting downtown from 28th Street, or heading uptown from 14th. A downtown train was no good. I was on the wrong side of Broadway. An uptown train was what I wanted.

The passenger called, 'Keep your hands where I can see them.'

I put one hand in my pocket. Partly to locate my MetroCard, and partly to see what would happen next. Agents are instructed to draw their weapons only in dire emergencies. There were innocent people all around.

The two agents drew their weapons. Glock pistols.

The passenger called, 'Don't move.'

The trash on the subway grates stirred. An uptown train. I stood up and walked to the head of the stairs. I went down one step at a time. Behind me I heard the agents coming after me. I turned my MetroCard in my pocket and pulled it out facing the right way round.

The fare control was high. Floor-to-ceiling bars, like a jail cell. There were two turnstiles. Both were narrow and full height. No need for a manned booth. I slid my card in and the last credit on it lit up the go light green and I pushed on through. Behind me the agents came to a dead stop. A regular turnstile, they would have jumped over. But the HEET entrance took away that option. And they weren't carrying MetroCards. They stood helplessly behind the bars. The first three cars were already round the curve. The train groaned and stopped and I stepped on without even breaking stride. The doors closed and the train bore me away.

I WAS ON AN R TRAIN. The R train follows Broadway to Times Square and then straightens a little until 57th Street and Seventh Avenue, where it hangs a tight right and stops at 59th and Fifth and then 60th and Lex before heading on under the river and east to Queens. I didn't want to go to Queens. I felt in my gut that the action lay in Manhattan, for sure. On the East Side, probably, and not far from 57th Street. Lila Hoth had used the Four Seasons as a decoy. Which put her real base somewhere close by. Not adjacent, but comfortably proximate.

And her real base was a town house. Because she had a crew with her, and they had to be able to come and go undetected.

I stayed on the train through Times Square. I got out at 59th and Fifth. I came up from under ground and saw no one looking for me.

I was three blocks west of where Susan Mark would have come up out of the 6 train, back at the beginning.

And right then I understood that Susan Mark had never been headed to the Four Seasons Hotel. Not dressed in black and ready for combat. Susan had been headed directly to the secret location, which had to be on a dark, discreet cross street. But which still had to be in the original sixty-eight-block box, between 42nd Street and 59th, between Fifth Avenue and Third.

I headed east across Fifth Avenue and resumed my aimless walking, watching for cars, staying in the shadows and prepared either to run or to fight, depending on who found me first.

I crossed Madison Avenue and headed for Park. Now I was directly behind the Four Seasons, which was two blocks due south. The street was mostly flagship retail stores and boutiques, all closed up. I turned south on Park and then east again on 58th. Some town houses. Some of them were consulates belonging to small nations. Some of them were offices for foundations and small corporations. Some of them were residential, but broken up into multiple apartments. All were fast asleep behind locked doors.

I strolled on, west and east, north and south, 58th, 57th, 56th, Lexington, Third, Second. Nothing jumped out at me.

It was close to three o'clock, and I got set to head west again. But twenty feet ahead of me a gold Chevy Impala jammed to a stop and Leonid climbed out of the back.

LEONID STOOD ON THE KERB and the car took off and then stopped again twenty feet behind me. The driver got out. Good moves. Leonid looked different. Still tall, still thin, but now he was in black shoes, black trousers and a black hooded sweatshirt. He looked alert and very dangerous. He looked like an ex-soldier.

I backed up against the wall of the building next to me so that I could watch both guys at once. The other guy was on my right, a squat man in his thirties. He looked Middle Eastern. Dark hair. He was dressed in cheap black sweats. A word lodged in my mind: disposable.

The guy took a step towards me. Leonid did the same.

Two choices, as always: fight or flight. We were on 56th Street's southern sidewalk. I could have run straight across the road and tried to get away. But Leonid and his pal were probably faster than me. So I stayed where I was.

On my left, Leonid took another step closer.

On my right, the short guy did the same thing.

Whatever the army had failed to teach me about staying out of sight, they had made up for by teaching me a lot about fighting. I was like a lot of military children. We had lived all over the world. We learned fighting from the locals. Martial arts from the Far East, full-on brawling from the seamier parts of Europe, blades and bottles from the seamier parts of the States. By the age of twelve we had it all boiled down to a kind of composite uninhibited ferocity. *Just do it*, was our motto, well before Nike started making shoes. Those of us who signed up for military careers of our own were offered further tuition. We thought we were tough when we were twelve. At eighteen, we thought we were unbeatable. We weren't. But we were very close to it by twenty-five.

I looked at Leonid and saw brass knuckles on his hand.

Same for the short guy.

Leonid sidestepped. So did the other guy. They were perfecting their angles. I was backed up against a building, which gave me a hundred and eighty degrees of empty space in front of me. Each one of them wanted forty-five degrees of that space on his right and forty-five on his left. That way, if I bolted, they had every exit direction equally covered.

First rule when you're fighting against brass knuckles: don't get hit. Especially not in the head. The best way not to get hit is to pull out a gun and shoot your opponents. But I was unarmed. The next best way is either to keep your opponents far away or crush them real close. Far away, they can swing all night and never connect. Real close, they can't swing at all. The way to keep them far away is to exploit superior reach, if you have it, or use your feet. My reach is spectacular. My instructors in the army were always making puns about it, based on my name. But I was facing two guys, and I wasn't sure if kicking was an option I could add. I had lousy shoes. Rubber gardening clogs.

I braced my right heel against the wall behind me.

I figured they would pile on together. The good news was that they wouldn't be trying to kill me. Lila Hoth wanted things from me. The bad news was that plenty of serious injuries fall short of fatal.

Leonid said, 'You don't have to get hurt. You can just come with us and talk to Lila.' His accent was rough.

I said, 'I'll take a pass. But you don't have to get hurt either. You can just tell Lila you never saw me.'

'But that wouldn't be true.'

'Don't be a slave to the truth, Leonid.'

The upside of a concerted attack by two opponents is that they have to communicate a start signal. I figured Leonid for the main man. The one who speaks first usually is. He would announce the attack. I watched his eyes, very carefully.

I said, 'Are you mad about what happened at the station?'

'I let you hit me. It was necessary. Lila said so.'

I said, 'Tell me about Lila.'

'She's a woman with a job to do.'

'What kind of a job?'

No answer. I watched Leonid. Saw his eyes widen and his head duck in a tiny nod. They came straight for me, together. I pushed off the wall behind me and put my fists against my chest and stuck my elbows out like airplane wings and charged them as hard as they were charging me. We met at a singular point like a collapsing triangle and my elbows caught both of them full in the face. On my right I felt the short guy's upper teeth punch out and on my left I felt Leonid's lower jaw give way.

I spun back and clubbed the short guy with a roundhouse right to the ear. His neck snapped sideways. I squelched back the other way in my lousy footwear and drove my elbow deep into Leonid's gut. I almost popped his spine out of his back. I used the bounce to jump back to the short guy again. I put a low right in his kidney. That spun him towards me. I butted him between the eyes. He went down like a sack. Leonid tapped me on the shoulder with his knuckle-duster. I wound up and dropped him with an uppercut to the jaw. His jaw was already broken. Now it broke a little more.

I took ten seconds to get my breath. Ten more to calm down. Then I hauled both guys across the sidewalk and into a sitting position against the wall where I had been standing. Their hooded sweatshirts stretched as I was hauling on them. Disposable, in case they had got soaked with my blood. Then I dislocated their right elbows. They were both right-handed. No permanent damage.

They had cellphones in their pockets. I took both of them. Both had my picture. There was nothing else. No money. No keys.

I dropped the brass knuckles down a storm drain.

Their car was still idling on the kerb. It had New York plates. No navigation system. Therefore no digital memory with a base location. I found a rental agreement in the door pocket made out to a name I had never heard and a London address I assumed was fake.

Then I stole their car and drove away.

I DROVE SOUTH on Second Avenue and took 50th Street all the way east to the end and dumped the car half a block from the FDR Drive. I hoped the guys from the 17th Precinct would find it and get suspicious and run some tests. If Lila's people had used that Impala to drive away from the hammer attack, then there would be some trace evidence inside.

I wiped the wheel and the gear stick and the door handles with the tail of my shirt. Then I dropped the keys down a grate and walked back to Second and looked for a cab. I was mindful of Theresa Lee's information: fake taxis, one guy in the front, two in the back. I waited for a cab that was empty apart from its driver and I flagged it down. I got out at Union Square and sat on a bench in the dark. At four o'clock I fell asleep.

At five o'clock one of the captured phones vibrated.

I woke up and fumbled the phone out of my pocket. The small window said: *Unknown caller*. I opened it up and said, 'Hello.'

Lila Hoth said, 'So, you decided to declare war.'

I said, 'Who are you exactly?'

'I'm your worst nightmare. As of about two hours ago. And you still have something that belongs to me.'

'So come and get it. Better still, send some more of your guys. Give me some more light exercise.'

She asked, 'Where are you?'

'Right outside your house.'

There was a pause. 'No, you're not.'

'Correct,' I said. 'But you just confirmed that you're living in a house. And that you're at a window.'

'Tell me where you are.'

'Close to you,' I said. 'Third Avenue and 56th Street.'

She started to reply, and then she stopped herself. Just a little *th* sound. Like, *that's not close to me*.

'Last chance,' she said. 'I want my property.' Her voice softened. 'We can make arrangements. Just leave it somewhere safe, and tell me where. I'll have it picked up. You could even get paid.'

'I'm not looking for work.'

'Are you looking to stay alive?'

'I'm not afraid of you, Lila.'

'That's what Peter Molina said.'

'Where is he?'

'Right here with us.'

'Alive? He left a message with his coach.'

'Or maybe I played a tape he made before he died. Maybe he told me his coach never answers the phone at dinner time.'

I asked, 'How long have you known Peter Molina?'

'Since I picked him up in the bar.'

'Is he still alive?'

'Come over and find out.'

I said, 'You're on borrowed time, Lila. You killed four Americans in New York. No one is going to ignore that.'

'I killed nobody.'

'Your people did.'

'People that have left the country. We're fireproof.'

'We?'

'You ask too many questions.'

'You'll never be fireproof from me. I'll find you.'

'I hope you do.' The phone went dead.

I got up off the bench and headed for the subway.

The Union Square subway station is a major hub. Multiple entrances, multiple exits, multiple lines, multiple tracks. I bought a new MetroCard, twenty rides plus three as a bonus. It was after five in the morning. The station was filling up with people. I passed a newsstand with squat bales of fresh tabloids ready for sale. Two separate titles. Both headlines were huge. One had three words: FEDS SEEK TRIO. The other had: FEDS HUNT TRIO. On balance I preferred *seek* to *hunt*.

I turned away and headed back for the street.

MADISON SQUARE PARK was seven blocks north. I had more than four hours to kill. I spent the time shopping and eating on Park Avenue South. It's always best to give pursuers what they don't expect. Fugitives are not supposed to dawdle through the immediate neighbourhood.

Delis and supermarkets and diners and coffee shops were all that was open. I started in a Food Emporium that had an entrance on 14th Street and an exit on 15th. I spent forty-five minutes in there. When I got bored I left the basket in a deserted aisle and slipped out through the back of the store.

Next stop was a diner four blocks north. I ate pancakes and bacon. Then I moved on to a French brasserie. More coffee and a croissant. Someone had left a *New York Times* on a chair. I read it from end to end. No mention of a manhunt.

I moved from a supermarket on the corner of Park and 22nd to a Duane Reade drugstore opposite and then to a CVS pharmacy. Then at twenty-five minutes to ten I looped round and took a careful look at my destination from the mouth of 24th Street. I saw nothing that worried me.

So at ten o'clock I stepped into Madison Square Park.

I FOUND THERESA LEE and Jacob Mark on a bench near a dog run. They looked rested but nervous. They were two of maybe a hundred people sitting peacefully in the sun.

I sat down next to Lee.

She said, 'Docherty was texting messages to me all night, while the phone was off.'

She took a sheaf of paper out of her back pocket.

I said, 'You took notes?'

She said, 'They were long messages. I didn't want to keep the phone on, if there were things I needed to review.'

'So what do we know?'

'The 17th Precinct checked transportation gateways. Standard procedure. Four men left the country three hours after the time of death. Through JFK. The 17th is calling them potential suspects.'

'The 17th Precinct is right,' I said. 'Lila Hoth told me so.'

'You met her?'

'She called me.'

'On what?'

'Another phone I took from Leonid. He and a pal found me.'

'She confessed?'

'More or less.'

'So where is she now?'

'I'm guessing east of Fifth, south of 59th. She used the Four Seasons as a front. Why travel?'

Lee said, 'There was a burnt-out rental car in Queens. The 17th thinks the four guys used it to get out of Manhattan. Then they used that elevated train thing to get to the airport. But here's the thing. The four guys were routed through to Tajikistan.'

'Which is where? Those new places confuse me.'

'Tajikistan is right next to Afghanistan. They share a border. Also with Pakistan.'

'You can fly direct to Pakistan.'

'Correct. Therefore either those guys were from Tajikistan or from Afghanistan. Tajikistan is where you go to get into Afghanistan without being too obvious about it. Kabul is not too far away.'

'OK.'

'And here's the other thing. Homeland Security has a protocol. Some kind of computer algorithm. They can trace groups of people through similar itineraries and linked bookings. Turns out those four guys entered the country three months ago from Tajikistan, along with some other folks, including two women with passports from Turkmenistan. One was sixty, and the other was twenty-six. They claimed to be mother and daughter. And Homeland Security is prepared to swear their passports were genuine.'

'OK.'

'So the Hoths were not Ukrainian. Everything they told us was a lie.'

I went through all the stuff Lila had told us and deleted it, item by item. Like pulling files from a drawer, and leafing through them, and then pitching them in the trash.

I asked, 'Where exactly is Turkmenistan?'

'Also next to Afghanistan. Afghanistan is surrounded by Iran, Turkmenistan, Uzbekistan, Tajikistan and Pakistan, clockwise from the Gulf.'

'Are Turkmenistan and Afghanistan ethnically similar?'

'Probably. All those borders are completely arbitrary. What matters are the tribal divisions.'

'Are you an expert?'

'The NYPD knows more about that region than the CIA. We've got better intelligence than anyone. You think the Hoths are from Afghanistan?'

'They knew a hell of a lot about the conflict with the Soviets.'

'Maybe they read books.'

'No, they got the feelings right. And the atmosphere. Like the ancient greatcoats. Details like that were not widely available. That's insider information. A lot of what the Hoths said sounded like first-hand information to me.'

'So?'

'Maybe Svetlana really did fight there. But on the other side.'

Lee paused. 'You think the Hoths are Afghan tribeswomen?'

'If Svetlana fought there, but not for the Soviets, then they must be,' I said.

'In which case Svetlana was telling the whole story from the other side. Everything was inverted. Including the atrocities.'

'Yes. Svetlana didn't suffer them. She committed them.'

We all went quiet. Jacob Mark had been staring at the ground. Finally he leaned forward, turned his head and looked at me. I thought, Here it comes.

'When Lila Hoth called, did she mention Peter?'

I nodded. 'She picked him up in the bar.'

'Where is he now?'

'She said he's here in the city.'

'Is he OK?'

'No, I don't think he's OK. I could be wrong.'

'What did she tell you?'

'I said I wasn't scared of her, and she said that's what Peter Molina had said.'

'Why would they want to mess with Peter?'

'To get to Susan, of course.'

'For what? The Pentagon is supposed to be helping Afghanistan.'

I said, 'If Svetlana was a fighting tribeswoman, then she was one of the mujahideen. And when the Russians went home, the mujahideen did not go back to tending their goats. Some of them became the Taliban, and the rest of them became al-Qaeda.'

Chapter Eight

J acob Mark said, 'You know that I have to go to the cops about Peter.'

'Think hard,' I said. 'Think about what the cops will do. They'll call the feds. The feds will lock you up again and put Peter on the back burner, because they've got bigger fish to fry.'

'I have to try.'

'Peter's dead, Jake.'

'There's still a chance.'

'Then the fastest way to find him is to find Lila. And we can do that better than those feds.'

'You think?'

'Look at their track record. They missed her once, and they let us break out of jail.' I looked at Theresa. 'Did you speak to Sansom?'

She shrugged. 'I spoke to him briefly. He said he might want to come up here. He said he would call me back to coordinate the where and the when. I said I was keeping the phone switched off. So he said he would call Docherty's cell, and I should pick up the message. So I did, and Docherty didn't answer. I tried the precinct switchboard. The dispatcher said Docherty was unavailable.'

'What does that mean?'

'I think it means he just got arrested.'

Which changed everything. Lee handed me her folded notes. She said, 'You understand, right? I have to turn myself in now. He's my partner. I can't let him face this madness alone.'

'You can't help anyone from a jail cell.'

'It's different for you. You can be gone tomorrow. I can't. I live here. And I won't turn my back on my partner.'

'What about Sansom? I need a time and a place.'

'I don't have that information. And you should take care with Sansom, anyway. He sounded weird on the phone.'

Then she gave me Leonid's first cellphone, and the emergency charger. She put her hand on my arm and squeezed. And right after that our temporary three-way partnership fell apart completely. Jacob Mark was on his feet. He said, 'I owe it to Peter. They might put me back in a cell, but at least they'll be out looking for him.'

I looked at them both and asked, 'Are you sure about this?'

They were sure about it. They walked out of the park to the sidewalk, where they stood looking for a police car, the same way people stand when they are trying to hail a cab. I sat alone for a minute, and then I got up and walked the other way.

Next stop, somewhere east of Fifth and south of 59th.

I TOOK THE BUS, which was a slow, lumbering vehicle, a counterintuitive choice for a wild-eyed fugitive, which made it perfect cover for me. A man on a bus is close to invisible.

I got out at 59th Street. Prime retail territory, therefore prime tourist territory, therefore a policemen on every corner. I found a line of vendors at the base of Central Park and bought a black T-shirt with *New York City* written on it, a pair of sunglasses and a black baseball cap with a red apple on it. I changed shirts in a hotel rest room and went to Madison. Nothing I could do about my height, but the new black upper body might let me slide by.

Finding a concealed hide-out in a big city is close to impossible. I was just following a geographic hunch. *The Four Seasons Hotel. Not adjacent, but comfortably proximate.* A two-minute drive? A five-minute walk? In which direction? Not south, I thought. Not across 57th Street, which is a major cross-town thoroughfare. Much more inviting to slip away to the north, to the quieter blocks.

I watched the traffic and thought: not a two-minute drive. Driving implied a lack of control, a lack of flexibility, and delays. Walking was better than driving in the city, whoever you were.

I took 58th Street and walked to the hotel's back entrance. There was a line of limousines waiting at the kerb. There was a loading dock, with a roll-up door, closed.

I stood with my back to the hotel door. Where would I go? Across the street was nothing but a solid line of high buildings. Mostly apartment houses. Directly opposite was an art gallery. I crossed the street and looked back from the far sidewalk.

To the left of the hotel, on the side nearer Park Avenue, there was nothing very interesting.

Then I looked to the right, and I got a new idea.

The hotel itself was a recent construction. Neighbouring buildings were all quiet and prosperous. But at the western end of the block there were three old piles in a row. Narrow, single-front, four-storey brick, somewhat decrepit, like three rotten teeth in a bright smile. One had an out-of-business restaurant for a ground-floor tenant. One had a hardware store. The third had an enterprise abandoned so long ago I couldn't tell what it had been. Each had a narrow door set alongside its commercial operation. Two of the doors had multiple bell pushes, signifying apartments. The door next to the old restaurant had a single bell push, signifying a sole occupier for the upper three floors.

Lila Hoth was not a Ukrainian billionaire. So she had a budget. A generous budget to allow for suites in the Four Seasons. But presumably not an infinite budget. And town houses in Manhattan run to many tens of thousands of dollars a month to rent.

Privacy could be achieved more cheaply in tumble-down mixed-use buildings like the three I was looking at. No doormen nearby.

I stood opposite the three old piles and stared at them. I reviewed my assumptions. The 6 train at 59th and Lexington was close by. The Four Seasons was close by. Third Avenue and 56th Street was not close by. *That's not close to me.* Anonymity was guaranteed. Cost was limited. Five out of five. Perfect. So I figured maybe I was looking for a place just like one of the three in front of me, located within a fan-shaped five-minute radius east or west of the hotel's back door. Not north, or Susan Mark would have parked in midtown and aimed to get out of the subway at 68th Street. Not south, because of 57th Street's psychological barrier.

A five-minute radius left or right out of the hotel's back door would end on either the exact block I was currently loitering on, or the next one to the east, between Park and Lex. And tumble-down mixed-use properties are rare on blocks like those.

It was possible I was looking at Lila Hoth's hide-out.

But unlikely. I believe in luck, but I'm not insane.

But I believe in logic too, and logic had led me to the spot. I went over it again, and ended up believing myself.

Because of one extra factor.

Which was that the same logic led someone else there, too.

Springfield stepped down into the gutter next to me and said, 'You think?'

SPRINGFIELD WAS WEARING the same suit I had seen him in before. It was creased and crumpled, like he slept in it. Which maybe he did.

He said, 'You think this is the place?'

I didn't answer. I was too busy checking all around me. I looked at hundreds of people and dozens of cars. But I saw nothing to worry about. Springfield was alone.

I asked, 'So what's the deal?'

'We should talk, maybe.'

'Where?'

'Your call,' he said. Which was a good sign. It meant that if there was going to be a trap in my immediate future, it was going to be improvised. Maybe even survivable.

'Make two lefts and go to 57 East 57th,' I said. 'I'll be ten minutes behind you. I'll meet you inside. We can get coffee.'

'OK,' he said. He crossed the street diagonally and turned left onto

Madison Avenue. I went the other way, just as far as the Four Seasons' back door on 58th Street. It was a block-through building. Its front door was at 57 East 57th. I would be inside about four minutes ahead of Springfield. I would know if he had brought a crew. I walked through to the lobby from the rear and waited.

Springfield came in alone, right on time, which was four minutes later. No time for hurried deployment out on the street.

He got his bearings and headed for the tearoom, where I had once met the Hoths. I gave it ten minutes, and then added two more. There was no back-up.

I walked into the tearoom and found Springfield in the same chair that Lila Hoth had used. The same waiter was on duty. He came over. Springfield asked for mineral water. I asked for coffee. The waiter nodded imperceptibly and went away again.

Springfield said, 'You met the Hoths here. Associating with them could be classed as a felony.'

'Because?'

'Because of the Patriot Act.'

'I also shot four federal agents with darts.'

'No one cares about them.'

'Who are the Hoths?' I asked.

'I can't volunteer information.'

'So why are we here?'

'You help us, we'll help you. We can make all your felonies disappear if you help us find what we lost.'

'The memory stick?'

Springfield nodded. The waiter came back with the mineral water and coffee. He arranged things on the table and backed away.

I said, 'I don't know where the memory stick is.'

'I'm sure you don't. But you got as close to Susan Mark as anyone. And she left the Pentagon with it, and it isn't in her house or her car or anywhere else she ever went. So we're hoping you saw something.'

'I saw her shoot herself. That was about all.'

'There must have been more,' he said.

'You had your chief of staff on the train. What did he see?'

'Nothing.'

'What was on the memory stick?'

'Why do you need to know?'

I said, 'I like to know at least the basic shape of the trouble I'm about to get myself into.'

'Then you should ask yourself a question.'

'What question?'

'The one you haven't asked yet, and the one you should have, right at the start. The key question.'

So I spooled back to the beginning, looking for the question I had never asked. The beginning was the 6 train, and passenger number four. Susan Mark, citizen, ex-wife, mother, sister, adoptee, resident of Annandale, Virginia. Susan Mark, civilian worker at the Pentagon.

I asked, 'What exactly was her job?'

Springfield took a long drink of water and then said, 'Slow, but you got there in the end. She was a systems administrator with responsibility for a certain amount of information technology.'

'I don't know what that means.'

'It means she knew a bunch of master passwords for the computers. Not the important ones. But obviously she was authorised for HRC records. And some of the archives.'

'But not the Delta archives, right? They're in North Carolina. At Fort Bragg. Not the Pentagon.'

'Computers are networked. Everything is everywhere and nowhere now. Systems administrators share common problems. They help each other. Apparently there was a defective line of code that made individual passwords less opaque than they should have been. So there was some leakage.'

I remembered Jacob Mark saying, *She was good with computers*.

I said, 'So she had access to Delta's archives?'

Springfield nodded.

I said, 'But you and Sansom quit five years before I did. Nothing was computerised then.'

Springfield said, 'The US Army as we know it is about ninety years old. We've got ninety years' worth of stuff all built up. Literally tons of paper. They've been cleaning house for the past ten years. The documents are scanned and preserved on computers.'

I nodded. 'And Susan Mark got in and copied one.'

'More than copied one,' Springfield said. 'She extracted one. Transferred it to an external drive, and then deleted the original.'

'The external drive being the memory stick?'

Springfield nodded. 'And we don't know where it is.'

'Why her?'

'Because she fitted the bill. The relevant part of the archive was traced through the medal award. HRC people keep the medal records. She was the systems administrator. And she was vulnerable through her son.'

'Why did she delete the original?'

'I don't know.'

'When was the document dug out and scanned?'

'A little over three months ago. Ten years into the programme and they're only up to the early 1980s.'

'Who does the work?'

'There's a specialist staff.'

'With a leak. The Hoths were over here immediately.'

'Evidently. Steps are being taken.'

'What was the document?'

'I can't volunteer information.'

'Who are the Hoths?'

He just smiled. *I can't volunteer information.* Four words, the third of which was perhaps the most significant.

I said, 'You could ask me questions. I could volunteer guesses. You could comment on them.'

He said, 'Who do you think the Hoths are?'

'I think they're native Afghans.'

He said, 'Go on.'

'Taliban or al-Qaeda sympathisers, or operatives.'

No reaction.

'Al-Qaeda,' I said. 'The Taliban mostly stay home.'

'Go on.'

'Operatives,' I said.

No reaction.

'Leaders?'

'Go on.'

'Al-Qaeda is using women leaders?'

'That's what they want us to think. They want us searching for men that don't exist. Go on.'

'OK, Svetlana fought with the mujahideen and knew you had captured the VAL rifle from Grigori Hoth. They used Hoth's name and story to get sympathy over here.'

'Because?'

'Al-Qaeda wants documentary proof of whatever else it was that you guys were doing that night.'

'Go on.'

'Which Sansom got a big medal for. So it must have looked pretty good, once upon a time. But now I'm assuming it wouldn't look so good.'

'Go on.'

'Sansom is miserable, but the government has got its knickers in a twist, too. So the trip was more political than military.'

'Obviously. We weren't officially at war with anyone.'

'You know the Hoths killed four people, and probably Susan Mark's son too, right?'

'We don't know it. But we suspect it.'

'So why haven't you busted them?'

'I work security for a congressman. I can't bust anyone.'

'Those feds could.'

'Apparently the feds consider the Hoths to be extremely dangerous, but not currently operational.'

'Which means what?'

'Which means that right now there's more to be gained by leaving them in place.'

'Which actually means they can't find them.'

'Of course.'

'You happy about that?'

'The Hoths don't have the memory stick, or they wouldn't still be looking for it. So I don't really care.'

'I think you should,' I said.

'You think that's their place? Where you were?'

'This block or the next.'

'I think this one,' he said. 'Those feds searched their hotel suite while they were out. They had shopping bags. Two from Bergdorf Goodman, and two from Tiffany. Those stores are about a block from those old buildings. If their base was on the block east of Park, they'd have gone to Bloomingdales instead. Because they weren't really shopping. They just wanted accessories in their suite, to fool people.'

'Good point,' I said.

'Don't go looking for the Hoths,' Springfield said.

'You worried about me now?'

'You could lose two ways round. They're going to think the same as us, that even if you don't have the stick, then somehow you know where it went. And they might be even more vicious and persuasive than we are.'

'And?'

'They might actually tell you what's on it. In which case from our point of view you would become a loose end.'

'How bad is it?'

'Major Sansom would be embarrassed.'

'And the United States.'

'That, too,' he said.

The waiter came back and enquired as to whether we needed anything else. Springfield said yes. He reordered for both of us. Which meant he had more to talk about. He said, 'Run through exactly what happened on the train.'

'Why weren't you there, instead of the chief of staff?'

'It came on us fast. I was in Texas, with Sansom.'

'Why didn't the feds have someone on the train?'

'They did. Two women. Undercover, borrowed from the FBI. Special Agents Rodriguez and Mbele. You blundered into the wrong car.'

'They were good,' I said. The Hispanic woman, small, hot, tired. The West African woman in the batik dress. 'But how did you all know she was going to take that train?'

'We didn't,' Springfield said. 'It was a huge operation. We knew she was in a car. So we had people waiting at the tunnels. The idea was to follow her from there.'

'Why wasn't she arrested on the Pentagon steps?'

'The feds wanted to roll up the whole chain in one go. And they might have.'

'If I hadn't screwed it up.'

'You said it.'

'She didn't have the memory stick.'

'She left the Pentagon with it, and it isn't in her house or her car.'

'What the hell was on that memory stick?'

Springfield didn't answer.

One of the captured phones in my pocket started to vibrate.

I PULLED all three phones out of my pocket and laid them on the table. One of them was skittering around. *Unknown caller*. I opened it up and put it to my ear and said, 'Hello?'

Lila Hoth asked, 'Are you still in New York?'

I said, 'Yes.'

'Are you near the Four Seasons?'

I said, 'Not very.'

'Go there. I left a package for you at the desk.'

The line went dead.

I glanced at Springfield and said, 'Wait here.' Then I hustled out to the lobby. I walked to the desk and gave my name and a minute later I had an envelope in my hands. I asked the desk clerk when it had been delivered. He said more than an hour ago.

I asked, 'Did you see who dropped it off?'

'A foreign gentleman.'

The envelope was padded, about six inches by nine. It had something stiff in it. Round, and maybe five inches in diameter. I carried it back to the tearoom and sat down again with Springfield. He said, 'From the Hoths?'

I nodded. I tore open the envelope. A disk spilled out.

'A DVD,' Springfield said.

It was a blank disk. The words *Watch This* had been written across the label side with a black marker.

I said, 'I don't have a DVD player.'

'You can play DVDs on a computer.'

'I don't have a computer.'

'Hotels have computers.'

'I don't want to stay here.'

'There are other hotels in the city.'

'Where are you staying?'

'The Sheraton. Where we were before.'

So Springfield paid our tearoom bill with a platinum credit card and we walked from the Four Seasons to the Sheraton.

Springfield opened the door to the business centre with his key card. He told me he would wait in the lobby. Three of the four work stations were occupied. I took the empty chair and found a slot on the tower unit. I pushed the disk in and a motor whirred and the unit sucked at the disk.

A big window opened on the screen. It had a graphic in the bottom corner. Play, pause, fast forward, rewind, skip. I moved the mouse and the pointer arrow changed to a chubby little hand.

The phone in my pocket started to vibrate.

I took the phone out of my pocket and opened it up. 'Hello.'

Lila Hoth asked, 'Have you got it yet?'

I said, 'Yes.'

'Have you watched it yet?'

'No.'

'I think you should. You'll find it educational.'

I asked, 'Is there sound on it?'

'No, it's a silent movie. Unfortunately. It would be better with sound.'

I didn't answer.

She asked, 'Where are you?'

'In a hotel business centre.'

'Can anyone else see the screen?'

I didn't answer.

'Play it,' she said. 'I'll do a commentary.'

I moved the mouse and put the chubby little hand over the play button. I clicked.

The blank window on the screen lit up. Then the picture settled to a wide-angle view of an outdoor space. It was night. The scene was brightly lit by halogen lights. Beaten earth, a dark khaki tone. One large rock. The rock was flat, bigger than a kingsize bed. It had been drilled and fitted with four iron rings. One at each corner.

There was a naked man tied to the rings. He was short and wiry. He had olive skin and a black beard. He was maybe thirty years old. He was on his back, stretched into a wide X shape. His head was jerking from side to side. He was screaming, but I couldn't hear him. It was a silent movie.

Lila Hoth asked, 'What are you seeing?'

I said, 'A guy on a slab. Who is he?'

'He *was* a taxi driver who ran an errand for an American journalist. Keep watching.'

Svetlana Hoth stepped into the frame. Unmistakable. She had a knife in her hand.

She crawled up on the rock and squatted beside the guy. She placed the tip of the blade on a spot about halfway between the guy's groin and his navel. She pressed down. The guy jerked uncontrollably. His mouth was forming words. *No!* and *Please!* are clear in any language.

'Where was this?' I asked.

Lila Hoth said, 'Not far from Kabul.'

Svetlana moved the blade up towards the guy's navel. Casual and practised and expert. The blade stopped above the guy's sternum. His belly was open, like a zipper had been pulled.

Svetlana put the knife down, slid off the rock and stepped out of the frame.

'You're crazy, you know that?'

'That's what Peter Molina said.'

'He saw this?'

'He's on it. Fast forward, if you like.'

I put the fat hand on the fast-forward button and clicked. The picture leaped into fast motion. The taxi driver's arms and legs twitched at double speed.

'You're sick,' I said. 'You're also dead. The truck hasn't hit you yet, but it's going to.'

'Are you the truck?'

'You bet your ass.'

'I'm glad. Keep watching.'

I clicked the fast-forward button again and again. The taxi driver stopped moving. Lila Hoth rushed into the frame. I hit the play button to get back to normal speed. Lila bent and felt for a pulse. Then she raised her head and smiled a happy smile.

Straight at me.

On the phone she asked, 'Is it over yet?'

I said, 'Yes.'

'Keep watching,' Lila said, in my ear.

The picture opened up on a new scene. An interior. A basement, maybe. There was a broad stone slab, like a table. Part of an old kitchen, possibly. A huge young man was tied to the slab.

He's three hundred pounds of muscle, Jacob Mark had said.

He was naked. Pale skin, tousled fair hair. His head was jerking back and forth and he was screaming.

I said, 'I'm not going to watch this.'

Lila Hoth said, 'You should. Maybe we let him go.'

'When was this?'

'We set a deadline and we kept it.'

I didn't reply.

'Watch it.'

I watched it. *Maybe we let him go.*

They didn't let him go.

AFTERWARDS I HUNG UP the phone, put the DVD in my pocket, made it to the lobby rest room and threw up in a stall. Not really because of the pictures. I have seen worse. But because of fury and frustration. I rinsed my mouth and washed my face.

Then I emptied my pockets. I kept my cash, and my passport, and my ATM card, and my subway card, and Theresa Lee's NYPD business card. I kept my toothbrush. I kept the phone that had rung. I dumped the other two phones in the trash, with the charger, and the business card from the four dead guys, and the notes Theresa Lee had made.

I dumped the DVD, too. And the Radio Shack memory stick. I didn't need a decoy anymore. Then I headed out to see Springfield.

He was in the lobby bar, in a chair. He had a glass of water on the table in front of him. He was relaxed, but he was watching everything. He said, 'You've gone pale.'

'It was two guys,' I said. 'They had their bellies slit open.'

'Who were the guys?'

'One was a taxi driver from Kabul and the other was Susan Mark's son.'

'Are the Hoths on the tape?'

I nodded. 'Like a confession.'

'Doesn't matter. They know we're going to kill them anyway. Doesn't really matter what we kill them for.'

'It matters to me.'

'Wise up, Reacher. That was the whole point of sending you the package. They want to make you mad and suck you in. They can't find you. So they want you to come find them.'

'Which I will.'

'Your future plans are your business. But you need to take care. You need to understand. Because this has been their tactic for two hundred years. That's why their abuse was always within earshot of the front lines. They wanted to bring out the rescue parties. Or provoke revenge attacks. They wanted a never-ending supply of prisoners. Ask the British. Or the Russians.'

'I'll take plenty of care.'

'I'm sure you'll try. But not until we've finished with you, about the train. It's in your interests to help us.'

'Not so far. All I have is promises.'

'All charges will be dropped when we have the memory stick in our possession.'

'Not good enough. I want the charges dropped now. I can't be looking out for cops the whole time.'

'I'll have to call Sansom.'

'Talk to him about Theresa Lee and Jacob Mark, too. And Docherty. I want a clean slate for all of them.'

'OK.'

'Two more things,' I said.

'You drive a hard bargain, for a guy with nothing to offer.'

'Homeland Security traced the Hoths coming in from Tajikistan with their crew. Three months ago. I want to know how many people were in the party.'

'To estimate the size of the opposing force?'

'Exactly.'

'And?'

'I want to meet Sansom again.'

'Why?'

'I want him to tell me what is on that memory stick.'

'Not going to happen.'

'Then I'll keep it and look for myself.'

'You've actually got the stick?'

'No,' I said. 'But I know where it is.'

Springfield asked, 'Where is it?'

I said, 'I can't volunteer information.'

'You're full of crap.'

I shook my head. 'Not this time.'

'You sure? You can take us there?'

'I can get you within fifteen feet. The rest is up to you. Call Sansom. Set up a meeting.'

Springfield finished what was left of his water and a waiter came by with the bill. Springfield paid with his platinum card, the same way he had for both of us at the Four Seasons. Which I had taken to be a good sign. So I chose to push my luck a little further.

'Want to get me a room?' I asked.

'Why?'

'Because it's going to take time to get me off the most-wanted list. And I was up all night. I want to take a nap.'

Ten minutes later we were in a room with a queensize bed. A nice space, but tactically unsatisfactory. Like all high-floor hotel rooms it had a window that was no good to me and therefore had only one way out. I could see that Springfield was thinking the same thing. He was thinking I was a lunatic to put myself in there.

I asked him, 'Can I trust you?'

He said, 'Yes.'

'Give me your gun.'

'Why do you want it?'

'You know why. So if you bring the wrong people to my door I can defend myself.'

I knew he would rather stick a needle in his eye than give up his weapon. But he reached under his suit coat and came out with a 9mm Steyr GB pistol. He handed it to me butt first. It had eighteen rounds in the magazine and one in the chamber.

'Thank you,' I said.

He walked out of the room. I double-locked the door after him, and put the chain on, and propped a chair under the handle. I emptied my pockets on the night stand. I put my clothes under the mattress to press. I took a long hot shower. Then I laid down and went to sleep, with Springfield's gun under the pillow.

I WAS WOKEN UP four hours later by a knock at the door. There was a full-length mirror on the wall inside the door. I wrapped a towel round my waist and collected the gun. I moved the chair and opened the door against the chain. Stood back and checked the view in the mirror.

Springfield, and Sansom.

They were alone, as far as I could tell. I took the slack out of the trigger and the chain off the door.

They came in. Sansom was in a navy suit with a white shirt and a red tie and he looked as fresh as a daisy. He took the chair I had been using under the door handle and carried it back to the table and sat down. Springfield closed the door and put the chain back on. I kept hold of the gun. I nudged the mattress with my knee and pulled my clothes out.

'Two minutes,' I said. 'Talk among yourselves.'

I dressed in the bathroom and came back out and Sansom asked, 'Do you really know where that memory stick is?'

'Yes,' I said. 'I really do.'

'Why do you want to know what's on it?'

'Because I want to know how embarrassing it is.'

'Why won't you tell me where it is right now?'

'Because I have something else to do first. And I need you to keep the cops out of my hair while I'm doing it. So I need a way of keeping your mind on the job.'

'You could be conning me.'

'I could be, but I'm not.'

'Is it here in New York?'

I didn't answer.

'Can I trust you?'

'Plenty of people have.'

He said, 'I saw your service record. It was mixed.'

'I tried my best. But I had a mind of my own.'

'Why did you quit?'

'I got bored. You?'

'I got old.'

'What's on that stick?'

He didn't answer. Springfield was standing mute, closer to the door than the window, invisible to an external sniper and close enough to the corridor to be all over an intruder the second the door swung open. Training stays with a person. I gave him his gun back. He took it without a word.

Sansom said, 'Tell me what you know so far.'

I said, 'You were probably airlifted from Bragg to Turkey, then Oman. Then India, probably. Pakistan, and then the North-West Frontier.'

He nodded. He had a faraway look in his eyes.

'Then Afghanistan,' I said.

'Go on,' he said.

'Probably you stayed on the flank of the Abas Ghar and headed south and west, following the line of the Korengal Valley.'

'Go on.'

'You stumbled over Grigori Hoth and took his rifle and let him wander away. Then you kept on walking, to wherever it was you had been ordered to go.'

He nodded.

I said, 'That's all I know so far.'

He asked, 'Where were you in March of 1983?'

'West Point.'

'What was the big news?'

'The Red Army was trying to stop the bleeding.'

He nodded again. 'It was an insane campaign. No one has ever beaten the tribesmen in the North-West Frontier. It was a slow-motion meat grinder. We were very happy about it, obviously.'

'We helped,' I said.

'We sure did. We gave the mujahideen everything they wanted. For free.'

'And?'

'When you're in the habit of giving people everything they want, it's very hard to stop.'

'What more did they want?'

'Recognition,' he said. 'Tribute.'

'So what was the mission?'

'We went to see the mujahideen's top boy. Bearing gifts from Ronald Reagan himself. We were his personal envoys. We were told to kiss ass at every opportunity.'

'It was twenty-five years ago.'

'So?'

'So who cares anymore? It's a detail of history. And it worked, anyway. It was the end of Communism.'

'But it wasn't the end of the mujahideen.'

'I know,' I said. 'They became the Taliban and al-Qaeda. But voters in North Carolina aren't going to remember the history.'

'Depends,' Sansom said.

'On what?'

'Name recognition.'

'What name?'

'The Korengal was where the Red Army met its end. Therefore the local mujahideen leader there was a really big deal. He was the one we were sent to meet. And we did.'

'Who was he?'

'He was a fairly impressive guy, initially. Young, tall, good-looking, intelligent, committed. He came from a billionaire family in Saudi. His father was a friend of Reagan's vice-president. But the guy quit the easy life for the cause.'

'Who was he?'

'Osama bin Laden.'

The room stayed quiet. Springfield sat down on the bed.

I said, 'Name recognition.'

Sansom said, 'It's a bitch.'

'But we've all read army reports,' I said.

'And?'

'They're very dry,' I said. 'Maybe they didn't mention you by name. Maybe they didn't mention *him* by name. Maybe it was all acronyms, all buried in three hundred pages of map references.'

Sansom said nothing. Springfield looked away.

I asked, 'What was he like?'

Sansom said, 'See? My whole life counts for nothing now, except I'm the guy who kissed Osama bin Laden's ass. He was a creep. He was clearly committed to killing Russians, which we were happy about at first, but pretty soon we realised he was committed to killing everyone who wasn't exactly the same as him. It was a very uncomfortable weekend.'

'You were there a whole weekend?'

'Honoured guests. Except not really. He lorded it over us the whole time.

We had to pretend to be impressed. I nearly puked. And not just because of the food.'

'You ate with him?'

'We were staying in his tent.'

'Which will be called their HQ in the report. It will be three hundred tedious pages about a rendezvous attempted and a rendezvous kept. People will die of boredom. Why are you worried?'

'The politics is awful. It's like we were subsidising him. Paying him, almost.'

I said, 'It's just words on a page.'

Sansom said, 'It's a big file.'

'The bigger the better. The bigger it is, the more buried the bad parts will be.'

'You ever used a computer?'

'I used one today.'

'What makes for the biggest files?'

'Long documents?'

'Wrong. Large numbers of pixels make the biggest files.'

'OK,' I said. 'I see. It's not a report. It's a photograph.'

Chapter Nine

Reagan wanted the photograph,' Sansom said. 'Partly because he was sentimental, and partly because he wanted to check we had followed his orders. I'm standing next to bin Laden with the mother of all grins on my face.'

Springfield said, 'With me on the other side.'

Sansom said, 'Bin Laden knocked down the Twin Towers. He attacked the Pentagon. He's the world's worst terrorist. That photograph will kill me in politics. Forever.'

I asked, 'Is that why the Hoths want it?'

He nodded. 'So that al-Qaeda can humiliate me, and the United States along with me. Or vice versa.'

'Hence the photograph in your book,' I said. 'And on your office wall. Donald Rumsfeld with Saddam Hussein, in Baghdad.'

'Yes,' Sansom said.

'Just in case. To show that someone else had done the same thing. Like a trump card. No one knew it was a trump.'

'It's not a trump,' Sansom said. 'It's like a lousy four of clubs. Because bin Laden is way worse than Saddam. And Rumsfeld wasn't looking to get elected to anything. There I am, grinning up at the world's most evil man.'

'You'll get the picture back.'

'When?'

'How are we doing with the felony charges?'

'Slow. There's good news and bad news.'

'Give me the bad news first.'

'It's very unlikely that the FBI will want to play ball. And it's certain the Department of Defense won't.'

'Those three guys?'

'They're off the case. One has a broken nose and one has a cut head. But they've been replaced.'

'So what's the good news?'

'We think the NYPD is prepared to be relaxed.'

'Terrific,' I said.

Sansom didn't reply.

I asked him, 'What about Theresa Lee and Jacob Mark? And Docherty?'

'They're back at work.'

'What are you going to do with the memory stick?'

'I'm going to check it's right, then I'm going to smash it up, and burn the pieces, and flush it down about eight toilets.'

'Suppose I asked you not to do that?'

'Why would you?'

'I'll tell you later.'

DEPENDING ON your point of view it was either late in the afternoon or early in the evening. But I had just woken up, so I figured it was time for breakfast. I called room service and ordered a big tray. About fifty bucks' worth. Sansom didn't bat an eye. He was seething with frustration and impatience.

The room-service guy brought my meal. Sansom took a cellphone call and confirmed that I was no longer a person of interest as far as the NYPD was concerned. But then he made a second call and told me the signs did not look good at the FBI. He made a third call and confirmed that the DoD definitely would not let go.

'End of story,' Sansom said.

'OK,' I said. 'As long as I know the shape of the battlefield.'

'It's not your battle, strictly speaking.'

'Jacob Mark will feel better with a little closure.'

'So are you doing it for Jacob Mark or for me?'

'I'm doing it for myself. They sent me that DVD.'

'Which was tactical. If you react, they win.'

'No, if I react, they lose.'

'Do you even know where they are?'

I said, 'I'm working on a couple of ideas.'

'Do you still have an open channel of communication?'

'I think she's going to call again.'

'One false step, and you're her prisoner. You'll end up telling her what she wants to know.'

I asked him, 'How many times have you flown commercial since September eleventh?'

He said, 'Hundreds.'

'And I bet every single time some small corner of your mind was hoping there were hijackers on board. So you could jump up and beat the hell out of them. Or die trying.'

Sansom gave a rueful little smile. 'You're right,' he said.

'Why?'

'I would want to protect the airplane.'

'And you would want to burn off your hate. I would. I liked the Twin Towers. I liked the way the world used to be. I have no political skills. So for a guy like me the chance to meet an al-Qaeda cell seems like all my birthdays and Christmases rolled into one.'

'You're crazy. This is not a thing to be done alone.'

'What's the alternative?'

'Homeland Security will find them eventually. They'll put something together. NYPD, FBI, SWAT teams.'

I said, 'Alone is always better.'

'Maybe not,' Springfield said. 'We checked on Homeland Security's computer algorithm. The Hoths brought a large party with them.'

'How many?'

'Nineteen men.'

I FINISHED MY BREAKFAST. The coffeepot was empty. So I finished a bottle of water and lobbed it towards the trash can. It struck the rim and bounced out and rolled away across the carpet. Not a good sign, if I were superstitious. But I'm not.

'Total of nineteen men,' I said. 'Four left the country and two are wounded with broken jaws and elbows. That leaves thirteen.'

Sansom said, 'Broken jaws and elbows?'

'They were out looking for me, but scuffling on the street seems not to be their main strength.'

'The FBI got a call from the Bellevue emergency room. Two unidentified foreigners were dumped there after a beating.'

'Punishment,' I said. 'The Hoths must have been displeased. So they gave them up, to encourage the others.'

'Ruthless.'

'Thirteen people,' I said.

'Plus the Hoths,' Springfield said. 'Fifteen.'

'We can't actively help you,' Sansom said. 'You understand that, right? This is going to end with a minimum of one and a maximum of fifteen homicides on the streets of New York City. We can't be a part of that. We can't be within a million miles of it.'

'I'm not asking for help.'

'The minimum one homicide would be you. In which case I wouldn't know where to look for my photograph.'

'So keep your fingers crossed for me.'

'Can I trust you? To keep your word.'

'What did you learn in Officer Candidate School?'

'That brother officers are to be trusted,' Sansom said.

'There you go, then.'

'But we were in different branches of the service.'

'You got that right. I was working hard while you were flying all over kissing terrorist ass. You didn't even get a Purple Heart.'

He said, 'I read your record. You got your Purple Heart for being blown up by that truck bomb in Beirut. The Marine barracks.'

'I remember it well.'

'You need to remember, that wasn't the Hoths.'

'I don't know who it was in Beirut. But whoever, they were the Hoths' brother officers.'

'You're motivated by revenge.'

'So?'

'So you might not be operating at peak efficiency.'

'Worried about me?'

'About myself, mainly. I want my photograph back.'

'You'll get it.'

'At least give me a clue where it is.'

'You know what I know. So you'll figure it out.'

He tried. He failed. He said, 'At least tell me why I shouldn't destroy it.'

'I'm sure you're a hell of a guy, Sansom. I'm sure you'd be a great senator. But at the end of the day any senator is just one out of a hundred. They're all fairly interchangeable.'

Sansom didn't say anything.

I asked him, 'Imagine a cave in the northwest of Pakistan. Imagine the al-Qaeda brass sitting there, right now. Are they saying we better not let John Sansom make it to the US Senate?'

He said, 'Probably not.'

'So why do they want the photograph?'

'The United States would be embarrassed.'

'But not very. Times change, things move on. It might destroy you personally, but destroying one American at a time isn't how al-Qaeda operates.'

'It would hurt Reagan's memory.'

'Who cares?'

'I think you're underestimating.'

'And I think you're overestimating.'

'The Defense Department is trying like crazy to get it back.'

'Is it? Then why did they give the job to their B team?'

'You think those guys were their B team?'

'I sincerely hope so.'

Sansom didn't answer.

'OK, it's bad for us. It's evidence of a strategic error. It's embarrassing. But that's all.'

'So al-Qaeda's expectations are too high?'

'No, I'm saying this whole thing is a little lopsided. Al-Qaeda fielded an A team and we fielded a B team. Therefore their desire to grab that photograph is just a little bit stronger than our desire to hold on to it.'

Sansom said nothing.

'And we have to ask, why wasn't Susan Mark just told to copy it? If their aim was to embarrass us, then copying it would have been better. Because when it came to light, and sceptics claimed it had been faked, then the original would still be on file.'

'OK.'

'But Susan Mark was told to steal it. With no trace left behind. Which added considerable risk and visibility. Which means they want to have it, and equally they want us *not* to have it.'

'I don't understand.'

'You need to cast your mind back. You need to figure out exactly what that camera saw. Because al-Qaeda stole the photograph because they want to suppress it.'

'Why would they?'

'Because however bad it is for you, there's something in it that's even worse for Osama bin Laden.'

Sansom and Springfield went quiet. They were casting their minds back to a dim tent above the Korengal Valley floor.

Sansom said, 'I don't remember.'

'Maybe it was us,' Springfield said. 'Maybe meeting with Americans looks like bad karma now.'

'No,' I said. 'It makes bin Laden look powerful and us look like patsies.'

'It was a zoo in there. Chaos and mayhem.'

'It has to be something that makes him look compromised, or weak, or deviant.'

'I don't remember. It was a long time ago.' Sansom went quiet. Eventually he said, 'I'm going to have to make a big decision.'

'I know you are.'

'If that picture hurts him more than it hurts me, I'm going to have to release it.'

'No, if it hurts him at all, you're going to have to release it. And then you're going to have to suck it up and face the consequences.'

'Where is it?'

I didn't answer.

'OK,' he said. 'I have to watch your back. But I know what you know. Which means I can figure it out. Which means the Hoths can figure it out too. Maybe they're picking it up right now.'

'Yes,' I said. 'Maybe they are.'

'And if they're going to suppress it, maybe I should just go ahead and let them.'

'If they're going to suppress it, that means it's a valuable weapon that could be used against them.'

'Go,' Sansom said. 'Go get the Hoths before they get the picture.'

I DIDN'T GO. Not right then. I had things to think about and plans to make. I was wearing rubber gardening clogs and blue trousers. I was unarmed. I wanted to go in the dead of night, dressed in black. With proper shoes. And weapons. The more the merrier.

I looked at Sansom. 'You can't actively help me, right?'

He said, 'No.'

I looked at Springfield. 'I'm heading out to a clothing store now. I figure on getting black trousers and a black T-shirt and black shoes. With a black windcheater, maybe triple-XL, kind of baggy. What do you think?'

Springfield said, ' We don't care. We'll be gone when you get back.'

I WENT TO THE STORE where I had bought the khaki shirt. I found black jeans, a black T-shirt, and a black cotton zip-up windcheater that ballooned way out in front.

Perfect, if Springfield had taken the hint.

I dressed in the changing cubicle and trashed my old stuff and paid the clerk fifty-nine dollars. Then I moved on to a shoe store. I bought a pair of sturdy black lace-ups and a pair of black socks.

Then I headed back through the gathering evening darkness to the hotel. I went up to my room and sat down on the bed to wait. I waited for close to four hours. I thought I was waiting for Springfield. But it was Theresa Lee who showed up.

She knocked on the door eight minutes before midnight. She was carrying a black gymnasium bag. Ballistic nylon. The way it hung from her hand I guessed it held heavy items. She put the bag on the floor and asked, 'Are you OK?'

'Are you?'

She nodded. 'We're all back on the job.'

'What's in the bag?'

'I have no idea. A man delivered it to the precinct.'

'Springfield?'

'No, the name he gave was Browning. He gave me the bag and said in the interests of crime prevention I should make sure you never got your hands on it.'

'But you brought it anyway?'

'I'm guarding it personally. Safer than leaving it around.'

'OK.'

She sat down on the bed. 'We raided those three old buildings on 58th Street.'

'Springfield told you about them?'

'He said his name was Browning. Our counterterrorism people went in two hours ago. The Hoths aren't there. They were, but they aren't anymore.'

'I know.'

'How do you know?'

'They turned in Leonid and his buddy. Therefore they've moved somewhere Leonid and his buddy don't know.'

She looked at me. 'Can you find them?'

'What are they doing for money?'

'We can't trace them that way. They stopped using credit cards and ATMs six days ago.'

'What else are your counterterrorism people doing?'

'Searching,' she said. 'With the FBI and the Department of Defense. There are six hundred people on the street right now.'

'OK.'

'Word is it's all about a Pentagon file on a USB memory stick.'

'Close enough.'

'Do you know where it is?'

'Close enough.'

'So go get it. Leave the Hoths for someone else.'

I didn't answer that.

She asked, 'When are you planning on setting out?'

'Two hours,' I said. 'Then another two hours to find them, and attack at four in the morning. My favourite time. Something we learned from the Soviets. People hit a low at four in the morning.'

'The missing file is about Sansom, right?'

'Partially.'

'Does he know you've got it?'

'I haven't got it. But I know where it is.'

'Does he know that?'

I nodded.

Lee said, 'So you made a bargain with him. Get me and Docherty and Jacob Mark out of trouble, and you'll lead him to it.'

'The bargain was designed to get myself out of trouble.'

'Didn't work for you. You're still on the hook with the feds.'

'It worked for me as far as the NYPD is concerned.'

'And it worked for the rest of us. For which I thank you.'

'You're welcome.'

She asked, 'How are the Hoths planning to get out of the country?'

'I don't think they are. I think that option disappeared. Now it's about finishing the job, do or die.'

'Like a suicide mission?'

'That's what they're good at.'

Lee got up from the bed. She told me to call her if I needed her, and wished me luck, then walked out through the door. She left the black bag on the floor near the bathroom.

I HEFTED THE BAG over to the bed. I unzipped it and looked inside. First thing I saw was a file folder.

It held twenty-one printed-out sheets. Immigration records. Two women, nineteen men. Citizens of Turkmenistan. They had entered the United States from Tajikistan three months ago. There were digital photographs and digital fingerprints, from the immigration booths at JFK. The photographs were in colour. I recognised Lila and Svetlana easily. And Leonid and his buddy. I didn't know the other seventeen. Four of them already had exit notations. I dropped their sheets in the trash and laid out the unknown thirteen on the bed.

All thirteen faces looked bored and tired. Small, wiry Middle Eastern men worn down to bone and muscle and sinew by climate and diet and culture. I looked hard at them.

Then I turned back to the bag.

At the minimum I was hoping for a decent handgun. At best I was hoping for a short submachine gun. My point to Springfield about the baggy jacket was to make him see that I would have room to carry something under it.

He had come through in fine style.

He had given me a *silenced* short submachine gun. A Heckler & Koch MP5SD. Just a pistol grip, a trigger, a housing for a curved 30-round magazine, and then a six-inch barrel radically fattened by a double-layered silencer casing. Nine-millimetre, fast, accurate and quiet. A fine weapon. It was fitted with a black nylon strap already reduced in length to its practical minimum. As if Springfield were saying, I heard you, pal.

On the left side of the gun was a combined safety and fire-selector switch. A plain white dot for safe, one little white bullet shape for single shots, three bullet shapes for three-round bursts, and a long string of bullet shapes for continuous automatic fire. I chose three-round bursts. My favourite.

I laid the gun on the bed.

He had supplied ammunition, too. Thirty rounds. Thirty rounds was not a lot, though. Not against fifteen people. But New York City is not easy. Not for me, not for Springfield.

I checked the bag again, in case there was more.

There wasn't. But there was a bonus of a kind. A knife.

A Benchmade 3300. Illegal in all fifty states unless you were active-service military or law enforcement, which I wasn't. I thumbed the release and the blade snapped out. A double-edged dagger with a spear point. Four inches long.

I closed it up and put it on the bed next to the H&K.

There were two final items in the bag. A single leather glove, black, for a large man's left hand. And a roll of black duct tape. I put them in line with the gun and the magazine and the knife.

Thirty minutes later I was all dressed up and locked and loaded and riding south on the R train.

THE R TRAIN uses older cars with some front- and rear-facing seats. But I was on a side bench, all alone. It was two o'clock in the morning. The train rocked on south. I looked back at myself in the dark window opposite and smiled.

Me against them.

I got out at 34th Street and sat on a wooden bench and walked myself through my theories one more time. I replayed Lila Hoth's history lesson from the British Empire: *When contemplating an offensive, the very first thing you must plan is your inevitable retreat.* Had her superiors back home followed that excellent advice? I was betting not. For two reasons. First, fanaticism. Start thinking rationally, and the whole thing falls apart.

And second, a plan for retreat carried with it the seeds of its own destruction. Inevitably. Six hundred agents were combing the streets. I guessed they would find nothing at all, because the planners back in the hills would have known that the only safe destination is an unplanned destination.

So now the Hoths were out in the cold. With their whole crew. They were crawling below the radar. They were in my world.

THE PHONE IN MY POCKET started to vibrate. I opened it.

Lila Hoth said, 'Well?'

I said, 'I can't find you.'

'I know.'

'So I'll deal. How much cash have you got?'

'Have you got the stick?'

'I can tell you exactly where it is.'

'But you don't actually have it?'

'No.'

'So what was the thing you showed us in the hotel?'

'A decoy.'

'Fifty thousand dollars.'

'A hundred.'

'I don't have a hundred thousand dollars.'

I said, 'You're trapped, Lila. Don't you want to die a success?'

'Seventy-five thousand.'

I said, 'Seventy-five, all of it tonight.'

'Sixty.'

'Deal.'

'Where are you?'

'Way uptown,' I lied. 'But I'll meet you in Union Square in forty minutes.'

'Where is that?'

'Broadway, between 14th Street and 17th.'

'I'll be there,' she said.

I MOVED ON to the north end of Madison Square Park and sat on a bench. I fished in my pocket for Theresa Lee's NYPD business card. I dialled her cell number.

'This is Reacher,' I said.

'What can I do for you?'

'Tell your counterterrorism people that forty minutes from now I'll be in Union Square and I'll be approached by a minimum of two and a maximum of maybe six of Lila Hoth's crew. Tell your guys they're theirs for the taking. But tell them to leave me alone.'

'Descriptions?'

'You looked in the bag, right? Before you delivered it?'

'Of course.'

'Then you've seen their pictures.'

'Where in the square?'

'I'll aim for the southwest corner.'

'Why are you meeting with her crew?'

'I set up a deal with her. But she'll send some of her people instead. It will help me if your guys grab them.'

NINE BLOCKS LATER I entered Union Square. I walked round it once. Saw nothing that worried me. I sat down near the statue of Gandhi.

Twenty minutes into my forty I saw the NYPD's counterterrorism squad begin to assemble. Good moves. They came in beat-up unmarked sedans and confiscated vans full of dents and scrapes. Altogether I counted sixteen men, and I was prepared to accept that I had missed maybe four or five others. If I didn't know better I would have suspected that a late session in a martial-arts gym had just got out. All the guys were young and fit and moved like trained athletes. They were all carrying gym bags.

I could tell they identified me. Then they melted into the scenery.

Thirty minutes into my forty I was feeling optimistic.

Five minutes later, I wasn't.

Because the feds showed up.

I pulled out the phone again and hit the green button to bring up Theresa Lee's number.

I said, 'The feds are here. How did that happen?'

'Either they're monitoring our dispatcher or one of our guys is looking for a better job.'

'Who takes precedence tonight?'

'They do. You should get the hell out of there.'

I closed the phone and put it back in my pocket. The eight guys from the Crown Vics stepped into the shadows.

I waited. Two minutes. Three.

Then thirty-nine minutes into my forty I saw figures moving through shadows and dim light. Seven men.

Good news. The more now, the fewer later.

All seven men were small, and neat, and wary. They weren't going to shoot me. Lila's need to know was like body armour. They saw me and paused. I sat still.

In theory this should have been the easy part. They approach me, the NYPD guys move in, I go about my business.

But not with the feds on the scene. At best they would want all of us. At worst they would want me more than them. I knew where the memory stick was. Lila's people didn't.

The seven men separated. Two stood still, anchored half-right of my position. Two scooted left. Three walked on, to get behind me.

I stood up. The two men on my right started to move in. The two on my left were halfway through their flanking manoeuvre. The three behind me were out of sight.

I ran.

Straight ahead, to the subway gazebo twenty feet in front of me. Down the stairs. I heard feet clattering after me. Probably close to forty people, all strung out in a crazy Pied Piper chase.

I made it into a tiled corridor and out again into the underground plaza. I changed direction and headed for the uptown R train. I jumped the turnstile and ran onto the platform and all the way to the end.

And stopped. And turned.

Behind me three separate groups followed one after the other. First came Lila Hoth's seven men. They raced towards me. They saw I had nowhere to go. They stopped. They turned suddenly and saw the NYPD counterterrorism squad right behind them.

Behind the NYPD guys were four of the eight federal agents.

No one else was on the platform. On the downtown platform opposite was a lone guy on a bench. Young. Maybe drunk. He was staring across at the sudden commotion.

It looked like a gang war. But what he was actually seeing was a fast and efficient takedown by the NYPD. They all piled in yelling with weapons drawn and badges visible and simply swamped the seven men. No contest. They slammed cuffs on their wrists and hauled them away. The guy opposite was still staring.

Then across the tracks I saw the other four federal agents arrive. They took up position directly opposite me. They all smiled a little, like they had made a smart move in a game of chess. The four agents on my side were between me and the exit. At my back was a blank white wall and the mouth of the tunnel.

Checkmate.

The agent nearest me took a gun out from under his coat.

He said, 'Raise your hands.'

Night-time schedules. Twenty-minute gaps between trains. We had been down there maybe four minutes. A maximum of sixteen minutes till the next train, and a minimum of no minutes at all.

The tunnel stayed dark and quiet.

'Raise your hands,' the agent called again. He was certainly ex-military, not FBI. Maybe this was an A team, not a B team.

'I'll shoot,' the lead agent called. But he wouldn't. They wanted the memory stick. I knew where it was.

Median delay before the next train, half of sixteen minutes. Eight minutes. The guy with the gun took a step forward. His three colleagues followed. Across the tracks the other four stood still.

The lead agent said, 'Just tell us where it is.'

I said, 'Where what is?'

'You know what. And you're missing one important factor. If you figured it out, we can figure it out too. Which means your continued existence would become surplus to requirements.'

'So go ahead,' I said. 'Figure it out.'

He raised his gun higher and straighter. It was a Glock 17. By far the lightest service pistol on the market. The guy could probably hold the pose indefinitely.

'Last chance,' he said.

Across the tracks the young guy walked away. He was prepared to waste a two-dollar MetroCard swipe in exchange for a quiet life.

No witnesses.

Median delay before the next train, maybe six minutes.

I said, 'I don't know who you are.'

The guy said, 'Federal agents.'

'Prove it.'

The guy nodded over his shoulder at the agent behind him, who put his hand in his inside jacket pocket and came back with a badge holder. He let it fall open. There were two separate pieces of ID in it. I couldn't read either one. They were too far away.

I stepped forward. I got within four feet of him and saw a standard Defense Intelligence Agency ID in the window of the wallet. In the lower window was some kind of a warrant that stated the holder was acting directly for the President of the United States.

'Very nice,' I said. 'Beats working for a living.'

I stepped back.

Median delay before the next train, five minutes.

The lead agent dropped the angle of his arm. Now he was aiming at my knees.

'I'll shoot,' he said. No witnesses.

If all else fails, start talking. 'Why do you want it?'

'National security.'

'Offence or defence?'

He said, 'I'll count to three.'

I said, 'Good luck with that.'

He said, 'One.'

Then the rails hissed in the track bed next to me. A train rushed into view, moving fast, and then the brakes bit down and the train pulled in right alongside us.

An uptown R train. Maybe fifteen cars.

Each with a handful of passengers. Witnesses.

The lead agent's Glock went under his coat.

The R train uses older cars. Each car has four sets of doors. The lead car was halted right next to us. I was in line with the first set of doors. The DIA guys were closer to sets three and four.

The doors opened, the whole length of the train.

I turned to face the train.

The DIA guys turned to face the train.

I stepped forward.

They stepped forward.

Choices: I could get on, whereupon they would get on. We could ride together all night. Or I could let the train go without me and spend a minimum twenty more minutes trapped with them on the same platform.

The doors stayed open.

I stepped into the car.

They stepped into the car.

I paused a beat and backed right out again.

They backed out.

The doors closed in front of me. Like a final curtain.

Five hundred tons of steel started to roll.

The R train uses older cars. They have toe boards and rain gutters. I hooked my fingers into the gutter and jammed my toes onto the board. I flattened myself against the metal and the glass. I hugged the car's exterior curve like a starfish. The MP5 dug into my chest. The train moved. The hard edge of the tunnel came right at me. I held my breath and laid my cheek against the glass.

IT WAS A NIGHTMARE RIDE. Incredible speed, howling blackness, battering noise, unseen obstructions hurtling straight at me, extreme physical violence. Wind tore at my clothes.

I rode nine blocks like that. Then we hit 23rd Street and the train braked hard. I hung on and was carried straight into the station's dazzling brightness at thirty miles an hour. I was clamped on the lead car like a limpet. It stopped at the north end of the station. I arched my body and the doors slid open under me. I stepped inside and collapsed into the nearest seat.

Nine blocks. Enough to cure me of subway surfing for life.

There were three other passengers in my car. None of them even looked at me. The doors sucked shut. The train moved on.

I got out at Herald Square. Ten to four in the morning. Still on schedule. I was twenty blocks and maybe four minutes north of where I got on the train in Union Square. Too far and too fast for organised DIA resistance. I came up from under the ground and walked.

Where did they go?

New York City. Two hundred and five thousand acres. Eight million separate addresses. I sorted possibilities like a machine.

I drew a blank. Then I smiled.

You talk too much, Lila.

I heard her voice in my head again. From the tearoom at the Four Seasons. She was talking about the old Afghan fighters, *The mujahideen were intelligent. They had a habit of doubling back to positions we had previously written off as abandoned.*

I set off back to Herald Square. To the R train. I could get out at Fifth and 59th. From there it was a short walk to the old buildings on 58th Street.

Chapter Ten

The old buildings on 58th Street were dark and quiet. Four thirty in the morning. There was crime-scene tape across the door with the single bell push. The one with the abandoned restaurant on the ground floor.

The crime-scene tape looked unbroken. Which meant there was a back door. Which was likely, with a restaurant on the premises.

I moved twenty yards south to widen my angle. Saw no open alleys. Next to the door with the crime-scene tape was the old restaurant's window. But next to that was another door.

Architecturally it was part of the restaurant building's neighbour. It was set into the ground floor of the next building along. It was wider than a normal door. It was black, a little scarred, and had no handle on the outside. Just a keyhole. Without a key it opened only from the inside. I made a bet with myself that it let out of a covered alley. I figured that the restaurant's neighbour was two rooms wide on the ground floor and three rooms wide above. At street level, there were passageways leading to rear entrances, all of them boxed in.

I pressed back in the darkness and waited.

The city that doesn't sleep was at least resting comfortably.

Three minutes later the phone in my pocket started to vibrate.

I kept my eyes on the restaurant building and opened the phone. Raised it to my ear and said, 'Yes?'

She asked, 'What happened?'

'You didn't show.'

'Did you expect me to? What happened to my people?'

'They're in the system.'

'We can still deal.'

'OK. But the price just went up. Seventy-five.'

'Where are you now?'

'Right outside your house.'

There was movement at a window. Third floor.

She said, 'No, you're not outside my house.'

But she didn't sound sure.

She said, 'Where do you want to meet?'

I said, 'What does it matter? You won't show.'

'I'll send someone.'

'You can't afford to. You're down to your last six guys.'

She started to say something and stopped.

I said, 'Times Square. Tomorrow morning at ten.'

'Why?'

'I want people around. Take it or leave it.'

She said, 'Stay on the line.'

'Why?'

'I have to check that I have seventy-five.'

I unzipped my jacket.

I heard Lila Hoth, breathing.

Fifty yards away the black door opened. The covered alley. A man stepped out. Small, dark, wiry.

I put the phone in my pocket. Still open. Still live.

I raised the MP5.

Submachine guns were developed for close-quarters combat, but the H&K was reliable out to at least a hundred yards. I moved the selector lever to single shot and put the front sight square on the guy's centre mass.

The guy stepped out to the kerb. Scanned right, scanned left. He saw the same nothing I was seeing. He stepped back to the door.

I waited until his momentum was set to move forward. Then I shot him in the back. Bull's-eye.

The guy pitched forward and went down. I put a second bullet into him for safety's sake and took the phone out of my pocket.

I said, 'You still there?'

She said, 'We're still counting.'

You're one short, I thought.

I zipped my jacket. Started walking. I hugged the far side of Madison and overshot 58th by a few yards. I crossed the avenue and came round the corner with my shoulder tight against the frontage of the buildings. I needed to keep below her line of sight.

I said from forty feet below her, 'I have to go now. Times Square, tomorrow morning at ten, OK?'

From forty feet above me she said, 'OK.'

I put the phone back in my pocket and dragged the dead guy all the way into the alley. I closed the door behind us.

There was a light in the alley. I recognised the dead guy from the photographs in Springfield's folder. He had been number seven of the original nineteen. I searched him. No ID. No weapon.

Then I found the inner door to the building, and unzipped my jacket. I wondered how long it would take for them to get worried about the missing guy.

They waited seven minutes and sent two men. The inner door opened and the first guy stepped out. Number fourteen on Springfield's list. He took a pace towards the alley door and the second guy stepped out. Number eight.

Then three things happened.

First, the first guy saw that the alley door was closed. It could not be opened from the outside without the key. Therefore the original searcher would have left it open. But it was closed. Therefore the original searcher was back inside.

The first guy turned round.

Second thing, the second guy also turned round.

Then the first guy saw me.

Third thing, I shot them both. Two three-round bursts.

The two guys went down.

Eight rounds gone. Twenty-two remaining. Seven men captured, three more down, three still walking. Plus the Hoths themselves.

I searched the new dead guys. No ID. No weapons. No keys, which meant the inner door wasn't locked.

Then I waited.

The phone vibrated in my pocket. I pulled it out. *Unknown caller.* Lila. I ignored her. I was all done talking.

I put my gloved fingers on the inner door's handle. I eased it down. Three men had gone out. If anyone was inside waiting, there would be a fatal split second of delay for recognition, friend or foe.

But no delay for me. Anyone I saw was my enemy.

I opened the door.

I was looking at an empty room. The abandoned restaurant's kitchen. It was dark and dismantled. There was a large stone table in the centre of the room. Cool, smooth, slightly dished from years of wear. Maybe once pastry had been rolled on it.

More recently Peter Molina had been murdered on it.

There was no doubt in my mind that it was the table I had seen in the DVD. I could see where the camera must have been positioned. I could see knots of frayed rope on the table legs, where Peter's wrists and ankles had been tied.

The phone vibrated in my pocket.

I ignored it. I moved on.

There were two swinging doors leading to the dining room. The doors had porthole windows. I peered through. Empty.

I stepped into the dining room. Turned left and left again. Found a back hallway with rest rooms.

Plus two more doors, one in each of the side walls. One would lead back to the kitchen. The other would lead to the stairwell.

I opened the stairwell door. Directly across from me was the door that led out to the street door with the crime-scene tape.

Out of the hallway rose a narrow staircase. I started up the stairs.

I came out in a first-floor hallway. One room to the left, one to the right and two dead ahead. Doors all closed.

The flutter I had seen had been at a third-floor window on the left, looking at the building from the outside. Which meant her room was the room on the right, looking at it from the inside. I doubted that there would be any significant difference in the floor plans. A walk through the first-floor room on the right would give me the lie of the land.

I squeezed the slack out of the MP5's trigger and put my gloved fingers on the door handle. I opened the door.

An empty studio apartment. A long, narrow space. A closet in the back, a bathroom, a kitchenette and a living area.

I walked to the window. The fire escape was a standard design. A narrow iron ladder came down from the floor above and gave onto a narrow iron walkway under the windows themselves.

The window was a sash design. The lower pane was designed to slide upwards inside the upper pane. Where the panes met they were locked together with a simple brass tongue in a slot. The window frames had been painted over many times.

I undid the lock and heaved. The frame shuddered upwards and stuck. I increased the pressure. The frame moved another eight inches and jammed. Total gap, about twenty inches.

I got one leg out, ducked through, got the other leg out.

The phone vibrated in my pocket.

I went up the iron ladder. Halfway up, my head was at the level of the second-floor sills and I could see both front-room windows.

Both had closed curtains. No light inside. No activity.

I moved on to the third storey. Closed curtains. I paused under the window where I had seen movement. I heard nothing.

I moved up to the fourth floor. No curtains. Empty rooms. The windows were locked. There was nothing I could do without busting the glass. Which would make a noise.

I got a foot up on the windowsill. I stepped up and grabbed the crumbling cornice high above my head. I heaved myself over it and sprawled face down on the roof. I got to my knees and looked around for a trap door. I found one right above where I judged the stairwell hallway would be. Presumably it was locked from below, probably with a hasp and a padlock.

The padlock would be strong, but the hasp would be screwed into the frame, and the frame would be weak from age and water damage.

Standard tactical doctrine for any assault: attack from the high ground.

I got my gloved fingers under the edge of the trap door opposite the hinge and yanked. No result. So I got serious. Two hands, bent legs, deep breath. I jerked the lid.

And the night started to unravel.

The padlock with the hasp still attached free-fell ten feet and thumped hard on the bare wooden floor below.

Not good.

I heard a door open down on the third floor.

I aimed the MP5.

A head came into view up the stairs. A man. He had a gun in his hand. He saw the padlock on the floor. He peered upwards. Number eleven on Springfield's list. He saw me. He hesitated. I didn't. I shot him through the top of his head. A burst of three. He went down with a loud clatter. I vaulted through the open trap door and landed feet first next to the guy.

Eleven rounds gone, nineteen remaining, two men still up.

Plus the Hoths.

The phone vibrated in my pocket.

I picked up the guy's gun and looked at the stairs.

No one came up.

The gun I had taken from the dead guy was a SIG SAUER P220, with a silencer on it. The same ammunition I was using. I thumbed the rounds out and dropped them loose into my pocket. I put the empty gun on the floor. Then I ducked into the front room on the right. It was empty. I paced out the studio layout. I made it to what I guessed was the centre of the living room and stamped down hard. I figured Lila was directly below me, listening.

The response came in the form of a bullet smashing up through the boards three feet to my right.

I fired back, a triple tap downward. Then I stepped to where I guessed their kitchen was.

Fourteen rounds gone. Sixteen remaining. Nine loose in my pocket. Another shot came up through the floor. I fired back. They fired back. I fired back one more time and crept out to the head of the stairs.

A guy was sneaking up on me. Number two on Springfield's list. He had another SIG P220 in his hand. He saw me. Fired once and missed. I didn't.

Twenty-three rounds gone. Seven left, plus nine loose.

One guy up, plus the Hoths themselves.

The phone vibrated in my pocket.

One last guy between them and me. How would they use him? They would send the guy up the fire escape. They would distract me with the phone and let the guy shoot me in the back.

Either immediately or much later. They would want me either surprised or bored.

They chose immediately.

I stepped back into the left-hand room. The iron ladder rose right-to-left from my perspective. I would see the guy's head as he came up from below.

I flattened myself against the window wall. Glanced out. Nothing. I flipped the window latch. Tried the handles. The window was stuck. I stepped in front of the glass, grabbed the handles and heaved. The window shot up and slammed open so hard the pane cracked. I backed up against the wall again.

I heard the dull, muted clang of rubber soles on iron. I let him get his head and shoulders in the room. He was number fifteen on Springfield's list. He saw me. I pulled the trigger. A triple tap.

I missed. He fired, then ducked back outside.

I went out after him. He made it back to the third floor and rolled on his back and raised his gun. I came down the ladder after him and stitched a triple tap into the centre of his face.

Six men down. Seven arrested. Four back home. Two in a locked ward. Nineteen out of nineteen.

The third floor window was open. The curtains were drawn back. Lila and Svetlana Hoth were standing together behind the kitchenette counter.

Twenty-nine rounds gone. One left.

I heard Lila's voice in my head again, *You must save the last bullet for yourself, because you do not want to be taken alive, especially by the women.*

I climbed over the sill and stepped into the room.

THE APARTMENT was laid out the same as the place on the first floor. Living room, then the kitchenette, then the bathroom, then the closet in the back. There were two lights burning. There was a folded-up bed against the wall in the living room. Plus two hard chairs. The kitchenette had two parallel counters and one wall cupboard. Lila and Svetlana were crammed hip-to-hip in it. Svetlana on the left, Lila on the right. Svetlana was in a brown housecoat. Lila was in black cargo trousers and a white T-shirt. She looked as beautiful as ever. Like a radical fashion photographer had posed his best model in a gritty urban setting.

I aimed the MP5. Black and wicked. It was hot. It stank of gunpowder and oil and smoke. I could smell it quite clearly.

I said, 'Put your hands on the counter.'

They complied. Four hands spread like starfish.

I said, 'You're not mother and daughter.'

Lila said, 'No, we're not.'

'So what are you?'

'Teacher and pupil.'

'Good. I wouldn't want to shoot a daughter in front of her mother. Or a mother in front of her daughter.'

The phone vibrated in my pocket.

I stared at Lila's hands. Flat. Empty. No phone.

She said, 'Perhaps you should answer that.'

I juggled the MP5 into my left hand and pulled out the phone. *Unknown caller*. I opened it and put it to my ear.

Theresa Lee said, 'Reacher? Where the hell have you been? I've been trying to call you for twenty minutes.'

'I've been busy. What's up?'

'Homeland Security got back to us. One of the Tajikistan party missed a connection in Istanbul. He came in through London and Washington instead. There are twenty men, not nineteen.'

The twentieth man stepped out of the bathroom.

SCIENTISTS MEASURE TIME all the way down to the picosecond. A trillionth of a regular second. What happened to me in the first few picoseconds was a whole bunch of things. First, I dropped the phone. By the time it was down level with my shoulder, lines of conversation with Lila were screaming in my head. I had said, *You're down to your last six guys*. She had started to reply, and then she had stopped. She had been about to say, *No, I've got seven*.

For once, she hadn't talked too much.

And I hadn't listened enough.

By the time the phone was down level with my waist I was focusing on the twentieth guy. He was holding a silenced handgun.

I was holding the MP5 left-handed. The magazine was empty. The last round was already chambered. I wanted to change hands.

To change hands would take too long. By the time the phone was down around my knees my right palm was slapping upwards to meet the barrel. Lila was stepping out into the room. My last round hit the twentieth guy in the face. Not bad for my left hand. Except that I had been aiming at his centre mass.

The phone hit the floor.

The twentieth guy went down in a clatter.

Lila kept on moving, ducking down. She came up with the dead guy's gun. Another SIG P220.

If Lila was scrambling for the gun, it was the only one in the apartment. It had been fired at least three times, through the ceiling.

Maximum six rounds left. Six versus zero.

Lila pointed the gun at me. I pointed mine at her.

Off to my left Svetlana said, 'Your gun is empty.'

I glanced at her. 'You speak English?'

'Fairly well.'

'I reloaded upstairs.'

'I can see from here. You're set to three-round bursts. But you fired only once. Therefore that was your last bullet.'

We stood like that for what seemed like a long time. The P220 was as steady as a rock in Lila's hand. She was fifteen feet from me. Svetlana was in the kitchen.

Svetlana said, 'Put your gun down.'

I said, 'You want the memory stick.'

'You don't have it.'

'But I know where it is.'

'So do we.'

I said nothing.

'As soon as you told us you knew where it was, we set about thinking. You spurred us on. You talk too much, Reacher. You made yourself disposable.'

Lila said, 'Put the gun down. Have a little dignity. Don't stand there like an idiot, holding an empty gun.'

I stood still.

Lila dropped her arm and fired into the floor between my feet. She hit a spot exactly equidistant between the toecaps of my shoes. Not an easy shot. She was a great markswoman.

Five rounds left.

I looped the strap up over my head. The gun was no longer any use to me.

Svetlana said, 'Throw it over here.'

I swung the gun slowly and let it go.

Svetlana said, 'Now take off your jacket.'

I shrugged the jacket off and threw it next to the MP5. Svetlana rooted through the pockets. She found the nine rounds and the roll of duct tape. She stood the rounds upright on the counter. She put the tape next to it.

She said, 'Shoes and socks.'

I threw them one after the other towards the pile.

Lila said, 'Take your shirt off.'

I kept my back against the wall and threw the shirt into the pile. Lila and Svetlana looked at my scars. They seemed to like them.

Svetlana said, 'Take your trousers off.'

I unbuttoned. I unzipped. I kicked the trousers towards the pile. Svetlana went through the pockets. Made a pile of my possessions on the kitchen counter.

The room went quiet. I stood there in my white boxers.

Svetlana balled up my gun and my shoes and my clothes into a tidy bundle and threw it behind the kitchen counter. She followed it with the two hard chairs. She picked up my phone, shut it off and tossed it away. She was clearing the space. The living room part of the studio was about twenty feet by twelve. I was backed up against the centre of one of the long walls. Lila tracked round in front of me, pointing the gun. She stopped in the far corner, by the window. Now she was facing me at a shallow angle.

Svetlana went into the kitchen. I heard a drawer rattle open. Saw Svetlana come back. With two knives.

They had steel blades. Wicked, wafer-thin cutting edges. Svetlana threw one of them to Lila. She caught it expertly. Svetlana moved to the corner opposite her. They had me triangulated.

Lila twisted her upper body and jammed the P220's silencer hard into the angle where the front wall met the side. She found the catch at the heel of the butt with her thumb and dropped the magazine. It fell out in the corner of the room. She threw the gun itself into the other corner, behind Svetlana. The gun and the magazine were now twenty feet apart.

Lila stepped forward a pace. Svetlana did the same. They held their knives low. Like street fighters.

I stood still.

Lila said, 'A delay is good. It heightens anticipation.'

Then I reached behind me and came out with my Benchmade 3300, from where it had been duct-taped to the small of my back.

I thumbed the release and the blade snapped out. A loud sound, in the silent room. I don't like knives. I have no real talent with them. But I have as much of an instinct for self-preservation as any guy. Maybe more than most.

I wanted to get to the kitchen, so I danced towards Svetlana, who was between me and it. Her blade hissed past my thigh. I jammed my ass back and my shoulders forward and clubbed her with an overarm left hook. It caught her full on the side of the nose.

She rocked back and Lila came in from my left. Concentrating hard. This was no longer a game. She ducked in, she ducked out. For a time we all danced like that.

I kept my hips back and my shoulders forward. I swung my blade hard for Lila's face. Lila ducked back. She knew the swing was going to miss, because she was going to make it miss. Svetlana knew it was going to miss, because she trusted Lila.

I knew it was going to miss, because I planned not to let it hit.

I stopped the manoeuvre, reversed direction and aimed a vicious backhand at Svetlana. I sliced her forehead. Open to the bone.

Within seconds blood was sheeting down into her eyes.

Lila came straight after me.

I dodged the arc of her blade. Left, right. I hit the wall behind me. Then Lila cut me.

She had figured out the reach issue. She was holding her knife in her fingertips way at the end of the handle. She lunged in. She stopped on a stiff front leg and leaned in and slashed at my stomach. And hit it.

A bad cut. It was a long diagonal slice below my navel.

I paused a beat. Disbelief. Then I did what I always do when someone hurts me. I stepped in, not away. Her momentum had carried her knife beyond my hip. My blade was low. I slashed backhand at her thigh and cut her deep and then pushed off my back foot and hit her in the face with my left fist. Bull's-eye. I barged on towards Svetlana. She swung her blade right. Then left. She opened up. I slashed down on the inside of her right forearm. I cut her to the bone. Her arm was useless. I spun her round and stabbed her in the kidney. All four inches, with a savage sideways jerk.

She went down to her knees. Lila was trying to clear her head. Her nose was broken. She charged me. I ducked away to the kitchenette. Stepped between the counters. Grabbed one of the hard chairs. I threw it left-handed at Lila. She ducked away and it smashed against her back.

I came out of the kitchen and stepped behind Svetlana and hauled her head back. Leaned round and cut her throat. I let go and she pitched forward.

I stepped away, panting. I said, 'One down.'

Lila said, 'One still up.'

Her thigh was bleeding badly. There was a neat slice in her trousers and blood was running down her leg. Her shoe was already soaked. My boxers were soaked. They had turned from white to red. I looked down and saw blood welling out of me. But my old scar had saved me. My shrapnel wound, from Beirut, long ago. The ridged white skin from the clumsy MASH stitches was tough and gnarled and it had slowed Lila's blade. Without it the cut would have been much longer and deeper. For years I had resented the hasty work by the emergency surgeons. Now I was grateful for it.

Lila's busted nose started to bleed. She coughed and spat.

My head buzzed. My blood pressure was falling.

Lila said, 'If you ask nicely I'll let you walk away.'

'I'm not asking.'

'You could kill a woman?'

'I just did.'

'One like me?'

'Especially one like you.'

She looked up at me with her amazing eyes. She said, 'If you mean it, this is where you do it.'

I meant it. So I did it. I was weak, but it was easy. Her leg was slowing her down. She was having trouble breathing. I took the second chair from the kitchen. Now my reach was unbeatable. I backed her into the corner with it and hit her with it twice until she dropped her knife and fell. I sat down beside her and strangled her. I didn't want to use the blade. I don't like knives.

Afterwards I crawled to the kitchen and rinsed the Benchmade under the tap. Then I used it to cut butterfly shapes out of the duct tape. I pinched my wound together with my fingers and used the butterflies to hold it together. A dollar and a half at any hardware store, but as much a part of standard-issue Special Forces equipment as thousand-dollar rifles and satellite radios. I struggled into my clothes. I reloaded my pockets. I put my shoes back on.

Then I sat down on the floor. A medical man would say I passed out. I prefer to think I just went to sleep.

I WOKE UP in a hospital bed. The clock in my head told me it was four in the afternoon. Ten hours. I had a clip on my finger. It had a wire. The wire must have been connected to a nurses' station. The clip must have detected some kind of an altered heartbeat pattern, because about a minute later a bunch of people came in. A doctor, then Jacob Mark, then Theresa Lee, then Springfield, then Sansom. The doctor was a woman.

The doctor fussed around, checking monitors. Then she told me I was in Bellevue Hospital and that my condition was satisfactory. The ER people had cleaned the wound and sutured it and filled me full of antibiotics and three units of blood. She told me to avoid heavy lifting for a month. Then she left.

I looked at Theresa Lee. 'What happened to me?'

'You don't remember?'

'Of course I remember. What's the official version?'

'You were found on the street in the East Village. Unexplained knife wound. They ran a tox screen and found traces of barbiturate. A dope deal gone bad.'

'How did I get to the East Village?'

'You didn't. We brought you straight here.'

'We?'

'Me and Mr Springfield.'

'How did you find me?'

'We triangulated the cellphone. The address was Mr Springfield's idea.'

Springfield said, 'A mujahideen leader told us about doubling back to abandoned hide-outs twenty-five years ago.'

I asked, 'Is there going to be any comeback?'

John Sansom said, 'No.'

Simple as that.

Sansom asked, 'Where is the memory stick?'

I looked at Jacob Mark. 'You OK?'

He said, 'Not really.'

I said, 'You're going to have to hear some stuff.'

He said, 'OK.'

I hauled myself into a sitting position. Didn't hurt at all. I guessed I was full of painkillers.

'We know the general shape of it,' I said. 'They planned for the best part of three months and then executed during the final week. They coerced Susan by using Peter as leverage. She drove up from Annandale, got stuck in a four-hour traffic jam, and then she arrived in Manhattan just before two in the morning. I assume we know exactly when she came out of the Holland Tunnel. So what we have to do is work backwards and figure out exactly where her car was jammed up at midnight.'

'How does that help us?'

'Because at midnight she threw the memory stick out of her car window.'

'How can you possibly know that?'

'Because when she arrived she didn't have a cellphone.'

Sansom glanced at Lee. Lee nodded. Said, 'Keys and a wallet. That was all. Not in her car. The FBI inventoried the contents.'

Jacob Mark said, 'She had one.'

Sansom said, 'So?'

'The Hoths set a deadline. Probably midnight. Susan didn't show, the Hoths went to work. They made a threat, and they carried it out. And they proved it. They phoned through a cellphone picture. Peter on the slab. Susan's life changed on the stroke of midnight. She was helpless in a traffic jam. The phone in her hand was suddenly repugnant. She threw it out the window. Followed it with the memory stick, which was the symbol of all her troubles. They're both still there, on the side of I-95. No other explanation.'

Nobody spoke.

I said, 'The median, probably. Susan would have put herself in the over-taking lane, because she was in a hurry. We could have triangulated the cellphone, but it's too late now. The battery will be dead.'

Silence in the room. A whole minute.

Sansom said, 'That's insane. The Hoths must have known they were losing control of the stick as soon as they phoned the picture through. They were giving up their leverage.'

'Two answers,' I said. 'The Hoths *were* insane, in a way. They could act the part in public, but underneath it was all black and white for them. A threat was a threat. Midnight was midnight. But their risk was minimal. They had a guy tailing Susan all the way.'

'Who?'

'The twentieth guy. It wasn't a missed connection in Istanbul. They suddenly realised that for a thing like this they needed someone on the ground in DC. So the twentieth guy followed Susan all the way up. Five or ten cars back. He didn't see what happened. But he stayed with her. He was on the train, wearing an NBA shirt. I thought he looked familiar, when I saw him again. But I couldn't confirm it, because I shot him in the face a second later.'

Sansom asked, 'So where was Susan at midnight?'

'You figure it out. Time, distance, average speed.'

Jacob Mark was from Jersey. He started talking about Troopers he knew. They patrolled I-95 night and day. They knew it like the backs of their hands. They had traffic cameras. Their recorded pictures could calibrate the paper calculations. Everyone got into a big conversation. They paid me no more attention. I laid back and they all started edging out of the room. Last out was Springfield. He paused in the doorway and looked back and asked, 'How do you feel about Lila Hoth?'

I said, 'I feel fine.'

'Really? I wouldn't. You nearly got taken down by two girls. It was sloppy. Things like that, you do them properly or not at all.'

'I didn't have much ammunition.'

'You had thirty rounds. You should have used single shots. Those triples were all about anger. You let emotion get in the way. I warned you about that.'

He looked at me for a long second with nothing in his face. Then he stepped out to the corridor and I never saw him again.

THERESA LEE CAME BACK two hours later. She had a shopping bag with her. She told me the hospital wanted its bed, so the NYPD was putting me in a hotel. She had bought clothes for me. Shoes, socks, jeans, boxers and a shirt, all sized exactly the same as the items the ER staff had burned.

'Thank you,' I said.

She told me the others were working on the maths problem. She told me they were arguing about the route Susan would have used from the Turnpike to the Holland Tunnel.

Then she said, 'They won't find the picture, you know.'

I said, 'You think?'

'Oh, they'll find the stick. But they'll say it was unreadable, or run over and damaged, or there was nothing sinister on it.'

I didn't answer.

Then she asked, 'How do you feel about things?'

I said, 'All in all, I'm regretting the approach on the train. With Susan. I wish I had given her a couple more stops.'

'I was wrong. She couldn't possibly have got over it.'

'The opposite,' I said. 'Was there a sock in her car?'

Lee thought back to the FBI inventory. Nodded.

'So think about Susan setting out. She's living a nightmare. But can't bring herself to believe it's as bad as she suspects. She's dressed in what she wore for work. Black trousers, white blouse. She's heading for an unknown situation. She's a woman on her own, she lives in Virginia, she's been around the military for years. So she takes her gun. It's probably still wrapped in a sock, like she stores it in her drawer. She puts it in her bag. She leaves. She gets stuck in the jam. Maybe the Hoths call her. They won't listen. They're fanatics and they're foreign. They think a traffic jam is a dog-ate-my-homework kind of thing.'

'Then she gets the midnight message.'

'And she changes. The point is, she has *time* to change. She's stuck in traffic. She can't go to the cops. She has to sit there and think. And she arrives at a decision. She's going to avenge her son. She makes a plan. She takes the gun out of the sock. She sees an old black jacket dumped on the back seat. She wants dark clothing. She puts it on. Eventually she drives on to New York.'

'What about the Israeli eleven-point list?'

'Maybe working round to killing someone else produces the same feelings as working round to killing yourself. That's what she was doing. She was climbing up on the plateau. But she wasn't quite there yet. I disturbed her too early. So she quit. She took the other way out. Maybe by 59th Street she would have been ready.'

'She had a six-shooter. There were twenty-two of them.'

I nodded. 'She'd have died, for sure. Maybe she would have died satisfied.'

A DAY LATER in the hotel Theresa Lee came to visit. She told me that Sansom had scoped out a target area about half a mile long and the Jersey highway people had closed it off. Three hours into the search they found Susan's cellphone. Four feet away, they found the memory stick.

It had been run over. It was crushed. It was unreadable.

I LEFT NEW YORK the next day. I moved south. I spent part of the next two weeks obsessing over what might have been in that picture. I came up with all kinds of speculations, some involving technical breaches of sharia law.

But by the time a month had passed I had forgot all of it. My cut had healed nicely. The scar was thin and white. The stitches were neat and tiny. My lower body was like a textbook illustration: this one is how it should be done, and that one is how it shouldn't. But I never forgot how those earlier, clumsier stitches had saved me. What goes around comes around. A benign legacy, from the truck bomb in Beirut, planned and paid for and driven there by persons unknown.

LEE CHILD

Early influence: Alistair MacLean
University degree: law
Addictions: books, music, baseball

Jack Reacher, the tall, honest drifter who stars in all thirteen of Lee Child's novels, has been dubbed 'the thinking reader's action hero', and was inspired by the kind of characters that Child always enjoyed reading about when he was younger, but which seemed to him to have been discarded by a new generation of writers. 'Maybe fifteen years before I started out, people had begun experimenting with "the flawed hero" and it had got out of hand. Heroes were becoming more and more miserable and dysfunctional.'

Lee Child puts his books squarely in the same class as his main character, describing them as 'straightforward, old-fashioned' adventures. However, in the opening scenes of *Gone Tomorrow*, he plunges Reacher into a very 21st-century situation: sitting opposite someone in a subway car who shows all the signs of being a suicide bomber. Without hesitation, Reacher challenges the suspect and becomes involved. 'Some people, and I think I'm one of them,' says Child, 'see a situation developing and can't just pass by on the other side. Reacher's like that.'

If this heroic, solitary ex-military policeman's code of justice seems to be that of a knight in shining armour, his attitude to women, whom he occasionally loves but always leaves, is perhaps less gallant? 'Reacher's core appeal comes down to wish fulfilment, pure and simple,' says Child. 'I think women wish that he would walk up their path and knock on their door, specifically because he *won't* stay very long. We all want a little bit of variety and adventure, but love affairs are generally very messy. Reacher will be a fun companion for three or four days, and then he will be gone. He's in your life and then out of your life. That's a very reassuring fantasy.'

Men are equally drawn to the Reacher character. 'Again, it's wish fulfilment. I've had so many guys—ordinary guys who have been working all day in a bank or on Wall Street or wherever—say to me at book signings, "Boy, I wish that I could live like Jack Reacher." That's because we all get burdened with responsibilities, bureacracy and chores, and wouldn't it be great just to get rid of it all and walk off into the sunset?'

AN INTERVIEW WITH JACK REACHER

Q: You always travel with your folding toothbrush, but what do you do about shaving?

A: When I feel the need I stop by a drug store and buy a three-pack of disposable razors and a small can of foam. Use once, throw away.

Q: You never seem to have a problem with pulling the ladies. What's your secret? Do you have a good chat-up line?

A: It's a secret to me too. I'm usually the last to know. I don't have chat-up lines. I just act like myself. I guess some like it, and some don't.

Q: Have you ever thought about settling down and having kids?

A: I like kids. And dogs. Wouldn't mind having some. I'd need help settling down. Haven't found anyone willing to undertake that project yet . . .

Q: I don't think you've ever been heard to swear in spite of your military background. What's your attitude to bad language?

A: It's because of, not in spite of. Officers don't swear. Part of the code. I don't mind it from other people.

Q: Why don't you carry a cellphone?

A: Who would I want to call? Who would want to call me?

Q: Do you play an instrument? Can you sing? How important is music to you?

A: I don't know if I can play an instrument. I never tried. I sing all the time. Not very well, but hey. I like music. Snatches on other people's radios cheer me up.

Q: You don't own a car—but if you did, what would it be?

A: A big sedan, battered on the outside but looked after underneath.

Q: Your perfect meal?

A: Soup, steak, bottled beer, pie, coffee.

Q: Significant date?

A: I was born October 29th. Didn't ask to be, but that's what started it all.

To read the full interview go to:
www.jackreacher.co.uk

Folly

Alan Titchmarsh

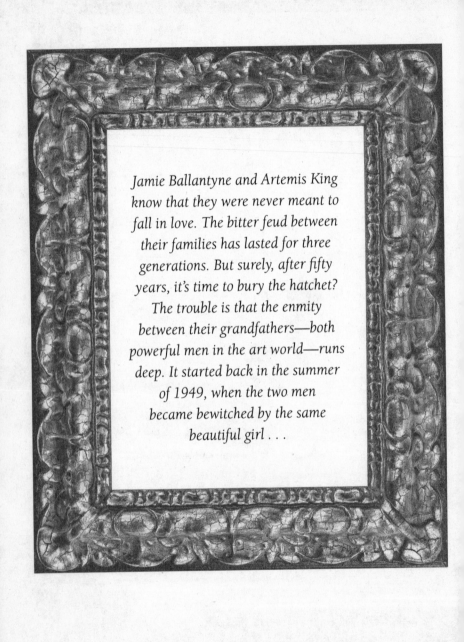

Jamie Ballantyne and Artemis King know that they were never meant to fall in love. The bitter feud between their families has lasted for three generations. But surely, after fifty years, it's time to bury the hatchet? The trouble is that the enmity between their grandfathers—both powerful men in the art world—runs deep. It started back in the summer of 1949, when the two men became bewitched by the same beautiful girl . . .

Chapter 1

Bath—November 2007

'Any more bids?'

In most salerooms this is not an anxious request. Brisk, yes, at times chivvying, but not anxious. It can even be delivered carelessly. But then the auctioneer on this occasion was not typical of his breed. Not the sort most usually found in a provincial saleroom—the tweedy sort with florid cheeks, a pair of half-moon spectacles and a voice owing its resonance to vintage port. No. He was in his thirties. Just. Slim. Quite good-looking. And at the moment he seemed a little uneasy. His name was James Ballantyne, which made him sound rather more confident than he really was, and he was the last in line (presently, at any rate) of a firm of auctioneers who had been established in Bath for three generations.

'Going once . . . going twice . . .' He scanned the room again. 'I'll have to let it go, then . . .' Those in the front row would have detected the merest hint of a wince in that muscle just above the top lip where involuntary reactions can often give the owner away.

And then, just as he was lifting his hammer, an arm was raised towards the back of the saleroom. That was all he could see—just an arm. He leaned sideways. The figure was partially obscured by a pillar. He could make out the slender frame of a fair-haired woman in a red jacket. She moved into his eye line and smiled at him.

Those who noticed the earlier flicker of the facial muscle would now have detected a movement of the jaw, which, but for the summoning of an iron will, would have dropped open. Instead it was turned rather neatly into a breath, and followed by a question: 'Was that a bid, madam?'

The woman nodded and raised her numbered paddle in confirmation.

It was a muscle in his cheek that now twitched involuntarily.

'With you at seven and a half thousand pounds, then . . . and against you, sir.' He looked in the direction of the fat dealer in the front row who had made the previous bid. The dealer stared pointedly at the floor.

James Ballantyne cleared his throat. 'This really is a nice little Herring; I don't want to have to let it go at this price, but I am selling . . .' He cast his eye once more in the direction of the long-legged thoroughbred—the one in the painting—a dark animal with wild eyes, set against a stable wall and a manger full of hay. He looked back at the young woman who had raised her arm. She fixed him with an unblinking stare, defying him to offer the painting to anyone else.

His loyalties were split now, between the bidder and his professional pride. John Frederick Herring was a respected artist, and the work was a good one; his mother would be disappointed it had not fared better. The woman was still staring at him, and now he could see the corners of her mouth breaking into a grin.

'The Herring's going, then . . .'

'Junior,' the dealer in the front row muttered to himself. 'Not worth it.'

'Selling, then, at seven and a half thousand pounds . . . All done?' He brought down the hammer and the customary soft murmur drifted around the saleroom. The blonde in the red jacket looked down as she recorded the price in her catalogue.

James noted her name in his ledger, his head filling with questions that he tried to put aside. Why was she here? Where had she been? But there was no time to dwell on them. He checked his notes. 'And so to lot two hundred and thirty-four—our final lot today. The Munnings.'

A man in a navy-blue overall manoeuvred the painting in its gilded frame onto an easel to the right of the auctioneer's desk.

James soldiered on. 'The highlight of today's sale. A lot of interest here. . .'

It was a simple painting of a woman on horseback, set against a leaden sky. It measured twenty inches by twenty-four inches. The horse was a grey, and the woman was seated sidesaddle in a riding habit and a wide-brimmed brown hat. She held the reins with her left hand. In her right hand rested a riding crop, and she gazed towards the artist with an expression on her face that seemed startlingly familiar.

The next few minutes he found hard to recall in detail later. The bidding had been brisk and competitive. Within what seemed like the blinking of an eye the picture had sold for £750,000 to the same woman who had bought the previous lot; the woman he had grown up with but had not set eyes on for the past five years. Her name had always had a magical ring to it. Artemis King. She had hated it herself, and as a consequence she had been known from childhood as Missy.

Like James she had been born into this world of artistic expression and high finance. Her grandfather had founded King's Fine Art fifty years ago, while Jamie's had established Ballantyne's, the auction house. Both old men were pillars of Bath society now. But it had not always been so. Once, they were simply grammar-school boys with grand ideas. How life had changed. How well they had done for themselves.

Oxford—April 1949

It was the most perfect April day. The sort of day that makes you forget things. Like the future. And exams. And earning a living. The long trails of willow wands were still unblemished by summer breezes and they sketched evanescent patterns on the water as the rowing boat nudged its way forward beneath them. The sky had been painted by Titian. At least, that's what Leo Bedlington claimed.

The rest of them just laughed. Three of them, anyway. The other simply curled his lip. Leo was reclining at the sharp end of the boat, trailing his hand over the side. He was wearing cricket flannels (not that he ever played), and the sleeves of a thick, milk-white jersey were draped over his shoulders. His fair hair, parted at the side, flopped over his eyes and he would throw it back from time to time and breathe deeply, murmuring 'Bliss, just bliss' to no one in particular.

Alongside him, leaning forward, John Macready was having none of it. 'What do *you* know about Titian?' The Glaswegian working-class tones sounded especially discordant on such a day. And then he stopped himself. 'Oh. But I suppose you've got a few?'

Leo's eyes were closed. 'Just the one.'

Their finals looming, the five students had put aside books and papers for the afternoon to make the most of the unseasonal weather.

'You see, Mac, you just walk into it, don't you?' Harry Ballantyne was on the starboard oar, grinning as he looked over his shoulder at the two men lounging in the bows of the boat.

Tall and dark, he cut an unlikely figure alongside the stocky, sandy-haired youth who sat beside him, and encouraged him to keep up. Richard King bit his bottom lip and pulled harder, beads of sweat glinting on his reddening brow. 'When are you going to do some work, Leo? It must be your turn.'

'Tomorrow.'

'And tomorrow and tomorrow,' muttered Richard, pulling on his oar.

'Does it matter? On a day like today, does it matter?'

The four men looked in the direction of the voice. It belonged to the woman sitting in the back of the boat. Her long and slender legs were neatly folded underneath her on the newly varnished wooden seat. She was dressed in cream slacks and a crisp white blouse and her head was topped with a broad-brimmed straw hat, around which daisies were threaded. Her pale features wore a reproachful frown and were framed by a bob of dark, shiny hair. She was every undergraduate's dream of a girl. Well, almost every undergraduate's.

'You're so right,' murmured Leo. 'No point in falling out.' He closed his eyes once more and leaned back towards the water.

Richard and Harry glanced sideways at each other and, with a brief nod, changed the direction of their stroke. The boat stopped abruptly, and with the deftness of a seal slipping from a rock into the waiting sea, the Honourable Leo Bedlington disappeared over the side.

Seconds later his head emerged from the ripples—'Bastards!'—and then he coughed up more river water before repeating the sentiment.

Mac leaned over the side and grabbed Leo's arm as the two oarsmen, now laughing uncontrollably, pulled in towards the bank and allowed him to clamber, dripping with water from the Cherwell, onto the grass.

'You are mean,' scolded the girl. 'Leo did bring the hamper.'

The oarsmen showed no sign of contrition, but busied themselves with the unpacking of the wicker basket and the unstoppering of the bottled beer.

'Beats me how he manages to get hold of all this,' muttered Mac. 'I mean, how many ration books does he have?'

'Probably comes from the family estate,' confided Harry, holding up to the light a clear glass jar filled with asparagus spears.

'Not unless the estate is called Fortnum and Mason,' said Richard, scrutinising the label on a tin of olives.

'Let's just be grateful, shall we?' whispered the girl, anxious that the provider of the luncheon should not overhear their ingratitude.

'You'll find a bottle of Pol Roger in there somewhere,' instructed Leo, from under the towel that the girl was using to dry his hair.

Eleanor Faraday had more than a little sympathy for Leo. The others might take the mickey out of him because of his life of privilege, but she had a gentler approach. Not that it would ever lead to anything. Leo was interested in women only as confidantes, not as companions. He didn't seem to have very much interest in men either. His eyes might alight on them from time to time but there never seemed to be 'a relationship'. He lived, apparently, entirely for art. But he was always good company, enjoying the social attention of both sexes, if not the intimacy of either.

Eleanor looked across at the other three, now intent on discovering what was for lunch. Mac, the Glaswegian, was the quietest of the trio. The son of a postal worker, he was a grammar-school boy like the other two, but he had managed to win a scholarship to Christ Church. Thanks to his artistic talents, he had become something of a local hero. Not that the role suited him. He rarely let his emotions show, and of the five of them was the one who was the hardest to read. Eleanor knew he liked her—or else why would he seek her company?—but of more than that she could not be sure. An enigma, that's what Mac was, she decided, for want of a more reasoned explanation. An enigma with a bit of a chip on his shoulder.

Richard King, on the other hand, was much easier to understand. Good-looking and athletic, he had the typical build of an Oxford blue if, at five feet nine inches, not quite the typical height. She admired his muscular frame, the pale green eyes and the way he had of making her feel that she mattered. There was no doubt that he was keen on her, but she wished sometimes that he were not quite so intense. He did have a sense of humour, but it surfaced only rarely. He liked fine art, fine wine and fine women, and had a will as strong as an ox.

And Harry? Well, Harry was just . . . Harry.

Tall and gangly, with dark hair and deep blue eyes and a vague, faraway look. There was an otherworldliness about Harry. His thoughts often seemed to be elsewhere. When questioned about it, he just shrugged and smiled a disingenuous smile that made her heart melt. Not that he seemed aware of it. What was he thinking? Probably nothing to do with her at all. Why were men so difficult to read? Except for Richard, of course, and even he had his moments . . .

Where Richard was intense, Harry was flippant. But sometimes, when he had had a glass or two of beer, she thought he looked at her in a way that meant something more than simple friendship. And then there was that one evening when they had kissed. She smiled to herself, then shook her head as if to clear it and asked, 'Is anybody going to bring me a drink?'

She knew who would be first off the mark. 'Beer or fizz?' asked Richard.

'Beer, I think. I'm thirsty.'

Before Richard had a chance to act, Harry flipped the stopper off a bottle and dangled it in front of her.

'Thank you.' She took the bottle and put it to her lips, slaking her thirst with the golden liquid.

'Good?' asked Harry.

Eleanor nodded, her mouth still filled with the frothing beer. She giggled and tried to swallow quickly. Then she lay on her side in the long grass, propping her head on her elbow and nestling the bottle of beer in a patch of clover by the now discarded straw hat.

The only sounds on that still, spring afternoon were the distant shouts of students punting on the river, the honk of alarmed geese fleeing for their lives and the gentle rustle of the willow leaves above the glassy water. For a moment the world seemed perfectly content to stand still, and their lives seemed to hang in the balance.

Mac looked across at Richard and Harry, and saw both of them gazing at Eleanor—Richard as though he were examining a fine painting and Harry as though he were regarding a cherished retriever. Mac pulled a drawing pad from a canvas bag stuffed under the seat of the boat. With a soft pencil he began to sketch out the scene in front of him. Deftly he traced the outline of Eleanor lying in the grass, and to her right the muscular frame of Richard, rising like a sideways 'Z' from the lush grass of the riverbank. He took his time sketching out Richard's face with a soft pencil: the short, fair hair, the prominent brow and the chiselled features. He framed the scene with a curtain of willow wands and, beyond them, with a single stroke, the undulating Oxford skyline.

Their collective mood was one of quiet thoughtfulness, but there was, seething beneath it, a hint of apprehension. With the end of term coming, it would not be long now before they would split up and go their separate ways, but relationships had been forged, or at least part-forged, and a question mark hung over the way in which matters would proceed. It was time for them all to take stock, to find some sense of direction, however vague.

Mac closed the cover of his sketch pad and turned to look at the river. He felt down among the grass for a pebble, located one and tossed it into the water. The plangent 'gloop' woke the others from their separate reveries. 'So what's next?' he asked of no one in particular.

'Today, tomorrow or in life?' responded Leo absently, as though talking in his sleep. His eyes were still closed.

'Let's go for the big one, shall we?'

'Do you mean, what do we want of it or what is it likely to bring?' asked Eleanor.

Mac fixed her with a cynical eye. 'Do you think the two can ever be the same?'

Eleanor took evasive action. She rolled onto her stomach and propped up her head in her hands, then looked at the two men—Harry and Richard— who were both watching her. 'I don't know,' she murmured. 'But it would be nice if they could be.'

'I think I'm expected to go and work for my uncle,' offered Richard.

'Doing what?' asked Eleanor.

'He's an estate agent,' he said. 'Says that when the boom comes, now that the war's over, he'll need a junior partner. I have other plans, too. For a gallery. One day.' He turned to Mac and asked, 'What about you, then?'

Mac shrugged. 'I'll go back home to say goodbye, but I'm not staying up there. Don't want to get stuck in some dead-end job just to earn money. Rather keep my independence.'

'Doing what?' asked Eleanor.

'Painting.'

'You think you can earn a living?' asked Harry doubtfully.

'I can bloody well try. Anything's better than going into the shipyard.'

Richard asked, 'You're not serious? They don't expect you to go into the shipyard now that you've been to Oxford?'

Mac looked gloomy. 'They didn't expect me to stay the course, so I'm buggered if I'm going to give them the satisfaction of seeing me go back now.'

'Where will you go?' asked Eleanor. 'Where will you live?'

Mac smiled. 'I haven't a clue. And, I'm not the only one, am I, Harry?'

'Mmm?' As usual, Harry had been lost in his own world.

'What are you going to do when you leave?'

'Travel.'

Eleanor looked anxious. 'What, for ever?'

'No. Just for a while.'

'Where will you go?' she asked, trying to sound detached. 'Venice? Rome? Florence?'

'Ah, the Grand Tour,' pronounced Leo.

'Hardly. I was thinking of Cheltenham or York. Somewhere like that.'

Richard grinned. 'You know how to live. Why do you want to go there?'

'To get a feel for the market, the auction market. I thought I might open a saleroom. Plenty of people looking for furniture now, and the market has to pick up soon.'

'That's my feeling, too,' said Richard. 'But I don't want to have to sell chests of drawers. The art market is poised for a revival, I'm sure of it.'

'So you're not going to be an estate agent, then?' asked Mac.

Richard shook his head. 'Not for long. No. I know exactly where I'm going, and I think I'll get there.'

The others sat in silence for a moment. Of them all, Richard was always the confident one, the one who seemed to have his life mapped out.

'I wish I was as sure,' murmured Eleanor.

Leo opened his eyes and sat up. 'Do you want Gypsy Rose Bedlington's prediction?'

Eleanor laughed. 'Yes. Go on, tell us what you think will become of us.'

Leo placed his champagne glass on the ground, grabbed a jersey and pulled it round his shoulders like a shawl. He began making circular motions over the glass with his hands as though it were a crystal ball.

'Hang on a minute,' said Harry, reaching into his pocket for a large red-and-white spotted handkerchief. He flapped it open, then tied it round Leo's head to complete the image of the fortune-telling gypsy.

'Oh, it's all too cloudy,' intoned Leo in the voice of the soothsayer. 'But it is clearing. Yes, it is clearing . . .'

Eleanor laughed again, then asked, 'What can you see?'

'I see a woman.'

'Well, that's a first,' muttered Harry.

Leo came out of character. 'Are you going to take this seriously or not?'

'Oh, yes, of course,' said Harry, with assumed gravitas. 'Do carry on.'

Leo frowned and stretched his arms out once more over the glass. 'I see a woman with a man.'

Harry drew breath to speak again, but a sharp glance from Leo made him keep silent.

'They are in an art gallery. Looking at a picture.'

'What sort of picture?' asked Eleanor.

Leo spoke more softly now and his face took on a look of intense concentration. 'A picture of a woman with an Arab.'

'Anyone we know?' asked Mac, leaning forward.

'Oh, yes,' breathed Leo.

'The woman, or the Arab?' asked Mac, under his breath.

Leo seemed not to hear him. 'And there is another man looking at the picture, a man who wants the picture very badly. But it is wrong. It's not what it is meant to be . . . not *who* it is meant to be.'

Harry glanced at Richard, then asked, 'What do you mean?'

Leo looked distressed. 'The people are all muddled up. The man and the woman . . .'

Eleanor noticed the colour draining from Leo's cheeks, and that he was beginning to sway from side to side. The sun was high in the sky. It was mid-afternoon and unseasonably warm.

'Harry, I think he's going to—' Before she could finish her sentence Leo's eyes had rolled in their sockets and he had slumped forwards, upsetting what was left of the champagne.

All four of them darted over and helped him to a sitting position. As Eleanor removed the handkerchief she was relieved to see the colour returning to Leo's cheeks. He opened his eyes and seemed dazed.

'A cold river and hot sunshine,' scolded Eleanor. 'No wonder you passed out.'

'Did I?' asked Leo.

'No,' said Richard. 'I reckon you were probably possessed.'

Harry grinned. 'Pissed more like.' Then he noticed Eleanor frowning at him and corrected himself. 'Possessed by spirits.'

'Never touch them,' murmured Leo. And then, partially recovering his composure, he asked, 'What were we doing?'

'Finding out what you thought the future would hold for us,' said Mac matter-of-factly. 'Through your crystal ball.'

'Oh. And did I know?'

Harry looked sceptical. 'Can't you remember?'

Leo shook his head. 'Not a thing. I remember falling in the water . . .'

Eleanor handed the handkerchief back to Harry. 'You must just have been a bit delirious. Cold water and hot sun and alcohol—fatal mixture. Strange what you were saying, though. Have you ever done that sort of thing before?'

'Never, no. I say, was I rather good at it? Shall I do it again?'

'I wouldn't bother,' muttered Mac. 'At least, not without an interpreter.'

Harry looked thoughtful. 'There is that rather sweet French girl—the one who keeps asking me to help her with her verbs.' His eyes brightened, and then he was suddenly aware of a tingling sensation down his spine. For a moment he wondered what it was, and then he looked up to see Eleanor pouring a bottle of beer down his neck.

Bath—November 2007

The saleroom began to clear, but at first he could not see her. Then he heard her voice.

'Jamie!'

He turned. She was walking towards him, her hands thrust deep into her jacket pockets, the catalogue under her arm. He looked down at her and the brilliance of her eyes almost dazzled him.

'Well, to what do we owe . . .?'

'The pleasure?' she asked mischievously.

He did not answer, but instead bent to kiss her on the cheek, then asked as levelly as he could, 'How long are you here for?'

Missy shrugged. 'Who knows? A while, I guess.'

Jamie chuckled.

'What?' she asked. 'What's the matter?'

'"I guess" . . .'

She looked at him quizzically.

'"I guess", rather than "I suppose". It shows where you've been.'

'Oh, I see.' Then she looked concerned. 'It's not that bad, is it?'

'Well, I've only heard half a dozen words so far. Five years across the pond. You could have turned into Dolly Parton.'

She hit him on the arm with her rolled-up catalogue. 'I might be blonde, but there the resemblance ends.'

Jamie looked her up and down. 'Oh, I don't know . . .'

Missy's eyes widened. 'You cheeky bugger!'

'Oh, no. Still very Anglo-Saxon. What a relief. Come on, I'd better buy you a coffee, seeing as how you must be spent up.'

'Not my money.'

'No, of course not.'

'Grandpa's. Fun, isn't it . . . spending other people's?'

'I wouldn't know,' he countered. 'I only sell the stuff.'

'Oh, poor you.' She looked at him with mock sympathy and put her arm through his.

'Do you mind not doing that here?' He extricated his arm.

'Oh. Too embarrassed to be seen fraternising with the enemy?'

He walked her towards the back of the room, past the cash desk, where half a dozen successful bidders were waiting to pay for their lots. The grumpy dealer from the front row, whose only successful bid had been for an Edgar Hunt painting of 'domestic fowl', opened his mouth to speak, but Missy beat him to it.

'Sorry I pipped you. Nice chickens, though.'

Jamie took her arm now and wheeled her past. 'Do you mind not upsetting the other clients? I'm hoping they'll come back.'

'Lovely word, "clients". Always sounds slightly suspicious.'

'Probably the company you keep,' he said, holding open the door to the small café at the back of the saleroom. The atmosphere in here was more intimate.

Jamie asked the waitress for two coffees and then sat down opposite Missy at a small table in the corner. He was beginning to relax now.

'Quite a morning that.'

'Yes. Better than your auctions used to be.'

'Hey! Just be careful. I am standing you a coffee.'

Missy frowned. 'After spending three-quarters of a million I should think you are. I'd hoped for at least a table at the Ivy.'

'If I'd known you were coming, I'd have booked.' He leaned back in his chair and breathed deeply. 'Anyway, I'm glad that's over.'

Missy smiled. 'You did well. You got a good price for the Munnings.'

'Yes. It made up for the Herring. *You* did rather well there.'

She did her best to look guilty, but failed. 'The old guy wasn't too pleased. Having to settle for a couple of hens.'

'He never is. Poor Mr Blunt. But then, he could have kept on bidding.'

'He doesn't think the Herring is a Senior.'

Jamie looked concerned. 'No. And I have an uneasy feeling that we didn't either. That might explain the low reserve on it. What do you think?'

'Oh, it's genuine all right. J. F. Herring Junior's stuff is much more fiddly.' She paused. 'The father's work is stronger. The son used to copy him. There was a great family row back in eighteen something or other.'

'Sounds familiar,' murmured Jamie.

She ignored him, warming to her subject. 'Beeswing took the Ascot Gold Cup in 1842. She was nine years old by then. Amazing horse. Won fifty-one out of her sixty-three starts between 1835 and 1842. Herring Senior painted her for her owner, a man called William Orde. You can see his initials on the rug in the stable.'

The waitress arrived with their coffees and the conversation was temporarily halted. Jamie had noticed the fire that shone in Missy's eyes when she got onto her pet subject and felt a little disappointed. He had hoped that some of her excitement was due to them meeting again, and not solely the result of her passion for sporting paintings. He made an effort to sound more interested. 'Mmm. So if it is a Herring Senior, what is your seven-and-a-half-thousand-pound painting worth?'

'We'll probably ask around seventy-five thousand and see how we do.'

'Bloody hell!'

Missy stirred her coffee; there was an expression of satisfaction on her face, but she was conscious of not wanting to appear too smug. 'I'm surprised there wasn't a higher reserve put on it.'

'I wasn't responsible for that. Not my bag, sporting paintings. Ben Nicholson's more in my line, if you remember. Peter Cathcart was meant to be doing this auction but he called in sick this morning. I had to step in at the last moment. I did as much homework as I could—checked all the reserves. The Herring went through bang on the nose.'

'Maybe the owner suspected that it wasn't the real thing. Or Peter Cathcart did.'

'Maybe.' Jamie continued to look thoughtful, then his face broke into a smile. 'At least I made you pay for the Munnings.'

'Bargain,' murmured Missy, doing nothing to disguise her relish.

'At seven hundred and fifty thousand, plus buyer's premium of twenty per cent and then the VAT, that's not much short of a million.'

'I know. But Munnings is top dollar now. You'd pay one and a half million pounds for that painting in one of the London galleries.'

Jamie leaned forward in his chair. 'OK, so what would you have gone to?'

Missy smiled. 'Ah, that's for me to know and you to wonder.'

'And you think you can make a decent profit on it?'

'Grandpa reckons he already has done. He's got a client lined up.'

'Lucky him. I just hope *my* grandfather doesn't get wind of me selling him such a bargain.'

'Oh, I should think three-quarters of a million will keep him happy, don't you? Especially when it's coming out of *my* grandfather's pocket.'

'I hope so.' He brightened. 'So your grandfather has called you back from the States, then?'

Missy nodded. 'More trade over here.'

'And there was nothing to keep you over there?'

She cocked her head on one side. 'Are you fishing?'

'Just catching up.'

Missy looked away. 'No. Nothing. Not now.'

Jamie felt guilty at having asked the question. Her grandfather had always been her guiding light. He was aware that more than a little jealousy had prompted him to ask the question. He offered an olive branch. 'I just wish your grandfather and mine could bury the hatchet. It's all so long ago now. I mean, they'll be eighty next year.'

Missy drained her cup. 'Yes.' She gazed into the middle distance. 'It would be good if they could get along a bit better. After all these years.'

They sat in silence for a few minutes, and then Missy said, 'Why don't we make them get on? Or at least *encourage* them to speak to one another.'

'And how do you think you are going to do that? They've been daggers drawn for close on sixty years.'

'We could rope in your mum and my dad,' she offered.

'Well, *they* barely tolerate one another either.'

'Yes, but if we worked on them a bit, made them see sense, maybe we could effect some kind of transformation.'

'You always were the optimist.'

Jamie knew Missy's terrier-like instincts. Once she had an idea in her head there was little point in trying to dislodge it. The fact that they had managed to stay friends at all was down to Missy's iron will, because there were times when even his loyalty nearly buckled under family pressure.

It was only during the last five years that their contact had been more sporadic. Immediately before that, it had seemed that their friendship might develop into something more, but then she had been sent to the States by her grandfather to run the King's Fine Art gallery in New York. Jamie had felt hurt at her apparent willingness to leave the country, but for the other members of both families it had been something of a relief, a temptation out of the way. And now here they were: a latter-day Romeo and Juliet, *sans* the romance, together again in the same city, for better or worse.

Jamie had finished his coffee and was getting up from the table. Missy, whose thoughts had been elsewhere, looked up. 'Going so soon?'

He was pleased to see that she seemed genuinely disappointed. 'I must. Sorry. I'll have to do a debrief. You know, explain myself.'

She saw the look of resignation on his face, then said, with a hint of mischief, 'Well, I hope I don't get you into any trouble.'

He looked at her with a curious expression. 'Since when did you ever do anything else?'

Chapter 2

Oxford—June 1949

April's weather continued through May with a heatwave, until June brought its usual capricious mixture of sunshine and showers, thunder and rain, and skies that had every art student in Oxford reaching for Payne's grey and Prussian blue, cadmium yellow and rose madder. While Leo and Eleanor turned to watercolours, Mac let rip with oils, filling canvas after canvas with rolling hills and angry skies, dramatic seas and vertiginous mountains.

Though Eleanor knew she should be concentrating on getting a job—in a London auction house, or an art gallery, or in that dreadful thing called 'education'—she had another problem on her mind, one that concerned both Richard and Harry. She could not let matters rumble on. She had to decide between the eager, attentive Richard and the engaging, if unpredictable, Harry. It did occur to her that she might be being presumptuous. Certainly in Harry's case. Over the next few weeks she would have to make some serious decisions about her future and whether it lay with one of them.

When she had arrived at Oxford she had seen herself as the archetypal bluestocking—keen to work, to be independent, to prove herself—but now that she had finished her course that early fire had abated. It made her feel slightly ashamed, but she knew she had no intention of becoming a career girl. Yes, she would look for a job, but it was no longer the focus of her life. What she wanted more than anything was the company of someone else of like mind, which would bring a different kind of freedom and a longed-for closeness. And a family. She wanted a family more than anything. The war had left her unsettled. It had also left her fatherless. A childhood of loss, of coming home and wondering if your house—let alone your family—would still be there, had left its mark. A house, a home, a family, these were her priorities now.

She was sitting on the window seat of Leo Bedlington's room, hunched up with her head on her knees, looking out over the city. The setting sun glinted on spire and dome, weathervane and cupola, and the scene seemed to match the wistful mood of her dreams. Leo was packing, in a desultory sort of way.

He looked across at her, silhouetted against the pale pink, early-evening sky, and said, 'You know, if I were that sort of man, I'd sweep you off your feet right now.'

She looked round. 'What?'

'You. There you sit in your shorts and plimsolls and your neat little blouse. You look like something out of a Hollywood movie.'

'Don't be ridiculous, Leo.'

'I'm not being ridiculous.' He walked over to where she sat and lightly stroked her hair. 'You really are quite beautiful, you know.'

'No, I'm not. My nose turns up too much, my eyes are too big, and—'

'And you have every student in Christ Church running after you.'

'No, I don't. Only one.'

'Why so sad, then?'

Eleanor looked up at Leo and he noticed the start of a tear in her eye. 'I don't know,' she said softly. 'Wrong one, perhaps.'

'Oh, I see.'

'I'm not sure you do.'

Leo eased in beside her on the window seat and put his arm round her shoulder. 'You mustn't think that I haven't noticed, you know.'

'Noticed what?'

'The fact that someone wants you more than you want him, and that the one you really want doesn't seem to notice.'

Eleanor sighed.

'Maybe he just needs a push,' said Leo.

Eleanor sat up. 'I can't do that!'

'No, I don't suppose you can. But I could.'

She turned to face him. 'Leo, you mustn't.'

'Why not? He thinks the world of you. He just needs encouragement.'

'You are not to do anything.' Eleanor turned away. 'You must think I'm such a fool.'

'No, not a fool. Just unlucky.'

'I've been over it so many times, imagining what *might* happen. What *could* happen. I know what I want, just not how to *make* it happen.' She turned back to Leo. 'What about you? You never talk about it yourself.'

Leo shrugged. 'Nothing to talk about.'

'Out of choice?'

He smiled weakly. 'Not entirely. But it's difficult when . . .' He trailed off, then, seeing she was waiting for more, said, 'When it's not quite as straight-forward as it should be.'

It was the first time he had ever admitted as much. Eleanor sat quietly, not wanting to interrupt.

'So, there you are. I do know how it feels. I've been there. Once. But the one I want doesn't want me, so . . . better to concentrate on other things. Don't want the family reading about me in the papers. And with Father being ill, it probably won't be long before I'm Lord Bedlington.'

'Don't say that.'

'Well, it's true, I'm afraid. He's not got long. Bloody war.'

'Mmm.'

He noticed that she was looking out of the window again, her eyes full of tears. 'I'm sorry,' he said. 'At least I still have mine. Just.'

'Yes.'

He laid his hand on her shoulder. 'What a war. What a waste of lives. But then . . . at least we had a chance to come here. That wouldn't have happened if we'd lost, would it? I mean the freedom.' He stroked her hair. 'I don't think you want a job, do you?'

She shook her head but did not speak.

'Just a man to look after you. And your babies.'

'Oh, Leo! Am I being really stupid?'

'No. I don't think so.'

'But all this . . .' She waved her arms around her and gestured out of the window. 'Such a waste if I only want to have a family.'

'It's never wasted,' said Leo. 'It helps make you who you are. Education isn't only useful in a job, you know. Look at me. I'll never have a job, not a proper one. Does that mean I don't deserve an education?'

She looked up at him and wiped away a tear.

'No. Don't answer that. As far as the rest of them are concerned, I'm a Hooray Henry. But I'll go back to Bedlington Park and it won't be long before I have to take charge of the place, and the staff. Worry about their housing and their wages. We're the largest local employer. Well, we were before the war. I'll have to try to build it up again. That's what I'm destined for—social work.' He smiled ruefully.

Eleanor waited, but nothing more was forthcoming. After a few moments she broke the silence. 'Anyway, we all go our separate ways soon.'

Leo brightened. 'Out into the wide blue yonder. And you don't know if you'll see either of them again?'

'Oh, Richard wants to see me. He's got all sorts of ideas.'

'And you? You do like him, don't you?'

'Yes, of course. He's very sweet, very attentive, hugely attractive . . .'

'I sense a "but" coming.'

'Yes.' Eleanor looked embarrassed.

'And Harry? Hasn't he said anything?'

'Not really, no. He's put his arms round me a few times, and we did kiss once—after a party, on the way home. That was all.'

'But enough to know?'

'Oh, yes.' Then she added, anxiously, 'I wouldn't want you to think . . .'

'I don't think anything. I just want you to be happy.'

'Unlikely, the way things are going.'

Leo stood up and threw a pile of clothing into a large, leather-bound trunk, then slammed it shut with a thud that startled Eleanor.

'Right!' he said. 'It's time we took your mind off things, gave you a good day out.'

'Where?'

'At the races.' He walked over to the battered mahogany desk, which was pushed against the wall. Above it hung a large picture of the Madonna and Child, and alongside that a smaller frame containing a brightly painted icon. He lifted the latter from the wall and handed it to Eleanor. 'There you are—you hold that while I find the *Racing Post*.'

Eleanor took the icon and asked, 'Why the *Racing Post*?'

'Because we're going to the races. Unless I'm very much mistaken . . .' He riffled through the pages until he found what he was looking for. 'Yes. Here we are. Newmarket, tomorrow.'

'What about it?'

'Black Tarquin. My uncle's horse. He's running tomorrow in the Princess of Wales's Stakes. Up against Lord Derby's horse—Dogger Bank. That should be worth seeing. Uncle Freddie can't stand Lord Derby. Looks likely to be a close-run thing. I think we should go and give him our support. We'll make a day of it—you, me, Mac, Harry and Richard.'

'Oh, but—'

'Now don't go all wobbly on me.'

'But I don't want you meddling . . .'

Leo held her by the shoulders. 'I'm not meddling, I promise. I just think that we could all do with a day out. It will get me away from this ghastly packing and it will take you out of yourself. It might also wake some people up to the fact that we won't always be together . . . unless we do something about it.'

'But . . .'

'I really don't think you can have any more "buts".' He pointed to the icon. 'You just hang onto that for a bit.'

'Who is it?'

'St Anthony of Padua. He is the patron saint of lost things.'

'Oh,' said Eleanor. 'I see.' She slipped the tiny icon into the pocket of her shorts, gave Leo a gentle kiss on the cheek and walked out of the room.

Bath—December 2007

Richard King held the painting in both hands and walked over to the window, manoeuvring it to catch the light. At first he looked troubled and Missy worried that he was not pleased with it, but then his anxiety seemed to evaporate. 'Well done,' he said softly. 'Very well done.'

'So you're happy with it?' Missy asked. Her grandfather had been away on business the day before and it was only now that she could show him the painting. It had spent the previous evening propped up on the bookshelf in her flat on the top floor of the Royal Crescent gallery.

He lowered the painting and turned round. 'Such a clever man,' he murmured, almost to himself.

'The best,' agreed Missy. Then she asked, 'Is it true that Augustus John used to criticise him? Said that if a horse was brown, then why not paint it brown instead of green?'

'Sorry?' Her grandfather's response was muted. He was still gazing intently at the painting.

Missy persisted. 'Munnings, the way he used reflected light. You know— when a horse was standing on grass, it would pick up the green.'

Richard replied without looking up. 'Yes. Yes, he was very good.'

Missy detected that something was troubling him. 'What is it?'

Her grandfather came out of his reverie. 'Nothing. Nothing at all. I was just remembering things.' He lowered the painting now and walked over to a corner of the room, where he leaned it face against the wall.

Missy was rather surprised that he did not want to hang it immediately and gaze at it, which was his usual *modus operandi* with a newly acquired painting. 'So where's it going off to?' she asked.

'Nowhere.'

'Oh, I thought you had a buyer.'

'I would have, ordinarily, but this one's different.'

'What's special about this one?'

Richard King shrugged. 'Just . . . sentimentality, really.'

'You know it, then? I mean, you've seen it before?'

'Yes. A long time ago.'

'It's funny,' said Missy, 'but the lady in the painting seems familiar.'

Her grandfather removed his spectacles, folded them and slipped them into the breast pocket of his jacket. Then he fixed her with the look she knew so well. He was a dapper man. Not tall, admittedly, but well dressed in grey trousers and a navy blazer, a silk handkerchief peeping out of the pocket into which he had just slipped his glasses. His hair was white now and his clean-shaven complexion that of a well-scrubbed schoolboy.

They stood together in the first-floor drawing room of the gallery in the Royal Crescent. He had always been anxious that clients should feel as though they were entering a well-furnished house rather than a purpose-built art gallery. The view from the tall sash windows was of the abbey nestling among Georgian terraces, and beyond that the city of Bath spread out before them like a theatre set.

Richard King had done well for himself. He had started with a small gallery in Bristol, where he'd struggled to pay the rent. But that was a long time ago now. By the time Missy was born he lived outside the city of Bath in Peel Place—a rambling Georgian rectory set in ten acres—and ran King's Fine Art from the house in the Royal Crescent. In his eightieth year he might be, but he still spent a part of every day there, still owned a fifty-one per cent share in the business. His wayward son, Patrick, had returned to the fold, but he seemed happiest spending most of his time wining and dining prospective clients, so it was helpful having Missy back. Though he found it hard to admit, he trusted his granddaughter more than his son—both in terms of judgment and reliability.

Missy waited for a response about the lady in the painting, but her grandfather said nothing, lost in thought once more. Then he asked absently, 'So what are you doing this evening? I thought we might . . .'

Missy hesitated. 'Ah. Well, I'm going out.'

Her grandfather was walking to the desk in the corner of the room. 'Anyone we know?' he asked, more out of politeness than curiosity.

'Jamie Ballantyne.'

During the ensuing silence Missy thought that she could hear her ears ringing. 'I met him at the auction. He sold me the picture. He telephoned me today and asked me out for a drink, so we could catch up. He's very nice, you know, and I haven't seen him for years.'

Her grandfather turned round to look at her and she saw the displeasure on his face. 'Jamie Ballantyne,' he murmured.

'Oh, Grandpa, you can't still be cross. Not after all these years.'

'Cross? Do I look cross?'

'You know what I mean. Come and sit down.' She gestured to an ornate sofa pushed against the wall, then sat down on it and gently patted the seat next to her, as if coaxing a favourite pet to join her. Richard did as he was bid. Missy took his hand in hers. 'Look, I know that you and Harry Ballantyne fell out at university, but what is it about the rest of the family? Surely you can't have anything against them?'

'Jamie's mother wasn't sorry to see you go to America.'

'No.'

'Dreadful, bossy woman.'

'Well, I know she didn't like me, and that she's a bit scary, but I wouldn't call her dreadful.'

'Well, she saw him off—her husband. After she'd made him change his name to hers.'

'What do you mean?'

'Why do you think she's called Ballantyne?'

'I imagined that after her husband left her she'd reverted to her maiden name.'

'No. Married Frank Bottomley and made him change his name to hers because she didn't like the sound of it. Then, after Frank pushed off, Emma got even more bossy. Devoted herself to the business. Business and baby, that's what she concentrated on. No time for a man.'

'But just because you don't like her—'

'It's a family thing,' Richard interrupted again. 'Been going on too long to do anything about it now.' He pushed himself up from the sofa. 'Just don't get involved with the Ballantynes.'

'WELL, I CAN'T SAY I'm pleased when I'm not.'

Jamie regretted telling his mother the moment he had done so. It was as if he were still tied to her apron strings and he could not help but feel resentful. 'I am thirty, Mum. Old enough to—'

'Old enough to know better than to get involved with the Kings.'

'You make it sound like a criminal offence.'

'Don't be ridiculous.' Emma Ballantyne was sitting at her desk in the office at the back of the saleroom. It was difficult to avoid her eye when his own desk faced hers.

'I'm only going out for a drink, not proposing.'

'Don't even joke about it!'

It was at times like this when he could see how easily people could be intimidated by her. There she sat in her large chair, determination seeping out of every pore, from the velvet Alice band on the top of her head to the black patent shoes on her feet. Her perfectly manicured hands, with their deep red nails, tapped the Cartier pen on the blotter in front of her.

'Well, don't be so bossy!' he scolded. 'I shall do what I want. Anyway, you were happy enough to take their money yesterday.'

'That's quite different. That's business.' Emma Ballantyne looked up from her catalogue and took off her spectacles. Time to try another tack. 'Oh, Jamie, you know I don't want to interfere. It's just that there are far more suitable girls . . .'

'Suitable? Excuse me, it's nothing to do with you, as far as I'm aware.'

His mother looked chastened. 'No. Of course not. It's just that—'

'No. I've heard enough. Missy's great fun and good company, and if she hadn't gone off to the States when she did . . .' He stopped himself from going on.

'Exactly. But then she did go off to the States, didn't she? Thanks to her grandfather. At least we shared the same sentiments there.'

'You think he sent her there to keep her away from me?'

'Probably. I think he was every bit as put out as I was.'

'Oh, "put out", eh? Don't tell me you're still harbouring a grudge.'

His mother leaned back in her chair. 'It's not a grudge, it's . . .'

'A way of life?'

Emma sighed. 'I suppose so, if I'm honest.'

'But why keep it going?' asked Jamie, with desperation in his voice.

'Because your grandfather would be upset if we started . . . well . . .'

'Fraternising with the enemy?' Jamie came and perched on the corner of her desk. 'Don't you ever bump into Patrick King?'

'Whenever he sees me he crosses the road to avoid me.'

'But don't you ever want to ask him why you both continue the feud?'

'I'm not sure that he'd know, to be honest.' Emma looked stern again.

'Anyway, I don't think I could ever strike up a conversation with a man who treated his own daughter as he did. I know that his wife dying like that was tragic, but there was really no reason to abandon Missy. If it hadn't been for her grandfather . . .'

Jamie seized his opportunity. 'There you are, you see, there is something good about him.'

Emma realised she was cornered. 'Yes, well . . .'

'Did you ever know Missy's mother?'

'Briefly. Before she was married, not after. Charlotte was a lovely girl. She and Patrick were married the same year as I was. Occasionally I'd notice them at parties. Then Patrick's best friend, Charlie Dunblane, was killed in a car smash. He was driving his MG too fast through the village lanes, hit a tree and died instantly. That really shook Patrick. Two weeks later Charlotte died while having Missy and he just flipped. Wouldn't have anything to do with the child who'd caused her mother's death.'

'Poor Missy.'

'Yes . . . But then Richard King took charge.'

'And Patrick went away?'

'Yes. It was years before we found out what had happened to him. Some people thought he might have run off with another woman; well, he and Charlie were both a bit fast and loose. I just thought it was all too much for him—losing his best friend and his wife in the space of a month. It turned out he was living in Umbria on his own. In some old farmhouse. Just left his daughter behind like a piece of luggage "not wanted on voyage".'

'And her grandfather just let him?'

'Oh, I think he would have had something to say about it. But when he saw it wasn't having any effect, he just brought Artemis up as his own.'

'Did he give her the name?' asked Jamie.

'Yes. I ask you. Poor little thing.'

'And then Patrick came back?'

'Eventually—twenty years later. A different woman on his arm every few weeks. But he's back in the firm, so Richard must have forgiven him.'

'And they get on now, then—Artemis and her dad?'

Emma got up from her chair and walked to the door. 'You'll have to ask her that tonight, won't you?' As she left the room, she turned to deliver her valediction. 'But don't raise your hopes too high.'

'What do you mean?'

'You do know your Greek mythology, don't you? Artemis was the daughter of Zeus and sister of Apollo.'

'I know,' said Jamie. 'You've told me before. She was a huntress.'

Newmarket—June 1949

The open-topped Talbot Ten bounced along the uneven turf, jolting the occupants to left and right and resulting in spilled beer and cries of disapproval directed at the driver.

'Don't blame me. I've never driven the bloody thing before!' cried Harry. He braced himself for another bump. It came and Leo, Mac, Richard and Eleanor momentarily left their seats again. 'Aaaaargh!' came the collective cry as they bumped down.

'Thought you'd have had a decent car, Leo. Like a Rolls,' said Mac.

'Don't be ridiculous. Far too showy. The Talbot has never let me down. Well, it's never let Osborne down.'

'Never driven yourself, then?'

'No need,' said Leo matter-of-factly. 'But there's no room for Osborne today, so—'

'So it's a good job that at least one of us can drive, isn't it?' There was a touch of irritation in Harry's voice.

They motored on past the grandstand and Harry steered the Talbot into a generous-sized gap between a Daimler and a Wolseley in the paddock reserved for parked cars. As he turned off the engine, the trio in the back gave a resounding cheer.

'What an ungrateful lot you are,' murmured Harry.

Eleanor reached over from the back seat, where she had been seated between Mac and Richard. She put her arms round Harry's shoulders and gave him a peck on the cheek. 'Not really. We're grateful to be out. Grateful to be away from Oxford. Aren't we, boys?'

'A bit too near Cambridge for my liking,' muttered Mac.

'Any more beer?' asked Richard, grinning.

'I should bloody well hope so,' said Harry. 'The driver's gasping.'

Leo slapped him on the back. 'Well done. Your reward will come in heaven.'

Harry looked disappointed. 'I was hoping not to have to wait quite that long.' Eleanor ruffled his hair and dropped a bottle of beer into his lap.

He turned towards her and smiled. 'Thank you. At least someone cares.'

Eleanor, caught unawares by the compliment, felt her face colouring and said, 'Right, come on. Which way do we go?' She turned away from Harry so that he could not see her face and busied herself with getting out of the car. When she looked up she was captivated by what she saw.

Around them were cars disgorging their passengers—smart couples from the town in racy MGs, small groups of friends who had crammed into assorted family saloons and vans, a motley collection of dark grey and black, burgundy and green. The June sunshine glinted on chrome head-lamps and radiator grilles, freshly polished paintwork and glass.

It was exactly as Eleanor had hoped it would be. In the distance she could hear the rallying cry of the loudspeaker, could see the fluttering bunting laced between the tall white posts. She could make out the top of the white-painted grandstand and was now desperate to see more.

Harry was draining his bottle of beer, and Mac, Leo and Richard were grouped round the back of the car, stretching their legs. They wore white flannels and striped blazers. The blazers were not their own, but brought by Leo, and though they weren't Mac, Richard or Harry's idea of racing apparel, they had gone along with it and entered into the spirit.

'Time we had a bit of colour,' said Leo. 'The war's over now, and we're not at Royal Ascot so there's no need for morning dress.'

'Come on, then!' pleaded Eleanor. 'I want to see what's going on.'

'But we haven't eaten yet,' wailed Richard.

'Oh!' Eleanor went to the hamper that lay in the now open boot of the Talbot. She undid the leather straps and removed the chequered tablecloth to reveal an assortment of comestibles that reminded her of the picnic scene in *The Wind in the Willows*. If nothing else, Leo was as brilliant at picnics as Water Rat, and an assortment of pies and loaves, pasties and sausage rolls, pâtés and cheeses lay there like some Elysian feast.

'Why don't we just grab something and bring it with us? Then we can go and explore,' Eleanor suggested.

'Walk around eating?' asked Leo incredulously.

Eleanor looked at him appealingly.

Leo shook his head. 'What would the family say?' He picked up a pie and bit into it. Then he smiled. 'Bugger the family; come on!' He held out his arm and Eleanor took it and walked with him towards the grandstand. Mac and Richard followed his lead, grabbing a chunk of bread and a piece of cheese, and sauntered off in the direction of the activity.

Harry, last to broach the hamper, asked, 'Do I lock the car or what?' but by then the others were gone. He shook his head, closed the boot and locked the doors, which seemed rather futile since the hood was down. Then he looked up at the sky and smiled. It would not rain. Not today.

ELEANOR SOMEHOW FELT that the day would turn out to be special. Good-humoured racegoers were all around and the four men she liked most in the world were close by. Richard put his arm round her shoulders as they stood by the rails watching the gleaming horses flash by on their way to the start, the jockeys' silks in pink and lime green, lemon yellow and scarlet dazzling in the afternoon sunshine.

Her eyes were drawn to Harry, carrying his blazer over his shoulder, his brown arms and face soaking up the sun. Richard was taking less kindly to the heat and his face was quite pink now. 'Why don't you take your blazer off?' she asked, and he did so without demur.

'We'd better get a bet on,' said Leo, 'or we're going to miss this race. What do you fancy?' He pulled a race card from his back pocket and ran his finger down the list of runners.

Eleanor leaned on his shoulder and looked at the list. 'That one.' She pointed to the fourth horse on the card, not bothering to look any further.

'Yes. I don't know why I asked, really,' said Leo softly. 'Come on, then, let's find a bookie. You coming, chaps?' He turned to the other three, who were hunched over the *Racing Post*.

'You go on—we haven't looked yet,' said Mac, who was already sketching a horse and jockey on his race card with a stubby pencil.

Leo took Eleanor by the hand and led her along the rails to where a row of bookies were standing under makeshift stands. 'Which one do you fancy?' he asked her.

Eleanor ran her eyes along the row, past Honest John and Billy Bingham to one she felt they should do business with. 'That one,' she said, pointing to a tall man in a grey check suit. 'He has a happy face.'

'You'd have a happy face if you'd won as much as he has,' grumbled Leo, but then he brightened and walked with Eleanor towards the board that said: TAFFY O'SHEA.

'What do we put on?' she asked.

'How flush are you feeling?'

Eleanor looked embarrassed. 'Not terribly.' She began to reach into the pocket of her skirt.

Leo patted her hand. 'You keep your money. Leo's treat.'

'But I couldn't possibly . . .'

Leo waved away her objections and hailed the bookmaker. 'A shilling each way on Tall Dark Stranger, please.' He looked at Eleanor, who smiled ruefully.

'A good choice, ma'am,' confirmed the bookie, flashing a warm smile at her. 'You'll have me bankrupted for sure.'

Eleanor glanced at the Gladstone bag open on the small table to his side and realised that it was unlikely. 'Let's go and see how he does,' she said to Leo, and they walked back to where they had left the others, but there was no sign of them now.

'Don't worry,' said Leo. 'They'll be back when they've placed their bets.'

But the other three did not return before the race had started, so Eleanor could cheer as loudly as she wanted at Tall Dark Stranger without fear of any sideways glances or suggestive remarks. Her horse got away well and seemed to be holding the lead, but then as the finish approached he could not quite maintain momentum and despite the encouragement of both Eleanor and the blue-silked jockey, Tall Dark Stranger came in second.

'Oh dear,' she said, as she looked up at Leo.

'Not to worry,' he said brightly. 'You had an each-way bet. Time to collect your winnings.' He escorted her back to Taffy O'Shea.

'And there was me thinking you were going to ruin me,' said the bookie. 'Three shillings and sixpence. There you go.' He handed Eleanor a half-crown and a shilling, which she attempted to give to Leo.

'No, no, no, your winnings. And there are more races. Come on.'

Eleanor looked across towards the winners' enclosure. 'What was the name of the winner?' she asked Leo.

'Let me look at your race card.'

'No point. Time to sort out the next one and to find the boys.' She was easily distracted and Leo was rather glad. It didn't do to set too much store by superstition when it came to the races.

It was easy to spot Mac, Richard and Harry, thanks to their blazers, now back on since the sun had gone behind a cloud, and because they seemed to be in such high spirits.

'Hello, you two!' shouted Richard, his eyes bright and his cheeks even redder than before. 'Ready to celebrate?'

'I suppose so,' said Eleanor. 'We came second. What about you?'

'We won!' said Mac, with a look of incredulity on his face. 'We bloody well won, and I'm surprised you didn't, too.'

'You mean you didn't back it?' asked Richard, looking disappointed.

'Back what?' asked Eleanor.

'The winner, King Dick.'

She felt a sinking feeling in her stomach, a feeling comprised partly of guilt and partly of disappointment. She did not see Harry glancing down at the *Racing Post* to check the name of the horse that had come second. Neither did she see him look up again, understanding dawning on his face.

'The only thing that I ask in this next race is that we have solidarity,' said Leo. 'It's Uncle Freddie's horse and we should stick by him, especially as he paid for our tickets.'

'Shouldn't we go and see him?' asked Eleanor.

'God, no! He'll be plastered by now and I don't want to embarrass you,' said Leo. 'We'll do our bit by backing Black Tarquin and leave it at that.'

'Mr O'Shea again?' asked Eleanor.

'If you like. Right, gentlemen, let me have your money and I'll put it on with the jolly Irishman,' said Leo.

But Mr O'Shea had even better luck in the Princess of Wales's Stakes, when Black Tarquin came in fourth to Lord Derby's Dogger Bank.

'We should have known by the weight,' complained Mac. 'Black Tarquin was carrying two stone more than Dogger Bank.'

'And Dogger Bank was number thirteen,' said Harry.

'Are you superstitious, then?' asked Mac.

'Not any more,' said Harry.

Leo felt it was time to change the subject. 'Anyone fancy a drive? I think we ought to motor along to the other end of the course—by Devil's Dyke. You get a different view from there.'

And so the quintet made their way back to the car and drove to the part of the heath known as Devil's Dyke—an ancient earthwork twenty feet high that stretched away across the county. There were fewer people here, and the landscape was open to the skies. Skylarks sang above them, and Eleanor sat on the running board of the Talbot, parked in the rough grass, and strained her eyes to see tiny specks of birds singing their hearts out, while the men made inroads into the picnic. The sun had come out again, and they lay back on the grass, eating and drinking and swapping silly remarks.

There was a different atmosphere here—less frantic. Eleanor could see haycocks in the field on the other side of the racecourse, and smell the wild thyme and herbs beneath her feet, mingled with the sweet-smelling grass.

'Isn't it lovely?'

She looked round as Harry sat down next to her on the running board.

'Yes,' she answered, turning back to gaze out over the heath.

They sat silently, side by side for several minutes, neither of them wanting to break the mood. Then Mac, who was sitting on the back seat of the Talbot, asked, 'Who's that over there?'

'Where?' asked Leo.

'On the end of the dyke. There's a man painting.'

They looked in the direction of his gaze and saw the distant figure, standing at an easel. He wore a nondescript jacket and trousers and a Panama hat on his head, and he seemed to be painting the scene in front of him.

'Let's go and look,' said Eleanor, getting to her feet. And before any of them could argue she was walking down the heath towards the man.

Mac glanced at Harry, who shrugged and got to his feet to follow her. The others did the same and within a few minutes were advancing quietly on the artist from behind, so as not to distract him. When they were a few yards from where he stood he said, without looking up, 'Lovely day!'

Eleanor, who was still ahead of the others, was taken by surprise and jumped a little before agreeing, 'Yes, lovely.'

The man turned to face her now and raised his hat politely. Eleanor nodded in acknowledgment as the others caught up with her.

'Having a good day?' the man asked, taking in the party.

Leo responded on their behalf. 'Yes. Mixed fortunes, though.'

'Ah, 'twas ever thus. You'll find it's calmer up here.' He seemed to be examining a particular part of the landscape.

Eleanor felt emboldened to enquire, 'Do you come up here a lot?'

The man nodded. 'Several times a year. More my bag than Ascot.'

'Always to paint?'

The man smiled. 'Yes, always.' He turned back to his canvas and made several sweeping strokes with his brush. He was clearly no amateur. He looked up again. 'Was there something . . .?'

The group were embarrassed now. 'Sorry,' blurted Mac. 'We're disturbing you . . . Only . . . we're art students.'

'Ah, I see.' The man laughed. 'Well, it's no use looking at what I do. Not everyone approves.'

Mac had edged closer now, riveted by the canvas. 'Oh my God!'

'Was that incredulity, young man, or just disbelief?'

'Er . . . no. . . . I mean, it's amazing.'

The man smiled again and said softly, 'Thank you.'

It was Richard who spoke next. 'You are, aren't you?' he asked.

'Now what am I meant to reply to that? I am or I am not what?'

'Munnings,' whispered Harry softly, almost under his breath, and then, having cleared his throat, 'Mr Munnings. I mean . . . Sir . . .'

'Yes,' said the man, and carried on painting.

Eleanor looked shocked. 'We must go,' she said.

'Oh, don't worry,' said the artist. He was wiping his brushes on an old rag now. 'I'm all but finished for today.' Carelessly he tossed the brushes into a paint-spattered wooden box and wiped his hands.

Munnings turned to face them and Eleanor was able to take in his appearance more fully. He was a tallish man, with fine yet craggy features and a face that lit up when he smiled. He had a faintly patrician air and looked as though his mood could change in the twinkling of an eye. He pushed the Panama to the back of his head and wiped his brow with a spotted handkerchief.

'So, you're art students. And whereabouts do you study your art?'

'Oxford,' blurted out Richard.

'Oh, goodness me, you're a long way from home. It's usually the other lot who drift around here.'

Eleanor was warming to him. She found him a little intimidating but quite compelling.

He directed his next question at her. 'And these four young men are squiring you for the afternoon, are they? Lucky chaps!'

Eleanor giggled. 'I don't know about that,' she murmured.

'So are you all painters?'

The other four turned in Mac's direction and said, almost as one, 'He is.'

Mac looked distinctly uncomfortable. 'Well, I—'

'Oils, or watercolour?' asked the artist.

'Both,' Mac stammered. 'But mainly oils.'

'Brave man.' He turned once more to Eleanor. 'So you don't paint?'

'A little. Watercolour. But I'm not that good.'

'Oh, we all think that. I don't know an artist worthy of the name who is satisfied with what he does. And I know a good many who shouldn't even call themselves artists.'

'Like Stanley Spencer?' offered Mac.

There was a brief silence. Mac wondered if he had gone too far. He had not meant to be rude, just to show that he knew to whom he was talking, and that he sympathised.

The artist's face broke into a grin. 'Have you been reading the papers?'

Mac nodded, relieved that his remark had not offended.

'Bloody modernists. Absolute junk. No time for 'em, and people pay fortunes for 'em. Fools.' His eyes were blazing now.

None of the five felt they should risk further comment. But Munnings's mood changed once more. 'So who do you admire, young man? I didn't catch your name . . .'

'John Macready, but everyone calls me Mac.'

'Well, who are your heroes, John Macready?'

'Turner.'

'Oh, he's everyone's hero.'

'And Reynolds. And Lawrence.'

'Portraitists, then?'

'Not always.' Mac looked embarrassed again. 'I like your work.'

'Thank you.' Munnings raised his Panama in appreciation.

'Particularly your horses.'

'Ah, yes.' Munnings was beginning to pack away his paints. 'Do you ever paint them?'

'I try. Bloody difficult.'

'Read your Stubbs?' asked the artist.

'*Anatomy of the Horse*? Yes. I've done lots of drawings.'

'Bought my copy when I was in my twenties. You've got to know what goes on *inside* to be able to paint the *outside*. Don't you think?'

'Yes.'

The artist had taken down the painting from the easel and handed it to Eleanor. 'Can you hold this for me a moment?'

Eleanor took the painting from him without speaking and held it out before her like some valuable religious artefact. The others gazed upon the still-wet landscape of Newmarket Racecourse as if they were in a trance.

Munnings folded up his easel. 'So how long have you left at university?'

It was Harry who replied. 'We go down this summer.'

'And if the rest of you don't paint, what will you do?'

Harry continued. 'I want to run an auction house, Richard wants his own gallery, Mac wants to paint, and Eleanor . . .' He paused, unsure what to say.

The artist helped him out. 'What does Eleanor want?' he asked.

'Eleanor's not sure yet,' interposed Leo.

'Oh. And your name is . . .?'

'Leo. Leo Bedlington.'

Mac stepped in. 'With any luck, Leo will just buy my paintings.'

Munnings's expression altered to one of recognition. 'Ah, Bedlington. Would that be of Bedlington Park?'

Leo nodded.

'In which case I shall be very nice to you. Lord Bedlington has helped swell the coffers. Which only leaves Eleanor, who isn't sure.' He looked again in Eleanor's direction. She tried to avoid his eyes. Munnings laughed. 'Not to worry. Plenty of time. And you have four young men to choose from.'

At which point none of the quintet felt able to say anything.

'Right, well, if I might have my painting back . . .'

Eleanor came back to earth. 'Yes. Of course.' She handed over the canvas, somehow sorry to be parted from it.

Mac, too, was riveted by the image, a fact which did not go unnoticed.

'So what will you do in the summer?' Munnings asked of Mac.

'Paint. I'm not sure where.'

'You should come and see me. Come down for a day or so and watch, if you like.'

'Well . . . if you're sure . . .'

'Oh, I'm sure. I might send you packing when I see what your painting's like, but if you're prepared to take the risk . . .'

'Yes. Well, yes . . . thank you . . .'

The artist fished in his pocket and pulled out a small white card. 'Here you are. Get in touch with me in a couple of weeks. I'll see what I can do.'

Mac held the card in both hands as though it were a fine jewel. 'Thank you very much,' he murmured.

Munnings turned away from them now, lifted his Panama to bid them farewell, then picked up the painting and paraphernalia and began to walk off. 'And you can bring Eleanor with you, if you like. Perhaps by then she'll have worked out what she's doing.'

Chapter 3

Bath—December 2007

Jamie deliberately put on the first clothes that came to hand, as if to convince himself that the evening would probably turn out to be nothing special and also that nothing was expected of it. Nothing serious, anyway. He had high hopes that she would still be as much fun as she used to be, would still make him laugh, but beyond that . . . Well, time would tell.

He had known her now for longer than he had known virtually anyone else, apart from family. Through some oversight on their parents' and grandparents' part, they had gone to the same nursery school. Then, later, when they went their separate ways—young James to the local grammar and Artemis to boarding school in Surrey—they had kept in touch through occasional letters and phone calls. Eventually they had both gravitated back to their family businesses in Bath.

HE PARKED HIS CAR opposite the Theatre Royal and walked along Upper Borough Wall before turning down Union Street towards the Pump Room. The shops were shut now, but there were still enough folk about to give the city a sense of bustle. There were chattering girls in skirts of ill-advised brevity, well-to-do couples smartly turned out and arms linked, men in suits making excuses into mobile phones. It was early December and unseasonably mild—little danger this year of a white Christmas, the weathermen said. In a week or two's time the shops would stay open later and be thronged with Christmas shoppers. In Bath Abbey churchyard there were men at work erecting the small wooden chalets that would turn the precincts of the Anglican abbey into something reminiscent of the Munich Christmas Market.

Jamie turned the corner and was embarrassed to find that she was already waiting for him. He looked at his watch. 'Am I late?'

'No. It's me. I'm always early. Sorry.'

'Oh, yes. I'd forgotten.' He leaned forward to kiss her on the cheek. Then he stepped back and stared at her. 'You look . . .'

'Different?' she asked, with a concerned expression.

'No, not different. Just . . . well . . . gorgeous.'

She smiled and looked relieved. 'Oh. That's nice.'

In that single moment he was aware of a complete change in his mood. He had been working so hard to convince himself of the unimportance of the evening that it came as a shock to discover a feeling that he had not experienced since before she had left for America: a sense of total relaxation, of complete ease in the company of another person. He looked at her and experienced once more the deep delight in her closeness to him. It made him laugh—an exclamation of a laugh—brief and quite involuntary.

'What is it?' she asked.

'It's just that . . . I mean . . . it doesn't seem . . . well . . .'

'As if we've ever been apart?' she asked, then felt worried that she had imputed too much into his hesitant attempt at an explanation.

'That's right.'

There was a brief silence now. It was not uncomfortable. It seemed like a moment in which they could tacitly acknowledge each other's presence. Then Jamie said, 'Shall we go and eat?'

'Yes, please,' said Missy. 'I'm starving.'

They found a corner table at a fish restaurant where they could see everything going on around them. Not that they appeared to notice. For most of the time they leaned in across the table and swapped stories about the intervening years—of Jamie's gradual taking on of more responsibility at Ballantyne's and Missy's exploits in the States.

'So did you like it there?' he asked.

'Some things, yes—the buzz, the art world, the shopping.'

'But not everything?'

She looked reflective. 'I missed the greenness, the countryside. And the architecture.' Then, brightening, 'How sad is that?'

'Not sad at all. I know what you mean. I was looking at the Christmas decorations going up and wondering what Beau Nash would have made of it all. And then I thought I ought to get a life.'

She reached across the table and put her hand on his. 'I'm glad you're still you.'

'Sad old me?'

'No. Just thoughtful old you.' She squeezed his hand and then let it go. 'Shall we order?'

Over a bottle of Sancerre and plates of fish they talked about the city and how it had changed—or not changed—since they had grown up.

'I mean, most people move away, don't they?' said Jamie.

'Where are you living now?' asked Missy.

'Batheaston.'

'Not too far out, then.'

'No. But I'd quite like to be in town. More buzz.'

Missy grinned.

'What is it?' he asked.

'Nothing. It's just that coming from New York, it seems funny to think of Bath as having a buzz.'

Jamie saw the funny side. 'I told you I'm sad. I ought to get out more.'

'Have you never wanted to?' asked Missy.

'Oh, I did a few years ago. I got a job with Christie's in London. Only stayed about six months. Couldn't stand it.'

'The job?'

'No. The place. Too big, too . . . unhappy. I just couldn't hack it. Then Mum and Granddad made me an offer I couldn't refuse.'

'A partnership in Ballantyne's?'

'Yes. So here I am.'

Missy fixed his eye. 'Exciting prospects, then?'

Jamie tried hard to suppress a grin. 'That depends.'

'Eat your fish,' said Missy. And then, raising her glass, 'Here's to—'

At which point Jamie cut in. 'Here's to us. Whatever happens.'

'Yes,' she agreed. 'Here's to us.'

They chinked glasses and each took a sip of wine. Then, as Missy lowered her glass, she said, 'By the way, the Munnings you sold me . . .'

'Yes?' Jamie put his glass down and looked concerned.

'Oh, don't worry, it's fine. It's just that . . . What do you know about its provenance?'

'Nothing. Not really. It came from a private collection.' Jamie looked thoughtful. 'If I remember rightly . . . Oh, but then I have to respect client confidentiality.'

Missy gave him her best 'oh, go on' look.

Jamie had always found her difficult to refuse. 'It was someone called Stephens or Stephenson or something. Not a name I recognised. Why do you want to know?'

'Oh, no reason. It's just that Grandpa has a particularly soft spot for it. Seemed very pleased to have it, and yet he didn't hang it on the wall.'

'Is that a problem?'

'Not exactly. It's just that he has a sort of routine when he gets a new picture. He always takes another one off the wall—the wall by the window, where there's a really good light—and then hangs up the new one and looks at it. You know, a bit like a child with a new toy. But this one he examined briefly—in both hands. Then he put it down and stood it with its face to the wall. I can't understand why.'

'Is that all?'

'No. It's the picture itself. The lady on the grey horse. Did she remind you of anybody?'

'That's funny. Because when the guys in the saleroom put the picture on the easel it gave me a bit of a shock.'

'Why?'

'Oh, probably just my imagination, or the fact that you were bidding for it and I hadn't seen you for however many years.'

'But . . .?'

'The lady in the picture looked just like you.'

Dedham—July 1949

They were not at all sure that it was a good idea. He had given Mac his card but it was on the spur of the moment and it was well known that Alfred Munnings was a temperamental old stick and just as likely to claim that he had done nothing of the sort.

There were only three of them in the Talbot this time. Leo had insisted they take it, in spite of the fact that his father had taken a turn for the worse the night before and he had had to stay behind at Bedlington Park. Richard was, to his great irritation, confined to bed in his lodgings with a heavy cold. With only a week to go before they left Oxford, he was reluctant to let Eleanor go without him, but she insisted that she would be well looked after by Mac and Harry. It crossed Richard's mind that she would be all too well looked after, but as he was powerless to win this particular argument, he had sloped off to bed.

It had been a long drive to Dedham, the village made famous by the paintings of John Constable on the Essex–Suffolk border. The clock on the tower of St Mary's Church struck one as they motored slowly down the high street in search of Castle House.

'Where do you suppose it is?' asked Eleanor.

'Not a clue,' confessed Mac. 'But I think it's a big house. At least it looks big in the painting of him and his missus out the back. She's on a horse, wearing a black riding habit and a silk top hat. There's a bow window, but I shouldn't think you can see that from the street.'

'He *is* expecting us, isn't he?' asked Harry.

'Well, I've had a postcard saying he is,' confirmed Mac. 'I just hope he remembers.'

'I think I'll stay in the car,' said Harry.

'You will not!' scolded Eleanor. 'I've come to give Mac moral support and you're here to give it to *me*.'

Harry smiled. 'Oh, that's nice, considering I'm only the driver.'

Eleanor flushed. 'You know what I mean.'

The village was long and winding, and the higgledy-piggledy rows of Georgian houses were more scattered now. After a mile or so, they spotted a likely house on the left-hand side of the road. A lane ran down one side of it and behind were paddocks where horses were grazing. The house was painted a warm shade of cream, and attached to it were an assortment of buildings, at least one of which could pass as a studio.

'Stop, stop!' exclaimed Mac. 'I think this is it.'

Harry pulled the Talbot up at the entrance to a short gravel drive. Mac leaped out and walked round the side of the house. They watched as he peered through the bushes and over the fence. He turned to them and nodded, then walked back to the car. 'I can see the bow window. This is it.'

The three of them looked at one another. 'Good luck,' murmured Harry as he manoeuvred the car into the short drive of Castle House.

Mac grabbed a large folio cover from the back seat, then they both walked up to the front door. Mac took a deep breath and rang the bell. Nothing happened. Then they heard a booming voice from above. 'If you're a bloody tradesman, use the tradesman's entrance!'

They looked, first at one another and then for an alternative door. They found it round the back of the house. By the time they got there, Sir Alfred James Munnings, KCVO, PRA, was standing in the doorway with his hands on his hips. His cheeks were highly coloured, and he wore a yellow riding stock at his neck and a rough, checked tweed jacket over grey flannels. He drew breath and let out a stream of invective. 'Can't a fella have a quiet bloody hour after his lunch on a summer's afternoon?'

None of them spoke. Instead they stared as if hypnotised at the man berating them for interrupting his afternoon nap. Only Mac was brave enough to offer, 'Well, you did tell us to come, sir. I'm sorry we're a bit late.'

'You cheeky young sod. What do you mean . . . ?' And then he caught sight of Eleanor hiding behind the two men.

'Ah! Oh, yes. Bugger me, so I did.' And then, directed at Eleanor, 'You must forgive a crotchety old man. Bad day. Glorious light, but bad day. Gout.' And then, recovering himself, 'Well, don't stand there like statues. Come on.'

He led them past lawns and brilliantly planted flowerbeds until eventually the party arrived at the building the artist used as his studio. 'In you go.' He motioned them inside. All three were amazed by what they saw. From the ceiling hung an assortment of racing silks in rainbow colours—yellow and violet, scarlet and blue, pink and orange. There were easels supporting half a dozen partly completed canvases, and paint-daubed palettes and pieces of board. Odd items of furniture—spattered stools and an assortment of tables—filled the rest of the space, along with riding crops and boots, a hunting horn, bridles and horse collars.

'Gosh!' exclaimed Eleanor.

'Yes. Sorry it's such a mess. In the middle of something, I'm afraid.'

'No,' murmured Mac, entranced by the scene in front of him. This was what he had spent his life dreaming about—becoming a real artist, painting real pictures, in a place like this.

The artist was pleased to see their reaction. 'Had it since 1906—the studio. The original, anyway. At Swainsthorpe where I used to be. Had it moved here lock, stock and barrel when I came to Dedham after the war, in 1919. It's twice as big now, but it's still the same place.'

Mac was examining a picture of a horse race—the brightly caparisoned jockeys vying for position against a background of bright green turf.

'Always the start, never the finish,' said Munnings. 'Impossible to capture the finish with any reality. The start is always a better bet.' Then he noticed Mac's folio, tucked under his arm. 'Come on, then. You've seen mine; let's have a look at yours.'

Mac demurred. 'Oh, I'm not sure it's really worth it.'

'Nonsense. That's what you came for, isn't it? Let's be having a look. I'll tell you what I think, mind. There's no point in me being kind if you haven't any talent. Let me look on that proviso.'

Mac hesitated, then handed his folio to the Master, who undid the ribbon ties that held it together and pulled out three paintings. There was a study of the Norfolk Broads—all water and sky—another of the Cherwell with a punt going by and a third of a grazing horse.

Having pored over each of them in turn, without saying a word, Munnings put the painting of the Norfolk Broads on a vacant easel. 'Right,' he said. 'This one—good sky, very good sky, but the water needs more work. You have to study it more carefully. See how the light plays; give your water depth *and* movement.' He took the painting down. 'Next, the river. The water here is better. You know it better, yes?'

Mac nodded.

'And then the horse.'

All three of them waited for the expected criticism. Munnings turned and looked directly at Mac. 'You have a talent. You've caught the anatomy well, plus the light. Your horse is alive. That's rare. Keep at it and, believe me, you'll be a fine painter.'

Mac hardly knew where to put himself.

'And now I've embarrassed you.'

'No, it's just . . .'

'Oh, I'm not an easy man to please, but you should be even harder on yourself. One day, when you're accepted into the Royal Academy . . .'

Mac shook his head.

'Oh, you will be, if you keep at it. On that day, walk right in there with your ticket and don't faint when you see how awful your picture looks. These are your youthful years, when the brain absorbs easily and learns quickly. Go and do some real study—outdoors. That's where your talent lies. And look at other artists' work—the good stuff, the stuff that leaves you breathless with admiration—and ask yourself, How did he do that? I do. Still.' The artist stopped.

The three stood silently, and then Mac said simply, 'Thank you.'

'Not at all. Now, then, how about you doing me a favour?'

The three students looked at each other; then Mac said, 'Yes, anything.'

'You see this painting?' He walked them over to an easel on which stood a partially completed painting of a grey, leaning forward and browsing. 'It needs a rider. My sitter failed to turn up this morning. A woman in the village. Her mother's gone down with influenza or something.' He turned to Eleanor. 'Have you ever ridden a horse?'

'Well, yes, but . . .'

'So you'll know how to sit. Perfect.'

'Oh, but . . .'

'No "buts". You hop up there into that saddle'—he gestured at a saddle wedged on top of the trestle—'and I'll use you as the model. There's a riding habit and boots behind that screen. Go and see if they fit.'

It seemed futile to argue. Munnings turned to Mac and the hitherto silent Harry and said, 'Go back to the house and ask the housekeeper for a beer apiece. You can come back in an hour when I've got started and see how it's going, but I don't want you peering over my shoulder for a while, is that understood?'

The two men nodded and walked quietly from the studio, allowing the former president of the Royal Academy to make the acquaintance of his new sitter. As they disappeared across the paddock, they could hear his voice ringing out behind them. 'What a go!' he said. 'What a go!'

Bath—December 2007

'Maybe that's why he bought the painting,' offered Jamie. 'Because he thought it looked like you.'

'Oh, I don't think Grandpa's that sentimental. Not to the tune of three quarters of a million, anyway. No, it would have been a business deal, nothing more.' She smiled wistfully. 'It would have been a nice thought, though, wouldn't it? That somebody loved you so much they had to buy a painting that looked like you?' She took another sip of her wine.

They were interrupted by the waiter. 'Would you like coffee, madam? Sir?'

Jamie looked across at Missy enquiringly.

'No, thanks.'

'Just the bill, then, please,' confirmed Jamie.

Missy said matter-of-factly, 'I thought you might like to come back to my place for a coffee. Unless you think that's too forward?'

'Well, it has taken you about twenty-five years to ask me, so at that rate we should be able to sleep together in 2109.'

'Oh,' she said. 'That soon?'

'BLOODY HELL,' exclaimed Jamie. 'You don't mean to tell me you live in the Royal Crescent!' They were walking along Brock Street towards the city's most prestigious address.

'Only a part of it,' replied Missy. 'A very little part of it.'

Jamie looked at the brass plaque beside the door of the lofty Georgian terrace house: KING'S FINE ART.

Missy turned her key in the lock and opened the front door. Before Jamie could say anything, he was pulled by the arm into the white-pillared Georgian hallway, to the accompaniment of a beeping alarm. Missy closed the door and punched a series of numbers into a small panel concealed behind a column that supported a bust of Sir Joshua Reynolds.

Jamie was standing in the hallway open-mouthed. He had been in some of these houses before, to value furniture, so he knew what to expect, but the fact that Missy should live in one came as a complete surprise.

'I thought you just had an ordinary flat,' he murmured.

'It is an ordinary flat. It's just in an extraordinary house.'

It then occurred to Jamie that there would be hell to pay if he were seen here. 'Look, don't you think I should go before your grandfather . . .?'

'No need to worry. He goes back to Peel Place every night now. That's why I can live here, in his old flat. I have the place to myself. Come on.'

She began to climb the majestic staircase with its ornate, white-painted balustrade. To Jamie, the sensation was of walking in Wonderland. To right and left of the staircase hung paintings of superb quality. At the top of the first staircase was a large landscape with horses—a grey and a bay—and the label beneath it confirmed his suspicions. It was a Stubbs.

'I know you're into more modern stuff, but even you must like that,' remarked Missy as they passed.

'Oh, yes. Bloody hell, it must be worth . . .'

'Don't go there. Anyway, it's not ours. We're trying to sell it for a client. Come on.' Missy slipped off her shoes now and padded further up the stairs until they reached a glazed door on the third floor. She slipped another key into the lock and pushed it open. What met Jamie's eyes then caused his jaw to drop once more.

The apartment was entirely white—the carpet, the curtains, the soft furnishings and the walls. The only colour to be seen was that from one enormous painting on the far wall. It was of three men on horses, three burly farmers intent on chasing a hare.

Jamie's face broke into a grin. 'Nice,' he said. 'Very nice.'

'Not the best painting, I'm afraid, but I've always liked it. Thomas Weaver. About 1818. The hare gets away, so it's OK.'

She moved from the sitting room through an archway that led to a kitchen. She punched some numbers into another keypad on the wall and the sound of soft chamber music filled the air.

'You really have got this sorted, haven't you?' conceded Jamie.

'I'm very lucky,' Missy admitted. 'But I don't take it for granted, and none of it really belongs to me.'

'You are a part of the firm now, though, aren't you?' he asked.

'Yes, but only a part. There's Grandpa, Patrick—my dad—and me.'

'Enough, then.'

She nodded and smiled. 'Enough.'

He watched her as she moved about the place making coffee, easy and relaxed in his company. Then he followed her back to the sitting room, where the various lamps were now dimmed.

Missy put down the tray on a low table and over coffee they chatted about his place in Batheaston. Then she asked him quite directly, 'So what about your love life?'

'Ah, yes, well . . . that will require a short answer.'

'You mean there isn't one?'

'Yes and no.'

'On and off, then?'

'Well, more off than on. Or to be honest, totally off.'

Missy curled her feet up underneath her as she sat on the white sofa, partially losing herself in the soft, deep cushions. She pushed her blonde bob behind her ears and took a sip of coffee.

Jamie sat on the sofa opposite. 'We met at Christie's. Quite a big thing for a while, but when I said I wanted to come back to Bath, she wasn't too pleased. Said that if I was serious I'd stay in town with her.'

'Well, she did have a point,' said Missy.

Jamie smiled ruefully. 'Anyway she's found another guy now, in China.'

'China?' asked Missy incredulously.

'Ceramics. It's a department at Christie's.'

Missy erupted in a burst of laughter. Then Jamie laughed, too. 'I suppose if I'm honest with myself, she wasn't the one for me.'

'Oh, come over here.' Missy patted the sofa beside her. Jamie rose from the opposite sofa and sat beside her. She squeezed his hand. 'Still the same old Jamie. Still a bit of an Eeyore.'

'Me? Nah. It's all a front designed to get sympathy from the opposite sex.' Then he looked at her enquiringly and asked, 'Do you think so?'

'Just a bit. But I wouldn't have you any other way.'

She leaned forward and kissed him very gently on the forehead. Then he put his arm round her shoulders and rested his head against hers.

'I'm glad you're back,' he said.

'So am I,' replied Missy. 'So am I.'

They sat silently for a while, he gently stroking her hair, she resting her hand on his arm. Then he asked, 'What about you? You said there was someone in the States. Has he gone away, too?'

''Fraid so. I found out he was seeing someone else as well as me. When I said it was her or me, he decided it was her. Simple as that.'

'So here you are, on the rebound.'

She pulled away from him. 'No!'

'Only teasing,' he said softly. 'Sorry. Unkind.'

He put his arm round her once more. 'And there's nobody else?' he asked.

'Well, yes.' Missy paused. 'There is, actually.'

Jamie withdrew his arm. 'Oh.' He did his best to sound unaffected.

'I don't know how to say this.'

'No, go on, please. It really doesn't matter.'

'It's been going on a long time now. I thought that when I went to the States, met new people in a new world, all those thoughts I had about him would disappear. I'd get over him.'

'And you didn't?'

Missy shook her head.

'I see.' Jamie did his best not to sound disappointed. 'So what's the situation now? Does he know you're back?'

'Oh, yes.'

'And has he made contact?'

'Yes. I've been out to dinner with him.'

She saw the look of abject disappointment on his face.

'And do you think there's a future in it?' he asked.

'I hope so. I really do hope so.'

'Good.' Jamie was quite still for a moment. Then he got to his feet. 'Well, I think I'd better be going.' He glanced at his watch. 'Busy day tomorrow, and my grandfather's summoned me. Don't know what all that's about.'

Missy remained seated, then looked up at him. 'You don't know who it is, do you?'

Jamie hesitated. 'No. No, I don't. But it doesn't matter. I think it's lovely that you've—'

'You silly man.'

Jamie saw that her eyes were beginning to fill with tears.

'I came back from the States because of you. Because however hard I try, I simply can't get you out of my head. You're so much a part of me that it hurts when I'm not near you. Wherever I am and whoever I'm with there is hardly a thought in my head that doesn't involve you.' She brushed away the tears that ran down her cheeks. 'And now I've probably made a complete fool of myself and all you'll want to do is get out of here and go home.'

Jamie stood motionless. The words echoed around his head for what seemed like an age. 'Me?'

Missy nodded.

'Come here,' he said softly. 'If you only knew how many times I've hoped you'd say something like that.'

Missy rose to her feet and went to where he stood. He put his arms round her and held her so close she felt she might melt into him.

Dedham—July 1949

Just across from the house, Harry and Mac sat in the shade of a monkey-puzzle tree, slaking their thirst with a mug of beer each.

'So, what do you make of him?' asked Harry.

'Rum bugger but a brilliant painter,' confessed Mac.

'What a place, though,' mused Harry, looking round at the rolling landscape. The land behind Castle House was divided up into lush paddocks in which six or seven horses grazed contentedly. In the distance they could hear the sound of farm workers cutting an early crop of hay. An occasional shout would echo across the still afternoon, and from time to time the sound of horses' hoofs pulling a farm cart would echo up the lane.

'How long do you think we ought to leave them?' asked Harry.

Mac glanced at his wristwatch. 'Another half-hour. Daren't risk upsetting him again.'

Harry planted his beer mug in the grass and leaned back on his hands, the better to take in the view. 'He seemed to like your painting, though.'

'Yes. Bloody surprise that. I thought he'd send me packing.'

Harry laughed.

'What?' asked Mac.

'You've no idea, have you?'

'About what?'

'About just how good you are.'

Mac shrugged.

Harry turned towards him. 'You've just been appraised by the country's finest equestrian painter, the finest painter of horses since George Stubbs, who's told you that you have a great talent, and you're still not convinced.'

'Maybe it's my Glaswegian bloody-mindedness.'

Harry shook his head. 'Well, you think what you want, but just promise me that you'll do what the old master said and give it a go. Work at it. Work bloody hard—and see what happens.'

'Oh, I'll do that all right. I can't do anything else. Sometimes I think I'll go mad if I don't paint.'

'Madder than you are already?' Harry chuckled and reached for his beer. He took a long gulp then said, 'I'd kill for your amount of drive and your talent. I feel a bit rudderless sometimes.'

'You're tired, that's all. Tired after three long years.'

'But look at Richard. He must be tired as well, and yet he's got it all sewn up. He'll have his own gallery in no time, just wait and see. He'll be selling your paintings before you can say "Alfred Munnings".'

'Funny you should say that.'

Harry looked more serious. 'He's asked you already, hasn't he?'

'Well, he's sort of hinted at it.'

'Wily bugger.'

'It's not a problem,' offered Mac. 'Richard can sell them at low prices when they're still wet, and you can flog them in your saleroom as Old Masters when I'm long gone. That way you get to make all the money.'

Harry smiled at the thought. 'Thank you, but I think those days are a long way off yet—certainly as far as the saleroom is concerned.'

'No money?' asked Mac.

'A bit put by. I'll have to rent to start with.' He slapped the ground with the flat of his hand. 'Oh, I'll manage somehow.'

'It's not that, though, is it?'

'Mmm?'

Mac said nothing for a moment. Then he said, quite softly, 'She's quite keen, you know.'

Harry shook his head. 'Oh, I don't think so.'

'She is, I tell you. And if you don't get your bloody act together, you'll lose her. She'll go off with Richard and that will be that.'

'I think she's already there, isn't she?'

'Only because she thinks you're not interested.'

'Hah!'

'Well, come on, you've not exactly given her much to go on, have you?'

'I wish . . . I wish I could . . .' Harry sighed. 'The thing is, as long as I put off asking her, there's a chance she might one day say yes. But if I do ask her and she says no, then it's all over. And I can't stand the thought of that. So there you are. I'm travelling hopefully and never arriving.'

'Travelling hopelessly more like. Look, I'm not exactly experienced in these matters, but I can read folk pretty well. I think she's waiting for you to make the first move.'

'I wish I shared your confidence. Anyway, why are you on my side and not Richard's?'

Mac stood up and thrust his hands into his pockets. 'Oh, for all sorts of reasons. Let's just say that I'm very fond of Richard, but I don't necessarily think that Eleanor is the girl for him, or that he's the man for her. At least you should find out how she feels about you so that you can resolve things one way or the other, that's all.'

'Simple as that?'

'Absolutely. What have you got to lose?'

Harry sighed. 'Well, Richard as a friend, for a start, but apart from that . . . We'll see. I should have made a move when I had the chance.'

'Oh, something will turn up, Harry. Come on, let's risk going back to the studio to see how they're getting on. I might be able to watch him paint.'

'You go back,' said Harry. 'I'll stay out here and look at the horses. Give myself time to think. I'll join you when I've finished my beer.'

MAC SLIPPED into the studio as quietly as he could and stood in the shadow of a large canvas propped on an easel.

'It's no use standing behind that,' boomed the artist. 'You won't see anything from there. Come over here and watch, but just be quiet.'

Mac did as he was bid and stood within a yard of the old man's shoulder, watching closely as he mixed his paints and applied them to the canvas. His deftness was astonishing, and his ability to create form out of a simple stroke or two left Mac in awe of the painter's talent. He looked across at Eleanor, sitting sidesaddle on the trestle. She smiled back at him nervously, hardly daring to move or say a word.

'Are you all right?' barked Munnings. 'Another half-hour and that should do it for today. My hand's playing me up. It's gout. I can hardly feel my left thumb in this palette. I'll need you again tomorrow to finish it off.'

Eleanor looked troubled. 'Oh, but we have to get back to Oxford.'

'What? No, no, no. We'll have a word with the Sun Hotel. They'll have rooms. They'll be able to put you up.'

'But—' Eleanor tried again.

'No "buts". It's a waste of a painting if I don't get you finished. You'll be able to get away by mid-afternoon.'

Eleanor looked pleadingly at Mac, but he seemed unconcerned. 'It's not a problem. We've nothing important to do tomorrow.'

'That's settled, then.' The artist noticed the worried look on Eleanor's face. 'If it's the bill you're worried about, don't even think of it. I'll take care of that. It's only fair when you've sat for me so beautifully.'

It was not the bill that Eleanor was thinking about. It was Richard, back in Oxford, confined to bed with a cold and wondering why she had not returned. Then again, she would probably not be seeing him for a day or so anyway, until his cold was better, so perhaps it wouldn't matter if she were out for the night with Harry and Mac. She brightened a little.

'That's better,' said Munnings. 'A much happier expression.' Eleanor's face broke into a smile. And so did Mac's.

Bath—December 2007

All thoughts of restraint, or of the inadvisability of their liaison, or of their being in bed together at the top of her grandfather's gallery were absent from Missy's mind as she lay in Jamie's arms. It did not matter what her family thought. Some pointless feud, caked in the dust of time, was not going to stop her from being with the man she had yearned for.

As dawn broke over the city, he was sleeping. She looked at the clock. It was seven minutes to eight. Her arm was across his chest. She lifted it and ran her fingers lightly over his skin. He was so beautiful. The tight, dark curls on his head were matched now by the gentle growth of early-morning stubble. She had never felt so deliciously happy, and tears of joy, tears of love, began to flow down her cheeks, landing on his skin and causing him to stir. She wondered what his reaction would be on waking. Would he regret having stayed?

Jamie opened his eyes, saw her and smiled. There was no suggestion of anything but contentment. 'Hello,' he murmured, then kissed her on the lips and they made the gentlest love once more.

Jamie left the Royal Crescent at a quarter past nine, forty-five minutes before the expected arrival of Missy's grandfather. He could not remember ever feeling happier. He knew there would be difficulties ahead, as far as the families were concerned, but they would have to be overcome. He had never felt more certain of anything in his life. His only surprise had been that Missy had been unaware of the depth of his feelings towards her.

He glanced at his watch. He had arranged to call on his grandfather at his house in the Circus at ten. Too early yet. He would go and get a paper.

The man in the paper shop in Queen Square picked up on his mood. 'You're cheery this morning, Mr Ballantyne.'

'No reason not to be, George. Lovely day.'

The weather was certainly in tune with his thoughts. The early December morning was bright and crisp, and a fine skein of mist wove through the city below. Ordinarily, Jamie would be dressed in a suit and tie at this time, clean-shaven and sitting at his desk in the auction house, but there seemed little point in going back to Batheaston to change and then coming all the way into town again. He had showered at Missy's and he was quite sure his grandfather wouldn't notice he hadn't shaved.

Jamie sat on a bench in the sunshine and riffled through the paper, wondering why his grandfather wanted to see him so urgently. He was usually much more vague about meeting and seemed happy for his grandson to just drop in from time to time, but yesterday on the phone he sounded as though there was something specific he wanted to discuss.

As Jamie turned the pages of *The Times* he noticed the obituary of a man that he had heard his grandfather mention from time to time. Someone called Lord Bedlington.

LEO RAVENSWING MALAHIDE BEDLINGTON, seventh Earl of Bedlington, has died aged 81. The earldom was established in 1738 when Thomas Malahide Bedlington was rewarded for his landscaping services to King George II. Since then the family fortunes have gone through many vicissitudes, not least during the Seventh Earl's own lifetime, when death duties of eighty per cent almost bankrupted him. His father, Hector Malahide Bedlington, an inveterate collector—from whom he inherited his love of art—achieved the rank of brigadier and fought with General Montgomery in the Battle of El Alamein. He died of his wounds some six years later, nursed at the end by his only son (his wife, Caroline, née Ravenswing, having died in childbirth). Only by selling most of the family's art treasures and Bedlington Park in Shropshire did Leo Bedlington manage to stave off total penury and settle instead for financial ruin. He studied art history at Christ Church, Oxford, just after the war and dabbled in the art world. He spent his latter years in the Villa Fabrice, near Menton on the Côte d'Azur.

He is fondly remembered by those who knew him as good-humoured and sociable, despite his dwindling fortune. He was unmarried and, at the end, alone; his companion of many years, the artist John Macready, having predeceased him in 1995 in a swimming accident.

Jamie folded the paper and placed it on his lap. He had no idea his grandfather had known a character who had led such a colourful life. He must ask him about those days at Oxford. What a time he must have had.

Chapter 4

Dedham—July 1949

There were three of them standing round the bar in the low-beamed back room of the Sun Hotel—Eleanor, Mac and Harry.

'So how did it feel?' Harry asked Eleanor. 'Being immortalised by the Master?'

'A bit strange, to be honest,' confessed Eleanor. Her face broke into a smile. 'And a bit silly—sitting sideways on top of that trestle thing and trying to pretend it was a horse.'

'Well, you looked fine,' said Harry, having a stab at a compliment. After finishing his beer he had rejoined the others in the studio before Munnings had called it a day. 'I actually saw the horse you were sitting on.'

'Oh, yes?' said Mac teasingly. 'What was it, then?'

'Well, as you saw in the painting, it was a grey, with a thick black mane.' Harry was warming to his subject. 'And it was nibbling grass. What I bet you didn't notice, though, was that when that other horse walked past—the mare—the grey began to look really interested. I thought for a moment that he might bolt.'

Eleanor threw back her head and laughed.

'Come on, drink up,' said Mac. 'Our supper will be ready in a minute and I've ordered a bottle of claret to go with it.'

'Claret? You're pushing out the boat!' exclaimed Harry.

'Nothing to do with me. The barmaid said that "'Im down the road said we 'ad to 'ave some bottles of the best wine in the 'ouse".'

'Red wine makes me tipsy,' said Eleanor.

'Oh, good,' retorted Mac. 'It's time you relaxed after all that riding.'

'The clothes were strange,' she said. 'Not sure about the riding habit.'

'Oh, I don't know,' said Harry absently. 'I find riding gear rather sexy.'

Eleanor blushed and Harry tried to make light of his comment, noticing the broad grin on Mac's face. 'Well, I just think it's flattering on a woman. Shows off her shape well.'

'You're getting in deeper,' murmured Mac, draining his glass.

Harry's further embarrassment was saved by the waitress, who arrived to show them to their table in the dining room. 'Would you like to follow me?' she asked. 'I'm afraid it's a bit of a limited menu tonight. Pea and ham soup, followed by rabbit pie, then orange jelly with real mandarins.'

'Pea and ham soup in July,' muttered Harry.

'And what's wrong with that?' asked Mac. 'If you came from the north, you'd be grateful for a drop of warming broth at any time of year.'

'We're in Essex,' said Harry, 'not the frozen north.'

'Why don't we go straight on to the rabbit pie, then?' Eleanor suggested.

Her diplomacy was cut short by the arrival of the claret, a dusty bottle from which the cork had already been extracted. Mac tasted it and pronounced it the best claret he had ever drunk.

Over the next hour and a half the wine flowed freely, thanks to the generosity of their host. They talked not so much of the future, but of the past: of punting on the Cherwell, of picnics in meadows, long evenings spent in student rooms overlooking grassy quads and of dreaming spires.

Eleanor watched as Harry and Mac sparred with one another. She was sorry that Leo was not here to enjoy the fun. Then she felt a pricking of conscience about Richard, who, while they were laughing and enjoying themselves, was probably sitting with his head over a bowl of Friar's Balsam, inhaling the curative fumes. Then she put such thoughts out of her head. She had considered him enough. The wine was good and she felt more relaxed than when they had arrived. And it was not as if she were committed to Richard. He had not claimed her as his own. He did, when she thought about it, take her rather for granted. Expected her to be there when he called round.

Well, she was still free, still unattached, and in the company of two good friends, one of whom she found especially attractive. She watched as Harry chatted relaxedly to Mac. Noticed the tilt of his head and the thick, dark hair that curled round the back of his ears. Occasionally he glanced over at her and her cheeks seemed to burn under his gaze. How she enjoyed simply being there with him. In the same room. At the same table.

At half past ten, Mac pushed back his chair and stood up. 'I'm done in. I'll leave you two to wash up.'

For a moment Eleanor took him seriously. 'Oh, do you think . . . ?' Then she saw the expression on his face. 'You're a dreadful man, John Macready, and one day you'll get your comeuppance.'

'Good night, both,' he said. 'Sleep well.' As he turned, he prodded Harry on the shoulder, unseen by Eleanor, who was reaching down for her cardigan, which had slipped to the floor.

Shortly after Harry had gone, the waitress came into the room once more. 'Oh, one of you's gone. I was going to ask if you wanted coffee in the snug.'

Eleanor and Harry glanced at each other, questioning whether the other would like to stay. Then, in perfect unison, they said, 'Yes, please.'

To begin with, Harry sat opposite her in an armchair, while Eleanor slipped off her shoes and tucked her feet underneath her on the sofa. The snug was a small, low-beamed room with a grandfather clock in the corner and a fire in the inglenook—three logs gently glowing to take away the chill of the summer evening and the sweet smoke of applewood filled the air. The Camp coffee was not to Eleanor's taste and she left it, untouched, on the round, brass Indian table.

Harry tasted his and winced. 'Not good, is it?' he whispered.

Eleanor shook her head. 'It doesn't matter.' She was smiling.

'Would you like something else instead? A nightcap?'

'Not for me. I've had enough wine. It was lovely.' She snuggled down into the sofa, gazing at the lazy flames that licked the logs in the grate.

Harry looked around. They were the only people left now, the locals having sloped off to their beds before another heavy day of haymaking.

'What a day,' murmured Harry, staring into the dying embers.

'Yes.' That was all Eleanor could manage. She could not recall the last time they had been alone. It seemed that she only ever met Harry in company—with Richard, with Mac or with Leo. Leo. She remembered his words that afternoon two weeks ago. 'Maybe he just needs a push.' But how could she 'give him a push' without appearing to be the sort of woman that Harry would not look twice at?

He seemed to be reading her thoughts, or at least one of them. 'I wonder how Leo's father is.'

'Not very good, I think.'

'Poor Leo. Just when he wanted a bit of freedom, it looks as though he's going to be saddled with everything, as well as losing his pa. Were they very close?'

'I don't think so. He was away fighting most of the time. In Africa, I believe.'

'Same as mine,' said Harry. 'But mine got off lightly. He's back selling insurance now. Not very glamorous, but at least he survived.' Then he realised his lack of tact. 'Do you miss yours?' he asked gently.

Eleanor nodded. 'Some days more than others.' She had not intended to cry. She had been feeling particularly happy, but at the mention of her father the tears welled up and she felt them tumbling down her cheeks.

Harry got up and crossed over to her. 'I'm so sorry. I didn't mean to . . .'

Eleanor smiled through the tears. 'No. So silly, I don't know why that happened.' She reached into her pocket and pulled out a handkerchief and dabbed at her eyes. 'You must think I'm very feeble,' she said.

'No, not feeble. Just . . . sensitive.'

'And feeble.' She laughed and dabbed again at the remaining tears.

'And beautiful.'

She was not sure that she had heard correctly. 'What do you mean?'

'I mean that you are the most beautiful girl I've ever met,' said Harry, reassured by the fact that she hadn't got up and walked away or slapped his face. He pushed back a wisp of hair that had fallen across her face.

She searched for a reply but could only manage, 'Really?'

Harry leaned over towards her and kissed her very gently on the lips. Then he moved his head away slightly and laid his hand on her shoulder. At first she did not know quite what to do. She looked into his deep blue eyes, as if searching for something. Then, at exactly the same moment, they both leaned forward and kissed again, more passionately this time. When their lips parted, she drew away briefly before twisting her body so that her head lay on his chest. He put his arm round her and they sat together on the sofa for several minutes before she said, 'This is nice.'

'Yes.'

Then they heard the iron sneck lift on the door behind them and the waitress came into the room. 'I'm locking up now, so . . .'

They both sprang to their feet. 'Yes, of course,' said Eleanor. 'We'll be going up.'

The waitress nodded and held the door open. The two walked through it like a pair of schoolchildren being called to the headmaster's study, and climbed the dark wooden stairs that led to the bedrooms above.

Their rooms were adjacent to one another. For a moment they both hesitated. 'I'd better say good night, then,' said Harry.

'Yes. Yes, I suppose so.' Eleanor tried not to sound disappointed even though she could not bear to let him go.

He seemed to read her confusion. 'Such a shame. We wait all this time and now . . . I've left it too late.'

Eleanor could feel her heart beating. She found it difficult to speak, aware that the next words she said would probably affect her whole future.

'You don't have to go,' she whispered softly.

Harry looked deep into her eyes. 'Are you sure?' he asked.

Bath—December 2007

Jamie rang the bell of his grandfather's house in the Circus, looking up as he always did to take in the carved stone frieze above the door with its serpents and its nautical emblems. He loved the Circus even more than the Royal Crescent. Begun in 1754, thirteen years earlier than the Crescent, it is a perfect circle composed of three arcs, each comprising eleven five-storey houses. William Pitt the Elder had lived at numbers seven and eight, number seventeen had played host to both Thomas Gainsborough and William Makepeace Thackeray, and Harry Ballantyne and his wife had moved to what was by then a dilapidated terraced house in the late 1960s.

Coming to see his grandparents in this house had always been a treat. As a child, he would be allowed to run up the staircases with his younger sister and would try to understand why so many of the walls were strangely angled, unlike those of their mother's house. The Circus had seemed a place of dreams, as magical as *The Lion, the Witch and the Wardrobe*—the book that his grandfather had given him for his seventh birthday.

The door was opened by Tilly, his grandfather's daily. 'Hello, Master Jamie.' He had always been 'Master Jamie' to Tilly, though he often thought he could detect a hint of irony in her voice when she said it nowadays. 'Mr Ballantyne's in the drawing room.' Tilly tilted her head towards the curving staircase behind her.

His grandparents had decorated the house when they took it on, but had done little since. Thanks to Tilly, the house was always clean and tidy, and the furniture gleaming and smelling of lavender polish, but the carpets were so threadbare now that they were verging on the embarrassing.

He pushed open the drawing-room door and saw the tall, slim figure of his grandfather standing looking out of the window across the Circus. He was wearing a lemon-yellow sweater and had his back to Jamie. It was not quite as ramrod straight as it had been, but his hair was still thick, even if it was iron grey rather than the black it had been forty or so years ago.

He turned on hearing Jamie enter. 'Ah, Master Jamie,' his grandfather teased. He was wearing an open-necked shirt. He hated ties, always had.

'Hello, Granddad.' Jamie walked over to where the old man stood and gave him a hug. 'Lovely day.'

His grandfather looked out of the window again. 'Yes. It won't last, though. It will be raining by lunchtime. Shame. Still, it is December.' He looked thoughtful for a moment, and then took in his grandson's mode of dress. 'You not working this morning?'

Jamie looked at his reflection in the gilt-framed overmantel. He did look more dishevelled than he would have liked. He spoke briskly, hoping that he would not be quizzed about why he should be unshaven at ten in the morning. 'I'm on my way to change. I had to see someone early about . . . something . . . and so I . . . Anyway, how are you?'

'As well as can be expected.' His grandfather smiled. 'Bloody leg doesn't get any better, but then I suppose I'm beginning to wear out.'

'And Gran?'

'Oh, she's fine. She's nipped down to the supermarket for something or other. Lunch, I suppose.' He looked pensive again.

Jamie was used to these spells of reverie on the part of his grandfather. He had learned that if he just let him drift for a moment or two, he would quickly come back to the matter in hand.

Harry Ballantyne soon recovered himself. 'Tilly's on the way up with coffee. At least, I hope she is.' He motioned Jamie to sit down in an easy chair and lowered himself carefully onto the edge of the leather-covered club fender that surrounded the fireplace. 'Easier to get up from here when she arrives,' he muttered by way of an excuse.

The door opened and Tilly entered with a tray bearing coffee and biscuits. 'I should pour it quickly, Mr Ballantyne—it's been standing for a few minutes so it should be strong enough, and I don't want it to go cold on you.'

Jamie's grandfather mumbled his appreciation and Tilly left the room. 'Coffee for you?' he asked.

Jamie nodded. 'So, what did you want to see me about?'

His grandfather did not speak but concentrated on pouring the coffee into two china cups. Jamie could not work out whether the silence was due to Harry's preoccupation with decanting from the cafetière or because he was considering what to say. It turned out to be the latter.

Harry handed Jamie a coffee and lowered himself carefully into the facing armchair. 'Your grandmother and I have lived in this house for more than forty years now,' he began. 'It's been a good place to bring up a family, even if that family was a small one, and . . . rather fragmented.'

The reference to Jamie's absent father did not go unnoticed, but Jamie was used to such comments. He realised that there was little bitterness in his grandfather's outbursts. He knew that it was more regret that Jamie's mother and father had not tried harder.

Jamie was right. Harry did not blame Frank Bottomley for pushing off. He might have done so himself, he reflected, had he been on the receiving end of Emma's tongue, but she was still his daughter and he loved her, even if she had driven him to distraction over the years.

'I've asked your mother if she wants to take on the house.'

'Oh?' The subject of his grandparents moving out of the Circus had never come up before, though if he had thought about it, Jamie would have realised that a five-storey house must have presented a challenge to two septuagenarians on the cusp of becoming octogenarians.

'But your mother seems happy where she is in the country—with her country friends and her little dinners. Doesn't want to move into town.'

It began to dawn on Jamie that a part of his life was about to be dismantled. He felt unsettled. 'But you've always lived here.'

'In your lifetime, yes, but we lived in more modest surroundings before you were born.'

'Yes, but . . . well . . . I suppose I just don't like the thought of the place not being a part of the family.'

'Nor I. That's why I'd like you to have it. There's no one else to leave it to. Your sister doesn't want it.'

'You mean you've asked her? Fran knows about this?'

His grandfather detected a little anger in Jamie's voice. 'I just wanted to make sure she didn't have a problem with it before I approached you. Fran wants to stay in Argentina, working with the horses. She will get her share.'

Jamie scratched his head. He had begun the day in a complete daze thanks to the events of the night before. Now here he was being offered a house of his own. 'But how will you . . . I mean . . . when . . . ?'

'As soon as you like. Your grandmother and I have found a serviced flat on the other side of town. Better for us than all these stairs.'

'I don't know what to say, Granddad. I mean, I'm not sure I can afford—'

'Don't worry about that. You won't have to pay us anything. It would have come to you anyway on our . . . so we'd rather you had it now.'

Jamie pulled himself together. 'Granddad, are you sure? I mean, is Mum happy with that? It's a big house for one person.'

'Well, you won't always be on your own, will you?'

The events of the previous night ricocheted around Jamie's head. 'Er, no. Well, I hope not.' Worried he sounded evasive, he quickly tried to change the subject. 'It'll be nice to have a bit more space, actually. Mind you, it'll take me a while to get this place sorted.' Then he realised he might have sounded rude. 'Oh, I mean . . . decorating and . . .'

'Don't worry. We'll give you a spot of cash to help you do it up.' He paused. 'You are pleased, aren't you? You would like to take on the place?'

Jamie shook his head and at first his grandfather thought he was refusing. 'I can't think of anything I'd rather do, anywhere I'd rather live. I just . . . I'm not sure that I deserve it.'

'Rubbish. You've worked hard. Taken on the lion's share of Ballantyne's over the past few years, and you'll need to keep working hard. They take a bit of upkeep, these old houses, but there should be enough left to avoid you going under when we're gone.'

'I do wish you wouldn't say that.'

'Well, I'm not going to be around for ever and it's nice to know that the place will be in good hands.' His face suddenly brightened. 'Oh, and you did rather well the other day.'

Jamie looked puzzled. 'Sorry?'

'With the Munnings.' Harry picked up the *Bath Chronicle* and pointed to an article that was headed: TOP PRICE PAID FOR SPORTING PICTURE.

'Oh, yes. I was quite pleased with that, and a bit surprised.'

His grandfather looked him in the eye. 'But not by who bought it?'

'You know, then?'

'I guessed.'

'It was a lovely painting,' Jamie offered.

'Yes, I know. I have a soft spot for Munnings.'

Jamie thought he detected a hint of sadness on his grandfather's face.

'Never wanted to own one, then?' he asked, as much to bring the old man out of his reverie as anything.

'Only one,' he murmured. 'Only one.'

Jamie watched as his grandfather seemed to lose himself completely in his thoughts. He seemed so very far away that Jamie felt unable to intrude, but then he remembered the morning paper.

'Oh, have you seen this morning's *Times*?'

'No. Not yet.'

'Well, I'm sorry to be the bearer of bad news, but there's an obituary of somebody you were at university with in the paper today. Lord Bedlington.'

'Good God! Has he died? Old Leo?'

'At his place in France, apparently.'

Harry Ballantyne looked out of the window again. 'Well, well, well.' Then his facial expression changed and he said very softly, 'That'll put the cat among the pigeons.'

Chapter 5

Dedham—July 1949

Harry woke up alone in his room at the Sun Hotel, stirred into consciousness by a coloratura blackbird performing in the elder tree outside his window. The events of the night before replayed in his mind. Had she planned to invite him to her room? Had Mac conspired with her to effect their being alone after supper? He did not know. He certainly could not ask. Eleanor had seemed happy to be with him, appeared finally to have put Richard from her mind. It was a strange and novel sensation, and one that he was happy to savour. Then he fell to wondering where it would lead. Whether it had been nothing but an impulsive moment.

He rose and washed at the basin in the corner of the room, then looked at himself in the mirror. The image reflected was not a pretty sight—half shaven and tousled. He splashed water on his hair to try to flatten it, with only partial success. He glanced at his watch—a quarter past eight—then dressed quickly and went downstairs to the room where they had dined last night. No longer was it warmly lit by candles, but flooded with the bright white light of a summer morning.

He squinted as the sun's rays caught him smack in the eye, and then heard a broad Glaswegian voice commenting, 'Ah, you're up! I was going to send a search party.' He turned to discover Mac sitting at the table in the corner, mopping up the remains of his breakfast egg with a crust of bread.

Harry wondered for a moment if he knew, but decided to play safe and say nothing. He sat down opposite Mac. The third chair at their table was still empty. He considered asking if Eleanor had come down, but was not confident that it was something he could achieve without looking sheepish, so he decided instead to give his order to the waitress, even if it did comprise only three words. He gestured towards Mac and said, 'The same, please.'

No sooner had the waitress taken his order than Eleanor appeared in the doorway looking fresh and radiant, her neatly brushed hair shimmering in shafts of sunlight that streamed in through the window. The two men stood on seeing her, and she seemed to glide towards the table before sitting down between them.

Harry gazed at her and she smiled at him. There was no embarrassment, no acknowledgment of what had gone before, and he wondered, for a moment, if it had all been a dream.

'What time are we expected?' Eleanor asked Mac.

'Half past nine. Are you all right with that?' he asked.

Eleanor nodded and turned to Harry. 'Are you?'

Harry hesitated. 'Er . . . yes. Yes, of course. I mean, I'm only . . .'

'The driver, I know.' Eleanor completed the sentence for him. 'But I just wanted to check, that was all.' She smiled at him.

He wanted to ask her if she was all right, if she had slept well, but in the presence of Mac such an enquiry would be unwise.

Eleanor ordered coffee and toast, and the conversation turned to what time Munnings would be finished with them and what time they thought they might arrive back in Oxford. There was a note of sadness in the air.

The two-day trip had come as a surprise to all three of them. For Mac, it had been an unexpected opportunity to watch the Master at work. For Eleanor, it had been her first experience of being an artist's model. And for Harry? For Harry, it might have been an evening that would change the course of his life. He only hoped that Eleanor felt the same way.

How could he find out? He hoped that having finished his breakfast Mac would leave them, even if just for a few moments, but he did not. He sat and waited for them to finish theirs, and then it was time to go back to Castle House for another tantalising day in her company. A day when he knew they would not have a single moment alone together.

At first Harry thought that Munnings would send them off again and that Mac might begin to question him about the night before, but today he operated rather differently. For a start, he greeted them warmly and was ready to start work almost immediately, having summoned the housekeeper to bring coffee for his guests. This was real coffee, unlike the chicory-based brew they had tasted the night before. Harry wondered how long it would be before rationing ceased. It had been four years now since the war had ended, and there were still times when certain things were in short supply, or priced beyond the reach of mere mortals.

While Eleanor slipped behind the screen to change into the riding habit, Munnings asked Harry what he wanted to do after graduating.

Harry smiled. 'I want to become an auctioneer.'

'Ah!' exclaimed Munnings. 'You want to make money off the back of the likes of me, eh?'

Harry stood his ground. 'Oh, I don't think I'll be there for a while yet, sir. More like bedroom furniture, chests of drawers, that sort of thing.'

'But eventually?'

Harry nodded thoughtfully. 'With any luck, yes.'

'Well, just make sure you deal with real artists. None of these Picasso fellas and Stanley Spencer—that sort of rubbish. Indecent, that's what they are. Indecent con artists,' he pronounced, warming to his subject. 'Don't be fooled. Art is about representation of mood and atmosphere and spirit, for sure, but it's about beauty and truth, too.'

The pair of them had fallen silent. Munnings noticed the look in their eyes, a cross between fear and awe, and laughed. 'Come on, let's get started. You, John Macready, you stand over here and watch. And, Mr Auctioneer, you can sit quietly on that chair and muse on the day when you'll be able to sell my paintings for far more than I ever will in my lifetime.'

Eleanor walked out from behind the screen and eased herself up onto the trestle. Munnings stepped forward to arrange the folds of her riding habit as they had been the day before. When he was satisfied, he stepped back to his easel and disappeared once more into his own world.

At seventeen minutes to two the artist threw down his brushes, laid his palette on a paint-spattered table and declared, 'There we are. That'll do. Enough.' The painting was finished.

He turned to look at Harry, who had sat silently against the far wall. 'Come on, Mr Auctioneer, come and have a look at the lady.'

Harry walked across to where Munnings and Mac were standing.

'What do you think?' asked the artist.

Harry examined the painting and marvelled at an image so full of life and vitality that it took his breath away. There were highlights of brilliant yellow and rich cream, shadows of green and grey and lavender blue, all applied with a virility and freshness that made him gasp. And there, atop the grey horse, sat Eleanor in her elegant riding habit, with that look in her eyes that seemed to see right through him. Munnings had caught it perfectly.

'Can I have a look?' she asked tentatively.

'Of course. How rude of me.' Munnings helped her down and she came to look at herself and the horse. She let out a little gasp. 'Oh, goodness!'

Munnings smiled. 'You've been very patient.' Then his face contorted into a frown and he rubbed his left thumb. 'Bloody gout! It'll be the end of me as an artist. Just pray it doesn't affect you, John Macready.'

Mac did not really hear. The tough Glaswegian was staring intently at the painting, and Harry noticed that there were tears in his eyes.

IT WAS A LONG, plodding journey back to Oxford. No sooner had they left Dedham than large spots of rain began to fall, spattering loudly on the black fabric hood that was the only thing that stood between them and a soaking.

The sky began to clear as they approached the city, and the spires and domes were illuminated by the soft evening light. Harry wound down the window as they motored down The High and inhaled the astringent scent of rain-washed pavements. His mind, too, was awash with thoughts—of the immediate past and the near future. What now? Where did they go from here? He was wondering what to do next when a voice from the back seat said, 'Here's fine.'

Harry came to. 'What? Sorry?'

'You can drop me here,' said Eleanor.

Harry had not noticed that they were alongside her hall of residence. Suddenly, he felt a rising sense of panic. There were things to say, things he wanted to clarify, not least being the time when he would see her again.

He pulled in at the side of the road, and before he could do anything Mac had leaped out of the passenger seat and was tipping his seat forward so that Eleanor could get out of the back. Harry opened his own door and walked round to where she stood. She was kissing Mac on the cheek. She turned to find him next to her. She said nothing for a moment, just looked up at him. Then she laid her hand on his arm and reached up to kiss him on the cheek just as she had done Mac. She squeezed his arm and said softly, 'Thank you.'

Harry took a deep breath and asked, 'When—'

That was the only word he managed to get out. The blaring of a horn and the raised voice behind him curtailed any further conversation. 'Move yer bloody motor, will you, mate? I'm trying to clean this bloody street.'

Harry looked up at the towering green lorry behind the Talbot, its stiff, circular brushes whirring in the gutter.

He looked pleadingly at Eleanor, then back at the now cursing road sweeper. Quickly he kissed her on the cheek, then offered her a look that he hoped said everything he wanted it to. He ran round the car, slipped back into the driver's seat and, with a brief wave, drove off.

'Oh,' said Mac, almost to himself. 'Well, I suppose I'll have to walk from here, too.' At that moment a sudden shower broke, and so, lifting his folio above his head, he called goodbye to Eleanor, who was now sheltering in the doorway, and ran off towards his lodgings.

He did not notice the bewilderment on her face, or the fact that it was a few minutes before she moved from where she stood, watching the Talbot disappear from view round a corner. It had all happened so fast. She had had no time to think, no time to say the things that she wanted to say. No time, really, to work out the significance of the past two days. But one thing she did know: tomorrow she would have to go and talk to Richard. It was only fair.

Bedlington Park—July 1949

Harry drove through the night and managed to get as far as the bottom of the drive at Bedlington Park before the Talbot finally ran out of petrol. Fearful of waking up the entire Bedlington household, he had bedded down in the back of the car under a plaid rug until he was woken by the early-morning light. He glanced in the rear-view mirror and was not heartened by the vision that gazed back. He now sported three days' stubble.

He glanced at the clock in the walnut dashboard. It was a quarter past seven. What time did earls get up? Then he remembered that Leo was nursing his father, and that the hours of the day would probably be meaningless.

He eased himself out of the car and onto the tree-lined drive. He shut the car door, stretched and began the long walk up the drive of Bedlington Park to seek assistance. A spot of breakfast would suit him, too. Then he fell once more to thinking about the previous day, and realised that it had now been more than twenty-four hours since they had breakfasted together. He wondered if they would ever do so again.

'What timing,' said Leo. He was standing in the doorway of Bedlington Park. He looked, if anything, even more dishevelled than Harry.

'I'm sorry. Have I woken you?' Harry asked.

Leo shook his head. 'No. I've been up all night.'

'How is he?'

Leo spoke evenly. 'He died at half past five this morning.'

'Oh, I'm so sorry.' Harry's own worries were, momentarily, put aside.

'No. It's a release, really. He's been ill for a long time. In the end I think it just wore him out.' Then Leo realised that his friend was still standing on the doorstep. 'Oh, I'm sorry, come in.'

Harry walked through the pair of large glazed doors in the centre of the Palladian portico and into the hall of Bedlington Park. The floor was of parchment-coloured limestone; the walls were painted creamy grey and hung with hunting trophies. The whole effect was rather oppressive. Leo led the way through a doorway to the left of the hall.

'Make yourself comfortable,' instructed Leo. 'I'll organise coffee.'

Harry perched on the arm of an easy chair and looked around. The drawing room was much less intimidating than the hall. Egg yolk-yellow walls were hung with a rich mixture of pictures, from the expected Georgian ancestors and a rather grubby Van Dyck to more modern works by Nash and Nicholson. There were pictures of horses, too, among them a large Herring of two racehorses approaching the finishing post.

A collection of chintz-covered chairs and sofas were dotted round the room and by the fireplace were two small paintings of Bedlington terriers. They made Harry smile. He fell to wondering what would happen to all this now that everything had been left to Leo, who, despite having never enjoyed a close relationship with his father, possessed a sense of duty and an awareness of the need for continuity. Within the week his friend had been transformed from a carefree young blade, who had nothing to do but enjoy himself, into a man of property and a landowner with obligations.

And then Harry saw the Munnings. It was hanging in an alcove. It was of a woman on a horse and not dissimilar in composition to the one of Eleanor riding sidesaddle. His thoughts returned to her. He should have run after her and asked when he could see her again, but the intervention of the road sweeper had thrown him and in the second or two it had taken to consider what he should do he had missed his opportunity.

His reverie was interrupted by the opening of the large mahogany door. Leo came into the room, followed by a butler who was stooping under the weight of a tray laden with tea and coffee, milk and sugar. The man put down the tray on the large, padded stool in front of one of the sofas, bowed respectfully from the neck and then exited without a word.

'I don't think Sands will ever get over it,' said Leo dejectedly, sitting down on the sofa and pouring the coffee. 'He's been here for thirty-odd years. Pa came and went, but Sands was always here, year after year. "The Sands of time" Pa used to call him. Sands kept the place going. Trouble is, I don't think he'll have the energy to carry on now.'

'So what will you do?' asked Harry, helping himself to milk and sugar.

'Stay and sort things out. There'll be lawyers to see—all that sort of thing—and until I've met them, I don't really know what will happen.' Leo stood up and walked over to one of the long windows that looked over the park. He sipped his coffee thoughtfully and then said, 'Look at all that. Two hundred years of history. It would be a tragedy if I were to lose it all now— even the bloody fountain. It's never worked properly.'

Harry stood up and walked to the window, standing beside Leo and looking out over the park. There were handsome clumps of oak, scattered seemingly at random, and great sweeps of grass, dotted with fallow deer. Right in front of the window was a large fountain of Neptune representing a trio of dolphins and raising his trident in the air. Water spurted from every orifice.

'Quite appalling,' murmured Leo, 'but I love it.' He turned to face into the room, and Harry could see that his eyes were filled with tears.

'Perhaps I should be going,' said Harry, draining his cup.

'You'll do no such thing,' insisted Leo. 'You've driven all this way. It was really good of you. If I'd thought about it, I could have sent Osborne to pick the car up, but I was a bit preoccupied . . . Anyway, there's no way I'm letting you leave this house looking like that. The locals would think standards have really slipped.' Leo glanced across at an ornate looking glass on the wall. 'Mind you, I'm one to talk. Come on, I'll get Sands to send someone up to run us baths and then we can catch up over breakfast. I want to know exactly what happened with Munnings. Take my mind off things.'

Over breakfast Harry told Leo of Munnings's hospitality, of his helpful attitude towards Mac and of his painting Eleanor on the horse.

'You've seen the one of Mama, of course?' asked Leo.

'In the drawing room?'

'Yes. Painted the year before I was born,' confided Leo. 'But then it would have been, wouldn't it . . . ?' He checked himself. 'Died having me, I'm afraid. Not much I could do about that, of course.' Harry saw in Leo's face a mixture of sadness and stoicism, an acquired ability to shrug off the most dreadful circumstances Then suddenly he brightened. 'So how is Eleanor? Has being an artist's model gone to her head?'

'Oh, I shouldn't think so. You know Eleanor.'

'Yes,' said Leo. 'But do you?'

Harry looked surprised. 'What do you mean?'

'She's quite soft on you, you know.' Leo's tone was casual.

'You think so?'

'I know so.'

'That's what Mac said, but I'm not so sure.'

Harry did not want to give away details of their evening together, to avoid embarrassing Eleanor.

'Why is it that some chaps can't see what's staring them in the face?' asked Leo. He popped a piece of toast and marmalade into his mouth and asked, 'So what are you going to do about it?'

Harry stood up and walked to the open door of the summer house. 'Go and see her before she leaves. Ask her . . .' His words trailed off as he gazed out over the green lawns of Bedlington Park.

'Ask her what?'

'If she'll marry me.'

Bath—December 2007

The letter came as a complete surprise. Jamie was sitting at his desk at Ballantyne's reading it through for the second time when his mother came into the office.

'You look worried. What's the matter?' she asked, bustling her way to her own desk and throwing off her cashmere cape.

'Not worried, just surprised. Did you see the paper this morning? The obituaries? One of Granddad's old university friends has died.'

'Which one?' Emma Ballantyne was busying herself with her shopping bag now, taking out of it an assortment of files and papers.

'Lord Bedlington.'

She carried on emptying her bag. 'Oh dear. Still, he must have been a good age, I suppose.'

'Eighty-one.' He walked over to her desk and dropped the letter in front of her on her blotter. 'This letter came this morning.'

Emma reached for her glasses and read out loud:

'Dear Sirs,

Re: the late Lord Bedlington

In the terms of the will of our client Leo, the late Lord Bedlington, the deceased requested that his goods and chattels, such as were not claimed directly by the two parties named therein, should be disposed of through the offices of Ballantyne's of Bath and the proceeds thereof distributed to the named beneficiaries of his will. Such goods and chattels are, at present, contained within the property known as Villa Fabrice, Menton, Côte d'Azur.

I would be grateful if you would be so good as to contact me at the address above so that our former client's wishes may be expedited.

Yours faithfully,

Edward Chesterman

for Chesterman, Chesterman and Paine, solicitors.'

Emma took off her glasses and looked up at her son. 'Well, I never. Why do you suppose he wanted *us* to sell it?'

'Maybe for old times' sake. But when I saw Granddad this morning and told him that Lord Bedlington had died, he said, "That'll put the cat among the pigeons." Why, do you think?'

Emma looked blank. 'I've absolutely no idea. But you'd better get onto'—she checked the letterhead again—'Chesterman, Chesterman and Paine and find out what they want us to do. As I recall, Leo Bedlington was all but penniless at the end, so I can't think there'll be much of interest. Ah, well. But I suppose we can do our bit for the old boy.'

'Did Granddad talk about him at all?' asked Jamie.

'Not much. But whenever he did it was always quite affectionately. I don't think they saw a lot of each other after their university days.'

'What about Richard King? Did he know him better?'

'Oh, as far as I'm aware, Leo Bedlington's relationship with Richard King was even less cordial than your grandfather's.'

'Why?'

His mother sighed deeply and pushed back her chair. 'Relationships then were not quite as simple as they are today, if you know what I mean.'

Jamie looked puzzled.

'Oh, Jamie! Young men in their late teens and early twenties are still finding out about life and about themselves.' She saw Jamie's eyebrows rise but continued with her explanation. 'I'm quite sure your grandfather and Richard King were completely certain about their own sexuality. But they would have had friends who might not have been.'

'Like Leo Bedlington?'

'Yes.'

'And what about his friend?' Jamie scanned the obituary column lying on his desk. 'John Macready—described as his "companion of many years". He died in a swimming accident.'

'I think your grandfather would be rather surprised by that.'

'His death, or the fact that they lived together?'

'Both.' Emma tapped her fingers on the desk impatiently. 'Why don't you ask him yourself? I'm sure he'd tell you about it.' She put down the letter and reached for the phone. 'Well, if you're not going to ring Chesterman, Chesterman and whoever, then I suppose I'd better.'

'I'll do it, I'll do it. I'm just a bit surprised, that's all. It's been a bit of a morning, all things considered.' He reached for the telephone, but paused before dialling the number, wondering what she might be doing now, up at the top end of town.

MISSY WAS WORKING on the catalogue for their next exhibition, writing descriptions of paintings, indicating their provenance and working out in her head exactly what would be hung where. The show would mark fifty years of King's Fine Art and would also be something of a personal celebration for Richard King at eighty. At the core of the exhibition would be the major equestrian artists of the eighteenth, nineteenth and early twentieth centuries, with a few modern pieces to broaden the appeal.

She straightened her back and looked up and directly ahead of her. Her grandfather had now hung the Munnings of the woman on the horse on the far wall. It stood alone. She must remember to ask him if he wanted it included in the exhibition. It would make a good counterpoint to the Stubbs that she planned to hang on the opposite side of the room.

She looked back at her laptop and tried hard to concentrate on the description of a Ben Marshall painting showing the chestnut colt Burleigh by the rubbing-down house at Newmarket, but her thoughts kept returning to the night before. He had not said anything before he left, but she did not feel anxious. Instead she felt a kind of inner calm—an echo of the sensation she had experienced the night before, lying there in his arms.

Her reverie was interrupted by her grandfather. The solid figure of Richard King pushed open the door and stood in front of her at the desk. Missy looked up. He was not his usual calm self. His cheeks were flushed and he drummed his fingers on the edge of the desk.

'What's the matter?' she asked.

'Oh, nothing, really. Just had a bit of a shock. Old university chum died. Leo, Lord Bedlington. Read it in the paper.'

'I'm so sorry.' Missy got up. 'Let me make you a cup of coffee.'

'No, no, it's all right.' Richard King turned away from the desk and walked over to the window. It was raining steadily now, more like December than it had been of late. More in tune with his mood.

'Did you know him very well?' Missy asked.

'Once. But we hadn't met for years.'

'But he would have been about your age, though?'

Her grandfather smiled ruefully. 'Old enough for it not to come as a shock?' he remarked.

'No . . . I didn't mean . . .' Missy was on sensitive ground.

'Oh, don't worry,' he said. 'Everyone of my age realises we're on borrowed time, it's just that we don't need to be reminded.'

'No.' Missy looked suitably contrite. 'Will there be a funeral?' she asked.

'I don't know. Probably over in France, I should think. That's where he lived at the end. Mind you, maybe they'll bring him back over here and bury him in the family vault.'

'Who was he?' asked Missy.

'Leo, Lord Bedlington. He was a friend at Christ Church back in the forties. He was just "the Honourable" back then, of course. A long time ago.'

'And you lost touch?'

'Yes.'

Missy flipped through Richard's copy of *The Times*. 'Here it is . . . the Earl of Bedlington. His father was a collector . . . Death duties . . .' Missy was speed-reading the obituary. 'He "dabbled in the art world".'

'Yes, well, it's probably all very boring to you.' Richard moved towards her as she finished the obituary.

'"His companion of many years, the artist John Macready—"' Missy lowered the paper. 'I didn't know that John Macready lived with him.'

'Well, there you are.'

'Did you know him as well, Grandpa?'

Richard King hesitated. 'Vaguely.'

'But didn't he study art at Christ Church, too?'

'Oh, probably. A lot of people studied art history at Christ Church. I didn't know them all.'

Missy was surprised at her grandfather's impatience. He was normally so imperturbable. Perhaps it was just the shock of his old friend dying.

'We've sold his pictures here—not recently, but over the years,' she continued. 'I just thought you might have encountered him.'

'Well, of course I encountered him, but that doesn't mean I knew him.'

'No, of course not. Sorry.' She began to wish that she had not asked about his past. Yet he had never seemed particularly sensitive about it before. Why should he be so nettled now?

'Well, if you'll excuse me, I've things to do.' He turned to leave. 'I'll probably be back late afternoon if anyone asks for me.'

'Fine. OK.' But she could not let it rest there. 'Grandpa, everything is all right, isn't it?'

He realised he had acted out of character, that his behaviour had alarmed her. 'Yes, of course. I'm sorry. Just a bit of a shock, that's all.' He bent forward and kissed the top of her head. 'Just a bit of a shock.' Then he smiled at her and left the room.

Oxford—July 1949

Richard was feeling bored and very sorry for himself. If he was honest with himself, his bones did not ache as much as they had done, and his nose was no longer a streaming torrent. He contemplated staying in bed, but the prospect of leaving Oxford the following day galvanised him into action.

He looked around the room at the scene of devastation—the piles of books and clothes lying everywhere, the trunks and cases open and ready to accept their load. By tomorrow he would have to be ready to go.

The knock at his door came as no surprise. He was waiting for Eleanor to return. He had expected her the previous day, but she had clearly left him to stew with his cold. He was a bit miffed by that, but then it was understandable—why should she risk catching it as well?

'Come in if you're healthy!' he yelled in the direction of the door.

The door opened and Mac put his head round. 'Any better?'

'A bit, thanks. It was a real bugger. Don't know where I picked it up.'

'Ah, well, you know colleges—always something doing the rounds.' Mac looked at the open trunks. 'You ready for the off, then?'

'Just about.'

'I've done mine. A life packed into suitcases.' He looked pensive for a moment, then said, 'Thought I'd go for a pint. Do you fancy one?'

Richard was not sure that drinking was a good idea after being confined to bed for two days, but then drowning his ailment in beer might be as good a way as any of ridding himself of it.

They sat at a table beside the river and the pint glasses began to pile up. Two, then three. They were on their fourth now.

'So when do you leave for Glasgow?' Richard asked Mac.

'Tomorrow morning. The early train.'

'What then?'

Mac shrugged. 'That depends. I just want some time to think, time to get myself sorted out.'

Richard lowered his glass to the table, where it landed with more of a thump than he had intended. 'That sounds a bit serious.'

Mac turned to look in the direction of a passing punt. 'I suppose so.'

There was a wistfulness in Mac's tone that Richard had not heard before. Maybe it was just the beer. 'Are you all right?' he asked. 'It's not a woman, is it? You haven't gone and found yourself a woman? Not after keeping yourself pure for the last three years . . .'

Mac shook his head, and then wished he hadn't. He held his head in his hands for a moment. 'No, I haven't gone and found myself a woman.'

'Too tied up in your painting, that's your trouble,' muttered Richard, reaching for his glass once more. 'You don't want to meet a hooker. You want a nice girl, a girl like Eleanor. Except not Eleanor. Another nice girl.'

'You reckon?' Mac's eyes were on the river, but his mind was elsewhere as he murmured, 'I wish it were that simple.'

'Whaddya mean?'

'As simple as finding the right girl.'

Richard looked up from his glass now and put his hands flat on the table, the better to steady himself. 'You see, all the years we've been here, you've never bothered, have you? You could have had lots of girls. You're not bad-looking. But now you're going back to Glasgow on your own and—'

'I'm not going back to Glasgow. Well . . . I'm not staying.'

'But you're on your own.'

'I wish you'd stop saying that as though it were some kind of disease.'

'Now there's no need to be rattled. It's a bit of a shame, that's all.' Richard tried to look sympathetic, but his eyes were red and watery.

Mac drained his glass and sighed. 'Are you happy?' he asked.

'I wish I hadn't got this cold. And that I hadn't had so many pints.'

'No, but are you happy generally, with the way things have turned out?'

'Ha! Well, they haven't turned out, have they? Not yet.'

'No.'

'And I don't know where she is. She said she'd come and see me, but she hasn't shown up yet and it's . . . it's . . . later than it should be.'

'Are you sure she's the one for you?' asked Mac.

'Yup. I think she thinks so, too. Got to sort things out today. Set the record straight.' Richard's brow furrowed with concentration, then he gave up. 'What about you? Are you happy? With your painting?'

Mac looked irritated. 'I wish you wouldn't keep going on as though my painting were the only thing worth living for.'

'Well, it is, isn't it? I mean, that's what you do. We all know that. You're far more dedicated than we are—and the best artist of the lot of us.'

'And that should be enough?'

Richard shrugged. 'I don't know. You tell me.'

'I wish I could,' murmured Mac. 'But it would be pointless.'

'And what's that supposed to mean? Nothing's pointless. Go on, tell me what you wished you could tell me.'

Mac shook his head. 'You've no idea, have you?'

'About what? I don't understand.'

'No, you wouldn't. I mean, why should you?'

Richard looked enquiringly at Mac, who was staring out across the river. In spite of the fact that Richard had had too much to drink, he could see that Mac's eyes were full of tears. Well, there was a turn-up for the books. Mac was the one who never showed emotion.

Mac spoke softly. 'If ever there's anything I can do, to help you, you will let me know, won't you?'

Richard smiled. 'You mean, when you're a successful painter, you'll let me sell your work for inflated prices and take a massive commission?'

'That's not what I mean.' He paused. 'You've never noticed, have you?'

'Noticed what?'

Mac turned to face him. 'About the girl thing?'

Richard was puzzled. 'What about it?'

'It was never an option. Never . . . an interest.'

The slow dawning of reality broke over Richard's face. 'You mean . . . not girls . . . but—'

Mac cut in gently, ''Fraid so.'

'Christ! And have you . . .?'

'God, no, never. Promiscuity never appealed. There was only one, you see. And I knew that was pointless. You've never given me any reason to believe that you felt the same way.'

He smiled, and the colour, so recently returned to Richard's cheeks, drained from them once more. He stared at Mac, unable to believe what he had heard, and then said, very softly, 'Oh, shit.'

'I'm sorry. I knew it would shock you. That's why I had to get pissed to tell you. But it was important somehow that I told you before we left.'

Never had so few words had such a sobering effect on Richard. 'I see,' he said softly.

'Well, there we are. Stupid, really.'

Richard's mind was whirring. He neither knew what to say nor how to behave. He was torn between wanting to hit Mac for daring to say such a thing and wanting to apologise to a man who had been a good friend, for being unable to return his feelings. The events of the past three years swirled around in his head. He searched in vain for things he might have said or done that could possibly have given Mac any reason to believe that there was the remotest chance that his feelings could be or would be reciprocated. He found none. Mac had been a friend, a really good friend. There was nothing remotely fey or effeminate about him. If anything, he was the most masculine of the four of them. Did Harry know? he wondered. That particular question was answered immediately.

'There's no need for anybody else to know, is there?' asked Mac.

Richard detected a note of fear in his voice—fear of being found out, fear of being spurned by the people he was closest to.

Richard shook his head. 'No, of course not,' he said.

'I'd better go,' said Mac. He stood up and swayed a little. Then he laid his hand on Richard's shoulder. 'Don't lose touch,' he said.

Richard could say nothing. He stared at the table, then, when he looked up to speak, Mac had gone. It may have been the note of despair in Mac's voice, or it may have been his own acute discomfort at the unexpected revelation, but, somehow, he knew that they would never meet again.

ELEANOR WAS QUITE DETERMINED. She had put off the evil moment long enough. It was unfair to leave things as they were, from everybody's point of view.

She took the long route to Richard's lodgings, along the banks of the Cherwell, the better to square in her mind what she wanted to say. She watched as students punted noisily up and down the river, remembering the times she had sat in the back of rowing boats and skiffs as attentive students vied for her attention. She knew now that there was only one of them that she really wanted to be a part of her life.

She passed Mac's digs on her way to see Richard. She would go and say her goodbyes there, too, before he left for Glasgow. As she rounded the corner by Richard's lodgings, in the next street, she did not see the lone figure in the distance, laden with suitcases, disappearing in the direction of the station. If she had done, she would have run after Mac, but she didn't. In that moment, he faded out of her life. Just as he had faded out of Richard's.

HARRY HOPED that Eleanor would be in her room, but when he got there, the cleaner said that she had left half an hour ago.

'Where was she going?' he asked.

'How should I know?' replied the cleaner. 'I just clean here.'

It was not a good start. He would just have to do the rounds of the various digs and lodgings and hope that somewhere along the way he would bump into her. He set off in the direction of Mac's, but when he found his rooms empty, he guessed that she must instead be with Richard. That could be tricky, he thought. Why had he left it until now? Why had he not told her earlier? Three long years he had shilly-shallied. How on earth could he have allowed himself to get into this ridiculous situation? Nobody else would leave it this late, would they?

MAC'S REVELATION had had a sobering effect on Richard King. He played their conversation over and over in his mind, still at a loss to understand how such a situation could have arisen.

Had Leo approached him, he could have understood. They all knew Leo's predilections, but the law being what it was, he had always been circumspect about such things. The situation had been tacitly understood and, as such, none of them had felt uncomfortable with it or inclined to dwell on it.

While he appreciated the courage it must have taken Mac to express his feelings towards him, Richard wished with all his heart that the Scotsman had kept his feelings to himself. However hard he tried, he could feel nothing except revulsion and embarrassment towards a man who, for the last three years, he had thought of as a friend. So deep was his preoccupation with these thoughts that at first he did not register when Eleanor put her head round his door.

'Hello?' she said questioningly, aware his mind was somewhere else.

He looked up and stared at her blankly.

'You look as though you've seen a ghost. Are you all right?'

Richard pulled himself together. He had promised Mac that he would say nothing. It was a promise he would have no problem keeping. 'I'm fine. I'm glad you came. I wanted to see you.'

'Yes. Me too.'

It pleased him that she needed to see him. It came as a relief after the events of the last hour, but it puzzled him that she seemed distracted.

'I need to talk to you,' Eleanor said.

'Yes.' Richard walked over to the chest of drawers. 'I need to talk to you, too.' He thought it best to get in first, do the right thing, override that last conversation with one that was more suitable. He slid open the top drawer, withdrew a small box and turned to face her. 'I have to ask you something.'

Eleanor looked uneasy.

Richard walked towards her. 'I wanted to do it earlier, but then I got that rotten cold and you were away for a couple of days.'

Suddenly she knew what was coming. 'I think you need to . . .'

He opened the box and held it towards her. It contained a small diamond-clustered ring. 'Will you marry me?'

'Oh, Richard!' she said.

Those were the only words that Harry heard. He was standing outside the door, choosing his moment to interrupt them. He was, he realised in that instant, the complete master of mistiming. He had, indeed, left it too late. She was Richard's. She was not his. He turned away, quietly retraced his steps down the stairs and walked to the river. He needed to think, to clear his head. There was no point in seeing her now. He would simply leave. He would just walk out of her life, as she had walked out of his.

IT WAS NOT EASY letting Richard down. She had explained that while she was very fond of him, she did not think she could marry him. He had not taken it well. She had not mentioned Harry, feeling that it would have been more than Richard could bear. Eventually she left him sitting alone and went to look for Harry, but he was nowhere to be found. His room was tidy and his cases were packed and waiting to go. She waited for half an hour, but when there was no sign of him, she wrote him a brief note:

Dear Harry,

I came looking for you and waited for half an hour, but you are obviously busy. I need to see you. Please get in touch at my hall. I'll wait there until I hear from you. It's very important.

Love, Eleanor x

ELEANOR'S CLEANER did not think to tell her that Harry had been looking for her. Why should she? She was having a rotten day—all these students going and new ones coming to take their place. What did she care?

It was early evening when Eleanor went once more to Harry's digs. The cases had gone and so had Harry. All that remained was the bed, the chest of drawers, a table and a chair. Beside the chair was a wastepaper bin; it was empty, she noticed, except for one scrap of screwed-up paper.

Chapter 6

Bath—December 2007

Missy was glad of the diversion, and particularly glad of the direction from which it had come. He had no time for a leisurely lunch, he had said, but, if she was free, they could meet for a quick bite at a sandwich bar round the back of the abbey at around 2 p.m.

They sat side by side on stools at a shelf that ran round the window, and if, as they say, we are what we eat, he was a double espresso and a BLT, and she was a hot chocolate and a tuna salad on foccacia. For a while neither said anything much of consequence, but then Jamie said, 'What is it, Missy? You seem distracted.'

Missy laid her head on his shoulder. 'It's nothing. I'm sorry. There's nothing wrong, really.'

'No, there is. You're worrying about something. Us?'

'No. Not us.'

'What, then?'

'Oh, just Grandpa. He's been a bit funny of late, uneasy, irritable. As if he's not totally in control.'

'Could just be his age. He is getting on a bit. They all are—the grandparents, I mean.'

'But Grandpa always seems to have been at ease with himself, well, confident, you know, self-assured.'

'Yes, you could say that.'

'Oh, I know some people interpret that as arrogance . . .'

Jamie raised an eyebrow.

'Yes, all right then, sometimes he is a bit arrogant, but he deserves to be—King's Fine Art has done really well over the years.'

'Mmm,' murmured Jamie.

Missy realised what he was driving at. 'And I know your grandfather has done really well, too. It's just that I've never got to know him. Doesn't he worry you, too, sometimes?'

'Not really, no. I suppose he's fairly self-contained. Nothing much rattles him. He mixes easily with everybody—well, with the odd exception.' He shot Missy a knowing glance, which was acknowledged. 'It's as if he's been through so much that nothing surprises him any more.'

'Oh. That sounds rather sad.'

'I don't think he's sad—far from it—but there is a sort of resignation about him now that didn't used to be there, a kind of acceptance of whatever the world might throw at him.'

'Maybe that's what happens.'

'Anyway, today he dropped a real bombshell. Told me he and Gran were moving into a flat and asked me if I'd like the house in the Circus.'

Missy's eyes widened. 'Bloody hell! What did you say?'

'Yes. Bloody hell indeed. And . . . well . . . I accepted.'

'Yesterday you were so impressed with my little flat in the Royal Crescent. Now I feel like a poor relation.'

'I just hope I can make it work.'

'A house in the Circus?' asked Missy, her voice shot through with irony. 'You'll make it work.'

'Well, it worked for Granddad all those years, so I hope so.'

Missy was stirring her hot chocolate and scooping up the frothy top with a long-handled spoon. 'Do you think he is happily married?'

'Yes. Well, I suppose so. I've never really thought about it. Nobody's ever suggested otherwise.' He looked thoughtful. 'Why do you ask?'

'Oh, I don't know. It's just that I wonder sometimes if my grandma and grandpa are really happy. He always seems to make the running. Asks her if she's got what she wants, makes her tea every morning, always checks to see where she is and how she's getting on.'

'Isn't that just normal married life?'

'I suppose.'

'Do you mean she doesn't seem happy to be fussed over?'

'No, it's not that. She's never unpleasant or ungrateful or anything; it's just that there's a certain sort of understanding between them.'

Missy saw the puzzled look on Jamie's face. 'I don't mean like our understanding. It's different.'

'Different how?'

'I can't really put my finger on it, but . . . there's not that real ease that you find between people who really, really love one another. I mean, I suppose they are quite comfortable together, but . . .'

'No spark?'

'No.'

'Maybe it disappears after fifty years of marriage.'

Missy looked disappointed. 'Do you think so?'

Jamie shrugged. 'Who knows?' Then he smiled. 'A bit early to worry about that.'

Missy blushed.

'Good Lord, the lady blushes.'

'You really are a dreadful man.'

Jamie glanced at his watch. 'Look, I'll have to be going. I've a client to see at three o'clock in Melksham, so I'll need to get my skates on.'

'Oh. That was a short lunch.'

'Well, I did warn you.'

'I suppose.' Missy put down the spoon and stepped down from her stool.

'But I never told you . . .' he said.

'Told me what?'

'That you look lovely.' He kissed her on both cheeks.

'That was very chaste,' she said.

'I'll be better tonight,' he promised.

She cocked her head on one side. 'Oh, there'll be a tonight, will there?'

'Unless you're busy,' he said, making for the door.

'I'll try to fit you in,' she said. 'My place at eight?'

'Perfect.'

BY THE TIME Missy got back to the gallery her grandfather had still not reappeared and so she returned to her cataloguing of the paintings for the forthcoming exhibition. At four o'clock the doorbell rang and the voice of a parcel courier came through on the intercom.

'I'll be right down.'

She opened the door to an overalled youth with spiky fair hair who had a flat parcel in one hand and an electronic touchpad in the other. He asked Missy to sign the screen and confirm receipt then handed her the parcel.

'I'm sorry I'm late. The van broke down.'

'No problem. I'm still here.'

'Lucky,' said the youth, giving her a smile. 'Enjoy your evening.'

Missy watched as he climbed into the cab of his van and flung it round the corner, clearly trying to impress. She found it hard not to smile. Then she looked at the package. It was addressed to her grandfather at King's Fine Art. She had better open it, just to check it was in one piece.

She tore away the brown paper and a good deal of Bubble Wrap, slicing through the parcel tape with a Stanley knife. Finally the gilt frame came into view and she turned the image to face her.

It was another Munnings. The label on the stretcher described it as *Gypsies in Hampshire*. The picture showed a group of colourfully caparisoned Romanies around their green-painted caravan, with a grey horse tethered to one side and a smoking campfire at the other. A white envelope had been slipped under the stretcher. Missy pulled it out, slit it open with a paper knife and removed the sheet of paper it contained. It bore no address and said, quite simply: *For you. With apologies, M.*

She stood the painting on the easel in front of the desk and examined it closely. She knew that Munnings had painted hop-pickers in Hampshire between the wars, but there was something about the painting that intrigued her. She had been a part of the art world for over ten years now, and in that time she had discovered that she had a sort of intuition which told her when something was 'not quite right'. The odd thing about this painting, was that it seemed, if anything, to be 'too Munnings', rather than the reverse.

She sat down in her chair and stared at it, willing the painting to give up its secrets.

It had the life, the vitality and the easy, almost slapdash paint application of Munnings, and yet, she just felt . . . doubtful.

Missy got up from her chair again and walked round the desk to look more closely at the painting. The signature seemed genuine enough, with that looping sweep under the tail of the final 's'. But signatures were easy to forge. No, it was more than that. What was it that made her suspicious? Perhaps it was the fact that the picture had arrived with no provenance, no indication of any part of its life to date. Somehow she felt she had seen it before.

She looked closely at the brushwork. It gave her every bit as much pleasure as the brushwork of the Master always did—so assured, so bold, so individual. The reflected colours on the coat of the horse could only be achieved by Sir Alfred Munnings. She shook her head and went back to her cataloguing. It was probably her imagination.

At a quarter to six she packed up for the day. There was still no sign of her grandfather; he had clearly thought better of returning to the office and had gone home to Peel Place. She was glad of that. Maybe tomorrow he would be his usual self again, and hopefully he would be able to shed some light on the Munnings that had just arrived.

She got up from the desk and stood the paintings she had catalogued in a row against the wall, to remind herself how far she had got. The next one in the ordered stack had its back to her, but when she saw the name of the artist on the stretcher she picked up the painting and turned it round.

She studied it carefully. It was a portrait of a single bay horse, its bridle held by a groom wearing jodhpurs, a hacking jacket and a flat cap. She removed the Munnings, placed the new painting on the easel and stood back a little. The sky was a refreshing confection of forget-me-not blue and creamy white—huge cumulus clouds building above the flowering elder trees that provided a background to the horse. It was an accomplished piece of work that any collector of equine art would be pleased to have in their collection. The artist's signature, in the bottom right-hand corner of the painting, was clearly visible: *J. Macready.*

She looked more closely at the work, admiring the artist's dexterity. Then, not really knowing why, she picked up the Munnings and placed it above the Macready on the easel.

For several minutes she stared at the two paintings, then went to the bookshelves behind her desk and pulled out *The Dictionary of British Equestrian Artists* and looked up John Macready. The entry was brief:

MACREADY, John Kelvin 1928–95

Glasgow-born artist who studied art history at Christ Church, Oxford, just after the Second World War. A self-taught painter of landscapes and equestrian subjects, he was an artist of considerable ability, a fact recognised by Sir Alfred Munnings, whom Macready had met while at Oxford. He seemed to spend the rest of his life emulating the Master until he died, tragically, in a swimming accident in the South of France.

Missy closed the book. Not much to go on. She looked again at the two paintings, and the words 'emulating the Master' echoed in her head.

What if? No. Not possible. A coincidence, nothing more.

She rubbed her eyes and stretched. It had been a long day. At eight Jamie would be here. She glanced in the mirror and flicked at her hair to give it some semblance of order. Behind her, in the reflection in the mirror, she saw the two paintings once more. The Munnings of the caravan and the gypsies suddenly looked familiar. She *had* seen it before? But where?

Impatiently, she ran her fingers along the shelf housing auction catalogues from sales going back over the years. Backwards and forwards her eyes ran over the catalogues, then, lighting on one from 2001, she pulled it out and flipped through the pages.

No. No. No . . . Then . . . yes! There it was. A painting of gypsies in Hampshire. A green caravan, a grey horse, a campfire gently smoking. A mirror image of the painting on the easel.

She steadied herself. This was not necessarily unusual. Artists often repeated a particular scene. Munnings was no exception. He had reproduced the famous portrait of himself painting, with his palette, and of his wife on her horse outside their house at Dedham several times—each one almost an exact copy of the first. *Almost* an exact copy.

She held the catalogue in front of her, while looking at the reflection of the Munnings in the mirror. It was identical, except that it was a mirror image. Why would Munnings have done that? If he were repeating the picture—as requested by a client—he would have painted it the same way round. And if one of the two paintings was a forgery, which one was it? And who had painted it?

Missy lay the open catalogue on her desk. The conclusion she felt bound to come to was not one that she wanted to believe. She could only hope she was wrong. If she were not, the consequences did not bear thinking about.

Chawton, Hampshire—November 1949

The wedding was arranged for the last day of November in the Church of St Nicholas at Chawton.

It was not the happiest of days for any of the parties concerned. Richard King's mother would rather he had found a better catch, someone with a title, perhaps. Richard's father had had to forego a trip to Cheltenham to the National Hunt meeting. Richard himself had hoped that his bride would be by his side because she knew that there was no one else in the world who meant so much to her, rather than because she was 'fond of him'. But at least she was marrying him.

For Eleanor, it was the saddest day of her life. She put a brave face on it; after all, she was grateful to Richard for being so persistent. Having turned him down the first time, she had no right to expect that he would ever ask her again. But he did, only two months later.

She accepted and asked if they might be married as soon as possible. Richard had agreed. They slept together almost from that moment onwards. Richard was surprised when she agreed, and equally surprised and not a little embarrassed when she very quickly fell pregnant, but then he knew she had always been desperate for a family.

Eleanor would never understand what had happened to Harry. Why, after that wonderful night together, had he never spoken to her again? Why had he gone away without responding to her note? Where had he gone? What had she done to so turn round his feelings towards her? Perhaps they had not been genuine feelings. Maybe he had never intended it to be anything more than a one-night stand. The very thought of it left her heartbroken.

Eleanor's mother watched the ceremony through a haze of tears, a nurse on either arm. After it was over, they would take her back to the hospital and she would not remember much at all. Eleanor glanced at her and wondered how it was possible for one person to bear so much grief.

Leo, who had given the bride away, watched the ceremony with an aching heart. How could the girl who just a few months ago seemed to be on the way to eternal happiness, have condemned herself to a life of ordinariness? Why had she changed her mind? Where was Harry? He had not seen him since that day at Bedlington Park when he had vowed that he was going back to Oxford to ask Eleanor to marry him. What had gone so terribly wrong? Why had he not contacted Leo to explain?

At first he had thought the worst: that Harry must have had an accident on the way back to Oxford, or had suddenly collapsed and died. It seemed that only something so dramatic could have stopped him from proposing to Eleanor. Then he had heard, a few weeks later, that Harry had been seen in York, in an auction room. So what had happened?

For each and every one of those present at the wedding there were unanswered questions.

The reception at a local hotel had been a low-key affair. In the absence of Eleanor's father, Leo made a speech. He was not at his sparkling best. How could he be? He knew this was not a marriage made in heaven, whatever the parson might have said. Oh, how it tore at his heart when he thought how different the day would have been had another groom been standing there. It was with a heavy heart that Leo journeyed back to Bedlington Park, to face the solicitors who were to tell him that in a matter of months his home and his fortune would be taken from him. The prospect for all of them, except Richard, seemed little short of bleak.

Chapter 7

York—November 1949

'You'll 'ave to be prepared to take the rough with the smooth and muck in, you know. I can't 'ave a fancy Oxford type thinking 'e's above the rest of us.' The full-bellied, tweed-suited partner of Fidler, Son and Bowker was sitting behind a large mahogany partners' desk with his arms folded over the vast acreage of his burgundy waistcoat.

Harry was perched on the stool that had been pulled up in front of the desk, convinced that his inquisitor was in danger, at any moment, of bursting out of his clothes and sending buttons flying to the four corners of the room. All three chins wobbled as he made his point, and his cheeks were the colour and shape of Worcester Pearmain apples. A fountain pen was clenched between pork-sausage fingers, and so fat were his thighs he had trouble getting them into the kneehole under the desk. It might have been a partners' desk, but, fortunately for Ernie Bowker, he was the only working partner left, Fidler having retired and the son of Fidler, after deciding that the family business was not for him, having become a sleeping partner.

'I'm very happy to . . . er . . . muck in,' confirmed Harry. 'That's what I'm here for—to get a handle on the business and work hard.'

'With a view to?' asked Ernie Bowker.

'Well, with a view to becoming a good auctioneer and valuer.'

'Right answer!' He banged his hands on the desk and Harry steadied himself to avoid falling off the stool during the subsequent earth tremor. 'Too many smart alecs come in 'ere, and when I ask 'em what sort of job they want, they say, "Yours." They think they're being funny. They're not. Mind you, there's nothing mysterious about auctioneering. It's a straightforward job. If an item's going to sell, it's going to sell.'

Harry raised an eyebrow.

'Oh, you can create a bit of an atmosphere, jolly folk along, but you'll not get 'em to pay a penny more than they want to, not up 'ere at any rate.'

Harry nodded to imply that he understood the northern way of things.

Ernie was getting into his stride now. 'Eyes and ears, those are your best assets. Do you wear glasses?'

'No.'

'Oh, pity. If you can look over 'em, it sometimes chivvies folk into speeding up a bit. Mind you, there's Ted and Wally to keep an eye out for any bids you miss. They'll shout soon enough if you don't spot 'em.'

'So do you think . . .?'

'Aye, you'll do. I'll give you a go. Why don't you come and work for a week for nowt just to see if you like it? If you do, I'll take you on. I can't say fairer than that. 'Ave you got any digs?'

'I'm lodging with Mrs Fairbrother in Coppergate.'

'Oh, well, the old lady'll fleece you every Friday so you'd better 'ave ten bob on account.' He reached into the inside pocket of his jacket with some difficulty and pulled out a battered black wallet from which he withdrew a ten-shilling note. Having flicked it a few times to make sure it was not adhering to any of its friends, he handed it over. 'Are you courtin'?' he said.

'No.'

'Just as well on what I'll be paying you. Now, then, you can make a start by looking through them catalogues over there.' Ernie pointed to a slithering pile of auction catalogues, those of Fidler, Son and Bowker as well as of London-based and other provincial auction houses. 'They're useful for working out values. Look at what things go for in London, divide by two and you'll get a rough idea of what your estimate should be up 'ere. Don't worry too much if it's on the low side—that encourages 'em to come and bid, and once you've a couple of keen bidders, they'll jack it up for you. With me so far?'

Harry nodded.

'Now, then, I've said it's straightforward, but there are a couple of things you can do to help the party along. Bids off the wall.' Harry looked suddenly anxious and Ernie noticed his change of expression. 'Now don't go all holy on me. Everybody does it and there's nothing wrong with it in moderation. We're here to get the best price for the vendor and it's our duty to find out what the maximum is that a bidder will pay. If you find that something's moving a bit slowly, you can help it along by spotting a bidder at the back of the room. But be careful. I don't mind you coming a cropper and buying the odd item yourself because you miscalculated, but more than once in an auction and I'll start charging you for it. Is that clear?'

Harry nodded again.

'That's for the good stuff. When it comes to the rubbish, try and embellish its 'istory a bit and you might get a few bob more, but not very often.' He leaned on the desk and pushed himself upright. 'I'm going for a spot of dinner down the Red Lion. You can go when I get back. All right?'

'Yes. Fine. Thank you.'

They were interrupted by a gentle tapping at the door.

'Ah, that'll be my dinner date.' The door opened to reveal a dark-haired young woman in a headscarf and a mackintosh. She smiled at them both and walked in, slipping off her headscarf as she did so and letting her dark, shiny hair tumble over her shoulders.

'It's bitter outside, Dad. You'll need a coat.'

'Not in this tweed I won't, and not with my lagging.' Ernie winked at Harry and then effected the introduction. 'This is Harry Ballantyne. He's coming to work with me, giving it a try at any rate, to see if we get on.'

The girl nodded in understanding.

'Harry, this is my daughter. My youngest unmarried. The rest have families now, but she's more into improving 'erself.'

Harry held out his hand.

'Sally Bowker,' she said, and Harry noticed that her eyes were almost as dark as her hair, and that her smile, flashed at him again, lit up the room.

She reminded him of someone else; someone he was trying to forget.

'Hello,' he managed.

'Are you coming to lunch?' she asked.

'It's dinner up 'ere,' corrected her father.

'Well, whatever it is, are you coming?'

'I . . . er . . . don't think . . .'

''E's got work to do,' insisted her father. 'Catalogues to sort through . . .'

'Oh, Dad, don't be such a meanie. If it's Harry's first day, you should at least take him out for lunch . . . dinner . . . whatever.'

Her father was clearly putty in her hands. 'Well, I suppose to seal the deal, though it's a bit premature . . .'

'Oh, I don't think so,' she said.

THE FIRST WEEK went well. The clients seemed to like Harry and he was even let loose for half an hour on an auction, which feat he accomplished without too many sniggers on the part of Ted and Wally. He confused a chiffonier with a commode, and a lowboy with a washstand, but these were minor misdemeanours that his employer seemed willing to overlook. The fact that his daughter had taken a shine to her father's prospective employee might have had something to do with it.

At the end of the week he was called into the office once more. Ernie Bowker looked at him over the top of his horn-rimmed half-moons, and told him to sit down.

'Well, 'ow was your first week, then?' he asked.

'All right, I think,' Harry said anxiously, waiting for reassurance.

His luck was in. 'Aye, you've not done bad. A couple of cock-ups, but nothing too serious. So if you still fancy it, I'll be 'appy to take you on.'

Harry smiled. 'Thank you.'

'But you're not there yet, mind. There's a lot to learn.'

'Yes, of course.'

Ernie leaned back in his chair and looked expansive. With his shape it was difficult to look anything else. 'You've enjoyed your first week, then?'

'Yes, very much.'

'Aye, well, you've caught Sally's eye, I'll say that for you. But be careful.'

Harry wondered where the conversation was leading.

'I'm not much of a one for mixing business with pleasure, and I've seen lads before trying it on with yon.' He nodded in the direction of the door, implying the direction in which Sally had last been seen going.

Harry was anxious to pre-empt any misgivings the father might have. 'Oh, please, I—'

'Nay, lad, don't worry. I've seen enough over the last week to know that you're a decent sort. Just don't break her heart, that's all. She's been to university like you—music she studied, in Manchester—doesn't need me watching over her like an 'awk. But you know what fathers are like with their daughters.'

Harry nodded. 'Of course.'

'Well, there we are, then. I'll be off for my dinner.'

Ernie squeezed past him and then turned before he walked through the door. He held out the sausage-like fingers. 'Welcome to Fidler, Son and Bowker. Play your cards right and you could become a partner one day.'

And that, in the fullness of time, is what happened. Harry became a partner in Fidler, Son and Bowker. He also married the boss's daughter.

Bath—December 2007

It took a while to track her father down. Patrick King had always been elusive, but Missy had become accustomed to his habits. Tonight, with any luck, he would be in the bar of the Boater in Argyle Street.

'To what do I owe the pleasure?' he asked with a grin, which quickly turned into a worried look. 'Everything all right?'

'I'm not sure. Can you spare me a few minutes at the gallery?'

He noticed the worried look on his daughter's face and drained what remained of his glass of red wine. 'See you tomorrow, Jack; I'm dining at the Hole in the Wall tonight so I won't be back.' He slipped his arm through Missy's as they walked out into the street.

They were an unlikely couple. Missy in her smart red jacket and black trousers, he in a baggy tweed jacket and corduroys, his unruly hair rather too long for a man of his age. 'What's the problem? Man trouble?'

'No,' she said scoldingly. 'Well, not in the way you think.'

'Oh. That's me put in my place, then.'

She could tell that the glass of wine he had drained was not his first.

'What do you know about John Macready?' she asked.

'I don't think there *is* much to know, is there?'

'How well did Grandpa know him?'

'Blowed if I know. He's never talked about him.'

'But he must have said something over the years. I mean, they were at university together.'

'Were they? He never said.'

They were walking over Pulteney Bridge now and her father glanced down at the water as the streetlights caught the shimmering surface. 'God! That looks cold tonight.'

She knew that his mind was elsewhere—probably with the woman he would be meeting at the Hole in the Wall. Missy sighed and tried to get back to the point. 'Has the gallery handled many of his paintings?'

'A few, over the years. He died, didn't he? Some kind of accident.'

'Swimming.'

Her father glanced once more at the water. 'Poor bugger. Rotten way to go.' He shuddered involuntarily and clasped her arm tighter as they walked towards the gallery.

As they turned into Brock Street, her father asked, 'How is your love life?'

'Fine, thank you.' She tried not to be rattled.

'Anyone we know?'

'That's none of your business.' She put the key in the lock and he walked in after her.

'Only taking an interest.' Again he saw the look she gave him. 'Yes, I know. Better late than never.'

Missy led the way to her office and flicked on the lights. The paintings were still on the easel in front of her desk. Her father walked over to them. 'Ah, Mr Munnings.' He leaned forward to look at the lower of the two paintings, then raised his eyes to the one above. 'Who's this one by?'

'John Macready.'

'Really? Bloody good, wasn't he?'

Missy walked to his side. 'Notice anything familiar about them?'

'I haven't seen them before, if that's what you mean.'

'Neither of them?'

Her father screwed up his eyes in concentration. 'Mmm. Well, we might have had this one a while.' He tapped the frame of the Macready with his finger. 'But I can't recall the Munnings.' He straightened up. 'Did you bring me all the way up here just to see if I can remember a couple of paintings?'

'No, not exactly. The Munnings arrived today addressed to Grandpa. But look at this.' She showed him the catalogue and the mirror-image painting.

For a few moments he said nothing, but read the catalogue description and the provenance thoroughly before straightening up and saying, in a tone more serious than before, 'I see.'

Missy looked at him enquiringly. 'What do you think?'

Her father walked over to the window. 'I think we've got a problem.'

Missy waited for more information.

Slowly he turned to face her. 'What's your take on it?' he asked.

Missy sat down on the chair behind her desk and folded her arms. 'Well, there are several options. The first is that Munnings painted another copy of the gypsy painting in mirror image, but that would be unusual. He would have been more likely to have painted the same composition as before, which we know he did with certain paintings.'

'The second option?'

'The second option is that it's a forgery by a hand unknown and we're in possession of a fake, which is bloody annoying, very costly and more than a little embarrassing if Grandpa has just bought it.'

'And the third?'

'Well, I think you know what the third option is, but, like me, you probably don't want to believe it. The canvas was painted by John Macready to be sold as a Munnings.'

'Not impossible, but why should that be any worse than option two?'

'Because Grandpa went to university with him and people are bound to make connections. Added to which, the note that came with it'—she handed her father the piece of paper—'was signed "M".'

Patrick King examined the note. 'Mmm. You don't really think Dad would be doing something like that?' he asked incredulously. 'Anyway, John Macready's dead.'

'Yes.' Missy paused, then said, 'Maybe it's just my overactive imagination, but look at the brushwork on the two paintings. It's so similar. John Macready was inspired by Munnings, was known to emulate him. Supposing he and Grandpa . . . oh, I hardly want to say it . . .'

'There's a world of difference between emulating somebody and forging his work.'

'I know, I know. But I just have this feeling. I can't put my finger on it.'

Her father smiled sympathetically. 'You'll need a little more than that.'

'I know.'

'And you haven't told Dad?'

'Heavens, no. And that's the other thing—when I was asking him if he knew John Macready, he got a bit shirty with me, said that he might have been at Christ Church at the same time but that he only knew him vaguely. I'd have expected him to have been interested at least.'

'So what are you going to do?'

'What do you think I should do?'

'I think you should put the so-called Munnings into the storeroom under lock and key and say nothing.'

'But he's probably expecting it to arrive.'

'Well, wait until he asks about it before you give it to him. I expect there'll be a perfectly rational explanation.' Patrick put his arm round his daughter's shoulders. 'Look, congratulate yourself on a bit of detective work, and be pleased that you spotted it before anyone else did. It won't be the first time we've had our fingers burned. Even King's Fine Art can come a cropper.'

'I guess.' Missy looked downcast.

'Perk up, old girl! Worse things have happened.' Patrick glanced at his watch. 'I'll have to dash. Business meeting at the Hole in the Wall.'

'Business?'

'Well, sort of.' Her father gave her one of his 'you know me' apologetic looks and made for the door. Then, with a cheery smile, he was gone.

'WHAT ON EARTH'S the matter with you?' asked Jamie.

Missy was holding the door open as he walked through. She reached up and planted a gentle kiss on his lips. 'Oh, just a long day, that's all.'

'You could tell me about it.'

'Maybe later. Come on, let's have a glass of wine.' She led the way to the flat above the gallery and again he was enveloped in its cool comfort.

Missy went to the kitchen and returned bearing a bottle of wine and two glasses.

'I hope I can make my place as nice as yours,' he said, sitting down at one end of the sofa while Missy poured the wine.

She handed him a glass. 'When do you think you'll move in?'

'Before Christmas.'

'What?'

Jamie grinned. 'I know. It's a bit sudden. A serviced flat has come up and Granddad wants to be in it as soon as possible. He rang this afternoon to say he and Gran are moving out next week.'

'But what about decorating and everything?'

'Well, I can move into the top floor, like you, while the plumber and the electrician do their stuff in the rest of the house. I'm in no rush.'

'No, I suppose not.'

He looked at her, standing in the archway that led to the kitchen, holding her glass of wine. She seemed dazed.

'Are you going to come and sit down?' he asked.

She came to. 'Yes. Sorry. It's just that . . .'

'It's all a bit sudden?'

'Yes.'

'Lucky me, eh?'

'Yes, lucky you.' She dropped onto the sofa beside him and raised her glass. 'Here's to you and the Circus.'

'You still haven't told me what's the matter,' said Jamie.

'Probably just me making a mountain out of a molehill.'

Jamie looked at her enquiringly.

'I came across a picture at the gallery today that I think is a forgery.'

'Oh dear. An expensive mistake?'

'Looks like it.'

'Embarrassing?'

'Very.' Missy sighed deeply, then asked, 'If you thought that a member of your family was being less than open with you, how would you handle it? I mean, would you pursue it like a terrier, or would you let it go?'

Jamie thought for a moment, then said, 'It depends on the seriousness of it, doesn't it? I mean, whether you *can* let it go or whether you feel you really do need to get to the bottom of it.'

'I suppose so.'

'So, who's being "less than open"?'

'I'm not sure. Grandpa, I think. Maybe Dad as well.'

'Are we talking about something that has legal implications? Or maybe even'—he hesitated for a moment—'criminal ones?'

Missy looked worried. 'I don't know.' She turned to him. 'Oh, I do hope not. Maybe it's just my vivid imagination . . . I'll probably turn up something that will prove that there's a perfectly straightforward explanation.'

'For a forgery?'

'Well, maybe just a copy.'

'There's a difference?'

Missy took a deep breath and explained to Jamie all of the possibilities surrounding the provenance of the painting: the fact that it could have been painted by an unknown artist, or by Munnings himself, unlikely as it seemed, or, even more unlikely, by John Macready.

'Do you think your grandfather might have colluded with him?'

'I don't know. I mean, why would he do that? He's always been scrupulously honest in his dealings. It's just that when I asked him about John Macready, he went all funny on me.'

'Have you been through all this with your father?'

'Yes. He told me to pack the painting up, stick it at the back of the store room and say nothing.'

'And you don't know if that's what you should do?'

'No.' Missy shook her head. 'You see why I've had a bit of a day?'

'I do. Time you unwound, I think.' Jamie took her glass of wine from her and put it beside his on the low table in front of the sofa. Then he took her head in his hands and kissed her tenderly on the lips.

'Oh, that's better,' she said softly. 'That's so much better.'

AT PEEL PLACE, on the outskirts of Bath, Richard King had shut himself in his study. It was unlike him. Normally when he returned from the gallery he poured himself a large Scotch and sat down in the drawing room to talk over the events of the day with his wife. Today was different. Eleanor King poured herself a gin and tonic and walked to the desk by the bay window.

On the blotter lay the day's post. She had been out since mid-morning Christmas shopping and so had missed its arrival. She sifted through the envelopes—nothing of particular interest. At the very bottom lay a small padded envelope. It had been sent by recorded delivery and signed for by the daily help. It had a French postmark. She took the paperknife and slit open the envelope, withdrawing a small object, which was further protected by a layer of Bubble Wrap. She pulled at the sticky tape that held it fast and then withdrew a small frame and picture that she had not seen for nearly sixty years. St Anthony of Padua gazed up at her with his wide, blue eyes, causing her heart to miss a beat. She sat down, then noticed the white envelope that had tumbled from the Bubble Wrap.

The envelope was neatly addressed in her maiden name: *Eleanor Faraday*. She opened the second envelope and withdrew the two sheets of paper that it contained. Unfolding them, she read the message:

Villa Fabrice, Menton, Côte d'Azur

My dear Eleanor,

You will receive this after my death. I wanted you to have it—there is precious little else left of my fabulous legacy! We had such happy times together at Oxford, and I think of you with nothing but fondness. By now you will be as old as me (well, almost) and it is time to set the record straight. I would hate to think that you, too, will pass away (dreadful euphemism) without knowing the truth.

It can change nothing now, of course, but you should hear it nevertheless. I know you believed that Harry Ballantyne deserted you for no apparent reason. I was puzzled myself at the time, but now I am convinced that he thought you had set your sights on Richard rather than him (even though it was clear to those of us close to you that the reverse was true). I am convinced, also, that he went away because he believed (wrongly) that you intended to accept Richard's proposal of marriage. His leaving was, in his eyes, I am sure, simply to spare you any pain. It is tragic that in reality it had the opposite effect.

To see you on your wedding day, and to give you away to a man I know you did not love, was the most heart-rending thing I have ever had to do. The loss of goods and chattels is as nought compared with the loss of true love. Believe me, I know.

Oh, it is too late for us all now, but try to find a little understanding in your heart for a man who clearly adored you and who, for whatever reason, made a hash of things. In our short lives we all make many mistakes. Mine has been full of them, not least those involving matters of the heart. Mac was a great companion, even if some of his actions were not always easy to understand. Yet I know that without his companionship my life would have been the poorer, in more ways than one.

Forgive my ramblings. I lack the ability to be as concise as I once was. What has not changed, however, is my love for you. Not, alas, the sort of love that a man can feel for a woman (ah, how I would have cherished you!), but the sort of love good friends can share.

Of what remains of my estate I have bequeathed one half to my only living relative—someone in America I have never met—and the other half to your granddaughter, Artemis. I never met her, but I have managed to keep an ear to the ground and know that in two respects we are alike. First, there is our love and respect for you and, second, the fact that we both had the misfortune to lose our mothers in childbirth. I wanted to make sure that your descendants benefited from your earlier kindnesses to me.

I hope you will not find it offensive, but I thought it fitting that Ballantyne's should handle the sale of my effects. Neat, don't you think? And Harry's family should make a tidy commission.

Do not be angry with me for telling you all this. It is done with the best intentions by a man who would have fought tooth and nail for your hand had life turned out rather differently.

I remain, my dear Eleanor, your affectionate friend,
Leo

Eleanor returned the letter to the envelope and slid it underneath the blotting pad and out of sight. She picked up the icon of St Anthony that she recognised from Leo's room in Christ Church. She stood it on the desk in front of her. Then she leaned forward onto the blotting pad, rested her head on her arms and wept.

York—March 1958

'But I thought he was a sleeping partner,' said Harry.

''E *is* a sleeping partner,' confirmed Ernie Bowker, 'but 'e's just woken up. 'E's had better things to do for years, but now 'e's decided that 'e'd like to be part of the firm.'

The two men were sitting at either side of the partners' desk in the office above the saleroom at Fidler, Son and Bowker. Harry, who had been made a partner five years earlier, was surprised and unnerved to discover that the 'Son' of Fidler, Son and Bowker, having wanted out for so many years, now wanted in. 'But what will he do?' he asked Ernie.

'Pretty much what 'e wants,' muttered his father-in-law bitterly.

'Has he any experience?'

'Not so's you'd notice. 'E's never wielded the 'ammer. But 'e's a collector. The worst sort—a dabbler. 'E thinks 'e knows everything when really 'e knows bugger all.'

'That sounds ominous.'

Ernie hauled himself up from behind the desk. 'I'm not a natural pessimist, as you know, 'Arry, but I can't say I'm looking forward to this association one bit.'

'Then why didn't you put your foot down?'

'Because Tom Fidler gave me a start in the business, like I gave you a start. I can't tell 'im I don't want 'is son just because I don't like 'im.'

THE ASSOCIATION LASTED six weeks, at the end of which time Harry knew that one of them would have to go. It was clearly not going to be Arnold Fidler, who was determined to claim his birthright.

'It hasn't been long,' said Sally. 'Can't you try a bit harder?'

They were sitting side by side on the sofa of their little house off Micklegate. 'I can't try harder than I am,' complained Harry. 'I enjoy the job, and I'd like to expand the firm, but with Arnold there, I seem to have lost my appetite for it. He's a sly bugger and I wouldn't trust him as far as I could throw him.'

'I could talk to Dad,' she offered.

'I don't want you fighting my battles for me. Besides, Ernie's over a barrel. Tom Fidler sees this as his son's right, and so does his son. As far as they're concerned, I'm the interloper.'

Sally sat quietly for a moment, then asked, 'So what do you want to do?'

'I think I'll have to look for another job.'

'But where? Who with? There's nothing round here.'

'I know.' He turned to face her. Her wide eyes were looking up at him, and every time she looked that way it reminded him of another time, another place, another woman. He had long since given up trying to erase the memory from his mind. Instead he had learned to live with it, told himself that it was a part of his life now. Eleanor would always be there, in his head, and sometimes the boundaries between the way he felt for her and the way he felt about Sally became blurred.

He and Sally would leave York early on Sunday mornings in their tiny Wolseley and travel up to the Dales. Wharfedale was Harry's favourite. He liked the terrain there more than the Vale of York. The moors were powerful, brooding even, but the River Wharfe, which flowed through the bottom of the dale, calmed his soul. They would paddle in the river at Burnsall and then go for lunch at Grassington or Bolton Abbey—maybe have afternoon tea before coming home and falling in bed exhausted but happy.

Sally was a good woman, and though there were moments when he hated himself for thinking that he'd settled for what some would call second best, he knew that life did not always turn out perfectly, that sometimes you had to make compromises. Over the years he had learned the difference between idealism and reality, and that reality was not so bad when you came down to it. And, anyway, there were other reasons why he had cause to be grateful. One of them was sleeping upstairs in the back bedroom. Emma was four years old. A bit of a character, her own person, spirited. Wilful, yes, but his own. Cherished. Loved. Like her mother. He did love Sally.

He looked at her now, her dark hair tied back in a ponytail, sitting at the small upright piano that he had bought from the saleroom for her last birthday, and playing a Mozart sonata of which she knew he was especially fond. It brought tears to his eyes, partly because of its beauty, partly because Sally was playing it for him, but also because it awoke uncomfortable feelings. It was only in those rare moments, when he probed deep within himself, and which he tried to avoid, that he could differentiate between loving someone and being 'in love'. It did not do to go there, though. Being 'in love' was for the young, for dreamers, he told himself. Contentment was more lasting. But now even that seemed to have been taken away. What could he do except grit his teeth and move on? But where?

IT WAS SALLY who saw the advertisement in *Country Life*. It was for a small saleroom in Bath. The old proprietor was retiring and the business 'with goodwill' was being sold.

At first Harry was dead against the idea. He knew little about Somerset and the West Country. But then he told himself that you had to take opportunities when they presented themselves. They would go and look around. He knew Bath was said to be beautiful, but would they be able to afford to live there? And yet, by the same token, it would be a good place to have a saleroom. It might even mean that he could sell better furniture than the run-of-the-mill stuff that came his way at Fidler, Son and Bowker. High time to go it alone, to sell his share in Fidler, Son and Bowker and open Ballantyne's of Bath.

He watched Sally's eyes glow as he outlined his plans. She was crouching in front of the fire, drying the dark tresses of her freshly washed hair in front of the glowing coals.

'Ballantyne's of Bath,' she murmured softly. 'It does have a nice ring to it, doesn't it? Sort of classy.'

He saw the reflection of the flickering flames in her eyes and it seemed to offer promise of a bright future. Of course it was the right thing to do.

ON MAY 31, 1958, Harry, Sally and Emma Ballantyne moved into a terraced house in Gay Street, Bath. Ernie had been more than generous and given Harry a payment that was rather over the odds for his brief partnership in the firm, but, he said, what was money for if not to look after your nearest and dearest?

He came to Bath just once, to check it over and see that it came up to his expectations. He found the hills rather steep after the flatness of the Vale of York, but he admired the architecture and approved of the move. He also enjoyed the local brew and told Harry that he would have plenty of places to go for his dinner. They took him to the Pump Room and gave him afternoon tea—as many scones and sandwiches as he could eat. He left them with a wink and a merry wave, but Harry knew that life with Arnold was taking its toll. Ernie had lost his sparkle.

Six months after Harry and Sally moved to Bath, Ernie retired from the business. Arnold had said that if the auction house was to survive it would need to change. 'Aye,' said Ernie. 'Well, there's one change that I can make. I'm buggering off, so you can run the bloody business yerself, and good luck to you.'

Sally's worry that her father would now have nothing to occupy him was justified. He got up late most mornings and had his 'dinner' down at the Red Lion. In the evenings he sat and looked at the small television he had bought—the first one in the street. On Christmas Day 1958, after watching the Queen's Christmas Message to the Commonwealth, Ernie died of a heart attack while sitting in his armchair.

He did have a telephone, though he didn't like using it, but it was when there was no reply on Christmas afternoon that Sally became concerned. Harry explained that he had probably gone out to see friends, but Sally knew when he had not returned by nine o'clock that something was wrong. First thing on Boxing Day morning they left Emma with a neighbour and motored up to York, where they found him in his armchair.

Sally blamed herself for not having had her father with them in Bath, but what was the point, asked Harry, when you knew he wouldn't come because of the hills?

It was not a promising start to their new life but, as the months passed, they came to look upon the West Country as home, and the visits to Harry's beloved Dales became less frequent. Ballantyne's of Bath grew slowly but steadily from a saleroom that dealt in everyday household goods to one that had occasional sales of finer furniture. These became more common and, to Harry's relief, more profitable.

By the mid-1960s the firm was on a high. It seemed that everything was rosy in Harry Ballantyne's garden—he owned a successful business, his wife ran the concert club, and his daughter Emma was doing well at school. And then a new art gallery opened in the Royal Crescent. Richard King moved his business to Bath, and with him came his wife.

Chapter 8

Glasgow—July 1959
On July 17, 1959, Sir Alfred James Munnings, KCVO, PRA, RWS, RP, the finest painter of horses since George Stubbs, died in his sleep at Castle House. He had ranted and railed about the perils of modern art to the end, and he forced himself to continue painting both indoors and out in all weathers and in spite of the stultifying pain of gout.

A private cremation took place at Colchester, and the following week a memorial service was held at St James's Church, Piccadilly. Among the mourners was Augustus John, who, after the service, pronounced that 'Munnings was greater than Stubbs. He made it move, had greater narrative quality, and his groupings are better.'

All of which was reported in *The Times*, where Mac read the story later that week. He folded the paper and lay it down by the side of his chair on top of the pile of *Glasgow Herald*s. In that moment the years fell away. He saw, in his mind's eye, the studio at Dedham, Eleanor sitting atop the 'wooden' horse, felt the warm, sweet grass beneath him and heard Harry asking about Eleanor's feelings for him. Then he thought about Richard, but then he often thought about Richard King. About how he had made a fool of himself with his pointless admission. How he had come here and shut himself away, not wanting to have to talk or explain or justify himself.

Then he thought about Leo and the catastrophe that had befallen him. How he used to tease that scion of the British aristocracy born with the silver-gilt spoon in his mouth, and how now they were both brought low by fate. Well, fate in Leo's case, bloody-mindedness in his own. He wondered what had happened to the others. He had lost contact with all of them. All except Leo, that is, who had sent him a note from somewhere in France.

Mac looked around the untidy attic room. He saw the canvases stacked against the grimy walls, many of them unfinished and all of them, to his eye, third rate. Something better must come of life than this, surely?

He pulled at the grizzled beard that now covered his chin and ran his hands through the thinning hair on his head. Time to make amends. Now that the artist who had so inspired him had gone, wasn't it time to fulfil the expectations of his mentor? He half laughed at the thought that a man he had known for just two days of his life could be regarded as a mentor. What did it matter? The important thing was to be fired up, and in recent months the fire had left him, except for the one he found in a bottle of Scotch. He had no one, no companion, except the stray tabby cat that turned up each morning on the steps of the seething Glasgow tenement. Glasgow, the city that he had been determined to leave.

He pushed himself up from the chair and went to the sink in the corner of the room. He turned on the tap and stuck his head under the stream of cold water that gushed from it, then glanced up and looked at himself in the broken mirror that hung on the tenement wall. There was nothing reassuring about the image that stared back. He slammed his hand on to the draining board with such force that the dirty dishes rattled and his cat, curled up in the corner of a filthy chair, shot out of the door and down the fire escape.

He picked up the bottle of Bell's and put it to his lips. Then he stopped. He did not throw back the liquid as he normally did, waiting for the comforting haze to blur his senses. Slowly and deliberately he eased the neck away from his mouth, tipped the contents down the sink and placed the empty bottle upright on the drainer.

Next he began to take off his clothes. He filled the sink with water and washed himself from top to toe, rubbing away the grime until his skin tingled. Naked and cleansed as well as cold water would allow, he walked to the battered chest of drawers at one end of the room and searched within it for a selection of clothing that, while not exactly clean, was less acrid-smelling than the garments he had removed.

He dressed, put down a saucer of food for the cat, then took a tin from the mantelpiece. It had once held toffee. Now it held an old letter and his savings. He laughed at the total. He put two one-pound notes under the empty whisky bottle, pushed the letter into the pocket of his trousers and set about gathering together his brushes and paints, stuffing them into a threadbare canvas holdall, along with the clothes he'd been wearing. Then he picked up the bag and walked to the door. He turned for a moment to take in the scene one last time. An artist's garret. All he had dreamed of once. A book lying on the bottom shelf where he stacked his paints caught his eye. He hesitated, then slowly crossed the room to where it lay. He picked it up and slid it into the bag and retraced his steps. He would leave the paintings for the landlord, who would curse him for running out, but then the canvases and the couple of pounds under the bottle should more than pay his dues.

Bath—June 1964

It came as a shock to both parties to discover their close proximity. Richard King had launched King's Fine Art in Bristol in 1958 and, once things were doing well, had decided that a move to Bath would make great sense.

The reason Richard had failed to notice that Ballantyne's of Bath was the main local auction house was that he had employed a firm of business analysts to report on the potential there, and their report had confirmed the presence of smaller galleries, which fed a healthy and expanding market, and a thriving saleroom that was a cut above the norm, without mentioning any names. It was as simple as that.

Eleanor King could remember the exact moment that she discovered she was living in the same city as Harry Ballantyne. She was leafing through the *Bath Chronicle* in search of a bicycle for Patrick. She had spotted the advertisement for the sale of household goods at Ballantyne's of Bath and at first she had thought it must be a coincidence. Then, when she had steeled herself to go to the saleroom and look, she had seen him in the office on the other side of the glass partition at the back of the main hall. The moment she saw his tall, ramrod-straight figure moving about the office, she had dodged behind a pillar, thinking she could escape without being seen. Her heart was thumping so loudly it surprised her that nobody could hear it. But the people around her continued to open drawers and look under chairs as though nothing untoward had happened.

She looked towards the exit. It was at the opposite side of the saleroom. She could not escape without coming into full view of the office window. In vain she scanned the room for tall furniture behind which she could make her escape unnoticed, but the wardrobes were arranged against the back wall. There was no cover.

Eleanor flopped down onto a striped Regency sofa and did her best to become invisible. She felt like a butterfly pinned to a board in the centre of the saleroom, in full view of the glass-walled office. She turned again to contemplate her means of escape, but she was too late. Harry had come out of the office and was walking across the saleroom towards her. Feverishly she began to examine the fabric on the sofa, running her hands over it.

'That's rather a good one, isn't it?' he said.

She could not help but look up, and as her eyes met his, there was on his face a sudden look of recognition that would live with her for the rest of her life. It might have been her imagination, but in that split second she thought he looked at her with those deep blue eyes in exactly the same way that he had in Dedham that evening fifteen years ago.

For a moment he could not speak. Then he said, quite straightforwardly, 'Oh, hello.'

Eleanor was surprised by the evenness of his tone. She expected him to be as overwhelmed with joy, with emotion, with confusion—but he did not appear to be. Her feelings were suddenly shot through with anger. How dare he be so unaffected at the sight of her. Why was *his* heart not beating faster as hers was? Why did *he* not have to sit down as she did?

He held out his hand to shake hers. She took it without thinking.

His expression was one of polite interest. 'What are you doing here?'

'Looking for a bicycle,' was all she could reply.

He seemed taken aback for a moment, then pointed to the back of the room. 'We leave them at the bottom of the stairs, so they don't put oil on the furniture.'

'Of course,' she murmured. All those years of wondering what he would say if they ever met again and never once had her thoughts come close to, 'oil on the furniture'. 'But . . . what are you doing in Bath?'

'We've moved here, moved the business here. We're opening the gallery in a couple of weeks. In the Royal Crescent.' At least he had the good grace to look bemused, she thought.

'I see. You must have done well.'

'We have. Well, Richard has. I just . . .'

He looked at her questioningly.

Oh, how she wanted to ask him where he had been, what he had been doing, but more than anything why he had gone and left her that day, the day after they had made love so tenderly in the hotel room at Dedham.

Suddenly, she felt an enormous welling of emotion and it took all of her strength to push herself up from the sofa. She took a deep breath, the better to speak steadily, and said, 'Well, I must go and look at bicycles.'

'Yes, of course.'

Harry watched Eleanor go. She had lost none of her beauty; if anything, she was even more devastating as a woman than she had been when she was a girl. He felt weak at the knees and sat down on the Regency sofa, his thoughts back in Dedham, reflecting on what had gone wrong fifteen years ago. How on earth was he going to carry on living in the same city as the woman he loved when she was married to someone else?

RICHARD KING SAT quite still when she told him. He said nothing, just gazed out of the window and over the city.

'It doesn't make any difference,' she said, though she did not for one minute believe the sentiment she was expressing.

'No. No difference at all,' he said, without turning round. Then he added, 'I shan't meet him if you don't mind.'

'Of course not,' said Eleanor. She could not recall ever feeling so empty, not since the day she had married.

Chapter 9

There were a surprisingly large number of crates of personal effects for someone who had supposedly died in penury, but then, thought Jamie, everything was relative. Penury to him would mean living in barely affordable rented accommodation, whereas penury to Lord Bedlington would mean not being able to live in a stately pile and cutting your staff by half.

As the storeroom beneath Ballantyne's saleroom began to fill with bureaux, chests, side tables and *fauteuils*, Jamie wandered back upstairs to the office, where his mother was standing behind her desk.

'Any good?' asked Emma Ballantyne.

'Oh, nothing special. Some elegant pieces, but I guess not especially good. There's quite a lot of it, though. I thought there would be less, somehow, seeing as he lost most of his money.'

His mother shot him a wry smile. 'Ah, well, that's the aristocracy for you. Always have a bit put by.'

'That's a surprisingly left-wing comment for you.'

'Not really. Just the voice of experience. The older I get, the more I realise that other people's values are not necessarily one's own. But I think my father was rather fond of him in a sneaky sort of way. Not that he'd ever admit it. A bit too shocking.'

'What, because Leo Bedlington was gay?'

'You must remember that society wasn't nearly so tolerant in those days. Homosexuality was illegal, for a start, which meant that those of that persuasion kept quiet about it.'

'Yes, but Granddad isn't . . . I mean . . . he's not homophobic, is he?'

'He's always been very open-minded, if that's what you mean. But he grew up in an era when men of that persuasion were called "queers".'

'What about Richard King?'

His mother shrugged. 'How would I know?' She looked thoughtful and then asked, 'Are you still seeing his granddaughter?'

'Does it matter?'

'It probably does to him.' She picked up her bag and made for the door.

'But not to you?'

Emma paused in the doorway. 'I can't approve, Jamie, but then I have no right to disapprove, either. I've been thinking about this—this feud that's been going on for so many years. To be perfectly honest, I think everyone would be better diverting their energies into today, rather than yesterday.'

'Oh.' Her reply rather took him aback.

'So there you are. You do what you want. You'll have no more trouble from me, but I wouldn't expect a smooth ride from those at the top of the hill.' She nodded her head in the direction of the Royal Crescent, then shot him a pitying look and said, 'I'm away home now. I'll see you tomorrow.'

'Yes. Right. Tomorrow.' Jamie looked puzzled and distracted. What had made her change her mind? He shook his head at her apparent reasonableness, then descended the stairs to the storeroom, which had now become an Aladdin's cave of Lord Bedlington's personal effects. From a cursory inspection, it seemed that the late earl had indeed been forced to part with all the best pieces in his collection.

'Any pictures?' he asked Len, one of the removal men.

'Over there against the wall, Guv,' the man in overalls replied.

Jamie weaved his way between the furniture to the pictures that were leaning against the end wall. There were a couple of large landscapes of sylvan scenes and half a dozen watercolours that had faded from being left in bright sunlight—the penalty for living in the South of France.

Then he saw a group of paintings stacked against the wall but facing away from him. Jamie picked up the one on the outside of the pile and turned it round so that he could see the subject. It was of the start of a race, with jockeys jostling for position in their bright silks. The sky was azure blue, and the flanks of the assorted horses seemed to shine in the sunlight, reflecting the green of the grass and the iridescent shades of the silks. He put down the painting and stepped back from it. The signature confirmed his suspicions; the work was by Sir Alfred Munnings. Wait until Missy saw it! How excited she would be.

There were other paintings to see as well, though. He turned over the next one and did a double-take. It was another Munnings, this time of a gypsy encampment. The third painting was similar—the label on the stretcher indicating that it had been painted at Epsom Races.

The fourth painting was superb—of a woman on horseback. The label on the back indicated that it was Lord Bedlington's mother and the landscape around her reflected the heat of a summer's day somewhere in the Cotswolds. It was as good an example of Munnings's work as he had seen. What a find!

The fifth and final painting in the group also lay facing the wall. He hardly dared turn it round. Would it be another Munnings or just a boring landscape? For a few moments he stood quite still, trying to regulate his breathing. Then he grasped the frame in both hands and slowly revolved it. When he took in the scene that met his eye, he had to steady himself to avoid dropping it. It was not possible. How could it be?

He propped the picture against the wall alongside the others. It was most certainly by the same hand. It was even signed by the artist. It was a sumptuous, beautifully executed painting of a woman on a grey horse. The only trouble was, it was exactly the same picture that he had sold to Missy just a few weeks ago.

'KING'S FINE ART.' She answered the phone in an assured manner, though self-assurance seemed to be conspicuously lacking in her at that moment. She had too many things to think about, too many things of which she was not sure whirling around in her head.

The voice at the other end of the line invaded her consciousness. 'Missy?'

'Yes?'

'It's Jamie.'

She was so relieved to hear him, so pleased that he should have called and had proved himself a constant in a world that seemed suddenly to be on the move.

'Hi! Is everything all right?' she asked.

'Yes. Well, no. I mean, there's something I need to see you about.'

'What is it?'

'It's just . . . there's something I want to ask your advice about.' He thought it best to give her no idea of what he really wanted to talk to her about until they met face to face. 'I thought you might like to come and see the house at the Circus,' he continued. 'Gran and Granddad will be out sizing up their new place and they said I could go in and measure up—that sort of thing. I'll come and pick you up at seven, if that's OK?'

'Yes. Seven. Fine. I'll see you then.' She hesitated. 'Everything is all right, isn't it? I mean, between us?'

'Yes. Course it is. Don't sound so worried. I'll see you at seven. I'll wait outside for you.'

Villa Fabrice, Menton, Côte d'Azur—August 1959–June 1965

Finding John Macready on his doorstep was not a scenario that Leo Bedlington had ever contemplated, especially since their final farewell ten years ago had been memorable only for its awkwardness.

At first he was unsure who the apparent stranger was. He took him for a tramp; this grizzled character with a fox-coloured beard and threadbare clothing. It was only when the man spoke that Leo had recognised his old college friend underneath the shabby coat and thinning hair. He'd been reaching into his pocket for a few francs to send the traveller on his way, but the Glaswegian tones stopped him in his tracks.

'Hello, Leo,' was all that Mac had said.

'Mac?'

'Aye. Here I am, then.'

It was as simple as that. For a few moments the two men stared at one another after the fashion of two tomcats stalking each other on a wall. Then Leo, aware of his temporary lapse in manners, said, 'Come in, come in. You must be exhausted. Where have you come from?'

Mac said but one word in reply. 'Oblivion.'

That night, in the warm Mediterranean air, they dined on the terrace of Villa Fabrice. The taciturn cook, Madame Farage, birdlike in both appearance and manner, brought them large bowls of homemade bouillabaisse and freshly baked bread. Leo watched as Mac fell upon the meal as if he had not eaten in a year, spooning up the nutritious broth as though his life depended on it. But then, thought Leo, it probably did.

In the lanterns that were strung along the blue-painted timbers of the villa, Leo could see how his friend had aged. His cheeks were sunken, his eyes seemed haunted, and the once-ruddy countenance was pallid now. Only his nose showed any colour, and that was obviously due to an overfondness for the bottle.

That night Mac declined a glass of wine, opting instead for water, as he would do for the rest of his life.

The serious business of eating over, Mac sat back in his chair and said, 'That was very good. And very necessary. Thank you.'

Leo smiled. He was reluctant to lunge into any kind of inquisition. He would wait until Mac was ready to talk. It did not take long.

After polite conversation about Madame Farage and her culinary skills, Mac gradually opened up. He had gone back to Glasgow to tell his family that he intended to support himself as an artist. He had rented a flat near the docks and set to work on his canvases. The results were, he thought, quite good, but failed to interest what few galleries there were in the city. He planned to move to Edinburgh—a city more supportive of the arts—but then, without warning, his father, a strapping postman, had collapsed and died, leaving Mac to support his mother and two sisters. It had not been easy, but he had travelled once a week to Edinburgh with his paintings, trying to make enough money to keep the family together. In the evenings he worked feverishly at his canvases, a glass of Scotch at his elbow to keep him going. But what he earned barely kept him supplied with materials and the family with food.

The two sisters married eventually, but, just when things should have been getting easier, Mac's mother was taken into hospital. She died there after a short illness. Now at last he found himself free to pursue his own life, but the glass of Scotch at his elbow of an evening had turned into two bottles a day. Gradually his few commissions dried up, and then the day arrived, in his grim attic room, when he realised that unless he made a fresh start, his life would not last much longer. The only possessions he had, apart from his paints and his brushes, were a book given to him by Munnings and a letter that Leo had sent him on his birthday the year after they had parted.

'Good God!' said Leo. 'I'd forgotten about that letter. I'm afraid I rather gave up on you when you didn't reply.'

'I'm not surprised. Yours was the only address I had. I've lost touch with the others.'

'We've not done very well at keeping up, have we?'

Mac shrugged. 'It happens.' He was tired of talking about himself. 'So what about you?' he asked.

'Oh, I think they call them "straitened circumstances".'

Mac looked around. 'Everything's relative.'

Leo felt suddenly guilty. 'Quite.'

'The house had to go, then?'

'Bedlington Park? 'Fraid so. And all the staff. I felt very bad about it, but there was nothing I could do with death duties at that rate.'

'Why here?'

'A bit like you: I wanted a fresh start, where I had no baggage.' He laughed at the appropriateness of his comment. 'So here we are, the two of us, with no baggage between us.'

Mac said nothing, but gazed out towards the sea. Leo endeavoured to fill the silence. 'You can stay as long as you want, you know. I'd be glad of the company. There's no one else here.'

Mac turned to face him. 'You didn't find anybody either?'

Leo looked down and shook his head. 'No,' he said softly. 'I didn't find anybody either.'

Mac did not meet his eye. 'You're very kind. Perhaps just until—'

'No,' Leo said emphatically. 'Don't set any constraints. Just stay for as long or as short a time as you want. The only thing I'll ask of you is that you give me a hand in the garden. There's a man who comes in, but he tends to be overzealous. I like it looking wild, so that it fits in with the view. He has a fondness for bedding plants; I do not.'

A flicker of a smile crossed Mac's face. It was the first glimmer of humour or ease that Leo had seen since he arrived. Perhaps Mac would find himself here, find his true painting skills, maybe even earn a living at it—there were plenty of little galleries in Cannes and Antibes.

'Well,' said Leo, pushing himself up from his chair, 'I tend to go to bed early. Stay up as long as you wish.' He pointed to the doorway. 'Your room's right at the end. Sleep well.' Then he looked up at the sky, studded with stars. 'It should be a nice day tomorrow, the nicest for a long while.'

IT WAS SEVERAL MONTHS before Mac could begin painting again. It took that long for his hands to stop shaking. Instead he gardened, and, mindful of Leo's entreaties, he pulled out the tangles of bindweed and allowed the wild flowers that Leo enjoyed to flourish. The following spring he planted up large terracotta pots with olives and myrtles and moon daisies, of which Leo approved. He shaved off his beard, and Madame Farage cut his hair once a month. Within a year Leo could hardly remember what life had been like without him, and Mac settled into life at Villa Fabrice with gratitude. In this way they rubbed along for six years—living together yet leading quite separate lives, amusing and irritating each other in equal measure.

Then, one morning in early summer 1965, a letter came that brought unwelcome news. Mac had just climbed up the garden to the terrace. He was an early riser and enjoyed a swim before breakfast. Leo was sitting at the table under the vines and holding the letter in his hands. They were trembling, Mac noticed.

'Bad news?' asked Mac, with his usual capacity for understatement.

'Very.'

'Want to share it?' Mac cocked his head on one side, waiting.

'The taxman needs more money.'

Mac was pouring himself a coffee with one hand and rubbing a towel through his hair with the other. 'I thought he'd bled you dry already.'

'He has,' said Leo.

Mac detected the quavering note in his voice. 'How much?' he asked.

'Another fifty thousand.'

'And it's taken them all this time to work it out?'

'Apparently.' Leo dropped the letter on the table. Mac could see that he was close to tears. 'It's not bloody fair. I mean, they've taken the Park and just about everything it contained. All that's left are the paintings.'

'Are they worth fifty thousand?'

'Oh, quite a lot more, but one of them's of my mother.' The composure that had always been so assiduously maintained finally failed. The dam burst and Leo's body was convulsed in heaving sobs.

Mac said nothing, but put his arm round Leo as his body shook and the sorrow of the last fifteen years flooded out. He held him silently until the torrent subsided.

'How can I keep giving them what I haven't got?' Leo said. 'I'm just a sad old queen who wants to get on with his life.' He reached into his pocket and pulled out a large, silk handkerchief. 'I'm so sorry. Not your problem. Very silly of me. No self-control.'

'Bollocks,' said Mac. 'And it's my problem, just as much as yours. I wouldn't be here if it weren't for you. I probably wouldn't even be alive, so don't start apologising.'

Leo blew his nose again and shook his head in despair.

'How badly do you want to keep those paintings?' asked Mac.

'What do you mean?'

'What I said. How badly do you want them?'

Leo was trying in vain to understand where the conversation was going. 'Very badly. They're all I have of Bedlington Park, of a heritage.'

'Has the taxman given you a deadline?'

Leo checked the letter. 'Six months.'

'That should be enough time for me to get to work.'

Leo looked bewildered. 'I don't understand.'

'Look, my paintings are selling now—not just down in Antibes, but the few I've sent back to Blighty.'

'Well, yes, but . . .'

'But they're not selling for the sort of money you need, I know. A Munnings or two, on the other hand, would bring in far more.'

Leo looked bewildered. 'I don't understand.'

'A Munnings or two painted by me.'

Leo stood quite still, trying to take in the significance of what Mac had said. 'You don't mean . . . forgery?'

'Exactly.'

Leo sat down abruptly and the colour drained from his cheeks. 'Oh, I don't think I could let you do that. The Bedlingtons are not dishonest.'

'And where has it got them?' asked Mac. 'I think it's time you gave the taxman a run for his money. He's had just about all you've got. I reckon you deserve to hang on to what little you have left.'

'Mac, it really is very kind of you, but in spite of the fact that I think you're a terribly good artist, I don't see how you could manage—'

Mac interrupted him with four words: 'Just let me try.'

THREE MONTHS LATER, Leo found himself standing in front of two paintings by Alfred Munnings, except that they were not by Alfred Munnings; they were by John Macready.

'It's incredible. You've even got the signature right.'

'Ha! That was the easiest bit. It's the brushwork that's the bugger.'

'Yes, of course.' Leo was bemused, entranced and, if he were honest with himself, rather excited at having two new Munningses in his house, even though they were identical to ones he already possessed. 'But do you think they'll fool the taxman, or, more importantly, the art world?'

'There's only one way to find out, isn't there?'

Leo could not pretend that he was happy. 'Well, I suppose so. But where do we sell them?'

Mac looked thoughtful. Then he said, 'There's an art gallery that's just opened in Bath. I think that might be a good place to try to sell them. Out of London, you know—not quite so much attention.'

'Yes. Perhaps that would be best.'

'I wonder if Madame Farage would mind handling it for us? Keep our names out of it altogether.'

'Yes, if you think so.'

Leo did not notice the mischievous glint in Mac's eye. He was too busy looking at the new picture of Eleanor on her horse.

'You never know. If they sell well, I could paint one or two more. The others could keep us going into our old age.'

Bath—December 2007

By the time six o'clock came, what little concentration Missy had been able to apply to her cataloguing at King's Fine Art had evaporated. She glanced over at the innocent-looking package. She would take her father's advice and slip it into the back of the storeroom before Jamie picked her up.

The store was a strongroom in the basement, climate-controlled and alarmed. She could never enter this vault without a frisson of excitement inspired by its astonishing treasure trove of art works, a potted history of the finest British painting over the last 300 years.

Part of her always felt guilty at presiding over such riches, as though she were a miser gloating over her spoils, but that feeling would be quickly replaced by one of awe and wonder at the skills of the artists who had captured such life and vitality, often several centuries previously.

She laid down the mirror-image Munnings on the desk beside the ledger and withdrew one of the racks, as she always did when she came down here, chiefly to keep up with the changing stock.

This one contained several drawings by Edward Lear—misty and mysterious evocations of the banks of the Nile and of Sintra. There was a Helen Allingham watercolour of a Surrey cottage. For her, the best picture on this particular rack was of mares and foals in a landscape by the Cumberland painter Sawrey Gilpin. It might have been painted more than 200 years ago, but it seemed to her so fresh and full of life that she could have been looking on the scene from a window of her house.

She smiled to herself. What was it about pictures of horses? Time after time she had attempted to analyse her fascination and had finally stopped trying. She loved them. It was as simple as that—as simple as loving Jamie. Her spirits lifted. She would be seeing him in less than an hour.

She slid the rack back and slowly the pictures disappeared from view. But when the rack was two-thirds of the way back it stopped abruptly. Normally the racks worked so efficiently. Missy assumed that one of the wheels must have come off its runner, but when she pulled the rack out again she could see that a large but slender cardboard box, which had presumably been slipped in between the racks until someone had time to hang up its contents, had jammed the mechanism. Missy slid out the adjoining racks until there was room for her to squeeze in and retrieve the box.

'Damn!' She was covered in dust now. The box was filthy. She looked more closely at it. It was sealed up with parcel tape and there was nothing on it to indicate what it could be.

Missy looked around her for something with which she could slit open the tape. There was a screwdriver in a toolbox on the shelves. That would do. She ran the sharp edge of the blade along the tape until the edge of the box flipped up, then she reached inside. She could feel several framed pictures and withdrew the first one.

It was a Munnings. As was the second one, and the third. There were four in all. Missy could feel her heart pounding in her chest. She steadied herself on the rack and took deep breaths, her mind reeling. Carefully she replaced the four paintings in their hiding place and slid the box alongside the last rack in the vault, pushing it out of sight.

She did not check the ledger. She knew that the paintings would not be recorded there. Instead she turned back to the mirror-image Munnings that she had brought down with her, tucked it under her arm and, locking the heavy door behind her, she climbed the stairs back to the first-floor gallery.

'I wondered where you were.'

Missy jumped.

'Sorry. Did I surprise you?' It was her grandfather. When Richard King noticed that the colour had drained from his granddaughter's cheeks he jumped up from behind his desk and hurried towards her. 'What on earth's the matter? Sit down for a minute—you look as white as a sheet.'

'Yes. No. I mean, I'm fine.'

'No, you're not. What is it?'

Missy shook her head. 'I don't know. I'm confused, that's all.'

'What about?'

'Everything.' Missy walked over to the sofa, flopped down among the cushions and lay the Munnings down beside her. 'The pictures.'

At first Richard King looked bemused. 'Which pictures?'

'The Munningses.' She rested her head in her hands.

He looked more concerned now. 'Which Munningses?'

Missy smiled sardonically. 'The ones hidden in the picture store, the one of the woman on horseback and the one that arrived yesterday. Six in all.'

'What do you mean, "the one that arrived yesterday"?'

Missy picked up the mirror-image painting and held it up. 'This one came with a note. What's going on, Grandpa? Why were the other pictures hidden. Why aren't they recorded? I know how meticulous you are about logging every painting. You've drummed it into me since I was little.'

'Because . . . because I'm not certain what they are.'

'*What* they are, or *whose* they are?' Missy asked, with a note of panic in her voice. 'Are they by John Macready?'

Richard King sighed heavily and seemed to diminish in stature at the same time. 'No, of course not.' Then he hesitated and sat down beside her, adding, 'I don't know.'

'But if they're not by Munnings, why have we got them? If you know they're not genuine, you wouldn't have them in the gallery. I mean, we can't sell them, can we? So why have we got them?'

Her grandfather looked flustered, uncomfortable. 'It's a long story.'

'Are you going to tell me? I think I ought to know. If we sold a Munnings as genuine and it's really a fake, then at best we'd be in deep trouble and at worst it would be the end of King's Fine Art. You've built this firm on respectability.' Missy stared at him uncomprehendingly. Her grandfather avoided her eyes.

'Grandpa, please! If we're to sort all this out, I need to know.'

Richard King sighed again. 'A long time ago—I suppose it's around sixty years now . . . I was at university in Oxford.' He murmured to himself, 'Goodness, where does the time go?' Missy watched as he collected his thoughts, then continued. 'I had a group of friends. Your grandmother was one of them, and John Macready was another.'

'And Harry Ballantyne?'

'Yes. And Leo Bedlington. Five of us. Well, after university we all went our own ways. Your grandmother and I never heard from any of them for years. And then, in the mid-sixties, a few years after Munnings's death, when we'd just arrived in Bath, I was sent a couple of his pictures to sell.'

'Genuine ones?' asked Missy.

'I thought so. They came from a collector in the South of France, not someone I knew.'

'And you sold them?'

'Yes. They fetched a tidy sum.'

'And that was that?'

'Not quite. Every few years another one would arrive. I thought nothing of it. Collectors do occasionally sell individual paintings, either to keep the wolf from the door or to reinvest in others. I bought five paintings from that collector over, I suppose, thirty years. All by Munnings. Then I came across some work by John Macready. I'd never been interested in his work myself, but I'd acquired one with a group of other paintings a few years earlier and I had that funny feeling . . .'

'Intuition?'

'Yes. I knew instinctively that the Munningses I'd sold were by Macready. Mac had met Munnings while he was at Oxford and Munnings though quite highly of Mac's work. Suddenly it all dropped into place: the fact that the paintings had come from the South of France, where Macready was living with Leo Bedlington, and that Leo Bedlington's father had owned paintings by Munnings. The alarm bells rang.'

Missy was wide-eyed now. 'So what did you do?'

'I tried to buy them back. I thought the only way I could save the firm would be to take them out of circulation.'

'And did you find them?'

'One or two of them.'

'But not all?'

'No. It took me a long time to locate them all, and of course the prices kept going up.'

'So why not just let them stay out there, in private collections?'

'Because when they came up for sale, the fact that this gallery had sold them as genuine would be a part of their provenance. I couldn't risk someone discovering that they were really fakes when they were originally sold by King's Fine Art. It would have ruined us . . . could still ruin us.'

'So the painting I bought in the auction last week . . . is that a fake?'

'I think so. The trouble is that I'm not quite so certain as I used to be. I bought that one back for sentimental reasons as much as to preserve the firm's name. It was not one that I should ever have sold. It was a sort of test, I suppose—a test that I failed. I think it was sent to me to see if love was more powerful than money.'

Missy looked bewildered. 'I don't understand.'

'It's a painting of your grandmother, when she was a student. It was painted the day she and Macready and Harry Ballantyne went to see Munnings. Well, the original one was.'

'Oh my goodness,' Missy murmured, remembering that Jamie had told her the painting reminded him of her. 'But if the one you've bought is a fake,' she continued, 'it means that you've effectively lost three-quarters of a million pounds.'

'Yes. I'm afraid I've lost rather more than that over the last few years.'

'Grandpa, are we in trouble?'

'Well, our finances are not as strong as they might be.'

'How much trouble?'

'We have a seven-million-pound overdraft.'

Missy slumped back on the sofa. 'Oh my God!'

'But we have almost enough stock to cover it.'

'And the gallery? And Peel Place?'

'Not quite that much. Mortgaged, I'm afraid.'

Missy got up and walked across the room, running over in her mind the possibilities and probabilities that could result from her grandfather's actions. 'So why did John Macready paint fake Munningses?'

'To make money, of course, for himself and Leo Bedlington. Leo had lost everything to death duties and Mac obviously saw it as a way of staving off further financial problems.'

'But why send the paintings to you? When he knew you'd get into trouble if they were found to be fake?'

'Ah, yes.' Richard King looked uncomfortable.

'Did you fall out?' asked Missy.

'In a manner of speaking, yes.'

She looked at him questioningly.

He lifted his hand and lowered it, then shifted in his chair until finally he said, 'I think John Macready was in love with me.'

Missy looked at him wide-eyed.

'Oh, I know it's difficult to believe, but it happened even then, you know, although we didn't speak about it as much.' He paused. 'I turned him down, and hell hath no fury . . .' Richard thought for a moment. 'The painting that arrived yesterday seems to be some kind of apology . . . if it's genuine. But why would it arrive now? Mac died more than ten years ago.'

'So did he sell you the paintings to get his own back? As revenge?'

'I think so. That and to avenge a friend of his whose true love I stole. I wasn't the only one who wanted your grandmother.'

'Harry Ballantyne?'

Her grandfather nodded. 'Yes,' he said softly.

'So that's why you don't want me going out with Jamie Ballantyne.'

Richard King got up from his desk. 'It's not just that, Artemis.'

Missy felt a shiver go down her spine. He only called her Artemis when he was being serious. She responded firmly, 'Grandpa, it really is my own life. I can't keep your feud going. I *won't* keep your feud going. Just because you and Harry Ballantyne fell out over a girl doesn't mean that this Montague–Capulet thing should be kept going for generations. We're not rivals any more. It's time we got on with our lives.'

'It's not quite as simple as that.'

'What do you mean?'

'Harry Ballantyne was your grandmother's lover at Oxford.' Richard was red in the face now. 'It's something that your grandmother and I have never talked about. Nobody knows it except the two of us, and we've never referred to it in fifty years.'

'What, for goodness' sake?'

'Your father is not my son. Your grandmother and I found we were unable to have children some time after Patrick was born. It was then that your grandmother told me that Patrick is Harry's son, not mine. You and Jamie Ballantyne have the same grandfather. Now do you see why I don't want you going out with him?'

Chapter 10

The South of France is mild in December. Mild, but not always warm, and the old woman slapped her hands against her sides to improve the circulation in her body; the rough woollen shawl seemed suddenly thin in the chill gust of air that blew up from the sea.

The Villa Fabrice was empty now, cleared of its furniture and its draperies, such as they were. She went from room to room with a broom, giving the place a final sweep. It broke her heart to think that they were both gone now. Both her men. She had washed and cleaned and cooked for them for almost fifty years.

Was it really that long? Had she really been here for almost fifty years? With a few hiccups, yes. A few rows and arguments. One or two broken pieces of china. But they were all, as Milord would say, '*Tempêtes en tasses*'. Silly man. Nice man. Kind man. Different from the other one. But then he was good in a different way. A man of few words in the same way that she was a woman of few words. When he was painting there was no talking to him. And he looked after Milord, in his own funny way. Acted as a kind of protector. She had thought, when she was young, that they might be lovers. But she soon learned that this was not the case.

Then there was the swimming accident. The day their lives changed for ever. It was she who had made Monsieur his breakfast. She who had remonstrated with him about swimming in the sea on a full stomach. But would he listen? Did he ever? She had watched as he walked down the winding path from the house that one last time, his towel over his shoulder.

It was she who found the towel on the beach two hours later, his shoes neatly placed beside it. But there was no sign of Monsieur. She sat with Milord all that day and through the night, but still Monsieur did not return.

Week after week they combed the beaches, and waited, the two of them, thinking that one day he would walk through the door and rebuke them for thinking anything unusual had happened. But he did not come back and gradually they learned to live their lives without him.

Milord changed from that day on. He was quietly angry for a while, and embittered, but then he became accepting. It broke her heart to see him like that. For ten years he lived quietly, seeing only the very occasional visitor. The end, when it came, was swift, praise God.

When he knew the end was coming he said he wanted to write some letters. She gave him pen and paper and summoned the notary, as he requested, so that he could finalise his will.

She brushed the last pile of dust out through the open French windows, where it was seized by the breeze and taken out towards the sea.

Gone. It was all gone now. She bolted the windows, turned the key in the lock and slipped it into her pocket. She would take it down to the notary later in the day. He would know what to do with it. It was he, after all, who had told her what to do with the parcel. She had found it tucked away behind Monsieur's bed when the bed had been removed by the owner of the local *brocante*. It had been wedged between the bedstead and the wall. It felt like a picture in a frame, but she did not open it because it was properly wrapped and addressed in Monsieur's hand. There was a letter with it, which the notary had translated. It said that the parcel was to be sent directly to the addressee and that a note for the recipient was already included. There were even some old franc notes to cover postage.

The notary had looked a little doubtful, but eventually suggested that Madame Farage should simply take it down to the *bureau de poste* and do as her former employer had asked of her. He would turn a blind eye.

And that was what she had done. It was over a week ago now and there had been no repercussions, so perhaps all was well. It was none of her business, anyway. And now her work here was finished. She began the slow walk back to her cottage at the top of the hill, muttering to herself. Bath. It was a strange name for a place. But then, so was Bains. Maybe she should use the money to go to Bath. But no. Paris would be more fun. Fun! The very idea. The fun was gone from her life, along with Monsieur and Milord. They had had fun. Once.

Bath—December 2007

Jamie sat in the car outside King's Fine Art, tapping the steering wheel. Oh, come on! Why was she so slow? He had so much to tell her, so much to show her.

She finally emerged from the house at twenty past seven.

'I'd almost given up on you,' he said, as she slipped into the passenger seat. She did not kiss him.

'Oh dear, bad day?' he asked gently.

Missy nodded. 'The worst.'

'Do you still want to see the house?'

She did her best to sound enthusiastic. 'Yes, of course.'

Jamie could not work out why she was so down, so uncommunicative. He told himself that this was real life, that he could not always expect her to be bright and bouncy, but deep down he did feel disappointed—he had not expected the bloom to wear off their love affair quite so quickly. Added to that, he was worried by her reaction to the paintings. What would she say?

It took only a couple of minutes to drive to the Circus. Jamie parked and went round to open her door. She got out and looked up at the imposing frontage. 'Impressive,' she said softly, but, he thought, without much feeling.

'Hang on,' he instructed. He went round to the boot of the car and lifted out one of the pictures, wrapped in a blanket. Then he picked up a cool bag and winked at her. 'Right, time for the private view.'

He took her through the rooms on each of the floors, hoping that she would feel as excited by it all as he did, but she only seemed to get quieter and quieter. Finally they reached the top floor and he put down the painting on an old chest of drawers and unzipped the cool bag. 'Champagne,' he said. 'To celebrate.'

'Oh,' she said. That was all.

'Look, I'm sorry if this is all a bit much,' he said, thinking that perhaps he was being too self-centred, too intent on showing her his world, and not listening to the reason why she had had a bad day. 'But there is something else, something that I'm rather concerned about.'

Missy heard the words, but her mind was elsewhere.

Jamie picked up the blanket-wrapped painting and slipped it from its cover. 'We're handling the auction of Lord Bedlington's estate and his pictures arrived this week. Here's one of them.'

Missy came out of her reverie. She looked at the painting and let out an involuntary gasp. It was an exact copy of one that she had found in the store room at King's Fine Art, except that she knew it was the real thing.

'Oh God!' she said.

'What do you think, Missy?' asked Jamie. He was worried now, worried by her reaction and worried by the implications. 'Is it real?' he asked.

'Almost certainly,' she murmured. 'Are there any more?'

'Yes. If you wait here, I'll go and bring them up.'

MISSY COULD NOT take her eyes off the paintings. They were all there: the start of the race, the gypsies at Epsom, the gypsy encampment, the woman on the bay and even the painting of her grandmother on the grey. Every last one of them she had seen in the last few days, but on different canvases. Her eyes ran from one to another as she explained to Jamie as well as she could from what her grandfather had told her.

'When our grandparents were at uni together,' she began, 'they had a bit of a thing about Munnings. Well, one of them did, a man called John Macready. He even went to see Munnings—in Dedham, where he lived. Macready was a painter, a good painter. Munnings thought very highly of him.'

Jamie listened attentively, but Missy did not meet his eye.

'My grandmother went with Macready and your grandfather to Dedham and ended up sitting for Munnings. That's her on the grey.'

'The one I sold to you?'

'No, the one you didn't sell to me.' She paused. 'Mine is a copy.'

'Oh God!'

'My grandfather didn't go. He was in bed with a cold. Anyway, to cut a long story short, this John Macready character didn't approve of Grandpa and Grandma marrying, so he decided to work a bit of mischief and at the same time help out Lord Bedlington, who he was now living with in the South of France. He painted copies of all Bedlington's Munningses over the space of about thirty years and sent them to Grandpa, who flogged them thinking they were real.'

'Just because he didn't approve of the marriage?'

'And because he and Leo Bedlington needed the money. Once Grandpa realised what had happened, he bought back every painting that he'd sold— often at inflated market prices.'

'That's dreadful. But why did Macready take it out on your grandfather?'

Missy shrugged. She so wanted to tell him, but something inside her was reluctant to give away all the secrets that she had been told. Least of all, she could not divulge the one secret that had been eating away at her heart from the moment that it had been shared with her.

'It's all a bit of a mess, isn't it?' offered Jamie.

'You can say that again.'

'So what do I do now?' asked Jamie, scratching his head.

'You sell them at auction, of course. They're all authentic. I have all the copies under lock and key in our strongroom. As far as everyone else in the world is concerned, they don't exist. Grandpa's bought his way out of trouble. It's cost him the business. You might as well enjoy your commission.' Then she added, 'You won't be able to sell the one of Grandma, of course, since you sold a copy to me last week. But in a year or two people will think it's just come on the market again, and you will be able to make even more money. At least you'll know it's of my grandmother.'

'But this is dreadful. Is King's Fine Art really in trouble?'

'Oh, yes. There's a seven-million-pound overdraft and every property is mortgaged to the hilt. There will be enough stock to stave off bankruptcy, but that's about all. We'll have to sell up.'

Jamie slumped down in a chair. 'I can't believe this.'

'Neither can I, but it's absolutely true.'

Jamie brightened a little. 'It's absolutely bloody awful, but at least we've still got each other. We'll find a way through somehow. It's not as if I'm without means now.'

Missy smiled. 'Oh, Jamie, you're so kind, but it's not going to work, is it?' She walked towards him. He had never seen her look so serious, so low. He was standing up now. She put her hands on his shoulders and looked into his eyes. 'I'd love to say it won't change anything, but it will. I can't be with you, Jamie—not with all this going on. I can't do it to the family.'

'Bugger the family. Bugger both families. I don't want to keep alive some old feud just to satisfy the pride of a couple of grandfathers. Just because they fell out when they were our age doesn't mean that we can't love each other. Does it?'

'I'm sorry.' She could not look at him now. She bowed her head.

Jamie could hardly believe what he was hearing. 'Tell me I'm imagining things. We said it was special. What happened to that "ease" we had with each other? Did it fly out of the window at the first little difficulty?'

'It's hardly a little difficulty,' said Missy.

'It's not insignificant, I know—it's massive—but we can overcome it. You're the most important thing to me and I don't want to lose you.'

She heard the desperate note in his voice and so wanted to throw herself into his arms and tell him that it would be all right, that they could sort it all out. But how could she, knowing what her grandfather had just told her? How could they be lovers if they were of the same blood? There was no way round the problem.

'Well?' asked Jamie.

'I'm sorry,' was all she could manage, trying to hold back the tears. She ran through the door and down the three flights of stairs, imperilling her life with her blurred vision. Out of the front door she ran, along Brock Street and into the Royal Crescent. The tears were flowing freely now and her body was wracked with sobs.

At the far end of the street, Jamie watched as the love of his life ran away from him, until he, too, could no longer see for the tears.

Rose Cottage, Bradford-on-Avon—Christmas 2007

'God rest ye, merry gentlemen,' intoned the carol singers on his mother's doorstep. He was not merry, and even God offered him little rest from his turbulent thoughts, but he gave them a fiver all the same before shutting the door and going back inside.

It should have been the best Christmas he had ever known. Instead it was the worst. She had not contacted him in the two weeks since that fateful day when she had told him it was all over. He had not called her, did not want to beg her to reconsider, but he had half hoped that she would call him to say that she was sorry, that it had all been a mistake. But the silence from her was deafening.

They had been together such a short while, but in that time his life had turned around; he had found it easier to get up in the morning knowing that at some point during the day he was likely to see her. And the nights. It made his heart sink to think of them now. His bed seemed the loneliest place in the world. And now it was Christmas Eve and the only thing in prospect was dinner with his mother and grandparents in Emma's cottage.

He knew he should snap himself out of it. He had faced rejection before and had got over it. But something in him did not want to shake it off this time. Why should he? What was the point? If he could not have Missy, then he would have nobody.

'You're very quiet.'

The voice was his mother's. Jamie was suddenly aware of the silence at the dinner table. They had been talking about heaven knows what and it had been easy enough to let them get on with it, but now all eyes were on him.

Sally Ballantyne reached out and took her grandson's hand. 'I think Jamie's mind is somewhere else.' She looked at him fondly.

Sally had always been the voice of common sense and reason in the Ballantyne household. Jamie put it down to her Yorkshire background. She, of all of them, thought the family feud a tiresome distraction, but in deference to her husband she avoided contact with the Kings. It was easier that way.

Harry had never levelled with her about his university days, and she had always put the acrimony between Richard and her husband down to male pride, nothing more. She had never pressed Harry for information on the intricacies of university life, aware that men got up to all kinds of things at that stage of their lives. In any event, it was nearly sixty years ago and of even less consequence now than it had been when she had got married.

Nevertheless, she was astute enough to know when a man's preoccupation was down to woman trouble, though she was not about to pry. She left that to her daughter. Emma did not disappoint.

'So what's Artemis King doing over Christmas?'

At the mention of her name, Sally Ballantyne's eyes widened and Harry sat bolt upright.

Jamie shrugged. 'No idea.'

'Ah!' exclaimed Emma. 'So that's it—lovers' tiff.' She seemed pleased that it was out in the open, relished sharing the news with her parents.

Jamie felt himself colouring up. 'Rather more than a tiff, actually. I've been dumped.' He saw little point in beating about the bush.

His grandmother's tone was sympathetic. 'Oh dear, how sad, and just before Christmas, too,' she said.

Harry was normally content to let the women do the talking when it came to affairs of the heart, but he was not about to sit idly by and watch his grandson being grilled, taunted or fussed over by these two women, whoever the third party. He himself had been totally unaware of the liaison. It surprised him and made him a little uneasy, but then he reasoned that if it was all over, there was little point in worrying about it.

'I don't think Jamie's love life has anything to do with the rest of us,' he offered.

'Thank you, Granddad,' was Jamie's heartfelt response.

'Whatever we might think.' He looked at Jamie over the top of the spectacles that he had been using to read a cracker motto, and the two women momentarily fell silent. 'Now, how about a cup of coffee?' asked Harry. 'Give Jamie and me a break from female conversation.'

Sally smiled indulgently. 'Come along,' she said in the direction of Emma. 'I think we'd better do as he says.'

The two women got up and carried out the plates and cutlery, leaving Jamie and his grandfather alone at the table.

'Do you fancy a cigar?' asked Harry.

'Not for me,' replied Jamie. 'They give me a sore throat, and even though I'm not working for the next few days, I'd rather not risk it.'

'Well, I'm on my own, then,' said Harry. 'My Christmas treat, though I don't think your grandmother approves.' He lit the cigar and inhaled the smoke luxuriantly. 'First of the year,' he murmured, 'and the last.'

Whatever else Harry Ballantyne was, he was not unaware of atmosphere and mood. He had been an auctioneer. It was his job to sense these things. He looked at Jamie, who was still sitting at the table. 'I didn't know you were hooked up with Artemis King.'

'Past tense,' shot back Jamie.

His grandfather ignored the reproachful reply. 'I expect you're waiting for me to say, "Just as well," or some such sentiment.'

'Everybody else has.'

'I can't say it thrills me, but then it's not really up to me. I choose not to have much to do with her grandfather. Our business paths cross from time to time and that's enough for me, if I'm honest.'

'Well, her family weren't too keen on us being together either, so I expect it's relief all round.'

'So that's that, then, is it?'

'Looks like it,' muttered Jamie.

'You're just going to let it go?'

'I don't have much choice. It was pretty final.'

'Any reason given?'

Jamie hesitated, then said, 'I think King's are about to go under.'

His grandfather dropped down into an easy chair by the fire. 'Good God! Are you sure?'

'That's what Missy says.' Jamie deliberated what to tell his grandfather. Not wanting to betray Missy's trust, he said, 'Something to do with some ill-advised buying. That's confidential, Granddad. Don't go telling anybody. I wouldn't want it to get out from us.'

'Well, I'll be . . . I thought they were as safe as houses. Did she say how it happened?'

Jamie shrugged, conscious that he had already said too much.

Harry thought for a few moments and then asked, 'And you think that's why she finished with you?'

Jamie nodded.

'Family pride,' murmured Harry. After a few moments he said, 'You look pretty cut up about it. She was the one for you, was she?'

'I thought so. I really thought so.'

'Well, you'd better do something about it, then, hadn't you?'

Jamie looked up, having been intent on studying the pattern of the Rajasthani rug. 'Not up to me, is it? She was the one who broke it off.'

'Mmm. Sounds a bit defeatist to me.'

'Granddad!' Jamie was both surprised and irritated at his grandfather's stance. Normally he was the last to interfere in his personal life. And the fact that he appeared to be encouraging him to take up with a King was totally unexpected.

'Oh, I know it's none of my business. Tell me to shut up if you want, but if you're sure that she's the one—and it seems that you are—then don't let her talk herself out of it. Unless you think she wouldn't be happy with you. That's different. But it sounds as if you think she's keen.'

'I thought she was, but circumstances seem to have changed things.'

Harry drew on his cigar and exhaled deeply. 'So you're just going to wait to see if she comes round?'

Jamie sighed.

Harry put down the cigar and looked across at his grandson. 'Don't lose her, Jamie, not if you know she's the one.'

Jamie looked up. 'Why are you so concerned?'

He watched as Harry got up and walked to the window. He was looking out over the wintry garden while he spoke. 'I've had a lovely life with your grandmother, lovely, but there was somebody before her. Somebody that I really, well . . .' He paused for a few moments, gathering his thoughts. 'I've always wondered . . . if things had been different . . . what it would have been like. It was very . . . strong.' He turned round to face his grandson. 'I wouldn't want you to go through the same—not knowing what might have been. That's all. Don't take it lying down.'

Peel Place, Corsham—Christmas 2007

Missy's Christmas was, if anything, even more deadly than Jamie's. At her grandfather's house in Wiltshire, the atmosphere was funereal. Only Patrick's presence would lift the gloom. Missy could not think why she should regard him as the only bright light in prospect this Christmas, bearing in mind their history. She knew she had every right to despise him for his cavalier attitude to her, but still he lifted her spirits whenever they met— exasperated and amused her in equal measure.

Richard still considered him a liability. Missy was a far better bet when it came to needing someone he could depend on, and look what had happened now: the firm he had hoped to hand on to her was on the brink of ruin. There really seemed no way out of it, and all because of his own shortcomings, his own stupidity and, from Mac's point of view, his own greed. If he had kept the painting of Eleanor on the horse, put his love of the woman in the picture above his desire to get on in life and make more money, then he never would have discovered it was a fake and Fate might have smiled on him. As it was, Fate, aided and abetted by John Macready, had dealt the final blow so late in life that he wondered if he would ever pick himself up. What was the point?

For most of Christmas Eve, Richard King had shut himself away in his study, leaving Missy and her grandmother to prepare the evening meal and wait to see if Patrick turned up. He had treated the news from his father with his usual equanimity. 'Not to worry,' he had said, before going off with his latest amour on a pre-Christmas cruise. So long as there was enough to pay the bills he would find something else to do. It did not seem to have crossed Patrick's mind that his daughter was now high and dry, without a job and with the prospect of not even having a roof over her head. But then, why should she be surprised? He had left her alone for the first twenty-odd years of her life. Why should he start caring what happened to her now?

Peeling Brussels sprouts with her grandmother was not how Missy had envisaged spending her Christmas Eve. She wanted to be sitting in front of a log fire with Jamie's arms round her, talking about their future.

'I know it's sad,' said Eleanor, 'but try not to blame your grandfather.'

'I don't blame him,' replied Missy, tossing another sprout into the saucepan. 'I just can't help thinking that it all seems such a waste.'

'Yes.'

'I mean, what will you do? Where will you live?'

Her grandmother was putting a brave front on it. 'Oh, we'll manage. We'll move into a flat, perhaps a little cottage with a garden, a small garden. We won't be destitute.' She smiled, but Missy was not being fooled.

'But Grandpa can't live in a small flat, or even a cottage. His whole life has been lived in big houses. That's what's important to him.'

'The first house in Bristol wasn't so big,' mused Eleanor. 'Maybe it's just what we've all got used to.'

'I suppose,' murmured Missy.

'You, too,' said her grandmother.

'Yes.'

'Your grandfather told me, you know,' Eleanor confided.

'Told you what?' Missy looked apprehensive.

'About Jamie Ballantyne.'

'I see.' Missy looked embarrassed. Her grandmother knew, then, that she had been told that Richard was not Patrick's real father, and that the elegant seventy-nine-year-old with whom she was at the moment peeling sprouts had had a love affair before she married; an affair with Harry Ballantyne.

'I'm sorry that he told you.'

'You mean you think I should have been kept in the dark?'

'No, of course not. I mean that *I* should have told you, not your grandfather. He's the one who's had to bear all the hurt.'

'Not you?' asked Missy pointedly.

Her grandmother put down the knife she was using to peel the sprouts. 'Shall we have a glass?'

Missy nodded. 'Yes, please. I could do with something.'

'Me too.'

'I'll get it.' Missy went to the fridge, took out a bottle of chilled Chablis and poured two generous measures of the wine. She handed one to her grandmother and took a small sip of her own.

'I expect you want to know how it happened?' offered Eleanor.

'Oh, Grandma, I—'

'No. You should know. It was a long time ago, but you ought to know about it. I'm really sorry, but it affects your life as well.'

'Yes.' Missy took a large gulp of wine to bolster her courage and asked, 'Was it a quick fling, then?'

Her grandmother tried to contain her surprise at the directness of the question. 'Well, yes, I suppose it was in a way.'

Missy looked at her sideways.

'Oh, don't look like that. It was not quite that straightforward. We were all at university together—me, your grandfather, Leo Bedlington, John Macready and Harry Ballantyne. Leo and Mac were never really interested in girls, but your grandfather and Harry were both keen on me, apparently.'

'And you?'

Eleanor looked across at the kitchen door, which was firmly closed. There were no sounds of activity in any other part of the house. 'I was very fond of your grandfather.'

'But you were in love with Harry?' Missy saw the trancelike look in her grandmother's eyes.

Eleanor nodded. 'Yes, I was.' She spoke as though she were far away.

'And he with you?'

'I never realised, not until the other week. When we were at university we went to see an artist, Alfred Munnings. We had to stay over. Your grandfather was back in Oxford with a cold—he said it was flu, but it was a cold.'

Missy smiled at her grandmother's ability to make a joke even when opening her heart.

'Harry finally melted. He'd never given me much hope that he had any feelings for me until then. Well, it was just a sort of torrent, I suppose—of emotion. We had one . . . wonderful . . . glorious night together.'

Missy saw a gleam in her grandmother's eyes and felt her own tears welling up. 'Oh, Grandma. So why didn't you carry on, with Harry, I mean?'

'Who knows? We had no chance to talk the following day. Mac was having breakfast with Harry when I came down. Then we went to see Munnings again and after that Harry drove us back to Oxford. He dropped me off. It was difficult to say anything, what with Mac being there and the traffic and things. We just had to say goodbye quite briefly.'

'So what happened after that?'

'Nothing, absolutely nothing. Harry just disappeared. He'd said he wanted to travel about the country—to look for somewhere to start up an auction business—so I suppose he went off and did it.'

'Without even saying goodbye?'

'Apparently. Mac was the same. I never got to say goodbye to him, either. I know why that was now. Your grandfather told me about Mac being in love with him, but only much later.'

'And nobody knew? About you and Harry?'

'Oh, I think Leo Bedlington knew, and probably Mac as well. Not about the baby, just about Harry and I being . . . well . . .'

'But what about Grandpa? Did he know?'

'Not at the beginning. He knew that Harry and I were attracted to one another, I suppose. The day after Harry and I had . . . been together . . . I went to tell him that I wanted to be with Harry, but before I could tell him he produced a ring and asked me to marry him.'

'So you just said yes?'

Eleanor saw the look of incredulity on Missy's face. 'No, of course not. I told him as gently as I possibly could that I was fond of him and I didn't want to hurt him, but that I just couldn't marry him.'

'How did he take it?'

'Oh, very much as you'd imagine. He was shocked and disappointed, and said that if I ever changed my mind, he'd be there for me. I didn't tell him about Harry. Not then.' Eleanor took a sip of wine and put down her glass before continuing. 'I went back to finish packing, expecting Harry to come and find me. Well, he didn't, so I went round to his room. I waited and waited, but he didn't come, so I wrote him a note and went back to my digs. He didn't respond and I went back to see if he'd returned. His bags were gone, and all I could see was my note screwed up in the waste-paper basket.'

'Oh, how dreadful!'

'Yes. It was very hard.' Eleanor seemed to lose herself in her thoughts for a while; then she murmured, 'Though Leo seemed to think that Harry really did love me . . . so why . . . ?'

Missy waited for a few moments before asking, 'And Grandpa?'

'Well, a few weeks later I found out that I was pregnant. I knew it was Harry's child. I hadn't been with anyone else. I didn't know what to do. I thought of getting rid of it, but I simply couldn't. And then your grandfather came back into my life, asked me again. He said that he understood that I didn't love him, but he hoped I would in time and that it was a chance he was prepared to take.'

'So you said yes?' asked Missy.

'I did.'

'Without telling him?'

Eleanor looked at her granddaughter with haunted eyes. 'Oh, I wanted to be honest with him, believe me I did. At least then I would have known he would be marrying me because of who I really was, rather than because he had put me on some kind of a pedestal. But I didn't. I thought at the time that it would have been folly to do so. That he would not have married me. I didn't tell him the truth until we found that we couldn't have children together, but by then, of course, he must have known.'

'And did you tell him that you were in love with Harry?'

'There are some things in life that don't need to be said. It was enough that he knew I had borne another man's child and that we could never have children together.'

'And he didn't mind?'

'Yes, he minded. It hurt him deeply. He was still prepared to stay with me, though, and that, in my mind, makes him a prince among men.'

'So is kindness more important than love?'

Eleanor shook her head. 'Oh, Artemis, in an ideal world love is worth more than anything, but I wasn't in an ideal world. I was in a nightmare world. I was about to be an unmarried mother at a time when only "trollops", as my mother would call them, did that sort of thing. I had no father and a mother who had all but lost her reason on account of the only man she had ever loved being killed in the war. I had two choices: break my mother's heart—what was left of it—and bring up the child on my own or agree to marry a man of whom I was very fond and who would be a father for my child. What would you have done?'

Missy looked away. 'I don't know.'

'No. Well, I did the best I could. What seemed right at the time.'

'And nobody knew?'

'I think Leo Bedlington suspected. He was always quite astute.'

'Does Dad know that Harry Ballantyne is his father?' She paused for a moment, then added, 'And that Emma is his half-sister?'

'We told him when we thought he was old enough to understand.' Eleanor looked enquiringly at Missy. 'I presume he didn't say anything to you when he knew you were going out with Jamie Ballantyne?'

'I didn't tell him about Jamie, and he never asked.'

'Yes, well, I can't say I'm surprised. Your father's very good at wrapping himself up in his own world.'

Missy's mind was reeling now, at the consequences of all the knowledge she had so recently acquired. 'So does Harry know that Patrick is his son?'

'No, certainly not.'

'And you didn't mind deceiving him?'

The accusation stung Eleanor. 'Of course I minded, but I had to think of what the knowledge would do to their family. What good could possibly have come of it?'

'But did Dad not want to talk to his real father?'

'To be honest, we discouraged it. I think he'd realised that it could cause more problems than it solved. Your grandfather has always been grateful to him for that. I think it's the reason he's been so forgiving of him, and losing your mother and his best friend in such a short time was a bitter blow.' Eleanor put her hand over Missy's. 'I'm sorry, Artemis. I'm sorry that the mess I made of my life has affected yours. I wish with all my heart that I could rewrite history, but I can't. Like it or not, Harry Ballantyne is *your* grandfather as well as Jamie's and there's nothing I can do about that. Believe me, if there was, I would do it.'

'Thank you,' said Missy, but it was hollow gratitude.

'There is one little ray of hope,' offered Eleanor.

Missy raised her eyes.

'Leo Bedlington has been rather kind to us in his will.'

'What do you mean?'

'Well, he lost almost everything to death duties—but half of the residue of his estate goes to some American relation and the other half to you.'

Missy looked at her blankly. 'To me? Why? He never even met me.'

'Oh, various reasons, I would guess. He was very fond of me, but I think he was also fond of your grandfather—your *real* grandfather, Harry—if he did suspect that was the case. Who knows? Anyway, I don't expect there will be much, but I thought you'd like to know.'

As the implication slowly dawned on her, Missy could not speak. She could not have Jamie, but she would have, instead, half the proceeds of the sale of the Munnings paintings that he had shown her. How cruel was Fate, to give with one hand and take away with the other.

Chapter 11

Bath—January 2008

As Jamie walked through the abbey churchyard, whipped mercilessly by the cold wind, he quickened his pace and thought about her again. He half laughed at the lack of novelty: he had thought about nothing else the entire holiday, though 'holiday' was an inappropriate word for the two weeks he had just endured. He had spent Christmas Day at his mother's, and Boxing Day with his grandmother and grandfather in their new flat. His familial obligations fulfilled, he had then knuckled down to sorting out the Circus, glad of the chance to be miserable alone.

And now it was back to work. He had let the electrician and the plumber in at 8 a.m., and having left them with an electric kettle and enough tea bags, milk and sugar to sustain the population of a small town, he had headed off for the office.

It was the practice of Ballantyne's to hold an auction in the last week of January and Jamie was grateful for the distraction. From behind his desk he glanced across the room to where the five Munnings paintings were propped against the wall. They should not be stored there, he knew, but for now he wanted to look at them. They seemed to offer him some kind of link with Missy, the only link he had, and in a couple of weeks they would be sold and even that link would disappear.

He leaned back in his chair and reflected on the words of his grandfather. His grandfather, who had so little time for the King family and yet had asked him to look into his heart and ask himself if she was worth fighting for. He reached for the phone. Quickly he dialled the number, before he had time to reconsider. The call was answered almost immediately.

'King's Fine Art.'

'Missy?'

'Yes.'

'It's me.'

For a moment the line went quiet. Then she said softly, 'Hello.'

'I just wondered how you were.'

'Oh, you know, battling on.'

There was a reserved note in her voice. He was unsure how to progress with the conversation. Half of him—the head half—wished he had not been so swift to dial her number, but the other half—the heart—was glad simply to hear her breathing at the other end of the line.

Before he had time to think properly, he heard himself asking, 'Do you fancy a coffee? Only, I'm up to my neck in a sale that we're having in a couple of weeks and I could do with a break. It would just be nice to see you, not having seen you over Christmas. Nothing serious. Just—'

'Yes.'

At first he did not hear the word. He was sure she would say no, was sure that she would give him the brush-off.

'Oh. Right. Well . . . the café by the abbey, the one with—'

'Yes. In half an hour? I'll see you there.'

HARRY BALLANTYNE was sitting in his armchair in the window of his flat when Tilly came in and gave him the envelope. She called in and 'did' a couple of mornings a week now. There was not nearly so much to attend to as there had been in the Circus, but she was grateful for that, what with her arthritis. It was good not to have to negotiate all those stairs.

Harry looked at his name and address on the front of the envelope. It was executed in Tilly's brother's handwriting. It had been good of Tilly to ask him to help out but then she was a good sort who would do Harry's bidding without too many questions. She appreciated that sometimes he needed to have things done quietly, and she was the mistress of discretion.

Once Tilly had left the room, Harry slit open the envelope and withdrew the handwritten note and the cheque. It was a sizeable sum—six figures. Not a fortune, but enough to help keep the wolf from the door.

Dear Mr Ballantyne,

I received the cheque from the auction house this morning. I have banked it and now enclose my own cheque for the same sum less the ten per cent you instructed me to take from it. I have done so very reluctantly. I am always happy to help out, since Tilly thinks so much

*of you, but it really was very kind of you to be so considerate of my
small part in the transaction.*

> *Yours sincerely,*
> *Edward Stephenson*

Harry got up and walked to the bureau that stood against the opposite
wall of the flat. From one of the small drawers he took out his chequebook
and set about filling in a deposit form from the back of the book. He tore it
out and tucked it into his wallet. Then he wrote out a cheque for the same
amount and slipped it into a plain envelope on which he carefully wrote the
name of the recipient. He did not write out an address; he would deliver the
cheque by hand.

He got up from the bureau and took the envelope with him into the hall.
With a look at the sky, which decided him against taking an umbrella, he
put on his overcoat and set out on the short walk into town.

Villa Fabrice, Menton, Côte d'Azur—August 1995

Madame Farage had gone home, leaving Leo to face the day alone. It mattered not that the sun shone from a cloudless sky, turning the sea into a
shimmering sheet of sapphires. Neither did he feel the benefit of the warm
breeze that played among the leaves of the acacia trees and whispered
through the needles of the pines. Such sensations were lost on him now. It
was all lost, and he had no one to blame but himself.

He went indoors to fetch a pen and writing paper, then settled himself in
the wicker armchair on the verandah once more and considered his options.
Did he really want to continue out here, on his own? He had been on his
own before Mac had arrived, so why could he not go back to being on his
own now? It was not as if they were lovers. Mac had made it quite clear that
that was out of the question. Leo had settled, instead, for an understanding,
an understanding of which he was now deprived.

It would not be so bad had he not known what had really happened. If he
had believed it was an accident, he could have wallowed in his grief for as
long as it took and then recovered and battled on. He was used to that, had
done it before. Maybe that was being selfish, though—not an accusation
that he could ever have levelled at Mac, except that, in a way, this was the
most selfish thing Mac had ever done.

During the weeks after his disappearance he had been convinced that

Mac had had an accident, that he had been caught out by the tide, or an attack of cramp. There were other times when jealousy raised its head. When he thought about the youth from the café in Menton, the youth for whom Mac seemed to have developed some kind of fascination. In moments of anguish he had fantasised about their relationship, about how Mac might simply have run off with him.

And then he had found the note, the note that had made it so hard to bear.

During the weeks before his disappearance their relationship had become strained. Mac had snapped at him more than usual, had been quiet and distant. It had happened before. Leo had put it down to artistic temperament, had told himself that Mac had a good heart—his kindness over the paintings had proved that. Oh, he was grudging about it from time to time, muttering to himself that he was betraying Munnings's trust, that hell and damnation must follow, but he had also said that the old man might be laughing up there in heaven at their audacity in fooling the art establishment, the very people that Munnings despised for their folly in raving about the kind of art that he considered worthless. That was what Mac had persuaded Leo to feel, and now he had gone, gone for all the wrong reasons and without ever sharing it all.

Suddenly Leo found his body shaking with tears. He could not remember having cried in years, and now he sobbed uncontrollably. Then he got up and shouted at the sea, at the flowers around him, at the gull that flew overhead and at everything that came into view until, exhausted, he slumped down in the chair and tried to breathe more evenly.

He mused on the futility of it all, of love. Who had ever done well out of it? Not him, that was for sure. Maybe Mac had—for a while—but even that had not lasted. Was anyone ever sure of love? Of trust? Of the durability of a relationship? Was it better never to love at all than to risk pouring everything into a relationship only to have it destroyed?

He remembered his college days. Richard, whom Mac had loved and failed to win; Eleanor, who had settled for Richard and not Harry, her true love. He could still remember the day Harry had come to see him at Bedlington Park, the day his father had died. He saw in Harry, that day, a man who had found the love of his life and who needed only an ounce of courage to make his dreams come true. Where had it all gone wrong? He knew that Eleanor loved him, so how could they end up without each other? In his heart he knew the answer: Fate. It was all down to Fate. The odds could be stacked in your favour, the future could seem assured, but one twist of Fate would be all that was needed to bring the world crashing down around you.

He took up his pen and began with the words: *Dear Harry . . .*

ONE MONTH LATER, Harry Ballantyne turned up on Leo's doorstep. He was on his way back from an antiques fair in Nice, he said. As they sat down on the verandah of Villa Fabrice, the years fell away and Harry was sorry that he had not been better disposed towards Leo's invitation. Now that he was here, he remembered with fondness Leo's kindnesses of nearly fifty years ago.

After the inevitable awkwardness of the preliminaries, the two men fell into the sort of conversation they might have had as young men. Conversation about dons and parties and, eventually, about relationships.

'So why did it never happen?' asked Leo eventually, topping up Harry's glass of wine.

'Why did what never happen?'

'You and Eleanor. She was mad about you, and I know how you felt about her. What went wrong?'

'She married Richard.'

'I know that. I was their best man,' Leo said reflectively. 'But why did she marry Richard when she was in love with you? When you left Bedlington Park the day my dad died, you said you were going to ask her to marry you. Why didn't you?'

'Because Richard beat me to it,' murmured Harry, gazing into his wine. 'I went to find her and ended up at Richard's digs. I was right outside the door when he proposed. It makes me go cold to remember it.'

'And you heard her say yes?'

'As good as.'

'Oh, Harry!'

'What? What do you mean?'

'I don't think she would have said yes. How could she have? She was probably trying to let him down gently.'

Harry butted in, 'Oh, you're very kind, but . . .'

'No. Not kind. Honest.' Leo shook his head.

Harry took a sip of his wine. 'Well, it's too late now, isn't it?'

'Reluctant as I am to admit it, I think you're probably right.'

Harry leaned back in the chair. 'I do think about her. Even now. And about how different it might have been.' He smiled. 'I see her occasionally, walking in the street. They live in Bath, you know. Not far from us.'

'That must be hard.'

'Yes, very.'

'And does she ever say anything?'

'No, we don't really communicate. I'm afraid that Richard King and I haven't spoken for years.'

'Because he got the girl?'

'I suppose so, but I think I could have learned to live with that. Strangely, all the animosity came from him. I don't know why.'

Leo looked hard at Harry, who was deep in thought. He considered giving an opinion, but thought better of it. Instead he stood up and said, 'There's something I want you to see.'

Harry looked up at him.

Leo motioned Harry to follow him indoors, into the drawing room of the villa. Above Leo's mahogany desk hung a painting, the sight of which took Harry's breath away.

'Oh my goodness, I haven't seen that for . . . nearly fifty years!'

'Eleanor, painted by Munnings,' confirmed Leo. 'The genuine article.'

'Yes. She was,' murmured Harry softly.

'I mean the painting,' said Leo.

Harry looked at him quizzically.

'There's something you ought to know,' confided Leo. 'About Munnings's paintings.' He took Harry by the arm and led him out onto the verandah again. 'You see, because I ran out of money, Mac had this idea. It was really a way of keeping the wolf from the door. It was a wicked thing to do, but it was the only way we could survive.'

It was half an hour before Harry spoke. It took Leo that long to explain.

'I see,' said Harry at last.

'And you think it was a dreadful thing to do?'

'Well, I certainly can't condone it.' Harry considered for a moment. 'So where are these paintings now?'

'Who knows? Scattered to the four corners of the earth, I suppose. Mac arranged to sell them through some gallery in England. Madame Farage did it all so that our names wouldn't come into it.'

'And you kept the real ones?'

'Yes.'

Harry shook his head in despair.

'And now you know, and you won't want to hear from me ever again,' muttered Leo.

'No. You shouldn't have done it, but then who am I to judge you?'

Leo got up and walked to the edge of the verandah, looking out across the sea. 'He didn't die by accident,' he said after a few minutes' silence.

'What?' said Harry, not following the change in the conversation.

'Mac. His death wasn't an accident.' Leo came and sat down in the wicker chair next to Harry. 'He took his own life.'

'No, not Mac—he wouldn't do that. I mean . . . he wasn't that selfish.'

'He didn't do it for himself. He did it for me.' Leo saw that Harry was not following him. 'He'd discovered that he was ill, terminally ill. What's the one thing that Mac would never have countenanced?'

'Being dependent on someone else,' murmured Harry.

'Exactly. He couldn't cope with being a burden on me, the man that he'd looked after for the past thirty-five years.'

Harry saw the tears building in Leo's eyes.

'What was he thinking, Harry?' Leo pulled a large white handkerchief from his pocket and blew his nose. 'Why did he think that I'd mind? He'd spent most of his life making sure that I was all right; why on earth did he think that I wouldn't do the same for him?'

Harry leaned sideways and put his hand on Leo's arm.

Leo looked up at him through the tears. 'We were never lovers, you know—just two people who lived together for mutual benefit, though heaven knows I had the lion's share of the benefits. All Mac did was paint to keep us alive, and now . . .' Leo looked up at him through the tears. 'But I did love him, Harry. I really did love him.'

Harry could not remember the last time he had hugged a man, except his grandson, which he did only rarely. Now he and Leo sat side by side with their arms round each other while Leo allowed the years of pent-up love to spill out, his aged body shaking uncontrollably.

Finally he eased away and blew his nose loudly. 'Thank you, Harry. It seems a long time since you poured your heart out to me about Eleanor. I had to wait forty-six years for my turn!'

Harry smiled at him. 'At least you had a long time together—you and Mac.' Then he said wistfully, 'More than me and Eleanor.'

'Yes.' Leo got to his feet and looked out to sea once more. Shafts of late-afternoon sunlight slanted onto the water, glinting on the crests of the shimmering waves. He turned to face Harry. 'That's why I want you to have the painting, the painting of Eleanor. You might have lost the real girl, but at least I can make sure you have the next best thing.'

Bath—January 2008

If asked why she had said yes to having coffee with him, her reply would have been brief and to the point: 'Because I wanted to see him.' She knew that. It was the only certainty in her life. She knew it was inadvisable, knew it would only lead to more heartache, but she so wanted to be in his company, even knowing that in the long term it was not possible for them to be together. She had tried keeping her distance, doing her best to get on, but she felt not one jot better now than she had three weeks ago. If anything, she felt worse.

What harm could come of talking to him over a cup of coffee, provided she stayed on an even keel and didn't say anything that would give him cause to hope?

She walked through the door of the café and across to where he sat. He stood up and leaned forward. Before she could make a decision whether or not to kiss him, he had already lightly brushed her cheek. She took a deep breath, sat down opposite him and said, 'Hi.'

'I've ordered you a hot chocolate. They said they'd bring it over when you came. Was that all right?'

She nodded. It was nice he had remembered.

Jamie, for his part, was so overwhelmed at her turning up that he had no idea how to begin the conversation.

'How was Christmas?' he asked eventually.

'Oh, not very good.' Missy smiled bravely. 'Grandpa wasn't himself. Hardly surprising, really.'

'So what . . .? I mean . . . is anything happening? With the business?'

'I'm not sure. I haven't really felt that I could ask, not just yet.'

The barista came over with her drink and Missy tried to change the subject. 'How about your house? How's it coming on?'

'Oh, nothing much has happened yet, really. The plumbers and electricians moved in this morning, so with any luck I might manage to get them out by next Christmas.' He smiled. 'What about you? Is the exhibition going ahead?'

'Yes. A last hurrah, I suppose. One final fling for King's Fine Art.'

'It might do better than you think,' he said encouragingly. 'It might net you enough to carry on.'

'I doubt it somehow.' Then, because she felt guilty at being so negative, she added, 'There is one little light at the end of the tunnel.'

'Yes?' He looked at her expectantly.

'Grandma told me that I'm due half the proceeds of your auction of Lord Bedlington's personal effects, including the Munnings paintings. I think he was rather fond of Grandma, and I think maybe he hoped it might make up for all that business with the copies. I guess he felt guilty about that.'

'So why didn't he leave them to her?'

'Oh, he said that he thought she had enough money already. He clearly had no idea how badly the firm had been hit. He imagined that Grandpa would have sold them on, I suppose, but obviously had no idea that he had bought them back and how much it had cost him. As far as I'm concerned, it doesn't really matter. I'll just use the proceeds to help reduce the overdraft.' She saw the hopeful look on Jamie's face. 'Don't get too excited—it won't be enough to cover our debts, but it should go some way towards keeping the bank happy for a while.'

'But that's brilliant. If I can get enough for them at auction, you'll be OK.'

'It's not really that simple, Jamie.'

'But it is, don't you see? I'll make certain that every single Munnings collector in the country gets the catalogue. I'll mail every London art dealer, and the provincial ones. By the end of the week there will be no one who's ever seen a horse on canvas who doesn't know that the finest set of Munnings paintings are about to go on the market.'

'Yes, but . . .'

Jamie motored on. 'What do you need? Seven million was the overdraft, wasn't it? Well, the five paintings won't get you that—and you only have a half-share—but if you do well with your exhibition and I do well on the platform, then at least we can drastically reduce your overdraft and you needn't go out of business.'

She watched his face as he enthused about the prospect of getting her out of the red and found it almost impossible not to break down. Oh, why could she not have this man? Clearly they were made for one another. It was all so desperately unfair.

He seemed to read her mind. 'Just let me try, that's all,' he said gently, aware that he might have sounded over-enthusiastic, proprietorial even.

'You're very kind. I don't really think I deserve your help, though.'

'That's for me to decide. Now, drink your hot chocolate and tell me what are the most exciting paintings in your exhibition. Then I'll do some sums.'

She could not help but smile. He was, without a shadow of a doubt, the most special man she had ever met in her whole life.

THE TAXI DROPPED HIM at the bottom of the tree-lined drive and he began to walk up the crunching gravel towards the house.

He had come unannounced. He saw little point in doing otherwise, but he reasoned that if it were early enough in the morning, the man he wanted to see would not yet have left for work, if indeed he still went to work.

The house was as imposing as he had imagined—with five bays and a central door, probably dating from around 1700. Supremely elegant, its mellow brickwork seemed to glow gently in the weak January sunshine. It was the sort of house people dream of, but then he had expected no less. He was nervous, but he hoped that the enmities of the past sixty years could finally be laid to rest. He was too old and too tired to keep up the silent feud. He could not bear to think that it would ruin the lives of another generation of their families. Things should be settled, for all of them.

He climbed the four wide, stone steps and rang the bell, checking once again that the envelope was in his pocket. It seemed only right to use this money, the proceeds from the sale of Leo's painting of Eleanor, to help salvage this whole mess. At that moment he knew it was too late to change his mind. There was no going back.

He heard a key turn in the lock on the other side of the door. It was opened quite smartly by a middle-aged man in a black jacket and tie and pinstripe trousers.

'Hello, Mr Ballantyne,' said the man. 'Please come in. Mr King is expecting you.'

This took Harry rather by surprise. He had assumed that if Richard King had known he was coming he would have made sure he was unavailable. He stepped into the hallway and the man closed the front door behind him.

'Would you care to come this way, sir?' The butler, for that was clearly what he was, led the way towards a pair of double doors at the back of the hall. He passed a white marble bust of Nelson on the way, but there was little time to take in the finer points of decoration, for the butler was now opening the double doors and saying, 'Mr Ballantyne, sir.'

Harry stepped forward into the book-lined room and saw the stocky, robust figure of Richard King, with his back to him, gazing out of the French windows. At the sound of his name, Richard swivelled round and the two men faced each other for the first time in nearly sixty years.

'Hello, Harry,' said Richard.

'Hello, Richard,' said Harry.

'Well, here you are, then.' Richard King motioned Harry to a chair in front of the large walnut desk that stood in the centre of what was clearly his study-cum-library. He did not attempt to shake hands.

'Your butler said you were expecting me?' said Harry questioningly.

'Yes. I was in the drawing room when you were coming up the drive. I saw you from there. I didn't want him to think your visit was a surprise. Which of course it is.'

'Yes.' Harry cleared his throat. 'I thought it was about time we called a halt to this feud. It was all so long ago and I really don't see why we should burden future generations with our differences, do you?'

Richard sat down in his chair and leaned forward on the desk. 'Why now? Why have you left it so long?'

Harry shrugged. 'Who knows? Why have either of us left it so long?'

Richard looked implacable. 'Maybe some of us prefer it that way.'

Harry was taken aback. He had hoped that Richard would be as eager as he was to put aside the animosity that had smouldered for so many years. It seemed that this was not the case. Harry continued, 'I know that my grandson and your granddaughter are'—he paused to choose his words carefully—'fond of one another, and I don't think that what happened with us all those years ago should get in their way, do you?'

Richard looked uncomfortable.

Harry persevered, 'If not for us, then for their sakes, let's set aside our differences. It simply isn't fair to expect them to continue our grievances.'

'It isn't fair,' said Richard slowly and softly. 'It isn't fair.' He was not looking at Harry now, but his eyes were focused on the middle distance. 'It isn't fair that I got Eleanor and you didn't. It isn't fair that your business is prospering and mine is about to go under. It isn't fair that your grandson and my granddaughter are probably in love with each other. It isn't fair.' He looked at Harry now. 'Life isn't fair, Harry. And you and I burying the hatchet now won't solve anything. It's all too late.'

'But it's not too late for Artemis and Jamie.'

'On the contrary, it's far too late. It was too late when they were born, for reasons you'll never understand.'

'What reasons? What reason can there possibly be why they should not be together, except for the pride of their aged grandparents?'

Richard King got up from his chair and walked round the desk. As he did so, the door of his study opened and he looked round to see Eleanor walking towards him. For a moment they just stared at each other.

'Harry,' she said absently.

Harry nodded. 'Hello, Eleanor.'

'Harry is just leaving,' said Richard.

'Oh, but—'

Richard interrupted his wife. 'We've had a brief meeting, but I think we've said everything we need to say.'

Eleanor looked troubled. Her eyes darted between the two men.

'Well, if that's how you feel,' said Harry.

'Yes, yes, it is. Thank you for coming. I'm sorry we can't do business.'

Eleanor looked confused. 'Would you at least like a cup of coffee?'

Richard was about to interrupt, but Harry got in first. 'No, thank you, I don't think so. I must be going.' He walked towards the double doors through which he had entered. They were opened as if by magic by the butler waiting on the other side. Harry turned in the doorway. 'I'm sorry things have turned out the way they have.' Then he turned to Eleanor. 'Goodbye, Eleanor. I'm sorry we didn't meet for longer. It would have been nice, but . . .'

Eleanor watched as he walked from the room and disappeared from view. Then she turned to Richard. 'What was all that about?'

Richard stood quite still for a moment, then said, 'Too little, too late.'

Harry waited at the bottom of the drive, pulling up the collar of his coat to keep out the bitter wind. It was half an hour before his taxi came. By the time he got home he was chilled to the marrow. Sally was out so he locked the envelope in the bureau, had a hot bath and then sat by the radiator. Still he did not seem to be able to get warm. All the time he could see Eleanor standing in front of him in Richard's study. She looked wonderful. Funny how after all these years she could still make his heart beat faster.

When Sally got home, she found Harry sitting in the chair by the radiator. He was so very cold. She held his hand for half an hour, but it never got any warmer. She lay her hand on his head and gently stroked his hair; then she called the ambulance.

Chapter 12

Bolton Abbey, Yorkshire—January 2008

They laid Harry Ballantyne to rest in his beloved Wharfedale, a reminder of the times when he and Sally had started out with nothing more than high hopes and a leg-up from her father. There were not many at the funeral. Well, Harry was nearly eighty after all, and Yorkshire is a long way from Bath. Sally didn't seem to mind, or to notice, even. Her heart was back with Harry in those early days when they would come up here in the Wolseley on a Sunday morning and paddle in the river at Burnsall.

Along with Sally, Emma and Jamie, and his sister, Fran, who had come over from Argentina, the mourners were a few locals who came out of respect for a man who loved this part of Yorkshire enough to be buried here. Among them was a man in his fifties who stood behind a pillar at the back of the church. Nobody seemed to notice him, but then he took care to make sure of that. Patrick King had come to say farewell to the father who had never known that he had a son. When the coffin had been carried out into the churchyard, he slipped quietly away.

The journey home was a quiet and sorrowful one. Harry had enjoyed a long and fulfilling life, but the fact that he had died so suddenly had left them all in a state of shock. Jamie left his grandmother with Emma and went back to the Circus. As he looked around the house it seemed to be filled with the spirit of his grandfather. He could see him in every room, standing by the windows in the drawing room, sitting on the fender by the fire, reading a book in his armchair, but the thoughts were all happy ones.

Late the following morning his grandmother called him and asked if he could come over to the flat. 'Of course,' he said. 'Is everything all right?'

She assured him it was and said, simply, that she had a few things she wanted him to sort out.

He found Sally sitting at her husband's bureau, going through his papers.

'I know what to do with most of what's here,' she said, 'but I can't understand what this is.'

She handed Jamie an envelope addressed to Harry Ballantyne in rather spidery handwriting. Jamie pulled out the letter. As he did so, a cheque fluttered to the floor. He read the letter, which was apparently from their housekeeper Tilly's brother, Edward Stephenson. Then he stooped and picked up the cheque. It was for the sum of £500,000. That alone would have made him gasp, but what really took his breath away was that it had been made out by his grandfather in favour of Richard King.

'What on earth?' exclaimed Jamie.

'That's what I said to myself,' said his grandmother. 'And there's this.' She picked up a bank statement and put on her glasses. 'There's an entry here for a week ago—a deposit in our bank account of exactly the same amount of money. I've rung the bank and asked about it. The cheque was made out by Tilly's brother. All quite above board, apparently.'

'So why did Tilly's brother pay Granddad so much money? And why did Granddad make out a cheque for half a million pounds to Richard King? I mean, they weren't even on speaking terms.'

'I was right to call you, wasn't I? It is important, isn't it?'

'Well, yes. I suppose so.' Jamie looked baffled. 'When is Tilly due next?' he asked.

Sally squinted at her watch. 'In about half an hour.'

'Have you been through the rest of Granddad's stuff?'

'All except the bureau. I thought I knew about everything.' Sally began to look tearful. 'Perhaps I didn't after all.'

Jamie made to comfort her. 'Oh, come on, Gran, I'm sure there's some perfectly simple explanation. Do you want me to look through the rest for you? I know it's private, but . . .'

'Oh, I've no secrets from you,' she said, wiping her eyes with a tissue. 'You go through it all and I'll make some tea.'

While Sally busied herself with the tea, Jamie turned out every drawer and every pigeonhole in search of anything that might offer a clue as to the reason for the cheque, but he found nothing.

There was only one place he had yet to look: in the centre of the bureau, in between the pigeonholes, was a tiny door. It was locked. 'Do you have a key for this?' Jamie asked his grandmother.

'Oh, yes. It's in a leather purse in the bottom drawer.'

'So that's what it was for.' He located the key, slipped it into the lock and turned it. The tiny door popped open and Jamie felt inside and pulled out a bundle of letters tied together with a piece of faded blue ribbon.

Sally took the bundle from him. 'They're the letters I wrote to your grandfather when we were going out.' She smiled as she remembered. Slipping off the ribbon, she sifted through them. 'Yes. Oh goodness, what a lot.' Then she stopped and turned one envelope over. 'No, this one isn't mine—not my handwriting.'

Jamie worried that his grandmother had discovered something that might upset her. 'Let me see . . .' He held out his hand and she passed it to him. He looked at the French postmark and stamp. 'Shall I open it?'

She nodded, and Jamie, his mind racing over what he should say if it proved to be unfortunate, withdrew the letter and read the contents. He had barely finished when there was a brief knock at the door and Tilly entered. She saw Jamie and his grandmother exchanging sideways glances and asked, 'What is it? What's the matter?'

Jamie got up. 'Tilly, sit down for a minute.'

Tilly looked apprehensive. 'I'm not sure I should. Too much to do.'

'No, really, sit down. There's something I need to ask you. It's about this.' Jamie handed her the letter that her brother had written.

'Oh, I see,' said Tilly in a low voice. 'It was nothing underhand, nothing dishonest, I promise,' she said.

'Just tell us, please, Tilly,' pleaded Jamie.

Tilly made an attempt to pull herself together. 'It was that picture of the beautiful young woman on the grey horse, the one that the Master had.'

Jamie looked at his grandmother. 'I didn't think we had a picture of a woman on a horse,' she said. 'Lots of ships, but no horses.'

'Master kept it in his dressing room at the Circus, wrapped in brown paper, behind his suits.'

'Oh.' Sally steadied herself and then sat down. The colour had drained from her cheeks.

Tilly continued, 'The Master had it for a few years—ten years p'r'aps. But then he decided he wanted to sell it, quietly, like. He explained to me that the Mistress knew nothing of its existence, that it had been his invest- ment, so to speak, and he couldn't sell it through Ballantyne's himself, not without everyone knowing it was his. So he asked if my brother would put it in the sale for him. He very kindly said he would make it worth his while.'

'I see,' said Jamie softly.

'Edward didn't want the money. He would happily have done it just for the Master, but the Master insisted, so . . .' She shrugged.

'So the painting was sold in the auction house,' said Jamie. 'By me, as it happens.'

'And then Edward sent the Master the proceeds, less the ten per cent that the Master had insisted he take.'

'Five hundred thousand pounds.'

Tilly's voice began to crack. 'It's a lot of money, I know, but . . .'

'Tilly, you mustn't get upset,' consoled Jamie. 'You only did what was asked of you.' He looked across at his grandmother and asked, 'May I hang onto this letter, the one we've just found? I've an idea that I might be able to make some sense of all this.'

Sally nodded. Then she asked in a quavering voice, 'Who was it from?'

Jamie smiled at her reassuringly. 'It was from Lord Bedlington.'

Bath—January 2008

That evening, in the quiet of his attic room, where he had made up a bed to be out of the way of the workmen on the floors below, Jamie read the letter and tried to piece together what he could from the information he had acquired over the last few weeks:

Dear Harry,

It was so good of you to come, especially at a time when I needed some solace from a true friend. As you suggested, I am sending the painting by courier. Hopefully it will bring back memories of your happy, if brief, affair with Eleanor at Oxford. I know that she loved you deeply.

As to Mac, I have come to terms with his actions. He wanted to spare me pain and so, apart from the pain that his loss has engendered, I cannot feel anything but a lasting love for him and a respect for his wishes. I like to think that is what he wanted.

It is no business of mine, but I do hope that you will make your peace with Richard, and he with you. That he landed Eleanor, and you did not, will be a lifelong regret for me, but I would hate to think that you both left this life without making peace with one another.

Anyway, the picture comes with much love. It was so lovely seeing you again and, in a funny sort of way, I feel I have laid to rest the ghosts of the past, getting all this off my chest. Neither should you worry about my well-being. I have just enough to see me out comfortably, and when the time comes, I shall know where to send what few goods and chattels that remain. The scandalous commission exacted by auction houses should help keep the wolf from your door! (This is meant as a joke, which I hope you will take in good spirits.) Anyway, hopefully that day is a way off yet, and I shall be able to find some peace before then.

Goodness, what a colourful life I have led, and how different from that which I thought I was going to lead that day when you came to Bedlington Park! I hear it is a retirement home now.

Enough. I have said all I need to, except that I shall always look upon you as a trusted friend who was there in my hour of need.

With fondest good wishes,

Leo

There was so much to take in. His grandfather had been Eleanor King's lover at Oxford, for a start. Well, the letter said *she* loved *him*, but did *he* love *her*? He must have done. Leo would not have given the painting to someone who had simply been a friend. Yet she had married Richard King. That must have been when the estrangement between the two men began.

Then there was the fact that the Munnings sold to Missy that day back in November had actually been put up for sale by his grandfather. At least that meant Missy's painting was, by the sound of it, genuine.

And what of John Macready, who had clearly not died accidentally but had taken his own life? The mirror-image picture that had been sent to Richard King was presumably some kind of posthumous apology. Did that mean that it, too, was real and not a fake? And then the cheque made out to

Richard King . . . Why would Harry do that? Unless . . . Jamie's head swam. He folded up the letter, slipped it into his jacket pocket, went down the stairs and out into the night. It was a short walk from the Circus to the Royal Crescent along Brock Street. He wanted to talk this over with Missy.

It was not long before he saw the lights blazing at King's Fine Art. He thought at first that something must be wrong, but then he remembered: it was the evening of the exhibition. The great and the good of Bath would be there, knocking back the Laurent Perrier and wolfing down the canapés. Some of them might look at the paintings. A few might even ask for some red dots to be placed on some of the tickets. He hoped so.

He walked along the pavement opposite, keeping in the shadows. The crystals of the chandelier in the hall shone like diamonds, their opulence belying the likely outcome of this last hurrah for King's Fine Art.

Jamie caught sight of Richard King's dapper figure through a window on the first floor, chatting with a well-dressed man and woman. Jamie imagined what must be going on inside his head.

MISSY KING HAD GREETED most of the guests herself, then directed them towards the waiters who were holding silver salvers laden with glasses of champagne.

After an hour she suddenly felt the need to escape. Her grandfather seemed as relaxed as she could hope, and Patrick had turned up, surprisingly, only half an hour late. She left the two of them holding court, knowing that she could not be gone for more than a few minutes, but desperately in need of a breath of air.

She slipped on her coat and strolled along to the end of the Crescent to look out over the city for a few minutes. This would, in all probability, be her last exhibition. But it was not the only sadness she felt. There was, if anything, a deeper sorrow within her: sorrow at the loss of the grandfather she had never known and who had not known her. She had sent Jamie a note, expressing her sympathy, but she knew that she could never tell him the truth; that a piece of history that was the fault of neither of them would always stand in their way. Oh, what a mess it all was.

She turned to look back at the gallery, shining like a jewel on the cold winter night. Below her, the golden lights of the city glinted and winked in the gloom, and then, without warning, the air was suddenly filled with large, white flakes. The streetlights, a moment ago casting their rays into the blackness, now illuminated a million tumbling stars. Missy turned her head to the sky and felt the ice-cold snowflakes falling onto her face and settling on her nose. The snow eddied about her and the freshness of the air was exhilarating—seemed to hold a promise of freedom. She sighed at the ridiculous thought, took a deep breath and headed back towards the brightly lit gallery.

In the denseness of the blizzard she almost fell over the figure huddled against the railings. 'I'm so sorry,' she exclaimed, putting out her hand to steady herself. Then she saw who it was. 'Jamie!'

'Hi.' He felt embarrassed at her finding him there like some stalker, embarrassed that she had fallen over him.

'I'm so sorry,' she said.

'No, I'm sorry,' he replied.

'About your grandfather, I mean. So very sorry.'

Jamie smiled weakly. 'Yes.'

Missy looked around her. 'What are you doing? I mean, out here?'

'Oh, just out for a breath of fresh air. Then it started to snow. Caught me by surprise, really.'

'Yes. Me too.'

Jamie looked at her standing in front of him with her collar pulled up, the flakes of snow swirling around her, and he could not remember ever seeing anything quite so beautiful. 'You look stunning,' he murmured.

Missy was caught unawares by the compliment and struggled to reply. 'Come inside,' she said. 'Come inside for a drink.'

'But I can't. I mean, your grandfather . . .'

'And my father. They're both in there. And Grandma. The whole family. Who cares? We're just friends, aren't we? If I can't invite *you* to the last exhibition at King's Fine Art, then who can I invite? Come on.' She took him by the arm and led him up to the front door of the gallery. 'Just don't say a word about this being our last show, that's all.'

'Yes. I mean, no. I mean . . . I'm not really dressed for this, am I?'

She looked down at the well-worn jeans and trainers, and then at the leather jacket. 'This is the art world—full of eccentrics. The ones in the suits are probably not the ones spending the money.'

In the doorway he watched as Missy slipped off her coat and handed it in to a cloakroom attendant, and then she took him by the hand and led him over to where a waiter was carrying a silver salver full of glasses filled with champagne.

Missy took one for herself and handed a second one to Jamie.

'Cheers!'

They clinked glasses and each took a rather larger sip than normal.

Missy smiled bravely and said, 'Dutch courage.'

'Do you need it?' Jamie asked.

'Oh, yes. Tonight more than ever.' Then she took him by the arm and said, 'Come with me. There's a painting I especially want you to see.'

Missy weaved between the chattering guests and up the stairs to the first floor, where yet more patrons were packed into the gallery. On the far wall, hanging in splendid isolation, was a painting of gypsies around a campfire.

'You remember the mirror-image painting I was worried about?'

Jamie nodded.

'This is it. But there's good news. The one in the catalogue—the one that was sold in the States—*that* was the forgery. This is the real McCoy.'

Jamie gazed at the painting and then said quietly, 'I thought so.'

Missy regarded him quizzically. 'What do you mean?'

'I need to talk to you. Not now, but tomorrow, after the auction.'

'Oh God!' she said. 'I'd forgotten, what with the exhibition and everything. It's tomorrow, isn't it? When you sell Lord Bedlington's stuff.'

'Yes, but I need to see you. I think you might be able to help me sort something out.'

'Me?' Missy looked apprehensive. 'OK.' She said hesitantly. 'What time?'

'Around four o'clock? Can you come to the Circus? Trust me. It's about the paintings, that's all.'

Missy's expression changed. She had looked worried and preoccupied, but now she looked determined. 'I'm sorry. You must think I'm really ungrateful. Come on, I want you to meet my father.'

'What?'

'And my grandfather. I've had enough of all this pussyfooting.' Missy took Jamie by the arm and propelled him across the room to where a man in a navy-blue blazer and open-necked, pink shirt was standing talking to three women who appeared to be hanging on his every word. 'Dad, this is Jamie, a very good friend of mine. Jamie Ballantyne.'

Patrick King turned towards Jamie. It appeared that he had not registered the name. 'Jamie?' he said absently. 'Jamie . . . Ballantyne?'

Jamie took a deep breath and held out his hand. 'Hello,' he said.

Patrick's face broke into a beaming smile. 'I'm delighted to meet you, Jamie. Thank you for coming.' He gesticulated around him. 'Seen anything that takes your fancy? Apart from these ladies, I mean!' The clutch of well-coiffed ladies dissolved into giggles. Jamie smiled politely and, to his surprise, Patrick King gave him a knowing wink and then said softly, 'Glad you came. Missy will be relieved to have your support.'

Before Jamie could reply, he felt Missy's hand on his elbow and heard her voice speak softly in his ear: 'One down, now . . . the big one.'

Jamie experienced a churning sensation in the pit of his stomach, which grew to epic proportions as Missy led him up to a short, dapper man dressed in a dark grey, pinstripe suit and blue shirt. He had seen him from a distance from time to time—you could not live in Bath and be unaware of the presence of Richard King—but he had never met him or even been this close. He detected the faint aroma of citrus as the owner of King's Fine Art turned to face him.

'Grandpa, this is Jamie Ballantyne.'

Richard King stared at Jamie for what seemed like an age. 'Is it, now?' was all he said.

'Good to meet you, sir,' Jamie said, and held out his hand.

For a moment it looked as though Richard King would ignore the gesture, but then, aware that he was surrounded by clients, and that he would appear ill-mannered were he not to respond, he shook Jamie's hand firmly and said, 'I was sorry to hear about your grandfather.'

'Thank you,' responded Jamie.

'We were at university together, you know.'

'Yes.'

Then Richard King turned back to the couple with whom he had been in conversation and it was clear to Jamie that his audience had ended.

He felt a hand on his side and heard a voice whisper in his ear, 'Well done. That's the hardest one out of the way.'

'You mean there's more?' he asked.

'Only Grandma.' Missy's heart was now beating rapidly in her chest. She wanted Jamie to meet the woman who had been his grandfather's lover and had borne his child, even though she could not tell Jamie that was so, or that it was the reason why she and he could never be together. She knew it was a rash thing to do, but deep inside she felt that introducing him to Eleanor would somehow lay a ghost to rest. It would clear the air, if nothing else. She was unaware that Jamie already knew that Eleanor and Harry had been lovers and, therefore, of the magnitude of this encounter.

The elderly lady sitting on the Louis Quinze sofa wore her thick, grey hair swept back off her face, and a triple row of pearls graced her neck. She had a poise and elegance that shone through her fragile frame, and her eyes glowed. On seeing Missy coming towards her, she rose to her feet and Jamie was surprised to discover that she was almost as tall as he was.

'Grandma, I want you to meet someone you haven't seen since he was very small, when we used to go to school together.'

'Hello,' said Jamie, this time not offering his hand, for fear of further embarrassment.

'Good heavens! Harry!' murmured Eleanor. 'I mean . . .'

'Jamie,' corrected Missy.

'Yes, of course,' agreed Eleanor. 'I'm so sorry. Just for a moment . . . how very strange.' With practised ease the old lady brushed aside her solecism and continued, 'Memory . . . silly tricks. Jamie. Of course.'

Jamie watched as Eleanor retrieved the situation, but saw, in that fleeting moment, the truth that shone in her eyes. For a split second she had looked at him as she must have looked at his grandfather, and he knew without a shadow of a doubt that they had indeed been lovers. In her eyes, he saw the same fire that he had seen in her granddaughter, the same fire that had captivated his grandfather all those years ago.

'Eleanor!' called a voice from across the room.

It was Richard King. 'The Bayntons are going.'

Eleanor replied almost without drawing breath, 'Coming, dear.'

'Do excuse me . . . er . . . Jamie. I must go and say goodbye to our guests. It's been lovely to see you after all these years.'

Eleanor held out her hand. Jamie took it and felt a tingling sensation, and then she was gone, sweeping elegantly across the floor in a wonderfully diaphanous dress that had clearly not come off the peg.

The waiter was at his elbow. 'Another glass of champagne, sir?'

He glanced sideways at Missy, but saw that she seemed distracted. He shook his head at the waiter, kissed Missy lightly on the cheek and with an aching heart quietly headed for home. He had begun the day looking for answers. He had ended the day with even more questions.

Chapter 13

Bath—January 2008

Before any auction, Jamie would always get a bit of a lift. The heart rate would climb slightly, the muscles tauten and the nerves sharpen. There were untold lots of furniture and assorted porcelain to get through before he arrived at the paintings—the star lots of this sale—and as a result the room was only moderately full at 10.30 a.m., when the sale began. Leo Bedlington's furniture made a respectable amount of money, but nothing that would assure the beneficiaries of early retirement.

Around noon the room began to fill up, and at a quarter to one Jamie took a sip of water, cleared his throat and announced the first of the paintings. 'Lot two hundred and ten, the first Munnings of the day, ladies and gentlemen. The property of the late Lord Bedlington. This is the first of two paintings of gypsies that I'll be auctioning this afternoon and I have a lot of interest already. I'm starting the bidding at a hundred thousand pounds. Any advance on one hundred?'

'One ten, one twenty, one thirty, one forty . . .'

From behind a pillar, where she had been the last time she attended an auction at Ballantyne's, Missy watched silently, hardly daring to breathe as rival bidders raised their paddles or their eyebrows.

'All done, then?' Jamie raised his gavel and scanned the room to make sure he had not missed any bids. 'If you're all finished, then, I'm selling at eight hundred and fifty thousand pounds.' Jamie brought down the hammer smartly on the desk. 'Number fifty-three. Thank you, sir,' he said, noting down the bidder number and the amount in his ledger.

Buoyed by the success of the first major lot, Jamie moved on to the second of the gypsy pictures. Interest was slightly less fervent here and the painting went for £600,000—still a huge amount for a provincial saleroom.

'Thank you, ladies and gentlemen, thank you.' Jamie had the unusual experience of having to quieten the room in between lots. The painting of the start of the race went next, for £730,000.

'And so, ladies and gentlemen, to our final lot: the painting of Lord Bedlington's mother on horseback and the star item in today's auction. This is one of Munnings's finest paintings and I have several commission bids. I'll start this one at five hundred thousand pounds.'

Missy's heart beat loudly in her chest. So did Jamie's, though he struggled to keep his voice steady. It seemed that the world and his wife wanted this painting. Jamie took his time, conducting the auction as though it were a symphony. First he would bring in this bidder and then that one; then he would glance at the girls on the telephones.

Finally, all the bidders in the room had fallen out and the competition was between two telephone bids. Hawklike, Jamie darted between the two—to the left, then to the right and back again. The room was silent now, except for the sounds of Jamie's voice and of a lone pigeon cooing on the glazed roof, as though expressing surprise at the rising price.

Eventually the right-hand telephone bidder dropped out and Jamie stared, gimlet-eyed, at the girl holding the handset. 'It's against you, then . . . and I'm selling . . .' He scanned the room once more to make sure that the final bid had been received. 'If you're all done, I'm selling at one million, eight hundred thousand pounds . . .' Bang! The hammer came down and the whole room erupted as though a winning goal had been scored in a cup final. A spontaneous round of applause followed, and Jamie could not resist a little bow. 'And that, ladies and gentlemen, concludes today's sale.'

He had not noticed Missy behind her pillar, and she was glad of that. She slipped out of the saleroom, making a mental note of the likely total and doing her best to work out its implications. Would it be enough, when taken with the proceeds of the exhibition, to save King's Fine Art?

Only one thing puzzled her: what would he do with the fifth painting, the one of her grandmother on the grey horse?

SHE ARRIVED on his doorstep at four fifteen, she who was normally never late. He kissed her lightly on the cheek and again felt a rise in his heart rate as he always did when she was around.

'Thank you so much for what you did this afternoon. I'd rather have you handling it than anyone else.'

'Oh, I think they would have sold well, anyway,' Jamie said as he led the way to the attic, where he'd done his best to create some sort of order out of the mess that was domestic-life-with-the-builders-in. He'd tossed a couple of throws over the sofa and armchair, and on a small table stood a tray carrying a bottle of champagne and two glasses.

He motioned her to sit down on the sofa as he uncorked the champagne. 'Have you told your grandfather yet?' he asked, handing her a glass.

Missy nodded.

'And?' asked Jamie expectantly.

'He didn't say much—just that the money was mine and I must do with it as I see fit. He's so bloody proud. Sometimes I want to shout at him.'

'I know the feeling.'

Missy brightened. 'But thank you for this.' She raised her glass.

'My pleasure. Happy to help.'

They both drank silently, allowing the bubbles to hit the backs of their throats and seal the day's proceedings. Then Missy asked, 'What will you do with the other painting, the one of Grandma on the horse?'

'I'll hang onto that one. It's the only one that isn't genuine.'

He explained about the bureau, about his grandfather and the cheque, about the letter from Leo Bedlington, and did his best to piece things together for her.

'So, you see, Granddad was given the real painting—the one you bought —shortly after Mac's death. Leo Bedlington wanted him to have it. The one I have is the fake. I'm sure of that now. That means you have another real Munnings to sell.'

'An *embarras de richesses*,' murmured Missy.

'Well, hopefully not an *embarras*,' chided Jamie.

Missy looked apprehensive. 'So now you know about my grandmother and your grandfather.'

'Yes. They were obviously lovers before Eleanor married Richard, and that was the start of the family feud.'

'Yes,' said Missy softly. It was the closest he had come to knowing the secret she would have to keep to herself. She felt her heart beating faster, felt the beads of perspiration beginning to form on her brow. 'And the mirror-image painting?' she asked, changing the subject. 'The one that we found was real . . .'

'Well, I should think John Macready sent that to your grandfather to say that he was sorry for using King's Fine Art to pass off his fakes.'

'But he died in 1995. Why has it only just arrived?'

Jamie shrugged. 'Maybe they only found it when Leo Bedlington died. Leo sent it on Macready's behalf. I don't expect we'll ever know for sure, but it looks as though it was some kind of peace offering.'

'Yes, and a way of telling Grandpa that, in spite of it all, he still loved him.'

'Loved him?'

'When they were at college, Mac told Grandpa that he loved him. Grandpa was horrified and just sort of cut himself off from Mac. I think Mac's actions in copying the Munningses were a way of getting back at Grandpa for turning him down, as much as to make money.'

'Then there's this,' said Jamie, pulling a cheque out of another envelope. 'It's made out for half a million pounds—in favour of Richard King.'

Missy took the cheque and looked at it. 'But it's from *your* grandfather.'

'Yes. It's the money Harry made from selling the painting of Eleanor. I think he felt that the money really belonged to your grandfather. Leo wanted my grandfather to have the painting for sentimental reasons, but, in spite of everything, Harry simply couldn't hang on to the money when he knew that your grandfather was in financial difficulties.'

'But he never delivered it?' asked Missy.

Jamie shrugged. 'Apparently not.'

'And now that he's died it won't be valid anyway,' she murmured.

'I've checked,' said Jamie evenly. 'Gran hasn't yet informed the bank of Granddad's death. I think she just forgot in the confusion of it all. If your grandfather presents it within the next few days, it should be honoured.'

'He won't do that,' countered Missy.

'It's what Granddad wanted,' said Jamie. 'Otherwise he wouldn't have gone to all the trouble of selling the painting. He never told Gran it had arrived. He kept it hidden for ten years and only took it out to sell it and help an old friend.'

'A friend who had married the girl he loved,' whispered Missy.

'Yes.'

Missy gazed into the middle distance. 'As long as I live I don't think I'll understand love,' she said.

'No,' agreed Jamie. 'Nor me.'

He saw her down the stairs, then kissed her softly on the cheek at the front door. He so wanted to take her in his arms and kiss her properly, and he thought he detected something in her look that wanted it too, but he did not want to spoil whatever it was that was left.

Bath—January 2008

The sadness she felt in her heart as she left him was of a depth she had not thought it possible She gripped the steering wheel of her car fiercely as she drove to her father's flat in the centre of Bath to tell him the day's news. With a heavy heart she climbed the stairs to the fourth floor.

'You should have taken the lift,' he scolded as he greeted her at the door. 'Fancy a drink?'

'No, I'd better not. I've already had a glass of champagne and I've got to drive home.'

'Oh? Have we cause to celebrate, then?'

'Who knows. I think we'll have made about two million all told.'

'*You'll* have made about two million, you mean.'

'It's not mine,' said Missy. 'Not really. I never knew the man.'

'No, but he knew your family—or a couple of members at any rate.'

'Yes, I suppose so.' She wanted to get up and go, having given him the news, but instead, to Patrick's surprise, her knees buckled underneath her and she collapsed onto the sofa.

'Hey! What the dickens . . . ? What's all this for? You should be pleased. You can save the firm now if it means so much to you.'

For several minutes he could get no sense out of her at all. She sat on the sofa with her head in her hands and sobbed.

Patrick came over, sat next to her and put a comforting arm round her shoulder. 'What is it?' he asked softly.

She shook her head, unwilling to share her woes with the man who had hardly been worth calling a father. 'Just . . . stuff.'

He still had his arm round her. 'What sort of stuff?'

She did not speak.

'Love stuff?' he asked.

She nodded.

'Anything to do with that man I met last night? Jamie Ballantyne?'

Again she nodded through the tears.

'I see.'

'But you don't see,' she said angrily. 'He's the loveliest, most gentle man I've ever met—will ever meet—and I can't have him because of . . .' Again she dissolved into tears.

'Because *his* grandfather is also *your* grandfather.'

'Y-e-s,' she wailed. 'And I don't think . . . I want to . . . live without him.' The words came out stertorously between the sobs. 'I tried hard not to want him. I went to America, not just because Grandpa sent me, but because I wanted to make a fresh start, to meet other people, other men. And I did, but there was no one to match Jamie.'

When the sobbing stopped she began to dry the tears with the back of her hand. 'I'm sorry. You don't want to hear all this. What is it to do with you?'

'Nothing really,' said Patrick calmly, 'but maybe that's an advantage.'

Missy looked at him questioningly.

'You never really forgave me for leaving you when you were a child, did you?'

Missy made to object.

'No, don't say it. I've been a lousy dad and you have every right to treat me like the shit I've always been when it came to bringing you up.'

Missy began to fill up once more. 'But it was because of Mum. How could you love me when she died having me? The woman you loved. What was I except the thing that caused you to lose her?'

Patrick's eyes also began to fill with tears. 'But it wasn't just that.'

'What, then? What else was there?'

'I had a friend, Charlie Dunblane. He died in a car crash two weeks before your mum gave birth.' Patrick brushed the tears from his eyes.

'Which made it even worse,' said Missy, who already knew about Charlie.

Patrick shook his head. 'Not for the reasons you think.' He put his other arm round her. 'The reason I went away, the reason I didn't want to know you was because you weren't my daughter. You were Charlie Dunblane's.'

The shock of hearing the words was enough to stop Missy's tears. She began to shake.

'He and your mum had a fling. He'd been drinking, so had she. I was away buying paintings for the gallery. Simple as that.'

'How did you find out?' she asked, trancelike.

'Your mother confessed, out of remorse. She didn't love him. It was just her way of getting me to take more notice of her. I always thought I had. I adored her . . .' He could not go on. Missy held onto him as they both wept. Finally Patrick took a deep breath and found the words to continue. 'And then when she had you, she lost a lot of blood and . . . well . . . It came as a double shock, you see. What a mess, eh?'

'Yes,' she murmured through the tears. 'What a mess.'

'I'm sorry. I know it must be just another shock in a long list of them, but you'll come to terms with it in time. Then perhaps you can stop hating me. Maybe, in a way, you'll see it was all for the best. You'll want to know all about Charlie. I can tell you that he wasn't a bad man; he was a good friend to me, in spite of the fact that he let me down in the worst way possible. I can't hate him; God knows I tried.'

Missy tried to dry her eyes with her hands as best she could. She sat up and looked at the man she had thought was her father.

'You look quite dreadful,' he said.

'You don't look so good yourself,' she replied.

'Don't hold it against me, Missy. Don't hate me for what I did. I might be a mixed-up old sod, but I do have some feelings. Too many for my own good, I think.'

Missy smiled through the tears. 'How could I hate you? You've just told me the best thing you possibly could: that Jamie and I aren't blood relations, so there's no reason . . .'

Patrick finished the sentence for her: 'Why you can't be together?'

There were tears of joy now. She hugged him so hard that the very breath seemed to be squeezed out of him.

Missy considered for a moment. 'Why did you never tell Harry he was your father?'

'Oh, I nearly did, several times. I wanted him to know, for revenge as much as anything. But then I realised how much it would upset Eleanor and Richard, and so I learned to live with it, as you'll have to. But you mustn't let it ruin your life like it did mine. Anyway,' he said, 'there's no reason to let it now, is there?'

'No,' said Missy. 'I suppose not. But I've lots of thinking to do.'

'It's a lot to take in,' said Patrick. 'But you'll cope. You always have.'

SHE DID NOT ring Jamie until the following morning. It was a Saturday, and he was wondering whether to bother getting up when the call came.

'I wondered if you fancied a walk in the snow?' she asked. 'I've got something to tell you. Well, quite a lot of things, actually. Some of them might surprise you, but it's a risk I've got to take. Only, the thing is, I don't want to have any secrets from you any more.'

He was not sure how to read her tone, or her words. He met her, as she had instructed, at the foot of Beckford's Tower, high up on Lansdown Hill. The city seemed to glisten way down in the distance as he waited in the silence that only snowfall can bring. In the deep, icy stillness he saw her climbing the slope below him, saw her smile and wave as she spotted his solitary figure at the top of the hill.

By the time she reached him she was panting, but her eyes were shining more than he could ever remember and her ice-cold cheeks were glowing as he bent to kiss her.

'Why this place?' he asked.

'Because you can see clearly from here,' she said.

'See what?'

Missy slipped her arms round his waist and looked over the city towards the hills. 'Out into the future.'

'Do you want to?' Jamie asked.

She turned to face him and looked searchingly into his eyes. 'Only if it's with you,' she said.

He bent to kiss her again, and in that moment felt more sure of himself and more certain of anything than he had ever done before. 'Do you believe in happy endings?' he asked.

'I'll start with a happy beginning,' she said.

ALAN TITCHMARSH

Born: Ilkley, Yorkshire, 1949
First job: apprentice gardener
Honours: MBE, RHS Victoria Medal

Britain's most famous gardener is now, among many other things, the author of seven best-selling novels, and *Folly*, a tale of romance, intrigue and two warring families, is his most ambitious to date. 'It's a romantic adventure and the first time that I've used a split time frame in a novel,' Alan Titchmarsh explains. 'The families are a bit like the Montagues and Capulets and Jamie and Artemis are like Romeo and Juliet. The setting is in the world of art and antiques. I tend to write about subjects I am passionate about and choose places that I love, so this one is set in Bath and Oxford, cities I adore.'

A Yorkshireman by birth, Titchmarsh has spent most of his adult life in southern England. He and his wife, Alison, and their two daughters, lived for several years in Barleywood in Hampshire, where, over a period of seven years, BBC television viewers would see him working in the garden as he presented *Gardeners' World*. The family still live in Hampshire, but now also have a home on the Isle of Wight where they spend a lot of their time. 'Alison and I fell in love with the island about ten years ago after I bought an old thirty-eight-foot trawler yacht; we used to pootle up and down the Solent and across to Cowes. We kept the boat at Chichester but, having liked the island so much, we decided to move her over and buy a flat in Cowes. We absolutely love it. There's a wonderful feeling of being a little distanced from the hurly-burly of life. For a small island, it has tremendously varied scenery—oh, and an amazing steam railway, which is one of my big things.'

In April 2008, Titchmarsh was appointed High Sheriff of the Isle of Wight for one year, a busy role that he takes very seriously. (Read his daily diary at www.highsheriff-iow.org.uk/diary.) It seems an almost full-time commitment, but this year he has also managed to see *Folly* through to publication, present *Melodies for You* on Sunday evening radio, as well as host his own daytime television show. And this doesn't even touch on the hours he gives to more than forty charities. 'These days I spend half my time meeting people who do voluntary work. It makes you realise that what you read, or see on the television news, is only a fraction of what's going on. All we are fed is gloom and disaster . . . There are an awful lot of good folk in the world just quietly getting on. Doing good stuff.'

It's these solid, unpretentious folk for whom Alan Titchmarsh writes. 'I am their man,' he says. 'I often say to Ali, when we've had a really good night somewhere with what someone else might call ordinary people, "Those are our folk." They're honest-to-goodness people who like reading a story or looking at gardening on the telly. They know who I am, and what I am, and they're happy with me. End of sermon.' The presenter's enormous popularity—people voted him among their fifty favourite television stars of all time—is testament to the fact that he speaks for a lot of people and represents what they believe in, or would like to believe in.

Titchmarsh is not one to talk about his Christian faith, but says that Christian values underpin what he does. His standards are also deeply rooted in the Yorkshire of his childhood. 'My mother would say, "If you can't say anything nice about someone, don't say anything," and, "Treat others as you like to be treated yourself." It's about goodness. It's under-rated.' But while his thoroughly down-to-earth goodness is beyond dispute, he still remains an intriguing contradiction—a man who loves to perform (he met his wife at an operatic society) but who also likes to spend his time alone, gardening, writing, or setting off somewhere new in a boat. 'Sailing. I love it. It's a great escape. When you're on a boat you're looking at nature in the raw. You can immerse yourself.'

SIR ALFRED MUNNINGS (1878–1959)

Alfred Munnings was born into a farming family in Mendham, Suffolk. He revealed early artistic talent and at fourteen was apprenticed to a Norwich printer as a poster artist, attending Norwich School of Art in his spare time. As highlighted in *Folly*, Munnings's fame is based on his paintings of horses, which many consider to rival those of Stubbs (1724–1806), but he was also an artist of great versatility, recording every aspect of rural life. In 1944, Munnings was elected president of the Royal Academy and awarded a knighthood. He died at his home, Castle House at Dedham in Essex (now the Sir Alfred Munnings Art Museum).

the
pyramid
henning
mankell

In the long watches of the night, Inspector Kurt Wallander lies awake and worries. About his elderly, increasingly eccentric father; his own solitary existence and failed marriage. And about his latest case: two mystery bodies found in the wreckage of a light aircraft in the Swedish countryside— a plane that doesn't officially exist. Soon, the crash appears to be related to two other crimes . . . forming a tantalising triple puzzle.

PROLOGUE

The aeroplane flew in over Sweden at a low altitude just west of Mossby Beach. The fog was thick out at sea but growing lighter closer to shore. Contours of the shoreline and the first few houses rushed towards the pilot. But he had already made this trip many times. As soon as he crossed the Swedish border and identified Mossby Beach and the lights along the road to Trelleborg, he made a sharp turn northeast and then another turn east. The plane, a Piper Cherokee, was obedient. He positioned himself along a route that had been carefully planned. An air corridor cut an invisible path over an area in Skåne where the houses were few and far between. It was a little before five o'clock on the morning of December 11, 1989. Around him there was an almost solid darkness. Every time he flew at night he thought about his first few years, when he had worked as a copilot for a Greek company that had transported tobacco at night and in secret from what had then been Southern Rhodesia, restricted by political sanctions. That had been in 1966 and 1967. It was when he had learned that a skilled pilot can fly even at night, with a minimum of aids, and in complete radio silence.

The plane was now flying so low that the pilot did not dare to take it any lower. He began to wonder if he would have to turn back without completing his mission. That happened sometimes. Safety always came first and visibility was still bad. But suddenly, right before the pilot would have been forced to make his decision, the fog lifted. He checked the time. In two minutes he would see the lights where he was supposed to make his drop. He turned round and shouted out to the man who was sitting on the only seat left in the cabin.

'Two minutes!'

The man behind him in the darkness directed a torch into his own face and nodded.

The pilot peered out into the black night. One minute to go now, he thought. And that was when he saw the spotlights that formed a square of 200 metres per side. He shouted to the man to make himself ready. Then he prepared for a left turn and approached the lighted square from the west. He felt the cold wind and light shaking of the fuselage as the man behind him opened the cabin door. He put his hand on the switch that glowed red in the back of the cabin. He had decreased his speed as much as possible. Then he threw the switch, the light changed to green, and he knew that the man back there was pushing out the rubber-clad container. The cold wind stopped when the door was closed. At that point, the pilot had already changed his course to the southeast. He smiled to himself. The package had landed now, somewhere between the spotlights. Someone was there to collect it. The lights would be turned off and loaded onto a truck, and then the darkness would become as impenetrable as before. A perfect operation, he thought. The nineteenth in a row.

He checked his watch. In nine minutes they would pass over the coast and leave Sweden again. At eight o'clock he would set his plane down on his private landing strip outside Kiel, and then get into his car and be on his way to Hamburg, where he lived.

The aeroplane lurched once. And then again. The pilot checked his instrument panel. Everything seemed normal. The headwind was not particularly strong, nor was there any turbulence. Then the plane lurched a third time, more strongly. The pilot worked the rudder, but the plane rolled onto its left side. He tried to correct it without success. The instruments were still normal. But something wasn't right. He could not straighten up. Although he was increasing his speed, the plane was losing altitude. He tried to think with complete calm. What could have happened? He always examined a plane before he took off. When he had arrived at the hangar at one o'clock in the morning, he had spent over half an hour examining it, going through all the lists that the mechanic provided, and then he had followed all the directions on the checklist before takeoff.

He struggled to straighten the plane, but the twisting continued. Now he knew the situation was serious. He increased his speed even more and tried to compensate with the rudder. The man in the back shouted and asked what was wrong. The pilot didn't reply. He had no answer. If he didn't manage to steady the plane they would crash in a few minutes. Just before they reached the sea. He was working with a pounding heart now. But nothing helped. Then came a brief moment of rage and hopelessness. He continued to pull on the levers and push the foot pedals until everything was over.

The Piper Cherokee struck the ground with vehement force at nineteen minutes past five. It immediately burst into flames. But the two men on board did not notice their bodies catching fire. They had died—torn into pieces—at the moment of impact.

The fog had come rolling in from the sea. It was 4°C and there was almost no breeze.

CHAPTER 1

Wallander woke up shortly after six o'clock on the morning of December 11. At the same moment that he opened his eyes, his alarm clock went off. He silenced it and lay staring out into the dark. Stretched his arms and legs, spread his fingers and toes. That had become a habit, to feel if the night had left him with any aches. He swallowed in order to check if any infection had sneaked into his respiratory system. He wondered sometimes if he was becoming a hypochondriac. But this morning everything seemed in order, and for once he was completely rested. He had gone to bed early the night before, at ten o'clock, and had fallen asleep immediately.

He got out of bed and walked into the kitchen. The thermometer read 6°C. Since he knew it showed the wrong temperature, he was able to calculate that he would greet the world at 4°C this day. He looked up at the sky. Ribbons of fog wafted by above the rooftops. No snow had fallen in Skåne yet this winter. But it is coming, he thought. Sooner or later, the snowstorms will arrive.

He made coffee and some sandwiches. As usual, his fridge was basically empty. Prior to going to bed he had written a shopping list that now lay on the kitchen table. While he ate breakfast he skimmed the *Ystads Allehanda* that he had picked up from the hall. He only paused when he reached the page with the advertisements. Somewhere in the back of his mind there was a vague longing for a house in the country. Where he could walk straight outside in the morning and piss on the grass. Where he could have a dog, and maybe—this dream was the most remote—a dovecote. There were several houses for sale, but none that interested him. Then he saw that some Labrador puppies were for sale in Rydsgård. I can't start at the wrong end, he thought. First a house, then a dog. Not the other way round. Otherwise I'll have nothing but problems, the work hours that I keep, as long as I don't live with anyone who could help out. It was now two months since Mona had definitively left him. Deep inside he still refused to accept what had happened. At the same time he didn't know what to do to get her to come back.

He was ready to leave at seven o'clock. He selected the sweater he usually wore when it was 0–8°C. He had sweaters for various temperatures and was very selective about what he wore. He hated being cold in the damp Skåne winter and he was annoyed the minute he started to sweat. He thought it affected his ability to think. Then he decided to walk to the station. When he stepped outside he felt a faint breeze from the sea. The walk from Mariagatan took him ten minutes.

While he walked he thought about the day ahead. If nothing in particular had occurred during the night, which was his constant prayer, he would question a suspected drug dealer who had been brought in yesterday. There were also constant piles on his desk with current investigations that he should do something about. Looking into the export to Poland of stolen luxury cars was one of the most thankless of his ongoing assignments.

He walked in through the glass doors of the station and nodded at Ebba sitting at the reception desk. He saw that she had permed her hair.

'Beautiful as always,' he said.

'I do what I can,' she replied. 'But you should watch out you don't start putting on weight. Divorced men often do.'

Wallander nodded. He knew she was right. After the divorce he had started to eat more irregularly and poorly. Every day he told himself he would break his bad habits, without any success so far. He walked to his office, hung up his coat and sat down at his desk.

The telephone rang at that moment. He lifted the receiver. It was

Martinsson. Wallander was not surprised. The two of them were the homicide division's earliest risers.

'I think we have to drive out to Mossby,' Martinsson said.

'What's happened?'

'A plane has crashed.'

Wallander felt a pang in his chest. His first thought was that it must be a commercial airliner coming in for landing or taking off from Malmö Sturup Airport. It meant a catastrophe, perhaps with many fatalities.

'A light aircraft,' Martinsson went on.

Wallander exhaled, while cursing Martinsson for not being able to provide him with a clear sense of the situation from the start.

'The call came in a while ago,' Martinsson said. 'The fire brigade is already on the scene. Apparently the plane was in flames.'

Wallander nodded into the receiver.

'I'm on my way,' he said. 'Who else do we have in the field?'

'No one, as far as I know. But the patrol units are there, of course.'

'Then you and I will go first.'

They met in the reception area. Just as they were about to leave, Rydberg walked in. He suffered from rheumatism, and looked pale. Wallander quickly told him what had happened.

'You two go on ahead,' Rydberg replied. 'I have to go to the bathroom before I do anything else.'

Martinsson and Wallander left the station and walked over to Martinsson's car. 'He looked ill,' Martinsson said.

'He is ill,' Wallander said. 'Rheumatism. And then there's something else. Something with his urinary system, I think.'

They took the coastal road going west.

'Give me the details,' Wallander said while he stared out at the sea.

'There are no details,' Martinsson said. 'The plane crashed some time around half past five. It was a farmer who called. Apparently the crash site is just north of Mossby, out in a field.'

'Do we know how many were in the plane?'

'No.'

'Sturup must have issued a dispatch about a missing plane. If the plane crashed in Mossby, surely the pilot would have been in radio contact with the air-traffic control tower in Sturup.'

'That was my thought too,' Martinsson said. 'That's why I contacted the control tower just before I called you.'

'What did they say?'

'They aren't missing any planes.'

Wallander looked at Martinsson. 'What does that mean?'

'I don't know,' Martinsson said. 'It should be impossible to fly in Swedish airspace without an assigned flight path and continuous radio contact with various towers.'

'Sturup received no emergency transmission? The pilot must have radioed if he ran into problems. Doesn't it usually take at least a couple of seconds before a plane hits the ground?'

'I don't know,' Martinsson answered. 'I don't know any more than what I've told you.'

Wallander shook his head. Then he wondered what sights lay in wait for them. He had seen a plane accident before, also a small plane. The pilot had been alone. The plane had crashed north of Ystad and the pilot had literally been torn to pieces, but the plane had not caught fire.

Wallander was filled with dread at the prospect of the crash scene. The day's morning prayer had been in vain.

When they got to Mossby Beach, Martinsson turned to the right and pointed. Wallander had already seen the pillar of smoke that rose to the sky.

They arrived a few minutes later. The plane had come down in the middle of a muddy field, about 100 metres from a farmhouse. The firefighters were still spraying foam on the wreck. Martinsson took a pair of wellingtons from the boot. Wallander looked unhappily down at his own shoes, a pair of winter boots, almost brand new. They started to make their way through the mud. The man in charge of the fire crew was Peter Edler. Wallander had met him on numerous occasions, and liked him. It was easy for them to work together. Apart from the two fire engines and the ambulance, there was also a patrol car.

Wallander nodded at Peters, a patrol officer. Then he turned to Edler. 'What do we have?' he asked.

'Two dead,' Edler replied. 'I have to warn you that it is not a pretty sight. That's what happens when people burn in petrol.'

'You don't have to warn me,' Wallander said. 'I know what that looks like.' Martinsson came up next to Wallander. 'Find out who made the call,'

Wallander said. 'Probably someone in that farm over there. Find out what the time was. And then someone has to have a serious talk with the control tower at Sturup.'

Martinsson nodded and set off towards the farm. Wallander approached the plane. It was lying on its left side, embedded in the mud. The left wing had been torn off and had broken into several parts that were strewn across the field. The right wing was still intact near the fuselage but had been broken off at the tip. Wallander observed that it was a single-engined plane. The propeller was bent and driven deep into the ground. He slowly circled the plane. It was black with soot and covered in foam. He waved Edler over.

'Is it possible to remove the foam?' he asked. 'Don't aeroplanes tend to have some kind of markings on the fuselage and under the wings?'

'I think we should let the foam stay on a while longer,' Edler said. 'You never know with petrol. There may still be some left in the fuel tank.'

Wallander knew he had to obey Edler's directives. He walked closer and peered into the plane. Edler had been right. It was impossible to discern any facial features. He circled the plane one more time. Then he lumbered out into the muddy field where the largest piece of wing lay. He crouched down. He could not make out any numbers or letter combinations. It was still very dark. He called out to Peters and asked for a torch. Then he studied the wing intently. Scraped the outside with his fingertips. It appeared to have been painted over. Could that mean that someone had wanted to conceal the identity of the plane?

He stood up. He was jumping to conclusions again. It was the job of Nyberg and his technical team to sort this out. He looked over absently at Martinsson, who was making his way to the farm with deliberate strides. Several cars with curious onlookers had pulled over on farmland. Peters and his partner were trying to convince them to keep going. Yet another police car had arrived, with Hansson, Rydberg and Nyberg. Wallander walked over and said hello. Explained the situation in brief and asked Hansson to cordon off the area.

'You have two bodies inside the plane,' Wallander repeated to Nyberg, who would be responsible for the preliminary forensic investigation.

Eventually, an accident commission would be appointed to investigate the cause of the crash. But at that point Wallander would no longer have to be involved.

'I think it looks as if the wing that was torn off had been repainted,' he said. 'As if someone wanted to eliminate all possibility of identifying the plane.'

Nyberg nodded mutely. He never wasted his words.

Rydberg appeared behind Wallander.

'One shouldn't have to tramp around in the mud at my age,' he said. 'And with this damned rheumatism.'

Wallander threw a quick glance at him. 'You didn't have to come out here,' he said. 'We can handle it.'

'I'm not dead yet,' Rydberg said with irritation. 'But who knows . . .' He didn't finish the sentence. Instead he made his way over to the plane, bent down and looked in. 'This one will have to be dental,' he said. 'I don't think there will be any other way of getting a positive ID.'

Wallander ran through the main points for Rydberg's benefit. They worked well together and never had to give each other lengthy explanations. Rydberg was also the one who had taught Wallander what he now knew about being a criminal investigator. They had worked together for many years, and Wallander had often thought that Rydberg must be one of the most skilful criminal investigators in Sweden. Nothing escaped him, no hypothesis was so outlandish that Rydberg did not test it. His ability to read a crime scene always surprised Wallander, who greedily absorbed it all.

Rydberg was single. He did not have much of a social life and did not appear to want one. Wallander, after all these years, was still not sure if Rydberg actually had any interests apart from his work.

On the occasional warm evening in early summer, they would sometimes get together and sit on Rydberg's balcony and drink whisky, often in a pleasant silence broken from time to time with some comment about work.

'Martinsson is trying to establish some clarity with regard to the time of the events,' Wallander said. 'Then it seems to me that we have to find out why the control tower at Sturup didn't raise the alarm.'

'You mean, why the pilot didn't raise the alarm,' Rydberg corrected him.

'Maybe he didn't have time?'

'It doesn't take many seconds to send an SOS,' Rydberg said. 'But you must be right. The plane would have been flying in an assigned air lane. If it wasn't flying illegally, of course.'

'Illegally?'

Rydberg shrugged. 'You know the rumours,' he said. 'People hear aeroplane noise at night. Low-flying, darkened planes slipping covertly into these areas close to the border. At least that's how it was during the Cold War. Perhaps it's not completely over yet. Sometimes we get reports about suspected espionage. And then you can always question if all drugs actually come in by sea. We will never know for sure about this plane. It may simply be our imagination. But if you fly low enough you escape the defence department's radar. And the control tower.'

'I'll drive in and talk to Sturup,' Wallander said.

'Wrong,' Rydberg said. 'I'll do that. I leave this mud to you, by the rights of my old age.'

Rydberg left. It was starting to get light. One of the technicians was photographing the wreck from various angles. Wallander saw Hansson talking to several reporters down on the farmland. He was happy not to have to do it himself. Then he spotted Martinsson tramping back through the mud. Wallander walked over to meet him.

'You were right,' Martinsson said. 'There's an old man in there who lives by himself. Robert Haverberg. Seventies, alone with nine dogs.'

'What did he say?'

'He heard the roar of a plane. Then it got quiet. And then the sound returned. But at that point it sounded more like a whine. And then he heard the crash.'

Wallander often felt that Martinsson was bad at formulating simple and clear explanations. 'Let's go over this again,' Wallander said. 'Robert Haverberg heard the engine noise?'

'Yes.'

'When was this?'

'He had just woken up. Sometime around five o'clock.'

Wallander frowned. 'But the plane crashed half an hour later?'

'That's what I said. But he was very firm on this point. First he heard the sound of a passing plane, at a low altitude. Then it grew quiet. He made some coffee. And then the sound returned, and then the explosion.'

Wallander reflected on this. 'How many minutes elapsed between the first time he heard the sound and the crash?'

'We worked out that it must have taken around twenty minutes.'

Wallander looked at Martinsson. 'How do you account for that?'

'I don't know.'

'Did the old man seem sharp?'

'Yes. He also has good hearing.'

'Do you have a map in your car?' Wallander asked.

Martinsson nodded. They walked up to where Hansson was still talking with the media. They got into Martinsson's car and unfolded the map. Wallander studied it in silence. He thought about what Rydberg had said, about aeroplanes on illegal missions.

'One could imagine the following,' Wallander said. 'A plane comes in low over the coast, passes by and continues out of earshot. Returns shortly thereafter. And then it goes straight down.'

'You mean it dropped something off somewhere? And then turned back?' Martinsson asked.

'Something like that.' Wallander folded the map back up. 'We know too little. Rydberg is on his way to Sturup. Then we have to try to identify the bodies, as well as the plane itself. We can't do any more at the moment.'

'I've always been a nervous flier,' Martinsson said. 'It doesn't exactly help to see things like this. But it's even worse when Teres talks about becoming a pilot.'

Teres was Martinsson's daughter. He also had a son. Martinsson was a real family man. He was always worried that something might have happened and called home several times a day. Often he went home for lunch. Sometimes Wallander was a little envious of his colleague's seemingly problem-free marriage.

'Tell Nyberg we're going now,' he said to Martinsson.

Wallander waited in the car. The landscape around him was grey and desolate. He shivered. Life goes on, he thought. I've just turned forty-two. Will I end up like Rydberg? A lonely old man with rheumatism?

Wallander shook off these thoughts.

Martinsson returned and they drove back to Ystad.

AT ELEVEN O'CLOCK Wallander stood up to go to the room where a suspected drug dealer by the name of Yngve Leonard Holm was waiting for him. At that moment Rydberg came in. He never bothered to knock. He sat down in the visitor's chair and got straight to the point. 'I've talked to an air-traffic controller by the name of Lycke,' he said. 'He claimed to know you.'

'I've spoken to him before, I don't remember the context.'

'He was very firm, in any case,' Rydberg continued. 'No single-engined plane was cleared to pass over Mossby at five o'clock this morning. Also, they have not received any emergency broadcast from any pilot. The radar screens have been empty. According to Lycke, the plane that crashed did not exist.'

'So you were right,' Wallander said. 'Someone was out there on an illegal mission.'

'We don't know that,' Rydberg objected. 'Someone was flying illegally. But if it was also an illegal mission, we don't know.'

'Who would be out there flying around in the dark without a particular reason?'

'There are so many idiots,' Rydberg said. 'You should know that.'

Wallander looked closer at him. 'You don't believe that, do you?'

'Of course not,' Rydberg said. 'But until we know who they were or identify the plane, we can't do anything. This has to go to Interpol. I'm willing to wager a pretty penny that the plane came from the outside.' Rydberg left.

Wallander mulled over what he had said. Then he stood up, took his papers and walked to the room where Yngve Leonard Holm was waiting with his lawyer. It was exactly a quarter past eleven when Wallander began his interrogation.

CHAPTER 2

Wallander turned off the tape recorder after an hour and ten minutes. He had had enough of Yngve Leonard Holm. Both because of the man's attitude and the fact that they were going to have to release him. Wallander was convinced that the man on the other side of the table was guilty of repeated and serious drug offences. But there was not one prosecutor in the world who would judge their evidence worthy of taking to court. Certainly not Per Åkeson, to whom Wallander was going to submit his report.

Yngve Leonard Holm was thirty-seven years old. He was born in Ronneby but had been registered as a resident of Ystad since the mid-1980s. He listed his profession as a paperback bookseller at outdoor summer markets. For the last few years he had declared a negligible income. At the same time, he was having a large villa built in an area close to the police station. The house was valued at several million kronor. Holm claimed to be financing the house with large gambling profits from horse racing. Predictably, he had no receipts for his wins. They had disappeared when the trailer where he had stored his financial records caught fire. The only receipt he could show was one for 4,993 kronor from a couple of weeks earlier.

Nothing of this altered Wallander's conviction that Holm was the final link in a chain that imported and sold significant amounts of drugs in southern Sweden. The circumstantial evidence was overwhelming. But Holm's arrest had been very poorly organised. The raids should have been synchronised to take place at the same time. One at Holm's house, the other at the warehouse in an industrial area in Malmö where he rented space for his paperbacks. It had been a coordinated operation between the police in Ystad and their colleagues in Malmö.

But something had gone wrong from the start. The warehouse space had been empty, except for a lone box of old, well-thumbed books. Holm had been watching TV in his house when they rang the bell. A young woman was curled up at his feet, massaging his toes, while the police searched the house. They found nothing. One of the sniffer dogs they had brought in had spent a long time sniffing a handkerchief they had found in the rubbish. Chemical analysis had only been able to establish that the cloth could have come into contact with a drug. In some way, Holm had been tipped off about the raid.

Wallander did not doubt that the man was both intelligent and good at covering up his activities. 'We have to let you go,' he said. 'But our suspicion of you remains. Or, to be precise, I'm convinced that you're involved in extensive drug trafficking in Skåne. Sooner or later, we will get you.'

The lawyer, who resembled a weasel, straightened up. 'My client doesn't have to put up with this,' he said. 'Slander of this kind against my client is inadmissible under the law.'

'Yes, of course it is,' Wallander said. 'You're very welcome to try to have me arrested.'

Holm, who was unshaven and appeared sick of the whole situation, stopped his lawyer from continuing. 'I understand that the police are simply doing their job,' he said. 'Unfortunately you made a mistake in directing your suspicions at me. I'm a simple citizen who knows a lot about horses and bookselling. Nothing else. Moreover, I regularly donate money to Save the Children.'

Wallander left the room. Holm would go home and have his feet massaged. Drugs would continue to stream into Skåne. We will never win this battle, Wallander thought as he walked down the corridor. The only room for hope is if future generations of young people reject it entirely.

It was now half past twelve. He felt hungry. He could see through the window that it had started to rain, and that there was snow mixed in with the rain. He pulled out a desk drawer and found the menu of a pizzeria that delivered. He eyed the menu without being able to decide on anything. Finally he closed his eyes and placed his index finger down at random. He called and ordered the pizza that fate had selected for him. Then he walked over to the window and stared at the water tower on the other side of the road.

The phone rang. He sat down at his desk and picked up. It was his father, calling from Löderup. 'I thought we had agreed that you would come here last night,' his father said.

Wallander sighed quietly. 'We didn't agree to anything.'

'Yes we did, I remember it very well,' his father said. 'You're the one who's starting to get forgetful. I thought the police had notepads. Can't you write down that you're planning to arrest me? Then maybe you'll remember.'

Wallander didn't have the energy to get angry. 'I'll come tonight,' he said. 'But we had *not* arranged that I was coming over last night.'

'It's possible I made a mistake,' his father replied, suddenly surprisingly meek.

'I'll be there around seven,' Wallander said. 'Right now I have a lot to do.' He hung up. My father engages in finely tuned emotional blackmail, he thought. And the worst thing about it is that he's continually successful.

The pizza arrived. Wallander paid and took the box back to the break room. Per Åkeson was sitting at a table eating some porridge. Wallander sat down across from him.

'I thought you were going to come and talk about Holm,' Åkeson said.

'And I will. But we had to release him.'

'That doesn't surprise me. The whole operation was exceedingly poorly executed.'

'You'll have to talk to Björk about that,' Wallander said. 'I wasn't involved.'

'I'm taking a sabbatical in three weeks,' Åkeson said.

'I haven't forgotten,' Wallander replied. 'I'm going to miss you.'

'Six months goes by fast. I have to admit that I'm looking forward to getting away for a while. I need to think.'

'I thought you were going to do some courses?'

'I am. But that won't stop me from thinking about the future. Should I continue as a public prosecutor for the rest of my life? Or is there something else I should do?'

'You could learn to sail and become a vagabond of the seas.'

Åkeson shook his head energetically. 'Nothing like that. But I am thinking about applying for something overseas. Perhaps in a project where one feels one is really making a difference. Perhaps I could be part of building a workable justice system where there was none before? In Czechoslovakia, for example.'

'I hope you write and tell me,' Wallander said. 'Sometimes I also wonder about the future, if I'm going to stay in this business until I retire. Or do something else.'

The pizza was tasteless. Åkeson, however, was tucking into his porridge with gusto. 'What's the story with that plane?' Åkeson asked.

Wallander told him what they knew.

'That sounds strange,' Åkeson said when Wallander had finished. 'Could it be drugs?'

'Yes, it could,' Wallander replied and regretted not having asked Holm if he owned a light aircraft. If he could afford to build a house he could probably afford to keep a private plane. Drug profits could be astronomical.

They stood at the sink together and cleaned their plates. Wallander had left half of his pizza uneaten. The divorce was still affecting his appetite.

'Holm is a criminal,' Wallander said. 'We'll get him sooner or later.'

'I'm not so sure of that,' Åkeson said. 'But of course I hope you're right.'

Wallander was back in his office a little after one o'clock. He considered calling Mona in Malmö. His daughter, Linda, lived with her right now. She was the one Wallander wanted to talk to. It had been almost a week since they talked last. She was nineteen and a little lost. Lately, she was back to thinking she wanted to become a furniture upholsterer.

Instead Wallander called Martinsson and asked him to come by. Together they went over the events of the morning. It was Martinsson who was going to write the report. 'People have called both from Sturup and the Department of Defence,' he said. 'There is something not right about that plane. It doesn't seem to have existed. And it seems you were right in thinking the wings and fuselage had been painted over.'

'We'll see what Nyberg comes up with,' Wallander said.

'The bodies are in Lund,' Martinsson went on. 'The only way we have of identifying them is through dental records. The bodies were so badly burned they fell to pieces when they were moved onto stretchers.'

'We'll have to wait and see, in other words,' Wallander said. 'I was going to suggest to Björk that you act as our representative in the accident commission. Do you have anything against that?'

'I'll always learn something new,' Martinsson said.

WHEN WALLANDER WAS alone again he ended up thinking about the difference between Martinsson and himself. Wallander's ambition had always been to become a good criminal investigator. And he had succeeded in this. But Martinsson had other ambitions. What tempted him was the post of chief of police in a not-too-distant future. To perform well in the field was for him only a step in his career.

Wallander dropped his thoughts about Martinsson, yawned, and listlessly pulled over the folder that was at the top of the pile on his desk. It still irritated him that he hadn't asked Holm about the plane. At least to get to see his reactions. But Holm was probably enjoying a delicious lunch at the Continental with his lawyer.

The folder remained unopened in front of Wallander. He decided he might as well talk to Björk, their chief of police, about Martinsson and the accident commission. He walked to the end of the corridor where Björk had his office. The door was open. Björk was on his way out.

'Do you have time?' Wallander asked.

'A few minutes. I'm on my way to a church to give a speech.'

Wallander knew that Björk was constantly giving lectures in the most unexpected settings. Apparently he loved performing in public, something that Wallander disliked intensely. Press conferences were a constant scourge. Wallander started to tell him about the morning's events, but apparently Björk had already been briefed. He had no objection to Martinsson's being appointed as police representative to the commission.

'I take it the plane was not shot down,' Björk said.

'Nothing so far indicates that it was anything other than an accident,' Wallander answered. 'But there is definitely something fishy about that flight.'

'We'll do what we can,' Björk said, indicating that the conversation was over. 'But we won't exert more of an effort than we have to. We have enough to do as it is.'

He left in a cloud of aftershave. Wallander shuffled back to his office. On the way he looked into Rydberg's and Hansson's offices. Neither was around. He got himself a cup of coffee and then spent some time reviewing an assault case that had occurred the week before in Skurup. New information had turned up that seemed to ensure that the man who had beaten up his sister-in-law could actually be charged with battery. Wallander organised the material and decided he would hand it over to Åkeson tomorrow.

It was a quarter to five. The police station seemed unusually deserted today. Wallander decided he would go home and get his car and then go shopping. He would still have time to make it to his father's by seven.

Wallander took his coat and walked home. The snow-slush had increased. When he got into his car he checked that he still had the grocery list in his pocket. The car was hard to start and he would soon have to get a new one. But where would he get the money? He managed to get the engine going and was about to put it in gear when he was struck by a thought. Even though he realised that what he wanted to do was meaningless, his curiosity proved too strong. He decided to put his shopping trip on hold. Instead he turned out onto Österleden and drove in the direction of Löderup.

The thought that had struck him was very simple. In a house just past the Strandskogen Forest, there lived a retired air-traffic controller Wallander had got to know a few years earlier. Linda had been friends with his youngest daughter. It occurred to Wallander that he might be able to answer a question that Wallander had been thinking about ever since he had stood next to the wrecked plane and listened to Martinsson's summary of his conversation with Haverberg.

Wallander turned into the driveway of the house where Herbert Blomell lived. As Wallander got out of his car, he saw Blomell standing on a ladder, in the process of repairing a gutter. He nodded pleasantly when he saw who it was and carefully climbed down onto the ground.

'A broken hip can be devastating at my age,' he said. 'How are things with Linda?'

'Fine,' Wallander said. 'She's with Mona in Malmö.'

They went in and sat in the kitchen.

'A plane crashed outside Mossby this morning,' Wallander said.

Blomell nodded and pointed to a radio on the windowsill.

'It was a Piper Cherokee,' Wallander continued. 'A single-engined plane. I know that you weren't just an air-traffic controller in your day. You also had a pilot's licence.'

'I've actually flown a Piper Cherokee a few times,' Blomell answered. 'A good plane.'

'If I put my finger on a map,' Wallander said, 'and then gave you a compass direction, and ten minutes, how far would you be able to fly the plane?'

'A matter of straightforward computation,' Blomell said. 'Do you have a map?' Wallander shook his head. Blomell stood up and left. Several minutes later he returned with a rolled-up map. They spread it out on the kitchen table. Wallander located the field that must have been the crash site.

'Imagine that the plane came straight in off the coast. The engine noise is heard here at one point. Then, at most, twenty minutes later, it returns. Of course, we cannot know that the pilot held the same course for the duration, but let us assume he did. How far did he go, then, in half that time? Before he turned round?'

'The Cherokee normally flies at around two hundred and fifty kilometres an hour,' Blomell said. 'If the load is of a normal weight.'

'We don't know about that.'

'Then let's assume maximum load and an average headwind.'

Blomell computed silently, then circled a spot north of Mossby. Wallander saw that it was close to Sjöbo.

'About this far,' Blomell said. 'But keep in mind that there are many unknowns included in this estimation.'

'Still, I know a lot more now than just a moment ago.' Wallander tapped his fingers on the table reflectively. 'Why does a plane crash?' he asked after a while.

'No two accidents are alike,' Blomell said. 'There may be basic reasons, such as errors in a plane's electrical wiring, or something. But in the end there is almost always some exceptional reason at the root of any given accident. And it almost always involves some degree of pilot error.'

'Why would a Cherokee crash?'

Blomell shook his head. 'The engine may have stalled. Poor maintenance. You'll have to wait and see what the accident commission comes up with.'

'The plane's identifying marks had been painted over, both on the fuselage and the wings,' Wallander said. 'What does that mean?'

'That it was someone who didn't want to be known,' Blomell said. 'There is a black market for aeroplanes just as for anything else.'

'I thought Swedish airspace was secure,' Wallander said. 'But you mean that planes can sneak in?'

'There is nothing in this world that is absolutely secure,' Blomell answered. 'Those who have enough money and enough motivation can always find their way across a border without interception.'

Blomell offered him a cup of coffee, but Wallander declined.

'I have to look in on my father in Löderup,' he said. 'If I'm late I'll never hear the end of it.'

'Loneliness is the curse of old age,' Blomell said. 'I miss my control tower with a physical ache. All night I dream of ushering planes through the air corridors. And when I wake up it's snowing and all I can do is repair a gutter.'

They took leave of each other outside. Wallander stopped at a grocery shop in Herrestad. He arrived at his father's house at three minutes to seven. The snow had stopped, but the clouds hung heavy over the countryside. Wallander saw the lights on in the little side building that his father used as a studio. He breathed in the fresh air as he walked across the yard. The door was ajar; his father had heard his car. He was sitting at his easel, an old hat on his head and his near-sighted eyes close to the painting he had just started. The smell of paint thinner always gave Wallander the same feeling of home. This is what is left of my childhood. The smell of paint thinner.

'You're on time,' his father observed without looking at him.

'I'm always on time,' Wallander said as he moved a couple of newspapers and sat down.

His father was working on a painting that featured a wood grouse. Just as Wallander had stepped into the studio he had placed a stencil onto the canvas and was painting a subdued sky at dusk. Wallander looked at him with a sudden feeling of tenderness. He is the last one in the generation before me, he thought. When he dies, I'll be the next to go.

His father put away his brushes and the stencil and stood up. They went into the main house. His father put on some coffee and brought some shot glasses to the table. Wallander hesitated, then nodded. He could allow himself one glass.

'Poker,' Wallander said. 'You owe me fourteen kronor from last time.'

His father looked closely at him. 'I think you cheat,' he said. 'But I still don't know how you do it.'

Wallander was taken aback. 'You think I'd cheat my own father?'

For once his father backed down. 'No,' he said. 'Not really. But you did win an unusual amount last time.'

The conversation died. They drank coffee. His father slurped as usual. This irritated Wallander as much as it always did.

'I'm going to go away,' his father said suddenly. 'Far away.'

'Where to?'

'To Egypt.'

'Egypt? What are you going to do there? I thought it was Italy you wanted to see.'

'Egypt and Italy. You never listen to what I say.'

'What are you going to do in Egypt?'

'I'm going to see the Sphinx and the pyramids. Time is running out. No one knows how long I will live. But I want to see the pyramids and Rome before I die.'

Wallander shook his head. 'Who are you going with?'

'I'm flying with Egypt Air, in a few days. Straight to Cairo. I'm going to stay in a very nice hotel called Mena House.'

'But you're going alone? Is it a charter trip? You can't be serious,' Wallander said in disbelief.

His father reached for some tickets on the windowsill. Wallander looked through them and realised that what his father said was true. He had a regular-fare flight ticket from Copenhagen to Cairo for December 14.

Wallander put the tickets down on the table. For once he was speechless.

WALLANDER LEFT Löderup at a quarter past ten. The clouds had started to break up. As he walked to the car he noticed that it had turned colder. This in turn would mean that the Peugeot would be harder to start than usual. But it wasn't the car that occupied his thoughts, it was the fact that he had not managed to talk his father out of taking the trip to Egypt. Or at least wait until a time when he could accompany him.

'You're almost eighty years old,' Wallander had insisted. 'At your age, you can't do this kind of thing.'

But his arguments had been hollow. There was nothing visibly wrong with his father's health. And even if he dressed unconventionally at times, he had a rare ability to adapt to new situations and the new people he met. When Wallander realised that the ticket included transfer from the airport to a hotel that was situated close to the pyramids, his concerns had slowly dissipated. He did not understand what drove his father to go to Egypt, to the Sphinx and the pyramids. But he couldn't deny that—many years ago now, when Wallander was still young—his father had actually told him many times about the marvellous structures on the Giza plateau, just outside Cairo.

Wallander paused with his hand on the car-door handle and drew in a breath of night air. I have a strange father, he thought. That's something I'll never escape.

Wallander had promised to drive him into Malmö on the morning of the 14th. He had made a note of the telephone number for Mena House, where his father would be staying. Since his father never spent money unnecessarily, he had not taken out any travel insurance, so Wallander was going to ask Ebba to take care of it tomorrow.

The car started reluctantly and he turned towards Ystad. He was back at Mariagatan shortly after eleven o'clock. When he unlocked the front door he saw that someone had slipped a letter through the letterbox. He opened the envelope and already knew who it was from. Emma Lundin, a nurse at the Ystad hospital. Wallander had promised to call her yesterday. She walked past his building on her way home to Dragongatan. Now she was wondering if something was wrong. Why had he not called her? Wallander felt guilty. He had met her a month before. They had fallen into conversation at the post office on Hamngatan. Then they had bumped into each other a few days later at the grocery shop and after only a couple of days they had started a relationship that was not particularly passionate on either side.

Emma was a year younger than Wallander, divorced with three children. Wallander had soon realised that the relationship meant more to her than to him. Without really daring to, he had started trying to extricate himself. As he stood in the hall now he knew why he hadn't called. He simply had no desire to see her. He put the letter down on the kitchen table and decided he had to end the relationship. It had no future, no potential. Wallander knew that he was looking for something completely different, someone completely different. Someone who would be able to replace Mona. If such a woman even existed. But above all it was Mona's return that he dreamed of.

He undressed and put on his old worn dressing gown. The phone rang. It was a quarter past eleven. He hoped that nothing serious had occurred that would make him have to get dressed again. It was Linda. As always, it made him happy to hear her voice.

'Where have you been?' she asked. 'I've been calling all evening.'

'You could have guessed,' he replied. 'And you could have called your grandfather. That's where I was.'

'I didn't think of that,' she said. 'You never go to see him.'

'I don't?'

'That's what he says.'

'He says a lot of things. By the way, he's going to fly to Egypt in a few days to see the pyramids.'

'Sounds fun. I wouldn't mind going along.'

Wallander said nothing. He listened to her lengthy narrative about how she had spent the past couple of days. He was pleased that she had now clearly committed herself to a career in upholstering furniture. He assumed that Mona was not home since she would normally get irritated when Linda talked so much and for so long on the phone. But he also felt a pang of jealousy. Even though they were now divorced, he could not reconcile himself to the thought of her seeing other men. The conversation ended with Linda promising to meet him in Malmö and see her grandfather off for his trip to Egypt.

ON THE MORNING of December 12, the temperature had sunk to –4°C. Wallander was sitting in the kitchen, just before seven o'clock, when the telephone rang. It was Blomell.

'I hope I didn't wake you,' he said.

'I was up,' Wallander said, coffee cup in hand.

'Something occurred to me after you left,' Blomell went on. 'I was thinking that for someone to hear the engine outside Mossby the plane must have been at a very low altitude. That should mean that others heard it. In that way you should be able to find out where it went. And perhaps you might even find someone who heard it turn round in the air and head back.'

Blomell was right. Wallander should have thought of it himself. But he did not say this. 'We're already on it,' he said instead.

'That was all,' Blomell said. 'How was your father?'

'He told me he's taking a trip to Egypt.'

'That sounds like a wonderful idea.'

Wallander didn't answer.

'It's getting colder,' Blomell concluded. 'Winter is on its way.'

'Soon we'll have snowstorms upon us,' Wallander said.

He went back to the kitchen, thinking about what Blomell had said. Martinsson could get in touch with colleagues in Tomelilla and Sjöbo. It might be possible to pinpoint the plane's route and destination by looking for people who were early risers and who had noticed an engine noise overhead, twice in a row if they were lucky. Surely there were still some dairy farmers around who were up at that time of day?

A little before eight o'clock Wallander walked in through the doors of the station. He was wearing the sweater he reserved for days of up to –5°C. He asked Ebba to arrange travel insurance for his father.

'That has always been my dream,' she said. 'To go to Egypt and see the pyramids.'

Everyone seems to be envious of my father, Wallander thought as he poured himself a cup of coffee and went to his office. No one even seems surprised. I'm the only one who's worried that something will happen. That he'll get lost in the desert, for example.

Martinsson had placed a report on his desk about the accident. Wallander eyed it quickly and thought that Martinsson was still far too verbose. Half as much would have been enough. He called Martinsson and told him about his conversation with Björk the day before. Martinsson seemed pleased. Then Wallander suggested a meeting. What Blomell had said was worth following up. Martinsson managed to locate Hansson and Detective Svedberg at half past eight. But Rydberg had still not arrived. They filed into one of the conference rooms.

'Has anyone seen Nyberg?' Wallander asked.

Nyberg walked in at that moment. As always, he appeared to have been up all night. His hair was standing on end. He sat in his usual seat, somewhat apart from the others.

'Rydberg seems ill,' Svedberg said, scratching his bald spot with a pencil.

'He is ill,' Hansson said. 'He has sciatica.'

'Rheumatism,' Wallander corrected. 'There's a big difference.'

Then he turned to Nyberg.

'We've examined the wings,' the latter said. 'And washed away the fire-retardant foam and tried to puzzle the pieces of the fuselage back together. The numbers and letters had not only been painted over, they had also been scraped away beforehand. The people on board definitely did not want to be traced.'

'I imagine there is a number on the engine,' Wallander said. 'And of course not as many planes are manufactured as cars.'

'We're getting in touch with the Piper factory in the United States,' Martinsson said.

'There are some other questions that need to be answered,' Wallander went on. 'How far can a plane like this fly on one tank of fuel? How common are additional fuel tanks?'

Martinsson wrote this down. 'I'll get the answers,' he said.

The door opened and Rydberg came in. 'I've been to the hospital,' he said curtly, 'and things always take a long time there.'

Wallander could see that he was in pain but said nothing.

Instead, he presented the idea of trying to find others who might have heard the engine noise. He felt a little ashamed that he did not give Blomell credit for this insight.

'This will be like in wartime,' Rydberg commented. 'When everyone in Skåne walked around and listened for planes.'

'It's possible it won't yield anything,' Wallander said. 'But there's no harm in checking with our colleagues in nearby districts. Personally I have trouble believing it could have been anything other than a drug transport. An arranged drop somewhere.'

'We should talk to Malmö,' Rydberg said. 'If they've noticed that the supply seems to have increased dramatically, there could be a connection. I'll call them.'

No one had any objections. Wallander brought the meeting to a close shortly after nine o'clock.

He spent the rest of the morning concluding work on the assault case in Skurup and presenting the findings to Per Åkeson. At lunchtime he went into the town centre and bought a hot-dog special from a stand. He was back at the station at a quarter past two. Everywhere still seemed deserted. Wallander continued to work through his pile of paper. After the assault in Skurup came a burglary in central Ystad, on Pilgrimsgatan. Someone had broken a window in the middle of the day and emptied the house of various valuables. Wallander shook his head as he read through Svedberg's report. It was unbelievable that none of the neighbours had seen anything.

Is this fear starting to spread even in Sweden? he wondered. The fear of assisting the police with the most elementary observations. If so, then the situation is far worse than I have wanted to believe.

Wallander struggled on with the material and made notes on who should be questioned and which searches should be made in the files. But he had no illusions that they would be able to solve the burglary case without a large dose of luck or reliable witnesses' accounts.

Martinsson walked into his office shortly before five. 'Sjöbo actually did have something to say,' Martinsson began. 'A man had been out looking for a lost bull calf all night. He called the police in Sjöbo that morning and said he had seen strange lights and heard an engine noise shortly after five.'

'Strange lights? What did he mean by that?'

'I've asked our Sjöbo colleagues to interview the man in more detail. Fridell was his name.'

Wallander nodded. 'Lights and engine noise. That could confirm our hypothesis about a scheduled drop.'

Martinsson spread out a map on Wallander's desk. He pointed. Wallander saw that it was in the area that Blomell had circled.

'Good work,' Wallander said. 'We'll have to see if it leads us anywhere.'

Martinsson folded up the map. 'It's terrible if it's true,' he said. 'If this really is the case then we're unprotected. If any old plane can come in across the border and drop off drugs without being sighted.'

'We have to get used to it,' Wallander said. 'But of course I agree with you.'

Martinsson left. Wallander left the station a little later. When he got home he cooked a real dinner for once, and had a shower while he waited for the potatoes to boil. At half past seven he sat down with a cup of coffee to watch the news. The phone rang as the top stories were being announced. It was Emma, just leaving the hospital. Wallander didn't really know what he wanted. Another evening alone. Or a visit from Emma. Without being sure that he really wanted to see her, he asked if she wanted to stop by. She said yes. Wallander knew this meant that she would stay until a little after midnight. Then she would get dressed and go home. In order to steel himself for the visit he had two glasses of whisky. He changed the sheets on the bed and threw the old bed linen into the wardrobe, which was already over-flowing with dirty laundry.

Emma arrived shortly before eight. Wallander cursed himself when he heard her on the stairs. Why couldn't he put an end to it, since it had no future?

She arrived, she smiled and Wallander asked her in. She had brown hair and beautiful eyes, and was short. He put on the kind of music he knew she liked. They drank wine and shortly before eleven they went to bed. Wallander thought of Mona.

Afterwards they both fell asleep. Neither of them had said anything. Just before he fell asleep, Wallander noticed a headache coming on. He woke up again when she was getting dressed, but he pretended to be asleep. When the front door had shut, he got out of bed and drank some water. Then he returned to bed, thought about Mona again, and fell back asleep.

The telephone started to ring deep inside his dreams. He woke immediately. Listened. The rings continued. He glanced at the clock on the bedside table. A quarter past two. That meant that something had happened. He lifted the receiver as he sat up in bed.

It was one of the officers who worked the night shift, Näslund.

'There's a fire on Möllegatan,' Näslund told him. 'Right on the corner of Lilla Strandgatan.'

'What's burning?'

'The Eberhardsson sisters' sewing shop.'

'That sounds like a case for the fire brigade and a patrol unit.'

'They're already there. It sounds like the house may have exploded. And the sisters live above the shop.'

'Did they get out?'

'It doesn't look like it.'

Wallander didn't need to think any further. He knew there was only one thing to do. 'I'm coming,' he said. 'Who else have you called?'

'Rydberg.'

'You could have let him sleep. Get Svedberg and Hansson.'

Wallander hung up. Checked the time again. Seventeen minutes past two. While he put his clothes on he thought about what Näslund had said. A sewing shop had been blown up. That sounded implausible. And it was serious if the two owners had not managed to escape.

He walked out onto the street and realised he had forgotten his car keys. He cursed, then ran back up the stairs, noticing how out of breath he became. I should start playing badminton with Svedberg again, he thought. I can't manage four flights without getting puffed.

Wallander pulled up on Hamngatan at half past two. The whole area had been blocked off. The smell of fire was perceptible before he even opened the car door. Flames and smoke were rising into the sky. The fire brigade had all their engines on the scene. Wallander ran into Peter Edler for the second time that week.

'It looks bad,' Edler shouted, raising his voice to be heard above the din. The whole house was in flames. The fire-fighters were spraying the surrounding buildings to restrict the damage.

'The sisters?' Wallander shouted.

Edler shook his head. 'No one has come out,' he replied. 'If they were home, they're still in there. We have a witness who says the building just blew up. It started to burn everywhere at once.'

Edler left to continue directing the operation. Hansson appeared at Wallander's side.

'Who the hell sets fire to a sewing shop?' he asked.

Wallander shook his head. He had no answer.

He thought about the two sisters who had worked in their sewing shop for as long as he had lived in Ystad. Once, he and Mona had bought a zip there for one of his suits.

Now the sisters were gone.

And if Edler was not completely mistaken, this fire had been started in order to kill them.

CHAPTER 3

Wallander rang in this St Lucia's Day, 1989, with lights other than those of a children's candlelit Lucia procession. He stayed at the scene of the blaze until dawn. By then he had sent home both Svedberg and Hansson. When Rydberg turned up, Wallander also told him to go home. The night cold would do nothing for his rheumatism. Peter Edler gave Wallander a cup of coffee. Wallander sat in the driver's cab in one of the fire engines and wondered why he didn't simply go home and sleep instead of staying here, waiting for the fire to be put out. He didn't manage to come up with a good answer. He thought back to the evening before, with discomfort. The erotic side of his relationship with Emma Lundin was completely devoid of passion. Hardly more than an extension of their earlier inane conversations.

I can't go on like this, he thought suddenly. Something has to happen in my life. Soon, very soon.

The fire was out at dawn. The building had burned to the ground. Nyberg arrived. They waited for Peter Edler to give the go-ahead for Nyberg to enter the smouldering remains with the fire brigade's own team of forensic technicians.

Then Björk turned up, impeccably dressed as usual, accompanied by a scent of aftershave that managed to overpower even the smoke.

'Fires are tragic,' he said. 'I hear the owners have died.'

'We don't know that yet,' Wallander said. 'But there are no indications to the contrary, unfortunately.'

Björk looked at his watch. 'I have to push on,' he said. 'I have a Rotary Club breakfast meeting.' He left.

Wallander and Nyberg stood quietly, waiting. Wallander felt cold and tired. The whole block was still closed to traffic, but a reporter Wallander recognised had managed to duck his way past the barriers. He was one of the reporters who usually wrote what Wallander actually said, so he was given the little information they had. They still could not confirm that anyone had died. The reporter let himself be satisfied with this.

Another hour went by before Edler could give them the green light. When Wallander had left home in the early hours that morning, he had been smart enough to put on rubber boots, and now he stepped carefully into the scorched rubble where beams and the remains of walls lay jumbled in a mess of water. Nyberg and some of the fire-fighters carefully made their way through the ruins. After less than five minutes, they stopped. Nyberg nodded for Wallander to come.

The bodies of two people lay a few metres away from each other. They were charred beyond the point of recognition. It occurred to Wallander that he had now experienced this sight for the second time in forty-eight hours. He shook his head.

'The Eberhardsson sisters,' he said. 'What were their first names?'

'Anna and Emilia,' Nyberg answered. 'But we don't yet know if it is actually them.'

'Who else would it be?' Wallander said. 'They lived alone in this house.'

'We'll find out,' Nyberg said. 'But it will take a couple of days.'

Wallander turned and went back out onto the street. Edler was smoking.

'You smoke?' Wallander said. 'I didn't know that.'

'Not very often,' Edler replied. 'Only when I'm very tired.'

'There must be a thorough examination of this fire,' Wallander said.

'I shouldn't jump to conclusions,' Edler said, 'but this looks like nothing less than deliberate arson. Though one may wonder why anyone wanted to take the lives of two old spinsters.'

Wallander nodded. He knew that Edler was an extremely competent fire chief.

'Two old ladies,' Wallander remarked. 'Who sold buttons and zips.'

There was no longer any reason for Wallander to stay. He left the scene, got in his car and went home. He made himself breakfast and conferred with the thermometer about which sweater to wear. He decided on the same one as yesterday. At twenty minutes past nine he was outside the police station, parking the car. Martinsson arrived at the same time.

They halted in the reception area and Ebba came over to them.

'Is it true what I hear?' she asked. 'That poor Anna and Emilia have burned to death?'

'That's what it looks like,' Wallander said.

Ebba shook her head. 'I've bought buttons and thread from them since 1951,' she said. 'They were always so friendly. If you needed anything extra, they always took care of it with no additional charge. Who on earth would want to take the lives of two old ladies in a sewing shop?'

'Is it a pyromaniac?' Martinsson asked.

'We'll have to wait and see,' Wallander replied. 'Has anything more come in about the crashed plane?'

'Not as far as I know. But Sjöbo was going to have another talk with the man who was looking for his calf.'

'Call the other districts just to be sure,' Wallander reminded him. 'It could turn out that they received calls about an engine noise too.'

Martinsson left. Ebba gave Wallander a piece of paper.

'The travel insurance for your father,' she said. 'Lucky man, he gets to leave this weather and see the pyramids.'

Wallander took the paper and went to his office. When he had hung up his coat, he called Löderup. There was no answer. His father must be out in the studio. Wallander put down the phone. I wonder if he remembers that he's supposed to travel tomorrow, he thought. And that I'm picking him up at seven o'clock. But Wallander was looking forward to spending a couple of hours with Linda. That always put him in a good mood.

He pulled over a pile of papers, this one about the burglary on Pilgrimsgatan. But he ended up lost in thought about other things. What if they had a pyromaniac on their hands? They had been spared that for the past couple of years. He forced himself to return to the burglary, but Nyberg called at ten thirty.

'I think you should come down here,' he said. 'To the scene of the fire.'

Wallander knew Nyberg would not have called unless it was important. It would be a waste of time to start asking questions over the phone. 'I'm on my way,' he said and hung up.

He picked up his coat and left the station. It took him only a couple of minutes by car to get downtown. Nyberg was waiting next to the ruins of the house, which were still smoking. He got straight to the point. 'This was not only arson,' he said. 'It was murder.'

'Murder?'

Nyberg gestured for him to follow. The two bodies in the ruin had now been dug out. They crouched down next to one and Nyberg pointed to the cranium with a pen. 'A bullet hole,' he said. 'She's been shot, assuming it is one of the sisters.'

They stood up and walked over to the second body.

'Same thing here,' he said and pointed. 'Just above the neck.'

Wallander shook his head in disbelief. 'Someone shot them?'

'Looks like it. What's worse is that it was execution-style. Two shots to the back of the head.'

Wallander had trouble taking in what Nyberg had just said. It was too preposterous, too brutal. But he also knew that Nyberg never said anything he wasn't absolutely sure about.

They walked back out to the street. Nyberg held up a small plastic bag in front of Wallander.

'We found one of the bullets,' he said. 'It was still stuck in the cranium. The other one exited through the forehead and has melted in the heat.'

Wallander looked at Nyberg while he tried to think. 'So we have a double murder that someone tried to cover up with a fire?'

Nyberg shook his head. 'That doesn't make sense. A person who executes people by shooting them in the back of the head most likely knows that fires normally leave skeletons intact. After all, it's not a crematorium.'

'What's the alternative?'

'The murderer may have wanted to conceal something else.'

'What can you conceal in a sewing shop?'

'That's your job to figure out,' Nyberg replied.

'I'll go and get a team together,' Wallander said. 'We'll start at one.' He checked his watch. It was eleven. 'Can you make it?'

'I won't be done here, of course,' Nyberg said. 'But I'll come by.'

Wallander returned to his car. He was filled with a feeling of unreality. Who could have a motive for executing two old ladies who sold needles and thread and one or two zips? This was beyond anything he had been involved in before.

When he reached the station he walked straight to Rydberg's office. It was empty. Wallander found him in the break room, where he was eating a dry-looking biscuit and drinking tea. Wallander sat down and told him what Nyberg had discovered.

'That's not good,' Rydberg said when Wallander was finished. 'Not good at all.'

Wallander stood up. 'I'll see you at one,' he said. 'For now, let Martinsson focus on the plane. But Hansson and Svedberg should be there. And try to get Åkeson. Have we ever had anything like this?'

Rydberg considered. 'Not that I can remember.'

Wallander lingered at the table.

'Execution-style,' he said. 'Not particularly Swedish.'

'And what is Swedish, exactly?' Rydberg asked. 'There are no longer any borders. Not for aeroplanes nor serious criminals. Once Ystad lay at the outskirts of something. What happened in Stockholm did not happen here. But that time is over.'

'What happens now?'

'The new era will need a different kind of police, particularly out in the field,' Rydberg said. 'But there will still be a need for those like you and me, the ones who can think.'

They walked together along the corridor. Rydberg walked slowly. They parted outside Rydberg's door.

'One o'clock,' Rydberg said. 'The double murder of two old ladies. Is that what we should call this? The case of the little old ladies?'

'I don't like it,' Wallander said. 'I don't understand why anyone would shoot two honourable old ladies.'

'That may be where we have to begin,' Rydberg said thoughtfully. 'By examining if they were actually as honourable as everyone appears to believe.'

Wallander was taken aback. 'What are you insinuating?'

'Nothing,' Rydberg said, and smiled suddenly. 'It's possible that one sometimes draws conclusions too quickly.'

Wallander stood by the window in his office and absent-mindedly watched some pigeons flapping around the water tower. Rydberg is right, he thought. As usual. If there are no witnesses, if we can't come up with any observations from outside, then this is where we have to start: who were they really, Anna and Emilia?

THEY WERE ALL assembled in the conference room at one o'clock. Wallander gave an account of the discovery that the two women had been shot. A sombre mood spread through the room. Evidently everyone had been to the sewing shop at least once. Then Wallander turned to Nyberg.

'We're still digging around in the rubble,' Nyberg said. 'But so far we haven't found anything of interest.'

'The cause of the fire?' Wallander asked.

'It's too early to tell,' he replied. 'But according to the neighbours there was a loud blast. Someone described it as a muted explosion. And then, within the span of a minute, the whole building was on fire.'

Wallander looked around the table. 'Since there is no immediately apparent motive, we have to begin by finding out what we can about these sisters. Is it true, as I believe, that they didn't have any relatives? Both were single. Had they ever been married? How old were they? I thought of them as old ladies already when I moved here.'

Svedberg answered that he was sure that Anna and Emilia had never been married, and that they had no children. But he would find out more in greater detail.

'Bank accounts,' said Rydberg, who had not said anything until then. 'Did they have money? Either stuffed under the mattress at home or at the bank. There are rumours about such things. Can that have been the reason for the murder?'

'That doesn't explain the execution-style method,' Wallander said. 'But we need to find out about this. We need to know.'

They divvied up the usual tasks among themselves. When it was a quarter past two, Wallander had only one more thing to say. 'We need to speak to the media,' he said. 'This will interest them. Björk should be present, of course. But I would be happy to get out of it.'

To everyone's surprise, Rydberg offered to speak to the reporters. Normally he was as reticent as Wallander on such occasions.

They broke up. Nyberg returned to the fire scene. Wallander and Rydberg stayed behind for a moment.

'I think we have to place some hope in the public,' Rydberg said. 'More than we usually do. It's clear that there must have been a motive for killing these sisters. And I have trouble thinking it could have been anything other than money.'

'We've encountered this before,' Wallander said. 'People who don't own a penny but who get attacked because there are rumours of wealth.'

'I have some contacts,' Rydberg said. 'I'll do a little investigating on the side.'

They left the room.

'Why did you take on the press conference?' Wallander asked.

'So that you wouldn't have to do it for once,' Rydberg said and went to his office.

Wallander managed to reach Björk, who was at home with a migraine. 'We're planning a press conference at five o'clock today,' Wallander said. 'We're all hoping you can be there.'

'I'll be there,' Björk said. 'Migraine or not.'

The investigative machine had been set in motion, slow but thorough. Wallander went back to the scene of the fire once more and talked to Nyberg, who was up to his knees in rubble. Then he returned to the station. But when the press conference started, he stayed away. He arrived home around six o'clock. This time his father answered when Wallander called.

'I've already packed,' his father said.

'I should hope so,' Wallander said. 'I'll be there at half past six. Don't forget your passport and tickets.'

Wallander spent the rest of the evening consolidating what they knew of the previous evening's events. He went to bed at midnight. He had trouble falling asleep even though he was very tired.

The thought of the two sisters who had been executed worried him.

Before he fell asleep at last, he had managed to convince himself that it would be a long and difficult investigation. If they did not have the good fortune of tripping over the answer at the very beginning.

THE FOLLOWING DAY he got up at five. At exactly half past six he turned into the driveway in Löderup.

His father was sitting outside on his suitcase, waiting.

They drove to Malmö in darkness. The daily commute from the Skåne region into Malmö had not yet begun in earnest. His father was wearing a suit and a strange-looking pith helmet. Wallander had never seen it before and thought that his father must have picked it up at a flea market or a second-hand shop. But he said nothing. He didn't even ask if his father had remembered to bring his tickets or his passport. 'You're really going,' was all he said.

'Yes,' his father replied. 'This is the day.'

Wallander could sense that his father did not want to talk. It gave him the opportunity to focus on his driving and lose himself in his own thoughts. He was worried about the recent developments in Ystad. Wallander tried to get a handle on it. Why someone would coldbloodedly shoot two old ladies in the back of the head. But he drew a blank. There was no context, no explanation. Only these brutal and incomprehensible executions.

As they turned into the small car park by the ferry terminal, they saw Linda already waiting outside. Wallander noticed that he didn't like how she greeted her grandfather first, then her father. She commented on her grandfather's pith helmet, saying she thought it suited him.

'I wish I had as nice a hat to show off,' Wallander said as he hugged his daughter.

They accompanied his father into the terminal. Wallander paid for his ferry ticket. Once he had climbed aboard, they stood in the darkness and watched the vessel chug out through the harbour.

'I hope I'll be like him when I'm old,' Linda said.

Wallander did not reply. To become like his father was something he feared more than anything.

They had breakfast together at the Central Station restaurant. Wallander watched his daughter, who talked almost continuously. She was not really beautiful in the traditional sense of the word. But there was something confident and independent about her manner. She did not belong among the scores of young women who did their utmost to please all the men they met. From whom she had inherited her loquaciousness he could not say. Both he and Mona were rather quiet. But he liked listening to her. It always raised his spirits. She continued to talk about going into the business of restoring furniture. Informed him of the possibilities in the field, what the challenges were, cursed the fact that the apprenticeship system had almost died out, and astonished him at the end by imagining a future where she set up her own shop in Ystad.

'It's too bad that neither you nor Mum have any money,' she said. 'Then I could have gone to France to learn.'

Wallander realised she was not in fact chastising him for not being wealthy. Nonetheless, he took it this way. 'I could take out a loan,' he said. 'I think a simple policeman can manage that.'

'Loans have to be paid back,' she said. 'And anyway, you are actually a detective inspector.'

Then they talked about Mona. Wallander listened, not without some satisfaction, to her complaints about Mona, who controlled her daughter in everything she did.

'And to top it off I don't like Johan,' she finished.

Wallander looked searchingly at her.

'Who's that?'

'Her new guy.'

'I thought she was seeing someone called Sören?'

'They broke up. Now his name is Johan and he owns two diggers.'

'And you don't like him?'

She shrugged. 'He's so loud. And I don't think he's ever read a book in his life. On Saturdays he comes over and he's bought some comic book. A grown man. Can you imagine?'

Wallander felt a momentary relief at the fact that he had never bought a comic book. 'That doesn't sound so good,' he said. 'I mean, that you and Johan don't get along.'

'It's not so much a question of us,' she said. 'It's more that I don't understand what Mum sees in him.'

'Come and live with me,' Wallander said impulsively. 'Your room is still there, you know that.'

'I've actually thought about it,' she said. 'But I don't think that would be a good idea.'

'Why not?'

'Ystad is too small. It would drive me crazy to live there. Maybe later, when I'm older. There are towns where you simply can't live when you're young.'

Wallander knew what she was talking about. Even for divorced men in their forties, a town like Ystad could start to feel cramped.

'What about you?' she asked.

'What do you mean?'

'What do you think? Women, of course.'

Wallander made a face. He didn't want to bring up Emma Lundin.

'You could put an ad in the paper,' she suggested. '"A man in his best years looking for a woman." You would get a lot of responses.'

'Sure,' Wallander said, 'and then it would take five minutes before we'd simply end up sitting there staring vacantly at each other, realising we have nothing to say.'

She surprised him again.

'You need to have someone to sleep with,' she said. 'It's not good for you to walk around with so much pent-up longing.'

Wallander winced. She had never said anything like that to him before. 'I have all I need,' he said evasively.

'Can't you tell me more?'

'There's not much to say. A nurse. A decent person. The problem is just that she likes me more than I like her.'

Linda did not ask any more questions. Wallander started to wonder about her sex life. But the very thought filled him with so many ambivalent feelings that he didn't want to get into it.

They stayed in the restaurant until it was past ten o'clock. Then he offered to drive her home, but she had errands to run. They parted in the car park, and Wallander gave her 300 kronor.

'You don't need to do this,' she said.

'I know. But take it anyway.'

Then he watched her walk off into the city. Thought that this was his family. A daughter who was finding her way. And a father who was right now sitting on a plane taking him to scorching-hot Egypt. He had a complicated relationship with both of them.

HE WAS BACK in Ystad at half past ten. When he walked into the reception area, Ebba called out to him. She looked a little tense. 'Björk wants to talk to you,' she said.

Wallander hung his coat up in his office, then walked to Björk's room. He was let in at once. Björk stood up behind his desk.

'I have to express my great dismay,' he said.

'With what?'

'That you go to Malmö on personal business when we are in the midst of a difficult murder case, one that you moreover are in charge of.'

Wallander could not believe his ears. Björk was actually reprimanding him. That had never happened before, even if Björk had often had ample reason to do so on previous occasions. Wallander thought about all the times that he had acted too independently during an investigation, without informing the others.

'This is extremely unfortunate,' Björk concluded. 'There will be no formal reprimand. But it was, as I said, a show of poor judgment.'

Wallander stared at Björk. Then he made an about-turn and left without saying a word. But when he was halfway back to his office, he turned and walked back, pulling open the door to Björk's office and saying, through clenched teeth, 'I'm not going to take any rubbish from you. Just so you know. Give me a formal reprimand if you want. But don't stand there talking nonsense. I won't take it.'

Then he left. He noticed that he was sweating. But he didn't regret it. The outburst had been necessary. And he was not at all worried about the consequences. His position at the station was strong.

He got a cup of coffee in the break room and then sat down at his desk. He knew that Björk had gone to Stockholm to take a leadership course of some kind. He had probably learned he should scold his colleagues from time to time in order to improve the climate of the workplace, Wallander thought. But if so, he had chosen the wrong person to start with.

Then he wondered who had passed on the fact that Wallander had spent the morning driving his father to Malmö. There were several possibilities. Wallander could not recall to whom he had mentioned his father's impending trip to Egypt.

The only thing he was sure of was that it was not Rydberg. The latter regarded Björk as a necessary administrative evil. Hardly anything more. And he was always loyal to those he worked with. His loyalty would never be corrupted, though of course he would not spare his colleagues if they acted irresponsibly. Then Rydberg would be the first to react.

Wallander was interrupted in this train of thought by Martinsson, who looked in. 'Is this a good time?'

Wallander nodded at his visitor's chair.

They began by talking about the fire and the murder of the Eberhardsson sisters. But Wallander soon realised that Martinsson had come in about something different.

'It's about the plane,' he said. 'Our Sjöbo colleagues have worked quickly. They've located an area just southwest of the village where lights were allegedly observed that night. From what I gather, it's a fairly uninhabited area. That could also corroborate the idea of an airdrop.'

'You mean that the lights would have been guiding lights?'

'That is one possibility. There's also a myriad of small roads through that area. Easy to get to, easy to leave.'

'That strengthens our theory,' Wallander said.

'I have more,' Martinsson went on. 'The Sjöbo team has checked to see who actually lives in that area. Most of them are farmers, of course, but they found one exception.'

Wallander sharpened his attention.

'A farm called Långelunda,' Martinsson said. 'For a couple of years it's been a haven for a variety of people who have caused problems for the Sjöbo police from time to time. People have moved in and out, the ownership has been unclear and there have been drug seizures. Not great quantities, but still.' He scratched his forehead. 'The colleague I spoke with, Göran Brunberg, gave me a few names. I wasn't paying that much attention, but when I hung up I started thinking. There was one name I thought I recognised. From a case we had recently.'

Wallander sat up. 'You don't mean that Yngve Leonard Holm lives up there? That he has a place there?'

Martinsson nodded.

'He's the one. It took a while for me to put it together.'

Damn it, Wallander thought. I knew there was something about him. But we had to let him go. 'We'll bring him in,' Wallander said and banged a fist firmly on his desk.

'That was exactly what I told our Sjöbo colleagues when I made the connection,' Martinsson said. 'But when they got out to Långelunda, Holm was gone.'

'What do you mean, "gone"?'

'Disappeared, gone, vanished. He did live there, even if he was registered in Ystad for the last couple of years. And built his mansion here. Our Sjöbo colleagues talked to a couple of other individuals living there. Rough types, from what I gather. Holm was there as recently as yesterday. But no one has seen him since then. I went to his house here in Ystad, but it's locked up.'

Wallander thought it over. 'So Holm doesn't usually disappear like this?'

'The people in the house actually seemed a little concerned.'

'In other words, there could be a connection,' Wallander said.

'I was thinking that Holm may have been intending to leave on the plane that crashed.'

'Not likely,' Wallander said. 'Then you're assuming the plane had somewhere to land and pick him up. And the Sjöbo police haven't found any place like that, have they? An improvised landing strip? It would also exceed the time frame.'

'A light aircraft with a skilled pilot might only need a small level area to land and take off from.'

Wallander hesitated. Martinsson could be right. 'We'll have to continue working on this,' he said. 'Unfortunately, you'll be more or less alone on it. The rest of us have to focus on the murdered sisters.'

'Have you found a possible motive?'

'We have nothing other than an incomprehensible execution and an explosive fire,' Wallander replied. 'But if there's anything to be found in the remains of the fire, Nyberg will get it.'

Martinsson left. Wallander noticed that his thoughts were alternating between the downed plane and the fire. It was two o'clock. His father would have landed in Cairo by now, if his plane had left on time from Kastrup. Then he thought about Björk's strange behaviour. He felt himself getting upset again and at the same time felt pleased that he had given his boss a piece of his mind.

Since he was having trouble concentrating on his paperwork he drove down to the scene of the fire. Nyberg was on his knees in the rubble together with the other technicians. The smell of smoke was still strong. Nyberg saw Wallander and made his way out onto the street.

'The fire burned with an intense heat, according to Edler's people,' he said. 'Everything appears to have melted. And that of course strengthens the suspicion of arson, about a fire started in several places at once. Perhaps with the help of petrol.'

'We have to get the people who did this,' Wallander said.

'That would be a good thing,' Nyberg said. 'One gets the feeling that this is the work of a madman.'

'Or the opposite,' Wallander said. 'Someone who really knew what he was after.'

'In a sewing shop? Run by two old unmarried sisters?'

Nyberg shook his head disbelievingly and returned to the ruins. Wallander walked down to the harbour. He needed some air. It was a couple of degrees below freezing and there was almost no breeze. He walked out onto the pier in the yacht harbour. A ferry to Poland was just leaving the large terminal that lay adjacent to it. Absent-mindedly he questioned how many cars were being smuggled out of Sweden this time.

He returned to the station at half past three. He wondered if his father had reached the hotel and settled in. And if he would receive a new reprimand from Björk for an unexplained absence.

At four o'clock he gathered with his colleagues in the conference room. They reviewed the findings of the day. Their collected material was still thin.

'Unusually thin,' Rydberg said. 'A building burns down in Ystad. And no one has noticed anything out of the ordinary.'

Svedberg and Hansson reported what they had found. Neither of the sisters had been married. There were a number of distant relatives, cousins and second cousins. But no one who lived in Ystad. The sewing shop yielded an unremarkable declared income. Nor had they uncovered any bank accounts with large savings. Hansson had located a safe-deposit box at Handelsbanken. But since they lacked keys, Per Åkeson would have to submit a request that the box be opened. Hansson calculated that it could be done by the following day.

Afterwards a heavy silence descended on the room.

'There has to be a motive,' Wallander said. 'Sooner or later we'll find it. If we only have patience.'

'Who knew these sisters?' Rydberg asked. 'They must have had friends and a bit of spare time now and again when they weren't working in the shop. Did they belong to any kind of organisation? Did they have a summer cabin? Did they take holidays? I still feel that we haven't scratched below the surface.'

Wallander thought Rydberg sounded irritable. He's probably in a lot of pain, Wallander thought. I wonder what is really wrong with him. If it isn't only rheumatism.

No one had anything to add to what Rydberg had said. They would go forward and delve deeper.

WALLANDER REMAINED in his office until close to eight o'clock. He made his own list of all the facts they had about the Eberhardsson sisters. As he read through what he had written he realised in earnest how thin it was. They had absolutely no leads to pursue.

Before leaving the office he called Martinsson at home. Martinsson told him that Holm had still not turned up.

Wallander went to his car. It took a long time for the engine to sputter into life. He angrily decided to take out a loan and get a new car as soon as he had the time.

When he came home he booked a time for the laundry room and then heated the contents of a can of stew. Just as he was about to sit down in front of the TV with his plate perched on his lap the phone rang. It was Emma. She asked if she could come by.

'Not tonight,' Wallander said. 'You've probably read about the fire and the two sisters. We're working round the clock right now.'

She understood. After Wallander hung up he wondered why he couldn't tell her the truth. That he didn't want to be with her any more. But of course it was inexcusable cowardice to say this over the phone. Therefore he had to steel himself to go over to her place some evening. He promised himself he would as soon as he had time.

He started to eat his food, which had already grown cold. It was nine o'clock. The telephone rang again. Annoyed, Wallander put the plate down and answered. It was Nyberg, who was still at the scene of the fire, calling from a patrol car.

'Now I think we've found something,' he said. 'A safe, the expensive kind that can withstand extreme heat.'

'Why didn't you find it earlier?'

'Good question,' Nyberg answered, without taking offence. 'The safe had been lowered into the foundations. We found an insulated trap door under all the rubble. When we managed to force it open we found a space underneath. And there was the safe.'

'Have you opened it?'

'With what? There are no keys. It will be difficult to force open.'

Wallander checked his watch. Five minutes past nine.

'I'm on my way,' he said. 'I wonder if you might have uncovered the lead we were looking for.'

When Wallander got down to the street he couldn't get the car to start. He gave up and walked to Hamngatan. At twenty minutes to ten he stood at Nyberg's side and studied the safe, illuminated by a lone spotlight.

At about the same time the temperature began to fall, and a gusty wind was moving in from the east.

CHAPTER 4

Shortly after midnight on December 15, Nyberg and his men had managed to lift up the safe with the help of a crane. It was loaded onto the back of a truck and immediately taken to the station. But before Nyberg and Wallander left the scene, Nyberg examined the space under the foundations.

'This was put in after the house was built,' he said. 'I have to assume it was constructed expressly to hold this safe.'

Wallander nodded without a reply. He was thinking about the Eberhardsson sisters. The police had searched for a motive. Now they may have found it, even if they didn't yet know what was in the safe. But someone else may have known, Wallander thought. Both that the safe existed. And what was inside.

Nyberg and Wallander left the scene of the fire and walked out to the street. 'Is it possible to cut into the safe?' Wallander asked.

'Yes, of course,' Nyberg answered. 'But it requires special welding equipment. This is not the kind of safe that a regular locksmith would dream of trying to crack open.'

'We have to open it as soon as possible.'

Nyberg pulled off his protective suit. He looked sceptically at Wallander. 'Do you mean that the safe should be opened tonight?'

'That would be best,' Wallander said. 'This is a double homicide.'

'Impossible,' Nyberg said. 'I can only get hold of people with the requisite welding equipment tomorrow at the earliest.'

'Are they here in Ystad?'

Nyberg reflected.

'There is a company that's a subcontractor for the armed forces,' he said. 'They probably have the equipment that would do the trick. I think their name is Fabricius. They're on Industrigatan.'

Nyberg looked exhausted. It would be insane to push him further right now. 'Seven o'clock tomorrow,' Wallander said.

Nyberg nodded.

Wallander looked around for his car. Then he remembered that it hadn't started. Nyberg could drop him off, but he preferred to walk. The wind was cold. He passed a thermometer outside a shop window on Stora Östergatan. Minus 6. Winter is creeping in, Wallander thought. Soon it will be here.

AT ONE MINUTE TO seven on the morning of December 15, Nyberg entered Wallander's office. Wallander had the telephone directory open on his desk. He had already inspected the safe, which was being stored in an empty room next to reception. One of the officers just going off the night shift told him that they had needed a fork-lift to get the safe inside. Wallander nodded. He had noticed the marks outside the glass doors and seen that one of the hinges was bent. That won't make Björk happy, he thought. But he'll have to live with it.

Nyberg called the company on Industrigatan. Wallander went to get some coffee. Rydberg arrived at the same time. Wallander told him about the safe.

'It was as I suspected,' Rydberg said. 'We know very little about these sisters.'

'We're in the process of trying to find a welder who can take on this kind of safe,' Wallander said.

'I hope you'll tell me before you open it,' Rydberg said. 'It will be interesting to be there.'

Wallander returned to his office and called Ebba to see who had come in.

'Martinsson phoned in to say that he was on his way to Sjöbo,' she answered. 'Svedberg hasn't arrived yet. Hansson is showering. He's apparently had a water leak at home.'

'We're going to open the safe soon,' Wallander said. 'That may get noisy.'

'I went in to take a look at it,' Ebba said. 'I thought it would be bigger.'

'One that size can hold a lot.'

Hansson appeared in the doorway. His hair was still wet.

'I've just talked to Björk,' he said cheerily. 'He pointed out that the doors of the station were damaged last night.'

Hansson had not yet heard about the safe. Wallander explained.

'That may provide us with a motive,' Hansson said.

'In the best-case scenario,' Wallander said. 'In the worst case, the safe is empty. And then we understand even less.'

'It could have been emptied by the people who shot the sisters,' Hansson objected. 'Perhaps he shot one of them and forced the other to open the safe?'

This had also occurred to Wallander. But something told him it was not what had actually happened.

At eight o'clock, under Ruben Fabricius's direction, two welders started the work of cutting open the safe. It was, as Nyberg had predicted, a difficult task.

'A special kind of steel,' Fabricius said.

'Can you blow it up?' Wallander asked.

'The risk would be that you'd take the whole building with you,' Fabricius answered. 'In that case I would first move the safe to an open field. But sometimes so much explosive is needed that the safe itself is blown to pieces. And the contents either burn or are pulverised.'

Fabricius was a large, heavyset man who punctuated each sentence with a short laugh. 'This kind of safe probably costs a hundred thousand kronor,' he said and laughed.

Wallander looked astonished. 'That much?'

'Easily.'

One thing at least is certain, Wallander thought as he recalled yesterday's discussion about the dead women's financial situation. The Eberhardsson sisters had much more money than they had reported to the authorities. They must have had undeclared income. But what can you sell of value in a sewing shop? Gold thread? Diamond-studded buttons?

The welding equipment was turned off at a quarter past nine. Fabricius nodded to Wallander and chuckled. 'All set,' he said.

Rydberg, Hansson and Svedberg had arrived. Nyberg had been following the work from the beginning. Using a crowbar, he now forced out the back piece that had been freed with a welding torch. Everyone crowded around. Wallander saw a number of plastic-wrapped bundles. Nyberg picked up one that lay on top. The plastic was white and sealed with tape. Nyberg placed the bundle on a chair and cut open the tape. Inside there was a thick wad of notes, hundred-dollar bills. There were ten wads, each a stack of ten thousand US dollars.

'A lot of money,' Wallander said. He carefully pulled out a bill and held it up to the light. It appeared genuine.

Nyberg took out the other bundles, one after another, and opened them.

'Let's take the rest to a conference room,' Wallander said. Then he thanked Fabricius and the two men who had cut open the safe.

'You'll have to send us a bill,' Wallander said. 'Without you, we would never have been able to get this open.'

'I think this one's on us,' Fabricius said. 'It was an experience for a tradesman. And a wonderful opportunity for professional training.'

'There is also no need to mention what was inside,' Wallander said.

Fabricius let out a short laugh and saluted him. Wallander understood that it was not intended to be ironic.

When all the bundles had been opened and the wads of notes counted, Wallander made a swift calculation. Most of it had been in US dollars. But there had also been British pounds and Swiss francs.

'I estimate it to be around five million kronor,' he said. 'No insignificant sum.'

'There wouldn't have been room for any more in the safe,' Rydberg said. 'And this means that if this cash was the motive then he or they who shot the sisters did not get what they had come for.'

'We nonetheless have some kind of motive,' Wallander said. 'This safe had been concealed. According to Nyberg, it appeared to have been there for a number of years. At some point the sisters must therefore have found it necessary to buy it because they needed to store and hide large sums of money. These were almost entirely new and unused dollar bills. Therefore it must be possible to trace them. Did they arrive in Sweden legally or not? We also need to find answers as quickly as possible to the other questions we're working on. Who did these sisters socialise with? What kind of habits did they have?'

'And weaknesses,' Rydberg added. 'Let us not forget about that.'

Björk entered the room at the end of the meeting. He gave a start when he saw all the money on the table. 'This has to be carefully recorded,' he said when Wallander explained in a somewhat strained manner what had happened. 'Nothing can be lost. Also, what has happened to the front doors?'

'A work-related accident,' Wallander said. 'When the fork-lift was lifting the safe.'

He said this so forcefully that Björk did not make any objections.

They broke up the meeting. Wallander hurried out of the room in order not to be left alone with Björk.

It had fallen to Wallander to contact an animal protection association where at least one of the sisters, Emilia, had been an active member, according to one of the neighbours. Wallander had been given a name and address by Svedberg: Tyra Olofsson, 11 Käringgatan.

Before Wallander left the station he called Arne Hurtig, the car sales-man he usually did business with. He explained the situation with his Peugeot. Hurtig gave him a few suggestions, all of which Wallander found too expensive. But when Hurtig promised a good trade-in price on his old car, Wallander decided to get another secondhand Peugeot. He hung up and called his bank. He had to wait several minutes until he could speak to the person who normally helped him. Wallander asked for a loan of 20,000 kronor. He was informed that this would not be a problem. He would be able to come in the following day, sign the loan documents and pick up the money.

The thought of a new car put him in a good mood. He stopped and inspected the damaged hinge on one of the front doors of the station. Since no one was around, he took the opportunity to give the door frame a kick. The damage became more noticeable. He walked away quickly, hunched over against the gusty wind.

Of course he should have called to make sure that Tyra Olofsson was in. But since she was retired, he took a chance. When he rang the doorbell, it opened almost at once. Tyra Olofsson was short and wore glasses that testi-fied to her myopia. Wallander explained who he was and held up his ID card, which she held near her glasses and studied carefully.

'The police,' she said. 'Then it must have to do with poor Emilia.'

'That's right,' Wallander said. 'I hope I'm not disturbing you.'

She invited him in. There was a strong smell of dogs in the hall. She led him out into the kitchen. Wallander counted fourteen food bowls on the floor. Worse than Haverberg, he thought.

'I keep them outside,' Tyra Olofsson said, having followed his gaze.

Wallander wondered briefly if it was legal to keep so many dogs in the city. He sat down at the table and looked in vain for something to write with. For once he had remembered to put a notepad in his pocket. But now he didn't have a pen. There was a small stump of a pencil lying on the windowsill, which he picked up.

'You're right, Mrs Olofsson,' he began. 'This is about Emilia Eberhardsson. We heard through one of the neighbours that she had been active in an animal protection association. And that you knew her well.'

'I can't say I knew Emilia well. I don't think anyone did.'

'Was her sister, Anna, ever involved in this work?'

'No.'

'Isn't that strange? I mean, two sisters, unmarried, who live together. I imagine they would develop similar interests.'

'That is a stereotype,' Tyra Olofsson said firmly. 'I imagine that Emilia and Anna were very different people. I worked as a teacher my whole life. Then you learn to see the differences in people. It's already apparent in young children.'

'How would you describe Emilia?'

Her answer surprised him.

'Snooty. The kind who always knows best. She could be very unpleasant. But since she donated money for our work, we couldn't get rid of her. Even if we wanted to.'

Tyra Olofsson told him about the animal protection group that she and a few other like-minded individuals had started in the 1960s. They had always worked locally and the impetus for the association was the increasing problem of feral cats. The association had always been small, with few members. One day in the early seventies, Emilia Eberhardsson had read about their work in the *Ystads Allehanda* and got in touch. She had given them money every month and participated in meetings and other events.

'But I don't think she really liked animals,' Tyra said unexpectedly. 'I think she did it so she would be thought of as a good person.'

'That doesn't sound like such a nice description.'

The woman on the other side of the table looked cheekily at him.

'I thought policemen always wanted to know the truth,' she said. 'Or am I wrong?'

Wallander changed the subject and asked about money.

'She donated a thousand kronor a month. For us that was a lot.'

'Did she give the impression of being rich?'

'She never dressed expensively. But I'm sure she had money.'

'You must have asked yourself where it came from. A sewing shop is hardly something one associates with a fortune.'

'I'm not particularly curious,' she answered. 'Where the money came from or how well their shop did, I know nothing about.'

Wallander hesitated for a moment, and then he told her the truth.

'It has been reported in the papers that the sisters burned to death,' he said, 'but it has not been reported that they were shot. They were already dead when the fire started.'

She sat up. 'Who could have wanted to shoot two old ladies? That's as likely as someone wanting to kill me.'

'That is exactly what we are trying to understand,' Wallander said. 'That's why I'm here. Did Emilia ever say anything about having enemies? Did she appear frightened?'

Tyra Olofsson did not have to reflect. 'She was always very sure of herself,' she said. 'She never said a word about her and her sister's life. And when they were away she never sent a postcard. Not once, even with all the wonderful postcards with animal motifs that you can get these days.'

Wallander raised his eyebrows. 'You mean they travelled a lot?'

'Two months out of every year. November and March. Sometimes in the summer.'

'Where did they go?'

'I heard it was Spain.'

'Who took care of their shop?'

'They always took turns. Perhaps they needed time apart.'

'Spain? What else do the rumours say? And where do these rumours come from?'

'I can't remember. I don't listen to rumours. Perhaps they went to Marbella. But I'm not sure.'

Wallander wondered if Olofsson was really as uninterested in gossip as she seemed. He thanked her and walked back to the station. He thought about what she had said. There had been no meanness in her voice, but her description of Emilia Eberhardsson had not been flattering.

WHEN WALLANDER REACHED the station, Ebba told him that Rydberg had been looking for him. Wallander went straight to his office.

'The picture is becoming clearer,' Rydberg said. 'I think we should get the others and have a short meeting. I know they're around.'

'What's happened?'

Rydberg waved a bunch of papers. 'VPC,' he said. 'And there's a great deal of interest in these papers.'

It took Wallander a moment to remember that VPC stood for the Swedish securities register centre, which, among other things, recorded stock ownership. 'For my part I've managed to establish that at least one of the sisters was a genuinely unpleasant person,' Wallander said.

'Doesn't surprise me in the least.' Rydberg chuckled. 'The rich often are.'

'Rich?' Wallander asked.

But Rydberg did not answer until they were all assembled in the conference room. Then he explained himself in detail. 'According to the Swedish securities register centre, the Eberhardsson sisters had stocks and bonds totalling close to ten million kronor. How they managed to keep this from being subject to wealth tax is a mystery. Nor do they appear to have paid income tax on their dividends. But I've alerted the tax authorities. It actually appears that Anna Eberhardsson was registered as a resident of Spain. But I'm not clear on the details of this yet. In any case, they had a large portfolio of investments both in Sweden and abroad.'

Rydberg put down the documents. 'We cannot exclude the possibility that what we see here is only the tip of the proverbial iceberg. Five million in a safe and ten million in stocks and bonds. This is what we have uncovered in the space of a few hours. What happens after we've been working for a week? Perhaps the amount will increase to one hundred million?'

Wallander reported on his meeting with Tyra Olofsson.

'The description of Anna isn't flattering either,' Svedberg said when Wallander had finished. 'I talked to the man who sold the sisters the house five years ago. That was when the market was getting soft. Until then they had always rented. Apparently it was Anna who negotiated. Emilia was never present. And the estate agent said Anna was the most difficult customer he ever had. Apparently she had discovered that his company was in trouble at that time, with regard to both solidity and liquidity. He said that she had been completely ice-cold and more or less blackmailed him.'

Svedberg shook his head. 'This isn't exactly how I would have imagined two old ladies who sold buttons,' he said and the room fell silent.

Wallander was the one who broke the silence.

'In a way this has been our breakthrough,' he started. 'We still have no leads on who killed them. But we have a plausible motive. And it is the most common of all motives: money. In addition, we know that the women committed tax fraud and concealed great sums of money from the authorities. We know that they were rich. It won't surprise me if we turn up a house in Spain. And perhaps other assets, in other parts of the world.'

Wallander poured himself a glass of mineral water before continuing.

'Everything we know now can be summed up in two points. Two questions. Where did they get the money? And who knew that they were rich?'

Wallander was about to lift the glass to his lips when he saw Rydberg flinch, as if he had been given a shock. Then his upper body slumped over the table. As if he was dead.

LATER, WALLANDER would remember that for a few seconds he had been entirely convinced that Rydberg had died. Everyone who was in the room when Rydberg collapsed thought the same thing: that Rydberg's heart had suddenly stopped. It was Svedberg who reacted first. He had been sitting next to Rydberg and could tell that his colleague was still alive. He grabbed the telephone and called for an ambulance. Wallander and Hansson lowered Rydberg onto the floor and unbuttoned his shirt. Wallander listened to his heart and heard it beating very quickly.

Then the ambulance arrived and Wallander accompanied it on the short drive to the hospital. Rydberg received immediate treatment, and after less than half an hour Wallander had been informed that it was not likely to have been a heart attack. Rather, Rydberg had collapsed for some as yet unknown reason. He was conscious at this point but shook his head when Wallander wanted to talk to him. He was judged to be in a stable condition and admitted to the hospital for observation. There was no longer any reason for Wallander to stay. A patrol car was waiting outside to drive him back to the station.

His colleagues had remained in the conference room. Even Björk was present. Wallander could inform them that the situation was under control.

'We work too hard,' he said and looked at Björk. 'We have more and more to do. But our numbers have not increased. Sooner or later what happened to Rydberg can happen to all of us.'

'It is a troubling situation,' Björk admitted. 'But we have limited resources.'

For the next half an hour the investigation was set aside. Everyone was shaken and talked about the working conditions. After Björk left the room, the words became sharper. About impossible planning, strange priorities and a continual lack of information.

At around two o'clock, Wallander felt they had to move on. Not least for his own sake. When he saw what had happened to Rydberg he had thought about what could happen to himself. How long would his own heart put up with the strain? All the unhealthy food, the frequently recurring bouts of broken and lost sleep? And, above all, his grief after the divorce.

'Rydberg would not approve of this,' he said. 'That we're wasting time talking about our situation. We'll have to do that later. Right now we have a double murderer to catch.'

They ended the meeting. Wallander went to his office and called the hospital. He was told that Rydberg was sleeping. It was still premature to expect an explanation for what had happened.

Wallander hung up the phone, and Martinsson walked in. 'What happened?' he asked. 'I've been in Sjöbo. Ebba was all shaken up out there.'

Wallander told him. Martinsson sat down heavily in the visitor's chair. 'We work ourselves to death,' he said. 'And who appreciates it?'

Wallander became impatient. He didn't want to think about Rydberg any more, at least not right now. 'Sjöbo,' he said. 'What do you have for me?'

'I've been out in a variety of muddy fields,' Martinsson replied. 'We've been able to pinpoint the location of those lights quite well. But there were no traces anywhere of either spotlights or marks from a plane landing or taking off. On the other hand, some information has turned up that probably explains why the aircraft couldn't be identified.'

'And what is it?'

'It simply doesn't exist.'

'What do you mean?'

Martinsson took a while to search through the papers he had taken out of his briefcase. 'According to the records of the Piper factory, this plane crashed in Vientiane in 1986. The owner back then was a Laotian consortium that used it to transport its managers to various agricultural centres around the country. The official cause of the crash was listed as a lack of fuel. No one was injured or killed. But the plane was wrecked and removed from all active registers and from the insurance company. This is what we know after looking up the engine registration number.'

'But that turned out not to be correct?'

'The Piper factory is naturally very interested in what has happened. It's not good for their reputation if a plane that no longer exists suddenly starts to fly again. This could be a case of insurance fraud and other things that we have no idea about.'

'And the men in the plane?'

'We're still waiting for them to be identified. I have a couple of good contacts in Interpol. They've promised to expedite the matter.'

'The plane must have come from somewhere,' Wallander said.

Martinsson nodded. 'That gives us yet another problem. Nyberg thinks he may have identified the remains of something that could have been a spare fuel tank. But we don't know yet. If this is the case, the plane could have come from virtually anywhere. At least Britain and Continental Europe.'

'But it must have been observed by someone,' Wallander insisted. 'You can't cross borders with complete impunity.'

'I agree,' Martinsson said. 'Therefore Germany would be an educated guess, because you fly over open water until you reach the Swedish border.'

'What do the German aviation authorities say?'

'It takes time,' Martinsson said. 'But I'm working on it.'

Wallander reflected for a moment. 'We actually need you on this double homicide,' he said. 'Can you delegate this work to someone else? At least while we wait on a positive identification of the pilots, and whether the plane came from Germany?'

'I was about to suggest the same thing,' Martinsson said.

Wallander checked the time. 'Ask Hansson or Svedberg to get you up to speed on the case.'

Martinsson got out of the chair. 'Have you heard from your father?'

'He doesn't call without a good reason.'

'My father died when he was fifty-five,' Martinsson said abruptly. 'He had his own business. A car-repairs garage. He had to work constantly to make ends meet. Right when things were starting to look up, he died. He would only have been sixty-seven now.'

Martinsson left. Wallander did his best to avoid thinking about Rydberg. Instead he again reviewed everything they knew about the sisters. They had a likely motive—money—but no trace of the killer. Wallander jotted a few words on his notepad.

The double life of the Eberhardsson sisters?

He pushed the pad away. When Rydberg was out, they lacked their best instrument. If an investigative team is like an orchestra, Wallander thought, we've lost our first violin. And then the orchestra doesn't sound as good.

At that moment he made up his mind to have his own talk with a neighbour who had provided some information about Anna Eberhardsson. He felt that Svedberg, who had interviewed the individual, was often too impatient when he talked to people about what they might have seen or heard. It's also a matter of finding out what people think, Wallander said to himself.

He found the name of the neighbour, Linnea Gunnér. Only women in this case, he thought. He dialled her phone number and heard her pick up. Linnea Gunnér was at home and happy to receive him. She gave him the code to the front door of her building and he made a note of it.

He left the station shortly after three o'clock, and kicked the damaged hinge again. The dent was getting worse. When he reached the scene of the fire, he saw that the ruins of the building were already being razed. There were still many curious onlookers gathered around the site.

Linnea Gunnér lived on Möllegatan. Wallander entered the door code and took the stairs to the first floor. The house dated back to the turn of the century and had beautiful designs on the walls of its stairwell. The woman who opened the door was the opposite of Tyra Olofsson in almost every way. She was tall, with a sharp gaze and a firm voice. She invited him into her apartment, which was filled with objects from all over the world. In the living room there was even a ship's figurehead. Wallander looked at it for a long time.

'This belonged to the barque *Felicia*, which sank in the Irish Sea,' Linnea Gunnér said. 'I bought it for an insignificant sum in Middlesbrough.'

'Then you've been at sea?' he asked.

'My whole life. First as a chef, then as a steward.'

She did not speak with a Skåne dialect. Wallander thought she sounded more as if she came from Småland or Östergötland.

'Where are you from?' he asked.

'Skänninge in Östergötland. About as far from the sea as one can get.'

'And now you live in Ystad?'

'I inherited this apartment from an aunt. And I have a view of the sea.'

She had put out coffee. Wallander thought it was probably the last thing his stomach needed. But he still said yes. He had immediately felt he could trust Linnea Gunnér. He had read in Svedberg's notes that she was sixty-six years old. But she appeared younger.

'My colleague Svedberg was here,' Wallander started.

'I told him about my impressions of Anna.'

'And Emilia?'

'They were different. Anna spoke in quick, choppy bursts. Emilia was quieter. But they were equally disagreeable. Equally introverted.'

'How well did you know them?'

'I didn't. Sometimes we bumped into each other on the street. Then we would exchange a few words. But never more than was necessary. Since I like to embroider, I often went to their shop. I always got what I needed. If something had to be ordered, it arrived quickly. But they were not pleasant.'

'Sometimes one needs time,' Wallander said. 'Time to allow one's memory to catch things one thought one had forgotten.'

'What would that be?'

'I don't know. You know. An unexpected event. Something that went against their habits.'

She thought about it. Wallander studied an impressive brass-inlaid compass on a bureau.

'My memory has never been good,' she said finally. 'But now that you mention it, I do remember something that happened last year. In the spring, I think it was. But I can't say if it's important.'

'Anything could be important,' Wallander said.

'One afternoon I needed some thread. I walked down to the shop. Both Emilia and Anna were behind the counter. Just as I was about to pay for the thread, a man entered the shop. I remember that he started, as if he hadn't been expecting anyone else to be in the shop. And Anna became angry. She gave Emilia a look that could kill. Then the man left. He had a bag in his hand. I paid for my thread and left.'

'Could you describe him?'

'He was not what one would call Swedish-looking. Swarthy, on the short side. A black moustache.'

'How was he dressed?'

'A suit. I think it was of good quality.'

'And the bag?'

'An ordinary black briefcase.'

'Nothing else?'

She thought back. 'Nothing that I can recall.'

'You only saw him that one time?'

'Yes.'

Wallander knew that what he had just heard was important. He could not yet determine what it meant. But it strengthened his impression that the sisters had led a double existence. He was slowly penetrating below the surface.

Wallander thanked her for the coffee.

'What was it that happened?' she asked when they were standing in the hall. 'I woke up with my room on fire. The light from the flames was so bright that I thought my own apartment was burning.'

'Anna and Emilia were murdered,' Wallander answered. 'They were dead when the fire started.'

'Who would have wanted to do something like that?'

'I don't think I'd be here if I knew the answer to that,' Wallander said and turned to leave.

When he stepped out onto the street he set off back in the direction of Hamngatan. In the building next to Linnea Gunnér's there was a travel agency. He stopped when he noticed a poster in the window that depicted the pyramids. His father would be home again in less than a week. Wallander felt he had been unfair. Why couldn't he be happy that his father was realising one of his oldest dreams? Wallander looked at the other posters in the window. Majorca, Crete, Spain.

Suddenly something occurred to him. He opened the door and walked in. Both of the sales agents were busy. Wallander sat down to wait. When the first of them, a young woman hardly older than twenty, became free he got up and sat down at her desk. He had to wait a couple of minutes longer as she answered the phone. He saw from a nameplate on the desk that her name was Anette Bengtsson. She put down the receiver and smiled.

'Do you want to get away?' she asked. 'There are still spaces left around Christmas and New Year.'

'My errand is of a different nature,' Wallander said and held up his ID card. 'You have of course heard that two old ladies burned to death across the street from here.'

'Yes, it's terrible.'

'Did you know them?'

He received the answer he had been hoping for.

'They booked their trips through us. It's so awful that they're gone. Emilia was planning to travel in January. And Anna in April.'

Wallander nodded slowly. 'Where were they going?' he asked.

'To the same place as always. Spain.'

'More precisely?'

'To Marbella. They had a house there.'

What she said next surprised Wallander even more.

'I've seen it,' she said. 'I went to Marbella last year. We have ongoing professional training. There's stiff competition between travel agencies these days. Once, when I had time, I drove out and looked at their house. I knew the address.'

'Was it large?'

'It was palatial. With a huge garden. High walls all around.'

'I would appreciate it if you could write down the address for me,' Wallander said, unable to conceal his eagerness.

She looked through her folders and then wrote it down.

'You said that Emilia was planning to travel in January?'

She entered something into her computer.

'The 7th of January,' she said. 'From Kastrup at five past nine in the morning, via Madrid.'

Wallander helped himself to a pencil from her desk and wrote the details on a pad. 'So she didn't take charter flights?'

'Neither of them did. They travelled first class.'

That's right, Wallander thought. These ladies were loaded.

She told him which airline Emilia had booked her flight with. Iberia, Wallander wrote.

'I don't know what happens now,' she said. 'The ticket has been paid for.'

'I'm sure it will sort itself out,' Wallander said. 'How did they pay for their travel, by the way?'

'Always in cash. In thousand-kronor notes.'

Wallander slipped his notepad into his pocket and got up.

'You've been a great help,' he said. 'The next time I travel anywhere I'll come and book my trip here. But for me that will mean charter.'

Wallander made it back to the station by twenty past four. Again he directed a ritual kick at the hinge. Ebba told him that Hansson and Svedberg were out. But, more important, she had called the hospital and been able to speak to Rydberg. He had said that he was feeling fine. But he was being kept in overnight.

'I'll go and see him.'

'That was the last thing he said,' Ebba replied. 'That under no circumstances did he want to have any visitors or phone calls. And absolutely no flowers.'

'Well, that doesn't surprise me,' Wallander said. 'If you think about how he is.'

'You all work too hard, eat too much junk and don't get enough exercise.'

Wallander leaned over towards her. 'That goes for you too,' he said. 'You aren't as slim as you once were, you know.'

Ebba burst into laughter. Wallander went to the break room and found half a loaf of bread that someone had left. He made several sandwiches and took them to his office, where he sat down and started to write a report on his conversations with Linnea Gunnér and Anette Bengtsson. He was done at a quarter past five. He read through what he had written and asked himself how they should proceed with the case from here. The money comes from somewhere, he thought. A man is on his way into the shop but turns round on the doorstep. They had a system of signs worked out.

The question is simply what is behind all this. And why were the women murdered all of a sudden? Something has been set in motion but then all at once it collapses.

He had just put his coat on to go home when Martinsson walked in.

'I think it's best that you sit down,' Martinsson said.

'I'm fine standing up,' Wallander said grumpily. 'What is it?'

Martinsson appeared confused. He was holding a telex message in his hand. 'This just came in from the Ministry of Foreign Affairs in Stockholm,' he said.

He handed the piece of paper to Wallander, who read the message without understanding anything. Then he sat down at his desk and read it again, word by word.

Now he understood what was written there, but he refused to believe it. 'It says here that my father has been arrested by the Cairo police, and that he will be brought before a judge if he does not immediately pay a fine of approximately ten thousand kronor. He has been accused of "unlawful entry and forbidden ascent". What the hell does "forbidden ascent" mean?'

'I called the foreign ministry,' Martinsson said. 'I also thought it seemed strange. Apparently he was trying to climb the Cheops pyramid. Even though it's against the law.'

Wallander stared helplessly at Martinsson.

'I think you're going to have to fly there and bring him home,' Martinsson said. 'There are limits to what the Swedish authorities can do.'

Wallander shook his head in disbelief.

CHAPTER 5

At ten past one the following day, Wallander sank down into a seat on an Scandinavian Airlines DC-9 aircraft called *Agne*. He sat in 19C, on the aisle, and he had a vague understanding that the plane, after stops in Frankfurt and Rome, would take him to Cairo. The arrival time was 10.15 p.m. Wallander still did not know if there was a time difference between Sweden and Egypt. In fact, he knew very little about what had jerked him out of his life in Ystad, from the investigation of a plane crash and a brutal double homicide, to an aircraft in Kastrup preparing for take-off, headed for North Africa.

The evening before, when the contents of the telex from the foreign ministry had actually sunk in, he had completely lost it. He had left the station without a word, and even though Martinsson accompanied him as far as the car park and offered to help, Wallander had not so much as answered him.

When he got home to Mariagatan, he had two large tumblers of whisky. Then he reread the crumpled telex several times in the hopes that there was an encoded message in it explaining that it was all an invention, a joke, one that perhaps even his own father had played on him. But he had realised that the Ministry of Foreign Affairs in Stockholm meant business. There was no way out for him other than to accept this as a fact: his demented father had started climbing a pyramid, with the result that he had been apprehended and was now being held in police custody in Cairo.

Shortly after eight o'clock, Wallander called Malmö. As luck would have it, Linda answered. He told her what had happened and asked for her advice. What should he do? Her answer had been very firm. He had no option but to travel to Egypt the following day and see to it that her grandfather was released. Finally he realised that she was right. She also promised him that she would find out what available connections there were to Cairo tomorrow.

Wallander slowly calmed himself. Tomorrow he was supposed to go to the bank to pick up a car loan for 20,000 kronor. No one would ask him what he was going to use the money for. He had enough money to buy a ticket and he could change the rest of the cash to British pounds or dollars in order to pay his father's fine. At ten o'clock Linda called and said that there was a flight the following day at ten past one. He also decided to ask Anette Bengtsson for help. Earlier that day, when he had promised to avail himself of the travel agency's services, he had not dreamed it would be so soon.

He tried to pack at around midnight, realising he knew nothing about Cairo. His father had gone there with an ancient pith helmet on his head. But he was unhinged and could not be taken seriously. Finally, Wallander tossed some shirts and underwear into a bag and decided that would be enough. He was not going to stay away any longer than necessary.

Then he had a couple more glasses of whisky, set his alarm clock to wake him at six and tried to sleep. A restless slumber carried him towards the dawn at an interminable crawl.

When the bank opened the following day he was the first customer to step through the doors. It took him twenty minutes to sign the loan documents, get his money and exchange half of it for British pounds. He hoped that no one would ask why half of the payment for the car was to be paid in pounds. From the bank he went straight to the travel agency. Anette Bengtsson couldn't believe her eyes when he walked in through the door. But she was immediately willing to help him book the ticket. The return had to remain open for now. He was astonished to hear the price. But he simply pulled out his thousand-kronor notes, took his tickets and left the agency.

Then he took a taxi to Malmö. He would never be able to afford a new car now. Perhaps he should consider getting a moped or a bike.

Linda met him by the ferry terminal. They only had a few minutes together. But she convinced him he was doing the right thing. And she asked if he had remembered his passport.

'You'll need a visa,' she said. 'But you can buy that at the airport in Cairo.'

Now he was sitting in 19C and felt how the aeroplane gathered speed and tilted up towards the clouds and the invisible air corridors, headed south. Frankfurt airport became a memory of an endless series of corridors and stairs. He took his aisle seat again and, when they came to Rome in order to make the last connection, he took off his coat, as it had suddenly become very warm. The plane thudded down at the airport outside Cairo, delayed by half an hour.

In order to lessen his worry, his fear of flying and his nervousness about what awaited him, Wallander had had far too much to drink during the flight. He was not drunk when he stepped out into the stifling Egyptian darkness, but he was not sober either. Most of the money was in a cloth bag squeezed in under his shirt. A tired passport controller directed him to a bank where he could buy a tourist visa. He ended up with a large number of dirty notes in his hand and was suddenly through both passport control and customs.

Many taxi drivers crowded round, prepared to drive him to any place in the world. But Wallander had the presence of mind to look around for a shuttle heading to Mena House Hotel, which he imagined to be quite large. His plan went this far: to stay at the same hotel as his father. In a minibus, sandwiched between some loud American women, he travelled through the city towards the hotel. He felt the warm night air on his face, discovered suddenly that they were crossing a river that might be the Nile, and then they were there.

When he stepped out of the bus he was sober again. From here on he did not know what to do. A Swedish policeman in Egypt could feel very insignificant, he thought gloomily as he stepped into the magnificent foyer of the hotel. He walked up to the reception desk, where a pleasant young man who spoke perfect English asked if he could be of service. Wallander explained his situation and said he had not reserved a room. The helpful young man looked concerned for a moment and shook his head. But then he managed to find a room.

'I think you already have a guest by the name of Wallander.'

The man searched in his electronic database and then nodded.

'That's my father,' Wallander said, and groaned inwardly over his poor English pronunciation.

'Unfortunately, I cannot give you a room close to his,' the young man said. 'We only have simple rooms left. Without a view of the pyramids.'

'That suits me fine,' Wallander said. He didn't want to be reminded of the pyramids more than was necessary.

He registered, was given a key and a small map, and then made his way through the labyrinthine hotel. He found his room and sat down on the bed. The air conditioning was cool. He took off his shirt, which was drenched in sweat. He looked at his face in the bathroom mirror.

'Now I am here,' he said out loud to himself. 'It's late at night. I need to eat something. And sleep. Above all, sleep. But I can't, since my crazy father is being held at a police station somewhere in this city.'

He put on a clean shirt, brushed his teeth and returned to the reception desk downstairs. The young man who had recently helped him was nowhere to be seen. Or else Wallander did not recognise him. He approached an older receptionist who was standing motionless and appeared to be surveying everything that happened in the lobby. He smiled when Wallander turned up in front of him.

'I have come here because my father has found himself in difficulty,' he said. 'His name is Wallander and he is an elderly man who arrived here several days ago.'

'What type of difficulty?' the receptionist asked. 'Has he become ill?'

'He appears to have tried to climb one of the pyramids,' Wallander answered. 'If I am right he chose the highest one.'

The receptionist nodded slowly. 'I have heard about it,' he replied. 'It was very unfortunate. The police and the Ministry of Tourism did not approve.'

He retreated behind a door and returned shortly with another man, also older. They spoke rapidly for a short while. Then they turned to Wallander. 'Are you the old man's son?' one of them asked.

Wallander nodded. 'Not only that,' he said, 'I am also a policeman.'

He displayed his identification, which clearly stated the word 'police'. But the two men did not appear to understand.

'You mean, you are not his son, you are police?'

'I am both,' Wallander said. '*Both* his son *and* police.'

They pondered what he had said for a while. Then they asked him to wait. They pointed to a group of sofas in the lobby. Wallander sat down. A veiled woman walked past. Scheherazade, Wallander thought. She could have helped me. Or Aladdin. I could have used someone in that league. He waited. An hour went by. The clock had struck twelve a long time ago. Wallander closed his eyes.

He jumped when someone touched his shoulder. When he opened his eyes the receptionist was there, together with a number of police officers in impressive uniforms. Wallander got up from the sofa. A clock on the wall read half past two. One of the police officers, who appeared to be about his own age and who was also wearing the most stripes on his uniform, saluted him.

'I hear you have been sent here by the Swedish police,' he said.

'No,' Wallander said. 'I *am* a police officer. But above all I am Mr Wallander's son.'

The policeman who had saluted him immediately exploded into an incomprehensible torrent of words directed at the receptionist. Wallander thought that the best thing he could do would be to sit down again. After about a quarter of an hour the policeman brightened.

'I am Hassaneyh Radwan,' he said. 'I now have a clear picture. It is a delight to meet a Swedish colleague. Come with me.'

They left the hotel. Wallander, surrounded by officers who were all carrying weapons, felt like a criminal. It was a very warm night. He sat down beside Radwan in the back of a police car that immediately revved into action and turned on its sirens. Just as they were driving away from the hotel grounds, Wallander saw the pyramids, illuminated by large spotlights.

It happened so fast he could not believe his eyes. But they were actually the pyramids that he had seen depicted so many times. And then he thought with dread about the fact that his father had tried to climb one.

They drove east, the same way he had come from the airport.

'How is my father doing?'

'He is a very determined man,' Radwan answered. 'But his English is unfortunately difficult to understand.'

He doesn't speak any English at all, Wallander thought helplessly.

They drove through the city at high speed. Wallander caught sight of some heavily loaded camels moving with slow dignity. They crossed the Nile.

Soon the police car slowed down. Wallander saw that the name of the street was Sadei Barrani. They were outside a large police station where armed guards stood in small sentry boxes outside the tall doors. Wallander followed Radwan to a room where garish neon tubes glowed in the ceiling. Radwan pointed to a chair. Wallander sat down and wondered how long he now had to wait. Before Radwan left, Wallander asked him if it would be possible to buy a soft drink. Radwan called over a young policeman.

'He will help you,' Radwan said and then left.

Wallander, who was extremely unsure of the value of his notes, gave the policeman a small wad of them.

'Coca-Cola,' he said.

The policeman looked wide-eyed at him. But he said nothing, he simply took the money and left. A little while later he returned with a carton of Coke bottles. Wallander counted fourteen in all. He opened two of them with his penknife and gave the rest to the policeman, who shared them with his colleagues.

It was half past four. Wallander watched a fly that was sitting still on one of the empty bottles. The sound of a radio came from somewhere.

Radwan came back and gave Wallander a sign to follow him. They walked down an endless succession of winding corridors, up and down stairs, and at last stopped outside a door where a policeman was standing guard. Radwan nodded and the door opened. Then he signalled for Wallander to step inside.

'I'll be back in half an hour,' he said and left.

Wallander entered the room, which was illuminated by the ubiquitous neon tubes. It was furnished with a table and two chairs. His father was sitting on one of the chairs, dressed in a shirt and trousers but barefoot. His hair was sticking up. Wallander suddenly felt pity for him.

'Hello, old man,' he said. 'How are you?'

His father looked at him without the slightest trace of surprise.

'I intend to protest,' he said.

'Protest what?'

'That they prevent people from climbing the pyramids.'

'I think we should wait on that protest,' Wallander said. 'The most important thing right now is for me to get you out of here.'

'I am not paying any fines,' his father replied angrily. 'I want to wait out my punishment instead. Two years, they said. That will go by quickly.'

Wallander quickly considered getting angry, but that could simply egg his father on. 'Egyptian prisons are probably not particularly comfortable,' he said carefully. 'No prisons are. I also doubt they would allow you to paint in your cell.'

His father stared back at him in silence. Apparently he had not considered this possibility.

He nodded and stood up.

'Let's go then,' he said. 'Do you have the money to pay the fine?'

'Sit down,' Wallander said. 'I don't think it's quite that simple. That you can just stand up and leave.'

'Why not? I haven't done anything wrong.'

'According to what I understand, you tried to climb the Cheops pyramid.'

'That was why I came here. Ordinary tourists can stand among the camels and look. I wanted to stand on the top.'

'That's not allowed. It's also very dangerous. And what would happen if everyone started to climb all over the pyramids?'

'I'm not talking about everyone else, I'm talking about me.'

Wallander realised it was futile to try to reason with his father. At the same time he couldn't help but be impressed with his intractability.

'I'm here now,' Wallander said. 'I'll try to get you out tomorrow. Or later today. I'll pay the fine and then it's over. We'll leave this place, go to the hotel and get your suitcase. Then we'll fly home.'

'I've paid for my room until the 21st.'

Wallander nodded patiently. 'Fine. I'm going home. You stay. But if you climb the pyramids one more time you're on your own.'

'I never got that far,' his father said. 'It was difficult. And steep.'

'Why did you want to get to the top?'

His father hesitated before answering.

'It's a dream I've had all these years. That's all. I think that one should be faithful to one's dreams.'

The conversation died away. Several minutes later Radwan returned. Wallander turned to him. 'I assume there's no possibility that I can take my father with me now?'

'He must appear before the court today at ten o'clock. The judge will most likely accept the fine.'

'Most likely?'

'Nothing is certain,' Radwan said. 'But we have to hope for the best.'

Wallander said goodbye to his father. Radwan followed him out to a patrol car that was waiting to take him back to the hotel. It was now six o'clock.

'I will send a car to pick you up a little after nine,' Radwan said as they parted. 'One should always help a foreign colleague.'

Wallander thanked him and got into the car. Once again he was thrown back against the seat as it sped off, sirens blaring.

At half past six Wallander ordered a wake-up call and collapsed naked on the bed. I have to get him out, he thought. If he ends up in prison he'll die.

Wallander sank into a restless slumber but was woken by the sun rising over the horizon. He had a shower and dressed. He was already down to his last clean shirt.

HE WALKED OUTSIDE. It was cooler now, in the morning. Suddenly he stopped as he caught sight of the pyramids. He stood absolutely still. The feeling of their enormity was overwhelming. He walked away from the hotel and up the hill that led to the entrance to the Giza plateau. Along the way he was offered rides on both donkeys and camels. But he walked. Deep down he understood his father. One should stay faithful to one's dreams. How faithful had he been to his own? He stopped close to the entrance and looked at the pyramids. Imagined his father climbing up the steeply inclined walls.

He ended up standing there for a long time before he returned to the hotel and had breakfast. At nine o'clock he was outside the hotel entrance, waiting. The patrol car arrived after several minutes. Traffic was heavy and the sirens were on as usual. Wallander crossed the Nile for the fourth time. He saw now that he was in a huge metropolis, incalculable, clamorous.

The court was on a street by the name of Al Azhar. Radwan was standing on the steps, smoking, as the car pulled up.

'I hope you had a few hours of sleep,' he said. 'It is not good for a person to go without sleep.'

They walked into the building. 'Your father is already here.'

'Does he have a defence lawyer?' Wallander asked.

'He has a court-assigned assistant. This is a court for minor offences.'

'But he could still receive two years in prison?'

'There is a big difference between a death sentence and two years,' Radwan said thoughtfully.

They walked into the courtroom. 'Your father's case is the first of the day,' Radwan said.

Then his father was led in. Wallander stared at him, horrified. His father was in handcuffs. Tears welled up in Wallander's eyes. Radwan glanced at him and put a hand on his shoulder.

A lone judge walked in and sat down. A prosecutor seemed to appear out of thin air and rattled off a long tirade that Wallander assumed to be the charges. Radwan leaned over.

'It looks good,' he whispered. 'He claims your father is old and confused.'

As long as no one translates that, Wallander thought. Then he really will go crazy.

The prosecutor sat down. The court assistant made a brief statement.

'He is making the case for a fine,' Radwan whispered. 'I have informed the court that you are his son and that you are a policeman.'

The assistant sat down. Wallander saw that his father wanted to say something, but the court assistant shook his head.

The judge struck the table with his gavel and uttered a few words. Then he banged the gavel again, got up and left.

'A fine,' Radwan said and patted Wallander on the shoulder. 'It can be paid here in the courtroom. Then your father is free to go.'

Wallander took out the bag inside his shirt.

Radwan led him to a table where a man calculated the sum from

Egyptian pounds into British pounds. Almost all Wallander's money disappeared. He received an illegible receipt for the amount. Radwan made sure his father's handcuffs were removed.

'I hope that the rest of your journey is pleasant,' Radwan said and shook both their hands. 'But it is not advisable for your father to attempt to climb the pyramids again.'

Radwan had a patrol car take them back to the hotel. Wallander made a note of Radwan's address. He realised that this would not have been so easy without Radwan's help. In some way he wanted to thank him. Perhaps it would be most appropriate to send him one of his father's paintings.

His father was in high spirits and commented on everything that they drove past. Wallander was simply tired.

'Now I will show you the pyramids,' his father said happily when they reached the hotel.

'Not right now,' Wallander said. 'I need to sleep for a few hours. You too. Then we'll look at the pyramids. When I've booked my return flight.'

His father looked intently at him.

'I must say that you surprise me. That you spared no expense in flying here and getting me out. I would not have thought that of you.'

Wallander did not answer. Then, 'Go to bed,' he said. 'I'll meet you here at two o'clock.'

Wallander did not manage to fall asleep. After writhing on his bed for an hour he went to the reception desk and asked them for help in booking his return flight. He was directed to a travel agency located in another part of the hotel. There he was assisted by a woman who spoke perfect English. She managed to get him a seat on the plane that was leaving Cairo the following day at nine o'clock. After he had confirmed his seat, it was only one o'clock. He sat down in a café next to the lobby and drank a cup of very hot coffee. At exactly two o'clock his father appeared, wearing his pith helmet.

Together they explored the Giza plateau in the intense heat. Wallander thought several times that he was going to faint. But his father seemed unaffected by the heat. Down by the Sphinx, Wallander at last found some shade. His father narrated and Wallander realised that he knew a great deal about the Egypt of old where the pyramids and the remarkable Sphinx had once been built.

It was close to six o'clock when they finally returned to the hotel. Since he was travelling very early the next morning they decided to eat dinner in the hotel, where there were several restaurants to choose from. At his father's suggestion they booked a table at an Indian restaurant and Wallander thought afterwards that he had rarely had such a good meal. His father had been pleasant the entire time and Wallander understood that he had now dismissed all thoughts of climbing the pyramids.

They parted at eleven. Wallander would be leaving the hotel at six.

'Of course I'll get up and see you off,' his father said.

'I'd rather you didn't,' Wallander said. 'Neither of us likes goodbyes.'

'Thank you for coming here,' his father said. 'You're probably right about it being hard to spend two years in prison without being able to paint.'

'Come home on the 21st and everything will be forgotten,' Wallander answered.

'The next time we'll go to Italy,' his father said and walked away towards his room.

That night Wallander slept heavily.

At six o'clock he sat in the taxi and crossed the Nile for the final time. The plane left on schedule and he was in Malmö at a quarter to four. He ran to the station and just made a train to Ystad. He strode home to Mariagatan, changed his clothes and walked in through the front doors of the station at half past six. The damaged hinge had been replaced. Martinsson's and Svedberg's offices were empty, but Hansson was in. Wallander told him about his trip in broad strokes. But first he asked how Rydberg was doing.

'He's supposed to be coming in tomorrow,' Hansson said. 'That was what Martinsson said.'

Wallander immediately felt relieved.

'And here?' he asked. 'The investigation?'

'There has been another important development,' Hansson said. 'But that has to do with the plane that crashed.'

'What is it?'

'Yngve Leonard Holm has been found murdered. In the woods outside Sjöbo.'

Wallander sat down.

'But that isn't all,' Hansson said. 'He hasn't just been murdered. He was shot in the back of the head, just like the Eberhardsson sisters.'

Wallander held his breath. He had not expected this. That a connection would suddenly appear between the crashed plane and the two murdered women who had been found in the remains of a devastating fire.

He looked at Hansson. What does it mean, he thought. What is the significance of what Hansson is telling me?

All at once the trip to Cairo felt very distant.

CHAPTER 6

At ten o'clock on the morning of December 19, Wallander called the bank and asked if he could increase his loan by another 20,000 kronor. He lied and said he had misheard the price of the car he intended to buy. The bank loan officer replied that it shouldn't present any difficulties. Wallander could come and sign the loan documents and collect the money later on that day. After Wallander hung up the phone, he called Arne, who was selling him the car, and arranged for him to deliver it to Mariagatan at one o'clock. Arne would also either try to bring the old one to life or tow it back to his garage.

Wallander made these two calls right after the morning meeting. They had met for two hours, starting at a quarter to eight. But Wallander had been at the station since seven o'clock. When he arrived, Rydberg was already there. They went to the break room, where they found several bleary-eyed officers who had just finished the night shift. Rydberg had tea and biscuits. Wallander sat down opposite him.

'I heard you went to Egypt,' Rydberg said. 'How were the pyramids?'

'High,' Wallander said. 'Very strange.'

'And your father?'

'He could have gone to prison. But I got him out by paying almost ten thousand kronor in fines. How are you feeling?'

'Something is wrong,' Rydberg said firmly. 'One doesn't collapse like that from rheumatism. Something is wrong. But I don't know what it is. And right now I'm more interested in this Holm who got a bullet in the back of his head.'

'I heard about it from Hansson yesterday.'

Rydberg pushed his teacup away.

'It is of course an incredibly compelling thought that the Eberhardsson sisters might turn out to have been involved in drug trafficking. Something like that would strike at the very foundations of the Swedish sewing supplies industry. Out with the embroidery, in with the heroin.'

'The thought has crossed my mind,' Wallander said. 'I'll see you in a while.'

As he walked to his office he thought that Rydberg would never have been as open about his health if he wasn't convinced that something was wrong. Wallander felt himself starting to worry.

Until a quarter to eight he went through some reports that had piled up on his desk during his absence. He had spoken to Linda the day before—just after he had got home and put his bag down. She had promised to go to Kastrup and meet her grandfather and make sure he made it home to Löderup. Wallander had not dared to hope that he would really be approved for a new loan and therefore be able to get a new car and pick up his father in Malmö.

The investigative meeting started with Wallander briefly describing his adventures in Cairo and the helpful police officer Radwan. Then they discussed Holm. The body had been found within the Sjöbo police district, but just a couple of hundred metres from the unmade road where Ystad's police district began. 'Our Sjöbo colleagues are happy to give him to us,' Martinsson said. 'We can symbolically carry the corpse across the boundary and then it is ours. Especially considering that we have already had dealings with Holm.'

Wallander asked for a timetable of events, which Martinsson was able to supply. Holm had gone missing shortly after he was brought in for questioning on the day that the aeroplane crashed. While Wallander was in Cairo, a man out walking in the woods had discovered the body. It had been lying at the end of a forest road. There were car tracks. But Holm still had his wallet, so it had not been a case of robbery-homicide. No observations of any interest had been called in to the police. The area was deserted.

Martinsson had just finished when the door to the conference room was opened. An officer popped his head in and said that a communication had arrived from Interpol. Martinsson went to get it. While he was gone, Svedberg told Wallander about the manic energy with which Björk had gone about getting the front doors repaired.

Martinsson returned. 'One of the pilots has been identified,' he said. 'Pedro Espinosa, thirty-three years old. Born in Madrid. He'd been imprisoned in Spain for embezzlement and in France for smuggling.'

'Smuggling,' Wallander said. 'That fits perfectly.'

'There's another thing that's interesting,' Martinsson said. 'His last known address is in Marbella. That's where the Eberhardsson sisters' villa is.'

The room fell silent. Wallander was clear on the point that it could still be a coincidence. A house in Marbella and a dead pilot who happened to have lived in the same place. But deep down he knew that they were in the process of uncovering a baffling connection.

'The other pilot is still unidentified,' Martinsson went on. 'But they're working on it.'

Wallander looked round the table.

'We need more help from the Spanish police,' he said. 'If they're as helpful as Radwan in Cairo, they should be able to search the Eberhardsson sisters' villa very soon. They should look for a safe. And they should look for drugs. Who did the sisters know down there? This is what we need to find out. And we need to find out soon.'

'Should one of us go down there?' Hanson asked.

'Not yet,' Wallander said. 'Your sunbathing will have to wait until next summer.'

They reviewed the material and assigned the tasks to be performed. Above all they were going to focus on Yngve Leonard Holm. Wallander noticed that the pace in the team had picked up. They ended the meeting at a quarter to ten.

After Wallander had made his telephone calls, he put down the receiver and closed the door. Slowly he went back through the material they had uncovered so far, regarding the plane that had crashed, Yngve Leonard Holm and the two Eberhardsson sisters. He drew a triangle on his notepad: each of the three components marked a corner. Five dead people, he thought. Two pilots, one of whom came from Spain. In an aeroplane that was literally a Flying Dutchman since it had supposedly been scrapped after an accident in Laos. An aeroplane that flew in across the Swedish border at night, turned round just south of Sjöbo and crashed next to Mossby Beach. Lights had been observed on the ground, which could mean that the plane had dropped something.

This is the first point of the triangle.

The second point is the two sisters, who ran their sewing shop in Ystad. They are killed with shots to the head and their building is burned down. They turn out to have been wealthy, with a safe built into the foundations and a villa in Spain. Wallander drew a line between Pedro Espinosa and the Eberhardsson sisters. There was a connection there. Marbella.

The third point consisted of Yngve Leonard Holm, who had been executed on a forest road outside Sjöbo. About him they knew that he was a notorious drug dealer who possessed an unusually well-developed ability to cover his tracks.

But someone caught up with him outside Sjöbo, Wallander thought.

He got up from the desk and studied his triangle. What did it say? He made a point in the middle of the triangle. A centre, he thought. Where was the centre, a midpoint? He continued to study his sketch. Then all at once he realised that what he had drawn could be interpreted as a pyramid. From a distance, a pyramid could look like a triangle.

Wallander sat down at the desk again. *Everything that I have in front of me tells me one thing. That something has happened that has disturbed a pattern. The most likely thing is the plane crash. It set a chain reaction in motion that has resulted in three murders, three executions.*

He started over from the beginning. He couldn't drop the thought of a pyramid. Could it be that a kind of strange power play had been enacted? Where the triangle points consisted of the Eberhardsson sisters, Yngve Leonard Holm and the downed plane? But where there was still an unknown centre?

Slowly and methodically he proceeded through all the known facts. Now and again he wrote down a question. Without him noticing the time pass, it was suddenly twelve o'clock. He dropped the pen, took his coat and walked down to the bank. It was a couple of degrees above zero and drizzling. He signed his loan documents and received another 20,000 kronor. Right now he did not want to think about all the money that had vanished in Egypt.

At exactly one o'clock the car salesman arrived with his 'new' Peugeot. The old one refused to start. Wallander did not wait for the tow truck. Instead he took a drive in the dark blue car. It was worn and reeked of smoke, but the engine was good. That was the most important thing. He drove towards Hedeskoga and was about to turn when he decided to continue. He was on the road to Sjöbo. Martinsson had explained in detail where Holm's body had been found. He wanted to see the place with his own eyes. And perhaps even stop by the house where Holm had lived.

The place where Holm had been found was still cordoned off. But there were no police. Wallander got out of the car. There was silence all around. He stepped over the police tape and looked about. If someone wanted to kill a person, this was an excellent location. He tried to imagine what had happened. Holm had arrived here with someone. According to Martinsson there were only tracks from one car.

A confrontation, Wallander thought. Certain goods are handed over, a payment is to be made. Then something happens. Holm is shot in the back of the head. He is dead before he falls to the ground. The person who has committed the murder vanishes without a trace.

A man, Wallander thought. Or more than one. The same person or people who killed the Eberhardsson sisters a few days earlier.

Suddenly he felt close to something. There was yet another connection here that he would be able to see if only he made an effort. That it had to do with drugs appeared obvious, even if it was still hard to accept that two sisters who owned a sewing shop would have been mixed up in something like that. But Rydberg's first comment had been right—what did they really know about the two sisters?

Wallander left the forest road and drove on. He could see Martinsson's map clearly in his head. He had to turn right at the large roundabout south of Sjöbo. Then another road, a gravel road, to the left, to the last house on the right, a red barn next to the road. A blue mailbox that was about to fall to the ground. Two junked cars and a rusty tractor on a field next to the barn. A barking dog of indeterminate breed in a dog run. He had no trouble finding it. He heard the dog before he even got out of the car. He stepped out and walked into the yard.

The paint on the main house was peeling. The gutters hung in pieces at the corners. The dog barked desperately and scratched at the fence. Wallander wondered what would happen if the fence gave way and the dog was let loose. He walked over to the door and rang a bell. Then he saw that the wiring was disconnected. He knocked and waited. Finally he banged on the door so hard that it opened. He called out to see if anyone was home. Still no answer.

I shouldn't go in, he thought. I will break many rules that pertain not only to the police but to all citizens. Then he pushed the door open further and went in. Peeling wallpaper, stale air, a mess. Broken couches, mattresses on the floor. Yet there was a large-screen television and a relatively new video recorder. A CD player with large speakers. He called out again and listened. No answer. There was indescribable chaos in the kitchen. Dishes piled up in the sink. Paper bags, plastic bags, empty pizza cartons on the floor to which various lines of ants led.

A mouse scuttled past in a corner. The place smelled musty. Wallander walked on. Stopped outside a door that had been spray-painted with the words 'Yngve's Church'. He pushed open the door. There was a real bed inside, but only a bottom sheet and a blanket on it. A chest of drawers, two chairs. A radio on the windowsill. Yngve Leonard Holm had lived here. While he was having a large house built in Ystad. On the floor there was a tracksuit top. He had been wearing it when Wallander questioned him. Wallander sat down gingerly on the edge of the bed, afraid that it would give way, and looked around. A person lived here, he thought. A person who lived by herding other people into various forms of drug hell. He shook his head with distaste. Then he leaned over and looked under the bed. Dust. A slipper and some porn magazines. He stood up and pulled out the chest drawers. More magazines with undressed, splay-legged women. Underwear, painkillers, plasters.

Next drawer. Piles of papers. Some photographs. Holm at a bar somewhere with a glass of beer in each hand. Drunk. Red-eyed. Another photograph: Holm naked on a beach. Grinning straight at the camera. Wallander continued to search among the papers. Stopped at an old aeroplane ticket. Took it over to the window. Copenhagen–Marbella, return. August 12, 1989. The return dated August 17. Five days in Spain, and not on a charter flight. He tucked it into his pocket and closed the drawer after a few more minutes of searching.

There was nothing of interest in the wardrobe. More clutter and chaos. Wallander sat back down on the bed. Wondered where the other people who lived in the house were. He walked into the living room. There was a telephone on the table. He called the station and spoke to Ebba. He asked her to look up the number of the travel agency where Anette Bengtsson worked. He made a mental note of it, finished his conversation with Ebba and dialled the agency. Anette picked up. He told her who it was.

'How was the trip to Cairo?' she asked.

'Good. The pyramids are very high. Remarkable, really.'

'You should have stayed longer.'

'I'll have to do that another time.'

Then he asked her if she could tell him if Anna or Emilia Eberhardsson had been in Spain between August 12 and 17.

'That will take a while,' she said.

'I'll wait,' Wallander said. She put the receiver down. Wallander again caught sight of a mouse in a corner. Winter is coming, he thought. The mice are on their way back into the house. Anette Bengtsson returned.

'Anna Eberhardsson left Ystad on the 10th of August,' she said. 'She returned at the beginning of September.'

'Thanks for the help,' Wallander replied. 'I would very much like to have an inventory of all the sisters' trips last year. For the investigation,' he added. 'I'll come in tomorrow.'

She promised to help him. He hung up. Thought that he would probably have fallen in love with her if he had been ten years younger. Now it would be senseless. He left the house and the dog barked like crazy. Wallander walked up to the dog run and it went quiet. As soon as he turned round and left it started to bark again. I should be grateful, he thought, that Linda doesn't live in a house like this. How many people in Sweden, how many normal, unthinking citizens, are familiar with these environments? Where people live in constant mists, misery, despair.

HE WAS BACK at the station at four o'clock. Wallander told Martinsson about his excursion and his conversation with Anette Bengtsson. He showed him the ticket. 'We now have another connection,' Wallander said. 'No one can still say this is a coincidence.'

That was also what he said at the case meeting at five o'clock. Then each of them went back to his tasks. Wallander called Linda and told her he now had a car that worked and could pick up her grandfather in Malmö. He went home a little before seven. Emma Lundin called. This time Wallander said yes. She stayed until just past midnight, as usual. Wallander thought of Anette Bengtsson.

The following day he stopped by the travel agency and picked up the information he had requested. There were many customers looking for seats for Christmas. Wallander would have liked to stay for a while and talk to Anette Bengtsson, but she didn't have time. He also stopped outside the old sewing shop. The rubble had now been cleared. He walked into town. Suddenly he realised there was only a week left until Christmas. The first one since the divorce.

That day nothing happened that took the investigation further. Wallander pondered his pyramid. The only addition he made was a thick line between Anna Eberhardsson and Yngve Leonard Holm.

The next day, December 21, Wallander drove to Malmö to pick up his father. He felt great relief when he saw him walk out of the ferry terminal. He drove him back to Löderup. His father talked nonstop about his wonderful trip. He appeared to have forgotten the fact that he had been in prison and that Wallander had actually also been to Cairo.

That evening Wallander went to the annual police Christmas function. He avoided sitting at the same table as Björk. But the toast the police chief made was unusually successful. He had taken the trouble to look into the history of the Ystad police. His account was both entertaining and well presented. Wallander chuckled on several occasions.

He was drunk when he came home. Before falling asleep he thought of Anette Bengtsson. And decided in the next moment to immediately stop thinking about her.

On December 22 they reviewed the state of the investigation. Nothing new had happened. The Spanish police had not found anything noteworthy in the sisters' villa. No hidden valuables, nothing. They were still waiting for the second pilot to be identified.

The next day they were able to add to the existing case data. Nyberg informed them that Holm had been shot with the same gun used on the Eberhardsson sisters. But there was still no trace of this weapon. Wallander made new lines in his sketch. The connections grew, but the top of the pyramid was still missing.

THE WORK WAS NOT supposed to stop during Christmas, but Wallander knew that it would lose momentum. Not least because it would be hard to track people down, hard to get information.

It rained in the afternoon on Christmas Eve. Wallander picked Linda up at the station and together they drove out to Löderup. She had bought her grandfather a new scarf. Wallander had bought him a bottle of cognac. Linda and Wallander made dinner while his father sat at the kitchen table and told them about the pyramids. The evening went unusually well, above all because Linda had such a good relationship with her grandfather. Wallander sometimes felt as if he were on the outside. But it didn't bother him. From time to time he thought about the dead sisters, Holm and the plane that had crashed into a field.

After Wallander and Linda had returned to Ystad they sat up and talked for a long time. Wallander slept late the following morning. He always slept well when Linda was in the apartment. Christmas Day was cold and clear. They took a long walk through Sand Forest. She told him about her plans. Wallander had given her a promise for Christmas. A promise to cover some of the costs, as much as he could afford, if she decided to pursue an apprenticeship in France. He accompanied her to the train station in the late afternoon. He had wanted to drive her to Malmö, but she wanted to take the train. Wallander felt lonely in the evening. He watched an old film on TV and then listened to *Rigoletto*. Thought that he should have called Rydberg to wish him a merry Christmas. But now it was too late.

WHEN WALLANDER LOOKED out of the window on Boxing Day, just after seven in the morning, a gloomy mix of snow and rain was falling over Ystad. He suddenly recalled the warm night air in Cairo. Thought that he should not forget to thank Radwan for his help in some way. He wrote it down on the pad of paper on the kitchen table. Then he cooked himself a substantial breakfast for once.

It was close to nine when he finally got to the police station. He talked to some of the officers who had worked during the night. Christmas had been unusually calm in Ystad this year. Now he would take up the murder investigations in earnest again. There were still technically two cases, even though he was convinced that the same person, or people, had killed the Eberhardsson sisters and Yngve Leonard Holm. It was not simply the same weapon and the same style. There was also a common motive.

He sat down with his notes. The pyramid with its base. He drew a large question mark in the middle. The apex, which his father had been aiming for, he now had to find himself.

After two hours of thinking, he was sure. They now had to concentrate their efforts on the missing link. A pattern, perhaps an organisation, had collapsed when the plane crashed. Then one or several unknown individuals had hastily stepped out of the shadows and acted. They had slain three people.

Silence, Wallander thought. Perhaps that is what all this is about? To prevent information from trickling out. Dead people do not speak.

That could be it. But it could also be something completely different.

He went over and stood by the window. The snow was falling more thickly now. This will take time, he thought. That's the first thing I'll say when we have our next meeting. We have to allow that it will take time to solve this case.

CHAPTER 7

That night Wallander had a nightmare. He was back in Cairo again, in the courtroom. Radwan was no longer at his side. But now he could suddenly understand everything that the prosecutor and judge were saying. His father had been sitting there at his side in handcuffs and Wallander had listened in horror as his father was sentenced to death. He had stood up in order to protest. But no one had heard him. At that point he had kicked himself out of the dream, up to the surface. When he woke up he was covered in sweat. He lay completely still, staring into the darkness.

The dream had made him so unsettled that he got out of bed and went to the kitchen. It was still snowing. The street lamp was swaying gently in the wind. It was half past four. He drank a glass of water, then stood for a while fingering a half-empty bottle of whisky. But he let it be. He thought about something that Linda had said; that dreams were messengers. Even if dreams were about other people, they consisted foremost of messages to the self. Wallander had always doubted the value of trying to interpret dreams. What could it mean for him to imagine that his father had been sentenced to death? Had the dreams pronounced a death sentence on him?

Perhaps it had to do with the concern he felt for Rydberg's health. He drank another glass of water and went back to bed.

But sleep would not come. His thoughts wandered. Mona, his father, Linda, Rydberg. And then he was back to his constant point of departure. Work. He thought about his sketch. The triangle with a question mark in the middle. But a pyramid also has different cornerstones, he thought in the darkness.

He tossed and turned until six o'clock. Then he got up, ran a bath and made a cup of coffee. He took his coffee cup with him into the bathroom. He lay and dozed in the warm water until close to six thirty. Thinking about going out into the weather was unpleasant. This endless slush. But now at least he had a car that would start.

He turned the key in the ignition at a quarter past seven. The engine started at once. He drove to the station and parked as close to the entrance as possible. Then he ran through the snow and slush and almost slipped on the front steps. Martinsson was in reception, skimming the police magazine. He nodded when he spotted Wallander.

'It says here that we're supposed to get better at everything,' he said with a note of despondency. 'Above all, we're supposed to improve our relations with the general public.'

'That sounds excellent,' Wallander said.

He had a recurring memory, something that had happened in Malmö over twenty years ago. He had been accosted by a girl at a café who accused him of hitting her with a baton at a Vietnam demonstration. He had never forgotten this moment. That she had been partly responsible for his almost being stabbed to death with a knife at a later time was of a lesser concern. It was her expression, her complete contempt, that he had never forgotten.

Martinsson threw the magazine onto the table. 'Don't you ever think about quitting?' he asked. 'Doing something else?'

'Every day. But I don't know what that would be.'

'One could apply to a private security company,' Martinsson said.

This surprised Wallander. He had always imagined that Martinsson nurtured a heady dream of one day becoming police chief.

Then he told him about his visit to the house that Holm had lived in. Martinsson expressed concern when he heard that only the dog had been at the house.

'At least two people live there,' Martinsson said. 'A girl of about twenty-five. I never saw her. But a man was there. Rolf was his name. Rolf Nyman, I think. I don't remember her name.'

'There was only a dog,' Wallander repeated. 'Outside in a run.'

They agreed to wait until around nine before meeting in the conference room. Martinsson was not sure if Svedberg was coming. He had called the night before and said that he had come down with a cold and a temperature.

Wallander walked to his office. As usual it was twenty-three steps away from the beginning of the corridor. Sometimes he wished that something would suddenly have happened. That the corridor would turn out to be longer or shorter. But everything was normal. He hung up his coat and removed a couple of hairs that had stuck to the back of the chair. He brushed his hand over his head. With every year he became more worried that he was going to lose his hair.

He heard rapid steps outside in the corridor. It was Martinsson, waving a piece of paper. 'The second pilot has been identified,' he said. 'This came just now from Interpol. Ayrton McKenna,' Martinsson read. 'Born 1945 in Southern Rhodesia. A helicopter pilot since 1964 in the then Southern Rhodesian military. Decorated many times during the 1960s. For what, one might ask. For bombing a lot of black Africans?'

Wallander only had a very vague sense of what had transpired in the former British colonies in Africa.

Martinsson continued to read. 'At some point after 1980, Ayrton McKenna moved to England. Between 1983 and 1985 he was in prison in Birmingham for drug smuggling. From 1985 on there are no records until he suddenly turns up in Hong Kong in 1987. There he is suspected of smuggling people from the People's Republic. He escapes from a prison in Hong Kong after shooting two guards to death and has been a wanted man ever since. But the identification is definitive. He was the one who crashed with Espinosa outside Mossby.'

Wallander mulled this over. 'What do we have?' he said. 'Two pilots, both with smuggling on their records. In an aeroplane that does not exist. They cross illegally over the Swedish border for a few short minutes and are probably on their way out again when the plane crashes. That leaves us with two possibilities. They were either leaving or collecting something. Since there are no signs that the plane landed, this seems to indicate that something was tossed out. What is dropped from a plane? Besides bombs?'

'Drugs.'

Wallander nodded. Then he leaned over the table.

'Has the accident commission begun its work yet?'

'Things have proceeded very slowly. But nothing indicates that the plane was shot down, if that's what you're getting at.'

'No,' Wallander said. 'I'm only interested in two things. Did the plane have extra fuel tanks, that is, from how far away could it have come? And was it an accident?'

'If it wasn't shot down, it could hardly have been anything other than an accident.'

'There is a possibility that it was sabotage. But perhaps that's remote.'

'It was an old plane,' Martinsson said. 'We know that. It crashed into the hillside outside Vientiane in 1986. And was then put back together again. It could, in other words, have been in bad shape.'

'When is this accident commission going to get started for real?'

'Tomorrow. The plane's been transported to a hangar in Sturup.'

'You should probably be there,' Wallander said. 'This matter of the extra fuel tanks is an important one.'

'I think it would need a great deal to be able to fly here from Spain without landing somewhere in between,' Martinsson said hesitantly.

'I don't believe that either. But I want to know if the flight could have originated from the other side of the sea. Germany. Or one of the Baltic States.'

Martinsson left. Wallander made some notes. Next to the name Espinosa he now wrote McKenna, unsure of the exact spelling.

The investigators met at half past eight. 'There was a stabbing incident last night,' Hansson said. 'Two brothers ended up in a fight with their father. Drunk, of course. One of the brothers and the father are in the hospital.'

'We'll have to deal with that when we have time,' Wallander said. 'Right now we have three murders on our plate. Or two, if we combine the sisters into one.'

'I don't really understand why Sjöbo can't deal with Holm on their own,' Hansson said with irritation.

'Because Holm has to do with us,' Wallander replied, just as irritated. 'If both of us investigate these things on our own we'll never get anywhere.'

Hansson did not back down. 'Do we know that Holm had anything to do with the Eberhardssons?'

'No,' Wallander said. 'But we know everything indicates that the same person killed them. I think that's enough of a connection to bind the cases and for us to lead a coordinated investigation from Ystad.' Wallander marked the end of this discussion with Hansson by turning to Rydberg.

'Do we have any updates on the drug trade?' he asked. 'Has anything happened in Malmö? Have the prices changed, or the supply?'

'I called,' Rydberg said, 'but there didn't appear to be anyone working there over Christmas.'

'Then we'll have to proceed with Holm,' Wallander decided. 'We need to dig deeper. Who was Holm? Who did he associate with? What was his position in the drug-trade hierarchy? Did he even have a position? And what about the sisters? We know too little.'

'Absolutely correct,' Rydberg said. 'Digging down usually takes one forward.'

They ended the meeting with Rydberg's words buzzing in their ears. Wallander drove down to the travel agency to speak to Anette Bengtsson. But to his disappointment she had taken time off over Christmas. Her colleague did, however, find an envelope to give to him.

ON THE WAY BACK to the station, Wallander suddenly remembered that he had signed up for the laundry room this morning. He stopped at Mariagatan, walked up to the apartment and carried down all the dirty laundry that had accumulated in his wardrobe. When he reached the laundry room there was a note taped to the front of the washing machine saying it was out of order. Wallander was so furious he carried all the laundry out to his car and threw it in the boot. There was a machine at the station. As he turned onto Regementsgatan he was almost hit by a motorcycle approaching at high speed. He pulled over to the side of the road, turned off the engine and closed his eyes. I'm stressed, he thought. If a broken washing machine almost causes me to lose control then there's something wrong with my life.

He knew what it was. Loneliness. The increasingly anaemic late-night hours with Emma Lundin.

Instead of driving to the station he decided to pay a visit to his father out in Löderup. It was always a risky proposition to arrive without prior notice. But right now Wallander felt the need to experience the smell of oil paints in the studio. The dream from last night still haunted him. He drove through the grey landscape and wondered where he should begin in order to achieve a change in his existence. Perhaps Martinsson was right and he should seriously consider whether or not he should remain a police officer for the rest of his life. Even my father has something that I lack, he thought as he turned into the driveway. The dreams that he has decided to stay faithful to. Even if they cost his only son a small fortune.

He got out of the car. A cat strutted out through the studio's half-open door and regarded him suspiciously. Wallander knocked and went in.

His father was leaning forward in front of his easel. 'You here?' he said. 'That's unexpected.'

'I was in the neighbourhood,' Wallander said. 'Am I disturbing you?'

His father pretended not to hear the question. Instead he talked of his trip to Egypt. As if it were a vivid but already very distant memory. Wallander sat down on an old sledge and listened.

'Now only Italy remains,' his father concluded. 'Then I can lie down to die.'

'I think we'll wait with that trip,' Wallander said. 'At least a couple of months.'

His father painted. Wallander sat quietly. Now and again they exchanged a few words. Then more silence. Wallander noticed that he was more relaxed. His head felt lighter. After about half an hour he stood up to leave. 'I'll come by for New Year,' he said.

'Bring a bottle of cognac,' his father replied.

Wallander returned to the police station, sat down in his office and reviewed the Eberhardsson sisters' trips during the past year. He tried to discern a pattern, without being sure of what he was really looking for. I know nothing about Holm, he thought. There are no fixed points, other than this single trip that Holm made at the same time as Anna Eberhardsson.

He put all the papers back into the envelope and put that into the folder where he kept all the documents having to do with the murder investigations. Then he wrote himself a reminder to buy a bottle of cognac.

It was already past noon. He felt hungry. In order to break his habit of downing a couple of hot dogs at a stand, he walked to the hospital and had a sandwich at the café. Then he leafed through a magazine that had been left on the table next to him. A pop star had almost died of cancer. An actor had fainted during a performance. Photographs from the parties of the rich. He tossed the magazine aside and started walking back to the station. He felt like an elephant lumbering around in a ring bounded by the city of Ystad. Something has to happen soon, he thought. Who executed these three people, and why?

When he got back to the station Rydberg was sitting in the reception area, waiting for him. Wallander sat down on a sofa next to him. As usual Rydberg got right to the point.

'Heroin is flowing into Malmö,' he said. 'In Lund, Eslöv, Landskrona, Helsingborg. I talked to a colleague in Malmö. He said that there were clear signs that the market had received a boost in supply. It could, in other words, coincide with a drug drop from the plane. In this case, there is only one important question.'

Wallander understood. 'Who was there to receive it?'

'If this is the case, we can play with several different scenarios,' Rydberg went on. 'No one counted on the fact that the plane would crash. A wreck of a plane from Asia that should have been junked a long time ago. Something must then have happened on land. Either the wrong person picked up the package that was dropped in the night. Or else there was more than one predator stalking this prey.'

Wallander nodded. He had also thought this far.

'Something went wrong,' Rydberg said. 'And this led to the execution-style slayings of the Eberhardsson sisters and subsequently Holm. With the same weapon and by the same hand, or hands.'

'But I still resist the thought,' Wallander said. 'We know by now that Anna and Emilia were not nice old ladies. And yet from there, the step of saying they were involved in narcotics feels too great.'

'I think so too,' Rydberg said. 'But nothing surprises me any longer. Greed knows no bounds when it sinks its claws into people. Perhaps the sewing shop was doing worse and worse. Perhaps they dreamed of a life in a sunny paradise. They could never have achieved this by selling press-studs and silk thread. Suddenly something happens. And they are caught in the web.'

'You can also look at it from the reverse perspective,' Wallander said. 'A better cover than two older women in a sewing shop can hardly be imagined. They were the personification of innocence.'

Rydberg nodded. 'Who was there that night to receive the package?' he repeated. 'And one more question: Who was behind all this? More precisely: Who is behind it?'

'We're still searching for a midpoint,' Wallander said. 'The apex of the pyramid.'

Rydberg yawned and got up from the sofa with some effort.

'We'll figure it out sooner or later,' he said.

THAT NIGHT WALLANDER slept heavily, without dreaming. The next day it was sunny and 5°C. He left the car at home and walked to the station. But when he was halfway there, he changed his mind. He thought of what Martinsson had told him, about the two people who lived in the house where Holm had a room. It was only a quarter past seven. He would have time to drive up there and see if they were in before going to his meeting at the station.

He turned into the front yard at a quarter to eight. The dog was in its fenced run, barking. Wallander looked around. The house appeared as abandoned as before. He walked up to the door and knocked. No answer. He felt the handle. It was locked. Someone must have been there.

He stepped away in order to walk round the house. Then he heard the front door open behind him. He jumped involuntarily. A man wearing a vest and sagging jeans was standing there staring at him. Wallander walked over and introduced himself.

'Are you Rolf Nyman?' he asked.

'Yes, that's me.'

'I need to speak to you.'

The man looked hesitant.

'The house is a mess,' he said. 'And the girl who lives here is sleeping.'

'My place is messy, too,' Wallander said. 'And we don't need to sit next to her bed.'

Nyman stepped aside and let Wallander in, then led him to the cluttered kitchen. They sat down. The man made no gesture to offer Wallander anything. But he appeared friendly. Wallander assumed he was embarrassed at the mess.

'The girl has big problems with drugs,' Nyman said. 'Right now she's trying to detox. I'm helping her as much as I can. But it's hard.'

'And you?'

'I never touch anything.'

'But isn't it strange then to live in the same place as Holm? If you want her to get over a drug addiction.'

Nyman's reply was swift and convincing.

'I had no idea he was involved with drugs. We lived here cheaply. He was nice. I had no idea what he did. To me he said he was studying astronomy. We used to stand outside in the garden in the evenings. He knew the name of every single star.'

'What do you do?'

'I can't hold down a permanent job until she gets better. I work at a disco from time to time.'

'You're a DJ?'

'Yes.'

Wallander thought he made a sympathetic impression. He did not appear anxious about anything other than disturbing the girl who was sleeping somewhere.

'Holm,' Wallander said. 'How did you meet him? And when was that?'

'In a disco in Landskrona. We started talking. He told me about this house. A couple of weeks later we moved in. The worst thing is that I don't have the energy to clean. I did earlier. Holm did too. But now all my time goes to taking care of her.'

'You never suspected what Holm was up to?'

'No.'

'Did he ever have visitors?'

'Never. He was usually gone during the day. But he always said when he was coming back. It was only the last time, when he didn't come back, that he said where he was going.'

'Had he appeared nervous that day?'

Rolf Nyman thought back. 'No, he was like normal.'

'And how was that?'

'Happy. But reserved sometimes.'

Wallander thought about how best to proceed.

'Did he have a lot of money?'

'He certainly didn't live in luxury. I can show you his room.'

'That won't be necessary. Are you sure he never had any visitors?'

'Never.'

'But there must have been telephone calls.'

Nyman nodded. 'It was as if he always knew when someone was going to call. Sat down next to the phone and it rang. If he wasn't at home, it never rang. That was the strangest thing about him.'

Wallander had reached the end of his questions and stood up.

'What will you do now?' he asked.

'I don't know. Holm rented the house from someone in Örebro. I guess we'll have to move.'

Rolf Nyman followed him out onto the front steps.

'Did you ever hear Holm mention the Eberhardsson sisters?'

'The ones who were killed? No, never.'

Wallander realised he had one final question.

'Holm must have had a car,' he said. 'Where is it?'

Rolf Nyman shook his head. 'I don't know.'

'What kind was it?'

'A black VW Golf.'

Wallander held out his hand and said goodbye. The dog was silent as Wallander walked to the car.

Holm must have concealed his business well, he thought as he drove back to Ystad. He pulled up and parked the car outside the station at a quarter to nine. Ebba was at her desk and said that Martinsson and the others were waiting for him in the conference room. He hurried over. Nyberg had also arrived.

'What's going on?' Wallander said before he had even sat down.

'Big news,' Martinsson said. 'Our Malmö colleagues have made a routine search of a well-known drug dealer. In his house they found a .38 calibre pistol.'

Martinsson turned to Nyberg. 'The forensic technicians have worked quickly,' he said. 'Both the Eberhardsson sisters and Holm were shot with a weapon of that calibre.'

Wallander caught his breath. 'What's the name of the dealer?'

'Nilsmark. But he's known as Hilton.'

'Is it the same pistol?'

'We can't answer that question yet. But the possibility exists.'

Wallander nodded. 'Good,' he said. 'This may be our breakthrough. And then we have a shot at wrapping this up before New Year.'

CHAPTER 8

They worked intensively for three days until New Year's Eve. Wallander and Nyberg drove into Malmö on the morning of December 28. Nyberg went to talk to the Malmö police technicians, Wallander to take part in the questioning of the drug dealer known as Hilton. He turned out to be a man in his fifties, overweight yet able to move with a surprising agility. He was dressed in a suit and tie and appeared bored. Before the start of his questioning, Wallander had been briefed on the man's history by a detective inspector named Hyttner.

Hilton had done some time at the beginning of the 1980s for dealing drugs. But Hyttner was convinced that the police and prosecutors had only been able to skim the surface that time and put him away for just a small portion of his criminal activities. He had clearly been able to retain control of his business from prison. During his absence, the Malmö police had not detected a power struggle among those who controlled the drug supply into the southern parts of Sweden.

When Hilton had got out of prison he had celebrated the event by getting divorced and marrying a young Bolivian beauty. Thereafter he had moved to a large estate just north of Trelleborg, extending his hunting-grounds as far as Ystad. On December 28, the police felt they had enough evidence against him to get a search warrant. That was when they found the gun.

Hilton had immediately confessed that he had no licence for the weapon. He explained that he had bought it in order to defend himself since his home was so isolated. But he had firmly denied any involvement in the murders of the Eberhardsson sisters and Yngve Leonard Holm.

Wallander sat in on the questioning of Hilton. Towards the end he posed some of his own questions, among them what exactly Hilton had been doing on the two dates in question. In the case of the Eberhardssons, the timetable was very precise. It was less certain when Holm had been shot. Hilton claimed to have been in Copenhagen when the Eberhardssons were killed. Since he had travelled alone, it would take time to confirm this claim. During the time that had elapsed between Holm going missing and when he had been found murdered, Hilton had done many different things.

After the session, Wallander had coffee with Hyttner. 'We've never been able to link him to any violent incidents before,' Hyttner said. 'He has always used other boys when needed. And they haven't always been the same ones. From what we can tell, he's brought in people from the Continent when he's had to break someone's leg who hasn't performed up to snuff.'

'All of them will have to be tracked down,' Wallander said, 'if it turns out that the weapon matches.'

'I have a hard time believing that it's him,' Hyttner said. 'He's not the type. He has no qualms about selling heroin to schoolkids. But he's also the kind who faints when he has to give a blood sample.'

Wallander returned to Ystad at the start of the afternoon. Nyberg remained in Malmö. Wallander noticed that he was hoping more than he believed that they were nearer to solving the case.

At the same time another thought had started to gnaw at him. Something he had overlooked. A conclusion he should have drawn, or an assumption he should have made. He searched his mind without finding an answer.

When Wallander got back to the station he bumped into Björk in the reception area.

'I hear you've solved those murders,' Björk said.

'No,' Wallander said firmly. 'Nothing has been solved.'

'Then we'll have to continue to hope.'

Björk left through the front doors. It is as if our confrontation had never taken place, Wallander thought. Or else he's more afraid of conflict than I am. Or nurses a grudge less.

Wallander gathered the squad together and reviewed the developments in Malmö.

'Do you think it's him?' Rydberg asked when Wallander was finished.

'I don't know,' Wallander answered.

'That means, in other words, that you don't think it's him?'

Wallander did not answer. He only shrugged somewhat despondently.

The rest of the day, nothing significant occurred. Everyone was waiting. Nyberg returned from Malmö. The forensic ballistics specialists were working at full speed on the weapon. Wallander walked to and fro in the corridor. He kept searching for the thought that was just out of reach. It continued to gnaw at his subconscious. He knew enough to realise it was only a detail that had flashed by. Perhaps a single word that he should have caught and examined more closely.

It was six o'clock. Together, Wallander and Martinsson reviewed everything they knew about Yngve Leonard Holm. He was born in Brösarp and, as far as they could tell, had never held down a real job in his life. Small-time stealing in his youth had led to increasingly serious crimes. But no violence. Just like Nilsmark/Hilton. At seven o'clock Wallander called Malmö and spoke to Hyttner. Nothing had happened there either.

Wallander went home. The washing machine had still not been repaired. And the dirty laundry was still in his car. He angrily returned to the station and stuffed the washing machine full. Then he sat doodling in his notebook. Thought about Radwan and the pyramids. By the time his laundry was dry it was past nine o'clock. He went home, heated a can of stew and ate in front of the TV while he watched an old Swedish film.

Before he went to bed he called Linda. This time it was Mona who answered. He could immediately tell from her voice that he had called at the wrong time. Linda was out. Wallander simply asked Mona to give Linda his greetings. The conversation was over before it had even begun.

THE FOLLOWING DAY, December 29, Wallander worked through his piles of paper. In the afternoon Per Åkeson came into his office and asked for an update on the latest developments. Wallander told him the truth, that they were just hoping they were on the right track. But there was still a great deal of groundwork to be done.

It was Åkeson's last day of work before his sabbatical.

'My replacement is a woman,' he said. 'You should be happy. Her name is Anette Brolin and she's coming down from Stockholm. She's much more attractive than I am.'

'We'll see,' Wallander said. 'But I expect we'll miss you.'

They wished each other a happy new year and promised to stay in touch. That evening Wallander talked to Linda for a long time on the phone.

She was planning to celebrate New Year's Eve with friends in Lund. Wallander was disappointed. He had thought, or at least hoped, that she would join them in Löderup.

'Two old men,' she said kindly. 'I can think of a more exciting way to spend the evening.'

After the call, Wallander realised that he had forgotten to buy the bottle of cognac his father had asked for. He ought to buy a bottle of champagne, too. He wrote two notes. He put one on the kitchen table and one in his shoe. That night he sat up for a long time listening to a recording of *Turandot* with Maria Callas. Only when it was nearly three did he fall asleep.

On the morning of December 30 there was a heavy snowfall over Ystad. It could be a chaotic New Year's Eve if the weather did not improve. But at ten o'clock the skies cleared and the snow started to melt away. Wallander wondered why the ballistics team was taking such an inordinate amount of time to decide whether it was the same weapon. Nyberg grew angry and said that forensic technicians did not earn their measly wages by performing substandard work. Wallander immediately crawled on his knees. They made up and then spent some time talking about the low wages of the police.

In the afternoon, the investigative squad assembled for what turned out to be a slow-moving meeting since there were so few new items. The police in Marbella had sent an impressively detailed report of their search of the Eberhardsson sisters' villa. They had even included a photograph. The picture was now passed round the table. The house really was palatial. But nonetheless the report did not yield anything new to the investigation. There was no breakthrough, only this waiting.

THEIR HOPES WERE dashed the next day. The forensic ballistics specialists were able to determine that the weapon that had been found in Nilsmark's home had not been the one used to kill either the Eberhardsson sisters or Holm. For a moment, the investigative squad was deflated. Only Rydberg and Wallander had suspected that the message would most likely be in the negative. The Malmö police had also been able to confirm Nilsmark's trip to Copenhagen. He could not have been in Ystad when the sisters were executed and their shop set on fire.

'That puts us back at square one,' Wallander said. 'In January we are going to have to start again at full speed. Review the material and work deeper.'

No one made any more comments. During the New Year's holiday, the investigation would be put on hold. Since they had no immediate leads Wallander felt that what they needed most was to rest. Then they wished one another a happy new year. Finally, only Rydberg and Wallander were left.

'We knew this,' Rydberg said. 'Both you and I. That it would have been too easy with that Nilsmark. Why the hell would he have kept the weapon? It was wrong from the start.'

'But we still had to look into it.'

'Police work often consists of doing what one knows from the start to be meaningless,' Rydberg said. 'But it is as you say. No stone can be left unturned.'

They talked briefly about New Year's Eve and shook hands, as if to mark the day as special. Then Wallander went to his office, put out a diary for 1990 and cleared out his desk. New Year's Eve was a good time to empty out drawers, to rid himself of old paper.

At seven o'clock he went home, had a shower and changed his clothes. Shortly after eight he was out in Löderup. His father had made a fish gratin that was surprisingly tasty. Wallander had managed to buy cognac and his father nodded approvingly when he saw that it was Hennessy. The bottle of champagne was put in the fridge. They drank beer with their dinner. His father had put on his old suit and tie for the occasion.

A little after nine they sat down and played poker. Wallander got three of a kind twice but threw one of his cards away each time so that his father could win. At around eleven, Wallander walked outside to relieve himself. It was clear and had grown colder. The stars were sparkling. Wallander thought of the pyramids. The fact that they were lit by strong spotlights meant the Egyptian night sky had been all but invisible. He went back inside. His father had downed several glasses of cognac and was starting to get drunk. Wallander only had small sips since he was driving back.

Linda called at half past eleven. They took turns talking to her. In the background Wallander heard the sounds of a stereo turned up very high. They had to shout at each other.

'You would have had a better time with us,' Wallander shouted.

'You don't know anything about it,' she yelled back.

They wished each other a happy new year. His father had yet another glass of cognac. He was starting to spill as he refilled his glass. But he was in good spirits. And that was the only thing that mattered to Wallander.

They sat in front of the TV at twelve and watched as the new year was rung in.

He went home a little before one. But first he had helped his father into bed. He had taken off his shoes and spread a blanket over him.

'We'll go to Italy soon,' his father said.

Wallander cleaned up in the kitchen. His father's snores were already rolling through the house.

ON THE MORNING of New Year's Day, Wallander woke up with a headache and a sore throat. He said as much to Emma Lundin when she came by at twelve o'clock. Since she was a nurse and Wallander was both hot and pale she didn't doubt that it was true. She checked his throat.

'A three-day cold,' she pronounced. 'Stay home.'

She made some tea that they drank in the living room, and then left at around three. Wallander spent the rest of the day in bed. For long periods of time he lay in a kind of half-stupor. The pyramids returned again and again in his thoughts. His father climbed and fell, or else he found himself deep down in a narrow passageway where enormous masses of stone were suspended above his head.

The following day he still felt ill. He called Martinsson and said he was planning to stay in bed. He was told that New Year's Eve had been a calm affair in Ystad but unusually troublesome in other parts of the country. At around ten o'clock he went out and bought groceries, since his fridge and pantry were almost empty. He also went to the chemist and bought some headache tablets. His throat felt better, but now his nose was running. He sneezed as he was about to pay for the painkillers. The cashier looked disapprovingly at him.

He went home to bed and fell asleep again.

Suddenly he woke up with a start. He had dreamed about the pyramids again. But it was something else that had woken him. Something that had to do with the thought that had eluded him.

What is it that I don't see? he wondered. He lay in absolute stillness and stared out into the darkened room. It had something to do with the pyramids. And with New Year's Eve at his father's in Löderup. When he had been standing out in the garden, staring up at the sky, he had seen the stars. Since it was dark all around him. The pyramids outside Cairo had been illuminated by strong lights. They had detracted from the light of the stars.

He finally grasped the thought that had nagged at him.

The plane that had sneaked in over the Swedish coast had dropped something. Lights had been observed beyond the woods. An area had been marked out in order for the plane to find it. Spotlights had been set up in the fields and then taken down again.

It was the spotlights that had nagged at him. Who had access to strong lights of this kind?

The idea was a long shot. Nonetheless he trusted his intuition. He thought about it for a while, sitting up in bed. Then he made up his mind, got up, put on his old dressing gown and called the police station. He wanted to talk to Martinsson.

'Do me a favour,' Wallander said. 'Call Rolf Nyman. The guy who shared that house with Holm outside Sjöbo. Call and make it sound like a routine enquiry. Some facts that need to be filled in. Nyman told me he worked as a DJ at various discos. Ask him in passing for the names of all the places where he's worked.'

'Why is this important?'

'I don't know,' Wallander said. 'But please do me this favour.'

Martinsson promised to get back to him. Wallander had already started to doubt himself. It was too much of a long shot. But it was as Rydberg always said: no stone should be left unturned.

The hours went by. It was already afternoon. Martinsson did not call. Wallander's fever was starting to go down, but he was still plagued by sneezing attacks. And a runny nose.

Martinsson called back at half past four. 'No one answered the phone until just now,' he said. 'But I don't think he suspected anything. I have a list here of the four discos. Two in Malmö, one in Lund, and one out in Råå, outside Helsingborg.'

Wallander wrote down the names. 'Good,' he said.

'I hope you realise that I'm curious.'

'It's just an idea I've had. We'll talk about it tomorrow.'

Wallander got dressed, let a couple of painkillers dissolve in a glass of water and had a cup of coffee. At a quarter past five he was on his way.

THE FIRST DISCO was housed in an old warehouse in the Malmö Frihamn area. Wallander was in luck. Just as he stopped the car, a man walked out of the closed disco. Wallander introduced himself and learned that the person in front of him was called Juhanen, and the owner of the disco Exodus.

'I want to ask you about Rolf Nyman,' Wallander said.

'Anything wrong?'

'No, just routine questions. He works for you sometimes?'

'He's good. Perhaps a little conservative in his choices. But skilled.'

'A disco lives on the high volume of its music and its light effects,' Wallander said, 'if I'm not completely mistaken?'

'Correct,' Juhanen said. 'I always stuff my ears, or I would have lost my hearing a long time ago.'

'Rolf Nyman never borrowed any lighting equipment, did he?' Wallander asked. 'Some of the high-intensity spotlights?'

'Why would he do that?'

'It's just a question.'

Juhanen shook his head firmly. 'I keep an eye on both the staff and the equipment,' he said. 'Nothing disappears around here. Or gets borrowed.'

'That's all I needed to know,' Wallander said. 'Also, I would rather you didn't mention this to anyone for now.'

Juhanen smiled. 'You mean, I shouldn't tell Nyman?'

'Exactly.'

'What's he done?'

'Nothing. But we have to snoop around in secret sometimes.'

Juhanen shrugged. 'I won't say anything.'

Wallander drove on. The second disco was located in the inner city. It was open. The volume hit Wallander's head like a club as he walked in the door. The disco was owned by two men, one of whom was present. Wallander convinced him to walk out onto the street. He also had a negative answer. Rolf Nyman had never borrowed any lights. Nor had any equipment gone missing.

Wallander got back in his car and blew his nose. This is meaningless, he thought. What I am doing right now is just a waste of effort. The only result will be that I'll end up staying ill longer.

Then he drove to Lund. The sneezing attacks came and went in waves. He was probably running a temperature again. The disco in Lund was called Lagårn—the Barn—and was in the eastern corner of the city. Wallander made several wrong turns before he found it.

The sign was not illuminated and the doors were locked. Lagårn was located in a building that had earlier been a dairy, Wallander was able to read from the façade. He wondered why the disco had not been given that name instead, the Dairy. He looked around. There was some light industry on either side of the disco. A little further away there was a house with a garden. Wallander walked over, opened the gate and rang the doorbell. A man around his own age opened it. Wallander heard opera music in the background.

Wallander showed him his police ID. The man let Wallander in.

'If I'm not mistaken, it's Puccini,' Wallander said.

The man looked more closely at him. 'That's right,' he said. '*Tosca*.'

'I'm actually here to talk about a different kind of music,' Wallander said. 'I'll keep this brief. I need to know who owns the disco next door.'

'How on earth would I know that?'

'Well, you are a neighbour,' said Wallander.

'Sorry. Why not ask your colleagues?' the man suggested. 'There are often fights outside. They would know.' The man pointed to a telephone on a table in the hall.

Wallander had the number of the Lund police memorised. After being transferred several times he got the information that the disco was owned by a woman with the last name Boman. Wallander made a note of her address and telephone number.

'It's easy to find,' the officer he spoke to said. 'She lives in the building that's across from the railway station.'

Wallander hung up. 'This is a very beautiful opera,' he said. 'The music, I mean. I have unfortunately never seen it performed.'

'I never go to the opera,' the man said. 'The music is enough for me.'

Wallander thanked him and left. Then he drove to the station in Lund. He parked in a no-parking zone, and walked across the street. He pressed the button with the name Boman. The door lock buzzed open and Wallander walked in. The apartment was on the second floor. Wallander looked around for a lift, but there wasn't one. Even though he walked slowly he got out of breath.

A woman who was very young, hardly twenty-five, was standing in a doorway waiting for him. She had very short hair and several rings in her ears. Wallander introduced himself and showed her his ID. She didn't even glance at it but asked him to come in. Wallander looked around with astonishment. There was almost no furniture in the apartment. The walls were bare. And yet it was cosy somehow. There was nothing in the way. It only contained what was absolutely necessary.

'Why do the police in Ystad want to speak with me?' she asked. 'I have enough trouble with the cops in Lund.'

He could tell that she was not overly fond of the police. She had sat down in a chair and was wearing a very short skirt. Wallander searched around for a spot next to her face where he could direct his gaze.

'I'll get right to the point,' Wallander said. 'Rolf Nyman.'

'What about him?'

'Nothing. But does he work for you?'

'I have him as a reserve. In case one of my regular DJs gets ill.'

'My question may strike you as strange,' Wallander said. 'But I have to ask it.'

'Why aren't you looking me in the eye?' she asked abruptly.

'That is probably because your skirt is so very short,' Wallander replied, surprised at his own directness.

She burst into laughter, reached for a blanket and laid it across her legs. Wallander looked at the blanket and then her face.

'Rolf Nyman,' he repeated. 'Has he ever borrowed any lighting equipment from your establishment?'

'Never.'

Wallander caught an almost imperceptible cloud of uncertainty that crossed her face. His attention sharpened at once. 'Never?'

She bit her lip. 'The question is odd,' she said. 'But the fact is that a number of lights disappeared from the disco about a year ago. We reported it to the police as a burglary. But they never found any leads.'

'When was that? Was it after Nyman started to work for you?'

She thought back. 'Exactly a year ago. In January. After he had started.'

'You never suspected that it could be an inside job?'

'No, actually.' She got up and quickly left the room. After a moment's absence she returned with a pocket calendar in her hand.

'The lights disappeared sometime between the 9th and 12th of January. And I can see that it was actually Rolf who was working then.'

'What kind of lights?' Wallander asked.

'Six spotlights. Not really useful for a disco. They're more for theatre work. Very strong, around two thousand watts. There were also a number of cables that went missing.'

Wallander nodded slowly.

'Why are you asking about this?'

'I can't tell you that right now,' Wallander said. 'But I have to ask you one thing, and I want you to regard it as an order. That you don't mention this to Rolf Nyman.'

'Request granted,' said Boman, 'as long as you have a word with your Lund colleagues and ask them to leave me alone.'

'I'll see what I can do.'

She followed him out into the hall.

'I don't think I ever asked you for your first name,' he said.

'Linda.'

'That's my daughter's name. Therefore it's a very beautiful name.'

Wallander was overcome by a sneeze. She drew back a few steps.

'I won't shake your hand,' he said. 'But you gave me the answer I had been hoping for.'

She was about to close the door when Wallander realised he had yet another question.

'Do you know anything about Rolf Nyman's private life?'

'No, nothing.'

'So, you don't know about his girlfriend who has a drug addiction?'

Linda Boman looked at him for a long time before she answered.

'I don't know if he has a girlfriend who takes drugs,' she said finally. 'But I do know that Rolf has serious problems with heroin. How long he'll manage to control it, I have no idea.'

Wallander went back down onto the street. The time was already ten o'clock and the night was cold.

We're there, he thought. Rolf Nyman. Surely he's the one.

CHAPTER 9

Wallander was almost back in Ystad when he decided not to go straight home. At the second roundabout on the edge of town he turned north instead. It was ten minutes to eleven. His nose continued to run, but his curiosity drove him on. He thought that what he was doing again—how many times now, he had no idea—was at odds with the most fundamental rules governing police work. Above all, the rule that forbade placing yourself in dangerous situations alone.

If it was true, as he was now convinced, that it was Rolf Nyman who had shot Holm and the Eberhardsson sisters, Nyman definitely counted as potentially dangerous. In addition, he had tricked Wallander. And he had done so effortlessly and with great skill. On his drive from Malmö, Wallander had been wondering what could be motivating Nyman. What was the crack that had appeared in the pattern? The answers he came up with pointed in at least two different directions. It could be a power struggle or about influence over the drug trade.

The point in the whole situation that worried him most was what Linda Boman had said about Nyman's own drug habit. That he was a heroin addict. Wallander had almost never come across drug dealers above the absolute bottom level who were also addicts. The question went round and round in Wallander's head. There was something that did not make sense, a piece that was missing.

Wallander turned by the road that led to the house where Nyman lived. He switched off the engine and the headlights. He took out a torch from the glove compartment. Then he carefully opened the door after first extinguishing the interior lights. Listened out into the darkness and then closed the car door as quietly as he could. It was about 100 metres to the yard entrance. He shielded the torch with one hand and directed the beam in front of him. When he reached the edge of the woods, he turned out the torch. One window in the house was lit up. Someone must be home. Now comes the dog, he thought. He walked back the way he had come, about fifty metres. Then he went into the woods and turned the torch back on. He was going to approach the house from the back. As far as he could recall, the room with the lighted window had windows both to the front and back of the house.

He moved slowly, trying to avoid stepping on twigs. He was sweating by the time he had reached the back of the house. He had also started to question himself more and more as to what he thought he was up to. In the worst-case scenario the dog would bark and give Rolf Nyman the first warning that someone was watching him. He stood still and listened. All he could hear was the sighing of the trees. Wallander waited until his breathing was back to normal before he carefully walked up to the house. He crouched down and held the torch only a few centimetres from the ground. Just before he entered the area lit up by the window, he turned off the torch and drew back into the shadows next to the house. The dog was still quiet. He listened with his ear pressed against the cold wall. No music, no voices, nothing. Then he cautiously peered in through the window.

Rolf Nyman was sitting at a table in the middle of the room. He was leaning over something that Wallander could not immediately see. Then he realised that Rolf Nyman was playing a game of patience. Wallander asked himself what he had been expecting. A man measuring out tiny bags of white powder on some scales?

I'm wrong, he thought. This is a mistake from beginning to end.

But he was still convinced. The man sitting at the table playing a game of patience had killed three people. Brutally executed them.

Wallander was just about to steal away from the house when the dog at the front started to bark. Rolf Nyman jumped. He looked straight at Wallander. For a second, Wallander thought he had been discovered. Nyman quickly stood up and walked to the front door, at which point Wallander was already on his way back into the woods. If he lets the dog loose I'm in trouble, he thought. He directed the torch at the ground that he was stumbling over. He slipped and felt a branch cut his cheek. In the background he could still hear the dog barking.

When he reached the car he dropped the torch but did not stop to pick it up. He turned the key and wondered what would have happened if he had had his old car. Now he was able to put the car in reverse without a problem and drive away. Just as Wallander got into the car he heard a tractor approach on the main road. If he could get the sound of his own engine to coincide with the sound of the other vehicle then he would be able to get away without Rolf Nyman hearing him. He stopped and quietly turned and sneaked slowly into third gear. When he got out onto the main road he saw the taillights of the tractor. Since he was going downhill he turned off the engine and let the car coast. There was no one in his rearview mirror. No one had come in pursuit. Wallander stroked his cheek and felt blood.

IT WAS ALREADY past midnight when he reached Mariagatan. The branch had made a deep cut in his cheek. Wallander briefly considered going to the hospital, but he settled for cleaning the wound himself and applying a large plaster. Then he put on a pot of strong coffee and sat down at the kitchen table with one of his many half-full notepads in front of him.

He reviewed his triangle-shaped pyramid once more and replaced the question mark in the middle with Rolf Nyman. He knew from the start that the material was very thin. The only thing that he could produce against Nyman was the suspicion that he had stolen the lights that were later used to mark the area for the plane drop.

But what else did he have? Nothing. What relationship had Holm and Nyman shared? Where did the plane and the Eberhardsson sisters fit in? They would need a more thoroughgoing investigation in order to move forward. He was also wondering how he could convince his colleagues that despite how it looked, he really had found the lead that they should concentrate on. How far could he go by simply citing his intuition again? Rydberg would understand, perhaps even Martinsson. But both Svedberg and Hansson would dismiss it.

It was two o'clock before he went to bed. His cheek ached.

IN THE MORNING it was cold and clear in Skåne. Wallander got up early and arrived at the station shortly before seven. He went to his office and poured himself some coffee. Then sat down and thought back to the events of the evening before.

His doubts from the previous day remained. Rolf Nyman could turn out to be a red herring. But there were still grounds for investigating him thoroughly. Wallander decided that they should put his house under discreet surveillance, not least in order to find out when Nyman would be out. They needed to get into the house. But there was an additional complication. Rolf

Nyman was not alone. There was also a woman, whom no one had seen, and who had been sleeping when Wallander stopped by.

Wallander wondered if the woman even existed. Much of what Nyman had told him had turned out not to be true. He looked at his watch. Twenty minutes past seven. It was probably very early for a woman who ran a disco. But he still searched around for Linda Boman's telephone number in Lund. She picked up almost immediately.

'I'm sorry if I woke you up,' he said.

'I'm awake.'

She is like me, Wallander thought. Doesn't like to admit that she has been woken up. Even if this is a perfectly decent hour to still be sleeping.

'I have some more questions about Rolf Nyman. You said that he had a serious heroin addiction. How do you know?'

'He told me. It took me by surprise. He didn't try to hide it, and that made an impression on me.'

'Does this mean that you never noticed that he had a problem?'

'He always did his job.'

'He never appeared high?'

'Not that I could tell.'

'And he never appeared nervous or anxious?'

'No more so than anyone else. I can also be nervous and anxious. Especially when the police in Lund bother me and the disco.'

Wallander sat quietly for a moment. 'Let me go through this one more time,' he said. 'You never saw him when he was under the influence. He only told you that he was a heroin addict.'

'I have a hard time believing that a person would lie about something like that.'

'I agree,' Wallander said. 'I have one more question,' he continued. 'You said that you never heard about a girlfriend.'

'No, I didn't.'

'You never saw him with one?'

'No, never.'

'So if we assume that he said he had a girlfriend you couldn't verify if this were true or not?'

'Your questions are getting stranger and stranger. Why wouldn't he have a girlfriend? He isn't worse-looking than other guys.'

'Then I have no more questions for the moment,' Wallander concluded. 'And what I said yesterday is still very much in effect.'

'I won't say anything. I'm going to sleep.'

'It's possible that I'll be in touch again,' Wallander said. 'Do you know, by the way, if Rolf has any close friends?'

'No.'

The conversation came to a close.

At half past eight Wallander informed his colleagues about the latest developments. About his conversation with Linda Boman and the missing lighting equipment. He did not, however, mention his night-time visit to the remote house outside Sjöbo. As he had predicted, Rydberg found the discovery important while Hansson and Svedberg had a number of objections. Martinsson said nothing.

'I know it's thin,' Wallander said after listening to the discussion. 'But I'm still of the opinion that we should concentrate on Nyman.' He argued that they needed to get into the house outside Sjöbo but without Nyman's knowledge, a view that was immediately greeted with new protests.

'We can't do that,' Svedberg said. 'That's illegal.'

'We have a triple murder on our hands,' Wallander said. 'If I'm correct, Rolf Nyman is very cunning. If we're going to find something, we have to observe him without his knowledge. When does he leave the house? What does he do? How long is he gone? But above all we have to find out if there really is a girlfriend.'

'Maybe I'll dress up as a chimney sweep,' Martinsson suggested.

'He'll see through it,' Wallander said, ignoring his ironic tone of voice. 'I had been thinking we would proceed more indirectly. With the help of the country postman. There is not one rural postman in this country who doesn't know what goes on in the houses in their district. Even if they never set foot in a house, they know who lives there.'

Svedberg was stubborn. 'Maybe that girl never receives any post?'

'It's not only about that,' Wallander replied. 'Postmen just know. That's how it is.'

Rydberg nodded in agreement. Wallander felt his support. It spurred him on. Hansson promised to contact the post office. Martinsson grudgingly agreed to organise surveillance of the house. Wallander said he would speak to Åkeson.

'Find out everything you can about Nyman,' Wallander said in closing. 'But be discreet. If he is the bear I think he is, we don't want to wake him.'

Wallander signalled to Rydberg that he wanted to speak to him in his office.

'Are you convinced?' Rydberg asked. 'That it's Nyman?'

'Yes,' Wallander said. 'But I'm aware that I could be wrong. That I could be steering this investigation in the wrong direction.'

'The theft of the lighting equipment is a strong indicator,' Rydberg said. 'For me that is the deciding factor. What made you think of it, by the way?'

'The pyramids,' Wallander answered. 'They're illuminated by spotlights. Except for one day a month, when the moon is full.'

'How do you know that?'

'My old man told me.'

Rydberg nodded thoughtfully. 'It's unlikely that drug shipments follow the lunar calendar,' he said. 'And they may not have as many clouds in Egypt as we have in Skåne.'

'The Sphinx was actually the most interesting,' Wallander said. 'Half man, half animal. Holding guard to make sure the sun returns every morning. From the same direction.'

'I think I've heard of an American security firm that uses the Sphinx as a symbol,' Rydberg said.

'That fits,' Wallander said. 'The Sphinx keeps watch. And we keep watch. Whether or not we're police officers or night guards.'

Rydberg burst into laughter. 'If you told new recruits about this kind of thing they would make fun of us.'

'I know,' Wallander said. 'But perhaps we should tell them anyway.'

Rydberg left. Wallander called Per Åkeson at home. He promised to inform his replacement, Anette Brolin.

'How does it feel?' Wallander asked. 'Not to have any criminal cases pending?'

'Good,' Åkeson said. 'Better than I could have imagined.'

THE INVESTIGATIVE SQUAD met twice more that day. Martinsson arranged the surveillance of the house. Hansson left in order to meet the rural postman. During this time the others continued with the task of establishing the facts of Rolf Nyman's life. He did not have a police record, something that made the process more difficult. He was born in 1957, in Tranås, and moved to Skåne with his parents in the mid-1960s. His father had been employed by a power plant as a systems operator, his mother stayed at home, and Rolf was an only child. His father had died in 1986 and his mother had then moved back to Tranås, where she had died the following year. Wallander had a growing feeling that Rolf Nyman had lived an invisible life. As if he had deliberately swept up any traces of himself.

Hansson returned, having spoken to the postal worker, whose name was Elfrida Wirmark. She had been very firm in stating that there were two people in the house, Holm and Nyman. Which meant there was only one person there these days, as Holm was in the mortuary, waiting to be buried.

They met in the conference room at seven that evening. According to the reports that Martinsson had received, Nyman had not left the house during the day other than to feed the dog. No one had come by to see him. Wallander asked if the officers who were keeping Nyman under surveillance had been able to tell if he was on his guard, but no such reports had been issued. Then Wallander made the final case review of the day. 'There are no indications that he is a heroin addict,' he started. 'That is his first lie. The second is that he has a girlfriend—he's alone in that house. If we want to get in there we have two choices. Either we wait until he leaves, which he has to do sooner or later, if for no other reason than to buy groceries. Or else we find a way to lure him out of the house.'

They decided to wait him out, at least for a few days. If nothing happened, they would revisit the situation.

They waited for two whole days. Nyman left the house twice in order to feed the dog. There were no indications that he had grown more watchful than before. During that time they continued to work on mapping his life. It was as if he had lived in a strange vacuum. Via the tax authorities they could see that he had a low annual income from his work as a DJ. He applied for a passport in 1986. He received his driver's licence in 1976. There did not appear to be any friends.

On the morning of January 5, Wallander sat down with Rydberg and closed the door. Rydberg said that they should probably continue for a couple more days, but Wallander presented an idea that would make it possible to lure Nyman out of the house. They decided to present this idea to the others that same afternoon.

Wallander called Linda Boman in Lund. The following evening the disco was going to be open, and a Danish DJ was scheduled that night. Wallander explained his idea. Linda Boman asked who would cover the extra costs since the DJ from Copenhagen had a contract with Linda's disco. Wallander told her she could send the bill to the Ystad police if need be. He promised to get back to her within a couple of hours.

At four o'clock in the afternoon, a bitingly cold wind had started to blow in. A snow front was passing from the east and could possibly nudge the southern tip of Skåne. Wallander gathered his team in the conference room. As succinctly as possible, he explained the idea that he had discussed with Rydberg earlier.

'We have to smoke out Rolf Nyman,' he said. 'Apparently he doesn't go anywhere unnecessarily. But it seems that he doesn't suspect anything.'

'Maybe the whole thing is too far-fetched,' Hansson interjected. 'Maybe because he has nothing to do with the murders?'

'That possibility does exist,' Wallander admitted. 'But we're assuming the opposite. And that means we need to get into the house without him finding out. The first thing that we have to do is find a way to get him out, but not for a reason that will arouse any suspicion.'

Then he laid out the plan. Linda Boman was going to call Nyman and tell him that the scheduled DJ had cancelled. Could Rolf cover for him? If he said yes, the house would be empty all evening. They could post someone at the disco who could keep in contact with the people inside the house. When Rolf Nyman returned to Sjöbo in the early morning, the house would be empty. No one except the dog would know they had been there.

'What happens if he calls his DJ colleague in Copenhagen?' Svedberg asked.

'We've thought of that. Linda Boman is going to tell the Dane not to answer the phone. The police will cover his regular fee. But we're happy to take that on.'

Wallander had expected more objections. But none came. He looked round the table. No one had anything more to add.

'Then we're agreed? The plan is to do this soon, tomorrow night.'

Wallander reached for the telephone on the table and called Boman. 'Let's do it,' he said, when she answered. 'Call me in an hour.' He hung up, checked his watch and then turned to Martinsson. 'Who's on surveillance?'

'Näslund and Peters.'

'Call them on the radio and tell them to be particularly observant at twenty past five. That's when Linda Boman is going to call Nyman.'

'What do you think might happen?'

'I don't know. I just want increased attentiveness.'

Then they talked through the programme. Linda Boman was going to ask Nyman to come into Lund early, at eight, in order to look over a number of new records. That meant he should leave Sjöbo around seven. The disco would stay open until three in the morning. As soon as the person posted at the disco confirmed that Nyman had entered, the others would go into the house. Wallander had asked Rydberg to come along. But Rydberg had in turn suggested Martinsson. So Martinsson it was.

'Martinsson and I will go into the house. Svedberg comes along and keeps watch. Hansson takes the disco in Lund. The rest remain here at the station. In case something happens.'

'What are we looking for?' Martinsson asked.

Wallander was about to ask when Rydberg raised his hand.

'We don't know,' he said. 'We're trying to find what we don't know that we're looking for. But eventually there will be a yes or a no. Was Nyman the one who killed Holm and the two sisters?'

'Drugs,' Martinsson said. 'Is that it?'

'Weapons, money, anything. Spools of thread bought in the Eberhardsson sisters' shop. Copies of plane tickets. We don't know.'

They sat round the table a little longer. Martinsson left in order to get in touch with Näslund and Peters. He returned, nodded, and sat down.

At twenty minutes past five, Wallander dialled Linda Boman's number. The line was busy. They waited.

Nine minutes later the phone rang. Wallander picked up the receiver. He listened and then hung up.

'Nyman has agreed,' he said. 'Now we're in business. Let's see if this leads us in the right or wrong direction.'

The meeting broke up. Wallander held Martinsson back.

'It's best for us to be armed,' he said.

Martinsson looked surprised.

'I thought Nyman was going to be in Lund?'

'Just in case,' Wallander replied. 'That's all.'

THE SNOWSTORM NEVER reached Skåne. The next day the sky was covered in clouds. A faint wind was blowing, there was rain in the air, and it was 4°C. Wallander stood indecisively in front of his sweaters for a long time before he was able to select one.

They met at six o'clock in the conference room. By then Hansson had already left for Lund. Svedberg was stationed behind a clump of trees where he had a view of the front of Nyman's house. Rydberg was doing crossword puzzles in the break room. Wallander had reluctantly taken out his gun and strapped on the holster that never quite fitted properly. Martinsson had his weapon in his coat pocket.

At nine minutes past seven they received a dispatch from Svedberg. *The bird has flown.* They waited. Six minutes to eight came Hansson's dispatch. *The bird has landed.* Rolf Nyman had driven slowly.

Martinsson and Wallander stood up. Rydberg looked up from his crossword puzzle and nodded.

They arrived at the house at half past eight. Svedberg greeted them. The dog barked. But the house was dark. 'I've checked the lock,' Svedberg said. 'A simple pass key is enough.'

Wallander and Svedberg held up their torches while Martinsson picked the lock. Svedberg left to resume his post as lookout.

They went in. Wallander turned on all the lights, which took Martinsson by surprise.

'Nyman is playing records at a disco in Lund,' Wallander said. 'Let's get started.'

They proceeded slowly and methodically through the house. They found no traces of a woman anywhere. Apart from the bed that Holm had used there was only one other single bed.

'We should have brought a sniffer dog,' Martinsson said.

'I think it's unlikely he keeps any supplies at home,' Wallander said.

They searched the house for three hours. Shortly before midnight Martinsson contacted Hansson on the police dispatch radio.

'There are a lot of people here,' Hansson said. 'And the music is thundering like hell. I'm staying outside. But it's cold.'

They continued to search. Wallander had started to worry. No drugs, no weapons. Nothing that indicated any involvement on Nyman's part. Martinsson had searched the basement and the outlying building. There was no lighting equipment. Nothing. Just the dog that was barking like crazy. Several times Wallander had felt an urge to shoot it. But he loved dogs, deep down. Even dogs that barked.

At half past one Martinsson got in touch with Hansson again. Still nothing.

'What did he say?' Wallander asked.

'That a lot of people were crowded around outside.'

At two o'clock they had got no further. Wallander had started to realise that he had made a mistake. There was no indication that Rolf Nyman was anything other than a DJ. The lie about a girlfriend could hardly be considered criminal. And they had also not found any indications that Nyman was a drug addict.

'I think we can wrap this up,' Martinsson said. 'We haven't found a thing.'

Wallander nodded. 'I'm staying behind for a while, but you and Svedberg can go home. Leave me the radio.'

Martinsson put the radio, which was turned on, on the table.

'Time to call it quits,' Wallander said. 'Hansson will have to wait until I call him, but everyone at the station can go home.'

'What do you think you'll find when you're on your own?'

Wallander caught the sarcastic tone in Martinsson's voice. 'Nothing,' he said. 'Perhaps I just need more time to realise that I've led us in the wrong direction.'

'We'll start over tomorrow,' Martinsson said. 'That's life.'

Martinsson left. Wallander sat down and looked around the room. The dog was barking. Wallander cursed. He was convinced he was right. It was Rolf Nyman who had killed the two sisters and Holm. But he had found no evidence. He remained seated for a while longer. Then he started to walk around and turn out the lamps.

The dog stopped barking.

Wallander froze. Listened. The dog was quiet. Immediately he sensed danger. Where it came from, he didn't know. The disco was supposed to be open until three. Hansson had not contacted him.

Wallander did not know what made him react. But suddenly he realised he was standing in a window that was clearly illuminated from the inside. He threw himself to the side. At that moment, the windowpane shattered. Wallander lay motionless on the floor. Confused thoughts went through his head. Someone had fired a shot. It could not be Nyman. Hansson would have told him. Wallander pressed himself against the floor while he tried to pull out his own gun. He tried to crawl deeper into the shadows but saw that he was about to enter the light again. The person who had fired the shot might have made it up to the window by now.

Overhead there was a ceiling light that was illuminating the room. He got out his weapon and aimed it at the bulb. When he pressed the trigger his hand was shaking so hard that he missed. He aimed again, holding it with two hands now. The shot shattered the bulb. The room became darker. He sat still, listening. His heart was pounding in his chest. What he needed most of all was the police radio. But it was on the table several metres away. And the table was in a pool of light.

The dog was still silent. He listened intently. Suddenly he thought he heard someone in the hall. Almost inaudible steps. He aimed the weapon at the doorway. His hands shook. But no one came in. How long he waited, he didn't know. He noticed that the table was on a rug. Carefully, without putting his gun down, he started to pull on the rug. The table was heavy. But it was moving. Then, just when he had the radio within reach, a second shot rang out. It hit the radio, which shattered. Wallander curled up into the corner. The shot had come from the front of the house.

Wallander realised that he would no longer be able to shield himself if the gunman walked round to the back of the house. I have to get out, he thought. If I stay here I'm dead. He tried desperately to come up with a plan. He had no chance of getting at the outside lights. The person out there would shoot him first.

He knew he had only one choice. A thought that was more repellent to him than anything. He took several deep breaths. Then he got to his feet, rushed out into the hall, kicked open the door, threw himself to the side, and aimed three shots into the dog run. A howl signalled that he had hit the mark. Every second that went by, Wallander expected to die. But the dog's howls gave him time to slip into the shadows. He saw Rolf Nyman standing in the middle of the yard, momentarily bewildered by the shooting of the dog. Then he spotted Wallander.

Wallander closed his eyes and fired two shots. When he opened his eyes again he saw that Rolf Nyman had fallen to the ground. Slowly Wallander walked up to him. He was alive. A bullet had caught him in the side.

Wallander took the weapon out of his hand, and then went up to the dog run. The dog was dead.

He could hear sirens approaching in the distance. His whole body shaking, he sat down on the front steps and waited. It had started to rain.

EPILOGUE

At a quarter past four, Wallander was sitting in the station break room drinking a cup of coffee. His hands were still shaking. After the first chaotic hour when no one had really been able to explain what had happened, the picture had finally cleared up. When Martinsson and Svedberg had left Nyman's home and contacted Hansson on the police dispatch, the police in Lund had stormed Linda Boman's disco, since they suspected that the number of people inside exceeded the legal limit.

In the general chaos that had ensued Hansson had misunderstood what Martinsson had said. He had believed that all the police officers had left Nyman's house. Then he had also realised too late that Nyman had sneaked out of a back door that he had missed when he had inspected the disco. He had asked an officer in charge where the employees were and had been told that they had been brought down to the Lund station for questioning. He had assumed that this group included Nyman.

Deciding there was no longer any reason for him to stay in Lund he had driven back to Ystad in the belief that Nyman's house had been empty for more than an hour.

During which time Wallander had lain on the floor, shot at the ceiling light, rushed out into the yard and killed a dog—and injured Rolf Nyman with a bullet to his side.

Wallander had thought several times since returning to Ystad that he should be furious. But he could decide for himself who he should blame. It had been an unfortunate series of misunderstandings that could have ended very badly, with not only a dog left dead. That had not happened. But it had been a close shave.

There is a time to live, and a time to die, Wallander thought. This was a mantra he had carried with him ever since the time he had been stabbed in Malmö many years ago. Now it had been a close call again.

Rydberg came into the break room.

'Rolf Nyman is going to be fine,' he said. 'You hit him in a good spot. He will suffer no permanent damage. The doctors seemed to think we could talk to him as early as tomorrow.'

'I could easily have missed,' Wallander said. 'Or hit him right between the eyes. I'm a terrible shot.'

'Most policemen are,' Rydberg said.

Wallander slurped more of the hot coffee.

'I talked to Nyberg,' Rydberg went on. 'He said that the weapon looked like a probable match with the one that was used to kill the Eberhardsson sisters and Holm. They've also found Holm's car. It was parked on a street in Sjöbo. Nyman probably drove it there.'

'So something has been solved,' Wallander said. 'But we still have no idea what's really behind all this.'

Rydberg had no answer to that.

IT WOULD TAKE several weeks for the whole picture to emerge. But when Nyman began to talk, the police were able to piece together a skilfully constructed organisation that managed the importation of large quantities of serious drugs into Sweden. The Eberhardsson sisters had been Nyman's ingenious camouflage. They organised the supply links in Spain, where the drugs—which had their origin in distant producers in both Central America and Asia—arrived on fishing boats. Holm had been Nyman's henchman. But then, at a moment that they were unable to pinpoint, Holm and the Eberhardsson sisters had joined forces in their greed and decided to oust Nyman.

When he had realised what was happening, he had struck back. The plane crash had occurred during this time. Drugs were being transported from Marbella to northern Germany. The night-time flights to Sweden had taken off from a private airstrip outside Kiel. The plane had always returned there, except this last time when it had gone down. The commission in charge of investigating the accident was not able to determine the actual cause. But there were indications that the plane was in such poor condition that several factors had worked together.

Wallander himself led the first questioning of Nyman. But when two other serious crimes occurred he had to hand the case over. Nonetheless he had understood from the start that Rolf Nyman was not the head of the pyramid that he had drawn. There were others above him—financiers, invisible men—who behind the façade of blameless citizens saw to it that the flood of drugs into Sweden did not dry up.

MANY EVENINGS WALLANDER thought about the pyramids. About the top that his father had been trying to reach. Wallander thought that this climb could stand as a symbol for his own work. He never reached the summit. There were always some who sat so high and far above everyone else that they could never be reached.

But this morning, January 7, 1990, Wallander was simply tired. At half past five he could no longer take it. Without saying a word to anyone he went home to the apartment on Mariagatan. He showered and crawled into bed without being able to fall asleep. Only when he managed to find a sleeping pill in an old bottle in the bathroom cabinet was he finally able to sleep, and he did not wake up until two o'clock in the afternoon.

He spent the rest of the day at the station and the hospital. Björk turned up and congratulated Wallander on his efforts. Wallander did not reply. He thought that most of what he had done had been wrong. It had been their luck, not their skill, that had finally felled Rolf Nyman.

Then he had had his first conversation with Nyman at the hospital. The man had been pale but collected. Wallander had expected Nyman to refuse to say a word. But he had answered many of Wallander's questions.

'The Eberhardsson sisters?' Wallander asked before he concluded the session. Rolf Nyman smiled.

'Two greedy old ladies,' he said. 'Who were tempted by the fact that someone rode into their lives and brought the scent of adventure.'

'That sounds implausible,' Wallander said. 'It's too big a step.'

'Anna Eberhardsson had lived a fairly wild life when she was younger. Emilia had always had to keep an eye on her. Perhaps deep down she had wanted to live the same life. What do we know about people? Other than that they have their weaknesses. And those are the things you need to know.'

'How did you meet them?'

The answer came as a surprise. 'I bought a zip. I saw those old ladies and had a crazy idea. That they could be useful. As a cover.'

'And then?'

'I started dropping by. Bought some thread. Talked about my travels around the world. How easy it was to make money. And that life is short. But that nothing was ever too late. I saw that they listened.'

'And then?'

Rolf Nyman shrugged. 'One day I made them an offer. How does that go again? An offer they couldn't refuse.'

Wallander wanted to ask more. But suddenly Nyman did not want to talk about it any more. Wallander changed the subject. 'And Holm?'

'He was also greedy. And weak. Too stupid to realise that he wouldn't be able to trick me.'

'How did you catch onto their plans?'

Rolf Nyman shook his head. 'I won't tell you that,' he said.

Wallander walked from the hospital to the station. A press conference was going on that to his relief he had managed to get out of. He wrote up a report on his first conversation with Rolf Nyman. Then he went home. Cooked some food, slept a few hours. Thought of calling Linda but didn't.

In the evening he listened to *La Traviata*. Thought that what he needed most right now was a couple of days off.

He only went to bed and fell asleep when it was close to two.

THE INCOMING CALL was registered by the Ystad police dispatcher on January 8 at 5.13 a.m. It was received by an exhausted policeman who had been on duty almost without a break since New Year's Eve. He had listened to the stammering voice on the phone and at first thought that it was a confused elderly person. But something nonetheless alerted his attention. He started to ask questions. When the conversation was over he only had to reflect for a moment before he lifted the receiver again and dialled a number he knew by heart.

When the telephone jerked Wallander from his slumber he had been deeply enmeshed in an erotic dream. He checked his watch as he reached his hand out for the receiver. A car accident, he thought quickly. An icy road, or someone driving too fast. People dead. Or clashes with refugees who arrived on the morning ferry from Poland.

He sat up in bed and pressed the receiver against his cheek, where his stubble stung.

'Wallander!' he barked.

'I didn't wake you, did I?'

'I was awake.'

Why do I lie? he wondered. Why don't I tell the truth? That most of all I would like to return to my sleep and catch a fleeting dream in the form of a naked woman.

'I thought I should call you. An old farmer called in from Lenarp. He claimed that a neighbouring woman was tied up on the floor and that some-one was dead.'

Wallander swiftly located Lenarp in his mind. Not so far from Marsvinsholm, in an unusually hilly area for Skåne.

'It sounds serious. I thought it was best to call you directly.'

'Who is available right now?'

'Peters and Norén are out looking for someone who broke a window at the Continental. Should I call them in?'

'Tell them to drive to the intersection of Kadesjö and Katslösa and wait until I get there. Give them the address. When did you receive the call?'

'A couple of minutes ago.'

'Are you sure it's not some drunk?'

'It didn't sound like it.'

Wallander got out of bed and dressed. The rest that he needed so much was not to be granted him.

He drove out of the city, passing the newly built furniture warehouse by the main road into town, and sensed the dark sea beyond it. The sky was covered in clouds.

The snowstorms are coming, he thought. Sooner or later they will be on top of us.

Then he tried to concentrate on whatever sight it was that he was about to encounter.

THE PATROL CAR was waiting for him by the road to Kadesjö.

It was still dark.

HENNING MANKELL

Born: Stockholm, 1948
Influenced by: John Le Carré
Homes: Sweden and Mozambique

Henning Mankell had a rocky start in life, in that his mother left a year after he was born and largely disappeared from his life until he was a teenager. The silver lining was that his father moved the family from Stockholm, to a part of the country and into a home situation where Henning's imagination and writing skills were nurtured.

He went with his father, Ivar—'a kind, strong man'—and his sister Helena, to Sveg, a quiet village in Härjedalen, central Sweden. Despite chilly winters and its remoteness from the capital, the Christmas-tree forests and unspoilt countryside were a perfect environment for a child to grow up in. Ivar's mother, a widow, moved nearby to help care for the children and she seems to have been a crucial influence in their early life. 'At school on Mother's Day we children were supposed to write letters to our mother, but we didn't have a mother, so we had to write to our grandmother instead. It made me feel a little awkward,' Helena recalls. Their grandmother taught Henning to write, and he clearly remembers the miracle of putting his first sentence together: 'The miracle that I could make a sentence, then more sentences, telling a story.'

Ivar Mankell was a judge, and he and the children lived in a flat above the local law courts. His son remembers having to keep quiet if the court was in session, and also being allowed to watch the occasional trial. Maybe these early encounters with the Swedish legal system explain his continuing preoccupation, as a writer, with fairness and justice, which he sees as being under threat in modern society. While his father worked, Henning read voraciously and loved the works of Mungo Park and other explorers of Africa, who opened up tantalising vistas of a world beyond Sweden. Africa was, to the young boy, 'The most exotic place I could conceive of—the end of the world.' He vowed that one day he would visit the continent.

By the time he was sixteen, he was disillusioned with school and left to join the merchant navy, a move that his father reluctantly supported, perhaps recognising a spirit of adventure in his son. Henning enjoyed being at sea for a time, ferrying coal and iron ore to Europe and across the Atlantic, and has referred to it as his 'real university'.

But after two years he'd had enough and, following a short, poverty-stricken spell in Paris, returned to Sweden where he got a job as a stagehand in a Stockholm theatre.

This was a second key turning point in his young life. He adored the theatre, although the job was badly paid, and, by the age of twenty, had written a first play. More were to follow. The African dream also continued to ferment in his imagination and by the end of 1972 he'd saved up enough money to pay a visit to Guinea-Bissau, a Portuguese colony in West Africa. It felt like a homecoming and he returned several times, eventually settling in Mozambique, where he was invited to found the country's first professional theatre, Teatro Avenida, and where he still lives today.

Henning Mankell's love life was turbulent for a long time; he had several affairs and four sons 'by previous relationships'. Today, however, he is happily married to Eva Bergman, daughter of Ingmar Bergman, the famous Swedish film director.

All Mankell's Wallander stories are coloured by his concern about the ills in society today. 'We know that if the system of justice doesn't work, democracy is doomed,' he once said in interview. 'Wallander is worried about that and so are many people in democracies. Maybe that's why he is so popular. I am a very radical person—as radical now as I was when I was younger. So my books all have in common my search for understanding of the terrible world we are living in and ways to change it.'

YSTAD—HOME TO SWEDEN'S EVERYMAN

Detective Inspector Kurt Wallander was introduced to Swedish readers in 1991 in *Faceless Killers*, a story about racism that won several prizes. Now his fame extends across the world, and in 2008 millions of Britons made his acquaintance in three BBC dramatisations of Mankell's crime novels starring Kenneth Branagh. The films were made on location in the tranquil town of Ystad in Skåne, southern Sweden, a region characterised by huge skies and long, windswept beaches (pictured), where Henning Mankell has a second home.

MARY ANN SHAFFER
GUERNSEY POSTAGE
GUERNSEY POSTAGE
The Guernsey Literary and Potato Peel Pie Society
DAWSEY ADAMS
Juliet

Guernsey is only a short hop from England, but it's a world away from bombed out London where Juliet Ashton is sitting in her flat, desperately trying to find inspiration for her next book.

Until, out of the blue, she receives a letter from islander Dawsey Adams. Cut off during the years of German Occupation, he and his friends are seeking good reading and lively discussion——the very things Juliet can provide.

It's a lifeline. In more ways than one . . . though Juliet doesn't know it yet.

Part One

Mr Sidney Stark, Publisher
Stephens & Stark Ltd
21 St James's Place
London SW1

8th January 1946

Dear Sidney,

Susan Scott is a wonder. We sold over forty copies of the book, which was very pleasant, but much more thrilling from my standpoint was the food. Susan managed to get hold of ration coupons for icing sugar and *real eggs* for the meringue. If all her literary luncheons are going to achieve these heights, I won't mind touring the country. Do you suppose that a lavish bonus could spur her on to butter? Let's try it—you may deduct the money from my royalties.

Now for my grim news. You asked me how work on my new book *English Foibles* is progressing. Sidney, it isn't. My head and my heart just aren't in it any longer. I don't want to write anything else under the name of Izzy Bickerstaff. I don't want to be considered a light-hearted journalist any more. I do acknowledge that making readers laugh—or at least chuckle—during the war was no mean feat, but I don't want to do it any more. I can't seem to dredge up any sense of proportion or balance these days, and God knows one can't write humour without them.

In the meantime, I am very happy that Stephens & Stark is making money on *Izzy Bickerstaff Goes to War*. It relieves my conscience over the debacle of my Anne Brontë biography.

My thanks for everything and love,
Juliet

From Sidney to Juliet

Miss Juliet Ashton
23 Glebe Place
Chelsea
London SW3

10th January 1946

Dear Juliet,
Congratulations! Susan Scott said you took to the audience at the luncheon like a drunkard to rum—and they to you—so please stop worrying about your tour next week. I have no doubt of your success. I know you will have every listener coiled round your little finger within moments.

Susan is looking forward to ushering you through bookshops from Bath to Yorkshire. And of course Sophie is agitating for an extension of the tour into Scotland. I've told her in my most infuriating older-brother manner that It Remains To Be Seen. She misses you terribly, I know, but Stephens & Stark must be impervious to such considerations.

I've just received *Izzy*'s sales figures from London and the Home Counties—they are excellent. Again, congratulations!

Don't fret about *English Foibles*. The crass commercial possibilities of the idea were attractive, but I agree that the topic would soon grow horribly fey. Another subject—one you'll like—will occur to you.

Dinner one evening before you go? Say when.
Love,
Sidney

From Juliet to Sidney

11th January 1946

Dear Sidney,
Yes, lovely—can it be somewhere on the river? I want oysters and champagne and roast beef, if obtainable; if not, a chicken will do. I am very happy that *Izzy*'s sales are good. Are they good enough for me not to have to pack a suitcase and leave London? As you and S&S have turned me into a moderately successful author, dinner must be my treat.
Love,
Juliet

From Juliet to her best friend, Sidney's sister Sophie Strachan

Mrs Alexander Strachan
Feochan Farm
by Oban
Argyll

12th January 1946

Dear Sophie,

Of course I'd adore to see you, but I am a soulless, will-less automaton. I have been ordered by Sidney on a book-signing tour of Bath, Colchester, Leeds and several other places I can't remember at the moment, and I can't just slope off to Scotland instead. Sidney's brow would lower, his eyes would narrow, he would stalk. You know how nerve-racking it is when Sidney stalks.

I wish I could sneak away to your farm and be coddled. You'd let me put my feet on the sofa, wouldn't you? And then you'd tuck me up in blankets and bring me tea. Would Alexander mind a permanent presence on his sofa? You've told me your husband is patient, but perhaps he would find it annoying.

Why am I so melancholy? I should be delighted at the prospect of reading *Izzy* to an entranced audience. You know how I love talking about books, and you know how I adore receiving compliments. I should be thrilled. But the truth is that I'm gloomy—gloomier than I ever felt during the war. Everything is so *broken*, Sophie: the roads, the buildings, the people. Especially the people.

It's probably the aftereffect of a horrid dinner party I went to last night. The food was ghastly, but that was to be expected. It was the guests who unnerved me—they were the most demoralising collection of individuals I've ever encountered. The talk was of bombs and starvation. Do you remember Sarah Morecroft? She was there, all bones and gooseflesh and bloody lipstick and now she's married to a doctor with grey skin who clicks his tongue before he speaks. And he was positively romantic compared to the man sitting next to me, who just happened to be single, presumably the last unmarried man on earth . . . I swear, Sophie, I think there's something wrong with me. Every man I meet is intolerable. Perhaps I should set my sights lower—not as low as the grey doctor who clicks, but a bit lower. I can't even blame it on the war—I was never very good at men, was I? Am I too choosy? I don't want to be married just for the sake of being married. I can't think of anything lonelier than spending the rest of my life with someone I can't talk to, or worse, someone I can't be silent with.

What a dreadful, complaining letter. You see? I've succeeded in making you feel relieved that I won't be visiting Scotland. But then again, I may—my fate rests with Sidney.

Kiss Dominic for me. Love to Alexander and even more to you,
Juliet

From Dawsey Adams, Guernsey, Channel Islands, to Juliet

Miss Juliet Ashton
81 Oakley Street
Chelsea
London SW3

12th January 1946

Dear Miss Ashton,

My name is Dawsey Adams, and I live on my farm in St Martin's Parish, Guernsey. I know of you because I have an old book that once belonged to you—*The Selected Essays of Elia*, by an author whose name in real life was Charles Lamb. Your name and address were written inside the front cover.

I will speak plain—I love Charles Lamb. My own book says *Selected*, so I wondered if that meant he had written other things to choose from. These are the pieces I want to read, and though the Germans are gone now, there aren't any bookshops left in Guernsey.

I want to ask a kindness of you. Could you send me the name and address of a bookshop in London? I would like to order more of Charles Lamb's writings by post. I would also like to ask if anyone has ever written his life story, and if they have, could a copy be found for me?

Charles Lamb made me laugh during the German Occupation, especially when he wrote about the roast pig. The Guernsey Literary and Potato Peel Pie Society came into being because of a roast pig we had to keep secret from the German soldiers, so I feel a kinship to Mr Lamb.

I am sorry to bother you, but I would be sorrier still not to know about him, as his writings have made me his friend.

Hoping not to trouble you,
Dawsey Adams

P.S. My friend Mrs Maugery bought a pamphlet that once belonged to you, too. It is called *Was There a Burning Bush? A Defence of Moses and the Ten Commandments*. She liked your margin note 'Word of God or crowd control???' Did you ever decide which?

From Juliet to Dawsey

Mr Dawsey Adams
Les Vaux Lavens
La Bouvée
St Martin's, Guernsey

15th January 1946

Dear Mr Adams,

I no longer live in Oakley Street, but I'm so glad that your letter found me and that my book found you. It was a sad wrench to part with *The Selected Essays of Elia*. I had two copies and a dire need of shelf-room, but I felt like a traitor selling it. You have soothed my conscience.

I wonder how the book got to Guernsey. Perhaps there is some secret sort of homing instinct in books that brings them to their perfect readers. How delightful if that were true.

I went at once to Hastings & Sons upon receiving your letter. I have gone to them for years, always finding the one book I wanted—and then three more I hadn't known I wanted. I told Mr Hastings you would like a good, clean copy of *More Essays of Elia*. He will send it to you by separate post (invoice enclosed) and was delighted to know you are also a lover of Charles Lamb. He said the best biography of Lamb was by E. V. Lucas, and he would hunt out a copy for you, though it may take a little while.

In the meantime, will you accept this small gift from me? It is his *Selected Letters*. I think it will tell you more about him than any biography ever could. E. V. Lucas sounds too stately to include my favourite passage from Lamb, 'Buz, buz, buz, bum, bum, bum, wheeze, wheeze, wheeze, fen, fen, fen, tinky, tinky, tinky, cr'annch! I shall certainly come to be condemned at last. I have been drinking too much for two days running. I find my moral sense in the last stage of a consumption and my religion getting faint.' You'll find that in the *Letters* (it's on page 244).

What I love about reading is that one tiny thing will interest you in a book, and that tiny thing will lead you on to another book, and another bit there will lead you on to a third book. It's geometrically progressive—all with no end in sight, and for no other reason than sheer enjoyment.

If you have time to correspond with me, could you answer several questions? Three, in fact. Why did a roast-pig dinner have to be kept a secret? How could a pig cause you to begin a literary society? And, most pressing of all, what is a potato peel pie—and why is it included in your society's name?

I am renting a flat in Chelsea, 23 Glebe Place, London SW3. My Oakley Street flat was bombed in 1945 and I still miss it. I could see the Thames out of three of my windows. I know that I am fortunate to have any place at all to live in London, but I much prefer whining to counting my blessings. I am glad you thought of me to do your *Elia* hunting.

Yours sincerely,

Juliet Ashton

P.S. I never could make up my mind about Moses—it still bothers me.

From Juliet to Sidney

18th January 1946

Dear Sidney,

This isn't a letter: it's an apology. Please forgive my moaning about the teas and luncheons you set up for *Izzy*. Did I call you a tyrant? I take it all back—I love Stephens & Stark for sending me out of London.

Bath is a glorious town: lovely crescents of white, upstanding houses instead of London's black, gloomy buildings or—worse still—piles of rubble that were once buildings. It is bliss to breathe in clean, fresh air with no coal smoke and no dust. The weather is cold, but it isn't London's dank chill. Even the people on the street look different—upstanding, like their houses, not grey and hunched like Londoners.

Susan said the guests at Abbot's book tea enjoyed themselves immensely. We are off tomorrow for bookshops in Colchester, Norwich, King's Lynn, Bradford and Leeds.

Love and thanks,

Juliet

From Juliet to Sidney

21st January 1946

Dear Sidney,

Night-time train travel is wonderful again! No standing in the corridors for hours, no being shunted off for a troop train to pass and, above all, no blackout curtains. All the windows we passed were lighted, and I could snoop once more. I missed it so terribly during the war. I felt we had all turned into moles scuttling along in our separate tunnels. I don't consider myself a real peeper—they go in for bedrooms, but it's families in sitting rooms or kitchens that thrill me. I can imagine their whole lives from a glimpse of book shelves, or desks, or burning candles, or bright cushions.

Sidney, do you know a man called Markham V. Reynolds, Junior? If you don't, will you look him up for me—*Who's Who*, the Domesday Book, Scotland Yard? Or he may simply be in the telephone directory. He sent a beautiful bunch of mixed spring flowers to me at the hotel in Bath, a dozen white roses to my train and heaps of red roses to Norwich—all with no message, only his card.

Come to that, how does he know where Susan and I are staying? What trains we are taking? All his flowers have been awaiting me on my arrival. I don't know whether to feel flattered or hunted.

Love,
Juliet

From Juliet to Sidney

23rd January 1946

Dear Sidney,

Susan's just given me the sales figures for *Izzy*—I can scarcely believe them. I honestly thought everyone would be so weary of the war that no one would want a remembrance of it—and certainly not in a book. Happily, and once again, you were right and I was wrong (though it half kills me to admit this).

Travelling, talking in front of a captive audience, signing books and meeting strangers *is* exhilarating. The women I've met have told me such wartime stories of their own, I almost wish I had my column back.

I love seeing the bookshops and meeting the booksellers—booksellers really are a special breed. No one in their right mind would take up work in a bookshop for the wages, and no one in their right mind would want to own one—the margin of profit is too small. So, it has to be a love of readers and reading that makes them do it—along with first goes at the new books.

Do you remember the first job your sister and I had in London? In crabby Mr Hawke's secondhand bookshop? How I loved him—he'd simply unpack a box of books, hand one or two to us and say, 'No cigarette ash, clean hands—and for God's sake, Juliet, none of your margin notes! Sophie, dear, don't let her drink coffee while she's reading.' And off we'd go with new books to read.

It was amazing to me then, and still is, that so many people who wander into bookshops don't really know what they're after—they want only to look around in the hope of seeing a book that will take their fancy. And then, being bright enough not to trust the publisher's blurb, they will ask the assistant: (1) What is it about? (2) Have you read it? (3) Was it any good?

Real dyed-in-the-wool readers—like Sophie and me—can't lie. Our faces always give us away. A raised brow or a curled lip means that it's a poor excuse for a book, and the clever customers ask for a recommendation instead, whereupon we frog-march them over to a particular volume and command them to read it. If they read it and despise it, they'll never come back. But if they like it, they're customers for life. Are you taking notes? You should—a publisher should send not just one reader's copy to a book-shop, but several, so that all the staff can read it, too.

Has Susan told you what else she has managed apart from our tour? Me. I hadn't known her half an hour before she told me that my make-up, my clothes, my hair and my shoes were drab, all drab. The war was over, hadn't I heard?

She took me to Madame Helena's for a haircut; it is now short and curly instead of long and lank. I had a light rinse, too—Susan and Madame said it would bring out the golden highlights in my 'beautiful chestnut curls'. But I know better; it's meant to cover any grey hairs (four, by my count) that have begun to creep in. I also bought a jar of face cream, a new lipstick and an eyelash curler—which makes my eyes cross whenever I use it.

Then Susan suggested a new dress. I reminded her that the Queen was very happy to wear her 1939 wardrobe, so why shouldn't I be? She said the Queen doesn't need to impress strangers—but I do. I felt like a traitor to my country: no decent woman has new clothes—but I forgot that the moment I saw myself in the mirror. My first new dress for four years, and what a dress! It is exactly the colour of a ripe peach and falls in lovely folds when I move. The shop assistant said it had 'Gallic chic' and I would too if I bought it. So I did. New shoes are going to have to wait, since I spent almost a year's worth of clothing coupons on the dress.

Between Susan, my hair, my face and my dress, I no longer look a listless, bedraggled thirty-two-year-old. I now look a lively, dashing, haute-coutured (if this isn't a French verb, it should be) thirty. But doesn't it seem shocking to have more stringent rationing after the war than during it?

I am still without any ideas for a book I want to write. It is beginning to depress me. Do you have any suggestions?

Since I am in what I consider to be the North I'm going to telephone Sophie in Scotland while I'm here. Any messages for your sister? Your brother-in-law? Your nephew?

Love,

Juliet

From Sidney to Juliet

Miss Juliet Ashton
The Queens Hotel
City Square
Leeds

26th January 1946

Dear Juliet,

I've just spoken to Susan about your going on to Scotland and have—though I know Sophie will never forgive me—decided against it. *Izzy's* sales figures are going up—right up—and I think you should come home.

The Times wants you to write a long piece for the supplement—one part of a three-part series they plan to publish in successive issues. I'll let them surprise you with the subject, but I can promise you three things now: they want it written by Juliet Ashton, *not by Izzy Bickerstaff*; the subject is a serious one; and the sum mentioned means you can fill your flat with fresh flowers every day for a year, buy a satin quilt (Lord Woolton says you no longer need to have been bombed out to buy new bed covers) and purchase a pair of real leather shoes—if you can find them. You can have my coupons.

The Times doesn't want the article until late spring, so we will have more time to think up a new book idea for you. All good reasons to hurry back, but the biggest one is that I miss you.

Now, about Markham V. Reynolds, Junior. I do know who he is, and the Domesday Book won't help—he's an American. He is the son and heir of Markham V. Reynolds, Senior, who used to have a monopoly on paper mills in America and now just owns most of them. Reynolds, Junior, being of an artistic bent, does not dirty his hands making paper—he prints on it instead. He's a publisher. *The New York Journal, The Word, View*—those are all his, and there are several smaller magazines as well. I knew he was in London. Officially, he's here to open the London office of *View*, but rumour has it that he's decided to begin publishing books, and he's here to beguile

England's finest authors with visions of plenty and prosperity in America. I didn't know his technique included roses, but I'm not surprised. He's always had more than his fair share of what we call cheek and Americans call can-do spirit. Just wait till you see him—he's been the undoing of stronger women than you, including my secretary. I'm sorry to say she's the one who gave him your itinerary *and* your address. The silly woman thought he looked so romantic, 'such a lovely suit and handmade shoes'. Dear God! She couldn't seem to grasp the concept of breach of confidentiality, so I had to dismiss her.

He's after you, Juliet, no doubt about it. Shall I challenge him to a duel? He would undoubtedly kill me, so I'd rather not. My dear, I can't promise you plenty or prosperity or even butter, but you do know that you're Stephens & Stark's—especially Stark's—most beloved author, don't you?

Dinner the first evening you are home?

Love,

Sidney

From Juliet to Sidney

28th January 1946

Dear Sidney,

Yes, dinner with pleasure. I'll wear my new dress and eat like a pig.

Thank you for tracing Markham V. Reynolds, Junior, to his source. So far, his blandishments are entirely floral, and I remain true to you and the Empire. However, I do have a pang of sympathy for your secretary—I hope he sent her some roses for her trouble—as I'm not certain that my scruples could withstand the sight of handmade shoes. If I ever do meet him, I'll be careful not to look at his feet—or I'll lash myself to a flagpole first and then peek, like Odysseus.

Bless you for telling me to come home. Am looking forward to *The Times*'s proposal for a series. Do you promise on Sophie's head it will not be a frivolous subject? They aren't going to ask me to write gossip about the Duchess of Windsor, are they?

Love,

Juliet

P.S. That man has sent me another bale of orchids. I'm getting a nervous twitch, waiting for him to come out of hiding and make himself known. Do you suppose this is his strategy?

From Dawsey to Juliet

31st January 1946

Dear Miss Ashton,

Your book came yesterday! I thank you with all my heart.

I have a job at St Peter Port harbour—unloading ships—so I can read during tea breaks. It is a blessing to have real tea and bread with butter, and now—your book. I like it too because the cover is soft and I can put it in my pocket everywhere I go, though I am careful not to use it up too quickly. And I value having a picture of Charles Lamb—he had a fine head, didn't he?

I would like to keep up our correspondence. I will answer your questions as well as I can. Though there are many who can tell a story better than I, I will tell you about our roast-pig dinner.

I have a cottage and a farm, left to me by my father. Before the war, I kept pigs and grew vegetables for the St Peter Port markets and flowers for Covent Garden. I also worked as a carpenter and roofer.

The pigs are gone now. The Germans took them away to feed their soldiers on the Continent, and ordered me to grow potatoes. We were to grow what they told us and nothing else. At first, before I knew the Germans as I came to later, I thought I could keep a few pigs hidden—for myself. But the Agricultural Officer nosed them out and carried them off. Well, that was a blow, but I thought I'd manage all right, for potatoes and turnips were plentiful, and there was still flour then. But it is strange how the mind turns to food. After six months of turnips and a lump of gristle now and then, I was hard put to think about anything but a fine, full meal.

One afternoon, my neighbour, Mrs Maugery, sent me a note. *Come quickly*, it said. *And bring a butcher's knife.* I tried not to get my hopes up— but I set out for the manor house at a great pace. And it was true! She had a pig, and she invited me to join in the feast with her and her friends!

That was the first meeting of the Guernsey Literary and Potato Peel Pie Society, even though we didn't know it then. The dinner was a rare treat, but the company was better. Talking and eating, we forgot about clocks and curfews until Amelia (Mrs Maugery) heard the chimes ring nine o'clock—we were an hour late. Well, the good food had strengthened our hearts, and when Elizabeth McKenna said we should strike out for our own homes instead of skulking in Amelia's house all night, we agreed. But breaking curfew was a crime—I'd heard of people being sent to prison camp for it— and keeping a pig was a worse one, so we whispered and picked our way through the fields as quietly as we could.

We would have come out all right if not for John Booker. He'd drunk more than he'd eaten at dinner, and when we got to the road, he forgot himself and broke into song! I grabbed hold of him, but it was too late: six German patrol officers suddenly rose out of the trees with their Lugers drawn and began to shout—Why were we out after curfew? Where had we been? Where were we going? I couldn't think what to do. If I ran, they'd shoot me. I knew that much. My mouth was as dry as chalk and my mind was blank, so I just held on to Booker and hoped.

Then Elizabeth stepped forward. She isn't tall, so those pistols were pointing at her eyes, but she didn't blink. She walked up to the officer in charge and started talking. You've never heard such lies. How sorry she was that we had broken curfew. How we had been attending a meeting of the Guernsey Literary Society, and the evening's discussion of *Elizabeth and Her German Garden* had been so delightful that we had all lost track of time. Such a wonderful book—had he read it?

None of us had the presence of mind to back her up, but the patrol officer couldn't help himself—he had to smile back at her. Elizabeth is like that. He took our names and then ordered us very politely to report to the Commandant the next morning. Then he bowed and wished us a good evening. Elizabeth nodded, gracious as could be, while the rest of us edged away, trying not to run like rabbits.

That is the story of our roast-pig dinner.

I'd like to ask you a question of my own. Ships are coming into St Peter Port harbour every day to bring us things Guernsey still needs: food, clothes, seed, ploughs, animal feed, tools, medicine—and most important, now that we have food to eat, shoes. I don't believe that there was a decent pair left on the island by the end of the war.

Some of the things being sent to us are wrapped up in old newspaper and magazine pages. My friend Clovis and I smooth them out and take them home to read—then we give them to neighbours who, like us, are eager for any news of the outside world in the past five years. Not just any news or pictures: Mrs Saussey wants to see recipes; Madame LePell wants fashion pictures (she is a dressmaker); Mr Brouard reads obituaries (he has his hopes, but won't say who); Mr Tourtelle wants to see beauty queens in bathing costumes; and my friend Isola likes to read about weddings.

There was so much we wanted to know during the war, but we weren't allowed letters or papers from England—or anywhere. In 1942, the Germans called in all the wireless sets—of course, there were hidden ones, listened to in secret, but if you were caught listening, you could be sent to the camps. That's why we don't understand so many things we can read about now.

I enjoy the wartime cartoons, but there is one that bewilders me. It was in a 1944 *Punch* and shows about ten people walking down a London street.

The chief figures are two men in bowler hats, holding briefcases and umbrellas, and one man is saying to the other, 'It is ridiculous to say these Doodlebugs have affected people in any way.' It took me several seconds to realise that every person in the cartoon had one normal ear and one *very large* ear on the other side of his head. Perhaps you could explain it to me?

Yours sincerely,

Dawsey Adams

From Juliet to Dawsey

3rd February 1946

Dear Mr Adams,

I am so glad you are enjoying Lamb's letters and the copy of his portrait. He did fit the face I had imagined for him, so I'm glad you agree.

Thank you very much for telling me about the roast pig, but don't think I didn't notice that you answered only one of my questions. I'm hankering to know more about the Guernsey Literary and Potato Peel Pie Society, and not merely to satisfy my idle curiosity—I have a professional duty to pry.

Did I tell you I am a writer? I wrote a weekly column for the *Spectator* during the war, and Stephens & Stark collected them together into a single volume and published them under the title *Izzy Bickerstaff Goes to War*. Izzy was the nom de plume the *Spectator* chose for me, and now, thank heavens, the poor thing has been laid to rest, and I can write under my own name again. I would like to write a book, but I am having trouble thinking of a subject I could live happily with for several years.

In the meantime, *The Times* has asked me to write an article for the literary supplement. They want to address the practical, moral and philosophical value of reading—spread out over three issues and by three different authors. I am to cover the philosophical side of the debate and so far my only thought is that reading keeps you from going gaga. You can see I need help.

Do you think your literary society would mind being included in such an article? I know that the story of the society's founding would fascinate *Times* readers, and I'd love to learn more about your meetings. But if you'd rather not, please don't worry—I will understand either way and, in any case, would like to hear from you again.

I remember the *Punch* cartoon you described very well and think it was the word *Doodlebug* that confused you. That was the name coined by the

Ministry of Information; it was meant to sound less terrifying than 'Hitler's V-1 rockets' or 'pilotless bombs'.

We were all used to bombing raids at night but these were unlike any bombs we had seen before. They came in the daytime, and they came so fast there was no time for an air-raid siren or to take cover. You could see them; they looked like slim, black, slanted pencils and made a dull, strangled sound above you—like a motor car running out of petrol. As long as you could hear them coughing and put-putting you were safe. You could think, Thank God, it's going past me. But when their noise stopped, it meant there was only thirty seconds before the thing plummeted. So, you listened for them. Listened hard for the sound of their motors cutting out.

I did see a Doodlebug fall once. I was quite some distance away when it hit, so I threw myself down in the gutter. Some women, in the top storey of a tall office building down the street, had gone to an open window to watch. They were sucked out by the force of the blast.

It seems impossible now that someone could have drawn a cartoon about Doodlebugs, and that everyone, including me, could have laughed at it. But we did. The old adage—humour is the best way to make the unbearable bearable—may be true.

Has Mr Hastings found the Lucas biography for you yet?

Yours sincerely,

Juliet Ashton

From Juliet to Markham Reynolds

Mr Markham Reynolds
63 Halkin Street
London SW1

4th February 1946

Dear Mr Reynolds,

I captured your delivery boy in the act of depositing a clutch of pink carnations onto my doorstep. I seized him and threatened him until he confessed your address—you see, Mr Reynolds, you are not the only one who can inveigle innocent employees. I hope you don't sack him; he seems a nice boy, and he really had no alternative.

Now I can thank you for the dozens of flowers you've sent me—it's been years since I've seen such roses, such orchids, and you can have no idea how they lift my heart in this shivering winter. Why I deserve to live in a bower, when everyone else has to be satisfied with bedraggled leafless trees and slush, I don't know, but I'm perfectly delighted to do so.

Yours sincerely,

Juliet Ashton

From Markham Reynolds to Juliet

5th February 1946

Dear Miss Ashton,

I didn't fire the delivery boy—I promoted him. He got me what I couldn't manage to get for myself: an introduction to you. The way I see it, your note is a figurative handshake and the preliminaries are now over. I hope you're of the same opinion, as it will save me the trouble of wangling an invitation to Lady Bascomb's next dinner party on the offchance you might be there. Your friends are a suspicious lot, especially that fellow Stark, who said it wasn't his job to reverse the direction of the lend-lease and refused to bring you to the cocktail party I threw at the *View* office.

God knows, my intentions are pure, or at least, non-mercenary. The simple truth of it is that you're the only female writer who makes me laugh. Your Izzy Bickerstaff columns were the wittiest work to come out of the war, and I want to meet the woman who wrote them.

If I swear that I won't kidnap you, will you do me the honour of dining with me next week? You pick the evening—I'm entirely at your disposal.

Yours,

Markham Reynolds

From Juliet to Markham Reynolds

6th February 1946

Dear Mr Reynolds,

I am no proof against compliments, especially compliments about my writing. I'll be delighted to dine with you. Thursday next?

Yours sincerely,

Juliet Ashton

From Markham Reynolds to Juliet

7th February 1946

Dear Juliet,
    Thursday's too far away. Monday?
    Claridge's? Seven?
    Yours,
    Mark
P.S. I don't suppose you have a telephone, do you?

From Juliet to Markham Reynolds

7th February 1946

Dear Mr Reynolds,
    All right—Monday, Claridge's, seven.
    I do have a telephone. It's in Oakley Street under a pile of rubble that used to be my flat. I'm only renting here, and my landlady, Mrs Olive Burns, possesses the sole telephone on the premises. If you would like to chat with her, I can give you her number.
    Yours sincerely,
    Juliet Ashton

From Dawsey to Juliet

7th February 1946

Dear Miss Ashton,
    I'm certain the Guernsey Literary Society would like to be included in your article for *The Times*. I have asked Mrs Maugery to write to you about our meetings, as she is an educated lady and her words will sound more at home in an article than mine. I don't think we are much like literary societies in London.
    Mr Hastings hasn't found a copy of the Lucas biography yet, but I had a

postcard from him saying, 'Hard on the trail. Don't give up.' He is a kind man, isn't he?

I'm heaving slates for the Crown Hotel's new roof. The owners are hoping that tourists may want to come back this summer. I am glad of the work but will be happy to be working on my land soon.

It is nice to come home in the evening and find a letter from you.

I wish you good fortune in finding a subject you would care to write a book about.

Yours sincerely,
Dawsey Adams

From Amelia Maugery to Juliet

8th February 1946

Dear Miss Ashton,

Dawsey Adams has just been to visit. I have never seen him as pleased with anything as he is with your gift and letter. He was so busy convincing me to write to you by the next post that he forgot to be shy. I don't believe he is aware of it, but Dawsey has a rare gift for persuasion—he never asks for anything for himself, so everyone is eager to do what he asks for others.

He told me of your proposed article and asked if I would write to you about the literary society we formed during—and because of—the German Occupation.

I will be happy to do so, but with a caveat.

A friend from England sent me a copy of *Izzy Bickerstaff Goes to War*—and I found your book as informative as it was entertaining and amusing—but it is the amusing tone I must quibble with. I realise that our name, the Guernsey Literary and Potato Peel Pie Society, is an unusual one and could easily be subjected to ridicule. Would you assure me you will not be tempted to do so? The Society members are very dear to me, and I do not wish them to be perceived as objects of fun by your readers.

Would you be willing to tell me of your intentions for the article and also something of yourself? If so, I should be glad to tell you about the Society.

I hope I shall hear from you soon.

Yours sincerely,
Amelia Maugery

From Juliet to Amelia

Mrs Amelia Maugery
Windcross Manor
La Bouvée
St Martin's, Guernsey

10th February 1946

Dear Mrs Maugery,
    Thank you for your letter. I am very glad to answer your questions.
    I did make fun of many wartime situations; the *Spectator* felt that humour would help to raise London's low morale. I am very glad *Izzy* served that purpose, but the need to be humorous against the odds is—thank goodness—over.
    I would never make fun of anyone who loved reading. Nor of Mr Adams—I was glad to learn one of my books fell into such hands as his.
    Since you should know something about me, I have asked the Reverend Simon Simpless, of St Hilda's Church near Bury St Edmunds, Suffolk, to write to you. He has known me since I was a child and is fond of me. I have asked Lady Bella Taunton to provide a reference, too. We were fire wardens together during the Blitz and she wholeheartedly dislikes me. Between the two of them, you may get a fair picture of my character.
    I am enclosing a copy of a biography I wrote of Anne Brontë, so you can see that I am capable of a different kind of work. It didn't sell very well—but I am much prouder of it than I am of *Izzy Bickerstaff Goes to War*.
    If there is anything else I can do to assure you of my goodwill, I will be glad to do so.
        Yours sincerely,
        Juliet Ashton

From Juliet to Sophie

12th February 1946

Dearest Sophie,
    Markham V. Reynolds, he of the roses, has finally materialised. Introduced himself, paid me compliments and invited me out to dinner—Claridge's, no less. I accepted regally—and then spent the next three days

fretting about my hair. It's lucky I have my lovely new dress, so I didn't have to waste precious fretting time on what to wear.

As Madame Helena said, 'The hairs, they are a disaster.' I tried a French roll; it fell down. A bun; it fell down. I was on the verge of tying an enormous red velvet bow on the top of my head when my neighbour Evangeline Smythe came to the rescue, bless her. She's a genius with my hair. In two minutes, I was a picture of elegance—she caught up all the curls and swirled them round at the back—and I could even move my head. Off I went, feeling perfectly adorable. Not even Claridge's marble lobby could intimidate *me*.

Then Markham V. Reynolds stepped forward and the bubble popped. He's dazzling.

Honestly, Sophie, I've never seen anything like him. Tanned, with blazing blue eyes. Ravishing leather shoes, elegant wool suit, blinding white handkerchief in breast pocket. Of course, being American, he's tall, and he has one of those alarming American smiles, all gleaming teeth and good humour, but he's not a genial American. He's quite impressive, and he's used to ordering people about—though he does it so easily they don't notice. He's got that way of believing his opinion is the truth, but he's not disagreeable about it. He's too sure he's right to bother about being disagreeable.

Once we were seated—in our own velvet-draped alcove—I asked him point-blank why he had sent me all those flowers without including any note.

He laughed. 'To make you interested. If I had written to you directly, asking you to meet me, how would you have replied?' I admitted I would have declined. He raised one pointed eyebrow at me. Was it his fault he could outwit me so easily?

I was awfully insulted to be so transparent, but he just laughed at me again. And then he began to talk about the war and Victorian literature—he knows I wrote a biography of Anne Brontë—and New York and rationing and, before I knew it, I was basking in his attention. I was, I admit, utterly charmed.

All our idle speculation as to the possible reasons why Markham V. Reynolds, Junior, was obliged to remain a man of mystery was to no avail. It's very disappointing, but we were completely wrong. He's not married. He's certainly not bashful. He doesn't have a disfiguring scar that causes him to shun the daylight. He doesn't seem to be a werewolf (no fur on his knuckles, anyway). And he's not a Nazi on the run (he'd have an accent).

Now that I think about it, maybe he *is* a werewolf. I can picture him lunging over the moors in hot pursuit of his prey, and I'm certain that he wouldn't think twice about eating an innocent bystander. I'll watch him closely at the next full moon. He's asked me to go dancing tomorrow—perhaps I should wear a high collar. Oh, that's vampires, isn't it?

I think I am a little giddy.

Love,

Juliet

From Lady Bella Taunton to Amelia

12th February 1946

Dear Mrs Maugery,

Juliet Ashton has written to me, and I am astonished. Am I to understand she wishes me to provide a character reference for her? Well, so be it! I cannot impugn her character—only her common sense. She hasn't any.

War, as you know, makes strange bedfellows, and Juliet and I were thrown together from the very first when we were paired off as fire wardens during the Blitz. When incendiary bombs fell, we would rush forth with stirrup pumps and buckets of sand to stifle any small blaze before it could spread.

Juliet and I did not chat, as less conscientious wardens would have done. I insisted on total vigilance at all times. Even so, I learned a few details of her life prior to the war.

Her father was a respectable farmer in Suffolk. Her mother, I surmise, was a typical farmer's wife, milking cows and plucking chickens, when not otherwise engaged in owning a bookshop in Bury St Edmunds. Juliet's parents were both killed in a motor-car accident when she was twelve and she went to live with her great-uncle in St John's Wood. There she disrupted his household by running away—twice.

In despair, he sent her to boarding school. Upon leaving, she shunned a higher education, came to London, and shared a flat with her friend Sophie Stark. She worked by day in bookshops. By night, she wrote a book about one of those wretched Brontë girls—I forget which one. I believe the book was published by Sophie's brother's firm, Stephens & Stark. Though it's biologically impossible, I can only assume that some form of nepotism was responsible for the book's publication.

Anyway, Juliet then began to publish feature articles for various of the magazines and newspapers. Her light, frivolous turn of mind gained her a large following among the less intellectually inclined readers—of whom, I fear, there are many.

She spent the very last of her inheritance on a flat in Chelsea, home of artists, models, libertines and socialists—completely irresponsible people all, just as Juliet proved herself to be as a fire warden.

I come now to the specifics of our association.

Juliet and I were two of several wardens assigned to the roof of the Inner Temple Hall of the Inns of Court. Let me say first that, for a warden, quick action and a clear head were imperative—one had to be aware of *everything* going on around one. *Everything.*

One night in May 1941, a high-explosive bomb was dropped through the roof of the Inner Temple Hall Library. The library was some distance away from Juliet's post, but she was so aghast by the destruction of her precious books that she sprinted *towards* the flames—as if she could single-handedly deliver the library from its fate! Of course, her delusions created nothing but further damage, for the firemen had to waste valuable minutes in rescuing her.

I believe Juliet suffered some minor burns in the debacle, but fifty thousand books were blown to Kingdom Come. Juliet's name was struck off the fire-warden list, and rightly so.

I discovered that she then volunteered her services to the Auxiliary Fire Services. On the morning after a bombing raid, the AFS would be on hand to offer tea and comfort to the rescue squads and the survivors: reuniting families, securing temporary housing, clothing, food, funds. I believe Juliet to have been adequate to that daytime task—causing no catastrophe among the teacups.

She was free to occupy her nights however she chose. Doubtless it included the writing of more light journalism, for the *Spectator* engaged her to write a weekly column under the name of Izzy Bickerstaff.

I read one of her columns and cancelled my subscription. She attacked the good taste of our dear (though dead) Queen Victoria. Doubtless you know of the huge memorial Victoria had built for her beloved consort, Prince Albert. It is the jewel in the crown of Kensington Gardens—a monument to the Queen's refined taste as well as to the Departed. Juliet applauded the Ministry of Food for having ordered peas to be planted in the grounds surrounding that memorial—commenting that no better scarecrow than Prince Albert existed in all England.

While I question her taste, judgment and inappropriate sense of humour, she does have one fine quality—she is honest. If she says she will honour the good name of your literary society, she will do so. I can say no more.

Sincerely yours,
Bella Taunton

From the Reverend Simon Simpless to Amelia

13th February 1946

Dear Mrs Maugery,

Yes, you may trust Juliet. I am unequivocal on this point. Her parents were my good friends as well as my parishioners at St Hilda's. Indeed, I was a guest at their home on the night she was born.

Juliet was a stubborn but nevertheless a sweet, considerate, joyous child—with an unusual bent for integrity in one so young.

I will tell you of one incident when she was ten years old. Juliet, while singing the fourth verse of 'His Eye Is on the Sparrow', slammed her hymnal shut and refused to sing another note. She told our choir master that the words cast a slur on God's character. We should not be singing it. He (the choir master, not God) didn't know what to do, so he escorted Juliet to my study for me to reason with her.

I did not fare very well. Juliet said, 'Well, he shouldn't have written, "His eye is on the sparrow"—what good was that? Did He stop the bird dying? Did He just say, "Oops"? It makes God sound like He's off birdwatching when real people need Him.'

I felt compelled to agree with Juliet on this matter—why had I never thought about it before? The choir has not sung 'His Eye Is on the Sparrow' since then.

Juliet's parents died when she was twelve and she was sent to live with her great-uncle, Dr Roderick Ashton, in London. Though not an unkind man, he was so mired in his Graeco-Roman studies he had no time to take any notice of the girl. He had no imagination, either—fatal for someone bringing up a child.

She ran away twice, the first time making it only as far as King's Cross Station. The police found her waiting, with a packed canvas bag and her father's fishing rod, to catch the train to Bury St Edmunds. She was returned to Dr Ashton—and she ran away again. This time, Dr Ashton telephoned me to ask for my help in finding her.

I knew exactly where to go—to her parents' former farm. I found her opposite the farm's entrance, sitting on a little wooded knoll, impervious to the rain—just sitting there, soaked—looking at her old (now sold) home.

I sent a telegram to her uncle and went back with her on the train to London the following day. Her uncle and I had a vigorous talk. He agreed that a boarding school might be best for Juliet—her parents had left ample funds for such an eventuality—and, fortunately, I knew of a very good one—St Swithin's. Academically fine, and with a headmistress not carved from granite. I am happy to tell you Juliet thrived there—she found her lessons stimulating, but I believe the true reason for Juliet's regained spirits was her friendship with Sophie Stark—and the Stark family. She often went to Sophie's home at half-term, and Juliet and Sophie came twice to stay with me and my sister at the Rectory. What jolly times we shared: picnics, bicycle rides, fishing. Sophie's brother, Sidney Stark, joined us once— though ten years older than the girls, and despite an inclination to boss them around, he was a welcome fifth to our happy party.

It was rewarding to watch Juliet grow up—as it is now to know her fully grown. I am very glad that she asked me to write to you of her character.

I have included our small history together so that you will realise I know whereof I speak. If Juliet says she will, she will. If she says she won't, she won't.

Very truly yours,
Simon Simpless

From Amelia to Juliet

18th February 1946

Dear Miss Ashton,

Thank you for taking my caveat so seriously. At the Society meeting last night, I told the members about your article for *The Times* and suggested that those who wished to do so should correspond with you about the books they have read and the joy they have found in reading.

The response was so vociferous that Isola Pribby, our Sergeant-at-Arms, was forced to bang her hammer for order (I admit that Isola needs little encouragement to bang her hammer). I think you will receive a good many letters from us, and I hope they will be of some help to your article.

Dawsey has told you that the Society was invented as a ruse to stop the Germans arresting my guests: Dawsey, Isola, Eben Ramsey, John Booker, Will Thisbee and our dear Elizabeth McKenna, who manufactured the story on the spot, bless her quick wits and silver tongue.

I, of course, knew nothing of their predicament at the time. As soon as they left, I made haste down to my cellar to bury the evidence of our meal. The first I heard about our literary society was the next morning when Elizabeth appeared in my kitchen and asked, 'How many books have you got?'

I had quite a few, but Elizabeth looked at my shelves and shook her head. 'We need more. There's too much gardening here.' She was right, of course—I do like a good garden book. 'I'll tell you what we'll do,' she said. 'After I've finished at the Commandant's Office, we'll go to Fox's bookshop and buy them out. If we're going to be the Guernsey Literary Society, we have to look literary.'

I was frantic all morning, worrying over what was happening at the Commandant's Office. What if they all ended up in the Guernsey prison? Or, worst of all, in a prison camp on the Continent? The Germans were erratic in dispensing their justice, so one never knew what sentence would be imposed. But nothing of the sort occurred.

Odd as it may sound, the Germans allowed—and even encouraged—artistic and cultural pursuits among the Channel Islanders. Their object was to prove to the British that the German Occupation was a model one. How this message was to be conveyed to the outside world was never explained, as the telephone and telegraph cable between Guernsey and London had been cut the day the Germans landed in June 1940. Whatever their skewed reasoning, the Channel Islands were treated much more leniently than the rest of conquered Europe—at first.

At the Commandant's Office, my friends were ordered to pay a small fine and submit the name and membership list of their society. The Commandant announced that he, too, was a lover of literature—might he, with a few like-minded officers, sometimes attend meetings?

Elizabeth told them they would be most welcome. And then she, Eben and I flew to Fox's, chose armloads of books and rushed back to the manor to put them on my shelves. Then we strolled from house to house—looking as carefree and casual as we could—in order to alert the others to come that evening and choose a book to read. Timing was vital, because Elizabeth feared the Commandant would appear at the next meeting, barely two weeks away. (He did not. A few German officers did attend over the years but, thankfully, left in some confusion and did not return.)

I knew all our members, but I did not know them all well. Dawsey had been my neighbour for over thirty years, and yet I don't believe I had ever spoken to him about anything more than the weather and farming. Isola was a dear friend, and Eben, too, but Will Thisbee was only an acquaintance and John Booker was nearly a stranger, for he had only just arrived when the Germans came. It was Elizabeth we had in common. Without her urging, I would never have thought to invite them to share my pig, and the Guernsey Literary and Potato Peel Pie Society would never have drawn breath. It was here Dawsey found his Charles Lamb and Isola fell upon *Wuthering Heights*. For myself, I chose *The Pickwick Papers*, thinking it would lift my spirits—it did.

Then each went home and read. We began to meet—for the sake of the Commandant at first, and then for our own pleasure. None of us had any experience of literary societies, so we made our own rules: we took turns to speak about the books we'd read. At the start, we tried to be calm and objective, but that soon fell away, and the purpose of the speakers was to goad the listeners into wanting to read the book themselves. Once two members had read the same book, they could argue, which was our great delight. We read books, talked books, argued over books and became dearer and dearer to one another. Other Islanders asked to join us, and our evenings together became bright, lively times—we could almost forget, now and then, the darkness outside. We still meet every fortnight.

Will Thisbee was responsible for the inclusion of Potato Peel Pie in our society's name. Germans or not, he wasn't going to go to any meetings unless there were eats! So refreshments became part of our agenda. Since there was scant butter, less flour and no sugar to spare on Guernsey then, Will concocted a potato peel pie: mashed potatoes for the filling, boiled beetroot for sweetness, and potato peelings for the crust. Will's recipes are usually dubious, but this one became a favourite.

I would love to hear from you again and to find out how your article progresses.

Yours most sincerely,
Amelia Maugery

From Isola Pribby to Juliet

19th February 1946

Dear Miss Ashton,

Amelia told us you would like to know about our book society and what we talk about at our meetings. She also said you have written a book about Anne Brontë, sister to Charlotte and Emily. I gave a talk on the Brontë girls once when it was my turn to speak. I'm sorry I can't send you my notes on Charlotte and Emily—I used them to kindle a fire in my stove—there being no other paper in the house. I'd already burned up my tide tables, the Book of Revelation and the story about Job.

You will want to know why I admired those Brontë girls. I like stories of passionate encounters. I myself have never had one, but now I can picture one. I didn't like *Wuthering Heights* at first, but the minute that spectre Cathy scratched her bony fingers on the windowpane I was grasped by the throat and not let go. With that Emily I could hear Heathcliff's pitiful cries upon the moors. I don't believe that after reading such a fine writer as Emily Brontë I will be happy to read again Miss Amanda Gillyflower's

Ill-Used by Candlelight. Reading good books ruins you for enjoying bad books.

I will tell you now about myself. I have a cottage and smallholding next to Mrs Maugery's manor house and farm. We are both situated by the sea. I tend my chickens and my goat, Ariel, and grow things. I have a parrot in my keeping, too—her name is Zenobia and she does not like men.

I have a stall at the market every week, where I sell my jam, vegetables and elixirs I make to restore manly ardour. Kit McKenna—daughter to my dear friend Elizabeth McKenna—helps me make my potions. She is only four and has to stand on a stool to stir my pot, but she is able to whip up quite a froth.

I do not have a pleasing appearance. My nose is big and was broken when I fell off the henhouse roof. One eyeball skitters upwards and my hair is wild and will not stay tamped down. I am tall and built of big bones.

I could tell you more about reading and how it perked up our spirits while the Germans were here, if you want me to.

The only time reading didn't help was after Elizabeth McKenna was arrested by the Germans. They caught her hiding one of those poor slave workers from Poland, and they sent her to prison on the Continent. There was no book that could lift my heart then, nor for a long time afterwards. It was all I could do not to slap every German I saw. For Kit's sake, I held myself in. She was only a little sprout then, and she needed us. Elizabeth hasn't come home yet. We are afraid for her, but, mind you, I say it's early days yet and she might still come home. I pray so, for I miss her sorely.

Your friend,
Isola Pribby

From Juliet to Dawsey

20th February 1946

Dear Mr Adams,

How did you know that I like white lilacs above all flowers? I always have, and now here they are, plumed over my desk. They are beautiful, and I love having them—the appearance, the delicious scent and the surprise of them. At first I thought, How on earth did he find these in February? and then I remembered that the Channel Islands are blessed by a warm Gulf Stream.

Due to your kind offices, I have received lovely long letters from Mrs Maugery and Isola Pribby. I hadn't realised that the Germans permitted *no outside news at all*, not even letters, in Guernsey. It surprised me so much. It shouldn't have—I knew the Channel Islands had been occupied, but I never, not once, thought what that might have entailed. Wilful ignorance is all I can call it.

So, I am off to the London Library to educate myself. The library suffered terrible bomb damage, but the floors are safe to walk on again. I know they have collected copies of *The Times* from 1900 to—yesterday. I shall mug up on the Occupation.

I want to find some travel or history books about the Channel Islands, too. Is it really true that on a clear day you can see the cars on the French coast roads? So it says in my encyclopedia, but I bought it secondhand for 4s and I don't trust it. There I also learned that Guernsey is 'roughly 7 miles long and 5 miles wide, with a population of 42,000'. Strictly speaking, very informative, but I want to know more than that.

Miss Isola Pribby told me that your friend Elizabeth McKenna has been sent to a prison camp on the Continent and has not yet returned. It knocked the wind out of me.

Ever since your letter about the roast-pig dinner, I had been imagining her there among you. Without even knowing it, I depended upon one day receiving a letter from her too. I am sorry. I will hope for her early return.

Thank you again for my flowers. It was a lovely thing for you to do.

Yours ever,

Juliet Ashton

From Juliet to Sidney

21st February 1946

Dearest Sidney,

I haven't heard from you for ages. Does your icy silence have anything to do with Mark Reynolds?

I have an idea for a new book. It's a novel about a beautiful yet sensitive author whose spirit is crushed by her domineering editor.

Do you like it?

Love always,

Juliet

From Juliet to Sidney

23rd February 1946

Dear Sidney,
    I was only joking.
    Love,
    Juliet

From Juliet to Sidney

25th February 1946

    Sidney?
    Love,
    Juliet

From Juliet to Sidney

26th February 1946

Dear Sidney,
    Did you think I wouldn't notice you'd gone? I did. After three notes went unanswered, I made a personal visit to St James's Place, where I encountered the iron Miss Tilley, who said you were out of town. Very enlightening. Upon pressing, I learned that you'd gone to Australia! Miss Tilley would not disclose your exact whereabouts—only that you were scouring the Outback, seeking new authors for Stephens & Stark's list. She would forward letters to you, at her discretion.
    Your Miss Tilley does not fool me. Nor do you—I know exactly where you are and what you are doing. You flew to Australia to find Piers Langley and are holding his hand while he sobers up. At least, I hope that's what you are doing. He is such a dear friend—and such a brilliant writer. I want him to be well again and writing poetry. I'd add forgetting all about Burma and the Japanese, but I know that's not possible.
    You could have told me, you know. I can be discreet when I really try.
    I liked your other secretary more. And you sacked her for nothing:

Markham Reynolds and I have met. All right, we've done more than meet. We've danced the rumba. But don't fuss. He hasn't mentioned *View*, except in passing, and he hasn't once tried to lure me to New York. We talk of higher matters, such as Victorian literature. He's not the shallow dilettante you would have me believe, Sidney. He's an expert on Wilkie Collins, of all things. Did you know that Wilkie Collins maintained two separate households with two separate mistresses and two separate sets of children? The organisational difficulties must have been shocking. No wonder he took laudanum.

I do think you would like Mark if you knew him better, and you may have to. But my heart and my writing hand belong to Stephens & Stark.

The article for *The Times* has turned into a lovely treat for me—now and ongoing. I have made a group of new friends from the Channel Islands—the Guernsey Literary and Potato Peel Pie Society. Don't you adore their name? If Piers needs distracting, I'll write you a nice fat letter about how they came by their name. If not, I'll tell you when you come home (when are you coming home?).

Love to you and Piers,
Juliet

From Juliet to Sophie

28th February 1946

Dearest Sophie,

I am as surprised as you are. He didn't breathe a word to me. On Tuesday, I realised I hadn't heard from Sidney for days, so I went to Stephens & Stark to demand attention and found he'd flown the coop. That new secretary of his is a fiend. To every one of my questions, she said, 'I really can't divulge information of a personal nature, Miss Ashton.' How I wanted to slap her.

Just as I was on the verge of concluding that Sidney had been approached by MI6 and was on a mission in Siberia, horrible Miss Tilley admitted that he'd gone to Australia. It all came clear then. He's gone to get Piers, who was going to drink himself steadily to death in that rest home unless someone came and stopped him. I can hardly blame him, after what he's been through—but Sidney won't allow it, thank God.

You know I adore Sidney with all my heart, but there's something terrifically freeing about Sidney *in Australia*. Mark Reynolds has been what your aunt Lydia would have called 'persistent in his attentions' for the past three weeks, but, even as I've gobbled lobster and guzzled champagne, I've been looking furtively over my shoulder for Sidney. He's convinced that Mark is trying to steal me away from London in general and Stephens & Stark in particular, and nothing I said could persuade him otherwise. I know he doesn't like Mark—*aggressive and unscrupulous* were the words he used last time I saw him—but really, he was a bit too King Lear about the whole thing. I am a grown woman—mostly—and I can guzzle champagne with whomever I choose.

When not checking under tablecloths for Sidney, I've been having the most wonderful time. I feel as though I've emerged from a black tunnel and found myself in the middle of a carnival. Mark gads about every night—if we're not going to a party (and we usually are), we're off to the cinema, or the theatre, or a nightclub, or a gin house of ill-repute (he says he's trying to introduce me to democratic ideals). It's very exciting.

Have you noticed there are some people—Americans especially—who seem untouched by the war, or at least unmangled by it? I don't mean to imply that Mark was a shirker—he was in their Air Corps—but he's simply not sunk under. And when I'm with him, I feel untouched by the war, too. It's an illusion, I know it is. But it's forgivable to enjoy myself a little—isn't it?

Is Dominic too old for a jack-in-the-box? I saw a diabolical one in a shop yesterday. It pops out, leering and waving, its oily black moustache curling above pointed white teeth, the very picture of a villain. Dominic would adore it, after he had got over his first shock.

Love,
Juliet

From Juliet to Isola

Miss Isola Pribby
Pribby Homestead
La Bouvée
St Martin's, Guernsey

28th February 1946

Dear Miss Pribby,
Thank you so much for your letter about yourself and Emily Brontë. I laughed when I read that Emily had caught you by the throat the second

poor Cathy's ghost knocked at the window. She got me at *exactly the same moment.*

Our teacher had assigned *Wuthering Heights* to be read over the Easter holidays. I went home with my friend Sophie Stark, and we whined for two days over the injustice of it all. Finally her brother Sidney told us to shut up and *get on with it.* I did, still fuming, until I got to Cathy's ghost at the window. I have never felt such dread as I did then. Monsters or vampires have never scared me in books—but ghosts are a different matter.

Sophie and I did nothing for the rest of the holidays but move from bed to hammock to armchair, reading *Jane Eyre, Agnes Grey, Shirley* and *The Tenant of Wildfell Hall.*

What a family the Brontës were—but I chose to write about Anne because she was the least known of the sisters, and, I think, just as fine a writer as Charlotte. God knows how Anne managed to write any books at all, influenced by such a strain of religion as her aunt Branwell possessed. Emily and Charlotte had the good sense to ignore their bleak aunt, but not poor Anne. Imagine preaching that God meant women to be Meek, Mild and Gently Melancholic. So much less trouble around the house—pernicious old bat!

I hope you will write to me again.

Yours,

Juliet Ashton

From Eben Ramsey to Juliet

28th February 1946

Dear Miss Ashton,

I am a Guernsey man and my name is Eben Ramsey. My fathers before me were tombstone cutters and carvers—lambs a speciality. These are things I like to do of an evening, but for my livelihood I fish.

Mrs Maugery said you would like to have letters about our reading during the Occupation. I was never going to talk—or think, if I could help it—about those days, but Mrs Maugery said we could trust to your judgment in writing about the Society during the war. If Mrs Maugery says you can be trusted, I believe it. Also, you had the kindness to send my friend Dawsey a book—and he all but unknown to you. So I am writing to you and hope it will be a help to your story.

We weren't a true literary society at first. Apart from Elizabeth, Mrs

Maugery and perhaps Booker, most of us hadn't had much to do with books since school. We took them from Mrs Maugery's shelves fearful we'd spoil the fine paper. I had no zest for such matters in those days. It was only by fixing my mind on the Commandant and jail that I could make myself lift the cover of the book and begin. It was called *Selections from Shakespeare.* Later, I came to see that Mr Dickens and Mr Wordsworth were thinking of men like me when they wrote their words. But most of all, I believe that William Shakespeare was. Mind you, I cannot always make sense of what he says, but it will come.

Do you know what sentence of his I admire the most? It is 'The bright day is done, and we are for the dark.' I wish I'd known those words on the day I watched those German troops land, planeload after planeload—and come off ships down in the harbour! If I could have thought those words, I'd have been consoled somehow and ready to go out and contend with circumstance—instead of my heart sinking to my shoes.

They came here on Sunday the 30th of June 1940, after bombing us two days before. They said they hadn't meant to bomb us; they mistook our tomato lorries on the pier for army trucks. How they came to think that strains the mind. They killed some thirty men, women and children—one among them was my cousin's boy. He had sheltered underneath his lorry when he first saw the planes dropping bombs, and it exploded and caught fire. They killed men in their lifeboats at sea. They strafed the Red Cross ambulances carrying our wounded. When no one shot back at them, they saw the British had left us undefended. They just flew in peaceably two days later and occupied us for five years.

At first, they were as nice as could be. They were that full of themselves they were thick enough to think it would just be a hop and a skip till they landed in London. When they found out that wasn't to be, they turned back to their natural meanness.

They had rules for everything—but they kept changing their minds; trying to seem friendly, like they were poking a carrot in front of a donkey's nose. But we weren't donkeys. So they'd get harsh again. For instance, they were always changing curfew—eight at night, or nine, or five in the evening if they felt really mean-minded. You couldn't visit your friends or even tend your stock.

We started out hopeful, sure they'd be gone in six months, but it stretched on and on. Food grew hard to come by, and soon there was no firewood left. Days were grey with hard work, and evenings were black with boredom. Everyone was sickly from so little nourishment, and bleak from wondering if it would ever end. We clung to books and to our friends; they reminded us that we had another part to us.

After D-Day, the Germans couldn't send any supply ships from France because of the Allied bombers. So they were finally as hungry as we were—and killing dogs and cats to give themselves something to eat. They would raid our gardens, rooting up potatoes—even the black rotten ones. Four soldiers died eating handfuls of hemlock, thinking it was parsley. I am not pointing a finger because some of us were doing the same. I think hunger makes you desperate when you wake to it every morning.

My grandson Eli was evacuated to England when he was seven. He is home now—twelve years old, and tall—but I will never forgive the Germans for making me miss his childhood.

I must go and milk my cow now, but I will write to you again if you like. I wish you good health,

Eben Ramsey

From Miss Adelaide Addison to Juliet

1st March 1946

Dear Miss Ashton,

Forgive the presumption of a letter from a person unknown to you, but a clear duty is imposed upon me. I understand from Dawsey Adams that you are to write a long article for *The Times* on the value of reading and you intend to feature the Guernsey Literary and Potato Peel Pie Society therein.

Perhaps you will reconsider when you learn that their founder, Elizabeth McKenna, is not even an Islander. Despite her fine airs, she is merely a jumped-up servant from the London home of Sir Ambrose Ivers, RA (Royal Academy). Surely, you know of him? He is a portrait painter of some note, though I've never understood why. In any event, Elizabeth McKenna was the daughter of his housekeeper, if you please.

While Elizabeth's mother dusted, Sir Ambrose let the child potter around in his London studio, and he kept her at school long after the normal leaving time for one of her station. Her mother died when Elizabeth was fourteen. Did Sir Ambrose send her to an institution to be properly trained for a suitable occupation? He did not. He kept her with him in his home in Chelsea. He proposed her for a scholarship to the Slade School of Fine Art, and doted upon her in a way that encouraged her besetting sin: lack of humility. The decay of standards is the cross of our times, and nowhere is this regrettable decline more apparent than in Elizabeth McKenna.

Sir Ambrose owned a home in Guernsey—on the clifftops near La Bouvée. He, his housekeeper and the girl summered here when she was a child. Elizabeth was a wild thing—roaming unkempt about the island, even on Sundays. No household chores, no gloves, no shoes, no stockings. Going out on fishing boats with rude men. Spying on decent people through her telescope. A disgrace.

When it became clear that the war was going to start in earnest, Sir Ambrose sent Elizabeth to close up his house. In the midst of her putting up the shutters, the German Army landed on her doorstep. However, the choice to remain here was hers, and, as is proven by certain subsequent events (which I will not demean myself to mention), she is not the selfless heroine that some people seem to think.

The so-called Literary Society is a scandal. There are some of true culture and breeding in Guernsey, and they will take no part in this charade (even if invited). There are only two respectable people in the Society—Eben Ramsey and Amelia Maugery. The other members include Dawsey Adams—a stuttering swineherd—and Isola Pribby—a practising witch, who, by her own admission, distils and sells potions. They collected a few others of their ilk along the way, and one can only imagine their 'literary evenings'.

You must not write about these people and their books—God knows what they saw fit to read!

Yours in Christian Consternation and Concern,
Adelaide Addison (Miss)

From Mark to Juliet

2nd March 1946

Dear Juliet,
I've just appropriated my music critic's opera tickets. Covent Garden at eight. Will you?
Yours,
Mark

From Juliet to Mark

Wonderful! I feel sorry for your critic, though. Those tickets are scarce as hens' teeth.
Juliet

From Mark to Juliet

He'll make do with standing room. He can write about the uplifting effect of opera on the poor, etc., etc.

I'll pick you up at seven.

Yours,

M.

From Juliet to Eben

Mr Eben Ramsey
Les Pommiers
Calais Lane
St Martin's, Guernsey

3rd March 1946

Dear Mr Ramsey,

It was so kind of you to write to me about your experiences during the Occupation, and I was glad to hear about your grandson Eli returning to you.

Does he live with you or with his parents? Did you receive no news of him at all during the Occupation? Did all the Guernsey children return at once? What a celebration, if they did!

I don't mean to inundate you with questions, but I have a few more, if you're in an answering frame of mind. I know you were at the roast-pig dinner that led to the founding of the Guernsey Literary and Potato Peel Pie Society—but how did Mrs Maugery come to have the pig in the first place? How does one hide a pig?

Elizabeth McKenna was brave that night! She truly has grace under pressure, a quality that fills me with hopeless admiration. I know you and the other members of the Society must worry as the months pass without word, but you mustn't give up hope. Friends tell me that Europe is like a hive broken open, teeming with thousands upon thousands of displaced people, all trying to get home. A dear old friend of mine, who was shot down in Burma in 1943, reappeared in Australia last month—not in the best of shape, but alive and intending to remain so.

Thank you for your letter.

Yours sincerely,

Juliet Ashton

From Eben to Juliet

10th March 1946

Dear Miss Ashton,

Thank you for your kind questions about my grandson Eli. He is the child of my daughter, Jane. Jane and her newborn baby died in hospital on the day that the Germans bombed us, the 28th of June 1940. Eli's father was killed in North Africa in 1942, so I have Eli in my keeping now.

Eli left Guernsey on the 20th of June along with the thousands of babies and schoolchildren who were evacuated to England. We knew the Germans were coming and Jane worried for his safety here. The doctor would not let Jane sail with the children, the baby's birth being so close.

We did not have any news of the children for six months. Then I got a postcard from the Red Cross, saying Eli was well, but not where he was situated—we never knew what towns our children were in, though we prayed not in a big city. An even longer time passed before I could send him a card in return, but I was of two minds about that. I dreaded telling him that his mother and the baby had died. I hated to think of my boy reading those cold words on the back of a postcard. But I had to do it. And then a second time, after I got word about his father.

Eli did not come back until the war was over—and they did send all the children home at once. That was a day! More wonderful even than when the British soldiers came to liberate Guernsey. Eli, he was the first boy down the gangway—he'd grown long legs in five years—and I don't think I could have stopped hugging him if Isola hadn't pushed me a bit so she could hug him herself.

I thank God that he was boarded with a farming family in Yorkshire. They were very good to him. Eli gave me a letter they had written to me—it was full of all the things I had missed. They told of his schooling, how he helped on the farm, how he tried to be steadfast when he got my postcards.

He fishes with me and helps me tend my cow and garden, but carving wood is what he likes best—Dawsey and I are teaching him how to do it. He fashioned a fine snake from a bit of broken fence last week, though it's my guess that the bit of broken fence was really a rafter from Dawsey's barn. Dawsey just smiled when I asked him about it, but spare wood is hard to find on the island now, as we had to cut down most of the trees—banisters and furniture, too—for firewood when there was no more coal or paraffin left. Eli and I are planting trees on my land now, but it is going to take a long time for them to grow—and we do all miss the leaves and shade.

I will tell you now about our roast pig. The Germans did fuss about bookkeeping. They kept track of every gallon we milked, weighed the cream, recorded every sack of flour. They left the chickens alone for a while, but then feed and scraps became so scarce they ordered us to kill off the older chickens, so the good egg layers could have enough feed to keep on laying.

They were especially fretful about meat because they didn't want any to go to the black market instead of feeding their own soldiers. If your sow had a litter, the German Agricultural Officer would come to your farm, count the piglets, give you a birth certificate for each one, and mark his record book. If a pig died a natural death, you told the AO and out he'd come again, look at the dead body and give you a death certificate.

They would make surprise visits to your farm, and your number of living pigs had better tally with their number of living pigs. One pig less and you were fined, one time more and you could be arrested and sent to jail in St Peter Port. If too many pigs went missing, the Germans thought you were selling on the black market, and you were sent to a labour camp in Germany. With the Germans you never knew which way they'd blow—they were a moody people. In the beginning, though, it was easy to fool the Agricultural Officer and keep a secret live pig for your own use. This is how Mrs Maugery came to have hers.

Will Thisbee had a sickly pig who died. The AO came out and wrote a certificate saying the pig was truly dead and left Will alone to bury the poor animal. But Will didn't—he raced off through the wood with the little body and gave it to Mrs Maugery. She hid her own healthy pig and called the AO, saying, 'Come quickly, my pig has died.'

The AO came out straight away and, seeing the pig with its toes turned up, never knew it was the same pig he'd seen earlier that morning. He inscribed his dead-animal book with one more dead pig.

Mrs Maugery took the same carcass over to another friend, and he pulled the same trick the next day. We could do this till the pig turned rank. The Germans caught on finally and began to tattoo each pig and cow at birth, so there was no more dead-animal swapping. But Mrs Maugery, with a live, hidden, fat and healthy pig, needed only Dawsey to come to kill it quietly. It had to be done quietly because there was a German battery by her farm, and it would not do for the soldiers to hear the pig's death squeal and come running.

Mrs Maugery's pig made us a fine dinner—there were onions and potatoes to fill out the roast. We had almost forgotten what it felt like to have full stomachs, but it came back to us. With the curtains closed, and food and friends at the table, we could make believe that none of it had happened.

You are right to call Elizabeth McKenna brave. She is that, and always was. She came from London to Guernsey as a little girl with her mother and

Sir Ambrose Ivers. She met my Jane her first summer here, when they were both ten, and they were ever staunch to one another since then.

When Elizabeth came back in the spring of 1940 to close up Sir Ambrose's house, she stayed longer than was safe because she wanted to stand by Jane. My girl had been feeling poorly since her husband, John, went to England to sign up—that was in December 1939—and she had a difficult time holding on to the baby till her time came. Dr Martin ordered her to bed, so Elizabeth stayed on to keep her company and play with Eli. Nothing Eli liked more than to play with Elizabeth. They were a threat to the furniture, but it was good to hear them laugh. I went over once to collect the two of them for supper and when I stepped in, there they were—sprawled on a pile of pillows at the foot of the staircase. They had polished Sir Ambrose's fine oak banister and come sailing down three floors!

It was Elizabeth who did what was needed to get Eli on the evacuation ship. We were given only one day's notice when the ships were coming from England to take the children away. Elizabeth worked like a whirligig, washing and sewing Eli's clothes and helping him to understand why he could not take his pet rabbit with him. When we set out for the school, Jane had to turn away so as not to show Eli a tearful face, so Elizabeth took him by the hand and said it was good weather for a sea voyage.

Even after that, Elizabeth wouldn't leave Guernsey when everyone else was trying to get away. 'No,' she said. 'I'll wait for Jane's baby to come, and, when it's fattened up enough, she and Jane and I will go to London. Then we'll find out where Eli is and go and get him.' For all her winning ways, Elizabeth was wilful. She'd stick out that jaw of hers and you could see it wasn't any use arguing with her about leaving. To tell the truth, I was glad she did not leave us. She was with me at the hospital when Jane and her new baby died. She sat by Jane, holding on hard to her hand.

After Jane died, Elizabeth and me, we stood in the hallway, numb and staring out of the window. It was then we saw seven German planes come in low over the harbour. They were just on one of the reconnaissance flights, we thought—but then they began dropping bombs—they tumbled from the sky like sticks. We didn't speak, but I know what we were thinking—thank God Eli was safely away.

Elizabeth stood by Jane and me in the bad time. I was not able to stand by Elizabeth, so I thank God her daughter, Kit, is safe and with us, and I pray for her to come home soon.

I was glad to hear of your friend who was found in Australia.

I hope you will correspond with me and Dawsey again, as he enjoys hearing from you as much as I do myself.

Yours sincerely,
Eben Ramsey

From Dawsey to Juliet

12th March 1946

Dear Miss Ashton,

I am glad you liked the white lilacs.

I am working several days a week now at the quarry, as well as at the port. Isola thought I looked tired and mixed up a balm for aching muscles—it's called Angel Fingers. Isola has a cough syrup called Devil's Suck and I pray I'll never need it.

Yesterday, Mrs Maugery and Kit came over for supper, and we took a blanket down to the beach afterwards to watch the moon rise. Kit loves doing that, but she always falls asleep before it is fully risen, and I carry her home. She is certain she'll be able to stay awake all night as soon as she's five.

Do you know much about children? I don't, and although I am learning, I think I am a slow learner. It was much easier before Kit learned to talk, but it was not so much fun. I try to answer her questions, but usually she has moved on to a new question before I can answer the first. Also, I don't know enough to please her. I don't know what a mongoose looks like.

I like getting your letters, but I often feel I don't have any news worth telling, so it is good to answer your questions.

Yours,

Dawsey Adams

From Adelaide Addison to Juliet

12th March 1946

Dear Miss Ashton,

I see you will not be advised by me. I came upon Isola Pribby at her market stall, scribbling a letter—in response to a letter from you! I tried to resume my errands calmly, but then I came upon Dawsey Adams posting a letter—to you!

Who will be next? I ask. This is not to be borne, and I seize my pen to stop you.

I was not completely candid with you in my last letter. In the interests of delicacy, I drew a veil on the true nature of that group and their founder, Elizabeth McKenna. But now, I see that I must reveal all: the Society members have colluded to raise the bastard child of Elizabeth McKenna and her

German paramour, Dr/Captain Christian Hellman. Yes, a German soldier! I don't wonder at your shock.

Now, I am nothing if not just. I do not say that Elizabeth was what the ruder classes called a Jerry-bag, cavorting around Guernsey with *any* German soldier who could give her gifts, like other Island hussies.

But the truth is bad enough. Herewith, the sorry facts: in April 1942, the UNWED Elizabeth McKenna gave birth to a baby girl—in her own cottage. Eben Ramsey and Isola Pribby were present at the birth—he to hold the mother's hand and she to keep the fire going. Amelia Maugery and Dawsey Adams (an unmarried man! For shame!) did the actual work of delivering the child, before Dr Martin could arrive.

The putative father? Absent! 'Ordered to duty on the Continent'—SO THEY SAID. The case is perfectly clear—when the evidence of their illicit connection was irrefutable, Captain Hellman abandoned his mistress and left her to her just deserts.

I could have foretold this scandalous outcome. I saw Elizabeth with her lover on several occasions—walking together, deep in talk. And once, I saw him put his hand on her face and follow her cheekbone down with his thumb.

Though I had little hope of success, I knew it was my duty to warn her of the fate that awaited her. I told her she would be cast out of decent society, but she did not heed me. In fact, she laughed. I bore it. Then she told me to get out of her house.

I take no pride in my prescience. It would not be Christian.

Back to the baby—named Christina, called Kit. Barely a year later, Elizabeth, as feckless as ever, committed a criminal act expressly forbidden by the German Occupying Force—she helped shelter and feed an escaped prisoner of the German Army. She was arrested and sentenced to prison on the Continent.

Mrs Maugery, at the time of Elizabeth's arrest, took the baby into her home. And since that night? The Literary Society has raised that child as its own—passing her around from house to house. The principal work of the baby's maintenance was undertaken by Amelia Maugery, with other Society members taking her out—like a library book—for several weeks at a time. They all cosseted her, and now that Kit can walk, she goes everywhere with one or another of them—holding hands or riding on their shoulders.

Such are their standards! You must not glorify such people in *The Times*!

You won't hear from me again—I have done my best.

On your head be it.

Adelaide Addison

Cable from Sidney to Juliet
20th March 1946
Dear Juliet, Trip home delayed. Fell off horse, broke leg. Piers nursing. Love, Sidney

Cable from Juliet to Sidney
21st March 1946
Oh God, which leg? Am so sorry. Love, Juliet

Cable from Sidney to Juliet
22nd March 1946
It was the other one. Don't worry—little pain. Piers excellent nurse. Love, Sidney

Cable from Juliet to Sidney
22nd March 1946
So happy it wasn't the one I broke. Can I send anything to help your convalescence? Books—recordings—poker chips—my life's blood?

Cable from Sidney to Juliet
23rd March 1946
No blood, no books, no poker chips. Just keep sending long letters to entertain us. Love, Sidney and Piers

From Juliet to Sophie
23rd March 1946

Dear Sophie,

I only got a cable from Sidney so you know more than I do. But it's absolutely ridiculous for you to consider flying off to Australia. What about Alexander? And Dominic? And your lambs? They'll pine away without you. Stop and think for a moment and you'll realise why you shouldn't fuss.

First: Piers will take excellent care of Sidney.

Second: better Piers than us—remember what a vile patient Sidney was last time? We should be glad he's thousands of miles away.

Third: Sidney has been stretched as tight as a bowstring for years. He needs a rest, and breaking his leg is probably the only way he'll allow himself to take one.

Most important of all, Sophie: *he doesn't want us there.*

I'm perfectly certain Sidney would prefer me to write a new book than to appear at his bedside in Australia, so I intend to stay right here in my dreary flat and cast about for a subject. I do have a tiny infant of an idea, but it's much too frail and defenceless to risk describing, even to you. In honour of Sidney's leg, I'm going to nurse it and feed it and see if I can make it grow.

Now, about Markham V. Reynolds (Junior).

Your questions regarding that gentleman are very delicate, very subtle, very much like being struck on the head by a mallet. Am I in love with him? What kind of a question is that? It's a tuba among the flutes, and I expect better of you.

The first rule of snooping is to come at it sideways—when you began writing me dizzy letters about Alexander, I didn't ask if you were in love with him, I asked instead what his favourite animal was. And your answer told me everything I needed to know about him—just how many men would admit that they loved ducks? (This brings up an important point: I don't know what Mark's favourite animal is. But I sincerely doubt if it's a duck.)

Would you care for a few suggestions? You could ask me who his favourite author is (Dos Passos! Hemingway!!). Or his favourite colour (blue, not sure what shade, probably royal). Is he a good dancer? (Yes, far better than I, never steps on my toes, but doesn't talk or even hum while dancing. Doesn't hum at all as far as I know.) Does he have brothers or sisters? (Yes, two older sisters, one married to a sugar baron and the other widowed last year. Plus one younger brother, dismissed with a sneer as an ass.)

So—now that I've done all your work for you, perhaps you can answer your own ridiculous question, because I can't. I feel addled when I'm with Mark, which might be love but might not. It certainly isn't restful. I'm rather dreading this evening, for instance. Another dinner party, very brilliant, with men leaning across the table to make a point and women gesturing with their cigarette holders.

Oh dear, I want to nuzzle into my sofa, but I have to get up and put on an evening dress.

Love aside, Mark is a terrible strain on my wardrobe.

Now, don't fret about Sidney. He'll be stalking around in no time.

Love,
Juliet

From Juliet to Dawsey

25th March 1946

Dear Mr Adams,

I have received a long letter (two, in fact!) from a Miss Adelaide Addison, warning me not to write about the Society. If I do, she will wash her hands of me for ever. I will try to bear that affliction with fortitude. She does work up quite a head of steam about Jerry-bags, doesn't she?

I have also had a wonderful letter from Isola Pribby. Between you all, Guernsey is virtually writing my article for me. Even Miss Adelaide Addison has done her bit—defying her will be such a pleasure.

I don't know as much about children as I would like to. I am godmother to Dominic, the three-year-old son of my friend Sophie. They live in Scotland and I don't see him very often. I am always astonished, when I do, by his increasing personhood—no sooner had I got used to carrying a warm lump of baby than he stopped being one and started rushing around on his own.

A mongoose, you may tell Kit, is a weaselly-looking creature with very sharp teeth and a bad temper. It is the only natural enemy of the cobra and is impervious to snake venom. Perhaps you could get her one for a pet?

Yours,

Juliet Ashton

P.S. I had second thoughts about sending this—what if Adelaide Addison is a friend of yours? Then I decided no, she couldn't possibly be—so off it goes.

P.P.S. Mr Hastings has found the E. V. Lucas biography. He has decided to send it at once. He said, 'A lover of Charles Lamb ought not to have to wait.'

From Juliet to Sidney and Piers

Mr Sidney Stark
Monreagle Hotel
Broadmeadows Avenue, 79
Melbourne
Victoria, Australia

31st March 1946

Dear Sidney and Piers,

No life's blood—just sprained thumbs from copying out the enclosed letters from my new friends in Guernsey. I love their letters and could not bear the thought of sending the originals to the bottom of the earth where they would undoubtedly be eaten by wild dogs.

I knew the Germans occupied the Channel Islands, but I barely gave them a thought during the war. I have since scoured *The Times* for articles and anything I can cull from the London Library on the Occupation. I also need to find a good travel book on Guernsey—one with descriptions, not timetables and hotel recommendations—to give me the feel of the Island.

Quite apart from my interest *in their interest* in reading, I have fallen in love with two men: Eben Ramsey and Dawsey Adams. I want Amelia Maugery to adopt me, and I want to adopt Isola Pribby. I will leave you to discern my feelings for Adelaide Addison (Miss) by reading her letters. The truth is, I am living more in Guernsey than I am in London at the moment—I pretend to work, with one ear cocked for the sound of the post dropping in the box. This must be how people felt when they gathered around the publisher's door to seize the latest instalment of *David Copperfield* as it came off the printing press.

To me, these people and their wartime experiences are fascinating and moving. Do you agree? Do you think there could be a book here? Don't be polite—I want your opinion (both of your opinions) unvarnished. And you needn't worry—I'll continue to send you copies of the letters even if you don't want me to write a book about Guernsey. I am (mostly) above petty vengeance.

Since I have sacrificed my thumbs for your amusement, you should send me one of Piers's latest pieces in return. So glad you are writing again, my dear.

My love to you both,
Juliet

From Dawsey to Juliet

2nd April 1946

Dear Miss Ashton,

Having fun is the biggest sin in Adelaide Addison's bible and I'm not surprised she wrote to you about Jerry-bags. Adelaide lives on her wrath.

There were few eligible men left in Guernsey and certainly no one exciting. Many of us were tired, scruffy, worried, shoeless and dirty—we were defeated and looked it. We didn't have the energy, time or money for fun. Guernsey men had no glamour—and the German soldiers did. They were tall, blond, handsome and tanned—like gods. They gave lavish parties, were jolly and zestful company, had cars and money and could dance all night long.

But some of the girls who went out with soldiers gave the cigarettes to their fathers and the bread to their families. They would come home from parties with rolls, pâté, fruit, meat pies and jellies stuffed into their bags, and their families would have a full meal the next day.

I don't think some Islanders ever credited the boredom of those years. Boredom is a powerful reason to befriend the enemy, and the prospect of fun is a powerful draw—especially when you are young.

There were many people who would have no dealings with the Germans—if you said so much as good morning you were abetting the enemy, according to their way of thinking. But circumstances were such that I could not abide by that with Captain Christian Hellman, a doctor in the Occupation forces and my good friend.

In late 1941, there wasn't any salt on the Island, and none was coming from France. Root vegetables and soups are listless without salt, so the Germans got the idea of using sea water to supply it. They carried it up from the bay and poured it into a big tanker set in the middle of St Peter Port. Everyone was to walk to town, fill up their buckets and carry them home again. Then we were to boil the water away and use the sludge in the bottom of the pan as salt.

That plan failed—there wasn't enough wood to waste building up a fire hot enough to boil the pot of water dry. So we decided to cook all our vegetables in the sea water itself.

That worked well enough for flavour, but there were many older people who couldn't manage the walk into town or to haul heavy buckets home. So I began to deliver water to some cottages. I exchanged a spare spade and some twine for Madame LePell's old pram, and Mr Soames gave me two small oak wine casks, each with a spigot. I sawed off the barrel tops to make moveable lids and fitted them into my pram—so now I had transport. Several of the beaches weren't mined, and it was easy to climb down the rocks, fill a cask with sea water, and carry it back up.

One day my hands were numb after I had climbed up from the bay with the first barrel of water. I was standing by my pram, trying to limber up my fingers, when Christian drove by. He stopped his car and asked if I wanted any help. I said no, but he got out anyway and helped me lift the barrel into my pram. Then, without a word, he went down the cliff with me, to help with the second barrel.

We slipped on the loose scree coming back up and fell against the hillside, losing our grip on the barrel. It tumbled down, splintered against the rocks and soaked us. God knows why it struck us both as funny, but it did.

We sagged against the cliffside, unable to stop laughing. That was when Elia's essays slipped out of my pocket, and Christian picked the book up, sopping wet. 'Ah, Charles Lamb,' he said, and handed it to me. 'He was not a man to mind a little damp.' My surprise must have shown, because he added, 'I read him often at home. I envy you your portable library.'

We climbed back up to his car. He wanted to know if I could find another barrel. I said I could and explained my water-delivery route. He nodded, and I started out with the pram. But then I turned back and said, 'You can borrow the book, if you like.' You would have thought I was giving him the moon. We exchanged names and shook hands.

After that, he would often help me carry up water, and then he'd offer me a cigarette, and we'd stand in the road and talk—about Guernsey's beauty, about history, about books, about farming—always things far away from the war. Once, as we were standing, Elizabeth rattled up the road on her bicycle. She had been on nursing duty all day and like the rest of us her clothes were more patches than cloth. But Christian broke off in mid-sentence to watch her coming. Elizabeth drew up to us and stopped. Neither said a word, but I saw their faces, and I left as soon as I could. I hadn't realised they knew each other.

Christian had been a field surgeon, until his shoulder wound sent him from Eastern Europe to Guernsey. In early 1942, he was ordered to a hospital in Caen; his ship was sunk by Allied bombers and he was drowned. Dr Lorenz, the head of the German Occupation hospital, knew we were friends and came to tell me of his death. He meant for me to tell Elizabeth, so I did.

The way that Christian and I met may have been unusual, but our friendship was not. I'm sure many Islanders grew to be friends with some of the soldiers. But sometimes I think of Charles Lamb and marvel that a man born in 1775 enabled me to make two such friends as you and Christian.

Yours truly,
Dawsey Adams

From Juliet to Amelia

4th April 1946

Dear Mrs Maugery,
The sun is out for the first time in months, and if I stand on my chair and crane my neck, I can see it sparkling on the river. I'm averting my eyes

from the mounds of rubble across the road and pretending London is beautiful again.

I've received a sad letter from Dawsey Adams, telling me about Christian Hellman, his kindness and his death. The war goes on and on, doesn't it? Such a good life—lost. And what a grievous blow it must have been to Elizabeth. I am thankful she had you, Mr Ramsey, Isola Pribby and Mr Adams to help her when she had her baby.

Spring is nearly here. I'm almost warm in my puddle of sunshine. And down the street—I'm not averting my eyes now—a man in a patched jumper is painting the door to his house sky blue. Two small boys, who have been walloping one another with sticks, are begging him to let them help. He is giving them a tiny brush each. So—perhaps there is an end to war.

Yours sincerely,
Juliet Ashton

From Mark to Juliet

5th April 1946

Dear Juliet,

You're being elusive and I don't like it. I don't want to see the play with someone else—I want to go with you. In fact, I don't give a damn about the play. I'm only trying to rout you out of that apartment. Dinner? Tea? Cocktails? Boating? Dancing? You choose, and I'll obey. I'm rarely so docile—don't throw away this opportunity to improve my character.

Yours,
Mark

From Juliet to Mark

Dear Mark,

Do you want to come to the British Museum with me? I've got an appointment in the Reading Room at two o'clock. We can look at the mummies afterwards.

Juliet

From Mark to Juliet
To hell with the Reading Room and the mummies. Come have lunch with me.
Mark

From Juliet to Mark
You consider that docile?
Juliet

From Mark to Juliet
To hell with docile.
M.

From Amelia to Juliet

10th April 1946

My dear Juliet,
I, too, have felt that the war goes on and on. When my son, Ian, died at El Alamein—side by side with Eli's father, John—visitors offering their condolences and meaning to comfort me said, 'Life goes on.' What nonsense. Of course it doesn't. It's death that goes on; Ian is dead now and will be dead tomorrow and next year and for ever. There's no end to that. But perhaps there will be an end to the sorrow of it. Sorrow has rushed over the world like the waters of the Deluge, and it will take time to recede. But already, there are small islands of—hope? Happiness? Something like that, anyway.

My greatest pleasure has been in resuming my evening walks along the clifftops. The Channel is no longer framed in rolls of barbed wire; the view is unbroken by huge *VERBOTEN* signs. The mines are gone from our beaches, and I can walk when, where and for as long as I like. If I stand on the cliffs and turn out to face the sea, I don't see the ugly cement bunkers behind me, or the land naked without its trees. Not even the Germans could ruin the sea. This summer, gorse will begin to grow around the fortifications, and by next year, perhaps, vines will creep over them. I hope they are soon covered. I will never be able to forget how they were made.

The Todt workers built them. I know you have heard of Germany's slave workers in camps on the Continent, but did you know that Hitler sent over sixteen thousand of them here, to the Channel Islands? Hitler was fanatical about fortifying these islands—England was never to get them back! His generals called it Island Madness. He ordered large-gun emplacements, anti-tank walls on the beaches, hundreds of bunkers and batteries, arms and bomb depots, miles and miles of underground tunnels, a huge underground hospital and a railway across the Island to carry materials. The coastal fortifications were absurd—the Channel Isles were better fortified than the Atlantic Wall built against an Allied invasion. The installations loomed over every bay. The Third Reich was to last one thousand years—in concrete.

So, of course, he needed the thousands of slave workers; men and boys were conscripted, some were arrested, and some were just picked up in the street—from cinema queues, cafés and from the country lanes and fields of any German Occupied territory. The Russian prisoners of war were treated the worst, perhaps because of their victory over the Germans on the Russian Front.

Most of these slave workers came to the Islands in 1942. They were marched all over the Island to their work sites: thin to the bone, dressed in ragged trousers with bare skin showing through, often no coats to protect them from the cold. No shoes or boots, their feet tied up in bloody rags. Young lads, fifteen and sixteen, were so weary and starved they could hardly put one foot in front of another. Islanders would stand by their gates to offer them what little food or warm clothing they could spare and sometimes the Germans guarding the Todt work columns would let the men break ranks to accept these gifts.

Thousands of those men and boys died here, and I have recently learned that their inhuman treatment was the deliberate policy of Himmler. He called his plan Death by Exhaustion. Work them hard, don't waste valuable food on them, and let them die. They could, and would, always be replaced by new slave workers from Europe's Occupied countries.

Some of the Todt workers were kept down on the common, behind a wire fence—they were white as ghosts, covered in cement dust; there was only one water standpipe for over a hundred men to wash themselves. Children sometimes went down there. They would poke walnuts and apples, sometimes potatoes, through the wire for the Todt workers.

No flowers or vines can cover such memories as these, can they?

I have told you the most hateful story of the war. Juliet, Isola thinks you should come and write a book about the German Occupation. She told me she did not have the skill to write it herself, but, as dear as Isola is to me, I am terrified she might buy a notebook and begin anyway.

Yours ever,
Amelia Maugery

From Susan Scott to Sidney

11th April 1946

Dear Sidney,

I'm as tender-hearted as the next girl, but damn it, if you don't get back here soon, Charlie Stephens is going to have a nervous breakdown. He's not cut out for work; he's cut out for handing over large wads of cash and letting you do the work. He actually turned up at the office *before ten o'clock* yesterday, but the effort exhausted him. He was deathly white by eleven, and had a whisky at eleven thirty. At noon, one of the innocent young things handed him a jacket to approve—his eyes bulged with terror and he began that disgusting trick with his ear—he's going to pull it right off one day. He went home at one, and I haven't seen him today (it's four in the afternoon).

In other depressing developments, Harriet Munfries has gone completely berserk; she wants to 'colour-coordinate' the entire children's list. Pink and red. I'm not joking. The boy in the post room (I don't even bother learning their names any more) got drunk and threw away all letters addressed to anyone whose name started with an S. Don't ask me why. Miss Tilley was so impossibly rude to Kendrick that he tried to hit her with her telephone. I can't say I blame him, but telephones are hard to come by and we can't afford to lose one. You must sack her the minute you come home.

If you need any further inducement to buy an aeroplane ticket, I can also tell you that I saw Juliet and Mark Reynolds looking very cosy at Café de Paris the other night. I could spy all the telltale signs of romance—he murmuring sweet nothings in her ear, her hand lingering in his beside the cocktail glasses, he touching her shoulder to point out an acquaintance. I considered it my duty (as your devoted employee) to break it up, so I elbowed my way to say hello to Juliet. She seemed delighted and invited me to join them, but it was apparent from Mark's smile that he didn't want company, so I retreated. He's not a man to cross, that one, with his thin smile, no matter how beautiful his ties are, and it would break my mother's heart if my lifeless body was found bobbing in the Thames.

In other words, get a wheelchair, get a crutch, get a donkey, but come home *now*.

Yours,
Susan

From Dawsey to Juliet

15th April 1946

Dear Miss Ashton,

I don't know what ails Adelaide Addison. Isola says she is a blight because she likes being a blight—it gives her a sense of destiny.

The biography of Charles Lamb came. I read it quickly—too impatient not to. But I'll go back and start again—reading more slowly this time, so I can take everything in. I did like what Mr Lucas said about him— that he could make any homely and familiar thing into something fresh and beautiful.

But what I cannot imagine is Charles coming home from work and finding his mother stabbed to death, his father bleeding and his sister, Mary, standing over both with a bloody knife. How did he make himself go into the room and take the knife away from her? After the police had taken her off to the madhouse, how did he persuade the judge to release her to his care and his care alone? He was only twenty-one years old, yet he promised to look after Mary for the rest of her life—and, once he put his foot on that road, he never stepped off it. It is sad he had to stop writing poetry, which he loved, and had to write criticism and essays, which he did not honour much, to make money.

I think of him working as a clerk at the East India Company, so that he could save money for the day, and it always came, when Mary would go mad again, and he would have to place her in a private home.

And even then he did seem to miss her—they were such friends. Picture them: he had to watch her like a hawk for the awful symptoms, and she could tell when the madness was coming on and could do nothing to stop it—that must have been worst of all. I imagine him sitting there, watching her on the sly, and her sitting there, watching him watching her. How they must have hated the way the other was forced to live.

But doesn't it seem to you that when Mary was sane there was no one saner—or better company? Charles certainly thought so, and so did all their friends: Wordsworth, Hazlitt, Leigh Hunt and, above all, Coleridge.

Perhaps I've written overlong about Charles Lamb, but I wanted you and Mr Hastings to know how much the books have given me to think about, and what pleasure I find in them.

Kit has taken against mongooses, now that she knows they eat snakes. She is hoping to find a boa constrictor under a rock.

Isola dropped in this evening and sent her best wishes—she says she will write to you as soon as she gets her crops in—rosemary, dill, thyme and henbane.

Yours,
Dawsey Adams

From Juliet to Dawsey

18th April 1946

Dear Mr Adams,

I am so glad you want to talk about Charles Lamb. I have always thought Mary's sorrow made Charles into a great writer—even if he had to give up poetry and work for the East India Company because of it. He had a genius for sympathy that not one of his great friends could touch. When Wordsworth chided him for not caring enough about nature, Charles wrote, 'I have no passion for groves and valleys. The rooms where I was born, the furniture which has been before my eyes all my life, a bookcase which has followed me about like a faithful dog wherever I have moved— old chairs, old streets, squares where I have sunned myself, my old school—have I not enough, without your Mountains? I do not envy you. I should pity you, did I not know, that the Mind will make friends of any thing.' A mind that can 'make friends of any thing'—I thought of that often during the war.

By chance, I came upon another story about him today. He often drank too much, far too much, but he was not a sullen drunk. Once, his host's butler had to carry him home, slung over his shoulder in a fireman's hold. The next day Charles wrote his host such a hilarious note of apology, the man bequeathed it to his son in his will.

Have you ever noticed that when your mind is awakened or drawn to someone new, that person's name suddenly pops up everywhere? My friend Sophie calls it coincidence, and Reverend Simpless calls it grace. He thinks that if one cares deeply about someone or something new, one throws a kind of energy out into the world, and 'fruitfulness' is drawn in.

Yours ever,
Juliet Ashton

From Isola to Juliet

18th April 1946

Dear Juliet,

Now that we are corresponding friends, I want to ask you some questions—they are highly personal. Dawsey said it would not be polite, but I say that's a difference between men and women. Dawsey hasn't asked me a personal question in fifteen years. I'd take it kindly if he would, but Dawsey's got quiet ways. I don't expect to change him, nor myself either.

I saw a picture of you on the cover of your book about Anne Brontë, so I know you are under forty years of age—how much under? Was the sun in your eyes, or does it happen that you have a squint? Is it permanent? It must have been a windy day because your curls were blowing about. I couldn't quite make out the colour of your hair, though I could tell it wasn't blonde—for which I am glad. I don't like blondes very much.

Do you live by the river? I hope so, because people who live near running water are much nicer than people who don't. I'd be cross as a snake if I lived inland. Do you have a serious suitor? I do not.

Is your flat cosy or grand? Be fulsome, so I can picture it in my mind. Would you like to visit us in Guernsey? Do you have a pet? What kind?

Your friend,
Isola

From Juliet to Isola

20th April 1946

Dear Isola,

I am glad you want to know more about me and am only sorry I didn't think of it myself, and sooner.

Present day first: I am thirty-two years old, and you were right—the sun was in my eyes. In a good mood, I call my hair chestnut with gold glints. In a bad mood, I call it mousy brown. It wasn't a windy day; my hair always looks like that. Naturally curly hair is a curse, and don't ever let anyone tell you different. My eyes are hazel. While I am slender, I am not tall enough to suit me.

I don't live by the Thames any more and that is what I miss the most— I loved the sight and sound of the river at all hours. I live now in a flat in Glebe Place. It is small and furnished and the owner won't be back from the United States until November, so I have the run of his house until then. I wish I had a dog, but the building management does not allow pets!

Kensington Gardens aren't far, so if I begin to feel cooped up I can walk to the park, hire a deck chair for a shilling, loll about under the trees, watch the passers-by and I am soothed—somewhat.

My home at 81 Oakley Street was demolished by a random V-1 just over a year ago. Most of the damage was to the row of houses behind mine, but three floors of Number 81 were shorn off, and my flat is now a pile of rubble. I hope Mr Grant, the owner, will rebuild—for I want my flat, or a facsimile of it, back again just as it was—with Cheyne Walk and the river outside my windows.

Luckily, I was away in Bury when the V-1 hit. Sidney Stark, my friend and now publisher, met my train that evening and took me home, and we viewed what was left of the building. With part of the wall gone, I could see my shredded curtains waving in the breeze and my desk, three-legged and slumped on the slanting floor that was left. My books were a muddy, sopping pile and although I could see my mother's portrait on the wall—half gouged out and sooty—there was no safe way to recover it.

The only intact possession was my large crystal paperweight—with *Carpe Diem* carved across the top. It had belonged to my father—and there it sat, whole and unchipped, on top of a pile of broken bricks and splintered wood. Sidney clambered over the rubble and retrieved it for me.

I was a fairly nice child until my parents died when I was twelve. I left our farm in Suffolk and went to live with my great-uncle in London. I was a furious, bitter, morose little girl. I ran away twice, causing my uncle no end of trouble—and at the time I was very glad to do so. I am ashamed now when I think about how I treated him. He died when I was seventeen so I was never able to apologise.

When I was thirteen, my uncle decided I should go away to boarding school. I went, mulish as usual, and met the headmistress, who marched me into the dining room. She led me to a table with four other girls. I sat, arms crossed, hands under my armpits, glaring like a moulting eagle, looking for someone to hate.

I hit upon Sophie Stark, Sidney's younger sister. Perfect, she had golden curls, big blue eyes and a sweet smile. She made an effort to talk to me. I didn't answer until she said, 'I hope you will be happy here.' I told her I wouldn't be staying long enough to find out.

That night I climbed out onto the dormitory roof, meaning to sit there and have a good brood in the dark. In a few minutes, Sophie crawled out—with a railway timetable for me.

Needless to say, I didn't run away. I stayed—with Sophie as my new friend. Her mother would often invite me to their house for the holidays, which was where I met Sidney. He was ten years older than me and was, of course, a god. He later changed into a bossy older brother and, later still, into one of my dearest friends.

Sophie and I left school and—wanting no more of academic life, but LIFE instead—we went to London and shared rooms Sidney had found for us. We worked together for a while in a bookshop, and at night I wrote—and threw away—stories.

Then the *Daily Mirror* sponsored an essay contest—five hundred words on 'What Women Fear Most' and the judges awarded me first prize. Five pounds and I was, at last, in print. The *Daily Mirror* received so many fan letters they commissioned me to write an article, then another one. I soon began to write feature stories for other newspapers and magazines. Then the war broke out, and I was invited to write a semi-weekly column for the *Spectator*, called 'Izzy Bickerstaff Goes to War'.

Sophie met and fell in love with an airman, Alexander Strachan. They married and Sophie moved to his family's farm in Scotland. I am godmother to their son, Dominic, and though I haven't taught him any hymns, we did pull the hinges off the cellar door last time I saw him—it was a Pictish ambush.

You ask if I have a suitor and I suppose I do, but I'm not really used to him yet. He's terribly charming and he plies me with delicious meals, but I sometimes think I prefer suitors in books rather than right in front of me. How awful, backward and cowardly that will be if it turns out to be true.

Sidney published a book of my Izzy Bickerstaff columns and I went on a book tour.

And then—I began writing letters to strangers in Guernsey, now friends, whom I would indeed like to come and see.

Yours,
Juliet

From Eli to Juliet

21st April 1946

Dear Miss Ashton,

Thank you for the blocks of wood. They are beautiful. I could not believe what I saw when I opened your box—all those sizes and shades, from pale to dark. How did you find all those different pieces of wood? You must have gone to so many places. I don't know how to thank you. They came at just the right time, too. Kit's favourite animal was a snake she saw in a book, and he was easy to carve, being so long and thin. Now she's mad about ferrets. She says she won't ever touch my knife again if I'll carve her a ferret. I don't think it will be too hard to make one, for they are pointy, too. Because of your gift, I have wood to practise with.

Is there an animal you would like to have? I want to carve a present for you, but I'd like it to be something you'd favour. Would you like a mouse? I am good at mice.

Yours truly,
Eli

From Eben to Juliet

22nd April 1946

Dear Miss Ashton,

Your box for Eli came on Friday—how kind of you. He sits and studies the blocks of wood—as if he sees something hidden inside them, and he can make it come out with his knife.

You asked if all the Guernsey children were evacuated to England. No—some stayed, and when I missed Eli, I looked at the little ones around me and was glad he had gone. The children here had a bad time, for there wasn't enough food to grow on.

In the middle of June 1940, when it became pretty certain we were in for it, the States, Guernsey's ruling body, got on the telephone to London and asked if they would send ships for our children and take them to England. They couldn't fly, for fear of being shot down by the Luftwaffe. London said yes, but the children had to be ready at once. The ships would have to hurry here and back again while there was still time.

It was a terrible thing to decide—send your children away to live among strangers, or let them stay with you. Maybe the Germans wouldn't come, but if they did, how would they treat us? But, come to that, what if they invaded England, too—how would the children manage without their families?

Jane knew her mind. She wanted Eli to go. Other ladies were in a dither—go or stay?—and they were frantic to talk, but Jane told Elizabeth to keep them away. 'I don't want to hear them fuss,' she said. 'It's bad for the baby.' Jane had an idea that babies knew everything that happened around them, even before they were born.

The time for dithering was soon over. Families had one day to decide, and five years to abide by it. School-age children and babies with their mothers went first on the 19th and 20th of June. The States gave out pocket money to the children, if their parents had none to spare. The littlest ones were all excited about the sweets they could buy with it. Some thought it was like a Sunday School outing, and they'd be back before dark. They were lucky in that. The older children, like Eli, knew better.

All the children were to be dropped off at the school by their parents. It was there we had to say our goodbyes. Buses came to take the children down to the pier. The boats, just back from Dunkirk, had to cross the Channel again for the children. There was no time to get a convoy together to escort them, no time to get enough lifeboats on board—or life jackets.

That morning we stopped first at the hospital for Eli to say goodbye to his mother. He couldn't do it. His jaw was clamped shut so tight, he could only nod. Jane held him for a bit, and then Elizabeth and I walked him down to the school. I hugged him hard and that was the last time I saw him for five years. Elizabeth stayed because she had volunteered to help get the children inside ready.

Isola told me that you might come to Guernsey. I would be glad to offer you hospitality.

Yours,
Eben Ramsey

From Isola to Juliet

24th April 1946

Dear Juliet,

Thank you for your life story. You have had such sadness with your mum and dad and your home by the river, for which I am sorry. But me, I am glad you have dear friends like Sophie and her mother and Sidney. As for Sidney, he sounds a very fine man—but bossy. It's a failing common in men.

I would like it if you came to see us. So would Eben and Amelia and Dawsey—and Eli, too. Kit is not so sure, but you mustn't mind that. She might come round. Your newspaper article will be printed soon, so you could come here and have a rest. You might find a story here you'd like to tell about.

Your friend,
Isola

From Dawsey to Juliet

26th April 1946

Dear Miss Ashton,

My temporary job at the quarry is over, and Kit is staying with me for a while. She is sitting under the table I'm writing on, whispering. What's that you're whispering? I asked, and there was a long quiet. Then she commenced whispering again, and I can make out my own name among the other sounds. This is what generals call a war of nerves, and I know who is going to win.

Kit doesn't resemble Elizabeth very much, except for her grey eyes and a look she gets when she is concentrating hard. But she is like her mother inside—fierce in her feelings. Even when she was tiny, she howled until the glass shivered in the windows, and when she gripped my finger in her little fist, it turned white.

I knew nothing about babies, but Elizabeth made me learn. She said I was fated to be a father and she had a responsibility to make sure I knew more than the usual run of them. She missed Christian, not just for herself, for Kit, too.

Kit knows her father is dead. Amelia and I told her that, but we didn't know how to speak of Elizabeth. In the end, we said that she'd been sent away and we hoped she'd return soon. Kit looked from me to Amelia and back, but she didn't ask any questions. She just went out and sat in the barn. I don't know if we did right.

Some days I wear myself out wishing for Elizabeth to come home. We have learned that her father was killed in one of the last bombing raids in London, and, as Elizabeth inherited his estate, his solicitors have begun a search for her. They must have better ways to find her than we have, so I am hopeful that Mr Dilwyn will get some word from her—or about her—soon. Wouldn't it be a blessed thing for Kit and for all of us if Elizabeth could be found?

Kit's stopped whispering. I've just peered under the table and she's asleep. It's later than I thought.

Yours,

Dawsey Adams

From Mark to Juliet

30th April 1946

Darling,

Just got in—the entire trip could have been avoided if Hendry had telephoned, but I smacked a few heads together and they've cleared the whole shipment through customs.

I feel as though I've been away for years. Can I see you tonight? I need to talk to you.

Suzette, at eight?

Love,

M.

From Juliet to Mark

Say please.

Yours,

J.

From Mark to Juliet

Pleased to see you at Suzette at eight.

Love,

M.

From Juliet to Mark

1st May 1946

Dear Mark,

I didn't refuse, you know. I said I wanted to think about it. You were so busy ranting about Sidney and Guernsey that perhaps you didn't notice— I only said I wanted time. I've known you *two months*. It's not long enough for me to be certain that we should spend the rest of our lives together, even if you are. I once made a terrible mistake and almost married a man I hardly knew (perhaps you read about it in the papers)—and at least in that case the war was an extenuating circumstance. I won't be such a fool again.

Think about it: I've never seen your home—I don't even know where it is, really. New York, but which street? What does it look like? What colour are your walls? Your sofa? Do you arrange your books alphabetically? (I hope not.) Are your drawers tidy or messy? Do you ever hum, and if so, what? Do you prefer cats or dogs? Or fish? What on earth do you eat for breakfast—or do you have a cook?

You see? I don't know you well enough to marry you.

I have one other piece of news that may interest you: Sidney is not your rival. I am not now nor have I ever been in love with Sidney, nor he with me. Nor will I ever marry him. Is that decisive enough for you?

Are you absolutely certain you wouldn't rather be married to someone more tractable?

Juliet

From Juliet to Sophie

1st May 1946

Dearest Sophie,

I wish you were here. I wish we still lived together in our lovely little studio and worked in dear Mr Hawke's shop and ate biscuits and cheese for supper every night. I want so much to talk to you. I want you to tell me whether I should marry Mark Reynolds.

He asked me last night—no bended knee, but a diamond as big as a pigeon's egg—at a romantic French restaurant. I'm not certain he still wants to marry me this morning—he's absolutely furious because I didn't give him an unequivocal yes. I tried to explain that I hadn't known him long enough and I needed time to think, but he wouldn't listen to me. He was certain that I was rejecting him because of a secret passion—for Sidney! They really are obsessed with each other, those two.

Thank God we were at his flat by then—he started shouting about Sidney and godforsaken islands and women who care more about strangers than men who are right in front of them (that's Guernsey and my new friends there). I kept trying to explain and he kept shouting until I began to cry from frustration. Then he felt remorseful, which was so unlike him and endearing that I almost changed my mind and said yes. But then I imagined a lifetime of having to cry to get him to be kind, and I went back to no again. We argued and I wept a bit more because I was so exhausted, and eventually he called his chauffeur to take me home. As he shut me into the car, he leaned in to kiss me and said, 'You're an idiot, Juliet.'

Maybe he's right. Do you remember those awful Cheslayne Fair novels we read the summer we were thirteen? My favourite was *The Master of Blackheath*. Do you remember Ransom—how he manfully hid his love for the girlish Eulalie so that she could choose freely, little knowing she had been mad about him ever since she fell off her horse when she was twelve? The thing is, Sophie—Mark Reynolds is exactly like Ransom. He's tall and handsome, with a crooked smile and a chiselled jaw. He shoulders his way through the crowd, careless of the glances that follow him. He's impatient and magnetic, and when I go to powder my nose I overhear other women talking about him. They can't help it. I used to get the shivers about Ransom. Sometimes I do about Mark, too—when I look at him—but I can't get over the nagging feeling that I'm no Eulalie. If I were ever to fall off a horse, it would be lovely to be picked up by Mark, but I don't think I'm likely to fall off a horse in the near future. I'm much more likely to go to Guernsey and write a book about the Occupation, and Mark can't abide the thought. He wants me to stay in London and marry him like a reasonable person.

Write and tell me what to do. Love to Dominic—and to you and Alexander,
Juliet

From Juliet to Sidney

3rd May 1946

Dear Sidney,

I may not be as distraught as Stephens & Stark is without you, but I do miss you and want you to advise me. Please drop everything you are doing and write to me at once.

I want to get out of London. I want to go to Guernsey. You know I've grown very fond of my Guernsey friends, and I'm fascinated by their lives under the Germans—and since. I've visited the Channel Islands Refugee Committee and read their files. I have read the Red Cross reports. I've read all I can find on Todt slave workers—there hasn't, so far, been much. I've interviewed some of the soldiers who liberated Guernsey and talked to Royal Engineers who removed the thousands of mines from the beaches. I've read all the 'unclassified' government reports on the state of the Islanders' health, or lack of it; their happiness, or lack of it; their food supplies, or lack of them. But I want to know more. I want to know the stories of the people who were there, and I can never learn those by sitting in a library in London.

For example—yesterday I was reading an article on the Liberation. A reporter asked a Guernsey Islander, 'What was the most difficult experience you had during the Germans' rule?' He made fun of the man's answer, but it made perfect sense to me. The Islander told him, 'You know they took away all our wirelesses? If you were caught with one, you'd get sent off to prison on the Continent. Well, those of us who had secret wirelesses, we heard about the Allies landing in Normandy. Trouble was, we weren't supposed to know it had happened! Hardest thing I ever did was walk around St Peter Port on the 7th of June, not grinning, not smiling, not doing anything to let those Germans know that I KNEW their end was coming. If they'd caught on, someone would be in for it—so we had to pretend not to know D-Day had happened.'

I want to talk to people like him (though he's probably off writers now) and hear about their war, because that's what I'd like to read, instead of statistics about grain. I'm not sure what form a book would take, or if I could even write one at all. But I would like to go to St Peter Port and find out.

Do I have your blessing?

Love to you and Piers,

Juliet

Cable from Sidney to Juliet

10th May 1946
Herewith my blessing! Guernsey is a wonderful idea, both for you and for a book. But will Reynolds allow it? Love, Sidney

Cable from Juliet to Sidney

11th May 1946
Blessing received. Mark Reynolds is not in a position to forbid or to allow. Love, Juliet

From Amelia to Juliet

13th May 1946

My dear,

I was delighted to receive your telegram yesterday and to learn that you are coming to visit us!

I spread the news at once—you have sent the Society into a whirlwind of excitement. The members instantly offered to provide you with anything you might need: bed, board, introductions, a supply of electric clothes pegs. Isola is ecstatic that you are coming and is already at work on behalf of your book. Though I warned her that it was only an idea so far, she is determined to find material for you. She has asked (perhaps threatened) everyone she knows in the market to send you letters about the Occupation; she thinks you'll need them to persuade your publisher that the subject is book-worthy. Don't be surprised if you are inundated with letters in the next few weeks.

Isola also went to see Mr Dilwyn at the bank this afternoon and asked him to let you rent Elizabeth's cottage. It is a lovely site, in a meadow below the Big House, and small enough to manage easily. Elizabeth moved there when the German officers confiscated the larger house for their use. You would be very comfortable there, and Mr Dilwyn need only stir himself to draw up a lease for you. Isola will see to everything else: airing the rooms, washing the windows, beating the rugs and killing spiders.

Please don't feel as though these arrangements place you under any obligation. Mr Dilwyn was planning in any case to assess the property for its rental possibilities. Sir Ambrose's solicitors have begun an inquiry into Elizabeth's whereabouts. They have found that there is no record of her arrival in Germany, only that she was put on a transport in France, with Frankfurt as the intended destination of the train. There will be further investigations, and I pray that they will lead to Elizabeth, but in the meantime, Mr Dilwyn wants to rent the property in order to provide income for Kit.

I sometimes think that we are morally obliged to begin a search for Kit's German relations, but I cannot bring myself to do it. Christian was a rare soul, and he detested what his country was doing, but the same cannot be true for many Germans, who believed in the dream of the Thousand-Year Reich. And how could we send our Kit away to a foreign—and destroyed—land, even if her relations could be found? We are the only family she's ever known.

When Kit was born, Elizabeth kept her paternity a secret from the authorities. Not out of shame, but because she was afraid that the baby would be taken from her and sent to Germany. There were dreadful rumours of such things. I wonder if Kit's heritage could have saved Elizabeth if she had made it known when she was arrested. But as she didn't, it is not my place to do so.

I will now turn to more cheerful subjects—such as last evening's meeting of the Society. After the uproar about your visit had subsided, the Society read your article about books in *The Times*. Everyone enjoyed it—not just because we were reading about ourselves, but because you brought us views we'd never thought to apply to our reading before. The article was delightful, and we were all so proud and pleased to be mentioned in it.

Will Thisbee wants to have a welcome party for you. He will bake a potato peel pie for the event and has devised a cocoa icing for it. He made a surprise pudding for our meeting last night—cherries flambé, which fortunately burned to a crisp so we did not have to eat it. I wish Will would leave cookery alone and go back to ironmongery.

We all look forward to welcoming you, and will be delighted to see you whenever you come. Just let us know the date and time of your arrival. Certainly, an aeroplane flight to Guernsey would be faster and more comfortable than the mail boat. But unless you are bedevilled by seasickness, I would catch the afternoon boat from Weymouth. There is no more beautiful approach to Guernsey than the one by sea—either with the sun going down, or with gold-tipped, black storm clouds, or the Island just emerging through the mist. This is the way I first saw Guernsey, as a new bride.

Fondly,
Amelia

From Dawsey to Juliet

16th May 1946

Dear Miss Ashton,

There's nothing left to do for your arrival except wait. Isola has washed, starched and ironed Elizabeth's curtains, looked up the chimney for bats, cleaned the windows, made up the beds and aired all the rooms.

Eli has carved a present for you; Eben has filled your woodshed and scythed your meadow—leaving, he says, the clumps of wild flowers for you to enjoy. Amelia is planning a supper party for you on your first evening.

I wish I could do more for your welcome—I hope it will be soon. I am glad you are coming.

Yours,
Dawsey Adams

From Juliet to Dawsey

19th May 1946

Dear Mr Adams,

I'll be there the day after tomorrow! I am far too cowardly to fly, so I shall come by the evening mail boat. There isn't anything you could do to make me feel more welcome in Guernsey than you already have. I'm having trouble believing that I am going to meet you all at last.

Yours,
Juliet Ashton

From Mark to Juliet

20th May 1946

Dear Juliet,

You asked me to give you time, and I have. You asked me not to mention marriage, and I haven't. But now you tell me that you're off to bloody Guernsey for—what? A week? A month? For ever? Do you think I'm going to sit back and let you go?

You're being ridiculous, Juliet. Any halfwit can see that you're trying to run away, but what nobody can understand is why. We're right together—you make me happy, you never bore me, you're interested in the things I'm interested in, and I hope I'm not deluded when I say I think the same is true for you. We belong together. In this case I do know best.

For God's sake, forget about that miserable island and marry me. I'll take you there on our honeymoon—if I must.

Love, Mark

From Juliet to Mark

20th May 1946

Dear Mark,

You're probably right, but, even so, I'm going to Guernsey tomorrow and *you can't stop me.*

I'm sorry I can't give you the answer that you want. I would like to be able to.

Love,
Juliet

P.S. Thank you for the roses.

From Mark to Juliet

Oh for God's sake. Do you want me to drive you down to Weymouth?
Love,
Mark

From Juliet to Mark

Will you promise not to lecture me?
Juliet

From Mark to Juliet

No lectures. However, all other forms of persuasion will be employed.
Mark

From Juliet to Mark

Can't scare me. What can you possibly do while driving?
Juliet

From Mark to Juliet

You'd be surprised. See you tomorrow.
M.

Part Two

From Juliet to Sidney

22nd May 1946

Dear Sidney,

There's so much to tell you. I've been in Guernsey only twenty hours, but each one has been so full of new faces and ideas that I've got reams to write. You see how conducive to writing island life is?

The voyage from Weymouth was ghastly, with the mail boat groaning and creaking and threatening to break to pieces in the waves. I almost wished it would, to put me out of my misery, except that I wanted to see Guernsey before I died. And as soon as we came in sight of the Island, I gave up the notion altogether because the sun broke beneath the clouds and set the cliffs shimmering into silver.

As the mail boat lurched into the harbour, I saw St Peter Port rising up from the sea, with a church at the top like a cake decoration, and I realised that my heart was galloping. However much I tried to persuade myself it was the thrill of the scenery, I knew better. All those people I've come to know and even love a little, waiting to see—me. And I, without any paper to hide behind. Sidney, in these past two or three years, I have become better at writing than living. On the page, I'm perfectly charming, but that's just a trick I've learned. It has nothing to do with me. At least, that's what I was thinking as the boat approached the pier. I had a cowardly impulse to pretend I was someone else.

I could see the faces of the people waiting—and then there was no going back. I knew them by their letters. There was Isola in a mad hat and a purple shawl pinned with a glittering brooch. She was smiling fixedly in the wrong direction and I loved her instantly. Next to her stood a man with a lined face and, at his side, a boy, all height and angles: Eben and his grandson, Eli. I waved to Eli and he smiled like a beam of light and nudged his grandfather—and then I went shy and lost myself in the crowd pushing down the gangplank.

Isola reached me first and pulled me up in a fierce hug that swung me off my feet. 'Ah, lovey!' she cried while I dangled. Wasn't that sweet? All my nervousness was squeezed out of me along with my breath. The others came towards me more quietly, but with no less warmth. Eben shook my hand and smiled. He manages to look grave and friendly at the same time. How does he do that? I found myself wanting to impress him.

Eli swung Kit up on his shoulders, and they came forward together. Kit has chubby little legs and a stern face—dark curls, big grey eyes—and she didn't take to me one bit. Eli's jersey was speckled with wood shavings, and he had a present for me in his pocket—an adorable little mouse with crooked whiskers, carved from walnut. I gave him a kiss on the cheek and survived Kit's malevolent glare. She has a very forbidding way about her for a four-year-old.

Then Dawsey held out his hands. I had been expecting him to look like Charles Lamb, and he does, a little—he has the same steady gaze. He is dark and wiry, and his face has a quiet, watchful look about it—until he smiles. Except for a certain sister of yours, he has the sweetest smile I've ever seen, and I remembered Amelia writing that he has a rare gift for persuasion—I can believe it. Like Eben—like everyone here—he is too thin. His hair is going grey, and he has deep-set brown eyes, so dark they look black. The lines around his eyes make him seem to be starting a smile even when he's not. I don't think he's more than forty. He is only a little taller than I am and limps slightly, but he's strong—he loaded all my luggage, me, Amelia and Kit into his cart with no trouble.

I shook hands with him and then he stepped aside for Amelia. She's one of those women who is more beautiful at sixty than she could possibly have been at twenty (oh, how I hope someone says that about me one day!). Small, thin-faced, lovely smile, grey hair in plaits wound round her head, she gripped my hand tightly and said, 'Juliet, I am glad you are here at last. Let's get your things and go home.' It sounded wonderful, as though it really was my home.

As we stood there on the pier, some glint of light kept flashing in my eyes, and then around the dock. Isola snorted and said it was Adelaide Addison, at her window with her opera glasses, watching every move we made. Isola waved vigorously at the gleam and it stopped. While we were laughing about that, Dawsey was gathering up my luggage and ensuring that Kit didn't fall off the pier and generally making himself useful. I began to see that this is what he does—and that everyone depends on him to do it.

Off we went out into the countryside. There are rolling fields, but they end suddenly in cliffs, and all around is the moist salt smell of the sea. As we drove, the sun set and the mist rose. You know how sounds become magnified by fog? Well, it was like that—every bird's cry was weighty and symbolic. Clouds boiled up over the cliffs, and the fields were swathed in grey by the time we reached the manor house, but I saw ghostly shapes that I think were the cement bunkers built by the Todt workers.

Kit sat beside me in the cart and sent me many sideways glances. I was not so foolish as to try to talk to her, but I played my severed-thumb trick—you know, the one that makes your thumb look as though it's been sliced in two. I did it over and over again, casually, not looking at her, while she watched me like a baby hawk. She was intent and fascinated and just said at last, 'Show me how you do that.'

She sat opposite me at supper and refused her spinach with a thrust-out arm, hand straight up like a policeman. 'Not for me,' she said, and I, for one, wouldn't care to disobey her. She pulled her chair close to Dawsey's and ate with one elbow planted firmly on his arm, pinning him in his place. He didn't seem to mind, even if it did make cutting his chicken difficult, and when supper was over, she climbed onto his lap. It is obviously her rightful throne, and though Dawsey seemed to be attending to the conversation, I spied him poking out a napkin-rabbit while we talked about food shortages during the Occupation.

I must have passed some test I didn't know I was being given, because Kit asked me to tuck her up in bed. She wanted to hear a story about a ferret. She liked vermin. Did I? Would I kiss a rat on the lips? I said, 'Never', and that seemed to win her over—I was plainly a coward, but not a hypocrite. I told her the story and she presented her cheek an infinitesimal quarter of an inch to be kissed.

What a long letter—and it only contains the first four hours of the twenty. You'll have to wait for the other sixteen.

Love,
Juliet

From Juliet to Sophie

24th May 1946

Dearest Sophie,

Yes, I'm here. Mark did his best to stop me, but I resisted him mulishly, right up to the bitter end.

It was only as the boat pulled away, and I saw him standing on the pier, tall and scowling—and somehow wanting to marry *me*—that I began to think perhaps I am a complete idiot. I know of three women who are mad about him—he'll be snapped up in a trice, and I'll spend my declining years in a grimy bedsit, with my teeth falling out one by one. Oh, I can see it all now: no one will buy my books, and I'll ply Sidney with tattered, illegible manuscripts, which he'll pretend to publish out of pity. Doddering and muttering, I'll wander the streets carrying my pathetic turnips in a string bag, with newspaper tucked into my shoes, and I'll boast to strangers that I was once nearly engaged to Markham Reynolds, the publishing tycoon. They'll shake their heads—the poor old thing's crazy as a coot, of course, but harmless.

Oh God. This way lies insanity.

Guernsey is beautiful and my new friends have welcomed me so generously, so warmly, that I hadn't doubted that I was right to come here—until just a moment ago, when I started thinking about my teeth. I'm going to stop thinking about them. I'm going to run through the wild-flower meadow outside my door and up to the cliff as fast as I can. Then I'm going to lie down and look at the sky and breathe in the warm scent of grass and pretend that Markham V. Reynolds doesn't exist.

I'm back indoors. It's hours later—the setting sun has rimmed the clouds in blazing gold and the sea is moaning below the cliffs. Mark Reynolds? Who's he?

Love always,
Juliet

From Juliet to Sidney

27th May 1946

Dear Sidney,

Elizabeth's cottage was plainly built for an exalted guest, because it's quite spacious. There is a big sitting room, a bathroom, a larder and a huge kitchen downstairs. There are three bedrooms, and, best of all, there are windows everywhere, so the sea air can sweep into every room.

I've shoved a writing table by the biggest window in my sitting room. The only flaw in this arrangement is the constant temptation to go outside and walk over to the cliff edge. The sea and the clouds don't stay the same for five minutes running and I'm frightened I'll miss something if I remain inside. When I got up this morning, the sea was full of sun pennies—and now it seems to be covered in lemon scrim. Writers ought to live far inland or next to the city dump if they are ever to get any work done. Or perhaps they need to be stronger-minded than I am.

If I needed any encouragement to be fascinated by Elizabeth, which I don't, her possessions would do it for me. The Germans arrived to take over Sir Ambrose's house and gave her only six hours to move her belongings to the cottage. Isola said Elizabeth brought only a few pots and pans, some cutlery and everyday china (the Germans kept the good china, silver, crystal and wine for themselves), her art supplies, an old wind-up gramophone, some records and armloads of books. So many books, Sidney, that they fill the living-room shelves and overflow into the kitchen. She even stacked some at one end of the sofa to use for a table—wasn't that brilliant?

In every nook, I find little things that tell me about her. She was a noticer, Sidney, like me: all the shelves are lined with shells, feathers, dried sea grass, pebbles, eggshells and the skeleton of something that might be a bat. They're just bits that anyone else would step over or on, but she saw they were beautiful and brought them home. I wonder if she used them for still lifes? I wonder if her sketchbooks are here somewhere. There's prowling to be done. Work first, but the anticipation is like Christmas Eve seven days a week.

The Big House (for want of a better name) is the one that Elizabeth came to close up for Ambrose. It is just up the drive from the cottage and is wonderful. Two-storeyed, L-shaped and made of beautiful blue-grey stone. It's slate-roofed with dormer windows and a terrace stretching from the crook of the L down its length. The top of the crooked end has a windowed turret and faces the sea. Most of the huge old trees had to be cut down for firewood, but Mr Dilwyn has asked Eben and Eli to plant new trees—chestnuts and oaks. The lawn is growing green and lush again, covering up the wheel ruts of German cars and trucks.

Escorted at different times by Eben, Eli, Dawsey or Isola, I have been round the Island's ten parishes in the past five days; Guernsey is very beautiful in all its variety. I have been told stories of her history (very lawless) with almost every new site and building. Guernsey pirates had superior taste—they built beautiful homes and impressive public buildings. These are sadly dilapidated and in need of repair, but their architectural splendour still shows through. Dawsey took me to a tiny church every inch of which is a mosaic of broken china and smashed pottery. One priest did this all by himself—he must have made pastoral visits with a sledgehammer.

My guides are as various as the sights. Isola tells me about cursed pirate chests bound with bleached bones washing up on the beaches. Eben describes how things used to look before the war, and Eli disappears suddenly, then returns with peach juice and an angelic smile on his face. Dawsey says the least, but he takes me to see wonders—like the tiny church. Then he stands back and lets me enjoy them for as long as I want. He's the most unhurrying person I've ever met. As we were walking along the road yesterday, I noticed that it cut very close to the cliffs and there was a path leading down to the beach below. 'Is this where you met Christian Hellman?' I asked. Dawsey seemed startled and said yes, this was the spot. 'What did he look like?' I asked, because I wanted to picture the scene.

I thought it was a futile request, given that men can't describe each other, but Dawsey surprised me. 'He looked like the German you imagine—tall, blond hair, blue eyes—except he could feel pain.'

With Amelia and Kit, I have walked into St Peter Port several times for tea. The harbour, with the town traipsing up steeply to the sky, must be one of the most beautiful in the world. The shop windows on the High Street and the Pollet are sparklingly clean and beginning to fill up with new goods. St Peter Port may be essentially drab at the moment—so many buildings need restoring—but it does not give off the dead-tired air poor London does. It must be because of the bright light that flows down on everything and the clean, clean air and the flowers growing everywhere—in fields, on verges, in crannies between paving stones.

You really have to be Kit's height to see this world properly. She's marvellous at pointing out things I would otherwise miss—butterflies, spiders, flowers growing tiny and low to the ground—they're hard to see when you're faced with a blazing wall of fuchsias and bougainvillea.

Kit carries a little box with her sometimes when we go to town—a cardboard box, tied up tightly with string and with a red-yarn handle. Even when we have tea, she holds it on her lap and is very protective of it. There are no air holes in the box, so it can't be a ferret. Or, oh Lord, perhaps it's a dead ferret. I'd love to know what's in it, but of course I can't ask.

I do like it here, and I've settled in well enough to start work now. I will, as soon as I come back from fishing with Eben and Eli this afternoon.

Love to you and Piers,

Juliet

From Juliet to Sidney

Mr Sidney Stark
Stephens & Stark Ltd
21 St James's Place
London SW1

6th June 1946

Dear Sidney,

I could hardly believe it was you, telephoning from London last night! How wise of you not to tell me you were flying home. You know how planes terrify me—even when they aren't dropping bombs. Wonderful to know you are no longer five oceans away, but only across the Channel. Will you come to see us as soon as you can?

Isola is better than a stalking horse. She has brought seven people over to tell me their Occupation stories—and I have a growing pile of interview notes. But for now, notes are all they are. I don't know yet if a book is possible—or, if possible, what form it should take.

Kit has taken to spending some of her mornings here. She brings rocks or shells and sits quietly on the floor and plays with them while I work. When I've finished we take a picnic lunch down to the beach. If it's too foggy, we play indoors; either hairdressers—brushing each other's hair until it crackles—or Dead Bride.

Dead Bride is not a complicated game like Snakes and Ladders; it's quite simple. The bride veils herself in a lace curtain and stuffs herself into the laundry basket, where she lies as though dead while the anguished bridegroom hunts for her. When he finally discovers her entombed in the laundry basket, he breaks into loud wails. Then and only then does the bride jump up, shout 'Surprise!' and clutch him to her. Then it is all joy and smiles and kisses.

Privately, I don't give that marriage much of a chance.

I know that all children are gruesome, but I don't know whether I am supposed to encourage them. I'm afraid to ask Sophie if Dead Bride is too morbid a game for a four-year-old. If she says yes, we'll have to stop playing, and I don't want to stop. I love Dead Bride.

So many questions arise when you are spending your days with a child. For instance, if one likes to cross one's eyes a lot, might they get stuck like that for ever, or is that a rumour? My mother said they would, and I believed her, but Kit is made of sterner stuff and doubts it.

I am trying hard to remember my parents' ideas about bringing up children but, as the child in question, I'm hardly one to judge. I know I was spanked for spitting my peas across the table at Mrs Morris, but that's all I can remember. Perhaps she deserved it. Kit seems to show no ill-effects from having been brought up piecemeal by Society members. It certainly hasn't made her fearful and retiring. I asked Amelia about it yesterday. She smiled and said there was no chance of a child of Elizabeth's being fearful and retiring.

I know it will take you a prodigious amount of time to catch up on your work. If you do have a moment to spare, could you find a book of paper dolls for me? One full of glamorous evening gowns, please.

I know Kit is growing fond of me—she pats my knee in passing.

Love,
Juliet

From Juliet to Sidney

10th June 1946

Dear Sidney,

I've just received a wonderful parcel from your new secretary. Is her name really Billee Bee Jones?

Never mind, she's a genius anyway. She found Kit two books of paper dolls, and not just any old paper dolls, either—Greta Garbo and *Gone with the Wind* paper dolls, pages of lovely gowns, furs, hats, boas . . . oh, they are wonderful. Billee Bee also sent a pair of blunt scissors, a piece of thoughtfulness that would never have occurred to me. Kit is using them now.

This is not a letter but a thank-you note. I'm writing one to Billee Bee, too. How did you find such an efficient person? I hope she's plump and motherly, because that's how I imagine her. She enclosed a note saying that eyes do not stay crossed permanently—it's an old wives' tale. Kit is thrilled and intends to cross her eyes until supper.

Love to you,

Juliet

P.S. I would like to point out that contrary to certain insinuating remarks in your last, Dawsey Adams makes no appearance in this letter. I haven't seen Mr Dawsey Adams since Friday afternoon, when he came to pick up Kit. He found us decked out in our finest jewels and marching around the room to the stirring strains of *Pomp and Circumstance* on the gramophone. Kit made him a tea-towel cape, and he marched with us. I think he has an aristocrat lurking in his genealogy: he can gaze into the middle distance just like a duke.

Letter delivered to Eben, 14th June 1946

To 'Eben' or 'Isola' or Any Member of a Book Society on Guernsey, Channel Islands

Dear Guernsey Book Society,

I greet you as those dear to my friend Elizabeth McKenna. I write to you so that I may tell you of her death in Ravensbrück Concentration Camp. She was executed there in March 1945.

In those days before the Russian Army arrived to free the camp, the SS carried truckloads of papers to the crematorium and burned them in the furnaces there. Thus I feared you might never learn of Elizabeth's imprisonment and death.

Elizabeth spoke often to me of Amelia, Isola, Dawsey, Eben and Booker. I recall no surnames, but believe the Christian names Eben and Isola to be unusual and thus hope you may be found easily on Guernsey.

I know that she cherished you as her family, and she felt gratitude and peace that her daughter, Kit, was in your care. Therefore I write so you and the child will know of her and the strength she showed to us in the camp. She could make us forget where we were for a small while, and in that place her friendship was all that aided one to remain human.

I reside now at the Hospice La Forêt in Louviers in Normandy. My English is yet poor, so Sister Touvier is improving my sentences as she writes them down.

I am twenty-four years old. In 1944, I was caught by the Gestapo in Brittany with a packet of forged ration cards. I was questioned and beaten and sent to Ravensbrück Concentration Camp. I was put in Block Eleven, and it was here that I met Elizabeth. She told me about your island of Guernsey and your book society. These things seemed like heaven to me. When Elizabeth spoke, I could imagine the good fresh sea air and the smell of fruit in the hot sun. Though it cannot be true, I don't remember the sun shining one day on Ravensbrück. I loved to hear, too, about how your book society came to be. I almost laughed when she told of the roasted pig, but I didn't. Laughter made trouble in the barracks.

Block Eleven held nearly four hundred women. In front of each barracks was a cinder path where roll call was held twice a day, at 5.30 a.m. and in the evening after work. The women from each barracks stood in squares of one hundred women each—ten women in ten rows. The squares would stretch so far to the right and left of ours we could often not see the end of them in the fog.

Our beds were on wooden shelves, built in platforms of three. There were pallets of straw to sleep on, sour-smelling and alive with fleas and lice. There were large yellow rats that ran over our feet at night. This was a good thing, for the overseers hated the rats and stench, so we would have freedom from them in the late nights.

There were several standpipes with cold water to wash in. Once a week we were taken for showers and given a piece of soap. This was necessary for us, for the thing we feared most was to be dirty, to fester. We dared not become ill, for then we could not work. We would be of no further use to the Germans and they would have us put to death.

Elizabeth and I walked out with our group each morning at six to the Siemens factory, where we worked. Once there, we pushed handcarts to the railway siding and unloaded heavy metal sheets onto the carts.

We were given wheat paste and peas at noon, and returned to camp for roll call at 6 p.m. and a supper of turnip soup.

I am perhaps saying too much, things you do not wish to hear. But I must do this to tell you how Elizabeth lived—and how she held on hard to her kindness and her courage. I would like her daughter to know this also.

Now I must tell you the cause of her death. Often, within months of being in the camp, most women stopped menstruating, but some did not. The camp doctors made no provision for the prisoners' hygiene during this time—no rags, no sanitary towels. The women just had to let the blood run down their legs. The overseers liked this: it gave them an excuse to scream, to hit. A woman named Binta was the overseer for our evening roll call and she began to rage at a bleeding girl and threaten her with her upraised rod. Then she began to beat the girl.

Elizabeth broke out of our line fast—so fast. She grabbed the rod from Binta's hand and turned it on her, hitting her over and over again. Guards came running and two of them struck Elizabeth to the ground with their rifles. They threw her into a truck and took her to the punishment bunker.

One of the guards told me that the next morning soldiers formed a guard around Elizabeth and took her from the cell. Outside the camp walls there was a grove of poplar trees. The branches of the trees formed a path and Elizabeth walked down this by herself, unaided. She kneeled on the ground and they shot her in the back of the head.

I will stop now. I know that I often felt my friend beside me when I was ill after the camp. I had fevers, and I imagined Elizabeth and I were sailing to Guernsey in a little boat. We had planned this in Ravensbrück—how we would live together in her cottage with her baby, Kit. It helped me to sleep. I hope you will come to feel Elizabeth by your side as I do. Her strength did not fail her, nor her mind—not ever—she just saw one cruelty too many.

Please accept my best wishes,
Remy Giraud

Note from Sister Cécile Touvier, in the envelope with Remy's letter

Sister Cécile Touvier, Nurse, writing to you. I have made Remy go to rest now. I do not approve of this long letter, but she insisted on writing it.

She will not tell you how ill she has been, but I will. In the few days before the Russians arrived at Ravensbrück, those filthy Nazis ordered anyone who could walk to leave. Opened the gates and turned them loose upon the devastated countryside. 'Go,' they ordered. 'Go—find any Allied troops that you can.'

They left those exhausted, starving women to walk miles and miles without any food or water. There were not even any gleanings left in the fields they walked past. Was it any wonder their walk became a death march? Hundreds of the women died on the road.

After several days, Remy's legs and body were so swollen with famine oedema she could not continue to walk. So she just lay down in the road to die. Fortunately, a company of American soldiers found her. They carried her to a field hospital, where she was given a bed, and quarts of water were drained from her body. After many months in hospital, she was well enough to be sent to this hospice. She weighed less than sixty pounds when she arrived here. Otherwise, she would have written to you sooner.

It is my belief that she will get her strength back once she can set about laying her friend to rest. You may, of course, write to her, but please do not ask her about Ravensbrück. It will be best for her to forget.

Yours truly,
Sister Cécile Touvier

From Amelia to Remy Giraud

Mademoiselle Remy Giraud
Hospice La Forêt
Louviers
France

16th June 1946

Dear Mademoiselle Giraud,

How good you were to write to us—it could not have been an easy task to call up your own terrible memories in order to tell us of Elizabeth's death. We had been praying that she would return to us, but it is better to know the truth than to live in uncertainty. We were grateful to learn of your friendship with Elizabeth and to think of the comfort you gave to one another.

May Dawsey Adams and I come and visit you in Louviers? We would like to, very much, but not if you would find our visit too disturbing. We want to know you and we have an idea to put to you. But again, if you'd prefer it that we didn't, we won't come.

Always, our blessings for your kindness and courage.

Sincerely,
Amelia Maugery

From Juliet to Sidney

16th June 1946

Dear Sidney,

How comforting it was to hear you say, 'God damn, oh God damn.' That's the only honest thing to say, isn't it? Elizabeth's death is an abomination and it will never be anything else.

It's odd, I suppose, to mourn someone you've never met. But I do. I have felt Elizabeth's presence in every room I enter, not just in the cottage but in Amelia's library, which she stocked with books, and Isola's kitchen, where she stirred up potions. Everyone always speaks of her—even now—in the present tense, and I wanted so much to know her. It's worse for everyone else.

When I saw Eben yesterday, he seemed older than ever. I'm glad he has Eli. Isola has disappeared. Amelia says not to worry: Isola does that when she's sick at heart.

Dawsey and Amelia have decided to go to Louviers to try to persuade Mademoiselle Remy Giraud to come to Guernsey. There was a heart-rending moment in her letter—Elizabeth used to help her go to sleep in the camp by planning their future in Guernsey. She said it sounded like heaven. The poor girl is due for some heaven: she has already been through hell.

I am to look after Kit while they're away. I am so sad for her—she will never know her mother—except by hearsay. I wonder about her future, too, as she is now—officially—an orphan. Mr Dilwyn said there is plenty of time to decide. 'Let us leave well alone at the moment.' He's not like any other banker or trustee I've ever heard of, bless his heart.

All my love,
Juliet

From Juliet to Mark

17th June 1946

Dear Mark,

I'm sorry that our conversation ended badly last night. It's very difficult to convey shades of meaning while roaring into the telephone.

It's true—I don't want you to come this weekend. But it has nothing whatsoever to do with you. My friends have just been dealt a terrible blow. Elizabeth was the centre of the circle here, and the news of her death has shaken us all. When I picture you reading that sentence, I see you wondering why this woman's death has anything to do with you or your plans for the weekend. It does. I feel as though I've lost someone very close to me.

I am in mourning.

Do you understand a little better now?

Yours,

Juliet

From Dawsey to Juliet

Miss Juliet Ashton
Grand Manoir, Cottage
La Bouvée
St Martin's, Guernsey

21st June 1946

Dear Juliet,

We are here in Louviers, though we have not been to see Remy yet. The trip has tired Amelia very much and she wants to rest for a night before we go to the hospice.

It was a dreadful journey across Normandy. Piles of blasted stone walls and twisted metal line the roads in the towns. There are big gaps between buildings, and the ones left look like black, broken-off teeth. Whole fronts of houses are gone and you can see in, to the flowered wallpaper and tilted bedsteads clinging somehow to the floors. I know now how fortunate Guernsey really was in the war.

Many people are still in the streets, removing bricks and stone in wheelbarrows and carts. Outside the towns are ruined fields with huge craters and broken hedges. It is grievous to see the trees. No big poplars, elms or chestnuts. What's left is pitiful, charred black and stunted—sticks without shade. German engineers apparently ordered the soldiers to fell whole woods and coppices. Then they stripped off the branches, smeared the tree trunks with creosote and stuck them upright in holes dug in the fields. The trees were called Rommel's Asparagus and were meant to keep Allied gliders from landing and soldiers from parachuting.

Of Louviers itself, the town is pretty in places, though much of it was bombed and the Germans set fire to it when they retreated. I cannot see how it will become a living town again.

I came back and sat on the terrace until dark, thinking about tomorrow.

Give Kit a hug from me.

Yours ever,

Dawsey

From Amelia to Juliet

23rd June 1946

Dear Juliet,

We met Remy yesterday. I felt unequal somehow to meeting her. But not, thank heavens, Dawsey. He calmly pulled up some garden chairs, sat us down under a shady tree, and asked a nurse if we could have some tea.

I wanted to learn more about Elizabeth, but I was frightened of Remy's fragility. She is very small and far too thin. Her dark curly hair is cut close to her head, and her eyes are enormous and haunted. You can see that she was a beauty in better times, but now—she is like glass and her hands tremble a good deal. She welcomed us as much as she was able, but she was very reserved until she asked about Kit—had she gone to Sir Ambrose in London?

Dawsey told her that Sir Ambrose had died and that we are bringing up Kit. He showed her the photograph of you and Kit that he carries. She smiled then and said, 'She is Elizabeth's child. Is she strong?' I couldn't speak, thinking of our lost Elizabeth, but Dawsey said yes, very strong, and told her about Kit's passion for ferrets. That made her smile again.

Remy is alone in the world. Her father died long before the war; in 1943, her mother was sent to Drancy for harbouring enemies of the government and later died in Auschwitz. Remy's two brothers have been missing since 1941 and she believes that they, too, must be dead.

Eventually I broached the subject of Remy coming to Guernsey. She went quiet, then explained that she was leaving the hospice very soon. The French government is offering allowances to concentration-camp survivors: for time lost, for permanent injuries and for recognition of suffering. There are also stipends for those wishing to resume their education. The government will help Remy pay the rent of a room or the cost of sharing a flat with other survivors, so she has decided to go to Paris and seek an apprenticeship in a bakery.

She was adamant about her plans, so I left the matter there, but I don't believe Dawsey is willing to do so. He thinks that looking after Remy is a moral debt we owe to Elizabeth. Perhaps he is right, or perhaps it is simply a way to relieve our sense of helplessness. In any case, he has arranged to take Remy for a walk tomorrow along the canal and visit a certain patisserie he saw in Louviers. Sometimes I wonder where our shy Dawsey has gone.

I feel well, though I am unusually tired—perhaps it is seeing my beloved Normandy so devastated.

I will be glad to be home, my dear.

A kiss for you and Kit,

Amelia

From Juliet to Sidney

28th June 1946

Dear Sidney,

What an inspired present you sent Kit—red satin tap shoes covered with sequins. Wherever did you find them? Where are mine?

Amelia has been tired since her return from France, so it seems best for Kit to stay with me, especially if Remy decides to come to Amelia's when she leaves the hospice. Kit seems to like the idea, too—heaven be thanked!

Kit knows now that her mother is dead. Dawsey told her. I'm not sure what she feels. She hasn't said anything, and I wouldn't dream of pressing her.

Sidney, I am in trouble with my book.

I have much of the data from the States' records and masses of personal interviews—but I can't make them come together in a structure that pleases me. Straight chronology is too tedious. Shall I send my pages to you? They need a finer and more impersonal eye than mine. Would you have time to look them over, or is the backlog from the Australian trip still so heavy? If it is, don't worry—I'm working anyway and something brilliant may yet come to me.

Love,

Juliet

From Sidney to Juliet

1st July 1946

Dear Juliet,

Don't bundle them up. I want to come to Guernsey myself. Does this weekend suit you? I want to see you, Kit and Guernsey—in that order. I have no intention of reading your work while you pace up and down in front of me—I'll bring the manuscript back to London.

I can arrive Friday afternoon on the five o'clock plane and stay until Monday evening. Will you book me a hotel room? Can you also manage a small dinner party? I want to meet Eben, Isola, Dawsey and Amelia. I'll bring the wine.

Love,
Sidney

From Juliet to Sidney

Wednesday

Dear Sidney,

Wonderful! Isola won't hear of you staying at the inn (she hints of bedbugs). She wants to put you up herself and needs to know if noises at dawn are likely to bother you. That is when Ariel, her goat, rises. Zenobia, the parrot, is a late sleeper.

Dawsey and I and his cart will meet you at the airfield. May Friday hurry up and get here.

Love,
Juliet

From Isola to Juliet, left under Juliet's door

Friday—close to dawn

Lovey, I can't stop, I must hurry to my market stall. I am glad your friend will be staying with me.

I've put lavender sprigs in his sheets. Is there one of my elixirs you'd like me to slip in his coffee? Just nod to me at the market and I'll know which one you mean.

XXX Isola

From Sidney to Sophie

Feochan Farm
by Oban
Argyll

3rd July 1946

Dear Sophie,

I am, at last, in Guernsey with Juliet and am ready to tell you three or four of the dozen things you asked me to find out.

First and foremost, four-year-old Kit seems as fond of Juliet as you and I are. She is a spirited little thing, affectionate in a reserved way (which is not as contradictory as it sounds) and quick to smile when she is with one of her adoptive parents from the Literary Society. She is adorable, too, with round cheeks, round curls and round eyes. The temptation to cuddle her is nearly overwhelming, but it would be a slight on her dignity, and I am not brave enough to try it. When she sees someone she doesn't like, she has a stare that would shrivel Medea.

I'll tell you one story about Kit and Juliet together. Dawsey (more about him later) dropped in to take Kit to watch Eben's fishing boat coming in. Kit said goodbye, flew out, then flew back in, ran up to Juliet, lifted her skirt a quarter of an inch, kissed her kneecap, and flew out again. Juliet looked dumbfounded—and then as happy as you or I have ever seen her.

I know you think Juliet seemed tired, frazzled and pale when you saw her last winter. She now looks as healthy as a horse and is full of her old zest. So full, Sophie, I think she may never want to live in London again—though she doesn't know it yet. Sea air, sunshine, green fields, flowers, the ever-changing sky and sea, and most of all the people, seem to have seduced her away from city life.

I can easily see why. It's such a welcoming place. Isola is the kind of hostess you always wish you'd come across on a visit to the country but never do. She rousted me out of bed the first morning to help her dry rose petals, churn butter, stir something (God knows what) in a big pot, feed her goat, Ariel, and go to the fish market to buy an eel.

Now, about Dawsey Adams. I have inspected him, as per instructions. I liked what I saw. He's quiet, capable, trustworthy—oh God, I've made him sound like a dog—and he has a sense of humour. In short, he is utterly unlike any of Juliet's other swains—praise indeed. He didn't say much at our first meeting—nor at any of our meetings since, come to think of it—but let him into a room and everyone in it seems to breathe a sigh of relief. I have never in my life had that effect on anyone; I can't imagine why not.

Juliet seems a bit nervous of him—his silence *is* slightly daunting—and she made a dreadful mess of the tea things when he came round to pick up Kit yesterday. But Juliet has always shattered teacups—remember what she did to Mother's Spode?—so that may not signify. As for him, he watches her with dark, steady eyes—until she looks at him and he glances away (I do hope you're appreciating my observational skills).

One thing I can say unequivocally: he's worth a dozen Mark Reynoldses, who is all charm and oil, and he gets what he wants. It's one of his few principles. Reynolds wants Juliet because she's pretty and 'intellectual' at the same time, and he thinks they'll make an impressive couple. If she marries him, she'll spend the rest of her life on display at theatres and restaurants and she'll never write another book. As her editor, I'm dismayed by that prospect, but as her friend, I'm horrified. It will be the end of our Juliet.

It's hard to say what Juliet is thinking about Reynolds, if anything. I asked her if she missed him, and she said, 'Mark? I suppose so,' as if he were a distant uncle, and not even a favourite one at that. I'd be delighted if she forgot all about him, but I don't think he'll allow it.

To return to minor topics, I was invited to accompany Juliet on visits to several Islanders this afternoon. Her interviews were about Guernsey's Day of Liberation on the 9th of May last year. What a morning that must have been! The crowds were lined up along St Peter Port harbour. Silent, absolutely silent: masses of people looking at the Royal Navy ships sitting just outside the harbour. Then when the Tommies landed and marched ashore, all hell broke loose. Hugs, kisses, crying, shouting. So many of the soldiers landing were Guernsey men. Men who hadn't seen or heard a word from their families for five years. You can imagine their eyes searching the crowds for family members as they marched—and the joy of their reunions.

When the soldiers emerged, they were carrying chocolates, oranges, cigarettes to toss to the crowd. Brigadier Snow announced that the cable to England was being repaired, and soon they'd be able to talk to their evacuated children and families in England, too. The ships also brought in food, tons of it, and medicine, paraffin, animal feed, clothes, cloth, seeds and shoes!

There must be enough stories to fill three books—it may be a matter of culling. But don't worry if Juliet sounds nervous from time to time—she should. It's a daunting task.

I must stop now and get changed for Juliet's dinner party. Isola is swathed in three shawls and a lace tablecloth—and I want to do her proud.

Love to you all,
Sidney

From Juliet to Sophie

7th July 1946

Dear Sophie,

Just a note to tell you that Sidney is here and we can stop worrying about him—and his leg. He looks wonderful: tanned, fit and without a noticeable limp. In fact, we threw his cane in the sea—I'm sure it's halfway to France by now.

I had a small dinner party for him—cooked by me, and edible, too. Will Thisbee gave me *The Beginner's Cook Book for Girl Guides*. It was just the thing; the writer assumes you know nothing about cookery and gives useful hints, 'When adding eggs, break the shells first.'

Sidney is having a lovely time as Isola's guest. Apparently they sat up late talking last night. Isola doesn't approve of small talk and believes in breaking the ice by stamping on it.

She asked him if he and I were engaged to be married. If not, why not? It was plain to everyone that we doted on each other. Sidney told her that indeed he did dote on me, always had and always would, but that we both knew that we could never marry—because he was a homosexual. Isola neither gasped, fainted nor blinked. She fixed him with her fish eye and asked, 'And Juliet knows?' When he told her yes, I had always known, Isola jumped up, swooped down, kissed his forehead and said, 'How nice—just like dear Booker. I'll not tell a soul; you can rely on me.'

Then she sat back down and began to talk about Oscar Wilde's plays. Weren't they a laugh? Sophie, wouldn't you have loved to have been a fly on the wall? I would.

Sidney and I are going shopping now for a present for Isola. I said she

would love a colourful shawl, but he wants to get her a cuckoo clock. Why???
  Love,
  Juliet
P.S. Mark doesn't write; he telephones. He rang me up only last week. It was one of those terrible connections that force you constantly to interrupt one another and bellow, 'WHAT?' However, I managed to get the gist of the conversation—I should come home and marry him. I politely disagreed. It upset me much less than it would have done a month ago.

From Isola to Sidney

8th July 1946

Dear Sidney,
  You are a very nice guest. I like you. So does Zenobia, or she would not have flown onto your shoulder and perched there so long.
  I'm glad you like to sit up late and talk. I like that myself of an evening. I am going to the manor now to find the book you told me about. How is it that Juliet and Amelia never made mention of Miss Jane Austen to me?
  I was lonely after you left, so I invited Dawsey and Amelia to tea yesterday. You should have seen how I didn't utter a word when Amelia said she thought you and Juliet would get married. I even nodded and slitted my eyes, like I knew something they didn't, to throw them off the scent.
  I do like my cuckoo clock. How cheering it is! I run into the kitchen to watch it. I am sorry Zenobia bit the little bird's head off—she has a jealous nature—but Eli said he'd carve me another one, as good as new.
  I hope you will come and visit us again. With fondness, your hostess,
  Isola Pribby

From Juliet to Sidney

9th July 1946

Dear Sidney,
  I knew it! I knew you'd love Guernsey. The next best thing to being here myself was having you here—even for such a short visit. I'm happy that

you know all my friends now, and they you. I'm particularly happy you enjoyed Kit's company so much. I regret to tell you that some of her fondness for you is due to your present, *Elspeth the Lisping Bunny*. Her admiration for Elspeth has caused her to take up lisping, and she is very good at it.

Dawsey has just brought Kit home—they have been visiting his new piglet. Kit asked if I was writing to Thidney. When I said yes, she said, 'Thay I want him to come back thoon.' Do you thee what I mean about Elspeth? That made Dawsey smile, which pleased me. I'm afraid you didn't see the best of Dawsey this weekend; he was extra-quiet at my dinner party. Perhaps it was my soup, but I think it more likely that he is preoccupied with Remy. He thinks she won't get better until she comes to Guernsey.

I am glad you took my pages home to read. God knows, I am at a loss to divine just *what exactly* is wrong with them. I only know something is.

What on earth did you say to Isola? She dropped in on her way to pick up *Pride and Prejudice* and to berate me for never telling her about Elizabeth Bennet and Mr Darcy. Why hadn't she known that there were love stories not riddled with ill-adjusted men, anguish, death and graveyards! What else had we been keeping from her?

I apologised for such a lapse and said you were absolutely right: *Pride and Prejudice* was one of the greatest love stories ever written—and she might actually die of suspense before she finished it.

Isola said that Zenobia is pining for you—she's off her feed. So am I, but I'm so grateful you could come at all.

Love,
Juliet

From Sidney to Juliet

12th July 1946

Dear Juliet,

I've read your chapters several times, and you're right—they won't do. Strings of anecdotes don't make a book. They need a centre—one person's voice to tell what was happening all around her. As written now, the facts, as interesting as they are, seem like random, scattered shots.

It would hurt like hell to write this letter to you if it wasn't for one thing: you already have the core—you just don't know it yet. I'm talking about Elizabeth McKenna. Have you noticed that everyone you've interviewed sooner or later mentions Elizabeth? Lord, Juliet: who thought up the lie about the Literary Society—and then made it true? Guernsey wasn't her home, but she adapted to it and to the loss of her freedom that she never, I gather, whined about. She went to Ravensbrück for sheltering a slave worker. Look at how she died, and why. Juliet, how did a young girl, an art student, who had never had a job in her life, turn herself into a nurse, working six days a week? She did have dear friends, but she had no one to call her own. She fell in love with an enemy officer and lost him; she had a baby alone during wartime. It must have been terrifying, despite all her good friends.

I'm returning the manuscript and your letters to me—read them again and see how often Elizabeth's name crops up. Ask yourself why. Talk to Dawsey and Eben. Talk to Isola and Amelia. Talk to Mr Dilwyn and to anyone else who knew her well.

I think you should focus on Elizabeth. I think Kit would greatly value a story about her mother—it would give her something to hang on to later. So, get to know Elizabeth well.

Think long and hard and let me know if you think she could be the heart of your book.

Love to you and Kit,

Sidney

From Juliet to Sidney

15th July 1946

Dear Sidney,

I don't need more time to think about it—the minute I read your letter, I knew you were right. Here I've been, wishing that I had known Elizabeth, and missing her as if I had—why did I never think of writing about her? I'll begin tomorrow.

Remy wants to come to Guernsey, after all. Dawsey has been writing to her, and I knew he'd be able to persuade her to come. He could talk an angel out of heaven if he chose to speak, which is not often enough for my liking.

Remy will stay with Amelia, so I'll keep Kit with me.

Undying love and gratitude,

Juliet

P.S. You don't suppose Elizabeth kept a diary, do you?

From Juliet to Sidney

17th July 1946

Dear Sidney,

No diary, but the good news is that she did draw while her paper and pencils lasted. I found some sketches stuffed into a large art folio on the bottom shelf of the sitting-room bookcase. Quick line drawings that seem marvellous portraits to me: Isola beating something with a wooden spoon; Dawsey digging the garden; Eben and Amelia with their heads together, talking.

As I sat on the floor, turning them over, Amelia dropped in. Together we pulled out several large sheets, covered with sketch after sketch of Kit. Kit asleep, on the move, on a lap, being rocked by Amelia, hypnotised by her toes. Perhaps every mother looks at her baby like that, with that intense focus, but Elizabeth put it on paper.

Then I found a sketch of a man with a good, strong, rather broad face; he's relaxed and appears to be looking over his shoulder, smiling at the artist. I knew at once that it was Christian—he and Kit have a double crown in exactly the same place. Amelia picked up the drawing and I asked her if she'd liked him.

'Poor boy,' she said. 'I was so against him. I thought Elizabeth was mad to have chosen him—an enemy, a German—and I was afraid for her. For the rest of us, too. I thought that he would betray her and us—so I told her that I thought she should break it off with him. I was very stern with her.

'Elizabeth just stuck out her chin and said nothing. But the next day he came to visit me. I was appalled. I opened the door and there was an enormous, uniformed German standing before me. I was sure my house was about to be requisitioned and I began to protest, when he thrust forward a bunch of flowers—limp from being clutched. I noticed he was very nervous, so I stopped scolding. "Captain Christian Hellman," he said, and blushed like a boy. I was still suspicious—what was he up to?—and asked him the purpose of his visit. He blushed more and said softly, "I've come to tell you my intentions."

'"For my house?" I snapped.

'"No, for Elizabeth," he said. And that's what he did—just as if I were the Victorian father and he the suitor. He perched on the edge of a chair in my drawing room and told me that he planned to come back to the Island the moment the war was over, marry Elizabeth, grow freesias, read and forget about war. By the time he'd finished, I was a little bit in love with him myself.'

Amelia was half in tears, so we put the sketches away and I made her some tea. Then Kit came in with a shattered gull's egg she wanted to glue together, and we were thankfully distracted.

Love,
Juliet

From Juliet to Sidney

19th July 1946

Dear Sidney,

Stories about Elizabeth are everywhere—not just among the Society members. Listen to this: Kit and I walked to the churchyard this afternoon. Kit was playing among the graves, and I was stretched out on a large tombstone—it's a table-top one with four stout legs—when Sam Withers, the ancient gravedigger, stopped beside me. He said I reminded him of Miss McKenna when she was a young girl. She used to take the sun right there on that very slab—brown as a walnut, she'd get. I sat up straight as an arrow and asked Sam if he'd known Elizabeth well.

Sam said, 'Well—not as to say real well, but I liked her. She and Eben's girl, Jane, used to come up here together to that very tombstone. They'd spread a cloth and eat their picnic—right on top of Mr Mulliss's dead bones.' He told me that the girls were always up to mischief—they tried to raise a ghost once and scared the living daylights out of the vicar's wife. Then he looked over at Kit at the church gate and said, 'That's surely a sweet little girl of hers and Captain Hellman's.'

I pounced on that. Had he known Captain Hellman? Had he liked him? He said, 'Yes, I did. He was a fine fellow, for all he was a German. You're not going to take that out on Miss McKenna's little girl, are you?'

'I wouldn't dream of it!' I said.

He wagged a finger at me. 'You'd better not, miss! You'd best learn the truth of certain matters before you go trying to write a book about the Occupation. I hated the Occupation, too. Some of those blighters was mean—they'd come into your house without knocking and push you to the ground. They was the sort to like having the upper hand, never having had it before. But not all of them was like that—not all, not by a long shot.'

Christian, according to Sam, was not. Sam liked Christian. 'To tell the truth,' he said, 'as long as the Occupation was to last, I met more than one nice German soldier. You would, you know, seeing some of them as much as every day for five years. You couldn't help but feel sorry for them—stuck here knowing their families at home were being bombed to pieces. Didn't matter then who started it in the first place. Not to me, anyway.

'Why, there'd be soldiers on guard in the back of potato lorries going to the army's mess hall—children would follow them, hoping potatoes would fall off into the street. Soldiers would look straight ahead, grim-like, and then flick potatoes off the pile—on purpose. They did the same thing with lumps of coal—those were precious when we didn't have enough fuel left.

'There were many such incidents: just ask Mrs Godfray about her boy. He had the pneumonia and she was worried half to death because she couldn't keep him warm nor give him good food to eat. One day there's a knock on her door, and it's an orderly from the German hospital. Without a word, he hands her a phial of that sulphonamide, tips his cap and walks away. He had stolen it from their dispensary for her. They caught him later, trying to steal some again, and they sent him off to prison in Germany— maybe hanged him. We'd not be knowing.'

He glared at me again suddenly. 'And I say that if some toffee-nosed Englishwoman wants to call being human Collaboration, they'll need to talk to me and Mrs Godfray first!'

I tried to protest, but Sam turned and walked away. I gathered Kit up and we went home. I felt I was beginning to know Kit's father—and to understand why Elizabeth must have loved him.

Next week Dawsey leaves for France to bring Remy to Guernsey.

Love,
Juliet

From Juliet to Sophie

21st July 1946

Dear Sophie,

Burn this letter: I wouldn't want it to appear among your collected papers.

I've told you about Dawsey, of course. You know that he was the first here to write to me; that he is fond of Charles Lamb; that he is helping to bring up Kit; that she adores him. What I haven't told you is that on the very first evening I arrived on the Island, the moment Dawsey held out both his hands to me at the bottom of the gangplank, I felt an unaccountable jolt of excitement. Dawsey is so quiet and composed that I had no idea if it was only me, so I've struggled to be reasonable and casual and *usual* for the past two months. And I was doing very nicely—until tonight.

Dawsey came over to borrow a suitcase for his trip to Louviers—he is going to collect Remy. What kind of man doesn't even own a suitcase? Kit was sound asleep, so we put my case in his cart and walked up to the cliffs. The moon was rising and the sky was coloured in mother-of-pearl, like the inside of a shell. The sea, for once, was quiet, with only silvery ripples, barely moving. No wind. I have never known the world to be so silent, and it dawned on me that Dawsey himself was exactly that silent too, walking beside me. I was as close to him as I've ever been, so I began to take particular note of his wrists and hands. I wanted to touch them, and the thought made me light-headed. There was a knife-edgy feeling—you know the one—in the pit of my stomach.

All at once, Dawsey turned. His face was shadowed, but I could see his eyes, very dark, watching me, waiting. Who knows what might have happened—a kiss?

Nothing—because in the next second we heard Wally Beall's horse-drawn carriage (our local taxi) outside my cottage, and Wally's passenger called out, 'Surprise, darling!' It was Mark—Markham V. Reynolds, Junior, resplendent in his exquisitely tailored suit, with a swathe of red roses over his arm.

I truly wished him dead, Sophie. But what could I do? I went to greet him—and when he kissed me all I could think was, Don't! Not in front of Dawsey! He deposited the roses on my arm and turned to Dawsey with his steely smile. So I introduced them, wishing I could crawl into a hole—and watched stupidly as Dawsey shook Mark's hand, turned to me, shook my hand and said, 'Thank you for the suitcase, Juliet. Good night.' He climbed into his cart and left, without a backward glance.

I could have cried. Instead I invited Mark in and tried to seem like a woman who had just received a delightful surprise. The cart and the introductions had awakened Kit, who looked suspiciously at Mark and wanted to know where Dawsey had gone—he hadn't kissed her good night. Me neither, I thought to myself.

I put Kit back to bed and persuaded Mark that my reputation would be in tatters if he didn't go to the Royal Hotel at once. Which he did, but with a very bad grace and many threats to appear on my doorstep the next morning at six.

Then I sat down and chewed my fingernails for three hours. Should I take myself over to Dawsey's house and try to pick up from where we had left off? But where *did* we leave off? I'm not sure. I don't want to make a fool of myself. What if he looks at me with polite incomprehension—or worse still, with pity?

And anyway, what am I thinking? Mark is here. Mark, who is rich and debonair and wants to marry me. Mark, whom I was doing very well without. Why can't I stop thinking about Dawsey, who probably doesn't give a fig about me? But maybe he does. Maybe I was about to find out what was on the other side of that silence. Damn, damn and damn.

It's two in the morning, I haven't a fingernail to my name and I look at least a hundred years old. Maybe Mark will be repulsed by my haggard appearance when he sees me. Maybe he will spurn me. I don't know that I will be disappointed if he does.

Love,
Juliet

From Juliet to Sophie

24th July 1946

Dear Sophie,

You should probably burn this letter as well as the last one. I've refused Mark finally and irrevocably, and my elation is indecent. If I were a properly brought-up young lady, I'd draw the curtains and brood, but I can't. I'm *free*! Today I bounced out of bed feeling frisky as a lamb, and Kit and I spent the morning running races in the field. She won, but that's because she cheats.

Yesterday was horrible. You know how I felt when Mark appeared, but the next morning was even worse. He turned up at my door at seven, radiating confidence and certain that we'd have a wedding date set by noon. He wasn't the slightest bit interested in the Island, or the Occupation, or Elizabeth, or what I'd been doing since I arrived—he didn't ask a single question about any of it.

Then Kit came down to breakfast. That surprised him—he hadn't really registered her the night before. He had a nice way with her—they talked about dogs—but after a few minutes it was obvious that he was waiting for her to clear off. I suppose, in his experience, nannies whisk the children away before they can annoy their parents. Of course, I tried to ignore his irritation and made Kit her breakfast as usual, but I could feel his displeasure billowing across the room.

At last Kit went outside to play, and the minute the door closed behind her, Mark said, 'Your new friends must be damned smart—they've managed to saddle you with their responsibilities in less than two months.'

He shook his head—pitying me for being so gullible.

I just stared at him.

'She's a cute kid, but she's got no claim on you, Juliet, and you're going to have to be firm about it. Get her a nice dolly or something and say goodbye before she starts thinking you're going to take care of her for the rest of her life.'

Now I was so angry I couldn't speak. I stood there, gripping Kit's porridge bowl with white knuckles. I didn't throw it at him, but I was close.

When I could speak again, I whispered, 'Get out.'

'Sorry?'

'I never want to see you again.'

'Juliet?' He had no idea what I was talking about.

So I explained. Feeling better by the minute, I told him that I would never marry him or anyone else who didn't love Kit and Guernsey and Charles Lamb.

'What the hell does Charles Lamb have to do with anything?' he shouted (as well he might).

I declined to elucidate. He tried to argue with me, then to coax me, then to kiss me, then to argue with me again, but it was over and he knew it.

For the first time in ages—since February, when I met him—I was absolutely sure that I had done the right thing. How could I ever have considered marrying him? One year as his wife and I'd have become one of those abject, quaking women who look at their husbands when someone asks them a question. I've always despised that type, but I see how it happens now.

Two hours later, Mark was on his way to the airfield, never (I hope) to return. And I, disgracefully un-heartbroken, was gobbling raspberry pie at Amelia's.

Last night, I slept the sleep of the innocent for ten blissful hours, and this morning I feel thirty-two again, instead of a hundred.

Kit and I are going to spend the afternoon at the beach, hunting for agates.

What a beautiful, beautiful day.

Love,

Juliet

P.S. None of this means anything with regard to Dawsey. Charles Lamb just popped out of my mouth by coincidence. Dawsey didn't even come to say goodbye before he left. The more I think about it, the more convinced I am that he turned to me on the cliff to ask if he could borrow my umbrella.

From Dawsey to Juliet

27th July 1946

Dear Juliet,

It will soon be time for me to collect Remy from the hospice, but as I have a few minutes, I will use them to write to you.

Remy seems stronger than she was last month, but she is very frail yet. Sister Touvier cautioned me that I must see to it that she gets enough to eat, that she stays warm, that she's not upset. She must be with people—cheerful people, if possible.

I've no doubt Remy will get nourishing food, and Amelia will see to it that she's warm enough, but how am I to serve up good cheer? Joking and suchlike is not natural to me. I didn't know what to say to the Sister, so I just nodded and tried to look jolly. I don't think it was very successful, because Sister glanced at me sharply.

I will do my best, but you, blessed as you are with a sunny nature and a light heart, would make a better companion for Remy than I. I don't doubt she will take to you as we all have, these past months, and you will do her good.

Give Kit a hug and kiss for me.

I will see you both on Tuesday.

Dawsey

From Juliet to Sophie

29th July 1946

Dear Sophie,

Please ignore everything I have ever said about Dawsey Adams. I am an idiot.

I have just received a letter from him praising the medicinal qualities of my 'sunny nature and light heart'. A sunny nature? A light heart? I have never been so insulted. Light-hearted is a short step from witless in my book.

A cackling buffoon—that's what I am to Dawsey.

I am also humiliated—while I was feeling the knife-edge of attraction as we strolled through the moonlight, he was thinking about Remy and how my light-minded prattle would amuse her.

No, it's clear that I was deluded and Dawsey doesn't give a fig for me. I am too irritated to write more now.

Love always,
Juliet

From Juliet to Sidney

1st August 1946

Dear Sidney,

Remy is here at last. She is petite and terribly thin, with short black hair and eyes that are nearly black, too. I had imagined that she would look wounded, but she doesn't, except for a little limp, which shows itself as a mere hesitancy in her walk, and a rather stiff way of moving her neck.

There is a grave intensity in her that is almost unnerving. She is not cold and certainly not unfriendly, but she seems to be wary of spontaneity. I suppose if I had been through her experience, I would be the same—somewhat removed from everyday life.

You can cross out all the above when Remy is with Kit. At first, she seemed inclined to follow Kit with her eyes instead of talking to her, but that changed when Kit offered to teach her how to lisp. Remy looked startled, but she agreed to take lessons and they went off to Amelia's greenhouse together. Her lisp is hampered by her accent, but Kit doesn't hold that against her and has generously given her extra instructions.

Amelia had a small dinner party the evening Remy arrived. Everyone was on their best behaviour. Eli shook her hand nervously and then retreated—I think he was afraid he'd hurt her accidentally. I was pleased to see that Remy gets on well with Amelia—they will enjoy each other's company—but Dawsey is her favourite. When he came into the sitting room a little later than the rest she relaxed visibly and even smiled at him.

Yesterday was cold and foggy, but Remy, Kit and I built a sandcastle on Elizabeth's tiny beach. We spent a long time on its construction, and it was a splendid, towering specimen. I had made a Thermos of cocoa, and we sat drinking and waiting impatiently for the tide to come in and knock the castle down.

Kit ran up and down the shore, inciting the sea to rush in farther and faster. Remy touched my shoulder and smiled. 'Elizabeth must have been like that once,' she said, 'the Empress of the seas.' I felt as if she had given me a gift—even a touch takes trust—and I was glad she felt safe with me.

While Kit danced in the waves, Remy talked about Elizabeth. She had meant to keep her head down, conserve the strength she had left, and come home as quickly as she could after the war. 'We thought it would be possible. We knew of the invasion; we saw all the Allied bombers flying over the camp. We knew what was happening in Berlin. The guards could not keep their fear from us. Each night we lay sleepless, waiting to hear the Allied tanks at the gates. We whispered that we could be free the next day. We did not believe we would die.'

There didn't seem to be anything else to say after that. I thought, If only Elizabeth could have held on for a few more weeks, she could have come home to Kit. Why, so close to the end, did she attack the overseer?

Remy watched the sea breathe in and out. Then she said, 'It would have been better for her not to have had such a heart.'

Yes, but worse for the rest of us.

Love,

Juliet

From Isola to Sidney

1st August 1946

Dear Sidney,

I am the new Secretary of the Guernsey Literary and Potato Peel Pie Society. I thought you might like to see a sample of my first minutes, being as how you are interested in anything Juliet is interested in. Here they are:

30th July 1946, 7.30 p.m.
Night cold. Ocean noisy. Will Thisbee was host. House dusted, but curtains need washing.

—Mrs Winslow Daubbs read a chapter from her autobiography, The Life and Loves of Delilah Daubbs. *Audience attentive—but silent afterwards. Except for Winslow, who wants a divorce. All were embarrassed, so Juliet and Amelia served the pudding, a lovely ribbon cake, on real china plates— which we don't usually run to.*

—Miss Minor then rose to ask if we were going to start being our own authors, could she read from a book of her very own thoughts? Her text is called The Common Place Book of Mary Margaret Minor. *Everybody already knows what Mary Margaret thinks about everything, but we said 'Aye' because we all like Mary Margaret. Will Thisbee ventured to say that*

perhaps Mary Margaret will edit herself in writing, as she has never done in talking, so it might not be so bad.

—I moved we have a specially called meeting next week so I don't have to wait to talk about Jane Austen. Dawsey seconded! All said 'Aye.' Meeting adjourned.

Miss Isola Pribby, Official Secretary to the Guernsey Literary and Potato Peel Pie Society.

Now that I'm Official Secretary, I could swear you in for a member if you'd like to be one. It's against the rules, because you're not an Islander, but I could do it in secret.

Your friend,
Isola

From Juliet to Sidney

3rd August 1946

Dear Sidney,

Someone—I can't imagine who—has sent Isola a present from Stephens & Stark. It was published in the mid-1800s and is called *The New Illustrated Self-Instructor in Phrenology and Psychiatry: with Size and Shape Tables and Over One Hundred Illustrations*. As if that were not enough, there's a subtitle, *Phrenology: the Science of Interpreting Bumps on the Head*.

Eben had Kit and me, Dawsey, Isola, Will, Amelia and Remy over for supper last night. Isola arrived with tables, sketches, graph paper, a measuring tape, callipers and a new notebook. Then she cleared her throat and read, 'You too can learn to read Head Bumps! Stun Your Friends, Confound Your Enemies with Indisputable Knowledge of Their Human Faculties or Lack of Them.' She thumped the book onto the table. 'I'm going to become an adept,' she announced, 'in time for Harvest Festival.'

She has told Reverend Elstone that she will no longer dress up in shawls and pretend to read palms. No, from now on she will see the future in a scientific way, by reading head bumps! The church will make far more money from head bumps than Miss Sybil Beddoes does with her stall, WIN A KISS FROM SYBIL BEDDOES.

Will Thisbee said she was absolutely right: Miss Beddoes wasn't a good kisser and he for one was tired of kissing her, even for charity's sake.

Sidney, do you realise what you have unleashed on Guernsey? Isola's already read the lumps on Mr Singleton's head (his stall is next to hers at the market) and told him his Love of Fellow Creatures Bump had a shallow trench right down the middle—which was probably why he didn't feed his dog enough. Do you see where this could lead? One day she'll find someone with a Latent Killer Knot, and he'll shoot her—if Miss Beddoes doesn't get her first.

One wonderful, unexpected thing did come from your present. After pudding, Isola began to read the bumps on Eben's head—dictating the measurements for me to write down. I glanced over at Remy, wondering what she would make of Eben's hair standing on end and Isola rummaging through it. Remy was trying to stifle a smile, but she couldn't manage it and burst out laughing. Dawsey and I stopped dead and stared at her! She's so quiet, not one of us could have imagined such a laugh. It was like water. I hope I'll hear it again.

Dawsey and I have not been as easy with each other as we once were, though he still comes often to visit Kit, or to bring Remy over. When we heard Remy laugh, our eyes met for the first time for a fortnight. But perhaps he was only admiring how my sunny nature had rubbed off on her. I do, according to some people, have a sunny nature, Sidney. Did you know that?

Love,
Juliet

From Isola to Sidney

5th August 1946

Dear Sidney,

I know it was you who sent *The New Illustrated Self-Instructor in Phrenology and Psychiatry: with Size and Shape Tables and Over One Hundred Illustrations*. It is a very useful book and I thank you for it.

I've been studying hard, so now I can finger through a whole headful of bumps without peeking into the book. I hope to make a mint for the church at Harvest Festival, as who would not desire to have their innermost workings—good and rotten—revealed by the Science of Phrenology?

I've found out more in the past three days than I knew in my whole life before. Mrs Gilbert has always been a nasty one, but now I know that she can't help it—she's got a big pit in her Benevolence spot. She fell into the quarry when she was a girl, and my guess is she cracked her Benevolence and was never the same since.

Even my friends are full of surprises. Eben is garrulous! I never would have thought it of him, but he's got bags under his eyes and there's no two ways about it. I broke it to him gently.

Juliet didn't want to have her bumps read at first, but she agreed when I told her that she was standing in the way of Science. She's awash in Amativeness. Also Conjugal Love. I told her it was a wonder she wasn't married, with such great mounds.

Will cackled, 'Your Mr Stark will be a lucky man, Juliet!' Juliet blushed red as a tomato, and I was tempted to say he didn't know much because Mr Stark is a homosexual, but I pulled myself together and kept your secret like I promised.

Dawsey up and left then, so I never got to his lumps, but I'll pin him down soon. I don't understand Dawsey sometimes. For a while he was downright chatty, but these days he doesn't have two words to rub together.

Thank you again for the fine book.

Your friend,

Isola

Telegram from Sidney to Juliet

6TH AUGUST 1946

BOUGHT A SMALL BAGPIPE FOR DOMINIC AT GUNTHER'S YESTERDAY STOP WOULD KIT LIKE ONE STOP LET ME KNOW SOONEST AS THEY HAVE ONLY ONE LEFT STOP HOW'S THE WRITING STOP LOVE TO YOU AND KIT STOP SIDNEY

From Juliet to Sidney

7th August 1946

Dear Sidney,

Kit would love a bagpipe. I would not.

I think the work is going splendidly, but I'd like to send you the first two chapters—I won't feel *settled* until you've read them. Do you have time?

Every day I learn something new about Elizabeth. How I wish I had known her myself!

As I write, I catch myself thinking of things she did as though I'd been there—she's so full of life that I have to remind myself that she's dead, and then I feel the wrench of losing her again.

I heard a story about her today that made me want to weep. We had supper with Eben, and afterwards Eli and Kit went out to dig for worms (a task best done by the light of the moon). Eben and I took our coffee outside, and for the first time he chose to talk about Elizabeth to me.

It happened at the school where Eli and the other children were waiting for the Evacuation ships. Eben wasn't there, because the families were not allowed, but Isola saw it happen, and she told him about it that night.

She said that the room was full of children, and Elizabeth was buttoning up Eli's coat when he told her he was scared of getting on the boat—leaving his mother and his home. If their ship *was* bombed, he asked, who would he say goodbye to? Isola said that Elizabeth took her time, studying his question. Then she pulled up her jumper and unpinned something from her blouse. It was her father's medal from the First War and she always wore it.

She explained to him that it was a magic badge, that nothing bad could happen to him while he wore it. Then she got Eli to spit on it twice to call up the charm. Isola saw Eli's face over Elizabeth's shoulder and told Eben that it had that beautiful light children have before the Age of Reason gets at them.

Of all the things that happened during the war, sending children away to try to keep them safe was surely the most terrible. It defies the animal instinct to protect your young. I see myself becoming bearlike around Kit. Even when I'm not actually watching her, I'm watching her. If she's in any sort of danger (which she often is, given her taste in climbing), my hackles rise—I didn't even know I *had* hackles before—and I run to rescue her.

When her enemy, the vicar's nephew, threw plums at her, I roared at him. And 'through some queer sort of intuition' I always know where she is, just as I know where my hands are—and if I didn't, I'd be ill with worry. This is how the species survives, I suppose, but the war put a spanner in all that. How did the mothers of Guernsey live, not knowing where their children were?

I can't imagine.

Love,

Juliet

P.S. What about a flute?

From Juliet to Sophie

9th August 1946

Darling Sophie,

What marvellous news—a new baby! Wonderful! I do hope you won't have to eat dry biscuits and suck lemons this time. I know you two don't care which/what/who you have, but I would love a girl. To that end, I am knitting a tiny matinee jacket and hat in pink wool. Of course Alexander is delighted, but what about Dominic?

I told Isola your news, and I'm afraid she may send you a bottle of her Pre-Birthing Tonic. Sophie—please don't drink it, and don't dispose of it where the dogs might find it. There may not be anything actually poisonous in it, but I don't think you should take any chances.

Your enquiries about Dawsey are misdirected. Send them to Kit—or Remy. I hardly see the man any more, and when I do, he's silent. Not in a romantic, brooding way, like Mr Rochester, but in a grave and sober way that indicates disapproval. I don't know what the matter is, I really don't. When I arrived in Guernsey, Dawsey was my friend. We talked about Charles Lamb and we walked all over the Island together. I enjoyed his company as much as that of anyone I've ever known. Then, after that appalling night on the cliffs, he stopped talking—to me, anyway. It's been a terrible disappointment. I miss the sense that we understood each other, but I'm beginning to think that was only my delusion all along.

Not being silent myself, I am wildly curious about people who are. As Dawsey doesn't talk about himself, I was reduced to questioning Isola about his head bumps in order to find out about his past. But Isola is beginning to fear that the bumps may lie after all, and she offered as proof the fact that Dawsey's Violence-Prone Node isn't as big as it should be, given that he nearly beat Eddie Meares, who gave/traded/sold information to the German authorities in exchange for favours, to death!!! Those exclamation marks are mine. Isola seemed to think nothing of it.

A week after Elizabeth was arrested, Meares was showing off a silver cigarette case, hinting that it was a reward for reporting some goings-on he'd seen. Dawsey heard about it and went to Mad Bella's pub the next night. According to Isola, he walked up to Eddie Meares, grabbed him by the shirt collar, lifted him up off his stool and began banging his head on the bar. Then they set to it on the floor. Dawsey was a mess: nose, mouth bleeding, one eye swollen shut, one rib cracked—but Eddie Meares was a bigger mess: two black eyes, two ribs broken and stitches. The Court sentenced Dawsey to three months in the Guernsey jail, though they let him out after one. The Germans needed the space for more serious criminals—

like black marketeers and thieves who stole petrol from army lorries.

Naturally I was agog and begged for more. As she's disillusioned with bumps, Isola moved on to actual facts. Dawsey didn't have a very happy childhood. His father died when he was eleven, and Mrs Adams, who'd always been sickly, grew odd. She became fearful, first of going into town, then of going into her own garden, and finally she wouldn't leave the house at all. She would just sit in the kitchen, rocking and staring out at nothing. She died shortly after the war began. Isola said that what with all this—his mother, farming and stuttering so badly—he'd always been shy, and never, except for Eben, had any ready-made friends. Isola and Amelia were acquainted with him, but that was about all.

That was how it was until Elizabeth came—and made him be friends. Forced him, really, into the Literary Society. And then, Isola said, how he blossomed! Now he had books to talk about instead of swine fever—and friends to talk to. The more he talked, the less he stuttered.

He's a mysterious creature, isn't he? Perhaps he *is* like Mr Rochester, and has a secret sorrow. Or a mad wife down in his cellar. Anything is possible, I suppose, but it would have been difficult to feed a mad wife on one set of ration coupons during the war. Oh dear, I wish we were friends again. (Dawsey and I, not the mad wife.)

Now I must rush to make myself presentable for tonight's meeting of the Society. I have one decent skirt to my name, and I have been feeling dowdy. Remy, for all she's so frail and thin, manages to look stylish at every turn. What is it about French women?

And when are you going to come and see me? Kit will do a tap dance in your honour and I will stand on my head. I still can, you know.

Just to torment you, I won't tell you any more news. You'll have to come and find out for yourself.

Love,
Juliet

From Juliet to Sophie

22nd August 1946

Dear Sophie,

Ever since I discovered that Elizabeth was dead and Kit was an orphan, I've been worried about her future—and about my own future without her. I think it would be unbearable. I'm going to make an appointment with Mr

Dilwyn when he and Mrs Dilwyn return from their holiday. He is her legal guardian, and I want to discuss my possible guardianship /adoption/foster-parenting of Kit. Of course, I want to adopt her, but I'm not sure Mr Dilwyn would consider a spinster of flexible income and no fixed abode a desirable parent.

I haven't said a word about this to anyone here, or to Sidney. There is so much to worry about. What would Amelia say? Would Kit like the idea? Is she old enough to decide? Where would we live? Can I take her away from the place she loves to London? A restricted city life instead of going about in boats and playing tag in churchyards? Kit would have you, me and Sidney, but what about Dawsey and Amelia and all the family she has here? It would be impossible to replace them. Can you imagine a London school-teacher with Isola's flair? Of course not.

I argue myself all the way to one end of the question and back again several times a day. One thing I am sure of, though, is that I want to look after Kit for ever.

Love,
Juliet

P.S. If Mr Dilwyn says no, not possible, I might just whisk Kit away and come and hide in your barn.

From Juliet to Sidney

23rd August 1946

Dear Sidney,

Called suddenly to Rome, were you? Have you been elected Pope? It had better be something at least as pressing, to excuse your not coming to visit.

At the Literary Society last night I was sorry you weren't in attendance at our meeting for the evening's speaker was a local man called Augustus Sarre, and he spoke on your favourite book, *The Canterbury Tales*. He chose to read 'The Parson's Tale' first because he knew what a parson did for a living—unlike those other fellows in the book: a Reeve, a Franklin or a Summoner. 'The Parson's Tale' disgusted him so much he could read no more.

Fortunately for you, I made careful mental notes, so I can give you the gist of his remarks. To wit: Augustus would never let a child of his read Chaucer; it would turn him against Life in general and God in particular. To hear the Parson tell it, life was a *cesspool*, where a man must wade through the muck as best he could; evil ever seeking him out, and evil ever finding him. (Don't you think Augustus has a touch of the poet about him? I do.)

'Think of it, friends,' Augustus said, 'a lifetime of misery with God not letting you draw one easy breath. Then in your last few minutes—POOF! you'd get Mercy. Thanks for nothing, I say.

'That's not all, friends: man must never think well of himself—that is called the sin of Pride. Friends, show me a man who hates himself, and I'll show you a man who hates his neighbours more! He'd have to—you wouldn't grant anyone else something you can't have for yourself—no love, no kindness, no respect! So I say, shame on the Parson! Shame on Chaucer!' Augustus sat down with a thump.

Two hours of lively discussion on Original Sin and Predestination followed. At last, Remy stood up to speak—she'd never done so before, and the room fell silent. She said softly, 'If there is Predestination, then God is the devil.' No one could argue with that—what kind of God would create Ravensbrück?

Isola is having several of us to supper tonight.

Love,
Juliet

From Juliet to Sophie

29th August 1946

Dear Sophie,

Mr Dilwyn is back from his holiday, and I must make an appointment to talk to him about Kit soon. I keep putting it off—I'm so dreadfully afraid that he'll refuse to consider it. I wish I looked more motherly—perhaps I could buy a fichu. If he asks for character references, will you give me one? Does Dominic know his alphabet yet? If so, he can write out this:

Dear Mr Dilwyn,

   Juliet Dryhurst Ashton is a very nice lady—sober, clean and responsible. You should let her be Kit McKenna's mother.

   Yours sincerely,
   James Dominic Strachan

I didn't tell you, did I, about Mr Dilwyn's plans for Kit's inheritance in Guernsey? He's engaged Dawsey, and a crew Dawsey is to select, to restore the Big House: banisters replaced; graffiti removed from the walls and paintings; windows put in; torn-out plumbing replaced with new; chimneys cleaned; wiring checked and terrace paving stones repointed—or whatever it is you do to old stones. Mr Dilwyn is not yet certain what can be done with the wooden panelling in the library—it had a beautiful carved frieze of fruit and ribbons, which the Germans used for target practice.

As no one will want to holiday on the Continent for the next few years, Mr Dilwyn is hoping that the Channel Islands will become a tourist haven again—and Kit's house would make a wonderful holiday home.

But on to stranger events: the Benoit sisters asked me and Kit to tea this afternoon. I had never met them, and it was quite an odd invitation. They asked if Kit had 'a steady eye and a good aim'. Did she like rituals? Bewildered, I asked Eben if he knew the Benoit sisters. Were they sane? Was it safe to take Kit there? Eben roared with laughter and said yes, the sisters were safe and sane. He said Jane and Elizabeth had visited them every summer for five years. The sisters always wore starched pinafores, polished court shoes and little lace gloves. We would have a lovely time, a lavish tea and entertainments afterwards, and we should go.

None of which told me what to expect. They are identical twins, in their eighties, dressed in ankle-length gowns of black georgette, larded with jet beads at bosom and hem, their white hair piled like swirls of whipped cream on top of their heads. So charming, Sophie. We did have a sinful tea, and I'd barely put my cup down when Yvonne (older by ten minutes) said, 'Sister, I do believe Elizabeth's child is too small yet.' Yvette said, 'I believe you're right, Sister. Perhaps Miss Ashton would help us?'

I think it was very brave of me to say, 'I'd be delighted,' when I had no idea what they were proposing.

'So kind, Miss Ashton. We denied ourselves during the war—so disloyal to the Crown, somehow. Our arthritis has grown very much worse; we cannot even join you in the rites. It will be our pleasure to watch!'

Yvette went to a drawer in the sideboard, while Yvonne opened one of the double doors between the drawing room and the dining room. Taped to a previously hidden panel was a full-page, full-length newspaper portrait in sepia of the Duchess of Windsor, *Mrs Wallis Simpson as was* (cut out, I gather, from the Society pages of the *Baltimore Sun* in the late 1930s).

Yvette handed me four silver-tipped, finely balanced, evil-looking darts. 'Go for the eyes, dear,' she said. So I did.

'Splendid! Three-for-four, Sister. Almost as good as dear Jane! Elizabeth always fumbled at the last moment! Shall you want to try again next year?'

It's a simple story, but sad. Yvette and Yvonne adored the Prince of Wales. 'So darling in his little plus fours.' 'How debonair in evening dress!' 'So admirable, so royal—until that hussy got hold of him.' 'Snatched him from the throne! His crown—gone!' It broke their hearts. Kit was enthralled—as well she might be. I am going to practise my aim—four-for-four being my new goal in life.

Don't you wish we had known the Benoit sisters while we were growing up?

Love and kisses,
Juliet

From Juliet to Sidney

2nd September 1946

Dear Sidney,

Something happened this afternoon; while it ended well, it was disturbing, and I can't get to sleep. I am writing to you instead of Sophie because she's pregnant and you're not. You don't have a delicate condition to be upset in, and Sophie does—I am losing my grip on grammar.

Kit was with Isola, making gingerbread men. Remy and I needed some ink and Dawsey needed some sort of putty for the Big House, so we all walked together into St Peter Port. We took the cliff walk by Fermain Bay. It's beautiful—a rugged path that wanders up and around the headlands. I was a little in front of Remy and Dawsey because the path had narrowed. A tall, red-haired woman walked around the large boulder at the path's turning and came towards us. She had a dog with her, a huge Alsatian. He wasn't on a lead and seemed overjoyed to see me. I laughed, and the woman called out, 'Don't worry. He never bites.' He put his paws on my shoulders, attempting a big, slobbering kiss.

Then, behind me, I heard an awful gulping gasp: a deep gagging that went on and on. I can't describe it. I turned and saw that it was Remy; she was bent over almost double and vomiting. Dawsey had caught her and was holding her as she went on vomiting in deep spasms, over both of them. It was terrible to see. Dawsey shouted, 'Get that dog away, Juliet! Now!'

I frantically pushed the dog away. The woman was apologising, almost hysterical herself. I held on to the dog's collar and kept saying, 'It's all right! It's all right! It's not your fault. Please go. Go!' At last she did, hauling her poor confused pet along by his collar. Remy was quiet then, only gasping for breath. Dawsey looked over her head and said, 'Let's get her to your house, Juliet. It's the nearest.' He picked her up and carried her, I trailing behind, helpless and frightened.

Remy was cold and shaking, so I ran her a bath, and once she was warm again, put her to bed. She was already half asleep, so I gathered her clothes into a bundle and went downstairs.

Dawsey was standing by the window, looking out. Without turning he said, 'She told me once that those guards used big dogs. Riled them up and deliberately let them loose on the lines of women standing for roll call—just to watch the fun. *Christ!* I've been ignorant, Juliet. I thought being here with us would help her forget. Goodwill isn't enough, is it? Not nearly enough.'

'No,' I said, 'it isn't.' He didn't say anything else, just nodded to me and left.

I telephoned Amelia to tell her where Remy was and why and then started the washing. Isola brought Kit back; we had supper and played Snap until bedtime.

But I can't sleep. I'm so ashamed of myself. I had wanted Remy to go home. But had I really thought her well enough to go home—or did I just want her out of the way? Did I think it was time for her to go back to France—to just get on with It, whatever It might be? I did—and it's sickening.

Love,
Juliet

P.S. As long as I'm confessing, I might as well tell you something else. Bad as it was to stand there holding Remy's awful clothes and smelling Dawsey's ruined ones, all I could think of was what he said, Goodwill isn't enough, is it? Does that mean that is all he feels for her? I've chewed over that errant thought all evening.

Night letter from Sidney to Juliet

4th September 1946

Dear Juliet,

All that errant thought means is that you're in love with Dawsey yourself. Surprised? I'm not. Don't know what took you so long to realise it—sea air is supposed to clear your head.

I want to come and see you but I can't get away till the 13th. Is that all right?

Love,
Sidney

Telegram from Juliet to Sidney

5TH SEPTEMBER 1946

YOU'RE INSUFFERABLE ESPECIALLY WHEN YOU'RE RIGHT STOP
LOVELY TO SEE YOU ANYHOW ON THE 13TH STOP LOVE JULIET

From Isola to Sidney

6th September 1946

Dear Sidney,

Juliet says you're coming to see us and I say it's about time.

I still cherish the head-bump book you sent me and I hope your feelings
are not hurt that I want to pursue another calling. I still trust the truth of
lumps; it's just that I've read the head bumps of everyone I care for, except
yours, and it can get tedious.

Juliet says you're coming next Friday. I could meet your plane and take
you to Juliet's. Eben is having a party on the beach the next evening, and he
says you are most welcome. Eben hardly ever gives parties, but he said this
one is to make a happy announcement to us all. A celebration! But of what?
Does he mean to announce nuptials? But whose? I hope he is not getting
married hisself; wives don't generally let husbands out by themselves of an
evening and I would miss Eben's company.

Your friend,
Isola

From Juliet to Sophie

7th September 1946

Dear Sophie,

At last, I mustered my courage and told Amelia that I wanted to adopt
Kit. Her opinion means a great deal to me—she loved Elizabeth so dearly;
she knows Kit so well—and me, almost well enough. I was anxious for her
approval, and terrified that I wouldn't get it. I choked on my tea but in the
end managed to get the words out. Her relief was so visible I was shocked.
I hadn't realised how worried she'd been about Kit's future.

She said, 'I think it would be a wonderful thing for both of you. It would be the best possible thing—' She broke off and pulled out a handkerchief. And then, of course, I pulled out my handkerchief. After we'd finished crying, we plotted. Amelia will come with me to see Mr Dilwyn. 'I have known him since he was in short trousers,' she said. 'He won't dare refuse me.' Having Amelia on your side is like having the Third Army at your back.

But something even more wonderful than having Amelia's approval has happened. My last doubt has shrunk to less than pinpoint-size. Do you remember my telling you about the little box Kit carried, tied up with string? The one I thought might hold a dead ferret? She came into my room this morning and patted my face until I woke up. She was carrying her box. Without a word, she began to undo the string. She took the lid off, parted the tissue paper and gave the box to me. Sophie—she stood back and watched my face as I turned over the things in the box and then lifted them all out onto the bed cover. A tiny, eyelet-covered baby pillow; a small photograph of Elizabeth digging in her garden and laughing up at Dawsey; a woman's linen handkerchief, smelling faintly of jasmine; a man's signet ring; and a small leather book of Rilke's poetry with the inscription *For Elizabeth, who turns darkness into light, Christian*. Tucked into the book was a much-folded scrap of paper. Kit nodded, so I carefully opened it and read, 'Amelia—kiss her for me when she wakes up. I'll be back by six. Elizabeth. P.S. Doesn't she have the most beautiful feet?'

She was showing me her treasures, Sophie—her eyes didn't once leave my face. We were both so solemn, and I, for once, didn't start crying; I just held out my arms. She climbed into them, and under the covers with me—and went straight to sleep. Not me! I couldn't. I was too happy planning the rest of our lives.

I don't care about living in London—I love Guernsey and I want to stay here, even after I've finished Elizabeth's book. I can't imagine Kit living in London, having to wear shoes all the time, having to walk instead of run, having no pigs to visit. No fishing with Eben and Eli, no visits to Amelia, no potion-mixing with Isola and, most of all, no time spent with Dawsey.

I think, if I become Kit's guardian, we could continue to live in Elizabeth's cottage. I could take my vast profits from *Izzy* and buy a flat for Kit and me to stay in when we visit London. Her home is here, and mine can be. Writers can write on Guernsey—look at Victor Hugo. The only things I'd really miss about London are Sidney and Susan, the nearness to Scotland, new plays and Harrods Food Hall.

Pray for Mr Dilwyn's good sense. I know he has it, I know he likes me, I know he knows Kit is happy living with me, and that I am solvent enough for two at the moment—and who can say better than that in these decadent times? Amelia thinks that if he does say no to adoption without a husband, he will gladly grant me guardianship.

Sidney is coming to Guernsey again next week. I wish you were coming, too—I miss you.

Love,
Juliet

From Juliet to Sidney

8th September 1946

Dear Sidney,

Kit and I took a picnic out to the meadow to watch Dawsey rebuilding Elizabeth's stone wall. It was a wonderful excuse to spy on him and his way of going at things. He studied each rock, felt the weight of it, brooded and placed it on the wall. Smiled if it accorded with the picture in his head. Took it off if it didn't and searched for a different stone. He is very calming to the spirit.

He grew so accustomed to our admiring gazes that he issued an unprecedented invitation to supper. Kit had a prior engagement with Amelia, but I accepted with unbecoming haste and then fell into an absurd twitter about being alone with him.

We were both a bit awkward when I first arrived, but he at least had the cooking to occupy him and retired to the kitchen, refusing help. I took the opportunity to snoop through his books. He hasn't got very many, but his taste is superior—Dickens, Mark Twain, Balzac, Boswell, Anne Brontë's novels (I wonder why he had those) and my biography of her. I didn't know he had that: he's never said a word—perhaps he loathed it.

Over supper, we discussed Jonathan Swift, pigs and the trials in Nuremberg. Doesn't that reveal a breathtaking range of interests? I think it does. We talked easily enough, but neither of us ate much—even though he had made a delicious sorrel soup (much better than I could). After coffee, we strolled down to his farmyard for a pig-viewing. Grown pigs don't improve on acquaintance, but piglets are a different matter—Dawsey's are spotted and frisky and sly. Every day they dig a new hole under his fence, ostensibly to escape, but really just for the amusement of watching Dawsey fill in the gap. You should have seen them grin as he approached the fence.

Dawsey's barn is extraordinarily clean. He also stacks his hay beautifully.

I believe I am becoming pathetic.

I'll go further. I believe that I am in love with a flower-growing, wood-carving quarryman/carpenter/pig farmer. In fact, I know I am. Perhaps tomorrow I will become entirely miserable at the thought that he doesn't love me back—may, even, care for Remy—but at this precise moment I am succumbing to euphoria. My head and stomach feel quite odd.

See you on Friday. Feel free to give yourself airs for discovering that I love Dawsey. You may even preen in my presence—this one time, but never again.

Love and XXXX,
Juliet

Telegram from Juliet to Sidney

11TH SEPTEMBER 1946

AM ENTIRELY MISERABLE stop SAW DAWSEY IN ST PETER PORT THIS AFTERNOON BUYING SUITCASE WITH REMY ON HIS ARM BOTH WREATHED IN SMILES stop IS IT FOR THEIR HONEY-MOON stop WHAT A FOOL I AM stop I BLAME YOU stop WRETCHEDLY JULIET

Detection Notes of Miss Isola Pribby
Private: Not to Be Read, Even after Death
Sunday

This book with lines in it is from my friend Sidney Stark. It came to me in the post yesterday. It had *PENSÉES* written in gold on the cover, but I scratched it off, because that's French for THOUGHTS and I am only going to write down FACTS. Facts gleaned from keen eyes and ears. I don't expect too much of myself at first—I must learn to be more observant.

Here are some of the observations I made today. Kit loves being in Juliet's company—she looks peaceful when Juliet comes into the room and she doesn't make faces behind people's backs any more. Also she can wiggle her ears now—which she couldn't before Juliet came.

My friend Sidney is coming to visit. He will stay with Juliet this time, because she's cleaned out Elizabeth's storeroom and put a bed in it for him.

Monday

Mrs Taylor has a rash on her arms. What, or who, from? Tomatoes or her husband? Look into further.

Tuesday

Nothing noteworthy today.

Wednesday

Nothing again.

Thursday

Remy came to see me today—she gives me the stamps from her letters from France—they are more colourful than English ones, so I stick them in my book. She had a letter in a brown envelope with a little open window in it, from the FRENCH GOVERNMENT. This is the fourth one she's got—what do they want from her? Find out.

I have been looking at a book about artists and how they size up a picture they want to paint. Say they want to concentrate on an orange—do they study the shape direct? No, they fool their eyes and stare at the banana beside it, or look at it upside-down, between their legs. They see the orange in a brand-new way. It's called getting perspective. So, I am going to try a new way of looking—not upside-down between my legs, but by not staring at anything direct or straight ahead. I can move my eyes slyly if I keep my lids lowered a bit. Practise this!!!

Friday

Not staring headlong works. I went with Dawsey, Juliet, Remy and Kit in Dawsey's cart to the airfield to meet dear Sidney. Here is what I observed: Juliet hugged him, and he swung her round like a brother would. He was pleased to meet Remy, and I could tell he was watching her sideways, like I was doing. Dawsey shook Sidney's hand, but he did not come in for apple cake when we got to Juliet's house. It was a little sunk in the middle, but it tasted good.

I had to put drops in my eyeballs before bed—it is a strain, always having to skitter them sideways. My eyelids ache from having to keep them halfway down, too.

Saturday

Remy, Kit and Juliet came with me down to the beach to gather firewood for an evening picnic. Amelia was out in the sun, too. She looks more rested and I am happy to see her so. Dawsey, Sidney and Eli carried Eben's big iron cauldron down. Dawsey is always nice and polite to Sidney, and Sidney is pleasant as can be to Dawsey, but he seems to stare at him in a wondering sort of way. Why is that?

Remy left the firewood and went over to talk to Eben, and he patted her on the shoulder. Why? Eben was never one to pat much. Then they talked for a while, but sadly out of my earshot.

When it was time to go home for lunch, Eli went off beachcombing. Juliet and Sidney each took hold of one of Kit's hands, and they walked her up the cliff path, playing that game of 'One Step. Two Steps. Three Steps—LIFT UP!' Dawsey watched them go up the path, but he did not follow. He walked down to the shore and just stood there, looking out over the water. It suddenly struck me that Dawsey is lonely. I think it may be that he has always been lonely, but he didn't mind before, and now he minds. Why now?

Saturday Night

I did see something at the picnic, something important—and like dear Miss Marple, I must act upon it. It was a brisk night and the sky looked moody. But that was fine—we bundled up in jumpers and jackets, eating lobster and laughing at Booker. He stood on a rock and gave an oration, pretending to be some Roman. I worry about Booker: he needs to read a new book. I think I will lend him Jane Austen.

I was sitting, senses alert, by the bonfire with Sidney, Kit, Juliet and Amelia. We were poking sticks in the fire when Dawsey and Remy walked up to Eben and the lobster pot. Remy whispered to Eben, he smiled, and picked up his big spoon and banged on the pot. 'Attention all,' Eben shouted, 'I have something to tell you.'

Everyone went quiet, except for Juliet, who drew in her breath so hard I heard her. She didn't let it out again, and went all over rigid—even her jaw. What could be the matter? I was so worried about her, having once been toppled by appendix myself, that I missed Eben's first few words.

'. . . and so tonight is a farewell party for Remy. She is leaving us next Tuesday for her new home in Paris. She will share rooms with friends and is apprenticed to the famous confectioner Raoul Guillemaux, in the city. She has promised that she will come back to Guernsey and that her second home will be with me and Eli, so we may all rejoice in her good fortune.'

What an outpouring of cheers from the rest of us! Everyone ran to gather round Remy and congratulate her. Everyone except Juliet—she let out her breath in a whoosh and flopped backwards onto the sand, like a gaffed fish!

I peered round, thinking I should observe Dawsey. He wasn't hovering over Remy—but how sad he looked. All of a sudden, IT CAME TO ME! I HAD IT! Dawsey didn't want Remy to go; he was afraid she'd never return. He was in love with Remy, and too shy in his nature to tell her so.

Well, I'm not. I would tell her of his affections, and then she, being *French*, would know what to do. She would let him know she'd find favour in his suit. Then they would marry, and she would not need to go off to Paris. What a blessing that I have no imagination and am able to see things clearly.

Sidney came up to Juliet and prodded her with his foot. 'Feel better?' he asked, and Juliet said yes, so I stopped worrying about her. Then he led her over to congratulate Remy. Kit was asleep in my lap, so I stayed where I was by the fire and thought carefully.

Remy, like most Frenchwomen, is practical. She would want evidence of Dawsey's feelings for her before she changed her plans willy-nilly. I would have to find the proof she needed.

A little bit later, when wine had been opened and toasts drunk, I walked up to Dawsey and said, 'Daws, I've noticed that your kitchen floor is dirty. I want to come and scrub it for you. Will Monday suit?'

He looked a little surprised, but he said yes. 'It's an early Christmas present,' I said. 'So you mustn't think of paying. Leave the door open for me.'

And so it was settled, and I said good night to all.

Sunday

I have laid my plans for tomorrow. I am nervous. I will sweep and scrub Dawsey's house, keeping a lookout for evidence of his love for Remy. Maybe a poem, 'Ode to Remy', screwed up in his wastepaper basket? Or doodles of her name all over his shopping list?

Miss Marple never really snooped so I won't either—I will not force locks. But once I have proof of his devotion to Remy, she won't get on the aeroplane to Paris on Tuesday. She will know what to do, and then Dawsey will be happy.

Monday: a Serious Error, a Joyous Night

I woke up too early and had to fiddle around with my hens until it was time for Dawsey to leave for work up at the Big House. Then, I cut along to his farm, checking every tree trunk for carved hearts. None.

With Dawsey gone, I went in with my mops, bucket and rags. For two hours I swept, scrubbed, dusted and waxed—and found nothing. I was beginning to despair, when I thought of his books. I began to clap dust out of them, but no loose papers fell to the floor. Suddenly I saw his little red book on Charles Lamb's life. What was it doing here? I had seen him put it in the wooden treasure box Eli carved for his birthday present. But if the red book was here on the shelf, what was in his treasure box? And where was it? I tapped the walls. No hollow sounds anywhere. I thrust my arm into his flour bin—nothing but flour. Would he keep it in the barn? What was left? His bed, under his bed!

I ran to his bedroom, fished under the bed and pulled out the treasure box. I lifted the lid and glanced inside. Nothing met my eye, so I was forced to dump everything out on the bed—still nothing: not a note from Remy, not a photograph of her, no handkerchief with the initial *R* in the corner. There was one, but it was one of Juliet's scented ones and had a *J* embroidered on it. He must have forgotten to return it to her. Other things were in there, but *nothing of Remy's*.

I put everything back in the box and straightened the bed. My mission had failed! Remy would get on that aeroplane tomorrow, and Dawsey would stay lonely. I was heartsore. I gathered up my mops and bucket.

I was trudging home when I saw Amelia and Kit—they were going bird-watching. They asked me to come along, but I knew that not even birdsong could cheer me up. But I thought Juliet could cheer me—she usually does. I wouldn't stay long and bother her writing, but maybe she would ask me in for a cup of coffee. Sidney had left this morning, so perhaps she'd be feeling bereft, too. I hurried down the road to her house.

I found Juliet at home, papers awhirl on her desk, but she wasn't doing anything, just sitting there, staring out of the window. 'Isola!' she said. 'Just when I've been wanting company!' She started to get up when she saw my mops and pail. 'Have you come to clean my house? Forget that and come and have some coffee.' Then she had a good look at my face and said, 'Whatever is the matter? Are you ill? Come and sit down.'

The kindness was too much for my broken spirits, and I—I admit it— I started to howl. I said, 'No, no, I'm not ill. I have failed—failed in my mission. And now Dawsey will stay unhappy.'

Juliet took me over to her sofa and she patted my hand. 'Now tell me, what was your mission? And why do you think you failed?'

So I told her all about it—my notion that Dawsey was in love with Remy, and how I'd looked for proof. If I'd found any I'd have told Remy he loved her, and then she'd want to stay. 'He is so shy, Juliet. He always has been— I don't think anybody's ever been in love with him, or he with anybody before, so he wouldn't know what to do about it. It'd be just like him to hide away mementos and never say a word. I despair for him, I do.'

Juliet said, 'A lot of men don't keep mementos, Isola. That doesn't necessarily mean a thing. What on earth were you looking *for*?'

'Evidence, like Miss Marple does. But no, not even a picture of her. There's lots of pictures of you and Kit, and several of you by yourself. One of you wrapped up in that lace curtain, being a Dead Bride. He's kept all your letters, tied up in that blue hair ribbon—the one you thought you'd lost. I know he wrote to Remy at the hospice, and she must have written back to him—but no, nary a letter from Remy. Not even her handkerchief— oh, he found one of yours. You might want it back—it's a pretty thing.'

She got up and went over to her desk. She stood there a while; then she picked up that crystal thing with Latin, *Carpe Diem*, or some such, etched on the top. She studied it.

'"Seize the Day",' she said. 'That's an inspiring thought, isn't it, Isola?'

'I suppose so,' I said, 'if you like being goaded by a bit of rock.'

Juliet did surprise me then—she turned round to me and gave me that grin she has, the one that made me first like her so much. 'Where is Dawsey? Up at the Big House, isn't he?'

At my nodding, she bounded out through the door and raced up the drive to the Big House.

Oh wonderful Juliet! She was going to give Dawsey a piece of her mind for shirking his feelings for Remy.

Miss Marple never runs anywhere; she follows after slowly, like the old lady she is. So I did, too. Juliet was inside the house by the time I got there.

I went on tippy-toes to the terrace and pressed myself into the wall by the library. The French windows were open. I heard Juliet open the door to the library. 'Good morning, gentlemen,' she said. I could hear Teddy Heckwith (he's a plasterer) and Chester (he's a joiner) say, 'Good morning, Miss Ashton.'

Dawsey said, 'Hello, Juliet.' He was on top of the big stepladder. I found that out later when he made so much noise coming down it.

Juliet said she would like a word with Dawsey, if the gentlemen could give her a minute. They said certainly, and left the room.

Dawsey said, 'Is something wrong, Juliet? Is Kit all right?'

'Kit's fine. It's me—I want to ask you something.'

Oh, I thought, she's going to tell him not to be a sissy. Tell him he must stir himself up and go and propose to Remy at once. But she didn't.

What she said was, 'Would you like to marry me?'

I liked to die where I stood.

There was quiet—complete quiet. Nothing! And on and on it went, not a word, not a sound.

But Juliet went on undisturbed, her voice steady—and me, I could not get so much as a breath of air into my chest. 'I'm in love with you, so I thought I'd ask.'

And then, Dawsey, dear Dawsey, swore. He took the Lord's name in vain. 'My God, yes,' he cried, and clattered down that stepladder; only his heels hit the rungs, which is how he sprained his ankle.

I kept to my scruples and did not look inside the room, tempted though I was. I waited. It was quiet in there, so I came on home to think. What good was training my eyes if I could not see things rightly? I had got everything wrong. Everything. It came out happy, so happy, in the end, but no thanks to me. I don't have Miss Marple's insight into the cavities of the human mind. That is sad, but best to admit it.

For now, I will ask Kit over for supper and to spend the night with me so that Juliet and Dawsey can have the freedom of the shrubbery—just like Mr Darcy and Elizabeth Bennet.

From Juliet to Sidney

17th September 1946

Dear Sidney,

Terribly sorry to make you turn round and come right back across the Channel, but I require your presence—at my wedding. I have seized the day, and the night, too.

Can you come and give me away in Amelia's back garden on Saturday?

Eben to be best man, Isola to be bridesmaid (she is manufacturing a gown for the occasion), Kit to throw rose petals.

Dawsey to be groom.

Are you surprised? Probably not—but I am. I am in a constant state of surprise these days. Actually, now that I calculate, I've been betrothed only one full day, but it seems as though my whole life has come into existence in the past twenty-four hours. Think of it! We could have gone on longing for one another and pretending not to notice *for ever*. This obsession with dignity can ruin your life if you let it.

Is it unseemly to get married so quickly? I don't want to wait—I want to start at once. I've always thought that the story was over when the hero and heroine were safely engaged—after all, what's good enough for Jane Austen ought to be good enough for anyone. But it's a lie. The story is about to begin, and every day will be a new piece of the plot.

Dawsey has just come down from the Big House and is demanding my immediate attention. His much-vaunted shyness has evaporated completely—I think it was a ploy to arouse my sympathies.

Love,

Juliet

P.S. I ran into Adelaide Addison in St Peter Port today. By way of congratulation, she said, 'I hear you and that pig farmer are about to regularise your connection. Thank the Lord!'

ANNIE BARROWS

Born: San Diego, California
Relationship to author: niece
Profession: writer

We talked to writer Annie Barrows, to ask her about her aunt's book, and the task of finishing it after unexpected illness interrupted Mary Ann Shaffer's writing in 2007. They are pictured here together. Mary Ann Shaffer died in February 2008.

RD: What is your most striking memory of Mary Ann?

AB: Without doubt, it's an image of her sitting at her dining-room table with a cup of cold coffee beside her and a book in her hand. She read more than anyone I ever met. But she was also a great talker and storyteller, plus being the only person I have ever seen fall out of a chair laughing.

RD: Can you tell us about the trip that inspired Mary Ann to write the book?

AB: She was visiting England in 1980 and, on a whim, decided to fly down to Guernsey. Once she was there, a fog enveloped the island and all ferry and plane service was shut down. Immured in the airport for seventy-two hours, Mary Ann passed the time warming herself under the hand-dryer in the men's restroom (the one in the women's restroom was broken) and reading all the books she could find in the airport bookstore. Apparently, in 1980, the subject of most of the available books was the German Occupation during World War Two. Mary Ann was riveted. When she was finally allowed to fly out, she brought half the contents of the bookstore in her suitcase. Her visit to Guernsey was short in duration, but lingering in effect.

RD: Have you been to the Channel Islands?

AB: Yes, I went to Guernsey this past summer, to make sure that all the things I said in the book were correct (they were!). I had a lovely time there—it reminded me of the craggy coast near my home in Northern California, but the land itself looked like Normandy. However, even as I was watching the bunnies leap through the grass and admiring the sea views, I was also noticing the marks that the German Occupation left on the island. After a few days I was inspecting every clump of wildflowers for a hidden gun emplacement. If I squinted out the trees, I could imagine what the island looked like during the Occupation.

RD: You're a published writer yourself, so you were well-qualified to complete the book. But did you find it hard to take up where Mary Ann had left off?

AB: No, it was surprisingly easy—or at least, not nearly as hard as I had imagined it would be. I discovered that all those years of stories and conversations and just hanging around with Mary Ann had left me with the sound of her voice inside my head. I already knew that we had read a lot of the same books, but I learned that we also told a story in the same way. Taking up her story was like having a long, complicated conversation—wonderful.

RD: Can you tell us a bit about your life—do you have family, are you working?

AB: I am married and have two daughters and two guinea pigs. At the moment, I am working like crazy, on my next novel for adults as well as the next book in my Ivy and Bean series for children.

RD: How and why did you start writing?

AB: It was a long process. I used to think that writers were not like me. They were magic beings who knew they were writers from an early age. They might suffer, they might agonise, but still, they were certain. There was nothing for them to learn, because they already knew it. After I worked in publishing and had edited several hundred books, my opinion changed. Sure, there are people who are natural, innate writers—I have encountered exactly one in my whole life—but most are simply people who write. They work at it, they mess up, they try to fix it, they just keep going.

RD: Have you ever been a member of a literary society of any kind?

AB: At one time, I belonged to a group of Dante-reading old ladies. I was the youngest member by about forty years, and I adored reading with them. Later in life, I used to meet with a group of disgruntled editors to read the *Iliad* in a bar across the street from our office. All those spears through breastplates were very satisfying at that point in my life. I don't know whether either of these experiences qualify as being in a literary society. I've never been in a book club because I like to follow my own whims in selecting what to read.

RD: And have you ever eaten any wartime delights such as Potato Peel Pie?

AB: Sad to say, I *have* eaten a Potato Peel Pie. First I made it (pretty simple, as there are only three ingredients) and then I ate it. It tasted like paste, because that's essentially what it is.

RD: If you could meet one of the characters from the book in real life, which one would you choose and why?

AB: Juliet would be my choice, because she's the most like Mary Ann, with the same wry wit and rueful view of life. And I miss my aunt.

COPYRIGHT AND ACKNOWLEDGMENTS

GONE TOMORROW: Copyright © Lee Child 2009.
Published at £18.99 by Bantam Press, an imprint of Transworld Publishers.
Condensed version © The Reader's Digest Association Limited, 2009.

FOLLY: Copyright © Alan Titchmarsh 2008.
Published at £18.99 by Hodder & Stoughton, an Hachette Livre UK Company.
Condensed version © The Reader's Digest Association Limited, 2009.

THE PYRAMID: Copyright © Henning Mankell 1999.
English translation of 'The Pyramid' by Ebba Segerberg, copyright © The New Press
1998. *The Pyramid* (The Kurt Wallander Stories) published at £17.99 by Harvill Secker,
an imprint of The Random House Group Limited.
Condensed version © The Reader's Digest Association Limited, 2009.

THE GUERNSEY LITERARY AND POTATO PEEL PIE SOCIETY: Copyright © 2008
by Mary Ann Shaffer.
Published at £10.99 by Bloomsbury Publishing Plc.
Condensed version © The Reader's Digest Association Limited, 2009.

The right to be identified as authors has been asserted by the following in accordance with
sections 77 and 78 of the Copyright, Designs and Patents Act, 1988: Lee Child, Alan
Titchmarsh, Henning Mankell, Mary Ann Shaffer.

Dustjacket spine: Photographer's Choice; illustrator: Trinette Reed. Back jacket: Alan
Titchmarsh © Isle of Wight County Press. 5 photograph of Mary Ann Shaffer © Stephanie
Mohan; 6–8 Dave Krieger/Stone; illustrator: Curtis Cozier; 4 and 164 © Johnny Ring.
166–8 © Daniel Berehulak/Getty/Corbis Art; illustrator: Claire Rankin; 4 and 330 © Niall
McDiarmid; 331 © Corbis/Hulton-Deutsch Collection. 332–4 © Sindre Ellingsen/Photographer's
Choice; illustrator: Narrinder Singh@velvet tamarind; 5 and 450 © Lina Ikse Bergman; 451
© Alamy/LOOK Die Bildagentur der Fotografen GmbH. 452–4 illustrator: Steve Carroll; 574
© Brook McCormick.

Printed and bound by GGP Media GmbH, Pössneck, Germany

020-259 DJ0000-1